THE LEOPARD HUNTS
IN DARKNESS
&
WHEN THE
LION FEEDS

Wilbur Smith was born in Central Africa in 1933. He was educated at Michaelhouse and Rhodes University.

He became a full-time writer in 1964 after the successful publication of *When the Lion Feeds*, and has since written thirty novels, all meticulously researched on his numerous expeditions worldwide. His books are now translated into twenty-six languages.

He owns a farm and game reserve and has an abiding concern for the peoples and wildlife of his native continent, an interest strongly reflected in his novels.

Also by Wilbur Smith

THE COURTNEYS
The Sound of Thunder
A Sparrow Falls
Birds of Prey
Monsoon
Blue Horizon

THE COURTNEYS OF AFRICA
The Burning Shore
Power of the Sword
Rage
A Time to Die
Golden Fox

THE BALLANTYNE NOVELS
A Falcon Flies
Men of Men
The Angels Weep

Also
The Dark of the Sun
Shout at the Devil
Gold Mine
The Diamond Hunters
The Sunbird
Eagle in the Sky
The Eye of the Tiger
Cry Wolf
Hungry as the Sea
Wild Justice
Elephant Song
River God
The Seventh Scroll
Warlock

WILBUR SMITH

The Leopard Hunts in Darkness

&

When the Lion Feeds

PAN BOOKS

The Leopard Hunts in Darkness first published 1984 by William Heinemann.
First published by Pan Books 1998
When the Lion Feeds first published 1964 by William Heinemann.
First published in paperback by Mandarin 1993. First published by Pan Books 1997

This omnibus edition published 2005 by Pan Books
an imprint of Pan Macmillan
A Division of Macmillan Publishers Limited
Pan Macmillan, 20 New Wharf Road, London N1 9RR
Basingstoke and Oxford
Associated companies throughout the world
www.panmacmillan.com

ISBN 978 0 330 44100 1

3 5 7 9 8 6 4 2

A CIP catalogue record for this book is available from
the British Library.

Printed and bound in the UK by
CPI Mackays, Chatham ME5 8TD

Visit **www.panmacmillan.com** to read more about all our
books and to buy them. You will also find features, author
interviews and news of any author events, and you can sign
up for e-newsletters so that you're always first to hear
about our new releases.

THE LEOPARD
HUNTS IN
DARKNESS

For Danielle
with all my love

This small wind had travelled a thousand miles and more, up from the great wastes of the Kalahari Desert which the little yellow Bushmen call 'the Big Dry'. Now when it reached the escarpment of the Zambezi valley, it broke up into eddies and backlashes amongst the hills and the broken ground of the rim.

The bull elephant stood just below the crest of one of the hills, much too canny to silhouette himself on the skyline. His bulk was screened by the new growth of leaves on the msasa trees, and he blended with the grey rock of the slope behind him.

He reached up twenty feet and sucked the air into his wide, hair-rimmed nostrils, and then he rolled his trunk down and delicately blew into his own gaping mouth. The two olfactory organs in the overhang of his upper lip flared open like pink rosebuds, and he tasted the air.

He tasted the fine peppery dust of the far deserts, the sweet pollens of a hundred wild plants, the warm bovine stench of the buffalo herd in the valley below, the cool tang of the water pool at which they were drinking and wallowing: these and other scents he identified, and accurately he judged the proximity of the source of each odour.

However, these were not the scents for which he was searching. What he sought was the other acrid offensive smell which overlaid all the others. The smell of native tobacco smoke mingled with the peculiar musk of the flesh-eater, rancid sweat in unwashed wool, of paraffin and carbolic soap and cured leather – the scent of man; it was there, as strong and close as it had been in all the long days since the chase had begun.

1

Once again the old bull felt the atavistic rage rising in him. Countless generations of his kind had been pursued by that odour. Since a calf he had learned to hate and fear it, almost all his life he had been driven by it.

Only recently there had been a hiatus in the lifelong pursuit and flight. For eleven years there had been surcease, a time of quiet for the herds along the Zambezi. The bull could not know nor understand the reason, that there had been bitter civil war amongst his tormentors, war that had turned these vast areas along the south bank of the Zambezi into an undefended buffer zone, too dangerous for ivory-hunters or even for the game rangers whose duties included the cull of surplus elephant populations. The herds had prospered in those years, but now the persecution had begun again with all the old implacable ferocity.

With the rage and the terror still upon him, the old bull lifted his trunk again and sucked the dreaded scent into the sinuses of his bony skull. Then he turned and moving silently he crossed the rocky ridge, a mere greyish blur for an instant against the clear blue of the African sky. Still carrying the scent, he strode down to where his herd was spread along the back slope.

There were almost three hundred elephant scattered amongst the trees. Most of the breeding cows had calves with them, some so young that they looked like fat little piglets, small enough to fit under their mothers' bellies. They rolled up their tiny trunks onto their foreheads and craned upwards to the teats that hung on swollen dugs between the dams' front legs.

The older calves cavorted about, romping and playing noisy tag, until in exasperation one of their elders would tear a branch from one of the trees and, wielding it in his trunk, lay about him, scattering the importunate youngsters in squealing mock consternation.

The cows and young bulls fed with unhurried delibera-tion, working a trunk deep into a dense, fiercely thorned thicket to pluck a handful of ripe berries then place them well back in the throat like an old man swallowing aspirin; or using the point of a stained ivory tusk to loosen the bark of a msasa tree and then strip ten feet of it and stuff it happily beyond the drooping triangular lower lip; or raising their entire bulk on their back legs like a begging dog to reach up with outstretched trunk to the tender leaves at the top of a tall tree, or using a broad forehead and four tons of weight to shake another tree until it tossed and whipped and released a shower of ripe pods. Further down the slope two young bulls had combined their strength to topple a sixty-footer whose top leaves were beyond even their long reach. As it fell with a crackle of tearing fibres, the herd bull crossed the ridge and immediately the happy uproar ceased abruptly, to be replaced by quiet that was startling in its contrast.

The calves pressed anxiously to their mothers' flanks, and the grown beasts froze defensively, ears outstretched and only the tips of their trunks questing.

The bull came down to them with his swinging stride, carrying his thick yellow ivories high, his alarm evident in the cock of his tattered ears. He was still carrying the man-smell in his head, and when he reached the nearest group of cows, he extended his trunk and blew it over them.

Instantly they spun away, instinctively turning down-wind so that the pursuers' scent must always be carried to them. The rest of the herd saw the manoeuvre and fell into their running formation, closing up with the calves and nursing mothers in the centre, the old barren queens surrounding them, the young bulls pointing the herd and the older bulls and their attendant askaris on the flanks, and they went away in the swinging, ground-devouring stride that they could maintain for a day and a night and another day without check.

As he fled, the old bull was confused. No pursuit that he had ever experienced was as persistent as this had been.

It had lasted for eight days now, and yet the pursuers never closed in to make contact with the herd. They were in the south, giving him their scent, but almost always keeping beyond the limited range of his weak eyesight. There seemed to be many of them, more than he had ever encountered in all his wanderings, a line of them stretched like a net across the southern routes. Only once had he seen them. On the fifth day, having reached the limits of forbearance, he had turned the herd and tried to break back through their line, and they had been there to head him off, the tiny upright sticklike figures, so deceptively frail and yet so deadly, springing up from the yellow grass, barring his escape to the south, flapping blankets and beating on empty paraffin tins, until his courage failed and the old bull turned back, and led his herds once more down the rugged escarpment towards the great river.

The escarpment was threaded by elephant trails used for ten thousand years by the herds, trails that followed the easier gradients and found the passes and ports through the ironstone ramparts. The old bull worked his herd down one of these, and the herd strung out in single file through the narrow places and spread out again beyond.

He kept them going through the night. Though there was no moon, the fat white stars hung close against the earth, and the herd moved almost soundlessly through the dark forests. Once, after midnight, the old bull fell back and waited beside the trail, letting his herd go on. Within the hour he caught again the tainted man-smell on the wind, fainter and very much more distant – but there, always there, and he hurried forward to catch up with his cows.

In the dawn they entered the area which he had not visited in ten years. The narrow strip along the river which had been the scene of intense human activity during the long-drawn-out war, and which for that reason he had avoided until now when he was reluctantly driven into it once again.

The herd moved with less urgency. They had left the pursuit far behind, and they slowed so that they could feed as they went. The forest was greener and more lush here on the bottom lands of the valley. The msasa forests had given way to mopani and giant swollen baobabs that flourished in the heat, and the old bull could sense the water ahead and he rumbled thirstily deep in his belly. Yet some instinct warned him of other danger ahead as well as that behind him. He paused often, swinging his great grey head slowly from side to side, his ears held out like sounding boards, his small weak eyes gleaming as he searched cautiously before moving on again.

Then abruptly he stopped once more. Something at the limit of his vision had caught his attention, something that glistened metallically in the slanted morning sunlight. He flared back with alarm, and behind him his herd backed up, his fear transmitted to them infectiously.

The bull stared at the speck of reflected light, and slowly his alarm receded, for there was no movement except the soft passage of the breeze through the forest, no sound but the whisper of it in the branches and the lulling chattering and hum of unconcerned bird and insect life around him. Still the old bull waited, staring ahead, and as the light altered he noticed there were other identical metal objects in a line across his front, and he shifted his weight from one forefoot to the other, making a little fluttering sound of indecision in his throat.

What had alarmed the old bull was a line of small square galvanized sheetmetal plaques. They were each affixed to the top of an iron dropper that had been hammered into the earth so many years ago that all man-smell had long ago dissipated. On each plaque was painted a laconic warning, which had faded in the brutal sunlight from crimson to pale pink. A stylized skull and crossbones above the words 'DANGER. MINEFIELD'.

The minefield had been laid years previously by the security forces of the now defunct white Rhodesian government, as a *cordon sanitaire* along the Zambezi river, an attempt to prevent the guerrilla forces of ZIPRA and ZANU from entering the territory from their bases across the river in Zambia. Millions of anti-personnel mines and heavier Claymores made up a continuous field so long and deep that it would never be cleared; the cost of doing so would be prohibitive to the country's new black government which was already in serious economic difficulties.

While the old bull still hesitated, the air became filled with a clattering roar, the wild sound of hurricane winds. The sound came from behind the herd, from the south again, and the old bull swung away from the minefield to face it.

Low over the forest tops rushed a grotesque dark shape, suspended on a whistling silver disc. Filling the sky with noise, it bore down upon the bunched herd, so low that the down-draught from its spinning rotors churned the branches of the tree-tops into thrashing confusion and flung up a fog of red dust from the earth's dry surface.

Driven by this new menace, the old bull turned and rushed forward beyond the sparse line of metal discs and his terror-stricken herd charged after him into the minefield.

He was fifty metres into the field before the first mine exploded under him. It burst upwards into the thick leather pad of his right hind foot, cut half of it away like an axe-stroke. Raw red meat hung in tatters from it and white bone gleamed deep in the wound as the bull lurched forward on three legs. The next mine hit him squarely in the right fore, and smashed his foot to the ankle into bloody mince. The bull squealed in agony and panic and fell back on his haunches pinned by his shattered limbs, while all around him his breeding herd ran on into the minefield.

The thump, thump of detonations was intermittent at first, strung out along the edge of the field, but soon they took on a broken staccato beat like that of a maniac drummer. Occasionally four and five mines exploded simultaneously, an intense blurt of sound that struck the hills of the escarpment and shattered into a hundred echoes.

Underlying it all, like the string section of some hellish orchestra, was the whistling clatter of the helicopter rotor as the machine dipped and swung and dropped and rose along the periphery of the minefield, worrying the milling herd like a sheepdog its flock, darting here to head off a bunch of animals that had broken back, racing there to catch a fine young bull who had miraculously run unscathed through the field and reached the clear ground of the river-bank, settling in his path, forcing him to stop and turn, then chasing him back into the minefield until a mine tore his foot away and he went down trumpeting and screaming.

Now the thunder of bursting mines was as continuous as a naval bombardment, and each explosion threw a column of dust high into the still air of the valley, so that the red fog cloaked some of the horror of it. The dust twisted and eddied as high as the tree-tops and transformed the frenzied animals to dark tormented wraiths lit by the flashes of the bursting mines.

One old cow with all four feet blown away lay upon her side and flogged her head against the hard earth in her attempts to rise. Another dragged herself forward on her belly, back legs trailing, her trunk flung protectively over the tiny calf beside her until a Claymore went off under her chest and burst her ribs outwards like the staves of a barrel, at the same instant tearing away the hindquarters of the calf at her side.

Other calves, separated from their dams, rushed squealing

7

through the dust fog, ears flattened against their heads in terror, until a clap of sound and a flash of brief fire bowled them over in a tangle of shattered limbs.

It went on for a long time, and then the barrage of explosions slowed, became intermittent once more, and then gradually ceased. The helicopter settled to earth, beyond the line of warning markers. The beat of its engine died, and the spinning rotor stilled. The only sound now was the screaming of the maimed and dying beasts that lay in the area of churned earth below the dust-coated trees. The fuselage hatch of the helicopter was open and a man dropped lightly from it to the earth.

He was a black man, dressed in a faded denim jacket from which the sleeves had been carefully removed, and tight-fitting tie-dyed jeans. In the days of the Rhodesian war, denim had been the unofficial uniform of the guerrilla fighters. On his feet he wore fancy, tooled, western boots, and pushed up on the top of his head gold-rimmed Polaroid aviator's sunglasses. These and the row of ballpoint pens clipped into the breast-pocket of his jacket were badges of rank amongst the veteran guerrillas. Under his right arm he carried an AK 47 assault rifle, as he walked to the edge of the minefield and stood for a full five minutes impass- ively watching the carnage lying out there in the forest. Then he walked back towards the helicopter.

Behind the canopy, the pilot's face was turned atten- tively towards him, with his earphones still in place over his elaborate Afro-style hairdo, but the officer ignored him and concentrated instead on the machine's fuselage.

All the insignia and identification numbers had been carefully covered with masking-tape, and then oversprayed with black enamel from a hand-held aerosol can. In one place the tape had come loose, exposing a corner of the identification lettering. The officer pressed it back into place with the heel of his hand, inspected his work briefly

8

but critically, and turned away to the shade of the nearest mopani.

He propped his AK 47 against the trunk, spread a handkerchief upon the earth to protect his jeans and sat down with his back to the rough bark. He lit a cigarette with a gold Dunhill lighter and inhaled deeply, before letting the smoke trickle gently over his full dark lips.

Then he smiled for the first time, a cool reflective smile, as he considered how many men, and how much time and ammunition it would take to kill three hundred elephant in the conventional manner.

'The comrade commissar has lost none of his cunning from the old days of the bush war – who else would have thought of this?' He shook his head in admiration and respect.

When he had finished the cigarette, he crushed the butt to powder between his thumb and forefinger, a little habit from those far-off days, and closed his eyes.

The terrible chorus of groans and screams from the minefield could not keep him from sleep. It was the sound of men's voices that woke him. He stood up quickly, instantly alert, and glanced at the sun. It was past noon.

He went to the helicopter and woke the pilot.

'They are coming.'

He took the loudhailer from its clamp on the bulkhead and waited in the open hatchway until the first of them came out from amongst the trees, and he looked at them with amused contempt.

'Baboons!' he murmured, with the disdain of the educated man for the peasant, of one African for another of a different tribe.

They came in a long file, following the elephant trail. Two or three hundred, dressed in animal-skin cloaks and ragged western cast-offs, the men leading and the women bringing up the rear. Many of the women were bare-

9

breasted, and some of them were young with a saucy tilt to the head and a lyrical swing of round buttocks under brief animal-tail kilts. As the denim-clad officer watched them, his contempt changed to appreciation: perhaps he would find time for one of them later, he thought, and put his hand into the pocket of his jeans at the thought. They lined the edge of the minefield, jabbering and screeching with delight, some of them capering and giggling and pointing out to each other the masses of great stricken beasts.

The officer let them vent their glee. They had earned this pause for self-congratulation. They had been eight days on the trail, almost without rest, acting in shifts as beaters to drive the elephant herd down the escarpment. While he waited for them to quieten, he considered again the personal magnetism and force of character that could weld this mob of primitive illiterate peasants into a cohesive and effective whole. One man had engineered the entire operation.

'He is a man!' the officer nodded, then roused himself from the indulgence of hero-worship and lifted the trumpet of the loudhailer to his lips.

'Be quiet! Silence!' He stilled them, and began to allocate the work that must be done.

He picked the butcher gangs from those who were armed with axe and panga. He set the women to building the smoking racks and plaiting baskets of mopani bark, others he ordered to gather wood for the fires. Then he turned his attention back to the butchers.

None of the tribesmen had ever ridden in an aircraft and the officer had to use the pointed toe of his western boot to persuade the first of them to climb into the hatch for the short hop over the mine-sown strip to the nearest carcass.

Leaning out of the hatchway, the officer peered down at the old bull. He appraised the thick curved ivory, and then saw that the beast had bled to death during the waiting hours, and he signalled the pilot lower.

He placed his lips close to the eldest tribesman's ear.

'Let not your feet touch the earth, on your life!' he shouted, and the man nodded jerkily. 'The tusks first, then the meat.'

The man nodded again.

The officer slapped his shoulder and the elder jumped down onto the bull's belly that was already swelling with fermenting gases. He balanced agilely upon it. The rest of his gang, clutching their axes, followed him down.

At the officer's hand signal the helicopter rose and darted like a dragonfly to the next animal that showed good ivory from the lip. This one was still alive, and heaved itself into a sitting position, reaching up with bloody dust-smeared trunk to try and pluck the hovering helicopter from the air.

Braced in the hatch, the officer sighted down the AK 47 and fired a single shot into the back of the neck where it joined the skull, and the cow collapsed and lay as still as the body of her calf beside her. The officer nodded at the leader of the next gang of butchers.

Balanced on the gigantic grey heads, careful not to let a foot touch the earth, the axemen chipped the tusks loose from their castles of white bone. It was delicate work, for a careless stroke could drastically diminish the value of the ivory. They had seen the officer in tie-dyed jeans, with a short, well-timed swing of the rifle-butt, break the jaw of a man who merely queried an order. What would he do with one who ruined a tusk? They worked with care. As the tusks were freed, the helicopter winched them up and then carried the gang to the next carcass.

By nightfall most of the elephant had died of their massive wounds or had been shot to death, but the screams of those who had not yet received the *coup de grâce* mingled with the hubbub of the gathering jackal and hyena packs to make the night hideous. The axemen worked on by the light of grass torches, and by the first light of dawn all the ivory had been gathered in.

Now the axemen could turn their attention to butchering and dismembering the carcasses. The rising heat worked more swiftly than they could. The stench of putrefying flesh mingled with the gases from ruptured entrails and drove the skulking scavengers to fresh paroxysms of gluttonous anticipation. The helicopter carried each haunch or shoulder as it was hacked free to the safe ground beyond the minefield. The women cut the meat into strips and festooned it on the smoking racks above the smouldering fires of green wood.

While he supervised the work, the officer was calculating the spoils. It was a pity they could not save the hides, for each was worth a thousand dollars, but they were too bulky and could not be sufficiently preserved, putrefaction would render them worthless. On the other hand, mild putrefaction would give the meat more zest on the African palate – in the same way that an Englishman enjoys his game high.

Five hundred tons of wet meat would lose half its weight in the drying process, but the copper mines of neighbouring Zambia with tens of thousands of labourers to feed, were eager markets for proteins. Two dollars a pound for the crudely smoked meat was the price that had already been agreed. That was a million U.S. dollars – and then of course there was the ivory.

The ivory had been ferried by the helicopter half a mile beyond the sprawling camp to a secluded place in the hills. There it had been laid out in rows, and a selected gang set to work removing the fat white coneshaped nerve mass from the hollow end of each tusk and cleansing the ivory of any blood and muck that might betray it to the sensitive nose of an oriental customs officer.

There were four hundred tusks. Some of those taken from immature animals weighed only a few pounds, but the old bull's tusks would go well over eighty pounds apiece. A good average was twenty pounds over the lot. The going price in Hong Kong was a hundred dollars a pound, or a total of eight hundred thousand dollars. The profit on the day's work would be over one million dollars, in a land where the average annual income of each adult male was less than six hundred dollars.

Of course, there had been the other small costs of the operation. One of the axemen had over-balanced and tumbled from his perch on an elephant carcass. He had landed flat on his buttocks, directly on top of an anti-personnel mine.

'Son of a demented baboon.' The officer was still irritated by the man's stupidity. It had held work up for almost an hour while the body was retrieved and prepared for burial.

Another man had lost a foot from an over-zealous axe-stroke, and a dozen others had lesser cuts from swinging pangas. One other man had died during the night with an AK 47 bullet through the belly when he objected to what the officer was doing to his junior wife in the bushes beyond the smoking racks – but when the profit was considered, the costs were small indeed. The comrade commissar would be pleased, and with good reason.

It was the morning of the third day before the team working on the ivory had completed their task to the officer's satisfaction. Then they were sent down the valley to assist at the smoking racks, leaving the ivory camp deserted. There must be no eyes to discover the identity of the important visitor who would come now to inspect the spoils.

He arrived in the helicopter. The officer was standing to attention in the clearing beside the long rows of

13

gleaming ivory. The down-draught of the rotors tore at his jacket, and fluttered the legs of his jeans, but he maintained his rigid stance.

The machine settled to earth and a commanding figure stepped down, a handsome man, straight and strong, with very white square teeth against the dark mahogany of his face, crisp kinky African hair cropped closely to the finely shaped skull. He wore an expensive pearl-grey suit of Italian cut over a white shirt and dark blue tie. His black shoes were hand-made of soft calf.

He held out his hand towards the officer. Immediately the younger man abandoned his respectful pose and ran to him, like a child to its father.

'Comrade Commissar!'

'No! No!' he chided the officer gently, still smiling. 'Not Comrade Commissar any longer, but Comrade Minister now. No longer leader of a bunch of unwashed bush fighters, but Minister of State of a sovereign government.' The minister permitted himself a smile as he surveyed the rows of fresh tusks. 'And the most successful ivory-poacher of all time – is that not true?'

C raig Mellow winced as the cab hit another pothole in the surface of Fifth Avenue just outside the entrance of Bergdorf Goodman. Like most New York cabs, its suspension would have better suited a Sherman tank.

'I've had a softer ride through the Mbabwe depression in a Land-Rover,' Craig thought, and had a sudden nostalgic twinge as he remembered that rutted, tortuous track through the bad lands below the Chobe river, that wide green tributary of the great Zambezi.

That was all so far away and long ago, and he pushed the memory aside and returned to brooding over the sense of slight that he felt at having to ride in a yellow cab to a luncheon meeting with his publisher, and having to pick up the tab for the ride himself. There had been a time when they would have sent a chauffeur-driven limousine for him, and the destination would have been the Four Seasons or La Grenouille, not some pasta joint in the Village. Publishers made these subtle little protests when a writer had not delivered a typescript for three years, and spent more time romancing his stockbroker and ripping it up at Studio 54 than at his typewriter.

'Well, I guess I've got it coming.' Craig pulled a face, reached for a cigarette, and then arrested the movement as he remembered that he had given it up. Instead he pushed the thick dark lock of hair off his forehead and watched the faces of the crowds upon the sidewalk. There had been a time when he found the bustle exciting and stimulating after the silences of the African bush, even the sleazy façades and neon frontings onto the littered streets had been different and intriguing. Now he felt suffocated and claustrophobic, and he longed for a glimpse of open sky, rather than that narrow ribbon that showed between the high tops of the buildings.

The cab braked sharply, interrupting his thoughts, and the driver muttered '16th Street' without looking round.

Craig pushed a ten-dollar bill through the slot in the armoured Perspex screen that protected the driver from his passengers. 'Keep it,' he said, and stepped out onto the sidewalk. He saw the restaurant immediately, all cutey ethnic awnings and straw-covered chianti bottles in the window.

When Craig crossed the sidewalk he moved easily, without trace of a limp, so that nobody watching him would have guessed at his disability. Despite his misgivings, it was cool and clean inside the restaurant and the smell of food was appetizing.

Ashe Levy stood up from a booth at the back of the room and beckoned to him.

'Craig, baby!' He put one arm around Craig's shoulders and patted his cheek paternally. 'You're looking good, you old hound dog, you!'

Ashe cultivated his own eclectic style. His hair was brush-cut and he wore gold-rimmed spectacles. His shirt was striped with a contrasting white collar, platinum cufflinks and tie pin, and brown brogues with a pattern of little holes punched in the toe caps. His jacket was cashmere with narrow lapels. His eyes were very pale, and always focused just a little to one side of Craig's own. Craig knew that he smoked only the very best Tihuana gold.

'Nice place, Ashe. How did you find it?'

'A change from boring old "Seasons",' Ashe grinned slyly, pleased that the gesture of disapproval had been noted. 'Craig, I want you to meet a very talented lady.'

She had been sitting well back in the gloom at the back of the booth, but now she leaned forward and held out her hand. The spotlamp caught the hand, and so it was the first impression that Craig had of her.

The hand was narrow with artistic fingers, but though the nails were scrubbed clean, they were clipped short and unpainted, the skin was tanned to gold with prominent aristocratic veins showing bluish beneath it. The bones were fine, but there were callouses at the base of those long straight fingers – a hand that was accustomed to hard work.

Craig took the hand and felt the strength of it, the softness of the dry cool skin on the back and the rough places on the palm, and he looked into her face.

She had dark thick eyebrows that stretched in an unbroken curve from the outer corner of one eye to the other. Her eyes, even in the poor light, were green with honey-coloured specks surrounding the pupil. Their gaze was direct and candid.

'Sally-Anne Jay,' Ashe said. 'This is Craig Mellow.'

16

Her nose was straight but slightly too large, and her mouth too wide to be beautiful. Her thick dark hair was scraped back severely from the broad forehead, her face was as honey-tanned as her hands and there was a fine peppering of freckles across her cheeks.

'I read your book,' she said. Her voice was level and clear, her accent mid-Atlantic, but only when he heard its timbre did he realize how young she was. 'I thought it deserved everything that happened to it.'

'Compliment or slap?' He tried to make it sound light and unconcerned, but he found himself hoping fervently that she was not one of those who attempted to demonstrate their own exalted literary standards by denigrating a popular writer's work to his face.

'Very good things happened to it,' she pointed out, and Craig felt absurdly pleased, even though that seemed to be the end of that topic as far as she was concerned. To show his pleasure he squeezed her hand and held it a little longer than was necessary, and she took it back from him and replaced it firmly in her lap.

So she wasn't a scalp-hunter, and she wasn't going to gush. Anyway, he told himself, he was bored with literary groupies trying to storm his bed, and gushers were as bad as knockers – almost.

'Let's see if we can get Ashe to buy us a drink,' he suggested, and slipped into the booth facing her across the table.

Ashe made his usual fuss over the wine list, but they ended up with a ten-dollar Frascati after all.

'Nice smooth fruit.' Ashe rolled it on his tongue.

'It's cold and wet,' Craig agreed, and Ashe smiled again as they both remembered the '70 Corton Charlemagne they had drunk the last time.

'We are expecting another guest later,' Ashe told the waiter. 'We'll order then.' And turning to Craig, 'I wanted an opportunity for Sally-Anne to show you her stuff.'

17

'Show me,' Craig invited, immediately defensive once again. The woods were full of them as wanted to ride on his strike – ones with unpublished manuscripts for him to endorse, investment advisers who would look after all those lovely royalties for him, others who would allow him to write their life stories and generously split the profits with him or sell him insurance or a South Sea Island paradise, commission him to write movie scripts for a small advance and an even smaller slice of any profits, all kinds gathering like hyenas to the lion's kill.

Sally-Anne lifted a hard-back portfolio from the floor beside her and placed it on the table in front of Craig. While Ashe adjusted the spotlight, Sally-Anne untied the ribbons that secured the folder and sat back.

Craig opened the cover and went very still. He felt the goose-bumps rise along his forearms, and the hair at the nape of his neck prickle – this was his reaction to greatness, to anything perfectly beautiful. There was a Gauguin in the Metropolitan Museum on Central Park; a Polynesian madonna carrying the Christ child on her shoulder. She had made his hair prickle. There were passages of T.S. Eliot's poetry and of Lawrence Durrell's prose that made his hair prickle every time he read them.

The opening bar of Beethoven's Fifth Symphony; those incredible *jeté* leaps of Rudolph Nureyev, and the way Nicklaus and Borg struck the ball on their good days – those things had made him prickle, and now this girl was doing it to him also.

It was a photograph. The finish was egg-shell grain so every detail was crisp. The colours clear and perfectly true.

It was a photograph of an elephant, an old bull. He faced the camera in the characteristic attitude of alarm, with his ears spread like dark flags. Somehow he portrayed the whole vastness and timelessness of a continent, and yet he was at bay, and one sensed that all his great strength was unavailing, that he was confused by things that were

18

beyond his experience and the trace memories of his ancestors, that he was about to be overwhelmed by change – like Africa itself.

With him in the photograph was shown the land, the rich red earth riven by wind, baked by sun, ruined by drought. Craig could almost taste the dust on his tongue. Then, over it all, the limitless sky, containing the promise of succour, the silver cumulo-nimbus piled like a snow-clad mountain range, bruised with purple and royal blue, pierced by a single beam of light from a hidden sun that fell on the old bull like a benediction.

She had captured the meaning and the mystery of his native land in the one hundredth of a second that it took the lens shutter to open and close again, while he had laboured for long agonizing months and not come anywhere near it, and secretly recognizing his failure was afraid to try again. He took a sip of the insipid wine that had been offered to him as a rebuke for this crisis of confidence in his own ability, and now the wine had a quinine after-taste that he had not noticed before.

'Where are you from?' he asked the girl, without looking at her.

'Denver, Colorado,' she said. 'But my father has been with the Embassy in London for years. I did most of my schooling in England.' That accounted for the accent. 'I went to Africa when I was eighteen, and fell in love with it,' she completed her life story simply.

It took a physical effort for Craig to touch the photograph and gently turn it face down. Beneath it was another of a young woman seated on a black lava rock beside a desert waterhole. She wore the distinctive leather bunny-ears headdress of the Ovahimba tribe. Her child stood beside her and nursed from her naked breast. The woman's skin was polished with fat and ochre. Her eyes were those from a fresco in a Pharaoh's tomb, and she was beautiful.

'Denver, Colorado, forsooth!' Craig thought and was

19

surprised at his own bitterness, at the depths of his sudden resentment. How dare a damned foreign girl-child encapsulate so unerringly the complex spirit of a people in this portrait of a young woman. He had lived all his life with them and yet never seen an African so clearly as at this moment in an Italian restaurant in Greenwich Village.

He turned the photograph with a suppressed violence. Beneath it was a view into the trumpet-shaped throat of the magnificent maroon and gold bloom of *kigelia Africana*, Craig's favourite wild flower. In the lustrous depths of the flower nestled a tiny beetle like a precious emerald, shiny iridescent green. It was a perfect arrangement of shape and colour, and he found he hated her for it.

There were many others. One of a grinning lout of a militia man with an AK 47 rifle on his shoulder and a necklace of cured human ears around his neck, a caricature of savagery and arrogance; another of a wrinkled witch-doctor hung with horns and beads and skulls and all the grisly accoutrements of his trade, his patient stretched out on the bare, dusty earth before him in the process of being crudely cupped, her blood making shiny dark serpents across her dark skin. The patient was a woman in her prime with patterns of tattoos on her breasts and cheeks and forehead. Her teeth were filed to points like those of a shark, a relic of the days of cannibalism, and her eyes, like those of a suffering animal, seemed filled with all the stoicism and patience of Africa.

Then there was another contrasting photograph of African children in a school-room of poles and rude thatch. They shared a single reader between three of them, but all their hands were raised eagerly to the young black teacher's questions and all their faces lit by the burning desire for knowledge – it was all there, a complete record of hope and despair, of abject poverty and great riches, of savagery and tenderness, of unrelenting elements and bursting fruitfulness, of pain and gentle humour. Craig could not bring himself to look at her again and he turned the stiff glossy sheets slowly, savouring each image and delaying the moment when he must face her.

Craig stopped suddenly, struck by a particularly poignant composition, an orchard of bleached bones. She had used black and white to heighten the dramatic effect, and the bones shone in the brilliant African sunlight, acres of bones, great femur and tibia bleached like driftwood, huge rib-cages like the frames of stranded ocean clippers, and skulls the size of beer barrels with dark caves for eye-sockets. Craig thought of the legendary elephant's graveyard, the old hunters' myth of the secret place where the elephants go to die.

'Poachers,' she said. 'Two hundred and eighty-six carcasses,' and now Craig looked up at her at last, startled by the number.

'At one time?' he asked, and she nodded.

'They drove them into one of the old minefields.'

Involuntarily, Craig shuddered and looked down at the photograph again. Under the table-top his right hand ran down his thigh until he felt the neat strap that held his leg, and he experienced a choking empathy for the fate of those great pachyderms. He remembered his own minefield, and felt again the slamming impact of the explosion into his foot, as though he had been hit by the full swing of a sledgehammer.

'I'm sorry,' she said softly. 'I know about your leg.'

'She does her homework,' Ashe said.

'Shut up,' Craig thought furiously. 'Why don't you both shut up.' He hated anyone to mention the leg. If she had truly done her homework, she would have known that – but it was not only mention of the leg, it was the elephants also. Once Craig had worked as a ranger in the game department. He knew them, had come to love them, and the evidence of this slaughter sickened and appalled him. It increased his resentment of the girl; she had inflicted

21

this upon him and he wanted to revenge himself; a childish urge to retaliate. But before he could do it, the late guest arrived, diverting them into a round of Ashe's introductions.

'Craig, I want you to meet a special sort of guy.' All of Ashe's introductions came with a built-in commercial. 'This is Henry Pickering. Henry is a senior vice-president of the World Bank – listen and you'll hear all those billions of dollars clashing around in his head. Henry, this is Craig Mellow, our boy genius. Not even excluding Karen Blixen, Craig is just one of the most important writers ever to come out of Africa, that's all he is!'

'I read the book,' Henry nodded. He was very tall and thin and prematurely bald. He wore a dark banker's suit and stark white shirt, with a little individual touch of colour in his necktie and twinkly blue eyes. 'For once you are probably not exaggerating, Ashe.'

He kissed Sally-Anne's cheek platonically, sat down, tasted the wine that Ashe poured for him and pushed the glass back an inch. Craig found himself admiring his style.

'What do you think?' Henry Pickering asked Craig, glancing down at the open portfolio of photographs.

'He loves them, Henry,' Ashe Levy cut in swiftly. 'He's ape over them – I wish you could have seen his face when he got his first look – loves them, man, loves them!'

'Good,' Henry said softly, watching Craig's face. 'Have you explained the concept?'

'I wanted to serve it up hot.' Ashe Levy shook his head. 'I wanted to hit him with it.'

He turned to Craig.

'A book,' he said. 'It's about a book. The title of the book is "Craig Mellow's Africa". What happens is you write about the Africa of your ancestors, about what it was and what it has become. You go back and you do an in-depth assessment. You speak to the people—'

'Excuse me,' Henry interrupted him, 'I understand that

you speak one of the two major languages – Sindebele, isn't it – of Zimbabwe?'

'Fluently,' Ashe answered for Craig. 'Like one of them.'

'Good,' Henry nodded. 'Is it true that you have many friends – some highly placed in government?'

Ashe fielded the question again. 'Some of his old buddies are cabinet ministers in the Zimbabwe government. You can't go much higher.'

Craig dropped his eyes to the photograph of the elephant graveyard. 'Zimbabwe,' he was not yet comfortable with the new name that the black victors had chosen. He still thought of it as Rhodesia. That was the country his ancestors had hacked out of the wilderness with pick and axe and Maxim machine-gun. Their land, once his land – by any name still his home.

'It's going to be top quality, Craig, no expense spared. You can go where you want to, speak to anybody, the World Bank will see to that, and pay for it.' Ashe Levy was running on enthusiastically, and Craig looked up at Henry Pickering.

'The World Bank – publishing?' Craig asked sardonically, and when Ashe would have replied again, Henry Pickering laid a restraining hand on his forearm.

'I'll take the ball a while, Ashe,' he said. He had sensed Craig's mood; his tone was gentle and placatory. 'The main part of our business is loans to underdeveloped countries. We have almost a billion invested in Zimbabwe. We want to protect our investment. Think of it as a prospectus, we want the world to know about the little African state that we would like to turn into a showpiece, an example of how a black government can succeed. We think your book could help do that for us.'

'And these?' Craig touched the pile of photographs.

'We want the book to have visual as well as intellectual impact. We think Sally-Anne can provide that.'

Craig was quiet for many seconds while he felt the

terror slither around deep inside him, like some loathsome reptile. The terror of failure. Then he thought about having to compete with these photographs, of having to provide a text that would not be swamped by the awesome view through this girl's lens. He had a reputation at stake, and she had nothing to lose. The odds were all with her. She was not an ally but an adversary, and his resentment came back in full force, so strong that it was a kind of hatred.

She was leaning towards him across the table, the spotlight catching her long eyelashes and framing those green-flecked eyes. Her mouth was quivering with eagerness, and a tiny bubble of saliva like a seed pearl sparkled on her lower lip. Even in his anger and fear, Craig wondered what it would be like to kiss that mouth.

'Craig,' she said. 'I can do better than those if I have the chance. I can go all the way, if you give me the chance. Please!'

'You like elephants?' Craig asked her. 'I'll tell you an elephant story. This big old bull elephant had a flea that lived in his left ear. One day the elephant crossed a rickety bridge, and when he got to the other side, the flea said in his ear, "Hoo boy! We sure rocked that bridge!"'

Sally-Anne's lips closed slowly and then paled. Her eyelids fluttered, the dark lashes beating like butterflies' wings, and as the tears began to sparkle behind them she leaned back out of the light.

There was a silence, and in it Craig felt a rush of remorse. He felt sickened by his own cruelty and pettiness. He had expected her to be tough and resilient, to come back with a barbed retort. He had not expected the tears. He wanted to comfort her, to tell her that he didn't mean it the way it sounded. He wanted to explain his own fear and insecurity, but she was rising and picking up the folio of photographs.

'Parts of your book were so understanding, so compassionate, I wanted so badly to work with you,' she said softly. 'I guess it was dumb to expect you to be like your book.' She looked at Ashe. 'I'm sorry, Ashe, I'm just not hungry any more.'

Ashe Levy stood quickly. 'We'll share a cab,' he said. Then softly to Craig, 'Well done, hero, call me when you've got the new typescript finished,' and he hurried after Sally-Anne. As she went through the door the sunlight back-lit her and Craig saw the shape of her legs through her skirt. They were long and lovely, and then she was gone.

Henry Pickering was fiddling with his glass, studying the wine thoughtfully.

'It's pasteurized Roman goat urine,' Craig said. He found his voice was uneven. He signalled the wine waiter and ordered a Meursault.

'That's better,' Henry understated it. 'Well, perhaps the book wasn't such a great idea after all, was it?' He glanced at his wrist-watch. 'We'd better order.'

They talked of other things – the Mexican loan default, Reagan's mid-term assessment, the gold price – Henry preferred silver for a quick appreciation and thought diamonds would soon be looking good again. 'I'd buy De Beers to hold,' he advised.

A svelte young blonde from one of the other tables came across while they were taking coffee.

'You're Craig Mellow,' she accused him. 'I saw you on TV. I loved your book. Please, please, sign this for me.'

While he signed her menu, she leaned over him and pressed one hard hot little breast against his shoulder.

'I work at the cosmetics counter in Saks Fifth Ave,' she breathed. 'You can find me there any time.' The odour of expensive, pilfered perfumes lingered after she had left.

'Do you always turn them away?' Henry asked a little wistfully.

25

'Man is only flesh and blood,' Craig laughed, and Henry insisted on paying the tab.

'I have a limo,' he offered. 'I could drop you.'

'I'll walk off the pasta,' Craig said.

'Do you know, Craig, I think you'll go back to Africa. I saw the way you looked at those photographs. Like a hungry man.'

'It's possible.'

'The book. Our interest in it. There was more to it than Ashe understood. You know the top blacks there. That interests me. The ideas you expressed in the book fit into our thinking. If you do decide to go back, call me before you do. You and I could do each other a favour.'

Henry climbed into the back seat of the black Cadillac, and then with the door still open he said, 'I thought her pictures were rather good, actually.' He closed the door and nodded to the chauffeur.

*B*awu was moored between two new commercially built yachts, a forty-five-foot Camper and Nicholson and a Hatteras convertible, and she stood the comparison well enough, although she was almost five years old. Craig had put in every screw with his own hands. He paused at the gates of the marina to look at her, but somehow today he did not derive as much pleasure as usual from her lines.

'Been a couple of calls for you, Craig,' the girl behind the reception desk in the marina office called out to him as he went in. 'You can use this phone,' she offered.

He checked the slips she handed him, one from his broker marked 'urgent', another from the literary editor of a mid-western daily. There hadn't been too many of those recently.

He phoned the broker first. They had sold the Mocatta

gold certificates that he had bought for three hundred and twenty dollars an ounce at five hundred and two dollars. He instructed them to put the money on call deposit.

Then he dialled the second number. While he waited to be connected, the girl behind the desk moved around more than was really necessary, bending over the lowest drawers of the filing-cabinet to give Craig a good look at what she had in her white Bermudas and pink halter-top.

When Craig connected with the literary editor, she wanted to know when they were publishing his new book.

'What book?' Craig thought bitterly, but he answered, 'We haven't got a firm date yet – but it's in the pipeline. Do you want to do an interview in the meantime?'

'Thanks, but we will wait until publication, Mr Mellow.'

'Long wait, my darling,' Craig thought, and when he hung up the girl looked up brightly.

'The party is on *Firewater* tonight.'

There was a party on one of the yachts every single night of the year.

'Are you coming across?'

She had a flat tight belly between the shorts and top. Without the glasses, she might be quite pretty – and what the hell, he had just made a quarter of a million dollars on the gold certificates and a fool of himself at the lunch table.

'I'm having a private party on *Bawu*,' he said, 'for two.' She had been a good patient girl and her time had come.

Her face lit up so he saw he had been right. She really was quite pretty. 'I finish in here at five.'

'I know,' he said. 'Come straight down.'

Wipe one out and make another happy, he thought. It should even out, but of course it didn't.

Craig lay on his back under a single sheet in the wide bunk with both hands behind his head and listened to the small sounds in the night, the creak of the rudder in its restrainer, the tap of a halyard against the mast and the slap of wavelets under the hull. Across the basin the party on *Firewater* was still in full swing, there was a faint splash and a distant burst of drunken laughter as they threw somebody overboard, and beside him the girl made regular little wet fluttering sounds through her lips as she slept.

She had been eager and very practised, but nevertheless Craig felt unrequited and restless. He wanted to go up on deck, but that would have disturbed the girl and he knew she would still be eager and he could not be bothered further. So he lay and let the images from Sally-Anne's portfolio run through his head like a magic-lantern show, and they triggered others that had long lain dormant but now came back to him fresh and vivid, accompanied by the smells and tastes and sounds of Africa, so that instead of the revels of drunken yachties, he heard again the beat of native drums along the Chobe river in the night; instead of the sour waters of the East river he smelled tropical raindrops on baked earth, and he began to ache with the bitter-sweet melancholy of nostalgia and he did not sleep again that night.

The girl insisted on making breakfast for him. She did so with not nearly the same expertise as she had made love, and after she had gone ashore it took him nearly an hour to clean up the galley. Then he went up to the saloon.

He drew the curtain across the porthole above his navigation and writing desk, so as not to be distracted by the activities of the marina, and settled down to work. He re-read the last batch of ten pages, and realized he would be lucky if he could salvage two of them. He set to it grimly and the characters baulked and said trite asinine

28

things. After an hour he reached up for his thesaurus from the shelf beside his desk to find an alternative word.

'Good Lord, even I know that people don't say "pusillanimous" in real conversation,' he muttered as he brought down the volume, and then paused as a slim sheaf of folded writing-paper fluttered out from between the pages.

Secretly welcoming the excuse to break off the struggle, he unfolded it, and with a little jolt discovered it was a letter from a girl called Janine – a girl who had shared with him the agonies of their war wounds, who had travelled with him the long slow road to recovery, had been at his side when he walked again for the first time after losing the leg, had spelled him at the helm when they sailed *Bawu* through her first Atlantic gale. A girl whom he had loved and almost married, and whose face he now had the greatest difficulty recalling.

Janine had written the letter from her home in Yorkshire, three days before she married the veterinary surgeon who was a junior partner in her father's practice. He re-read the letter slowly, all ten pages of it, and realized why he had hidden it away from himself. Janine was only bitter in patches, but some of the other things she wrote cut deeply.

' – You had been a failure so often and for so long that your sudden success clean bowled you—'

He checked at that. What else had he ever done besides the book – that one single book? And she had given him the answer.

' – You were so innocent and gentle, Craig, so lovable in a gawky boyish way. I wanted to live with that, but after we left Africa it dried up slowly, you started becoming hard and cynical—'

' – Do you remember the very first day we met, or almost the very first, I said to you, "You are a spoilt little boy, and you just give up on everything worthwhile"? Well, it's true, Craig. You gave up on our relationship. I don't just mean the other little dolly-birds, the literary scalp-hunters with no elastic in their drawers, I mean you gave up on the caring. Let me give you a little advice for free, don't give up on the only thing that you've ever done well, don't give up on the writing, Craig. That would be truly sinful—'

He remembered how haughtily he had scoffed at that notion when he had first read it. He didn't scoff now – he was too afraid. It was happening to him, just as she had predicted.

'I truly came to love you, Craig, not all at once, but little by little. You had to work very hard to destroy that. I don't love you any more, Craig, I doubt I'll ever love another man, not even the one I'll marry on Saturday – but I like you, and I always will. I wish you well, but beware of your most implacable enemy – yourself.'

Craig refolded the letter, and he wanted a drink. He went down to the galley and poured a Bacardi – a large one, easy on the lime. While he drank it he re-read the letter and this time a single phrase struck him.

'After we left Africa it seemed to dry up inside you – the understanding, the genius.'

'Yes,' he whispered. 'It dried up. It all dried up.'

Suddenly his nostalgia became the unbearable ache of homesickness. He had lost his way, the fountain in him had dried up, and he wanted to go back to the source.

He tore the letter to tiny pieces and dropped them into the scummy waters of the basin, left the empty glass on the coamings of the hatch and crossed the gangplank to the jetty.

He didn't want to have to talk to the girl, so he used the pay phone at the gate of the marina.

It was easier than he expected. The girl on the switchboard put him through to Henry Pickering's secretary.

'I'm not sure that Mr Pickering is available. Who is calling, please?'

30

'Craig Mellow.' Pickering came on almost immediately.

'There is an old Matabele saying, "The man who drinks Zambezi waters must always return to drink again",' Craig told him.

'So you're thirsty,' Pickering said. 'I guessed that.'

'You said to call you.'

'Come and see me.'

'Today?' Craig asked.

'Hey, fellow, you're hot to trot! Hold on, let me check my diary – what about six o'clock this evening? That's the soonest I can work it in.'

Henry's office was on the twenty-sixth floor and the tall windows faced up the deep sheer crevasses of the avenues to the expansive green swathe of Central Park in the distance.

Henry poured Craig a whisky and soda and brought it to him at the window. They stood looking down into the guts of the city and drinking in silence, while the big red ball of the sun threw weird shadows through the purpling dusk.

'I think it's time to stop being cute, Henry,' Craig said at last. 'Tell me what you really want from me.'

'Perhaps you're right,' Henry agreed. 'The book was a little bit of a cover-up. Not really fair – although, speaking personally, I'd like to have seen your words with her pictures—'

Craig made an impatient little gesture, and Henry went on.

'I am vice-president in charge of the Africa division.'

'I saw your title on the door,' Craig nodded.

'Despite what a lot of our critics say, we aren't a charitable institution, we are one of the bulwarks of capitalism. Africa is a continent of economically fragile states. With the obvious exceptions of South Africa and the oil-producers further north, they are mostly subsistence agricultural societies, with no industrial backbone and very few mineral resources.'

31

Craig nodded again.

'Some of those who have recently achieved their independence from the old colonial system are still benefiting from the infrastructure built up by the white settlers, while most of the others – Zambia and Tanzania and Maputo, for instance – have had long enough to let it run down into a chaos of lethargy and ideological fantasy. They are going to be hard to save.' Henry shook his head mournfully and looked even more like an undertaker stork. 'But with others, like Zimbabwe, Kenya and Malawi, we have got a fighting chance. The system is still working, as yet the farms haven't been totally decimated and handed over to hordes of peasant squatters, the railroads work, there are some foreign exchange earnings from copper and chrome and tourism. We can keep them going, with a little luck.'

'Why bother?' Craig asked. 'I mean you said you are not in the charity game, so why bother?'

'Because if we don't feed them, then sooner or later we are going to have to fight them, it's as simple as that. If they begin to starve, guess into whose big red paws they are going to fall.'

'Yes. You're making sense.' Craig sipped his whisky.

'Returning to earth for a moment,' Henry went on, 'the countries on our shortlist have one exploitable asset, nothing tangible like gold, but many times more valuable. They are attractive to tourists from the west. If we are ever going to see any interest on the billions that we have got tied up in them, then we are going to have to make good and sure that they stay attractive.'

'How do you do that?' Craig turned to him.

'Let's take Kenya as an example,' Henry suggested. 'Sure it's got sunshine and beaches, but then so have Greece and Sardinia, and they are a hell of a lot closer to Paris and Berlin. What the Mediterranean hasn't got is African wildlife, and that's what the tourists will fly those extra

32

hours to see, and that's the collateral on our loan. Tourist dollars are keeping us in business.'

'Okay, but I don't see how I come in,' Craig frowned.

'Wait for it, we'll get there in time,' Henry told him. 'Let me lay it out a little first. It's like this – unfortunately, the very first thing that the newly independent black African sees when he looks around after the white man flies out is ivory and rhinoceros horn and meat on the hoof. One rhinoceros or bull elephant represents more wealth than he could earn in ten years of honest labour. For fifty years a white-run game department has protected all these marvellous riches, but now the whites have run to Australia or Johannesburg; an Arab sheikh will pay twenty-five thousand dollars for a dagger with a genuine rhinoceros-horn handle and the victorious guerrilla fighter has an AK 47 rifle in his hands. It's all very logical.'

'Yes, I've seen it,' Craig nodded.

'We had the same thing in Kenya. Poaching was big business and it was run from the top. I mean the very top. It took us fifteen years and the death of a president to break it up. Now Kenya has the strictest game laws in Africa – and, more important, they are being enforced. We had to use all our influence. We even had to threaten to pull the plug, but now our investment is protected.' Henry looked smug for a moment, then his melancholia overwhelmed him again. 'Now we have to travel exactly the same road again in Zimbabwe. You saw those photographs of the kill in the minefield. It's being organized again, and once again we suspect it's somebody in a very high place. We have to stop it.'

'I'm still waiting to hear how it affects me.'

'I need an agent in the field. Somebody with experience – perhaps even somebody who once worked in the game and wildlife department, somebody who speaks the local language, who has a legitimate excuse for moving around and asking questions – perhaps an author researching a new book, who has contacts high up in government. Of course, if my agent had an international reputation, it would open even more doors, and if he were a dedicated proponent of the capitalist system and truly believed in what we are doing, he would be totally effective.'

'James Bond, me?'

'Field investigator for the World Bank. The pay is forty thousand dollars a year, plus expenses and a lot of job-satisfaction, and if there isn't a book in it at the end, I'll stand you to lunch at La Grenouille with the wine of your choice.'

'Like I said at the beginning, Henry, isn't it time to stop being cute and level with me completely?'

It was the first time Craig had heard Henry laugh, and it was infectious, a warm, throaty chuckle.

'Your perception confirms the wisdom of my choice. All right, Craig, there is a little more to it. I didn't want to make it too complicated – not until you had got your feet wet first. Let me freshen your drink.'

He went to the cocktail cabinet in the shape of an antique globe of the world, and while he clinked ice on glass he went on.

'It is vitally important for us to have a complete picture of what's going on below the surface in all of the countries in which we have an involvement. In other words, a functioning intelligence system. Our set-up in Zimbabwe isn't nearly as effective as I'd like it to be. We have lost a key man lately – motor car accident – or that's what it looked like. Before he went, he gave us a hint – he had picked up the rumours of a *coup d'état* backed by the Ruskies.'

Craig sighed. 'We Africans don't really put much store in the ballot box any more. The only things that count are tribal loyalties and a strong arm. *Coup d'état* makes better sense than votes.'

34

'Are you on the team?' Henry wanted to know.

'I take it that "expenses" include first-class air tickets?' Craig demanded wickedly.

'Every man has his price,' Henry darted back, 'is that yours?'

'I don't come that cheap,' Craig shook his head, 'but I'd hate like hell to have a Soviet stooge running the land where my leg is buried. I'll take the job.'

'Thought you might.' Henry offered his hand. It was cool and startlingly powerful. 'I'll send a courier down to your yacht with a file and a survival kit. Read the file while the courier waits and send it back. Keep the kit.'

Henry Pickering's survival kit contained an assortment of press cards, a membership of the TWA Ambassadors Club, an unlimited World Bank Visa credit card, and an ornate metal and enamel star in a leather case embossed 'Field Assessor – World Bank'.

Craig weighed it in his palm. 'You could beat a man-eating lion to death with it,' he muttered. 'I don't know what else it will be good for.'

The file was a great deal more rewarding. When he finished reading it, he realized that the alteration of name from Rhodesia to Zimbabwe was probably one of the least drastic changes that had swept over the land of his birth since he had left it just a few short years before.

C raig nursed the hired Volkswagen over the undulating golden grass-clad hills, using an educated foot on the throttle. The Matabele girl at the Avis desk at the Bulawayo airport had cautioned him.

'The tank is full, sir, but I don't know when you will get another tankful. There is very little gasoline in Matabeleland.'

In the town itself he had seen the vehicles parked in

long queues at the filling-stations, and the proprietor of the motel had briefed Craig as he signed the register and picked up the keys to one of the bungalows.

'The Maputo rebels keep hitting the pipeline from the east coast. The hell of it is that just across the border the South Africans have got it all and they are happy to deal, but our bright laddies don't want politically tainted gas, so the whole country grinds to a halt. A plague on political dreams – to exist we have to deal with them and it's about time they accepted that.'

So now Craig drove with care, and the gentle pace suited him. It gave him time to examine the familiar countryside, and to assess the changes that a few short years had wrought.

He turned off the main macadamized road fifteen miles out of town, and took the yellow dirt road to the north. Within a mile he reached the boundary, and saw immediately that the gate hung at a drunken angle and was wide open – the first time he had ever seen it that way. He parked and tried to close it behind him, but the frame was buckled and the hinges had rusted. He abandoned the effort and left the road to examine the sign that lay in the grass.

The sign had been pulled down, the retaining bolts ripped clear out. It lay face up, and though sun-faded, it was still legible:

> King's Lynn Afrikander Stud
> Home of 'Ballantyne's Illustrious IV'
> Grand Champion of Champions.
> Proprietor: Jonathan Ballantyne.

Craig had a vivid mental image of the huge red beast with its humped back and swinging dewlap waddling under its own weight of beef around the show-ring with the blue rosette of the champion on its cheek, and

Jonathan 'Bawu' Ballantyne, Craig's maternal grandfather, leading it proudly by the brass ring through its shiny wet nostrils.

Craig walked back to the VW and drove on through grassland that had once been thick and gold and sweet, but through which the bare dusty earth now showed like the balding scalp of a middle-aged man. He was distressed by the condition of the grazing. Never, not even in the four-year drought of the fifties, had King's Lynn grass been allowed to deteriorate like this, and Craig could find no reason for it until he stopped again beside a clump of camel-thorn trees that threw their shade over the road.

When he switched off the engine, he heard the bleating amongst the camel-thorns and now he was truly shocked.

'Goats!' he spoke aloud. 'They are running goats on King's Lynn.' Bawu Ballantyne's ghost must be without rest or peace. Goats on his beloved grassland. Craig went to look for them. There were two hundred or more in one herd. Some of the agile multi-coloured animals had climbed high into the trees and were eating bark and seed-pods, while others were cropping the grass down to the roots so that it would die and the soil would sour. Craig had seen the devastation that these animals had created in the tribal trustlands.

There were two naked Matabele boys with the herd. They were delighted when Craig spoke to them in their own language. They stuffed the cheap candy that he had brought with him for just such a meeting into their cheeks, and chattered without inhibition.

Yes, there were thirty families living on King's Lynn now, and each family had its herd of goats – the finest goats in Matabeleland, they boasted through sticky lips, and under the trees a horned old billy mounted a young nanny with a vigorous humping of his back. 'See!' cried the herdboys, 'they breed with a will. Soon we will have more goats than any of the other families.'

'What has happened to the white farmers that lived here?' Craig asked.

'Gone!' they told him proudly. 'Our warriors drove them back to where they came from and now the land belongs to the children of the revolution.'

They were six years old, but still they had the revolutionary cant word-perfect.

Each of the children had a slingshot made from old rubber tubing hanging from his neck, and around his naked waist a string of birds that he had killed with the slingshot: larks and warblers and jewelled sunbirds. Craig knew that for their noon meal they would cook them whole on a bed of coals, simply letting the feathers sizzle off and devouring the tiny blackened carcasses with relish. Old Bawu Ballantyne would have strapped any herdboy that he caught with a slingshot.

The herdboys followed Craig back to the road, begged another piece of candy from him and waved him away like an old dear friend. Despite the goats and songbirds, Craig felt again the overwhelming affection for these people. They were, after all, his people and it was good to be home again.

He stopped again on the crest of the hills and looked down on the homestead of King's Lynn. The lawns had died from lack of attention, and the goats had been in the flower-beds. Even at this distance, Craig could see the main house was deserted. Windows were broken, leaving unsightly gaps like missing teeth, and most of the asbestos sheets had been stolen from the roof and the roof-timbers were forlorn and skeletal against the sky. The roofing sheets had been used to build ramshackle squatters' shacks down near the old cattle-pens.

Craig drove down and parked beside the dip tank. The tank was dry, and half-filled with dirt and rubbish. He went past it to the squatters' encampment. There were half a dozen families living here. Craig scattered the yapping cur dogs that rushed out at him with a few well-aimed stones, then he greeted the old man who sat at one of the fires.

'I see you, old father.' Again there was delight at his command of the language. He sat at the fire for an hour, chatting with the old Matabele, the words coming more and more readily to his tongue and his ear tuning to the rhythm and nuances of Sindebele. He learned more than he had in the four days since he had been back in Matabeleland.

'They told us that after the revolution every man would have a fine motor-car, and five hundred head of the best white man's cattle.' The old man spat into the fire. 'The only ones with motor-cars are the government ministers. They told us we would always have full bellies, but food costs five times what it did before Smith and the white men ran away. Everything costs five times more – sugar and salt and soap – everything.'

During the white regime a ferocious foreign exchange control system and a rigid internal price control structure had isolated the country from the worst effects of inflation, but now they were experiencing all the joys of re-entering the international community, and the local currency had already been devalued twenty per cent.

'We cannot afford cattle,' the old man explained, 'so we run goats. Goats!' He spat again into the fire and watched his phlegm sizzle. 'Goats! Like dirt-eating Shona.' His tribal hatred boiled like his spittle.

Craig left him muttering and frowning over the smoky fire and walked up to the house. As he climbed the steps to the wide front veranda, he had a weird premonition that his grandfather would suddenly come out to meet him with some tart remark. In his mind's eye he saw again the old man, dapper and straight, with thick silver hair, skin like tanned leather and impossibly green Ballantyne eyes, standing before him.

'Home again, Craig, dragging your tail behind you!'

However, the veranda was littered with rubble and bird-droppings from the wild pigeons that roosted undisturbed in the rafters.

He picked his way along the veranda to the double doors that led into the old library. There had been two huge elephant tusks framing this doorway, the bull which Craig's great-great-grandfather had shot back in the 1860s. Those tusks were family heirlooms, and had always guarded the entrance to King's Lynn. Old grandpa Bawu had touched them each time he passed, so that there had been a polished spot on the yellow ivory. Now there were only the holes in the masonry from which the bolts holding the ivory had been torn. The only family relics he had inherited and still owned were the collection of leather-bound family journals, the laboriously hand-written records of his ancestors from the arrival of his great-great-grandfather in Africa over a hundred years before. The tusks would complement the old books. He would search for them, he promised himself. Surely such rare treasures must be traceable.

He went into the derelict house. The shelving and built-in cupboards and floor-boards had been stripped out by the squatters in the valley for firewood, the window-panes used as targets by small black boys with slingshots. The books, the portrait photographs from the walls, the carpets and heavy furniture of Rhodesian teak were all gone. The homestead was a shell, but a sturdy shell. With an open palm Craig slapped the walls that great-great-grandfather Zouga Ballantyne had built of hand-hewn stone and mortar that had had almost a hundred years to cure to adamantine hardness. His palm made a solid ringing tone. It would take only a little imagination and a deal of money to transform the shell into a magnificent home once again.

Craig left the house and climbed the kopje behind it to

the walled family cemetery that lay under the msasa trees beneath the rocky crest. There was grass growing up between the headstones. The cemetery had been neglected but not vandalized, as had many of the other monuments left from the colonial era.

Craig sat on the edge of his grandfather's grave and said, 'Hello, Bawu. I'm back,' and started as he almost heard the old man's voice full of mock scorn speaking in his mind.

'Yes, every time you burn your arse you come running back here. What happened this time?'

'I dried up, Bawu,' he answered the accusation aloud and then was silent. He sat for a long time and very slowly he felt the tumult within him begin to subside a little.

'The place is in a hell of a mess, Bawu,' he spoke again, and the little blue-headed lizard on the old man's head-stone scuttled away at the sound of his voice. 'The tusks are gone from the veranda, and they are running goats on your best grass.'

Again he was silent, but now he was beginning to calculate and scheme. He sat for nearly an hour, and then stood up.

'Bawu, how would you like it if I could move the goats off your pasture?' he asked, and walked back down the hill to where he had left the Volkswagen.

I t was a little before five o'clock when he drove back into town. The estate agency and auctioneering floor opposite the Standard Bank was still open for business. The sign had even been repainted in scarlet, and as soon as Craig entered, he recognized the burly red-faced auction-eer in khaki shorts and short-sleeved, open-necked shirt.

'So you didn't take the gap, like the rest of us did, Jock,' Craig greeted Jock Daniels.

'Taking the gap' was the derogatory expression for

emigrating. Out of 250,000 white Rhodesians, almost 150,000 had taken the gap since the beginning of hostilities, and most of those had left since the war had been lost and the black government of Robert Mugabe had taken control.

Jock stared at him. 'Craig!' he exploded. 'Craig Mellow!' He took Craig's hand in a horny brown paw. 'No, I stayed, but sometimes it gets hellish lonely. But you've done well, by God you have. They say in the papers that you have made a million out of that book. People here could hardly believe it. Old Craig Mellow, they said, fancy Craig Mellow of all people.'

'Is that what they said?' Craig's smile stiffened, and he took his hand back.

'Can't say I liked the book myself.' Jock shook his head. 'You made all the blacks look like bloody heroes – but that's what they like overseas, isn't it? Black is beautiful – that's what sells books, hey?'

'Some of my reviewers called me a racist,' Craig murmured. 'You can't keep all the people happy all of the time.'

Jock wasn't listening. 'Another thing, Craig, why did you have to make out that Mr Rhodes was a queer?'

Cecil Rhodes, the father of the white settlers, had been dead for eighty years, but the old-timers still called him Mr Rhodes.

'I gave the reasons in the book,' Craig tried to placate him.

'He was a great man, Craig, but nowadays it's the fashion for you young people to tear down greatness – like mongrels snapping at the heels of a lion.' Craig could see that Jock was warming to his subject, and he had to divert him.

'How about a drink, Jock?' he asked, and Jock paused. His rosy cheeks and swollen purple nose were not solely the products of the African sun.

'Now, you're making sense.' Jock licked his lips. 'It's been a long thirsty day. Just let me lock up the shop.'

'If I fetched a bottle, we could drink it here and talk privately.'

The last of Jock's antagonism evaporated. 'Damn good idea. The bottle store has a few bottles of Dimple Haig left – and get a bucket of ice while you are about it.'

They sat in Jock's tiny cubicle of an office and drank the good whisky out of cheap thick tumblers. Jock Daniels' mood mellowed perceptibly.

'I didn't leave, Craig, because there was nowhere to go. England? I haven't been back there since the war. Trade unions and bloody weather – no thanks. South Africa? They are going to go the same way that we did – at least we've got it over and done with.' He poured again from the pinch bottle. 'If you do go, they let you take two hundred dollars with you. Two hundred dollars to start again when you are sixty-five years old – no bloody thanks.'

'So what's life like, Jock?'

'You know what they call an optimist here?' Jock asked. 'It's somebody who believes that things can't get any worse.' He bellowed with laughter and slapped his bare hairy thigh. 'No. I'm kidding. It's not too bad. As long as you don't expect the old standards, if you keep your mouth shut and stay away from politics, you can still live a good life – probably as good as anywhere in the world.'

'The big farmers and ranchers – how are they doing?'

'They are the elite. The government has come to its senses. They've dropped all that crap about nationalizing the land. They've come to face the fact that if they are going to feed the black masses, then they need the white farmers. They are becoming quite proud of them: when they get a state visitor – a communist Chinese or a Libyan minister – they give him a tour of white farms to show him how good things are looking.'

'What about the price of land?'

'At the end of the war, when the blacks first took over and were shouting about taking the farms and handing them over to the masses, you couldn't give the land away.' Jock gargled with his whisky. 'Take your family company for instance, Rholands Ranching Company – that includes all three spreads: King's Lynn, Queen's Lynn and that big piece of country up in the north bordering the Chizarira Game Reserve – your uncle Douglas sold the whole damned shooting match for quarter of a million dollars. Before the war he could have asked ten million.'

'Quarter of a million.' Craig was shocked. 'He gave it away!'

'That included all the stock – prize Afrikander bulls and breeding cows, the lot,' Jock related with relish. 'You see, he had to get out. He had been a member of Smith's cabinet from the beginning and he knew that he would have been a marked man once the black government took over. He sold out to a Swiss-German consortium, and they paid him in Zürich. Old Dougie took his family, and went to Aussie. Of course, he already had a few million outside the country, so he could buy himself a nice little cattle station up in Queensland. It's us poor buggers with everything we have tied up here that had to stay.'

'Have another drink,' Craig offered, and then steered Jock back to Rholands Ranching. 'What did the consortium do with Rholands?'

'Cunning bloody Krauts!' Jock was slurring a little by now. 'They took all the stock, bribed somebody in government to give them an export permit and shipped them over the border to South Africa. I hear they sold for almost a million and a half down there. Remember, they were the very top breeding-stock, champions of champions. So they cleared over a million, and then they repatriated their profit in gold shares and made another couple of million.'

'They stripped the ranches and now they have abandoned them?' Craig asked, and Jock nodded weightily.

'They're trying to sell the company, of course. I've got it on my books – but it would take a pile of capital to restock the ranches and get them going again. Nobody is interested. Who wants to bring money into a country which is tottering on the brink? Answer me that!'

'What is the asking price for the company?' Craig enquired airily, and Jock Daniels sobered miraculously, and fastened Craig with a beady auctioneer's eye.

'You wouldn't be interested?' And his eye became beadier. 'Did you really make a million dollars out of that book?'

'What are they asking?' Craig repeated.

'Two million. That's why I haven't found a buyer. Lots of the local boys would love to get their paws on that grazing – but two million. Who the hell has that kind of money in this country—'

'Supposing they could be paid in Zürich, would that make a difference to the price?' Craig asked.

'Do a Shona's armpits stink!'

'How much difference?'

'They might take a million – in Zürich.'

'A quarter of a million?'

'No ways, never – not in ten thousand years,' Jock shook his head emphatically.

'Telephone them. Tell them the ranches are over-run with squatters, and it would cause a political hoo-ha to try and move them now. Tell them they are running goats on the grazing, and in a year's time it will be a desert. Point out they will be getting their original investment out intact. Tell them the government has threatened to seize all land owned by absentee landlords. They could lose the lot.'

'All that is true,' Jock grumped. 'But a quarter of a million! You are wasting my time.'

'Phone them.'

'Who pays for the call?'

'I do. You can't lose, Jock.'

Jock sighed with resignation. 'All right, I'll call them.'

'When?'

'Friday today – no point in calling until Monday.'

'All right, in the meantime can you get me a few cans of gas?' Craig asked.

'What do you wants gas for?'

'I'm going up to the Chizarira. I haven't been up there for ten years. If I'm going to buy it, I'd like to look at it again.'

'I wouldn't do that, Craig. That's bandit country.'

'The polite term is political dissidents.'

'They are Matabele bandits,' Jock said heavily, 'and they'll either shoot your arse full of more holes than you can use, or they will kidnap you for ransom – or both.'

'You get me some gas and I'll take the chance. I'll be back early next week to hear what your pals in Zürich have to say about the offer.'

It was marvellous country, still wild and untouched – no fences, no cultivated lands, no buildings – protected from the influx of cattle and peasant farmers by the tsetse-fly belt which ran up from the Zambezi valley into the forests along the escarpment.

On the one side it was bounded by the Chizarira Game Reserve and on the other by the Mzolo Forest Reserve, both of which areas were vast reservoirs of wildlife. During the depression of the 1930s, old Bawu had chosen the country with care and paid sixpence an acre for it. One hundred thousand acres for two thousand five hundred pounds. 'Of course, it will never be cattle country,' he told Craig once, as they camped under the wild fig trees beside a deep green pool of the Chizarira river and watched the sand-grouse come slanting down on quick wings across the setting sun to land on the sugar-white sandbank beneath the far bank. 'The grazing is sour, and the tsetse will kill anything you try to rear here – but for that reason it will always be an unspoiled piece of old Africa.'

The old man had used it as a shooting lodge and a retreat. He had never strung barbed-wire nor built even a shack on the ground, preferring to sleep on the bare earth under the spreading branches of the wild fig.

Very selectively Bawu had hunted here – elephant and lion and rhinoceros and buffalo – only the dangerous game, but he had jealously protected them from other rifles, even his own sons and grandsons had been denied hunting rights.

'It's my own little private paradise,' he told Craig, 'and I'm selfish enough to keep it like that.'

Craig doubted that the track through to the pools had been used since he and the old man had last been here together ten years before. It was totally overgrown, elephant had pushed mopani trees down like primitive road-blocks, and heavy rains had washed it out.

'Eat your heart out, Mr Avis,' said Craig, and put the sturdy little Volkswagen to it.

However, the front-wheel drive vehicle was light enough and nippy enough to negotiate even the most unfriendly dry river-beds, although Craig had to corduroy the sandy bottoms with branches to give it purchase in the fine sand. He lost the track half a dozen times, and only found it after laboriously casting ahead on foot.

He hit one ant-bear hole and had to jack up the front end to get out, and half the time he was finding ways around the elephant road-blocks. In the end he had to leave the Volkswagen and cover the last few miles on foot. He reached the pools in the last glimmering of daylight.

He curled up in the single blanket that he had filched from the motel, and slept through without dreaming or stirring, to wake in the ruddy magic of an African dawn.

He ate cold baked beans out of the can and brewed coffee, then he left his pack and blanket under the wild figs and went down along the bank of the river.

On foot he could cover only a tiny portion of the wide wedge of wild country that spread over a hundred thousand acres, but the Chizarira river was the heart and artery of it. What he found here would allow him to judge what changes there had been since his last visit.

Almost immediately he realized that there were still plenty of the more common varieties of wildlife in the forest: the big, spooky, spiral-horned kudu went bounding away, flicking their fluffy white tails, and graceful little impala drifted like roseate smoke amongst the trees. Then he found signs of the rarer animals. First, the fresh pug-marks of a leopard in the clay at the water's edge where the cat had drunk during the night, and then, the elongated teardrop-shaped spoor and grapelike droppings of the magnificent sable antelope.

For his lunch he ate slices of dried sausage which he cut with his clasp-knife and sucked lumps of tart white cream of tartar from the pods of the baobab tree. When he moved on he came to an extensive stand of dense wild ebony bush, and followed one of the narrow twisting game trails into it. He had gone only a hundred paces when he came on a small clearing in the midst of the thicket of interwoven branches, and he experienced a surge of elation.

The clearing stank like a cattle-pen, but even ranker and gamier. He recognized it as an animal midden, a dunghill to which an animal returns habitually to defecate. From the character of the faeces, composed of digested twigs and bark, and from the fact that these had been churned and scattered, Craig knew immediately that it was a midden of the black rhinoceros, one of Africa's rarest and most endangered species.

Unlike its cousin the white rhinoceros, who is a grazer on grassland and a lethargic and placid animal, the black rhinoceros is a browser on the lower branches of the thick bush which it frequents. By nature it is a cantankerous, inquisitive, stupid and nervously irritable animal. It will charge anything that annoys it, including men, horses, lorries and even locomotives.

Before the war, one notorious beast had lived on the escarpment of the Zambezi valley where both road and railway began the plunge down towards the Victoria Falls. It had piled up a score of eighteen lorries and buses, catching them on a steep section of road where they were reduced to a walking pace, and taking them head-on so that its horn crunched through the radiator in a burst of steam. Then, perfectly satisfied, it would trot back into the thick bush with squeals of triumph.

Puffed up with success, it finally over-reached itself when it took on the Victoria Falls express, lumbering down the tracks like a medieval knight in the jousting lists. The locomotive was doing twenty miles per hour and the rhinoceros weighed two tons and was making about the same speed in the opposite direction, so the meeting was monumental. The express came to a grinding halt with wheels spinning helplessly, but the rhinoceros had reached the end of his career as a wrecker of radiators.

The latest deposit of dung on the midden had been within the preceding twelve hours, Craig estimated with delight, and the spoor indicated a family group of bull and cow with calf at heel. Smiling, Craig recalled the old Matabele myth which accounted for the rhino's habit of scattering its dung, and for its fear of the porcupine – the only animal in all the bush from which it would fly in snorting panic.

The Matabele related that once upon a time the rhino had borrowed a quill from the porcupine to sew up a tear caused by a thorn in his thick hide. The rhino promised to return the quill at their next meeting. After repairing the rent with bark twine, the rhino placed the quill between his lips while he admired his handiwork, and inadvertently swallowed it. Now he is still searching for the quill, and assiduously avoiding the porcupine's recriminations.

The total world-wide population of the black rhinoceros probably did not exceed a few thousand individuals, and to have them still surviving here delighted Craig and made his tentative plans for the area much more viable.

Still grinning, he followed the freshest tracks away from the midden, hoping for a sighting, and had gone only half a mile when just beyond the wall of grey impenetrable bush that flanked the narrow trail, there was a sudden hissing, churring outcry of alarm calls and a cloud of brown ox-peckers rose above the scrub. These noisy birds lived in a symbiotic relationship with the larger African game animals, feeding exclusively on the ticks and bloodsucking flies that infested them, and in return acting as wary sentinels to warn of danger.

Swiftly following the alarm, there was a deafening chuffing and snorting like that of a steam engine: with a crash, the bush parted and Craig got his longed-for sighting as an enormous grey beast burst out onto the path not thirty paces ahead of him and, still uttering blasts of affronted indignation, peered short-sightedly over its long polished double horns for something to charge.

Aware that the beast's weak eyes could not distinguish a motionless man at more than fifteen paces, and that the light breeze was blowing directly into his face, Craig stood frozen but poised to hurl himself to one side if the charge came his way. The rhino was switching his grey bulk from side to side with startling agility, the din of his ire unabated, and in Craig's fevered imagination his horn seemed to grow longer and sharper every second. Stealthily he reached for the clasp-knife in his pocket. The beast sensed the movement and trotted a half dozen paces closer, so that Craig was on the periphery of his effective vision and in serious danger at last.

Using a short underhanded flick, he tossed the knife high over the beast's head into the ebony thicket behind it, and there was a loud clatter as it struck a branch.

Instantly the rhino spun around and launched its huge grey body in a full and furious charge at the sound. The bush opened as though before a centurion tank, and the clattering, crashing charge dwindled swiftly as the rhinoceros kept going up the side of the hill and over the crest in search of an adversary. Craig sat down heavily in the middle of the path, and doubled over with breathless laughter in which were echoes of mild hysteria.

Within the next few hours, Craig had found three of the pans of stinking, stagnant water that these strange beasts prefer to the clean running water of the river, and he had decided where to site the hides from which his tourists could view them at close range. Of course, he would furnish salt-licks beside the waterholes to make them even more attractive to the beasts, and bring them in to be photographed and gawked at.

Sitting on a log, beside one of the waterholes, he reviewed the factors that favoured his plans. It was under an hour's flight from here to the Victoria Falls, one of the seven natural wonders of the world, that already attracted thousands of tourists each month. It would be only a short detour to his camp here, so that added little to the tourists' original airfare. He had an animal that very few other reserves or camps could offer, together with most of the other varieties of game, concentrated in a relatively small area. He had undeveloped reservations on both boundaries to ensure a permanent source of interesting animal life.

What he had in mind was a champagne and caviar type of camp, on the lines of those private estates bordering the Kruger National Park in South Africa. He would put up small camps, sufficiently isolated from each other so as to give the occupants the illusion of having the wilderness to themselves. He would provide charismatic and knowledgeable guides to take his tourists by Land-Rover and on foot close to rare and potentially dangerous animals and make an adventure of it, and luxurious surroundings when they returned to camp in the evening – air-conditioning and fine food and wines, pretty young hostesses to pamper them, wildlife movies and lectures by experts to instruct and entertain them. And he would charge them outrageously for it all, aiming at the very upper level of the tourist trade.

It was after sunset when Craig limped back into his rudimentary camp under the wild figs, his face and arms reddened by the sun, tsetse-fly bites itching and swollen on the back of his neck, and the stump of his leg tender and aching from the unaccustomed exertions. He was too tired to eat. He unstrapped his leg, drank a single whisky from the plastic mug, rolled into his blanket and was almost immediately asleep. He woke for a few minutes during the night, and while he urinated he listened with sleepy pleasure to the distant roaring of a pride of hunting lions, and then returned to his blanket.

He was awakened by the whistling cries of the green pigeons feasting on the wild figs above his head, and found he was ravenously hungry and happy as he could not remember being for years.

After he had eaten, he hopped down to the water's edge, carrying a rolled copy of the *Farmers' Weekly* magazine, the African farmers' bible. Then, seated in the shallows with the coarse-sugar sand pleasantly rough under his naked backside and the cool green waters soothing his still aching stump, he studied the prices of stock offered for sale in the magazine and did mental arithmetic with the figures.

His ambitious plans were swiftly moderated when he realized what it would cost to restock King's Lynn and Queen's Lynn with thoroughbred bloodstock. The consortium had sold the original stud for a million and a half, and prices had gone up since then.

He would have to begin with good bulls, and grade cows – slowly build up his blood lines. Still, that would cost plenty, the ranches would have to be re-equipped, and the development of the tourist camp here on the Chizarira river was going to cost another bundle. Then he would have to move the squatter families and their goats off his grazing – the only way to do that was to offer them financial compensation. Old grandfather Bawu had always told him, 'Work out what you think it will cost, then double it. That way you will come close.'

Craig threw the magazine up onto the bank, and lay back with only his head above water while he did his sums.

On the credit side, he had lived frugally aboard the yacht, unlike a lot of other suddenly successful authors. The book had been on the bestseller lists on both sides of the Atlantic for almost a year, main choice of three major book-clubs, translations into a number of foreign languages, including Hindi, Reader's Digest condensed books, the TV series, paperback contracts – even though, at the end, the taxman had got in amongst his earnings.

Then again he had been lucky with what was left to him after these depredations. He had speculated in gold and silver, had made three good coups on the stock exchange, and finally had transferred most of his winnings into Swiss francs at the right time. Added to that, he could sell the yacht. A month earlier he had been offered a hundred and fifty thousand dollars for *Bawu*, but he would hate to part with it. Apart from that, he could try hitting Ashe Levy for a substantial advance on the undelivered novel and hock his soul in the process.

He reached the bottom line of his calculations and decided that if he pulled out all the stops, and used up all his lines of credit, he might be able to raise a million and a half, which would leave him short of at least as much again.

'Henry Pickering, my very favourite banker, are you ever in for a surprise!' He grinned recklessly as he thought of how he was planning to break the first and cardinal rule of the prudent investor and put it all in one basket. 'Dear Henry, you have been selected by our computer to be the lucky lender of one and a half big Ms to a one-legged dried-up sometime scribbler.' That was the best he could come up with at the moment, and it wasn't really worth worrying seriously until he had an answer from Jock Daniels' consortium. He switched to more mundane considerations.

He ducked down and sucked a mouthful of the sweet clear water. The Chizarira was a lesser tributary of the great Zambezi, so he was drinking Zambezi waters again, as he had told Henry Pickering he must. 'Chizarira' was a hell of a mouthful for a tourist to pronounce, let alone remember. He needed a name under which to sell his little African paradise.

'Zambezi Waters,' he said aloud. 'I'll call it Zambezi Waters,' and then almost choked as very close to where he lay a voice said clearly. 'He must be a mad man.'

It was a deep melodious Matabele voice. 'First, he comes here alone and unarmed, and then he sits amongst the crocodiles and talks to the trees!'

Craig rolled over swiftly onto his belly, and stared at the three men who had come silently out of the forest and now stood on the bank, ten paces away, watching him with closed, expressionless faces.

They were, all three of them, dressed in faded denims – the uniform of the bush fighters – and the weapons they carried with casual familiarity were the ubiquitous AK 47s with the distinctive curved black magazine and laminated woodwork.

Denim, AK 47s and Matabele – there was no doubt in

Craig's mind who these were. Regular Zimbabwean troops now wore jungle fatigues or battle-smocks, most were armed with Nato weapons and spoke the Shona language. These were former members of the disbanded Zimbabwe People's Revolutionary Army, now turned political rebels, men subject to no laws, nor higher authority, forged by a long murderous and bloody bush war into hard, ruthless men with death in their hands and death in their eyes. Although Craig had been warned of the possibility, and had indeed been half-expecting this meeting, still the shock made him feel dry-mouthed and nauseated.

'We don't have to take him,' said the youngest of the three guerrillas. 'We can shoot him and bury him secretly – that is good as a hostage.' He was under twenty-five years of age, Craig guessed, and had probably killed a man for every year of his life.

'The six hostages we took on the Victoria Falls road gave us weeks of trouble, and in the end we had to shoot them anyway,' agreed the second guerrilla, and they both looked to the third man. He was only a few years older than they were, but there was no doubt that he was the leader. A thin scar ran from the corner of his mouth up his cheek into the hairline at the temple. It puckered his mouth into a lopsided, sardonic grin.

Craig remembered the incident that they were discussing. Guerrillas had stopped a tourist bus on the main Victoria Falls road and abducted six men, Canadian, Americans and a Briton, and taken them into the bush as hostages for the release of political detainees. Despite an intensive search by police and regular army units, none of the hostages had been recovered.

The scarred leader stared at Craig with smoky dark eyes for long seconds, and then, with his thumb, slid the rate-of-fire selector on his rifle to automatic.

'A true Matabele does not kill a blood brother of the tribe.' It took Craig an enormous effort to keep his voice steady, devoid of any trace of his terror. His Sindebele was so flawless and easy that it was the leader of the guerrillas who blinked.

'Hau!' he said, which is an expression of amazement. 'You speak like a man – but who is this blood brother you boast of?'

'Comrade Minister Tungata Zebiwe,' Craig answered, and saw the instant shift in the man's gaze, and the sudden discomfiture of his two companions. He had hit a chord that had unbalanced them, and had delayed his own execution for the moment, but the leader's rifle was still cocked and on fully automatic, still pointed at his belly.

It was the youngster who broke the silence, speaking too loudly, to cover his own uncertainty. 'It is easy for a baboon to shout the name of the black-maned lion from the hilltop, and claim his protection, but does the lion recognize the baboon? Kill him, I say, and have done with it.'

'Yet he speaks like a brother,' murmured the leader, 'and Comrade Tungata is a hard man—'

Craig realized that his life was still at desperate risk, a little push either way was all that was needed.

'I will show you,' he said, still without the slightest quaver in his voice. 'Let me go to my pack.'

The leader hesitated.

'I am naked,' Craig told him. 'No weapons – not even a knife – and you are three, with guns.'

'Go!' the Matabele agreed. 'But go with care. I have not killed a man for many moons – and I feel the lack.'

Craig stood up carefully from the water and saw the interest in their eyes as they studied his leg foreshortened halfway between knee and ankle, and the compensating muscular development of the other leg and the rest of his body. The interest changed to wary respect as they saw how quickly and easily Craig moved on one leg. He reached his pack with water running down the hard flat muscles of chest and belly. He had come prepared for this meeting, and from the front pocket of his pack he pulled out his wallet and handed a coloured snapshot to the guerrilla leader.

In the photograph two men sat on the bonnet of an ancient Land-Rover. They had their arms around each other's shoulders, and both of them were laughing. Each of them held a beer can in his free hand and with it was saluting the photographer. The accord and camaraderie between them was evident.

The scarred guerrilla studied it for a long time and then slipped the selector on his rifle to lock. 'It is Comrade Tungata,' he said, and handed the photograph to the others.

'Perhaps,' conceded the youngster reluctantly, 'but a long time ago. I still think we should shoot him.' However, this opinion was now more wistful than determined.

'Comrade Tungata would swallow you without chewing,' his companion told him flatly, and slung his rifle over his shoulder.

Craig picked up his leg and in a moment had fitted it to the stump – and instantly all three guerrillas were intrigued, their murderous intentions set aside as they crowded around Craig to examine this marvellous appendage.

Fully aware of the African love of a good joke, Craig clowned for them. He danced a jig, pirouetted on the leg, cracked himself across the shin without flinching, and finally took the hat of the youngest, most murderous guerrilla from his head, screwed it into a ball and with a cry of 'Pele!' drop-kicked it into the lower branches of the wild fig with the artificial leg. The other two hooted with glee, and laughed until tears ran down their cheeks at the youngster's loss of dignity as he scrambled up into the wild fig to retrieve his hat.

Judging the mood finely, Craig opened his pack and

brought out mug and whisky bottle. He poured a generous dram and handed the mug to the scar-faced leader.

'Between brothers,' he said.

The guerrilla leaned his rifle against the trunk of the tree and accepted the mug. He drained it at one swallow, and blew the fumes ecstatically out of his nose and mouth. The other two took their turn at the mug with as much gusto.

When Craig pulled on his trousers and sat down on his pack, placing the bottle in front of him, they all laid their weapons aside and squatted in a half circle facing him.

'My name is Craig Mellow,' he said.

'We will call you Kuphela,' the leader told him, 'for the leg walks on its own.' And the others clapped their hands in approbation, and Craig poured each of them a whisky to celebrate his christening.

'My name is Comrade Lookout,' the leader told him. Most of the guerrillas had adopted *noms-de-guerre*. 'This is Comrade Peking.' A tribute to his Chinese instructors, Craig guessed. 'And this,' the leader indicated the youngest, 'is Comrade Dollar.' Craig had difficulty remaining straight-faced at this unlikely juxtaposition of ideologies.

'Comrade Lookout,' Craig said, 'the *kanka* marked you.'

The *kanka* were the jackals, the security forces, and Craig guessed the leader would be proud of his battle scars.

Comrade Lookout caressed his cheek. 'A bayonet. They thought I was dead and they left me for the hyena.'

'Your leg?' Dollar asked in return. 'From the war also?'

An affirmative would tell them that he had fought against them. Their reaction was unpredictable, but Craig paused only a second before he nodded. 'I trod on one of our own mines.'

'Your own mine!' Lookout crowed with delight at the joke. 'He stood on his own mine!' And the others thought it was funny, but Craig detected no residual resentment.

'Where?' Peking wanted to know.

'On the river, between Kazungula and Victoria Falls.'

'Ah, yes,' they nodded at each other. 'That was a bad place. We crossed there often,' Lookout remembered. 'That is where we fought the Scouts.'

The Ballantyne Scouts had been one of the elite units of the security forces, and Craig had been attached to them as an armourer.

'The day I trod on the mine was the day the Scouts followed your people across the river. There was a terrible fight on the Zambian side, and all the Scouts were wiped out.'

'Hau! Hau!' they exclaimed with amazement. 'That was the day! We were there – we fought with Comrade Tungata on that day.'

'What a fight – what a fine and beautiful killing when we trapped them,' Dollar remembered with the killing light in his eyes again.

'They fought! Mother of Nkulu kulu – how they fought! Those were real men!'

Craig's stomach churned queasily with the memory. His own cousin, Roland Ballantyne, had led the Scouts across the river that fateful day. While Craig lay shattered and bleeding on the edge of the minefield, Roland and all his men had fought to the death a few miles further on. Their bodies had been abused and desecrated by these men, and now they were discussing it like a memorable football match.

Craig poured more whisky for them. How he had loathed them and their fellows – 'terrs', they called them, terrorists – loathed them with the special hatred reserved for something that threatens your very existence and all that you hold dear. But now, in his turn, he saluted them with the mug, and drank. He had heard of RAF and Luftwaffe pilots meeting after the war and reminiscing as they were doing, more like comrades than deadly enemies.

'Where were you when we rocketed the storage tanks in Harare and burned the fuel?' they asked.

'Do you remember when the Scouts jumped from the sky onto our camp at Molingushi? They killed eight hundred of us that day – and I was there!' Peking recalled with pride. 'But they did not catch me!'

Yet now Craig found that he could not sustain that hatred any longer. Under the veneer of cruelty and savagery imposed upon them by war, they were the true Matabele that he had always loved, with that irrepressible sense of fun, that deep pride in themselves and their tribe, that abounding sense of personal honour, of loyalty and their own peculiar code of morals. As they chatted, Craig warmed to them, and they sensed it and responded to him in turn.

'So what makes you come here, Kuphela? A sensible man like you, walking without even a stick into the leopard's cave? You must have heard about us – and yet you came here?'

'Yes, I have heard about you. I heard that you were hard men, like old Mzilikazi's warriors.'

They preened a little at the compliment.

'But I came here to meet you and talk with you,' Craig went on.

'Why?' demanded Lookout.

'I will write a book, and in the book I will write truly the way you are and the things for which you are still fighting.'

'A book?' Peking was suspicious immediately.

'What kind of book?' Dollar backed him.

'Who are you to write a book?' Lookout's voice was openly scornful. 'You are too young. Book-writers are great and learned people.' Like all barely literate Africans, he had an almost superstitious awe of the printed word, and reverence for the grey hairs of age.

'A one-legged book-writer,' Dollar scoffed, and Peking giggled and picked up his rifle. He placed it across his lap and giggled again. The mood had changed once more. 'If he lies about this book, then perhaps he lies about his friendship with Comrade Tungata,' Dollar suggested with relish.

Craig had prepared for this also. He took a large manila envelope from the flap of his pack and shook from it a thick sheaf of newspaper cuttings. He shuffled through them slowly, letting their disbelieving mockery change to interest, then he selected one and handed it to Lookout. The serial of the book had been shown on Zimbabwe television two years previously, before these guerrillas had returned to the bush, and it had enjoyed an avid following throughout its run.

'Hau!' Lookout exclaimed. 'It is the old king, Mzilikazi!'

The photograph at the head of the article showed Craig on the set with members of the cast of the production. The guerrillas immediately recognized the black American actor who had taken the part of the old Matabele king. He was in a costume of leopard-skin and heron-feathers.

'And that is you – with the king.' They had not been as impressed, even by the photograph of Tungata.

There was another cutting, a photo taken in Double-day's bookstore on Fifth Avenue, of Craig standing beside a huge pyramid of the book, with a blow-up of his portrait from the back cover riding atop the pyramid.

'That is you!' They were truly stunned now. 'Did you write that book?'

'Now do you believe?' Craig demanded, but Lookout studied the evidence carefully before committing himself.

His lips moved as he read slowly through the text of the articles, and when he handed them back to Craig, he said, seriously, 'Kuphela, despite your youth, you are indeed an important book-writer.'

Now they were almost pathetically eager to pour out their grievances to him, like petitioners at a tribal *indaba* where cases were heard and judgement handed down by the elders of the tribe. While they talked, the sun rose up across a sky as blue and unblemished as a heron's egg, and reached its noon and started its stately descent towards its bloody death in the sunset.

What they related was the tragedy of Africa, the barriers that divided this mighty continent and which contained all the seeds of violence and disaster, the single incurable disease that infected them all – tribalism.

Here it was Matabele against Mashona.

'The dirt-eaters,' Lookout called them, 'the lurkers in caves, the fugitives on the fortified hilltops, the jackals who will only bite when your back is turned to them.'

It was the scorn of the warrior for the merchant, of the man of direct action for the wily negotiator and politician.

'Since great Mzilikazi first crossed the river Limpopo, the Mashona have been our dogs – *amaholi*, slaves and sons of slaves.'

This history of displacement and domination of one group by another was not confined to Zimbabwe, but over the centuries had taken place across the entire continent. Further north, the lordly Masai had raided and terrorized the Kikuyu who lacked their warlike culture; the giant Watutsi, who considered any man under six foot six to be a dwarf, had taken the gentle Hutu as slaves – and in every case, the slaves had made up for their lack of ferocity with political astuteness, and, as soon as the white colonialists' protection was withdrawn, had either massacred their tormentors, as the Hutu had the Watutsi, or had bastard-ized the doctrine of Westminster government by discarding the checks and balances that make the system equitable, and had used their superior numbers to place their erst-while masters into a position of political subjugation, as the Kikuyu had the Masai.

Exactly the same process was at work here in Zimbabwe. The white settlers had been rendered inconsequential by the bush war, and the concepts of fair play and integrity that the white administrators and civil servants had imposed upon all the tribes had been swept away with them.

'There are five dirt-eating Mashona for every one Matabele *indoda*,' Lookout told Craig bitterly, 'but why should that give them any right to lord it over us? Should five slaves dictate to a king? If five baboons bark, must the black-maned lion tremble?'

'That is the way it is done in England and America,' Craig said mildly. 'The will of the majority must prevail—'

'I piss with great force on the will of the majority,' Lookout dismissed the doctrine of democracy airily. 'Such things might work in England and America – but this is Africa. They do not work here – I will not bow down to the will of five dirt-eaters. No, not to the will of a hundred, nor a thousand of them. I am Matabele, and only one man dictates to me – a Matabele king.'

Yes, Craig thought, this *is* Africa. The old Africa awakening from the trance induced in it by a hundred years of colonialism, and reverting immediately to the old ways.

He thought of the tens of thousands of fresh-faced young Englishmen who for very little financial reward had come out to spend their lives in the Colonial Service, labouring to instil into their reluctant charges their respect for the Protestant work-ethic, the ideals of fair play and Westminster government – young men who had returned to England prematurely aged and broken in health, to eke out their days on a pittance of a pension and the belief that they had given their lives to something that was valuable and lasting. Did they, Craig wondered, ever suspect that it might all have been in vain?

The borders that the colonial system had set up had been neat and orderly. They followed a river, or the shore of a lake, the spine of a mountain range, and where these did not exist, a white surveyor with a theodolite had shot a line across the wilderness. 'This side is German East

Africa, this side is British.' But they took no cognizance of the tribes that they were splitting in half as they drove in their pegs.

'Many of our people live across the river in South Africa,' Peking complained. 'If they were with us, then things would be different. There would be more of us, but now we are divided.'

'And the Shona is cunning, as cunning as the baboons that come down to raid the maize fields in the night. He knows that one Matabele warrior would eat a hundred of his, so when first we rose against them, he used the white soldiers of Smith's government who had stayed on—'

Craig remembered the delight of the embittered white soldiers who considered they had not been defeated but had been betrayed, when the Mugabe government had turned them loose on the dissenting Matabele faction.

'The white pilots came in their aeroplanes, and the white troops of the Rhodesian Regiment—'

After the fighting the shunting-yards at Bulawayo station had been crowded with refrigerated trucks each packed from floor to roof with the bodies of the Matabele dead.

'The white soldiers did their work for them, while Mugabe and his boys ran back to Harare and climbed shaking and snivelling under their women's skirts. Then, after the white soldiers had taken our weapons, they crawled out again, shook off the dust of their retreat, and came strutting back like conquerors.'

'They have dishonoured our leaders—'

Nkomo, the Matabele leader, had been accused of harbouring rebels and accumulating caches of weapons, and driven in disgrace by Mashona-dominated government into enforced retirement.

'They have secret prisons in the bush where they take our leaders,' Peking went on. 'There they do things to our men that do not bear talking of.'

'Now that we are deprived of weapons, their special units move through the villages. They beat our old men and women, they rape our young women, they take our young men away, never to be seen or heard of again.'

Craig had seen a photograph of men in the blue and khaki of the former British South Africa police, so long the uniform of honour and fair play, carrying out interrogations in the villages. In the photograph they had a naked Matabele spread-eagled on the earth, an armed and uniformed constable standing with both booted feet and his full weight on each ankle and wrist to pin him, while two other constables wielded clubs as heavy as baseball bats. They were using full strokes from high above the head, and raining blows on the man's back and shoulders and buttocks. The photograph had been captioned 'Zimbabwe Police interrogate suspect in attempt to learn whereabouts of American and British tourists abducted as hostages by Matabele dissidents'. There had been no photographs of what they did to the Matabele girls.

'Perhaps the government troops were looking for the hostages which you admit you seized,' Craig pointed out tartly. 'A little while ago you would have been quite happy to kill me or take me hostage as well.'

'The Shona began this business long before we took our first hostage,' Lookout shot back at him.

'But you *are* taking innocent hostages,' Craig insisted. 'Shooting white farmers—'

'What else can we do to make people understand what is happening to our people? We have very few leaders who have not been imprisoned or silenced, and even they are powerless. We have no weapons except these few we have managed to hide, we have no powerful friends, while the Shona have Chinese and British and American allies. We have no money to continue the struggle – and they have all the wealth of the land and millions of dollars of aid from these powerful friends. What else can we do to make the world understand what is happening to us?'

Craig decided prudently that this was neither the time nor the place to offer a lecture on political morality – and then he thought wryly, 'Perhaps my morality is old-fashioned, anyway.' There was a new political expediency in international affairs that had become acceptable: the right of impotent and voiceless minorities to draw violent attention to their own plight. From the Palestinians and the Basque separatists to the bombers from Northern Ireland blowing young British guardsmen and horses to bloody tatters in a London street, there was a new morality abroad. With these examples before them, and from their own experience of successfully bringing about political change by violence, these young men were children of the new morality.

Though Craig could never bring himself to condone these methods, not if he lived a hundred years, yet he found himself in grudging sympathy with their plight and their aspirations. There had always been a strange and sometimes bloody bond between Craig's family and the Matabele. A tradition of respect and understanding for a people who were fine friends and enemies to be wary of, an aristocratic, proud and warlike race that deserved better than they were now receiving.

There was an elitist streak in Craig's make-up that hated to see a Gulliver rendered impotent by Lilliputians. He loathed the politics of envy and the viciousness of socialism which, he felt, sought to strike down the heroes and reduce every exceptional man to the common greyness of the pack, to replace true leadership with the oafish mumblings of trade-union louts, to emasculate all initiative by punitive tax schemes and then gradually to shepherd a numbed and compliant populace into the barbed-wire enclosure of Marxist totalitarianism.

These men were terrorists – certainly. Craig grinned.

Robin Hood was also a terrorist – but at least he had some style and a little class.

'Will you see Comrade Tungata?' they demanded with almost pitiful eagerness.

'Yes. I will see him soon.'

'Tell him we are here. Tell him we are ready and waiting.'

Craig nodded. 'I will tell him.'

They walked back with him to where he had left the Volkswagen, and Comrade Dollar insisted on carrying Craig's pack. When they reached the dusty and slightly battered VW, they piled into it with AK 47 barrels protruding from three windows.

'We will go with you,' Lookout explained, 'as far as the main Victoria Falls Road, for if you should meet another of our patrols when you are alone, it might go hard for you.'

They reached the macadamized Great North Road well after darkness had fallen. Craig stripped his pack and gave them what remained of his rations and the dregs of the whisky. He had two hundred dollars in his wallet and he added that to the booty. Then they shook hands.

'Tell Comrade Tungata we need weapons,' said Dollar.

'Tell him that, more than weapons, we need a leader.' Comrade Lookout gave Craig the special grip of thumb and palm reserved for trusted friends. 'Go in peace, Kuphela,' he said. 'May the leg that walks alone carry you far and swiftly.'

'Stay in peace, my friend,' Craig told him.

'No, Kuphela, rather wish me bloody war!' Lookout's scarred visage twisted into a dreadful grin in the reflected headlights.

When Craig looked back, they had disappeared into the darkness as silently as hunting leopards.

'I wouldn't have taken any bets about seeing you again,' Jock Daniels greeted Craig when he walked into the auctioneer's office the next morning. 'Did you make it up to the Chizarira – or did good sense get the better of you?'

'I'm still alive, aren't I?' Craig evaded the direct question.

'Good boy,' Jock nodded. 'No sense messing with those Matabele *shufta* – bandits the lot of them.'

'Did you hear from Zürich?'

Jock shook his head. 'Only sent the telex at nine o'clock local time. They are an hour behind us.'

'Can I use your telephone? A few private calls?'

'Local? I don't want you chatting up your birds in New York at my expense.'

'Of course.'

'Right – as long as you mind the shop for me, while I'm out.'

Craig installed himself at Jock's desk, and consulted the cryptic notes that he had made from Henry Pickering's file.

His first call was to the American Embassy in Harare, the capital three hundred miles north-east of Bulawayo.

'Mr Morgan Oxford, your cultural attaché, please,' he asked the operator.

'Oxford.' The accent was crisp Boston and Ivy League.

'Craig Mellow. A mutual friend asked me to call you and give you his regards.'

'Yes, I was expecting you. Won't you come in here any time and say hello?'

'I'd enjoy that,' Craig told him, and hung up.

Henry Pickering was as good as his word. Any message handed to Oxford would go out in the diplomatic bag, and be on Pickering's desk within twelve hours.

His next call was to the office of the minister of tourism and information, and he finally got through to the minister's secretary. Her attitude changed to warm co-operation when he spoke to her in Sindebele.

'The comrade minister is in Harare for the sitting of Parliament,' she told him, and gave Craig his private number at the House.

Craig got through to a parliamentary secretary on his fourth attempt. The telephone system had slowly begun deteriorating, he noticed. The blight of all developing countries was lack of skilled artisans; prior to independence all linesmen had been white, and since then most of them had taken the gap.

This secretary was Mashona and insisted on speaking English as proof of her sophistication.

'Kindly state the nature of the business to be discussed.' She was obviously reading from a printed form.

'Personal. I am acquainted with the comrade minister.'

'Ah yes. P-e-r-s-o-n-n-e-l.' The secretary spelled it out laboriously as she wrote it.

'No – that's p-e-r-s-o-n-a-l,' Craig corrected her patiently. He was beginning to adjust to the pace of Africa again.

'I will consult the comrade minister's schedule. You will be obliged to telephone again.'

Craig consulted his list. Next was the government registrar of companies, and this time he was lucky. He was put through to an efficient and helpful clerk who made a note of his requirements.

'The Share Register, Articles and Memorandum of Association of the company trading as Rholands Ltd, formerly known as Rhodesian Lands and Mining Ltd.' He heard the disapproval in the clerk's tone of voice. 'Rhodesian' was a dirty word nowadays, and Craig made a mental resolution to change the company's name, if ever he had the power to do so. 'Zimlands' would sound a lot better to an African ear.

'I will have Roneoed copies ready for you to collect by four o'clock,' the clerk assured him. 'The search fee will be fifteen dollars.'

Craig's next call was to the surveyor general's office, and again he arranged for copies of documents – this time the titles to the company properties – the ranches King's Lynn, Queen's Lynn and the Chizarira estates.

Then there were fourteen other names on his list, all of whom had been ranching in Matabeleland when he left, close neighbours and friends of his family, those that grandpa Bawu had trusted and liked.

Of the fourteen he could contact only four, the others had all sold up and taken the long road southwards. The remaining families sounded genuinely pleased to hear from him. 'Welcome back, Craig. We have all read the book and watched it on TV.' But they clammed up immediately he started asking questions. 'Damned telephone leaks like a sieve,' said one of them. 'Come out to the ranch for dinner. Stay the night. Always a bed for you, Craig. Lord knows, there aren't so many of the old faces around any more.'

Jock Daniels returned in the middle of the afternoon, red-faced and sweating. 'Still burning up my telephone?' he growled. 'Wonder if the bottle store has another bottle of that Dimple Haig.'

Craig responded to this subtlety by crossing the road and bringing back the pinch bottle in a brown paperbag.

'I forgot that you have to have a cast-iron liver to live in this country.' He unscrewed the cap and dropped it into the waste-paper basket.

At ten minutes to five o'clock he telephoned the minister's parliamentary office again.

'The Comrade Minister Tungata Zebiwe has graciously consented to meet you at ten o'clock on Friday morning. He can allow you twenty minutes.'

'Please convey my sincere thanks to the minister.'

That gave Craig three days to kill and meant he would have to drive the three hundred miles to Harare.

'No reply from Zürich?' He sweetened Jock's glass.

'If you made me an offer like that, I wouldn't bother to answer either,' Jock grumped, as he took the bottle from Craig's hand and added a little more to the glass.

Over the next few days Craig availed himself of the invitations to visit Bawu's old friends, and was smothered with traditional old Rhodesian hospitality.

'Of course, you can't get all the luxuries – Crosse and Blackwell jams, or Bronnley soap – any more,' one of his hostesses explained as she piled his plate with rich fare, 'but somehow it's fun making do.' And she signalled the white-robed table servant to refill the silver dish with baked sweet potatoes.

He spent the days with darkly tanned, slow-speaking men in wide-brimmed felt hats and short khaki trousers, examining their sleek fat cattle from the passenger seat of an open Land-Rover.

'You still can't beat Matabeleland beef,' they told him proudly. 'Sweetest grass in the whole world. Of course, we have to send it all out through South Africa, but the prices are damned good. Glad I didn't run for it. Heard from old Derek Sanders in New Zealand, working as a hired hand on a sheep station now – and a bloody tough life too. No Matabele to do the dirty work over there.'

He looked at his black herders with paternal affection. 'They are just the same, under all the political claptrap. Salt of the bloody earth, my boy. My people, I feel that they are all family, glad I didn't desert them.'

'Of course, there are problems,' another of his hosts told him. 'Foreign exchange is murder – difficult to get tractor spares, and medicine for the stock – but Mugabe's government is starting to wake up. As food-producers we are getting priority on import permits for essentials. Of course, the telephones only work when they do and the trains don't run on time any longer. There is rampant inflation, but the beef prices keep in step with it. They have opened the schools, but we send the kids down south across the border so they get a decent education.'

'And the politics?'

'That's between black and black. Matabele and Mashona. The white man's out of it, thank God. Let the bastards tear each other to pieces if they want to. I keep my nose clean, and it's not a bad life – not like the old days, of course, but then it never is, is it?'

'Would you buy more land?'

'Haven't got the money, old boy.'

'But if you did have?'

The rancher rubbed his nose thoughtfully. 'Perhaps a man could make an absolute mint one day if the country comes right, land prices what they are at the moment – or he could lose the lot if it goes the other way.'

'You could say the same of the stock exchange, but in the meantime it's a good life?'

'It's a good life – and, hell, I was weaned on Zambezi waters. I don't reckon I would be happy breathing London smog or swatting flies in the Australian outback.'

On Thursday morning Craig drove back to the motel, picked up his laundry, repacked his single canvas holdall, paid his bill and checked out.

He called at Jock's office. 'Still no news from Zürich?'

'Telex came in an hour ago.' Jock handed him the flimsy, and Craig scanned it swiftly.

'Will grant your client thirty-day option to purchase all Rholands company paid-up shares for one half million US dollars payable Zürich in full on signature. No further offers countenanced.' They did not come more final than that. Bawu had said double your estimate, and so far he had it right.

Jock was watching his face. 'Double your original offer,' he pointed out. 'Can you swing half a million?'

'I'll have to talk to my rich uncle,' Craig teased him. 'And anyway I've got thirty days. I'll be back before then.'

'Where can I reach you?' Jock asked.

'Don't call me. I'll call you.'

He begged another tankful from Jock's private stock and took the Volkswagen out on the road to the north-east, towards Mashonaland and Harare and ran into the first road-block ten miles out of town.

'Almost like the old days,' he thought, as he climbed down onto the verge. Two black troopers in camouflage battle-smocks searched the Volkswagen for weapons with painstaking deliberation, while a lieutenant with the cap-badge of the Korean-trained Third Brigade examined his passport.

Once again Craig rejoiced in the family tradition whereby all the expectant mothers in his family, on both the Mellow and Ballantyne side, had been sent home to England for the event. That little blue booklet with the gold lion and unicorn and *Honi Soit Qui Mal y Pense* printed on the cover still demanded a certain deference even at a Third Brigade road-block.

It was late afternoon when he crested the line of low hills and looked down on the little huddle of skyscrapers that rose so incongruously out of the African veld, like headstones to the belief in the immortality of the British Empire.

The city that had once borne the name of Lord Salisbury, the foreign secretary who had negotiated the Royal Charter of the British South Africa Company, had reverted to the name Harare after the original Shona chieftain whose cluster of mud and thatch huts the white pioneers had found on the site in September 1890 when they finally completed the long trek up from the south.

The streets also had changed their names from those commemorating the white pioneers and Victoria's empire to those of the sons of the black revolution and its allies – 'a street by any other name' – Craig resigned himself.

Once he entered the city he found there was a boom-town atmosphere. The pavements thronged with noisy black crowds and the foyer of the modern sixteen-storied Monomatapa Hotel resounding to twenty different languages and accents, as tourists jostled visiting bankers and businessmen, foreign dignitaries, civil servants and military advisers.

There was no vacancy for Craig until he spoke to an assistant manager who had seen the TV production and read the book. Then Craig was ushered up to a room on the fifteenth floor with a view over the park. While he was in his bath, a procession of waiters arrived bearing flowers and baskets of fruit and a complimentary bottle of South African champagne. He worked until after midnight on his report to Henry Pickering, and was at the parliament buildings in Causeway by nine-thirty the next morning.

The minister's secretary kept him waiting for forty-five minutes before leading him through into the panelled office beyond, and Comrade Minister Tungata Zebiwe stood up from his desk.

Craig had forgotten how powerful was this man's presence, or perhaps he had grown in stature since their last meeting. When he remembered that once Tungata had been his servant, his gunboy, when Craig was a ranger in the Department of Game Conservation, it seemed that it had been a different existence. In those days he had been Samson Kumalo, for Kumalo was the royal blood line of the Matabele kings, and he was their direct descendant. Bazo, his great-grandfather, had been the leader of the Matabele rebellion of 1896 and had been hanged by the settlers for his part in it. His great-great-grandfather, Gandang, had been half-brother to Lobengula, the last king of the Matabele whom Rhodes' troopers had ridden to an ignoble death and unmarked grave in the northern wilderness after destroying his capital at GuBulawayo, the place of killing.

Royal were his blood-lines, and kingly still his bearing. Taller than Craig, well over six foot and lean, not yet running to flesh, which was often the Matabele trait, his physique was set off to perfection by the cut of his Italian silk suit, shoulders wide as a gallows tree and a flat greyhound's belly. He had been one of the most successful bush fighters during the war, and he was warrior still, of that there was no doubt. Craig experienced a powerful and totally unexpected pleasure in seeing him once more.

'I see you, Comrade Minister,' Craig greeted him, speaking in Sindabele, avoiding having to choose between the old familiar 'Sam' and the *nom de guerre* that he now used, Tungata Zebiwe, which meant 'the Seeker after Justice.'

'I sent you away once,' Tungata answered in the same language. 'I discharged all debts between us – and sent you away.' There was no return light of pleasure in his smoky dark eyes, the heavily boned jaw was set hard.

'I am grateful for what you did.' Craig was unsmiling also, covering his pleasure. It was Tungata who had signed a special ministerial order allowing Craig to export his self-built yacht *Bawu* from the territory in the face of the rigid exchange-control laws which forbade the removal of even a refrigerator or an iron bedstead. At that time the yacht had been Craig's only possession, and he had been crippled by the mine blast and confined to a wheel-chair.

'I do not want your gratitude,' said Tungata, yet there was something behind the burnt-honey-coloured eyes that Craig could not fathom.

'Nor the friendship I still offer you?' Craig asked gently.

'All that died on the battlefield,' Tungata said. 'It was washed away in blood. You chose to go. Now why have you returned?'

'Because this is my land.'

'Your land—' he saw the reddish glaze of anger suffuse the whites of Tungata's eyes. 'Your land. You speak like a white settler. Like one of Cecil Rhodes' murdering troopers.'

'I did not mean it that way.'

'Your people took the land at rifle-point, and at the point of a rifle they surrendered it. Do not speak to me of your land.'

'You hate almost as well as you fought,' Craig told him, feeling his own anger begin to prickle at the back of his eyes, 'but I did not come back to hate. I came back because my heart drew me back. I came back because I felt I could help to rebuild what was destroyed.'

Tungata sat down behind his desk and placed his hands upon the white blotter. They were very dark and powerful. He stared at them in a silence that stretched out for many seconds.

'You were at King's Lynn,' Tungata broke the silence at last, and Craig started. 'Then you went north to the Chizarira.'

'Your eyes are bright,' Craig nodded. 'They see all.'

'You have asked for copies of the titles to those lands.' Again Craig was startled, but he remained silent. 'But even you must know that you must have government approval to purchase land in Zimbabwe. You must state the use to which you intend to put that land and the capital available to work it.'

'Yes, even I know that,' Craig agreed.

'So you come to me to assure me of your friendship.' Tungata looked up at him. 'Then, as an old friend, you will ask another favour, is that not so?'

Craig spread his hands, palms upward in gesture of resignation.

'One white rancher on land that could support fifty Matabele families. One white rancher growing fat and rich

76

while his servants wear rags and eat the scraps he throws them,' Tungata sneered, and Craig shot back at him.

'One white rancher bringing millions of capital into a country starving for it, one white rancher employing dozens of Matabele and feeding and clothing them and educating their children, one white rancher raising enough food to feed ten thousand Matabele, not a mere fifty. One white rancher cherishing the land, guarding it against goats and drought, so it will produce for five hundred years, not five—' Craig let his anger boil over, and returned Tungata's glare, standing stiff-legged over the desk.

'You are finished here,' Tungata growled at him. 'The kraal is closed against you. Go back to your boat, your fame and your fawning women, be content that we took only one of your legs – go before you lose your head as well.'

Tungata rolled his hand over and glanced at the gold wrist-watch.

'I have nothing more for you,' he said, and stood up. Yet, behind his flat, hostile stare, Craig sensed that the undefinable thing was still there. He tried to fathom it – not fear, he was certain, not guile. A hopelessness, a deep regret, perhaps, even a sense of guilt – or perhaps a blend of many of these things.

'Then, before I go, I have something else for you.' Craig stepped closer to the desk, and lowered his voice. 'You know I was on the Chizarira. I met three men there. Their names were Lookout, Peking and Dollar and they asked me to bring you a message—'

Craig got no further, for Tungata's anger turned to red fury. He was shaking with it, it clouded his gaze and knotted the muscles at the points of his heavy lantern jaw.

'Be silent,' he hissed, his voice held low by an iron effort of control. 'You meddle in matters that you do not understand, and that do not concern you. Leave this land before they overwhelm you.'

77

'I will go,' Craig returned his gaze defiantly, 'but only after my application to purchase land has been officially denied.'

'Then you will leave soon,' Tungata replied. 'That is my promise to you.'

In the parliamentary parking lot the Volkswagen was baking in the morning sun. Craig opened the doors and while he waited for the interior to cool, he found he was trembling with the after-effects of his confrontation with Tungata Zebiwe. He held up one hand before his eyes and watched the tremor of his fingertips. In the game department after having hunted down a man-eating lion or a crop-raiding bull elephant, he would have the same adrenalin come-down.

He slipped into the driver's seat, and while he waited to regain control of himself, he tried to arrange his impressions of the meeting and to review what he had learned from it.

Clearly Craig had been under surveillance by one of the state intelligence agencies from the moment of his arrival in Matabeleland. Perhaps he had been singled out for attention as a prominent writer – he would probably never know – but his every move had been reported to Tungata.

Yet he could not fathom the true reasons for Tungata's violent opposition to his plans. The reasons he had given were petty and spiteful, and Samson Kumalo had never been either petty or spiteful. Craig was sure that he had sensed correctly that strange mitigating counter-emotion beneath the forbidding reception, there were currents and undercurrents in the deep waters upon which Craig had set sail.

He thought back to Tungata's reaction to his mention of the three dissidents he had met in the wilderness of Chizarira. Obviously Tungata had recognized their names, and his rebuke had been too vicious to have come from a clear conscience. There was much that Craig still wanted to know, and much that Henry Pickering would find interesting.

Craig started the VW and drove slowly back to the Monomatapa down the avenues that had been originally laid out wide enough to enable a thirty-six-ox span to make a U-turn across them.

It was almost noon when he got back to the hotel room. He opened the liquor cabinet and reached for the gin bottle. Then he put it back unopened and rang room service for coffee instead. His daylight drinking habits had followed him from New York, and he knew they had contributed to his lack of purpose. They would change, he decided.

He sat down at the desk at the picture window and gazed down on the billowing blue jacaranda trees in the park while he assembled his thoughts, and then picked up his pen and brought his report to Henry Pickering up to date – including his impressions of Tungata's involvement with the Matabeleland dissidents and his almost guilty opposition to Craig's land-purchase application.

This led logically to his request for financing, and he set out his figures, his assessment of Rholands' potential, and his plans for King's Lynn and Chizarira as favourably as he could. Trading on Henry Pickering's avowed interest in Zimbabwe tourism, he dwelt at length on the development of 'Zambezi Waters' as a tourist attraction.

He placed the two sets of papers in separate manila envelopes, sealed them and drove down to the American Embassy. He survived the scrutiny of the marine guard in his armoured cubicle, and waited while Morgan Oxford came through to identify him.

The cultural attaché was a surprise to Craig. He was in his early thirties, as Craig was, but he was built like a college athlete, his hair was cropped short, his eyes were a penetrating blue and his handshake firm, suggesting a great deal more strength than he exerted in his grip.

He led Craig through to a small back office and accepted the two unaddressed manila envelopes without comment.

'I've been asked to introduce you around,' he said. 'There is a reception and cocktail hour at the French ambassador's residence this evening. A good place to begin. Six to seven – does that sound okay?'

'Fine.'

'You staying at the Mono or Meikles?'

'Monomatapa.'

'I'll pick you up at 17.45 hours.'

Craig noted the military expression of time, and thought wryly, 'Cultural attaché?'

Even under the socialist Mitterrand regime, the French managed a characteristic display of *élan*. The reception was on the lawns of the ambassador's residence, with the tricolour undulating gaily on the light evening breeze and the perfume of frangipani blossom creating an illusion of coolness after the crackling heat of the day. The servants were in white ankle-length *kanza* with crimson fez and sash, the champagne, although non-vintage, was Bollinger, and the *foie gras* on the biscuits was from the Périgord. The police band under the spathodea trees at the end of the lawn played light Italian operetta with an exuberant African beat, and only the motley selection of guests distinguished the gathering from a Rhodesian governor-general's garden party that Craig had attended six years previously.

The Chinese and the Koreans were the most numerous and noticeable, basking in their position of special favour with the government. It was they who had been most constant in aid and material support to the Shona forces during the long bush war, while the Soviets had made a rare error of judgement by courting the Matabele faction, for which the Mugabe government was now making them atone in full measure.

Every group on the lawn seemed to include the squat figures in the rumpled pyjama suits, grinning and bobbing their long lank locks like mandarin dolls, while the Russians formed a small group on their own, and those in uniform were junior officers – there was not even a colonel amongst them, Craig noted. The Russians could only move upstream from where they were now.

Morgan Oxford introduced Craig to the host and hostess. The ambassadress was at least thirty years younger than her husband. She wore a bright Pucci print with Parisian chic. Craig said, '*Enchanté, madame,*' and touched the back of her hand with his lips; when he straightened, she gave him a slow speculative appraisal before turning to the next guest in the reception line.

'Pickering warned me you were some kind of cocks-man,' Morgan chided him gently, 'but let's not have a diplomatic incident.'

'All right, I'll settle for a glass of bubbly.'

Each of them armed with a champagne flute, they surveyed the lawn. The ladies from the central African republics were in national dress, a marvellous cacophony of colour like a hatching of forest butterflies, and their men carried elaborately carved walking-sticks or fly-whisks made from animal tails, and the Muslims amongst them wore embroidered pill-box fezes with the tassels denoting that they were *hadji* who had made the pilgrimage to Mecca.

'Sleep well, Bawu,' Craig thought of his grandfather, the arch-colonist. 'It is best that you never lived to see this.'

'We had better make your number with the Brits, seeing that's your home base,' Morgan suggested, and introduced him to the British High Commissioner's wife, an iron-jawed lady with a lacquered hair style modelled on Margaret Thatcher's.

'I can't say I enjoyed all that detailed violence in your

book,' she told him severely. 'Do you think it was really necessary?'

Craig kept any trace of irony out of his voice. 'Africa is a violent land. He who would hide that fact from you is no true story-teller.' He wasn't really in the mood for amateur literary critics, and he let his eye slide past her and rove the lawn, seeking distraction.

What he found made his heart jump against his ribs like a caged animal. From across the lawn she was watching him with green eyes from under an unbroken line of dark thick brows. She wore a cotton skirt with patch pockets that left her calves bare, open sandals that laced around her ankles and a simple T-shirt. Her thick dark hair was tied with a leather thong at the back of her neck, it was freshly washed and shiny. Although she wore no make-up, her tanned skin had the lustre of abounding health and her lips were rouged with the bright young blood beneath. Over one shoulder was slung a Nikon FM with motor drive and both her hands were thrust into the pockets of her skirt.

She had been watching him, but the moment Craig looked directly at her, she lifted her chin in a gesture of mild disdain, held his eye for just long enough and then turned her head unhurriedly to the man who stood beside her, listening intently to what he was saying and then showing white teeth in a small controlled laugh. The man was an African, almost certainly Mashona, for he wore the crisply starched uniform of the regular Zimbabwean army and the red staff tabs and stars of a Brigadier-General. He was as handsome as the young Harry Belafonte.

'Some have a good eye for horse flesh,' Morgan said softly, mocking again. 'Come along, then, I'll introduce you.'

Before Craig could protest, he had started across the lawn and Craig had to follow.

'General Peter Fungabera, may I introduce Mr Craig Mellow. Mr Mellow is the celebrated novelist.'

'How do you do, Mr Mellow. I apologize for not having read your books. I have so little time for pleasure.' His English was excellent, his choice of words precise, but strongly accented.

'General Fungabera is Minister of Internal Security, Craig,' Morgan explained.

'A difficult portfolio, General.' Craig shook his hand, and saw that though his eyes were penetrating and cruel as a falcon's, there was a humorous twist to his smile, and Craig was instantly attracted to him. A hard man, but a good one, he judged.

The general nodded. 'But then nothing worth doing is ever easy, not even writing books. Don't you agree, Mr Mellow?'

He was quick and Craig liked him more, but his heart was still pumping and his mouth was dry so he could concentrate only a small part of his attention on the general.

'And this,' said Morgan, 'is Miss Sally-Anne Jay.' Craig turned to face her. How long ago since he had last done so, a month perhaps? But he found that he remembered clearly every golden fleck in her eyes and every freckle on her cheeks.

'Mr Mellow and I have met – though I doubt he would remember.' She turned back to Morgan and took his arm in a friendly, familiar gesture. 'I am so sorry I haven't seen you since I got back from the States, Morgan. Can't thank you enough for arranging the exhibition for me. I have received so many letters—'

'Oh, we've had feed-back also,' Morgan told her. 'All of it excellent. Can we have lunch next week? I'll show you.' He turned to explain. 'We sent an exhibition of Sally-Anne's photographs on a tour of all our African consular offices. Marvellous stuff, Craig, you really must see her work.'

'Oh, he has.' Sally-Anne smiled without warmth. 'But unfortunately Mr Mellow does not have your enthusiasm for my humble efforts.' And then without giving Craig a chance to protest, she turned back to Morgan. 'It's wonderful, General Fungabera has promised to accompany me on a visit to one of the rehabilitation centres, and he will allow me to do a photographic series—' With a subtle inclination of her body she effectively excluded Craig from the conversation, and left him feeling gawky and wordless on the fringe.

A light touch on his upper arm rescued him from embarrassment and General Fungabera drew him aside just far enough to ensure privacy.

'You seem to have a way of making enemies, Mr Mellow.'

'We had a misunderstanding in New York.' Craig glanced sideways at Sally-Anne.

'Although I did detect a certain arctic wind blowing there, I was not referring to the charming young photographer, but to others more highly placed and in a better position to render you disservice.' Now all Craig's attention focused upon Peter Fungabera as he went on softly. 'Your meeting this morning with a cabinet colleague of mine was,' he paused, 'shall we say, unfruitful?'

'Unfruitful will do very nicely,' Craig agreed.

'A great pity, Mr Mellow. If we are to become self-sufficient in our food supplies and not dependent on our racist neighbours in the south, then we need farmers with capital and determination on land that is now being abused.'

'You are well informed, General, and far-seeing.' Did everyone in the country already know exactly what he intended, Craig wondered?

'Thank you, Mr Mellow. Perhaps when you are ready to

make your application for land-purchase, you will do me the honour of speaking to me again. A friend at court, isn't that the term? My brother-in-law is the Minister for Agriculture.'

When he smiled, Peter Fungabera was irresistible. 'And now, Mr Mellow, as you heard, I am going to accompany Miss Jay on a visit to certain closed areas. The international press have been making a lot of play regarding them. Buchenwald, I think one of them wrote, or was it Belsen? It occurs to me that a man of your reputation might be able to set the record straight, a favour for a favour, perhaps – and if you travelled in the same company as Miss Jay, then it might give you an opportunity to sort out your misunderstanding, might it not?'

I t was still dark and chilly when Craig parked the Volkswagen in the lot behind one of the hangars at New Sarum air force base, and, lugging his hold-all, ducked through the low side-entrance into the cavernous interior.

Peter Fungabera was there ahead of him, talking to two airforce non-commissioned officers, but the moment he saw Craig he dismissed them with a casual salute and came towards Craig, smiling.

He wore a camouflage battle-smock and the burgundy-red beret and silver leopard's head cap-badge of the Third Brigade. Apart from a holstered sidearm, he carried only a leather-covered swagger-stick.

'Good morning, Mr Mellow. I admire punctuality.' He glanced down at Craig's hold-all. 'And the ability to travel lightly.'

He fell in beside Craig and they went out through the tall rolling doors onto the hard-stand.

There were two elderly Canberra bombers parked before

the hangar. Now the pride of the Zimbabwe airforce, they had once mercilessly blasted the guerrilla camps beyond the Zambezi. Beyond them stood a sleek little silver and blue Cessna 210, and Peter Fungabera headed towards it just as Sally-Anne appeared from under the wing. She was engrossed in her walk-around checks and Craig realized she was to be their pilot. He had expected a helicopter and a military pilot.

She was dressed in a Patagonia wind-cheater, blue jeans and soft leather mosquito boots. Her hair was covered by a silk scarf. She looked professional and competent as she made a visual check of the fuel level in the wing tanks and then jumped down to the tarmac.

'Good morning, General. Would you like to take the right-hand seat?'

'Shall we put Mr Mellow up front? I have seen it all before.'

'As you wish,' she nodded coolly at Craig. 'Mr Mellow,' and climbed up into the cockpit. She cleared with the tower and taxied to the holding point, pulled on the hand-brake and murmured, 'Too much pork for good Hebrew education causes trouble.'

As a conversational opener it took some following. Craig was startled, but she ignored him and only when her hands began to dart over the controls setting the trim, checking masters, mags and mixture, pushing the pitch fully fine, did he understand that the phrase was her personal acronym for pre-take-off, and the mild misgivings that he had had about female pilots began to recede.

After take-off, she turned out of the circuit on a north-westerly heading and engaged the automatic pilot, opened a large-scale map on her lap and concentrated on the route. Good flying technique, Craig admitted, but not much for social intercourse.

'A beautiful machine,' Craig tried. 'Is it your own?'

'Permanent loan from the World Wildlife Trust,' she answered, still intent on the sky directly ahead.

'What does she cruise at?'

'There is an air-speed indicator directly in front of you, Mr Mellow,' she crushed him effortlessly.

It was Peter Fungabera who leaned over the back of Craig's seat and ended the silence.

'That's the Great Dyke,' he pointed out the abrupt geological formation below them. 'A highly mineralized intrusion – chrome, platinum, gold—' Beyond the dyke, the farming lands petered out swiftly and they were over a vast area of rugged hills and sickly green forests that stretched endlessly to a milky horizon.

'We will be landing at a secondary airstrip, just this side of the Pongola Hills. There is a mission-station there and a small settlement, but the area is very remote. Transport will meet us there but it's another two hours' drive to the camp,' the general explained.

'Do you mind if we go down lower, General?' Sally-Anne asked, and Peter Fungabera chuckled.

'No need to ask the reason. Sally-Anne is educating me in the importance of wild animals, and their conservation.'

Sally-Anne eased back the throttle and went down. The heat was building up and the light aircraft began to bounce and wobble as it met the thermals coming up from the rocky hills. The area below them was devoid of human habitation and cultivation.

'Godforsaken hills,' the general growled. 'No permanent water, sour grazing and fly.'

However, Sally-Anne picked out a herd of big beige hump-backed eland in one of the open vleis beside a dry river-bed, and then, twenty miles further on, a solitary bull elephant.

She dropped to tree-top level, pulled on the flaps and did a series of steep slow turns around the elephant, cutting him off from the forest and holding him in the open, so he was forced to face the circling machine with ears and trunk extended.

'He's magnificent!' she cried, the wind from the open window buffeting them and whipping her words away. 'A hundred pounds of ivory each side,' and she was shooting single-handed through the open window, the motor drive on her Nikon whirring as it pumped film through the camera.

They were so low that it seemed the bull might grab a wingtip with his reaching trunk, and Craig could clearly make out the wet exudation from the glands behind his eyes. He found himself gripping the sides of his seat.

At last Sally-Anne left him, levelled her wings and climbed away. Craig slumped with relief.

'Cold feet, Mr Mellow? Or should that be singular, foot?'

'Bitch,' Craig thought. 'That was a low hit.' But she was talking to Peter Fungabera over her shoulder.

'Dead, that animal is worth ten thousand dollars, tops. Alive, he's worth ten times that, and he'll sire a hundred bulls to replace him.'

'Sally-Anne is convinced that there is a large-scale poaching ring at work in this country. She has shown me some remarkable photographs – and I must say, I am beginning to share her concern.'

'We have to find them and smash them, General,' she insisted.

'Find them for me, Sally-Anne, and I will smash them. You already have my word.'

Listening to them talking, Craig felt again an old-fashioned emotion that he had been aware of the very first time he had seen these two together. There was no missing the accord between them, and Fungabera was a dashingly handsome fellow. Now he darted a glance over his shoulder, and found the general watching him closely and speculatively, a look he covered instantly with a smile.

'How do you feel about the issue, Mr Mellow?' he said, and suddenly Craig was telling him about his plans for Zambezi Waters on the Chizarira. He told them about the black rhinoceros and the protected wilderness areas surrounding it, and he told them how accessible it was to Victoria Falls, and now Sally-Anne was listening as intently as the general. When he finished, they were both silent for a while, and then the general said, 'Now, Mr Mellow, you are making good sense. That is the kind of planning that this country desperately needs, and its profit-potential will be understood by even the most backward and unsophisticated of my people.'

'Wouldn't Craig be easier, General?'

'Thank you, Craig – my friends call me Peter.'

Half an hour later Craig saw a galvanized iron roof flash in the sunlight dead ahead, and Sally-Anne said, 'Tuti Mission Station,' and began letting down for a landing. She banked steeply over the church and Craig saw tiny figures around the cluster of huts waving up at them.

The strip was short and narrow and rough, and the wind was across, but Sally-Anne crabbed in and kicked her straight at the moment before touch-down, then held the port wing down with a twist of the wheel. She was really very good indeed, Craig realized.

There was a sand-coloured army Land-Rover waiting under a huge marula tree off to one side of the strip, and three troopers saluted Peter Fungabera with a stamping of boots that raised dust and a slapping of rifle-butts. Then while Craig helped Sally-Anne tie down the aircraft, they loaded the meagre baggage into the Land-Rover.

As the Land-Rover drew level with the mission school-house beside the church, Sally-Anne asked, 'Do you think they have a girls' room here?' and Peter tapped the driver on the shoulder with his swagger-stick and the vehicle stopped.

Goggle-eyed black children crowded the veranda and the school-mistress came out to greet Sally-Anne as she climbed the steps, and gave her a little curtsey of welcome. The teacher was about the same age as Sally-Anne, with long slim legs under her simple cotton skirt. Her dress was surgically clean and crisply ironed, and her white gym shoes were spotless. Her skin was glossy as velvet, and she had the typical moon face, shining teeth and gazelle eyes of the Nguni maiden, but there was a grace in her carriage, an alert and intelligent expression and a sculpturing of her features that was truly beautiful.

She and Sally-Anne talked for a few moments and then she led the white girl through the door.

'I think you and I should understand each other, Craig.' Peter watched the two girls disappear. 'I have seen you looking at Sally-Anne and me. Let me just say, I admire Sally-Anne's accomplishments, her intelligence and her initiative – however, unlike many of my peers, miscegenation has no attraction for me whatsoever. I find most European women mannish and overbearing, and white flesh insipid. If you will pardon my plain speaking.'

'I am relieved to hear it, Peter,' Craig smiled.

'On the other hand, the little schoolteacher there strikes me as – you are the wordmaster, give me a word for her, please.'

'Toothsome.'

'Good.'

'Nubile.'

'Even better,' Peter chuckled. 'I really must find time to read your book.' And then he was serious again as he went on, 'Her name is Sarah. She has four A levels and a high-school teacher's diploma; she has qualifications in nursing, she is beautiful and yet modest, respectful and dutiful with traditional good manners – did you see how she did not

look directly at us men? – that would have been forward.'
Peter nodded approval. 'A modern woman with old-fashioned virtues. Yet her father is a witch-doctor who dresses in skins, divines by throwing the bones, and does not wash from one year to the next. Africa,' he said. 'My wonderful, endlessly fascinating ever-changing never-changing Africa.'

The two young women returned from the outhouses behind the school and were chatting animatedly to each other, while Sally-Anne clicked away with her camera, capturing images of the children with their teacher who seemed not much older than they. The two men watched them from the Land-Rover.

'You strike me as a man of action, Peter – and I cannot believe you lack the bride-price.' Craig asked. 'What are you waiting for?'

'She is Matabele, and I am Mashona. Capulet and Montague,' Peter explained simply. 'And that is an end of it.'

The children, led by Sarah, sang them a song of welcome from the veranda and then at Sally-Anne's request recited the alphabet and the multiplication tables, while she photographed their intent expressions. When she climbed back into the Land-Rover, they trilled their farewells and waved until the billowing dust hid them.

The track was rough and the Land-Rover bounced over the deep ruts formed in the rainy season in black glutinous mud and dried now to the consistency of concrete. Through gaps in the forest they glimpsed blue hills on the northern horizon, sheer and riven and uninviting.

'The Pongola Hills,' Peter told them. 'Bad country.' And then as they neared their destination, he began telling them what they might expect when at last they arrived.

'These rehabilitation centres are not concentration camps – but are, as the name implies, centres of reeducation and adaptation to the ordinary world.'

91

He glanced at Craig. 'You, as well as any of us, know that we have lived through a dreadful civil war. Eleven years of hell, that have brutalized an entire generation of young people. Since their early teens, they have known no life without an automatic rifle in their hands, they have been taught nothing but destruction and learned nothing except that a man's desires can be achieved simply by killing anybody who stands in his way.'

Peter Fungabera was silent for a few moments, and Craig could see that he was reliving his own part in those terrible years. Now he sighed softly.

'They, poor fellows, were misled by some of their leaders. To sustain them in the hardships and privations of the bush war they were made promises that could never be kept. They were promised rich farming land and hundreds of head of prime cattle, money and motor-cars and many wives of their choice.' Peter made an angry gesture. 'They were built up to great expectations, and when these could not be met, they turned against those who made the promises. Every one of them was armed, every one a trained soldier who had killed and would not hesitate to kill again. What were we to do?' Peter broke off and glanced at his wrist-watch. 'Time for lunch and a stretch of the legs,' he suggested.

The driver parked where the track crossed a high earthen causeway and a timber bridge over a river-bed in which cool green waters swirled over the rippled sand-banks and tall reeds nodded their heads from either bank. The escort built a fire, roasted maize cobs over it and brewed Malawi tea, while Peter walked his guests in leisurely fashion along the causeway and went on with his lecture.

'We Africans once had a tradition. If one of our young people became intractable and flouted the tribal laws, then he was sent into bush camp where the elders licked him back into shape. This rehabilitation centre is a modernized version of the traditional bush camp. I will not attempt to hide anything from you. It is no Club Med holiday home that we are going to visit. The men in it are tough, and only hard treatment will have any effect on them. On the other hand, they are not extermination camps – let us rather say that they are equivalent to the detention barracks of the British army—' Craig could not help but be impressed by Peter Fungabera's honesty ' – you are free to speak to any of the detainees, but I must ask you not to go wandering off into the bush on your own – that applies to you especially, Sally-Anne,' Peter smiled at her. 'This is a very isolated and wild spot. Animals like hyenas and leopards are attracted by offal and sewage, and become fearless and bold. Ask me if you want to leave the camp, and I will provide you with an escort.'

They ate the frugal lunch, husking the scorched maize with their fingers and washing it down with the strong, black, over-sweetened tea.

'If you are ready, we will go on.' Peter led them back to the Land-Rover, and an hour later they reached Tuti Rehabilitation Centre.

During the bush war it had been one of the 'protected villages' set up by the Smith government in an attempt to shield the black peasants from intimidation by the guerrillas. There was a central rocky kopje that had been cleared of all vegetation, a pile of large grey granite boulders on top of which had been built a small, sandbagged fort with machine-gun embrasures, firing platforms, communication trenches and dugouts. Below this was the encampment, orderly rows of mud-and-thatched huts, many with half-walls to allow air circulation, built around a dusty open space which could have been parade ground or football field, for there were rudimentary goal posts set up at each end, and, incongruously, a sturdy whitewashed wall at the side nearest the fort.

A double fence of barbed-wire, sandwiching a deep

ditch, surrounded the camp. The wire was ten-foot high and tightly woven. The floor of the ditch was armed with closely planted, sharpened wooden stakes, and there were high guard-towers on bush poles at each corner of the stockade. The guards at the only gate saluted the Land-Rover, and they drove slowly down the track that skirted the parade ground.

In the sun, two or three hundred young black men, dressed only in khaki shorts, were performing vigorous calisthenics to the shouts of uniformed black instructors. In the thatched open-walled huts hundreds more were sitting in orderly rows on the bare earth, reciting in chanted unison the lesson on the blackboard.

'We'll do a tour later,' Peter told them. 'First we will get you settled.'

Craig was allocated a dugout in the fort. The earthen floor had been freshly swept and sprinkled with water to cool it and lay the dust. The only furnishings were a plaited-reed sleeping-mat on the floor and a sacking screen covering the doorway. On the reed mat was a box of matches and a packet of candles. Craig guessed that these were a luxury reserved for important guests.

Sally-Anne was allocated the dugout across the trench from his. She showed no dismay at the primitive conditions, and when Craig glanced around the screen, he saw her sitting on her reed mat in the lotus position, cleaning the lens of her camera and reloading film.

Peter Fungabera excused himself and went up the trench to the command post at the hilltop. A few minutes later an electric generator started running and Craig could hear Peter on the radio talking in rapid Shona which he could not follow. He came down again half-an-hour later.

'It will be dark in an hour. We will go down and watch the detainees being given the evening meal.'

The detainees lined up in utter silence, shuffling forward to be fed. There were no smiles nor horseplay. They did not show even the slightest curiosity in the white visitors and the general.

'Simple fare,' Peter pointed out. 'Maize-meal porridge and greens.'

Each man had a dollop of the fluffy stiff cake spooned into his bowl, and topped by another of stewed vegetable.

'Meat once a week. Tobacco once a week – both can be withheld for bad behaviour.' Peter was telling it exactly as it was. The men were lean, ribs racked out from under hard-worked muscle, no trace of fat on any of them. They wolfed the food immediately, still standing, using their fingers to wipe the bowl clean. Lean, but not emaciated, finely drawn but not starved, Craig judged, and then his eyes narrowed.

'That man is injured.' The purple bruising showed even over his sun-darkened skin.

'You may speak to him,' Peter invited, and when Craig questioned him in Sindebele, the man responded immediately.

'Your back – what happened?'

'I was beaten.'

'Why?'

'Fighting with another man.'

Peter called over one of the guards and spoke quietly to him in Shona, then explained. 'He stabbed another prisoner with a weapon made of sharpened fencing wire. Deprived of meat and tobacco for two months and fifteen strokes with a heavy cane. This is precisely the type of anti-social behaviour we are trying to prevent.'

As they walked back across the parade ground past the whitewashed wall, Peter went on, 'Tomorrow you have the run of the camp. We will leave the following morning early.'

They ate with the Shona officers in the mess, and the fare was the same as that served to the detainees with the addition of a stew of stringy meat of indeterminate origin and dubious freshness. Immediately they finished eating, Peter Fungabera excused himself and led his officers out of the dugout leaving Craig and Sally-Anne alone together.

Before Craig could think of anything to say, Sally-Anne stood without a word and left the dugout. Craig had reached the limit of his forbearance and was suddenly angry with her. He jumped up and followed her out. He found her on the firing platform of the main trench, perched up on the sandbag parapet, hugging her knees and staring down on the encampment. The moon was just past full and already well clear of the hills on the horizon. She did not look round as Craig stepped up beside her, and Craig's anger evaporated as suddenly as it had arisen.

. 'I acted like a pig,' he said.

She hugged her knees a little tighter and said nothing.

'When we first met I was going through a bad time,' he went on doggedly. 'I won't bore you with the details, but the book I was trying to write was blocked and I had lost my way. I took it out on you.'

Still she showed no sign of having heard him. Down in the forest beyond the double fence there was a sudden hideous outcry, shrieks of mirthless laughter rising and falling, sobbing and wailing, taken up and repeated at a dozen points around the camp perimeter, dying away at last in a descending series of chuckles and grunts and agonized moans.

'Hyena,' said Craig, and Sally-Anne shivered slightly and straightened up as if to rise.

'Please.' Craig heard the desperate note in his own voice. 'Just a minute more. I have been searching for a chance to apologize.'

'That isn't necessary,' she said. 'It was presumptuous of me to expect you to like my work.' Her tone was not in the least conciliatory. 'I guess I asked for it – and did you ever let me have it!'

'Your work – your photographs—' his voice dropped ' – they frightened me. That was why my reaction was so spiteful, so childish.'

Now she turned to look at him for the first time and the moon silvered the planes of her face. 'Frightened you?' she asked.

'Terrified me. You see, I wasn't able to work. I was beginning to believe that it had been only a one-off thing, that the book was a fluke, and there was no real talent left in me. I kept going back to the cupboard and each time it was bare—' she was staring at him now, her lips slightly parted and her eyes mysterious cups of darkness ' – and then you hit me with those damned photographs, and dared me to match them.'

She shook her head slowly.

'You might not have meant that, but that's what it was – a challenge. A challenge I didn't have the courage to accept. I was afraid, I lashed out at you, and I have been regretting it ever since.'

'You liked them?' she asked.

'They shook my little world. They showed me Africa again, and filled me with longing. When I saw them, I knew what was missing in me. I was struck with homesickness like a little boy on his first lonely night at boarding-school.' He felt a choking in his throat, and was unashamed of it. 'It was those photographs of yours that made me come back here.'

'I didn't understand,' she said, and they were both silent. Craig knew that if he spoke again, it might come out as a sob, for the tears of self-pity were prickling the rims of his eyelids.

Down in the encampment below them someone began to sing. It was a fine African tenor voice that carried faint but clear to the hilltop, so that Craig could recognize the words. It was an ancient Matabele regimental fighting chant, but now it was sung as a lament, seeming to capture all the suffering and tragedy of a continent; and not even the hyena cried while the voice sang:

> 'The Moles are beneath the earth,
> "Are they dead?" asked the daughters of Mashobane.
> Listen, pretty maids, do you not hear
> Something stirring, in the darkness?'

The singer's voice died away at last, and Craig imagined all the hundreds of other young men lying in wakeful silence on their sleeping-mats, haunted and saddened by the song as he was.

Then Sally-Anne spoke again. 'Thank you for telling me,' she said. 'I know what it must have cost you.' She touched his bare upper arm, a light brush of her fingertips which thrilled along his nerve ends and made his heart trip.

Then she uncurled her legs and dropped lightly off the parapet and slipped away down the communication trench. He heard the sacking flap fall over the entrance to her dugout and the flare of a match as she lit a candle.

He knew he would be unable to sleep, so he stayed on alone listening to the African night and watching the moon. Slowly he felt the words rising up in him, like water in a well that has been pumped down to the mud. His sadness fell away, and was replaced by excitement.

He went down to his own dugout and lit one of the candles, stuck it in a niche of the wall and from his hold-all took his notebook and ballpoint pen. The words were bubbling and frothing in his brain, like boiling milk. He put the point of the pen to the lined white paper – and it sped away across the page like a living thing. Words came spurting out of him in a joyous, long-pent-up orgasm and spilled untidily over the paper. He stopped only to relight fresh candles from the guttering stump.

In the morning his eyes were red and burning from the strain. He felt weak and shaky as though he had run too far and too fast, but the notebook was three-quarters filled and he was strangely elated.

His elation lasted him well into the hot brilliant morning, enhanced by Sally-Anne's change of attitude towards him. She was still reserved and quiet, but at least she listened when he spoke and replied seriously and thoughtfully. Once or twice she even smiled, and then her too-large mouth and nose were at last in harmony with the rest of her face. Craig found it difficult to concentrate on the plight of the men that they had come to study, until he realized Sally-Anne's compassion and listened to her speaking freely for the first time.

'It would be so easy to dismiss them as brutish criminals,' she murmured, watching their expressionless faces and guarded eyes, 'until you realize how they have been deprived of all humanizing influences. Most of them were abducted from their schoolrooms in their early teens and taken into the guerrilla training-camps. They have nothing, have never had any possession of their own except an AK 47 rifle. How can we expect them to respect the persons and properties of others? Craig, please ask that one how old he is.'

'He does not know,' Craig translated for her. 'He does not know when he was born, nor where his parents are.'

'He does not even have a simple birthright,' Sally-Anne pointed out, and suddenly Craig remembered how churlishly he could reject a wine that was not exactly to his taste, or how thoughtlessly he could order a new suit of clothing, or enter the first-class cabin of an airliner – while these men wore only a ragged pair of shorts, without even a pair of shoes or a blanket to protect them.

'The abyss between the haves and the have-nots of this world will suck us all into destruction,' Sally-Anne said as she recorded through her Nikon lens that dumb-animal resignation that lies beyond despair. 'Ask that one how he is treated here,' she insisted, and when Craig spoke to him the man stared at him without comprehension, as though the question was meaningless, and slowly Craig's sense of well-being burned off like mist in the morning.

In the open huts the lessons were political orientation, and the role of the responsible citizen in the socialist state. On the blackboards, diagrams showed the relationship of parliament to the judiciary and the executive branches of the state. They had been copied onto the boards in a laboured, semi-literate hand by bored instructors and were recited parrot-fashion by the rows of squatting detainees. Their obvious lack of comprehension depressed Craig even more.

As they trudged back up the hill to their quarters, a thought struck Craig and he turned to Peter Fungabera.

'All the men here are Matabele, aren't they?'

'That is true,' Peter nodded. 'We keep the tribes segregated – it reduces friction.'

'Are there any Shona detainees?' Craig insisted.

'Oh, yes,' Peter assured him. 'The camps for them are up in the eastern highlands – exactly the same con-ditions—'

At sunset the generator powering the radio was started and twenty minutes later Peter Fungabera came down to the dugout where Craig was re-reading and correcting his writing of the previous night.

'There is a message for you, Craig, relayed by Morgan Oxford at the American Embassy.'

Craig jumped to his feet eagerly. He had arranged for Henry Pickering's reply to be passed on to him as soon as it was received. He took the sheet of notepaper on which Peter had jotted the radio transmission, and read; 'For

Mellow. Stop. My personal enthusiasm for your project not shared by others. Stop. Ashe Levy unwilling to advance or guarantee. Stop. Loans Committee here requires substantial additional collateral before funding. Stop. Regrets and best wishes. Henry.'

Craig read the message once fast and then again very slowly.

'None of my business,' Peter Fungabera murmured, 'but I presume this concerns your plans for the place you call Zambezi Waters?'

'That's right – and it puts the kibosh on those, I'm afraid,' Craig told him bitterly.

'Henry?'

'A friend, a banker – perhaps I relied on him too much.'

'Yes,' Peter Fungabera said thoughtfully, 'it looks that way, doesn't it?'

Even though he had missed the previous night, Craig had difficulty sleeping. His mat was iron-hard and the hellish chorus of the hyena pack in the forest echoed his sombre mood.

On the long drive back to the airstrip at Tuti Mission, he sat beside the driver and took no part in the conversation of Peter and Sally-Anne in the seat behind him. Only now did he realize how much store he had set on buying Rholands, and he was bitterly angry with Ashe Levy who had refused his support and with Henry Pickering who had not tried hard enough, and his damned Loans Committee who could not see the ends of their own noses.

Sally-Anne insisted on stopping once again at the mission schoolhouse to renew her acquaintance with Sarah, the Matabele teacher. This time Sarah was prepared and offered her visitors tea. In no mood for pleasantries, Craig found a seat on the low veranda wall well separated from the others, and began scheming without real optimism how he might circumvent Henry Pickering's refusal.

Sarah came to him demurely with an enamel mug of tea

on a carved wooden tray. As she offered it, her back was turned to Peter Fungabera.

'When the man-eating crocodile knows the hunter is searching for him, he buries himself in the mud at the bottom of the deepest pool,' she spoke softly in Sindebele, 'and when the leopard hunts, he hunts in darkness.'

Startled, Craig looked into her face. Her eyes were no longer downcast, and there was a fierce and angry glow in their dark depths.

'Fungabera's puppies must have been noisy,' she went on just as softly, 'they could not feed while you were here. They would have been hungry. Did you hear them, Kuphela?' she asked, and this time Craig started with surprise. Sarah had used the name that Comrade Lookout had given him. How had she known that? What did she mean by Fungabera's puppies?

Before Craig could reply, Peter Fungabera looked up and saw Craig's face. He rose to his feet easily but swiftly, and crossed the veranda to Sarah's side. Immediately the black girl dropped her gaze from Craig's face, bobbed a little curtsey and retired with the empty tray.

'Do not let your disappointment depress you too much, Craig. Do come and join us.' Peter placed a friendly hand on Craig's shoulder.

On the short drive from the mission station to the airstrip Sally-Anne suddenly leaned forward and touched Craig's shoulder.

'I have been thinking, Craig. This place you call Zambezi Waters can only be about half an hour's flying time from here. I found the Chizarira river on the map. We could make a small detour and fly over it on the way home.'

'No point.' Craig shook his head.

'Why not?' she asked, and he passed her the sheet of notepaper with Pickering's message.

'Oh, I am so sorry.' It was genuine, Craig realized, and her concern comforted him a little.

'I would like to see the area,' Peter Fungabera cut in suddenly, and when Craig shook his head again, his voice hardened. 'We will go there,' he said with finality, and Craig shrugged his indifference.

Craig and Sally-Anne pored over her map. 'The pools should be here, where this stream joins the main river-course.' And she worked swiftly with callipers and her wind-deflection computer.

'Okay,' she said. 'Twenty-two minutes' flying time with this wind.'

While they flew, and Sally-Anne studied the terrain and compared it to her map, Craig brooded over the Matabele girl's words. 'Fungabera's puppies.' Somehow it sounded menacing, and her use of the name 'Kuphela' troubled him even more. There was only one explanation: she was in touch with, and was probably a member of, the group of dissident guerrillas. What had she meant by the leopard and crocodile allegory, and Fungabera's puppies? And whatever it was, just how unbiased and reliable would she be if she were a guerrilla sympathizer?

'There is the river,' said Sally-Anne as she eased the throttle closed and began a shallow descending turn towards the glint of waters through the forest-tops.

She flew very low along the river-bank, and despite the thick cloak of vegetation, picked out herds of game animals, even once, with a squeal of glee, the great rocklike hulk of a black rhinoceros in the ebony thickets.

Then suddenly she pointed ahead. 'Look at that!'

In a loop of the river, there was a strip of open land hedged in with tall riverine trees, where the grass had been grazed like a lawn by the zebra herds who were already raising dust as they galloped away in panic from the approaching aircraft.

'I bet I could get down there,' Sally-Anne said and pulled on the flaps, slowing the Cessna and lowering the nose to give herself better forward vision. Then she let down the landing-gear.

She made a series of slow passes over the open ground, each lower than the previous one, until at the fourth pass her wheels were only two or three feet above the ground and they could see each individual hoofprint of the zebra in the dusty earth.

'Firm and clear,' she said, and on the next pass touched down, and immediately applied maximum safe braking that pulled the aircraft to a dead stop in less than a hundred and fifty paces.

'Bird lady,' Craig grinned at her and she smiled at the compliment.

They left the aircraft and set off across the plain towards the forest wall, passed through it along a game trail and came out on a rocky bluff above the river.

The scene was a perfect African cameo. White sand-banks and water-polished rock glittering like reptiles' scales, trailing branches decked with weaver birds' nests over deep green water, tall trees with white serpentine roots crawling over the rocks – and beyond that, open forest.

'It's beautiful,' said Sally-Anne, and wandered off with her camera.

'This would be a good site for one of your camps,' Peter Fungabera pointed at the great lumpy heaps of elephant dung on the white sandbank below them.

'Grandstand view.'

'Yes, it would have been,' Peter agreed. 'It seems too good to pass up – at that price. There must be millions of profit in it.'

'For a good African socialist, you talk like a filthy capitalist,' Craig told him morosely.

Peter chuckled and said, 'They do say that socialism is the ideal philosophy – just as long as you have capitalists to pay for it.'

Craig looked up sharply, and for the first time saw the glitter of good old western European avarice in Peter Fungabera's eyes. Both of them were silent, watching Sally-Anne in the river-bed, as she made compositions of tree and rock and sky and photographed them.

'Craig.' Peter had obviously reached a decision. 'If I could arrange the collateral the World Bank requires, I would expect a commission in Rholands shares.'

'I guess you would be entitled to it.' Craig felt the embers of his dead hopes flicker, and at that moment Sally-Anne called, 'It's getting late and we have two and a half hours' flying to Harare.'

Back at New Sarum air force base Peter Fungabera shook hands with both of them.

'I hope your pictures turn out fine,' he said to Sally-Anne, and to Craig, 'You will be at the Monomatapa? I will contact you there within the next three days.'

He climbed into the army jeep that was waiting for them, nodded to his driver, and saluted them with his swagger-stick as he drove away.

'Have you got a car?' Craig asked Sally-Anne, and when she shook her head, 'I can't promise to drive as well as you fly – will you take a chance?'

She had an apartment in an old block in the avenues opposite Government House. He dropped her at the entrance.

'How about dinner?' he asked.

'I've got a lot of work to do, Craig.'

'Quick dinner, promise – peace offering. I'll have you home by ten.' He crossed his heart theatrically, and she relented.

'Okay, seven o'clock here,' she agreed, and he watched

the way she climbed the steps before he started the Volkswagen. Her stride was businesslike and brisk, but her backside in the blue jeans was totally frivolous.

Sally-Anne suggested a steakhouse where she was greeted like royalty by the huge, bearded proprietor, and where the beef was simply the best Craig had ever tasted, thick and juicy and tender. They drank a Cabernet from the Cape of Good Hope and from a stilted beginning their conversation eased as Craig drew her out.

'It was fine just as long as I was a mere technical assistant at Kodak, but when I started being invited on expeditions as official photographer and then giving my own exhibitions, he just couldn't take it,' she told him, 'first man ever to be jealous of a Nikon.'

'How long were you married?'

'Two years.'

'No children?'

'Thank God, no.'

She ate like she walked, quickly, neatly and efficiently, yet with a sensuous streak of pleasure, and when she was finished she looked at her gold Rolex.

'You promised ten o'clock,' she said, and despite his protestations, scrupulously divided the bill in half and paid her share.

When he parked outside the apartment, she looked at him seriously for a moment before she asked, 'Coffee?'

'With the greatest of pleasure.' He started to open the door, but she stopped him.

'Right from the start, let's get it straight,' she said. 'The coffee is instant Nescafé – and that's all. No gymnastics – nothing else, okay?'

'Okay,' he agreed.

'Let's go.'

Her apartment was furnished with a portable tape recorder, canvas-covered cushions and a single camp-bed on which her sleeping-bag was neatly rolled. Apart from the cushions, the floor was bare but polished, and the walls were papered with her photographs. He wandered around studying them while she made the coffee in the kitchenette.

'If you want the bathroom, it's through there,' she called. 'Just be careful.'

It was more dark-room than ablution, with a light-proof black nylon zip-up tent over the shower cabinet and jars of chemicals and packets of photographic paper where in any other feminine bathroom there would have been scents and soaps.

They lolled on the cushions, drank the coffee, played Beethoven's Fifth on the tape, and talked of Africa. Once or twice she made passing reference to his book, showing that she had read it with attention.

'I've got an early start tomorrow—' at last she reached across and took the empty mug out of his hand. 'Good night, Craig.'

'When can I see you again?'

'I'm not sure, I'm flying up into the highlands early tomorrow. I don't know how long.' Then she saw his expression and relented. 'I'll call you at the Mono when I get back, if you like?'

'I like.'

'Craig, I'm beginning to like you – as a friend, perhaps, but I'm not looking for romance. I'm still hurting – just as long as we understand that,' she told him as they shook hands at the door of the apartment.

Despite her denial, Craig felt absurdly pleased with himself as he drove back to the Monomatapa. At this stage he did not care to analyse too deeply his feelings for her, nor to define his intentions towards her. It was merely a pleasant change not to have another celebrity boffer trying to add his name to her personal scoreboard. Her powerful physical attraction for him was made more poignant by her reluctance, and he respected her talents and accomplishments and was in total sympathy with her love of Africa and her compassion for its peoples.

'That's enough for now,' he told himself as he parked the Volkswagen.

The assistant manager met him in the hotel lobby, wringing his hands with anguish, and led him through to his office.

'Mr Mellow, I have had a visit from the police special branch while you were out. I had to open your deposit box for them, and let them into your room.'

'God damn it, are they allowed to do that?' Craig was outraged.

'You don't understand, here they can do whatever they like,' the assistant manager hurried on. 'They removed nothing from the box, Mr Mellow – I can assure you of that.'

'Nevertheless, I'd like to check it,' Craig demanded grimly.

He thumbed through his travellers' cheques and they tallied. His return air-ticket was intact, as was his passport – but they had been through the 'survival kit' that Henry Pickering had provided. The gilt field assessor's identification badge was loose in its leather cover.

'Who could order a search like this?' he asked the assistant manager as they relocked the box.

'Only someone pretty high up.'

'Tungata Zebiwe,' he thought bitterly. 'You vicious, nosy bastard – how you must have changed.'

Craig took his report of his visit to Tuti Rehabilitation Centre for Henry Pickering up to the embassy, and Morgan Oxford accepted it and offered him coffee.

'I might be here a longer time than I thought,' Craig told him, 'and I just can't work in an hotel room.'

'Apartments are hell to find,' Morgan shrugged. 'I'll see what I can do.'

He phoned him the next day. 'Craig, one of our girls is going home on a month's vacation. She is a fan of yours, and she will sub-let her flat for six hundred dollars. She leaves tomorrow.'

The apartment was a bed-sitter, but it was comfortable and airy. There was a broad table that would do as a writing-desk. Craig set a pile of blank Typex bond paper in the centre of it with a brick as a paper-weight, his Concise Oxford Dictionary beside that and said aloud: 'Back in business.'

He had almost forgotten how quickly the hours could pass in never-never land, and in the deep pure joy of watching the finished sheets of paper pile up at the far end of the table.

Morgan Oxford phoned him twice during the next few days, each time to invite him to diplomatic parties, and each time Craig refused, and finally unplugged the telephone. When he relented on the fourth day and plugged the extension in again, the telephone rang almost immediately.

'Mr Mellow.' It was an African voice. 'We have had great difficulty finding you. Hold on, please, for General Fungabera.'

'Craig, it's Peter.' The familiar heavy accent and charm. 'Can we meet this afternoon? Three o'clock? I will send a driver.'

Peter Fungabera's private residence was fifteen miles out of town on the hills overlooking Lake Macillwane. The house had originally been built in the 1920s by a rich remittance man, black sheep younger son of an English aircraft manufacturer. It was surrounded firstly by wide verandas and white fretwork eaves and then by five acres of lawns and flowering trees.

A bodyguard of Third Brigade troopers in full battledress checked Craig and his driver carefully at the gate before allowing them up to the main house. When Craig climbed the front steps, Peter Fungabera was waiting for him at the top. He was dressed in white cotton slacks and a crimson short-sleeved silk shirt, which looked magnificent against his velvety black skin. With a friendly arm around Craig's shoulders, he led him down the veranda to where a small group was seated.

'Craig, may I introduce Mr Musharewa, governor of the Land Bank of Zimbabwe. This is Mr Kapwepwe, his assistant, and this is Mr Cohen, my attorney. Gentlemen, this is Mr Craig Mellow, the famous author.'

They shook hands. 'A drink, Craig? We are drinking Bloody Marys.'

'That will do very well, Peter.'

A servant in a flowing white *kanza*, reminiscent of colonial days, brought Craig his drink and when he left, Peter Fungabera said simply, 'The Land Bank of Zimbabwe has agreed to stand as your personal surety for a loan of five million dollars from the World Bank or its associate bank in New York.'

Craig gaped at him.

'Your connection with the World Bank is not a particularly closely guarded secret, you know. Henry Pickering is well known to us too,' Peter smiled, and went on quickly. 'Of course, there are certain conditions and stipulations, but I don't think they will be prohibitive.' He turned to his white attorney. 'You have the documents, Izzy? Good, will you give Mr Mellow a copy, and then read through them for us, please.'

Isadore Cohen adjusted his spectacles, squared up the thick pile of documents on the table in front of him and began.

'Firstly, this is a land purchase approval,' he said. 'Authority for Craig Mellow, a British subject and a citizen of Zimbabwe, to purchase a controlling interest in the land-owning private company, known as Rholands (Pty) Ltd. The approval is signed by the state president and countersigned by the minister of agriculture.'

Craig thought of Tungata Zebiwe's promise to quash that approval and then he remembered that the minister of agriculture was Peter Fungabera's brother-in-law. He glanced across at the general, but he was listening intently to his lawyer's recitation.

As he came to each document in the pile, Isadore Cohen read through it carefully, not omitting even the preamble, and pausing at the end of each paragraph for questions and explanations.

Craig was so excited that he had difficulty sitting still and keeping his expression and voice level and business-like. The momentary panic he had felt at Peter's sudden mention of the World Bank was forgotten and he felt like whooping and dancing up and down the veranda: Rholands was his, King's Lynn was his, Queen's Lynn was his, and Zambezi Waters was his.

Even in his excitement there was one paragraph that rang with a hollow note when Isadore Cohen read it out.

'What the hell does that mean – *enemy of the state and the people of Zimbabwe?*' he demanded.

'It's a standard clause in all our documentation,' Isadore Cohen placated him, 'merely an expression of patriotic sentiment. The Land Bank is a government institution. If the borrower were to engage in treasonable activity and was declared an enemy of the state and people, the Land Bank would be obliged to repudiate all its obligations to the guilty party.'

111

'Is that legal?' Craig was dubious, and when the lawyer reassured him, he went on, 'Do you think the lending bank will accept that?'

'They have done so already on other contracts of surety,' the bank governor told him. 'As Mr Cohen says, it's a standard clause.'

'After all, Craig,' Peter Fungabera smiled, 'you aren't intending to lead an armed revolution to overthrow our government, are you?'

Craig returned his smile weakly. 'Well, okay, if the American lending bank will accept that, then I suppose it must be kosher.'

The reading took almost an hour, and then Governor Musharewa signed all the copies, and both his assistant and Peter Fungabera witnessed his signature. Then it was Craig's turn to sign and again the witnesses followed him, and finally Isadore Cohen impressed his seal of Commissioner of Oaths on each document.

'That's it, gentlemen. Signed, sealed and delivered.'

'It only remains to see if Henry Pickering will be satisfied.'

'Oh, did I forget to mention it?' Peter Fungabera grinned wickedly. 'Governor Kapwepwe spoke to Pickering yesterday afternoon, 10 a.m. New York time. The money will be available to you just as soon as the surety is in his hands.' He nodded to the hovering house servant. 'Now you can bring the champagne.'

They toasted each other, the Land Bank, the World Bank, and Rholands Company, and only when the second bottle was empty did the two black bankers take reluctant leave.

As their limousine went down the drive, Peter Fungabera took Craig's arm. 'And now we can discuss my raising fee. Mr Cohen has the papers.'

Craig read them, and felt the blood drain from his face.

'Ten per cent,' he gasped. 'Ten per cent of the paid-up shares of Rholands.'

'We really must change that name.' Peter Fungabera frowned. 'As you see, Mr Cohen will hold the shares as my nominee. It might save embarrassment later.'

Craig pretended to re-read the contract, while he tried to muster a protest. The two men watched him in silence. Ten per cent was robbery, but where else could Craig go?

Isadore Cohen slowly unscrewed the cap of his pen and handed it to Craig.

'I think you will find a cabinet minister and an army commander a most useful sleeping partner in this enterprise,' he said, and Craig accepted the pen.

'There is only one copy.' Craig still hesitated.

'We only need one copy,' Peter was still smiling, 'and I will keep it.' Craig nodded.

There would be no proof of the transaction, shares held by a nominee, no documentation except in Peter Fungabera's hands. In a dispute it would be Craig's word against that of a senior minister – but he wanted Rholands. More than anything in his life, Craig wanted Rholands.

He dashed his signature across the foot of the contract and on the other side of the table the two men relaxed visibly and Peter Fungabera called for a third bottle of champagne.

U p to now, Craig had needed only a pen and a pile of paper, and time had been his to squander or use as the fancy led him.

Suddenly, he was faced with the enormous responsibility of ownership and time telescoped in upon him. There was so much to do and so little time to do it that he felt crippled with indecision, appalled by his own audacity, and despairing of his own organizational skills.

He wanted comfort and encouragement, and he thought immediately of Sally-Anne. He drove around to her apartment, but the windows were closed, the mail overflowed her box, and there was no answer to his knock.

He returned to the bed-sitter, sat at his table and pulled a blank sheet from the pile and headed it, 'Work to be done,' and stared at it.

He remembered what a girl had once said of him. 'You have only done one thing well in your life.' And writing a book was a far cry from getting a multi-million-dollar ranching company back on its feet. He felt panic rising within him and crushed it back. His was a ranching family – he had been raised with the ammoniacal smell of cow dung in his nostrils, and had learned to judge beef on the hoof when he was small enough to perch up on Bawu's saddle-pommel like a sparrow on a fence pole.

'I can do it,' he told himself fiercely, and began to work on his list. He wrote:

1) Ring Jock Daniels. Accept offer to purchase Rholands.
2) Fly to New York.
   a) World Bank meeting.
   b) Open checking account and deposit funds.
   c) Sell *Bawu*.
3) Fly Zürich.
   a) Sign share purchase.
   b) Arrange payment to sellers.

His panic began to subside. He picked up the telephone and dialled British Airways. They could get him out on the Friday flight to London, and then Concorde to New York.

He caught Jock Daniels in his office. 'Where the hell you been?' He could hear Jock had made a good start on the evening's drinking.

'Jock, congratulations – you have just made yourself twenty-five grand commission,' Craig told him and enjoyed the stunned silence.

Craig's list began to stretch out, ran into a dozen pages:

39) Find out if Okky van Rensburg is still in the country.

Okky had been the mechanic on King's Lynn for twenty years. Craig's grandfather had boasted that Okky could strip down a John Deere tractor and build up a Cadillac and two Rolls-Royce Silver Clouds from the spare parts. Craig needed him.

Craig laid down his pen, and smiled at his memory of the old man. 'We are coming home, Bawu,' he said aloud. He looked at his watch and it was ten o'clock, but he knew he would not be able to sleep.

He put on a light sweater and went out to walk the night streets, and an hour later he was standing outside Sally-Anne's apartment. His feet had made their own way, it seemed.

He felt a little tingle of excitement. Her window was open and her light burning.

'Who is it?' Her voice was muffled.

'It's me, Craig.' There was a long silence.

'It's nearly midnight.'

'It's only just eleven – and I have something to tell you.'

'Oh, okay – door is unlocked.'

She was in her dark-room. He could hear the splash of chemicals.

'I'll be five minutes,' she called. 'Do you know how to make coffee?'

When she came out, she was dressed in a sloppy cable-knit jersey that hung to her knees and her hair was loose on her shoulders. He had never seen it like that, and he stared.

'This had better be good,' she warned him, fists on her hips.

'I've got Rholands,' he said, and it was her turn to stare.

'Who or what is Rholands?'

'The company that owns Zambezi Waters. I own it. It's mine. Zambezi Waters is mine. Is that good enough?'

She started to come to him, her arms rising to embrace him, and he mirrored the movement, and instantly she caught herself and stopped, forcing him to do the same. They were two paces apart.

'That's marvellous news, Craig. I am so happy for you. How did it happen? I thought it was all off.'

'Peter Fungabera arranged a surety for a loan of five million dollars.'

'My God. Five million. You're borrowing five million? How much is the interest on five million?'

He had not wanted to think about that. It showed on his face, and she was immediately contrite.

'I'm sorry. That was insolent. I'm truly happy for you. We must celebrate—' Quickly she moved away from him.

In the cabinet in the kitchenette, she found a bottle of Glenlivet whisky with an inch left in the bottom and added it to the steaming coffee.

'Here's success to Zambezi Waters,' she saluted him with the mug. 'Now first tell me all about it – and then I've got news for you also.'

Until after midnight he elaborated his plans for her: the development of the twin ranches in the south, the rebuilding of the homestead and the restocking with blood cattle, but mostly he dwelt upon his plans for Zambezi Waters and its wildlife, knowing that that was where her interest would centre.

'I was thinking – I'd need a woman's touch in planning and laying out the camps, not just any woman, but one with an artistic flair and a knowledge and love of the African bush.'

116

'Craig, if that is meant to describe me, I'm on a grant from the World Wildlife Trust, and I owe them all my time.'

'It wouldn't take up much time,' he protested, 'just a consultancy. You could fly up for a day whenever you could fit it in.' He saw her weaken. 'And then, of course, once the camps were running, I'd want you to give a series of lectures and slide-shows of your photographs for the guests—' and he saw that he had touched the right key. Like any artist, she relished an opportunity to exhibit her work.

'I'm not making any promises,' she told him sternly, but they both knew she would do it, and Craig felt his new burden of responsibility lighten appreciably.

'You said you had news for me,' he reminded her at last, grateful for the chance to draw the evening out further. But he was not prepared for her sudden change to deadly seriousness.

'Yes, I've got news,' she paused, seemed to gather herself, and then went on, 'I have picked up the spoor of the master poacher.'

. 'My God! The bastard who wiped out those herds of jumbo? That is real news. Where? How?'

'You know that I have been up in the eastern highlands for the last ten days. What I didn't tell you is that I am running a leopard study in the mountains for the Wildlife Trust. I have people working for me in most of the leopardy areas of the forest. We are counting and mapping the territories of the cats, recording their litters and kills, trying to estimate the effect of the new human influx on them – all that sort of thing – which brings me to one of my men. He is a marvellously smelly old Shangane poacher, he must be eighty years old and his youngest wife is seventeen and presented him with twins last week. He is a complete rogue, with a tremendous sense of humour, and a taste for Scotch whisky – two tots of Glenlivet and he gets talkative.

117

We were up in the Vumba mountains, just the two of us in camp, and after the second tot he let it slip that he had been offered two hundred dollars a leopard-skin. They would take as many as he could catch, and they would supply the steel spring traps. I gave him another tot, and learned that the offer had come from a very well-dressed young black, driving a government Land-Rover. My old Shangane told the man he was afraid that he would be arrested and sent to gaol, but he was assured that he would be safe. That he would be under the protection of one of the great chiefs in Harare, a comrade minister who had been a famous warrior in the bush war and who still commanded his own private army.'

There was a hard cardboard folder on the camp-bed. Sally-Anne fetched it and placed it in Craig's lap. Craig opened it. The top sheet was a full list of the Zimbabwe Cabinet. Twenty-six names, each with the portfolio set out beside it.

'We can narrow that down immediately – very few of the Cabinet did any actual fighting,' Sally-Anne pointed out. 'Most of them spent the war in a suite at the Ritz in London or in a guest dacha on the Caspian Sea.'

She sat down on the cushion beside Craig, reached across and turned to the second sheet.

'Six names.' She pointed. 'Six field commanders.'

'Still too many,' Craig murmured, and saw that Peter Fungabera's name headed the six.

'We can do better,' Sally-Anne agreed. 'A private army. That must mean dissidents. The dissidents are all Matabele. Their leader would have to be of the same tribe.'

She turned to the third sheet. On it was a single name.

'One of the most successful field commanders. Matabele. Minister of Tourism, and the Wildlife Department comes under him. It's an old chestnut, but those set to guard a treasure, are too often those who loot it. It all fits.'

Craig read the name aloud softly, 'Tungata Zebiwe,' and

found that he didn't want it to be true. 'But he was with me in the Game Department, he was my ranger—'

'As I said, the keepers have more opportunity to despoil than any other.'

'But what would Sam do with the money? The master poacher must be coining millions of dollars. Sam lives a very frugal life, everybody knows that, no big house, no expensive cars, no gifts for women nor privately owned land – no other expensive indulgences.'

'Except, perhaps, the most expensive of all,' Sally-Anne demurred quietly. 'Power.'

Craig's further protestation died unuttered, and she nodded. 'Power. Don't you see it, Craig? Running a private army of dissidents – takes money, big, big money.'

Slowly the pattern was shaking itself into place, Craig admitted. Henry Pickering had warned him of an approaching Soviet-backed coup. The Russians had supported the Matabele ZIPRA faction during the war, so their candidate would almost certainly be Matabele.

Still Craig resisted it, clinging to his memories of the man who had been his friend, probably the finest friend of his entire lifetime. He remembered the essential decency of the man he had then known as Samson Kumalo, the mission-educated Christian of integrity and high principles, who had resigned with Craig from the Game Department when they suspected their immediate superior of being involved in a poaching ring. Was he now the master poacher himself? The man of fine compassion who had helped Craig when he was crippled and broken to take his single possession, his yacht, with him when he left Africa. Was he now the power-hungry plotter?

'He is my friend,' Craig said.

'He was. But he has changed. When last you saw him, he declared himself your enemy,' Sally-Anne pointed out. 'You told me that yourself.'

Craig nodded, and then suddenly remembered the

search of his deposit box at the hotel by the police on high orders. Tungata must have suspected that Craig was an agent of the World Bank, would have guessed that he had been detailed to gather information on poaching and power-plotting – all that could have accounted for his unaccountably violent opposition to Craig's plans.

'I hate it,' Craig muttered. 'I hate the idea like hell, but I think that you just may be right.'

'I am sure of it.'

'What are you going to do?'

'I'm going to Peter Fungabera with what evidence I have.'

'He will smash Sam,' Craig said, and she came back quickly, 'Tungata is evil, Craig, a despoiler!'

'He is my friend.'

'He *was* your friend,' Sally-Anne contradicted him. 'You don't know what he has become – you don't know what happened to him in the bush. War can change any human being. Power can change him even more radically.'

'Oh God, I hate it.'

'Come with me to Peter Fungabera. Be there when I put the case against Tungata Zebiwe.' Sally-Anne took his hand, a small gesture of comfort.

Craig did not make the mistake of returning her grip.

'I'm sorry, Craig.' She squeezed his fingers. 'I truly am,' she said, and then she took her hand away again.

Peter Fungabera made time for them in the early morning, and they drove out together to his home in the Macillwane Hills.

A servant showed them through to the general's office, a huge sparsely furnished room that overlooked the lake and had once been the billiard room. One wall was covered with a blown-up map of the entire territory. It was flagged with multi-coloured markers. There was a long table under the windows, covered with reports and despatches and parliamentary papers, and a desk of red African teak in the centre of the uncarpeted stone floor.

Peter Fungabera rose from the desk to greet them. He was barefooted, and dressed in a simple white loin-cloth tied at the hip. The bare skin of his chest and arms glowed as though it had been freshly oiled, and the muscles moved beneath it like a sackful of living cobras. Clearly Peter Fungabera kept himself in a warrior's peak of fighting condition.

'Excuse my undress,' he smiled as he came to greet them, 'but I really am more at ease when I can be completely African.'

There were low stools of intricate carved ebony set in front of the desk.

'I will have chairs brought,' Peter offered. 'I have few white visitors here.'

'No, no.' Sally-Anne settled easily on one of the stools.

'You know I am always pleased to see you, but I am due in the House at ten hundred hours—' Peter Fungabera hurried them.

'I'll come to it without wasting time,' Sally-Anne agreed. 'We think we know who the master poacher is.'

Peter had been about to seat himself at the desk, but now he leaned forward with his fists on the desk-top, and his gaze was sharp and demanding.

'You said I had only to give you the name and you would smash him,' Sally-Anne reminded him, and Peter nodded.

'Give it to me,' he ordered, but Sally-Anne related her sources and her deductions, just as she had to Craig. Peter Fungabera heard her out in silence, frowning or nodding thoughtfully as he followed her reasoning. Then she gave her conclusion, the last name left on her list.

'Comrade Minister Tungata Zebiwe,' Peter Fungabera

repeated softly after her, and at last he sank back onto his own chair and picked up his leather-covered swagger-stick from the desk. He stared over Sally-Anne's head at the map-covered wall, slapping the baton into the rosy pink palm of his left hand.

The silence drew out until Sally-Anne had to ask, 'Well?'

Peter Fungabera dropped his gaze to her face again.

'You have chosen the hottest coal in the fire for me to pick up in my bare hands,' he said. 'Are you sure that you have not been influenced by Comrade Zebiwe's treatment of Mr Craig Mellow?'

'That is unworthy,' Sally-Anne told him softly.

'Yes, I suppose it is.' Peter Fungabera looked at Craig. 'What do you think?'

'He was my friend, and he has done me great kindness.'

'That was once upon a time,' Peter pointed out. 'Now he has declared himself your enemy.'

'Still I like and admire him.'

'And yet—?' Peter prodded gently.

'And yet, I believe Sally-Anne may be on the right spoor,' Craig conceded unhappily.

Peter Fungabera stood up and crossed the floor silently to stand before the vast wall-map.

'The whole country is a tinder-box,' he said, staring at the coloured flags. 'The Matabele are on the point of a rebellion. Here! Here! Here! Their guerrillas are gathering in the bush.' He tapped the map. 'We have been forced to nip the plotting of their more irresponsible leaders who were moving towards armed revolt. Nkomo is in forced retirement, two of the Matabele Cabinet members have been arrested and charged with high treason. Tungata Zebiwe is the only Matabele still in the Cabinet. He commands enormous respect, even outside his own tribe, while the Matabele look upon him as their only remaining leader. If we were to touch him—'

'You are going to let him go!' Sally-Anne said hopelessly. 'He will get away with it. So much for your socialist paradise. One law for the people, another for the—'

'Be silent, woman,' Peter Fungabera ordered, and she obeyed.

He returned to his desk. 'I was explaining to you the consequences of hasty action. Arresting Tungata Zebiwe could plunge the entire country into bloody civil war. I didn't say that I would not take action, but I certainly would do nothing without proof positive, and the testimony of independent witnesses of impeccable impartiality to support my actions.' He was still staring at the map across the room. 'Already the world accuses us of planning tribal genocide against the Matabele, while all we are doing is maintaining the rule of law, and searching for a formula of accommodation with that warlike, intractable tribe. At the moment Tungata Zebiwe is our only reasonable and conciliatory contact with the Matabele, we cannot afford to destroy him lightly.' He paused, and Sally-Anne broke her silence.

'One thing I have not mentioned, but which Craig and I have discussed. If Tungata Zebiwe is the poacher, then he is using the profits to some special end. He gives no visible evidence of extravagance, but we know there is a connection between him and dissidents.'

Peter Fungabera's expression had set hard, and his eyes were terrible. 'If it's Zebiwe, I'll have him,' he promised himself more than her. 'But when I do, I'll have proof for the world to see – and he will not escape me.'

'Then you had best move pretty damned quickly,' Sally-Anne advised him tartly.

'Well, you've picked a good time to sell.' The yacht-broker stood in *Bawu*'s cockpit and looked nautical in his double-breasted blazer and marine cap with golden anchor device – seven hundred dollars from Bergdorf Goodman. His tan was even and perfect – sun-lamp at the N.Y. Athletic Club. There was a fine web of wrinkles around his piercing blue eyes – not from squinting through a sextant nor from tropical suns on far oceans and coral beaches, Craig was certain, but from perusing price-tags and cheque figures.

'Interest rates right down – people are buying yachts again.'

It was like discussing the terms of a divorce with a lawyer, or the arrangements with a funeral director. *Bawu* had been part of his life for too long.

'She is in good nick, all tight and shipshape, and your price is sensible. I'll bring some people to see her tomorrow.'

'Just make sure I'm not here,' Craig warned him.

'I understand, Mr Mellow.' The man could even sound like an undertaker.

Ashe Levy also sounded like an undertaker when Craig telephoned. However, he sent an office messenger down to the marina to collect the first three chapters Craig had completed in Africa. Then Craig went to lunch with Henry Pickering.

'It really is good to see you.' Craig had forgotten how much he had grown to like this man in just two short meetings.

'Let's order first,' Henry suggested, and decided on a bottle of the Grands Echézeaux.

'Courageous fellow,' Craig smiled. 'I am always too

afraid to pronounce it in case they think I am having a sneezing fit.'

'Most people have the same reluctance. Must be why it is the least known of the world's truly great wines – keeps the price down, thank God.'

Appreciatively they nosed the wine and gave it the attention it deserved. Then Henry set his glass down.

'Now tell me what you think of General Peter Fungabera,' he invited.

'It's all in my reports. Didn't you read them?'

'I read them, but tell me just the same. Sometimes a little thing may come out in conversation that just didn't get into a report.'

'Peter Fungabera is a cultivated man. His English is remarkable – his choice of words, his power of expression – but it all has a strong African accent. In uniform he looks like a general officer in the British army. In casual clothes he looks like the star of a TV series, but in a loin-cloth he looks what he really is, an African. That's what we tend to forget with all of them. We all know about Chinese inscrutability, and British phlegm, but we seldom consider that the black African has a special nature—'

'There!' Henry Pickering murmured smugly. 'That wasn't in your reports. Go on, Craig.'

'We think them slow-moving by our own bustling standards, and we do not realize that it is not indolence but the deep consideration they bring to any subject before acting. We consider them simple and direct – when really they are the most secretive and convoluted of people, more tribally clannish than any Scot. They can maintain a blood feud over a hundred years, like any Sicilian—'

Henry Pickering listened intently, prodding him with a leading question only when he slowed. Once he asked, 'Something that I still find a little confusing, Craig – the

125

subtle difference between the term Matabele, Ndebele and Sindebele. Can you explain?'

'A Frenchman calls himself a Français, but we call him a Frenchman. A Matabele calls himself an Ndebele, but we call him a Matabele.'

'Ah,' Henry nodded, 'and the language he speaks is Sindebele, isn't it?'

'That's right. Actually the word Matabele seems to have acquired colonial connections since independence—'

Their talk ranged on easily, relaxed and free-flowing, so that it was with a start of surprise that Craig realized that they were almost the last party left in the restaurant and that the waiter was hovering with the bill.

'What I was trying to say,' Craig concluded, 'is that colonialism has left Africa with a set of superimposed values. Africa will reject them and go back to its own.'

'And probably be the happier for it,' Henry Pickering finished for him. 'Well, Craig, you have certainly earned your wage. I'm truly pleased that you are going back. I can see that you will soon be our most productive field agent in that theatre. When do you return?'

'I only came to New York to pick up a cheque.'

Henry Pickering laughed that delightful purring laugh of his. 'You hint with a sledge-hammer – I shudder at the prospect of a direct demand from you.' He paid the bill and stood up. 'Our house lawyer is waiting. First you sign away your body and soul and then I give you drawing rights up to the total of five million dollars.'

The interior of the limousine was silent and cool, and the suspension ironed out most of the trauma of the New York street surfaces.

'Now enlarge on Sally-Anne Jay's conclusions regarding the head of the poaching ring,' Henry invited.

'At this stage, I don't see any alternative candidate for the master poacher, perhaps even the leader of the dissidents.'

126

Henry was silent for a moment. Then he said, 'What do you make of General Fungabera's reluctance to act?'

'He is a prudent man, and an African. He will not rush in. He will think it out deeply, lay his net with care, but when he does act, I think we will all be surprised at how devastatingly swift and decisive it will be.'

'I would like you to give General Fungabera all the assistance you can. Full co-operation, please, Craig.'

'You know Tungata was my friend.'

'Divided loyalty?'

'I don't think so, not if he is guilty.'

'Good! My board is very happy with your achievements so far. I am authorized to increase your remuneration to sixty thousand dollars per annum.'

'Lovely,' Craig grinned at him. 'That will be a big help on the interest payment on five million dollars.'

I t was still light when the cab dropped Craig at the gates of the marina. The smog of Manhattan was transformed by the low angle of the sun to a lovely purple mist which softened the grim silhouettes of the great towers of concrete.

As Craig stepped on the gangplank, the yacht dipped slightly under his weight, and alerted the figure in the cockpit.

'Ashe!' Craig was taken by surprise. 'Ashe Levy, the fairy princess of struggling authors.'

'Baby.' Ashe came down the deck to him with a landlubber's uncertain steps. 'I couldn't wait, I had to come to you right away.'

'I am touched.' Craig's tone was acid yellow. 'Always when I don't need help you come at a gallop.'

Ashe Levy ignored it, and put a hand on each of Craig's

shoulders. 'I read it. I read it again – and then I locked it in my safe.' His voice sank. 'It's beautiful.'

Craig checked his next jibe, and searched Ashe Levy's face for signs of insincerity. Instead he realized that behind the gold-rimmed spectacles, Ashe Levy's eyes were steely with tears of emotion.

'It's the best stuff that you have ever done, Craig.'

'It's only three chapters.'

'It hit me right in my guts.'

'It needs a lot of polishing.'

'I doubted you, Craig. I'll admit that. I was beginning to believe that you didn't have another book in you, but this – it was just too much to take in. I've been sitting here for the last few hours going over it in my mind, and I find I can recite parts of it by heart.'

Craig studied him carefully. The tears might be a reflection of the sunset off the water. Ashe removed his spectacles, and blew his nose loudly. The tears were genuine, yet Craig could still scarcely believe them, there was only one positive test.

'Can you advance on it, Ashe?'

Now he didn't need money, but he needed the ultimate reassurance.

'How much do you need, Craig? Two hundred grand?'

'You really like it, then?' Craig let go a small sigh, as the writer's eternal doubts were dispelled for a brief blessed period. 'Let's have a drink, Ashe.'

'Let's do better than that,' said Ashe. 'Let's get drunk.'

Craig sat in the stern with his feet up on the rudder post, watching the dew form little diamonds on the glass in his hand, and no longer really listening to Ashe Levy enthusing about the book. Instead he let his mind out to roam, and thought that it would be best not to have all one's good fortunes at the same time – but to spread them out and savour each more fully.

He was inundated with delights. He thought about King's Lynn and in his nostrils lingered the odour of the loams of the Matabele grassland. He thought about Zambezi Waters and heard again the rush of a great body in the thorn brush. He thought about the twenty chapters which would follow the first three, and his trigger finger itched with anticipation. Was it possible, he wondered, that he might be the happiest man in the world at that moment?

Then abruptly he realized that the full appreciation of happiness can only be achieved by sharing it with another – and he found a small empty space down deep inside him, and a shadow of melancholy as he remembered strangely flecked eyes and a firm young mouth. He wanted to tell her about it, he wanted her to read those three chapters, and suddenly he longed with all his soul to be back in Africa where Sally-Anne Jay was.

Craig found a second-hand Land-Rover in Jock Daniels' used car lot that backed onto his auctioneering floor. He closed his ears to Jock's impassioned sales *spiel* and listened instead to the motor. The timing was out, but there was no knocking or slapping. The front-wheel transmission engaged smoothly, the clutch held against the brakes. When he gave it a run in an area of erosion and steep dongas on the outskirts of town, the silencer box fell off, but the rest held together. At one time he had been able to take his other old Land-Rover down into its separate parts and reassemble it over a weekend. He knew he could save this one. He beat Jock down a thousand dollars and still grossly overpaid, but he was in a hurry.

Into the Land-Rover he loaded everything he had saved from the sale of the yacht: a suitcase full of clothing, a dozen of his favourite books and a leather trunk with brass bindings, his heaviest piece of luggage, that contained the family journals.

These journals were his entire inheritance, all that Bawu had left him. The rest of the old man's multi-million-dollar estate, including the Rholands shares, had gone to his eldest son Douglas, Craig's uncle, who had sold out and cut for Australia. Yet those battered old leatherbound, hand-written texts had been the greater treasure. Reading them had given Craig a sense of history and a pride in his ancestral line, which had armed him with sufficient confidence and understanding of period to sit down and write the book, which had in turn brought him all this: achievement, fame and fortune, even Rholands itself had come back to him through that box of old papers.

He wondered how many thousands of times he had driven the road out to King's Lynn – but never like this, never as the *patron*. He stopped just short of the main gate, so that his feet could touch his own earth for the first time.

He stood upon it and looked around him at the golden grassland and the open groves of flat-topped acacia trees, at the lines of blue grey hills in the distance and the unblemished blue bowl of the sky over it all, then he knelt like a religious supplicant. It was the only movement in which the leg still hampered him a little. He scooped up the earth in his cupped hands. It was almost as rich and as red as the beef that it would grow. By eye he divided the handful into two parts, and let a tenth part spill back to earth.

'That's your ten per cent, Peter Fungabera,' he whispered to himself. 'But this is mine – and I swear to hold it for all my lifetime and to protect and cherish it, so help me God.'

Feeling only a little foolish at his own theatrics, he let the earth fall, dusted his hands on the seat of his pants and went back to the Land-Rover.

On the foothills before the homestead he met a tall lanky figure coming down the road. The man wore an oily unwashed blanket over his back and a brief loin-cloth; over his shoulder he carried his fighting-sticks. His feet were thrust into sandals cut from old car tyres, and his earrings were plastic stoppers from acid jars embellished with coloured beads that expanded his earlobes to three times normal size. He drove before him a small herd of multi-coloured goats.

'I see you, elder brother,' Craig greeted him, and the old man exposed the gap in his yellow teeth as he grinned at the courtesy of the greeting and his recognition of Craig.

'I see you, Nkosi.' He was the same old man that Craig had found squatting in the outbuildings of King's Lynn.

'When will it rain?' Craig asked him, and handed him a packet of cigarettes that he had brought for precisely such a meeting.

They fell into the leisurely question and answer routine that in Africa must precede any serious discussions.

'What is your name, old man?' A term of respect rather than an accusation of senility.

'I am called Shadrach.'

'Tell me, Shadrach, are your goats for sale?' Craig could at last ask without being thought callow, and immediately a craftiness came into Shadrach's eyes.

'They are beautiful goats,' he said. 'To part with them would be like parting with my own children.'

Shadrach was the acknowledged spokesman and leader of the little community of squatters who had taken up residence on King's Lynn. Through him, Craig found he could negotiate with all of them, and he was relieved. It would save days and a great deal of emotional wear and tear.

He would not, however, deprive Shadrach of an opportunity to show off his bargaining skill, nor insult him by trying to hasten the proceedings, so these were extended

131

over the next two days while Craig reroofed the old guest cottage with a sheet of heavy canvas, replaced the looted pump with a Lister diesel to raise water from the borehole and set up his new camp-bed in the bare bedroom of the cottage.

On the third day the sale price was agreed and Craig found himself the owner of almost two thousand goats. He paid off the sellers in cash, counting each note and coin into their hands to forestall argument, and then loaded his bleating acquisitions into four hired trucks and sent them into the Bulawayo abattoirs, flooding the market in the process and dropping the going price by fifty per cent for a net loss on the entire transaction of a little over ten thousand dollars.

'Great start in business,' he grinned, and sent for Shadrach.

'Tell me, old man, what do you know about cattle?' – which was rather like asking a Polynesian what he knew about fish, or a Swiss if he had ever seen snow.

Shadrach drew himself up in indignation. 'When I was this high,' he said stiffly, indicating an area below his right knee, 'I squirted milk hot from the cow's teat into my own mouth. At this height,' he moved up to the kneecap, 'I had two hundred head in my sole charge. I freed the calves with these hands when they stuck in their mothers' wombs; I carried them on these shoulders when the ford was flooded. At this height,' two inches above the knee, 'I killed a lioness, stabbing her with my assegai when she attacked my herd—'

Patiently Craig heard out the tale as it rose in small increments to shoulder height and Shadrach ended, 'And you dare to ask me what I know about cattle!'

'Soon on this grass I will graze cows so sleek and beautiful that to look upon them will dim your eyes with tears. I will have bulls whose coats shine like water in the sun, whose humps rise like great mountains on their backs and whose dewlaps, heavy with fat, sweep the earth when they walk as the rain-winds sweep the dust from the drought-stricken land.'

'Hau!' said Shadrach, an expletive of utter astonishment, impressed as much by Craig's lyricism as by his declaration of intention.

'I need a man who understands cattle – and men,' Craig told him.

Shadrach found him the men. From the squatter families he chose twenty, all of them strong and willing, not too young to be silly and flighty, not too old to be frail.

'The others,' said Shadrach contemptuously, 'are the products of the unions of baboons and thieving Mashona cattle-rustlers. I have ordered them off our land.'

Craig smiled at the possessive plural, but was impressed with the fact that when Shadrach ordered, men obeyed.

Shadrach assembled his recruits in front of the rudely refurbished cottage, and gave them a traditional *giya*, the blood-rousing speech and mime with which the old Matabele indunas primed their warriors on the eve of battle.

'You know me!' he shouted. 'You know that my great-great-grandmother was the daughter of the old king, Lobengula, "the one who drives like the wind".'

'Eh – he!' They began to enter into the spirit of the occasion.

'You know that I am a prince of the royal blood, and in a proper world I would rightfully be an induna of one thousand, with widow-bird feathers in my hair and oxtails on my war shield.' He stabbed at the air with his fighting-sticks.

'Eh – he!' Watching their expressions, Craig saw the real respect in which they held the old man, and he was delighted with his choice.

'Now!' Shadrach chanted. 'Because of the wisdom and far-sightedness of the young Nkosi here, I am indeed become an induna. I am the induna of King's Lynn,' he pronounced it 'Kingi Lingi', 'and you are my *amadoda*, my chosen warriors.'

'Eh – he!' they agreed, and stamped their bare feet on the earth with a cannon-fire clap.

'Now, look upon this white man. You might think him young and unbearded – but know you, that he is the grandson of Bawu and the great-grandson of Taka Taka.'

'Hau!' gasped Shadrach's warriors, for those were names to conjure with. Bawu they had known in the flesh, Sir Ralph Ballantyne only as a legend: Taka Taka was the onomatopoeic name the Matabele had given Sir Ralph from the sound of the Maxim machine-gun which the old free-booter had wielded to such effect during the Matabele war and the rebellion.

They looked upon Craig with new eyes.

'Yes,' Shadrach urged them, 'look at him. He is a warrior who carried terrible scars from the bush war. He killed hundreds of the cowardly, women-raping Mashona—' Craig blinked at the poetic licence Shadrach had taken unto himself – 'he even killed a few of the brave lion-hearted Matabele ZIPRA fighters. So you know him now as a man – not a boy.'

'Eh – he!' They showed no rancour at Craig's purported bag of their brethren.

'Know also that he comes to turn you from goat-keeping women, sitting in the sun scratching your fleas, into proud cattle-men once more, for—' Shadrach paused for dramatic effect ' – soon on this grass will graze cows so sleek and beautiful that to look upon them—'

Craig noted that Shadrach could repeat his own words perfectly, displaying the remarkable memory of the illiterate. When he ended with a high stork-like leap in the air and a clatter of his fighting-sticks, they applauded him wildly, and then looked to Craig expectantly.

'One hell of an act to follow,' Craig told himself as he

stood before them. He spoke quietly, in low, musical Sindebele.

'The cattle will be here soon, and there is much work to be done before they arrive. You know about the wage that the government has decreed for farm-workers. That I will pay, and food rations for each of you and your families.' This was received without any great show of enthusiasm. 'And in addition,' Craig paused, 'for each year of service completed, you will be given a fine young cow and the right to graze her upon the grass of Kingi Lingi, the right also to put her to my great bulls so that she might bear you beautiful calves—'

'Eh – he!' they shouted, and stamped with joy, and at last Craig held up both hands.

'There might be some amongst you who will be tempted to lift that which belongs to me, or who will find a shady tree under which to spend the day instead of stringing fencing-wire or herding the cattle.' He glared at them, so they quailed a little. 'Now this wise government forbids a man to kick another with his foot – but, be warned, I can kick you without using my own foot.'

He stooped and in one deft movement plucked off his leg, and stood before them with it in his hand. They gaped in amazement.

'See, this is not my own foot!' Their expressions began to turn sickly, as though they were in the presence of terrible witchcraft. They began to shuffle nervously and look around for escape.

'So,' Craig shouted, 'without breaking the law, I can kick who I wish.' Making two swift hops, he used the momentum to swing the toe of the boot of his disembodied leg into the backside of the nearest warrior.

For a moment longer the stunned silence persisted, and then they were overwhelmed by their own sense of the ridiculous. They laughed until their cheeks were streaked with tears. They staggered in circles beating their own heads, they hugged each other, heaving and gasping with laughter. They surrounded the unfortunate whose backside had been the butt of Craig's joke, and abused him further, prodding him and shrieking with laughter. Shadrach, all princely dignity discarded, collapsed in the dust and wriggled helplessly as wave after wave of mirth overcame him.

Craig watched them fondly. Already they were his people, his special charges. Certainly, there would be rotters amongst them. He would have to weed them out. Certainly, even the good ones would at times deliberately test his vigilance and his forbearance as was the African way, but in time also they would become a close-knit family and he knew that he would come to love them.

The fences were the first priority. They had fallen into a state of total disrepair: there were miles of barbed-wire missing, almost certainly stolen. When Craig tried to replace it, he realized why. There was none for sale in Matabeleland. No import permits had been issued that quarter for barbed-wire.

'Welcome to the special joy of farming in black Zimbabwe,' the manager of the Farmers' Co-operative Society in Bulawayo told him. 'Somebody wangled an import permit for a million dollars' worth of candy and milk chocolate, but there was none for barbed-wire.'

'For God's sake.' Craig was desperate. 'I've got to have fencing. I can't run stock without it. When will you receive a consignment?'

'That rests with some little clerk in the Department of Commerce in Harare,' the manager shrugged, and Craig turned sadly back to the Land-Rover, when suddenly an idea came to him.

'May I use your telephone?' he asked the manager.

He dialled the private number that Peter Fungabera had given him, and after he had identified himself, a secretary put him straight through.

'Peter, we've got a big problem.'

'How can I help you?'

Craig told him, and Peter murmured to himself as he made notes. 'How much do you need?'

'At least twelve hundred bales.'

'Is there anything else?'

'Not at the moment – oh yes, sorry to bother you, Peter, but I've been trying to find Sally-Anne. She doesn't answer the telephone or reply to telegrams.'

'Phone me back in ten minutes,' Peter Fungabera ordered, and when Craig did so, he told him, 'Sally-Anne is out of the country. Apparently she flew up to Kenya in the Cessna. She is at a place called Kitchwa Tembu on the Masai Mara.'

'Do you know when she will be back?'

'No, but as soon as she re-enters the country again I'll let you know.'

Craig was impressed at the reach of Peter Fungabera's arm, that he could follow a person's movements even outside Zimbabwe. Obviously, Sally-Anne was on some list for special attention, and the thought struck him that he himself was probably on that very same list.

Of course, he knew why Sally-Anne was at Kitchwa Tembu. Two years previously Craig had visited that marvellous safari camp on the Mara plains at the invitation of the owners, Geoff and Jorie Kent. This was the season when the vast herds of buffalo around the camp would start dropping their calves and the battles between the protective cows and the lurking packs of predators intent on devouring the newborn calves provided one of the great spectacles of the African veld. Sally-Anne would be there with her Nikon.

On his way back to King's Lynn, he stopped at the post

137

office and sent her a telegram through Abercrombie and Kent's office in Nairobi: 'Bring me back some tips for Zambezi Waters. Stop. Is the hunt still on. Query. Best Craig.'

Three days later a convoy of trucks ground up the hills of King's Lynn and a platoon of Third Brigade troopers offloaded twelve hundred bales of barbed-wire into the roofless tractor sheds.

'Is there an invoice to pay?' Craig asked the sergeant in charge of the detail. 'Or any papers to sign?'

'I do not know,' he answered. 'I know only I was ordered to bring these things – and I have done so.'

Craig watched the empty trucks roar away down the hill, and there was an indigestible lump in his stomach. He suspected that there would never be an invoice. He knew also that this was Africa, and he did not like to contemplate the consequences of alienating Peter Fungabera.

For five days he worked with his Matabele fencing gangs, bared to the waist, with heavy leather gloves protecting his hands; he flung his weight on the wire-strainers and sang the work chants with his men – but all that time the lump of conscience was heavy in his belly, and he could not suffer it longer.

There was still no telephone on the estate, so he drove into Bulawayo. He reached Peter at the Houses of Parliament.

'My dear Craig, you really are making a fuss about nothing. The quarter-master general has not yet invoiced the wire to me. But if it makes you feel better, then send me a cheque and I will see that the business is settled immediately. Oh, Craig, make the cheque payable "Cash", will you?'

Over the next few weeks, Craig discovered in himself the capacity to live on much less sleep than he had ever believed possible. He was up each morning at four-thirty and chivvied his Matabele gangs from their huts. They emerged sleepily, still blanket-wrapped and shivering at the chill, coughing from the wood-smoke of the watch-fire, and grumbling without any real malice.

At noon, Craig found the shade of an acacia, and slept through the siesta as they all did. Then, refreshed, he worked through the afternoon until the ringing tone of the gong of railway-line suspended from the branch of a jacaranda tree below the homestead sounded the hour and the cry of 'Shayile! It has struck!' was flung from gang to gang and they trooped back up the hills.

Then Craig washed off the sweat and dust in the concrete reservoir behind the cottage, ate a hasty meal and by the time darkness fell, he was sitting at the cheap deal table in the cottage in the hissing white light of the gas lantern with a sheet of paper in front of him and a ballpoint pen in his hand, transported into the other world of his imagination. Some nights he wrote through until long after midnight, and then at four-thirty was out in the dewy not-yet dawn again, feeling alert and vigorous.

The sun darkened his skin and bleached the cowlick of hair over his eyes, the hard physical work toned up his muscles and toughened his stump so he could walk the fences all day without discomfort. There was so little time to spare, that his cooking was perfunctory and the bottle of whisky remained in his bag with the seal unbroken – so that he grew lean and hawk-faced.

Then one evening as he parked the Land-Rover under the jacaranda trees and started up towards the cottage, he was forced to stop. The aroma of roasting beef and potatoes was like running into a brick wall. The saliva spurted from under his tongue and he started forward again, suddenly ravenous.

In the tiny makeshift kitchen a gaunt figure stood over the wood fire. His hair was soft and white as cotton wool, and he looked up accusingly as Craig stood in the doorway.

'Why did you not send for me?' he demanded in Sindebele. 'Nobody else cooks on Kingi Lingi.'

'Joseph!' Craig cried, and embraced him impetuously. The old man had been Bawu's cook for thirty years. He could lay a formal banquet for fifty guests, or whip up a hunters' pot on a bush fire. Already there was bread baking in the tin trunk he had improvised as an oven and he had gleaned a bowl of salad from the neglected garden.

Joseph extricated himself from Craig's embrace, a little ruffled by this breach of etiquette. 'Nkosana,' Joseph still used the diminutive address, 'your clothes were filthy and your bed was unmade,' he lectured Craig sternly. 'We have worked all day to tidy the mess you have made.'

Only then did Craig notice the other man in the kitchen.

'Kapa-lala,' he laughed delightedly, and the houseboy grinned and bobbed with pleasure. He was at work with the heavy black smoothing-iron filled with glowing coals. All Craig's clothes and bed-linen had been washed and were being ironed to crisp perfection. The walls of the cottage had been washed down and the floor polished to a gloss. Even the brass taps on the sink shone like the buttons on a marine's dress uniform.

'I have made a list of the things we need,' Joseph told Craig. 'They will do for the time being, but it is unfitting that you should live like this in a hovel. Nkosi Bawu, your grandfather, would have disapproved.' Joseph the cook had a definite sense of style. 'Thus, I have sent a message to my senior wife's uncle who is a master thatcher, and told him to bring his eldest son who is a bricklayer, and his nephew, who is a fine carpenter. They will be here tomorrow to

140

begin repairing the damage that these dogs have done to the big house. As for the gardens, I know a man—' and he ticked off on his fingers what he considered necessary to restore King's Lynn to some sort of order. 'Thus we will be ready to invite thirty important guests to Christmas dinner, like we used to in the old days. Now Nkosana, go and wash. Dinner will be ready in fifteen minutes.'

With the home paddocks securely fenced and the work on the restoration of the outbuildings and main homestead well in hand, Craig could at last begin the vital step of restocking. He summoned Shadrach and Joseph, and gave King's Lynn into their joint care during his absence. They accepted the responsibility gravely. Then Craig drove to the airport, left the Land-Rover in the car park and boarded the commercial flight southwards.

For the next three weeks he toured the great cattle stud ranches of Northern Transvaal, the province of South Africa whose climate and conditions most closely resembled those of Matabeleland. The purchases of blood cattle were not transactions that could be hurried. Each was preceded by days of discussion with the seller, and study of the beasts themselves, while Craig enjoyed the traditional hospitality of the Afrikaner country folk. His hosts were men whose ancestors had trekked northwards from the Cape of Good Hope, drawn by their oxen, and had lived all their lives close to their animals. So while Craig purchased their stock, he drew upon their accumulated wisdom and experience and came from each transaction with his own knowledge and understanding of cattle immensely enriched. All he learned reinforced his desire to follow Bawu's successful experiments with cross-breeding the indigenous Afrikaner strain, known for its hardiness and disease- and drought-resistance, with the quicker-yielding Santa Gertrudis strain.

He bought young cows that had been artificially inseminated and were well in calf. He bought bulls of fine pedigree from famous blood-lines, and laboured through the documentation and inspection and inoculation and quarantine and insurance that were necessary before they could be permitted to cross an international border. In the meantime he arranged for road transportation northwards to King's Lynn by contractors who specialized in carrying precious livestock.

He spent almost two million of his borrowed dollars before flying back to King's Lynn to make the final preparations for the arrival of his cattle. The deliveries of the blood-stock were to be staggered over a period of months, so that each consignment could be properly received and allowed to settle down before the arrival of the next batch.

The first to arrive were four young bulls, just ready to take up their stud duties. Craig had paid fifteen thousand dollars for each of them. Peter Fungabera was determined to make an important occasion out of their arrival. He persuaded two of his brother ministers to attend the welcoming ceremony, though neither the prime minister nor the minister of tourism, Comrade Tungata Zebiwe, was available on that day.

Craig hired a marquee tent, while Joseph happily and importantly prepared one of his legendary *al fresco* banquets. Craig was still smarting from having paid out two million dollars, so he went cheap on the champagne, ordering the imitation from the Cape of Good Hope rather than the genuine article.

The ministerial party arrived in a fleet of black Mercedes, accompanied by their heavily armed bodyguards, all sporting aviator-type sunglasses. Their ladies were dressed in full-length safari prints, of the wildest and most improbable colours. The cheap sweet champagne went down as though a plug had been pulled out of a bath, and they were all soon twittering and giggling like a flock of glossy starlings. The minister of education's senior wife unbuttoned her blouse, produced a succulent black bosom, and gave the infant on her hip an early lunch while herself taking on copious quantities of champagne. 'Refuelling in flight,' one of Craig's white neighbours, who had been an RAF bomber-pilot, remarked with a grin.

Peter Fungabera was the last to arrive, wearing full dress, and driven by a young aide, a captain in the Third Brigade whom Craig had noticed on several other occasions. This time Peter introduced him.

'Captain Timon Nbebi.'

He was so thin as to appear almost frail. His eyes behind the steel-rimmed spectacles were too vulnerable for a soldier, and his grip was quick and nervous. Craig would have liked to have spoken to him, but, by this time the transporter carrying the bulls was already grinding up the hills.

It arrived in a cloud of fine red dust before the enclosure of split poles that Craig had built to receive the bulls. The gangplank was lowered, but before the tailgate was raised Peter Fungabera climbed up onto the dais and addressed the assembly.

'Mr Craig Mellow is a man who could have chosen any country in the world to live in and, as an internationally bestselling writer, would have been welcomed there. He chose to return to Zimbabwe, and in doing so has declared to all the world that here is a land where men of any colour, of any tribe – black or white, Mashona or Matabele – are free to live and work, unafraid and unmolested, safe in the rule of just laws.'

After the political commercial, Peter Fungabera allowed himself a little joke. 'We will now welcome to our midst these other new immigrants, in the sure knowledge that they will be the fathers of many fine sons and daughters, and contribute to the prosperity of our own Zimbabwe.'

Peter Fungabera led the applause as Craig raised the gate and the first new immigrant emerged to stand blinking in the sunlight. He was an enormous beast, over a ton of bulging muscles under the glistening red-brown hide. He had just endured sixteen hours penned up in a noisy, lurching machine. The tranquillizers he had been given had worn off, leaving him with a drug hangover and a bitter grudge against the entire world. Now he looked down on the clapping throng, on the swirling colours of the women's national costumes, and he found at last a focus for his irritation and frustration. He let out a long ferocious bellow, and, dragging his handlers behind him, he launched himself like an avalanche down the gangplank.

The handlers released their hold on the restrainers, and the split-pole barrier exploded before his charge, as did the ministerial party. They scattered like sardines at the rush of a hungry barracuda. High officials overtook their wives, in a race for the sanctuary of the jacaranda trees; infants strapped on the women's backs howled as loudly as their dams.

The bull went into one side of the luncheon marquee, still at a dead run, gathering up the guy ropes on his massive shoulders, so the tent came down in graceful billows of canvas, trapping beneath it a horde of panic-stricken revellers. He emerged from the further side of the collapsing marquee just as one of the younger ministerial wives sprinted, shrilling with terror, across his path. He hooked at her with one long forward-raked horn, and the point caught in the fluttering hem of her dress. The bull jerked his head up and the brightly coloured material unwrapped from the girl's body like the string from a child's top. She spun into an involuntary pirouette, caught her balance, and then, stark naked, went bounding up the hill with long legs flashing and abundant breasts bouncing elastically.

'Two to one, the filly to win by a tit,' howled the RAF

bomber-pilot ecstatically. He had also fuelled up on the cheap champagne.

The gaudy dress had wrapped itself around the bull's head. It served to goad him beyond mere anger into the deadly passion of the corrida bull facing the matador's cape. He swung his great armed head from side to side, the dress swirling rakishly like a battle ensign in a high wind, and exposing one of his wicked little eyes – which lighted on the honourable minister of education, the least fleet-footed of the runners, who was making heavy weather of the slope.

The minister was carrying the burden of flesh that behoves a man of such importance. His belly wobbled mountainously beneath his waistcoat. His face was grey as last night's ashes, and he screamed in a girlish falsetto of terror and exhaustion, 'Shoot it! Shoot the devil!'

His bodyguards ignored the instruction. They were leading him by fifty paces and rapidly widening the gap.

Craig watched helplessly from his grandstand position on the transporter, as the bull lowered his head and drove up the slope after the fleeing minister. Dust spurted from under his hooves, and he bellowed again. The blast of sound, only inches from the ministerial backside, seemed physically to lift and propel the honourable minister the last few paces, and he turned out to be a much better climber than sprinter. He went up the trunk of the first jacaranda like a squirrel and hung precariously in the lower branches with the bull directly beneath him.

The bull bellowed again in murderous frustration, glaring up at the cowering figure, tore at the earth with his front hooves, and gored the air with full-blooded swings of his vicious, white-tipped horns.

'Do something!' shrieked the minister. 'Make it go away!'

His bodyguards looked back over their shoulders and,

seeing the *impasse*, regained their courage. They halted, unslung their weapons and began cautiously closing in on the bull and his victim.

'No!' Craig yelled over the rattle of loading automatic weapons. 'Don't shoot!' He was certain that his insurance did not cover 'death by deliberate rifle-fire', and, quite apart from the fifteen thousand dollars, a volley would sweep the area behind the bull, which included the marquee and its occupants, a scattering of fleeing women and children and Craig himself.

One of the uniformed bodyguards raised his rifle and took aim. His recent exertions and terror did nothing for the steadiness of his hand. The muzzle of his weapon described widening circles in the air.

'No!' Craig bellowed again and flung himself face down on the floor of the trailer. At that moment a tall, skinny figure stepped between the wavering rifle-muzzle and the great bull.

'Shadrach!' whispered Craig thankfully, as the old man imperiously pushed up the rifle-barrel and then turned to face the bull.

'I see you, Nkunzi Kakhulu! Great bull!' he greeted him courteously.

The bull swung its head to the sound of his voice, and very clearly he saw Shadrach also. He snorted and nodded threateningly.

'Hau! Prince of cattle! How beautiful you are!' Shadrach advanced a pace towards those vicious pike-sharp horns.

The bull pawed at the earth and then made a warning rush at him. Shadrach stood him down and the bull stopped.

'How noble your head!' he crooned. 'Your eyes are like dark moons!'

The bull hooked his horns towards him, but the swing was less vicious and Shadrach answered with another step forward. The shrieks of terror-struck women and children

146

died away. Even the most faint-hearted stopped running, and looked back at the old man and the red beast.

'Your horns are sharp as the stabbing assegai of great Mzilikazi.'

Shadrach kept moving forward and the bull blinked uncertainly and squinted at him with red-rimmed eyes.

'How glorious are your testicles,' Shadrach murmured soothingly, 'like huge round boulders of granite. Ten thousand cows will feel their weight and majesty.'

The bull backed up a pace and gave another half-hearted toss of his head.

'Your breath is hot as the north wind, my peerless king of bulls.' Shadrach stretched out his hand slowly, and they watched in breathless silence.

'My darling,' Shadrach touched the glossy, wet, chocolate-coloured muzzle and the bull jerked away nervously, and then came back cautiously to snuffle at Shadrach's fingers. 'My sweet darling, father of great bulls—' gently Shadrach slipped his forefinger into the heavy bronze nose-ring and held the bull's head. He stooped and placed his mouth over the gaping, pink-lined nostrils and blew his own breath loudly into them. The bull shuddered, and Craig could clearly see the bunched muscle in his shoulders relaxing. Shadrach straightened and, with his finger still through the nose-ring, walked away – and placidly the bull waddled after him with his dewlap swinging. A weak little cheer of relief and disbelief went up from his audience, and subsided as Shadrach cast a withering contemptuous eye around him.

'Nkosi!' he called to Craig. 'Get these chattering Mashona monkeys off our land. They are upsetting my darling,' he ordered, and Craig hoped fervently that none of his highly placed guests understood Sindebele.

Craig marvelled once again at the almost mystical bond that existed between the Nguni peoples and their cattle. From that age, long obscured by the mists of time, when

147

the first herds had been driven out of Egypt to begin the centuries-long migrations southwards, the destinies of black man and beast had been inexorably linked. This hump-backed strain of cattle had originated in India, their genus *bos indicus* distinct from the European *bos taurus*, but over the ages had become as African as the tribes that cherished and shared their lives with them. It was strange, Craig pondered, that the cattle-herding tribes seemed always to have been the most dominant and warlike: people such as the Masai and Bechuana and Zulu had always lorded it over the mere tillers of the earth. Perhaps it was their constant need to search for grazing, to defend it against others and to protect their herds from predators, both human and animal, that made them so bellicose.

Watching Shadrach lead the huge bull away, there was no mistaking that lordly arrogance now, master and beast were noble in their alliance. Not so the minister of education, still clinging, catlike, to his perch in the jacaranda. Craig went to add his entreaties to those of his bodyguards, who were encouraging him to descend to earth once more.

Peter Fungabera was the last of the official party to leave. He accompanied Craig on a tour of the homestead, sniffing appreciatively the sweet odour of the golden thatching grass that already covered half the roof area.

'My grandfather replaced the original thatch with corrugated asbestos during the war,' Craig explained. 'Your RPG-7 rocket shells were hot little darlings.'

'Yes,' Peter agreed evenly. 'We started many a good bonfire with them.'

'To tell the truth, I am grateful for the chance to restore the building. Thatch is cooler and more picturesque, and both the wiring and plumbing needed replacing—'

'I must congratulate you on what you have accomplished in such a short time. You will soon be living in the

148

grand manner that your ancestors have always enjoyed since they first seized this land.'

Craig looked at him sharply, searching for malice, but Peter's smile was as charming and easy as always.

'All these improvements add vastly to the value of the property,' Craig pointed out. 'And you own a goodly share of them.'

'Of course,' Peter laid a hand placatingly on Craig's forearm. 'And you still have much work ahead of you. The development of Zambezi Waters, when will you begin on that?'

'I am almost ready to do so – as soon as the rest of the stock arrives, and I have Sally-Anne to assist with the details.'

'Ah,' said Peter. 'Then you can begin immediately. Sally-Anne Jay flew into Harare airport yesterday morning.' Craig felt a tingle of rising pleasure and anticipation.

'I'll go into town this evening to phone her.'

Peter Fungabera clucked with annoyance. 'Have they not installed your telephone yet? I'll see you have it tomorrow. In the meantime you can patch through on my radio.'

The telephone linesman arrived before noon the following day, and Sally-Anne's Cessna buzzed in from the east an hour later. Craig had a smudge pot of old engine oil and rags burning to mark the disused airstrip and give her the wind direction, and she touched down and taxied to where he had parked the Land-Rover.

When she jumped down from the cabin, Craig found he had forgotten the alert, quick way she moved, and the shape of her legs in tight-fitting blue denim. Her smile was of genuine pleasure and her handshake firm and warm. She was wearing nothing beneath the cotton shirt. She noticed his eyes flicker down and then guiltily up again, but she showed no resentment.

149

'What a lovely ranch, from the air,' she said.

'Let me show you,' he offered, and she dropped her bag on the back seat of the Land-Rover and swung her leg over the door like a boy.

It was late afternoon when they got back to the homestead.

'Kapa-lala has prepared a room for you, and Joseph has cooked his number-one dinner. We have the generator running at last, so there are lights and the hot-water donkey has been boiling all day, so there is a hot bath – or I could drive you in to a motel in town?'

'Let's save gas,' she accepted with a smile.

She came out on the veranda with a towel wrapped like a turban round her damp hair, flopped down in the chair beside him and put her feet up on the half-wall.

'God, that was glorious.' She smelled of soap and she was still pink and glowing from the bath.

'How do you like your whisky?'

'Right up and lots of ice.'

She sipped and sighed, and they watched the sunset. It was one of those raging red African skies that placed them and the world in thrall; to speak during it would have been blasphemous. They watched the sun go in silence, and then Craig leaned across and handed her a thin sheaf of papers.

'What is this?' She was curious.

'Part-payment for your services as consultant and visiting lecturer at Zambezi Waters.' Craig switched on the light above her chair.

She read slowly, going over each sheet three or four times, and then she sat with the sheaf of papers clutched protectively in her lap and stared out into the night.

'It's only a rough idea, just the first few pages. I have suggested the photographs that should face each text,' Craig broke the silence awkwardly. 'Of course, I've only seen a few. I am certain you have hundreds of others. I thought we would aim at two hundred and fifty pages, with the same number of your photographs – all colour, of course.'

She turned her head slowly towards him. 'You were afraid?' she asked. 'Damn you, Craig Mellow – now I am scared silly.'

He saw that there were tears in her eyes again. 'This is so—' she searched for a word, and gave up. 'If I put my photographs next to this, they will seem – I don't know – puny, I guess, unworthy of the deep love you express so eloquently for this land.'

He shook his head, denying it. She dropped her eyes to the writing and read it again.

'Are you sure, Craig, are you sure you want to do this book with me?'

'Yes – very much indeed.'

'Thank you,' she said simply, and in that moment Craig knew at last, for sure, that they would be lovers. Not now, not tonight, it was still too soon – but one day they would take each other. He sensed that she knew that too, for though after that they spoke very little, her cheeks darkened under her tan with shy young blood whenever he looked across at her, and she could not meet his eyes.

After dinner Joseph served coffee on the veranda, and when he left Craig switched out the lights and in darkness they watched the moon rise over the tops of the msasa trees that lined the hills across the valley.

When at last she rose to go to her bed, she moved slowly and lingered unnecessarily. She stood in front of him, the top of her head reaching to his chin, and once again said softly, 'Thank you,' tilted her head back, and went up on tiptoe to brush his cheek with soft lips. But he knew she was not yet ready, and he made no effort to hold her.

By the time the last shipment of cattle arrived, the second homestead at Queen's Lynn five miles away was ready for occupation and Craig's newly hired white overseer moved in with his family. He was a burly, slow-speaking man who, despite his Afrikaner blood, had been born and lived in the country all his life. He spoke Sindebele as well as Craig did, understood and respected the blacks and in turn was liked and respected by them. But best of all, he knew and loved cattle, like the true African he was.

With Hans Groenewald on the estate, Craig was able to concentrate on developing Zambezi Waters for tourism. He chose a young architect who had designed the lodges on some of the most luxurious private game ranches in southern Africa, and had him fly up from Johannesburg.

The three of them, Craig, Sally-Anne and the architect, camped for a week on Zambezi Waters, and walked both banks of the Chizarira river, examining every inch of the terrain, choosing the sites of five guest-lodges, and the service complex which would support them. At Peter Fungabera's orders they were guarded by a squad of Third Brigade troopers under the command of Captain Timon Nbebi.

Craig's first impressions of this officer were confirmed as he came to know him better. He was a serious, scholarly young man, who spent all his leisure studying a correspondence course in political economics from the University of London. He spoke English and Sindebele, together with his native Shona, and he and Craig and Sally-Anne held long conversations at night over the camp-fire, trying to arrive at some solution of the tribal enmities that were racking the country. Timon Nbebi's views were surprisingly moderate for an officer in the elite Shona brigade, and he seemed genuinely to desire a working accommodation between the tribes.

'Mr Mellow,' he said, 'can we afford to live in a land

divided by hatred? When I look to Northern Ireland or the Lebanon and see the fruits of tribal strife, I become afraid.'

'But you are a Shona, Timon,' Craig pointed out gently. 'Your allegiance surely lies with your own tribe.'

'Yes,' Timon agreed. 'But first I am a patriot. I cannot ensure peace for my children with an AK 47 rifle. I cannot become a proud Shona by murdering all the Matabele.'

These discussions could have no conclusion, but were made more poignant by the very necessity of an armed bodyguard even in this remote and seemingly peaceful area. The constant presence of armed men began to irk both Craig and Sally-Anne, and one evening towards the end of their stay at Zambezi Waters, they slipped their guards.

They were truly at ease with each other at last, able to share a friendly silence, or to talk for an hour without pause. They had begun to touch each other, still brief, seemingly casual contacts of which they were both, however, intensely aware. She might reach out and cover the back of his hand with hers to emphasize a point, or brush against him as they pored together over the architect's rough sketches of the lodges. Though she was certainly more agile than he was, Craig would take her elbow to help her jump across a rock-pool in the river or lean over her to point out a woodpecker's nest or a wild beehive in the tree-top.

This day, alone at last, they found a clay anthill which rose above the level of the surrounding ebony and overlooked a rhino midden. It was a good stand from which to observe and photograph. Seated on it, they waited for a visit from one of the grotesque prehistoric monsters. They talked in whispers, heads close together, but this time not quite touching.

Suddenly Craig glanced down into the thick bush below them and froze. 'Don't move,' he whispered urgently. 'Sit very still!'

Slowly she turned her head to follow his gaze, and he heard her little gasp of shock.

'Who are they?' she husked, but Craig did not reply.

There were two that he could see, for only their eyes were visible. They had come as silently as leopards, blending into the undergrowth with the skill of men who had lived all their lives in hiding.

'So, Kuphela,' one of them spoke at last, his voice low but deadly. 'You bring the Mashona killer dogs to this place to hunt us.'

'That is not so, Comrade Lookout,' Craig answered him in a hoarse whisper. 'They were sent by the government to protect me.'

'You were our friend – you did not need protection from us.'

'The government does not know that.' Craig tried to put a world of persuasion into his whisper. 'Nobody knows that we have met. Nobody knows that you are here. That I swear on my life.'

'Your life it may well be,' Comrade Lookout agreed. 'Tell me quickly why you are here, if not to betray us.'

'I have bought this land. That other white man in our party is a builder of homes. I wish to make a reserve here for tourists to visit. Like Wankie Park.'

They understood that. The famous Wankie National Park was also in Matabeleland, and for minutes the two guerrillas whispered together and then looked up at Craig again.

'What will become of us?' Comrade Lookout demanded. 'When you have built your houses?'

'We are friends,' Craig reminded him. 'There is room for you here. I will help you with food and money, and in return you will protect my animals and my buildings. You will secretly watch over the visitors who come here, and there will be no more talk of hostages. Is that an agreement between friends?'

'How much is our friendship worth to you, Kuphela?'

'Five hundred dollars every month.'

'A thousand,' Comrade Lookout counter-offered.

'Good friends should not argue over mere money,' Craig agreed. 'I have only six hundred dollars now, but the rest I will leave buried beneath the wild fig tree where we are camped.'

'We will find it,' Comrade Lookout assured him. 'And every month we will meet either here or there.' Lookout pointed out two rendezvous, both prominent hillocks well distanced from the river, their peaks only bluish silhouettes on the horizon. 'The signal of a meeting will be a small fire of green leaves, or three rifle shots evenly spaced.'

'It is agreed.'

'Now, Kuphela, leave the money in that ant-bear hole at your feet and take your woman back to camp.'

Sally-Anne stayed very close beside him on the return, even taking his arm for reassurance every few hundred yards and looking back fearfully over her shoulder.

'My God, Craig, those were real *shufta*, proper dyed-in-the-wool guerrillas. Why did they let us go?'

'The best reason in the world – money.' Craig's chuckle was a little hoarse and breathless even in his own ears, and the adrenalin still buzzed in his blood. 'For a miserly thousand dollars a month, I have just hired myself the toughest bunch of bodyguards and gamekeepers on the market. Pretty good bargain.'

'You're doing a deal with them?' Sally-Anne demanded. 'Isn't that dangerous? It's treason or something, surely?'

'Probably, we just have to make sure that nobody finds out about it, won't we?'

The architect turned out to be another bargain. His designs were superb; the lodges would be built of natural stone, indigenous timber and thatch. They would blend unobtrusively into the chosen sites along the river. Sally-Anne worked with him on the interior layouts and the furnishings, and introduced charming little touches of her own.

During the next few months, Sally-Anne's work with the World Wildlife Trust took her away for long periods at a time, but on her travels she recruited the staff that they would need for Zambezi Waters.

Firstly, she seduced a Swiss-trained chef away from one of the big hotel chains. Then she chose five young safari guides, all of them African-born, with a deep knowledge and love of the land and its wildlife and, most importantly, with the ability to convey that knowledge and love to others.

Then she turned her attention to the design of the advertising brochures, using her own photographs and Craig's text. 'A kind of dress rehearsal for our book,' she pointed out when she telephoned him from Johannesburg, and Craig realized for the first time just what he had taken on in agreeing to work with her. She was a perfectionist. It was either right or it wasn't, and to get it right she would go to any lengths, and force him and the printers to do the same.

The result was a miniature masterpiece in which colour was carefully co-ordinated and even the layout of blocks of print balanced her illustrations. She sent out copies to all the African travel specialists around the world, from Tokyo to Copenhagen.

'We have to set an opening date,' she told Craig, 'and make sure that our first guests are newsworthy. You'll have to offer them a freebie, I'm afraid.'

'You aren't thinking of a pop star?' Craig grinned, and she shuddered.

'I telephoned Daddy at the Embassy in London. He may be able to get Prince Andrew – but I'll admit it's a big "may be". Henry Pickering knows Jane Fonda—'

'My God, I never realized what an up-market broad you are.'

'And while we are on the subject of celebrities, I think I can get a best-selling novelist who makes bad jokes and will probably drink more whisky than he is worth!'

When Craig was ready to commence actual construction on Zambezi Waters, he complained to Peter Fungabera about the difficulty of finding labourers in the deep bush. Peter replied, 'Don't worry, I'll fix that.' And five days later, a convoy of army trucks arrived carrying two hundred detainees from the rehabilitation centres.

'Slave labour,' Sally-Anne told Craig with distaste.

However, the access road to the Chizarira river was completed in just ten days, and Craig could telephone Sally-Anne in Harare and tell her, 'I think we can confidently set the opening date for July 1st.'

'That's marvellous, Craig.'

'When can you come up again? I haven't seen you for almost a month.'

'It's only three weeks,' she denied.

'I have done another twenty pages on our book,' he offered as bait. 'We must go over it together soon.'

'Send them to me.'

'Come and get them.'

'Okay,' she capitulated. 'Next week, Wednesday. Where will you be, King's Lynn or Zambezi Waters?'

'Zambezi Waters. The electricians and plumbers are finishing up. I want to check it out.'

'I'll fly up.'

She landed on the open ground beside the river where Craig's labour gangs had surfaced a strip with gravel to make an all-weather landing ground and had even rigged a proper windsock for her arrival.

The instant she jumped down from the cockpit Craig could see that she was furiously angry.

'What is it?'

'You've lost two of your rhino.' She strode towards him. 'I spotted the carcasses from the air.'

'Where?' Craig was suddenly as angry as she was.

'In the thick bush beyond the gorge. It's poachers for certain. The carcasses are lying within fifty paces of each other. I made a few low passes, and the horns have been taken.'

'Do you think they are Charlie and Lady Di?' he demanded.

From the air Craig and Sally-Anne had done a rhino count, and had identified twenty-seven individual animals on the estate, including four calves and nine breeding pairs of mature animals to whom they had given names. Charlie and Lady Di were a pair of young rhinoceros who had probably just come together. On foot Craig and Sally-Anne had been able to get close to them in the thick jessie bush that the pair had taken as their territory. Both of the animals carried fine horns, the male's much thicker and heavier. The front horn, twenty inches long and weighing twenty pounds, would be worth at least ten thousand dollars to a poacher. The female, Lady Di, was a smaller animal with a thinner, finely curved pair of horns, and she had been heavily pregnant when last they saw her.

'Yes. It's them. I'm sure of it.'

'There is some rough going this side of the gorge,' Craig muttered. 'We won't get there before dark.'

'Not with the Land-Rover,' Sally-Anne agreed, 'but I think I have found a place where I can get down. It's only a mile or so from the kill.'

Craig unslung his rifle from the clips behind the driver's seat of the Land-Rover and checked the load.

'Okay. Let's go,' he said.

The poachers' kill was in the remotest corner of the

estate, almost on the rim of the rugged valley wall that fell away to the great river in the depths. The landing-ground that Sally-Anne had spotted was a narrow natural clearing at the head of the river gorge, and she had to abort her first approach and go round again. At the second attempt, she sneaked in over the tree-tops, and hit it just right.

They left the Cessna in the clearing, and started down into the mouth of the gorge. Craig led, with the rifle cocked and ready. The poachers might still be at the kill.

The vultures guided them the last mile. They were roosting in every tree around the kill, like grotesque black fruit. The area around the carcasses was beaten flat and open by the scavengers, and strewn with loose vulture feathers. As they walked up, half a dozen hyena went loping away with their peculiar high-shouldered gait. Even their fearsomely toothed jaws had not been able completely to devour the thick rhinoceros hide, though the poachers had hacked open the belly cavities of their victims to give them easy access.

The carcasses were at least a week old, the stench of putrefaction was aggravated by that of the vulture dung which whitewashed the remains. The eyes had been picked from the sockets of the male's head, and the ears and cheeks had been gnawed away. As Sally-Anne had seen from the air, the horns were gone, the hack marks of an axe still clearly visible on the exposed bone of the animal's nose.

Looking down upon that ruined and rotting head, Craig found that he was shaking with anger and that the saliva had dried out in his mouth.

'If I could find them, I would kill them,' he said, and beside him Sally-Anne was pale and grim.

'The bastards,' she whispered, 'the bloody, bloody bastards.'

They walked across to the female. Here also the horns had been hacked off and her belly cavity opened. The hyena had dragged the calf out of her womb, and devoured most of it.

Sally-Anne squatted down beside the pathetic remains. 'Prince Billy,' she whispered. 'Poor little devil.'

'There's nothing more we can do here.' Craig took her arm and lifted her to her feet. 'Let's go.'

She dragged a little in his grip as he led her away.

F rom the peak of the hill that Craig had arranged as the rendezvous with Comrade Lookout, they looked out across the brown land to where the river showed as a lush serpentine sprawl of denser forest almost at the extreme range of their vision.

Craig had lit the signal fire of smoking green leaves a little after noon, and had fed it regularly since then. Now the sky was turning purple and blue and the hush and chill of evening fell over them, so that Sally-Anne shivered.

'Cold?' Craig asked.

'And sad.' Sally-Anne tensed but did not pull away when he put his arm around her shoulders. Then slowly she relaxed and pressed against him for the warmth of his body. Darkness blotted out their horizon and crept in upon them.

'I see you, Kuphela.' The voice was so close as to startle them both, and Sally-Anne jerked away from Craig almost guiltily. 'You summoned me.' Comrade Lookout stayed outside the feeble glow of the fire.

'Where were you when somebody killed two of my *bejane* and stole their horns?' Craig accused him roughly. 'Where were you who promised to stand guard for me?'

There was a long silence out in the darkness.

'Where did this thing happen?'

Craig told him.

'That is far from here, far also from our camp. We did

not know.' His tone was apologetic, obviously Comrade Lookout felt he had failed in a bargain. 'But we will find the ones who did this. We will follow them and find them.'

'When you do, it is important that we know the name of the person who buys the horns from them,' Craig ordered.

'I will bring the name of that person to you,' Comrade Lookout promised. 'Watch for our signal fire on this hill.'

Twelve days later, through his binoculars, Craig picked up the little grey feather of smoke on the distant whaleback of the hill. He drove alone to the assignation for Sally-Anne had left three days previously. She had wanted desperately to stay, but one of the directors of the Wildlife Trust was arriving in Harare and she had to be there to greet him.

'I guess my grant for next year depends on it,' she told Craig ruefully as she climbed into the Cessna, 'but you phone me the minute you hear from your tame bandits.'

Craig climbed the hill eagerly and on the crest he was breathing evenly and his leg felt strong and easy. He had grown truly hard and fit in these last months, and his anger was still strong upon him as he stood beside the smouldering remains of the signal fire.

Twenty minutes passed before Comrade Lookout moved silently at the edge of the forest, still keeping in cover and with the automatic rifle in the crook of his arm.

'You were not followed?' Craig shook his head reassuringly. 'We must always be careful, Kuphela.'

'Did you find the men?'

'Did you bring the money?'

'Yes.' Craig drew the thick envelope from the patch pocket of his bush-jacket. 'Did you find the men?'

'Cigarettes,' Comrade Lookout teased him. 'Did you bring cigarettes?'

Craig tossed a pack to him, and Comrade Lookout lit one and inhaled deeply. 'Hau!' he said. 'That is good.'

161

'Tell me,' Craig insisted.

'There were three men. We followed their spoor from the kill – though it was almost ten days old, and they had tried to cover it.' Comrade Lookout drew on his cigarette until sparks flew from the glowing tip. 'Their village is on the escarpment of the valley three days' march from here. They were Batonka apes,' the Batonka are one of the primitive hunter-gatherer tribes that live along the valley of the Zambezi, 'and they had the horns of your rhinoceros with them still. We took the three of them into the bush and we spoke to them for a long time.' Craig felt his skin crawl as he imagined that extended conversation. He felt his anger subside to be replaced with a hollow feeling of guilt: he should have cautioned Comrade Lookout on his methods.

'What did they tell you?'

'They told me that there is a man, a city man who drives a motor-car and dresses like a white man. He buys the horns of rhinoceros, the skins of leopards and the teeth of ivory, and he pays more money than they have ever seen in their lives.'

'Where and when do they meet him?'

'He comes in each full moon, driving the road from Tuti Mission to the Shangani river. They wait on the road in the night for his coming.'

Craig squatted beside the fire and thought for a few minutes, then looked up at Comrade Lookout. 'You will tell these men that they will wait beside the road next full moon with the rhinoceros horns until this man comes in his motor-car—'

'That is not possible,' Comrade Lookout interrupted him.

'Why?' Craig asked.

'The men are dead.'

Craig stared at him in utter dismay. 'All three of them?'

162

'All three,' Comrade Lookout nodded. His eyes were cold and flat and merciless.

'But—' Craig couldn't bring himself to ask the question. He had set the guerrillas onto the poachers. It must have been like setting a pack of fox-terriers onto a domesticated hamster. Even though he had not meant it to happen, he was surely responsible. He felt sickened and ashamed.

'Do not worry, Kuphela,' Comrade Lookout reassured him kindly. 'We have brought you the horns of your *bejane*, and the men were only dirty Batonka apes anyway.'

Carrying the bark string bag of rhinoceros horns over his shoulder, Craig went down to the Land-Rover. He felt sick and weary and his leg hurt, but the draw-string bag cutting into his flesh did not gall him as sorely as his own conscience.

T he rhinoceros horns stood in a row on Peter Fungabera's desk. Four of them – the tall front horns and the shorter rear horns.

'Aphrodisiac,' Peter murmured, touching one of them with his long, tapering fingers.

'That's a fallacy,' Craig said. 'Chemical analysis shows they contain no substance that could possibly be aphrodisiac in effect.'

'They are nothing more than a type of agglutinated hair mass,' Sally-Anne explained. 'The effects that the failing Chinese roué seeks when he crushes it to powder and takes it with a draught of rose-water is merely sympathetic medicine – the horn is long and hard, *voilà!*'

'Anyway, the Arab oil men will pay more for their knife-handles than the cunning old Chinese will pay for their personal daggers,' Craig pointed out.

'Whatever the final market, the fact is that there are

163

two less rhino on Zambezi Waters than there were a month ago, and in another month how many more will have gone?'

Peter Fungabera stood up and came around the desk on bare feet. His loin-cloth was freshly laundered and crisply ironed. He stood in front of them.

'I have been pursuing my own lines of investigation,' he said quietly. 'And all of it seems to point in the same direction as Sally-Anne's own reasoning led her. It seems absolutely certain that there is a highly organized poaching ring operating across the country. The tribesmen in the game-rich areas are being enticed into poaching and gathering the valuable animal products. They are collected by middlemen, many of whom are junior civil servants, such as district officers and game department rangers. The booty is accumulated in various remote and safe caches until the value is sufficient to warrant a large single consignment being sent out of the country.'

Peter Fungabera began to pace slowly up and down the room.

'The consignment is usually exported on a commercial Air Zimbabwe flight to Dar-es-Salaam on the Tanzania coast. We are not sure what happens at that end, but it probably goes out on a Soviet or Chinese freighter.'

'The Soviets have no qualms about wildlife conservation,' Sally-Anne nodded. 'Sable-fur production and whaling are big foreign-exchange-earners for them.'

'What portfolio do Air Zimbabwe operations fall under?' Craig asked suddenly.

'The portfolio of the minister of tourism, the honourable Tungata Zebiwe,' Peter replied smoothly, and they were all silent for a few moments before he went on. 'When a consignment is due, the products are brought into Harare, all on the same day, or night. They are not stored, but go directly onto the aircraft under tight security conditions and are flown out almost immediately.'

'How often does this happen?' Craig asked and Peter Fungabera glanced enquiringly at his aide who was standing unobtrusively at the back of the room.

'That varies,' Captain Timon Nbebi replied. 'In the rainy season the grass is long and the conditions in the bush are bad. There is little hunting activity, but during the dry months the poachers can work more efficiently. However, we have learned through our informant that a consignment is almost due and will in fact go out within the next two weeks—'

'Thank you, Captain,' Peter Fungabera interrupted him with a small frown of annoyance; obviously he had wanted to deliver that information himself. 'What we have also learned is that the head of the organization often takes an active part in the operation. For instance, that massacre of elephant in the abandoned minefield,' Peter looked across at Sally-Anne, 'the one that you photographed so vividly – well, we have learned that a government minister, we do not know for certain which one, went to the site in an army helicopter. We know that on two further occasions a high government official, reputedly of ministerial rank, was present when consignments were brought in to the airport for shipment.'

'He probably does not trust his own men not to cheat him,' Craig murmured.

'With the bunch of cut-throats he's got working for him, who can blame him?' Sally-Anne's voice was hoarse with her outrage, but Peter Fungabera seemed unaffected.

'We believe that we will be forewarned of the next consignment. As I have intimated, we have infiltrated a man into their organization. We will watch the movements of our suspect as the date approaches and, with luck, catch him red-handed. If not, we will seize the consignment at the airport, and arrest all those handling it. I am certain we will be able to convince one of them to turn state's evidence.'

Watching his face, Craig recognized that same cold, flat, merciless expression that he had last seen when Comrade Lookout reported the death of the three poachers. It was only a fleeting glimpse behind the urbane manner and then Peter Fungabera had turned back to his desk.

'For reasons that I have already explained to you, I require independent and reliable witnesses to any arrest that we might be fortunate enough to make. I want both of you to be there. So I would be obliged if you could hold yourselves ready to move at very short notice, and if you could inform Captain Nbebi where you may be contacted at all times over the next two or three weeks.'

As they rose to leave, Craig asked suddenly, 'What is the maximum penalty for poaching?' and Peter Fungabera looked up from the papers he was rearranging on his desk.

'As the law stands now, it is a maximum of eighteen months' hard labour for any one of a dozen or so offences under the act—'

'That's not enough.' Craig had a vivid mental image of the violated and rotting carcasses of his animals.

'No,' Peter agreed. 'It's not enough. Two days ago in the House I introduced an amendment to the bill, as a private member's motion. It will be read for the third time on Thursday, and I assure you it has the full support of the party. It will become law on that day.'

'And,' Sally-Anne asked, 'what are the new penalties to be?'

'For unauthorized dealing in the trophies of certain scheduled wild game, as opposed to mere poaching or hunting, for buying and reselling and exporting, the maximum penalty will be twelve years at hard labour and a fine not exceeding one hundred thousand dollars.'

They thought about that for a moment, and then Craig nodded.

'Twelve years – yes, that is enough.'

P eter Fungabera's summons came in the early morning, when Craig and Hans Groenewald, his overseer, had just returned to the homestead from the dawn patrol of the pastures. Craig was in the middle of one of Joseph's gargantuan breakfasts when the telephone rang, and he was still savouring the homemade beef sausage as he answered it.

'Mr Mellow, this is Captain Nbebi. The General wants you to meet him as soon as possible at his operational headquarters, the house at Macillwane. We are expecting our man to move tonight. How soon can you be here?'

'It's a six-hour drive,' Craig pointed out.

'Miss Jay is already on her way to the airport. She should be at King's Lynn within the next two hours to pick you up.'

Sally-Anne arrived within the two hours, and Craig was waiting on the airstrip. They flew directly to Harare airport and Sally-Anne drove them out to the house in the Macillwane hills.

As they drove through the gates, they were immediately aware of the unusual activity in the grounds. On the front lawn stood a Super Frelon helicopter. The pilot and his engineer were leaning against the fuselage, smoking and chatting to each other. They looked up expectantly as Sally-Anne and Craig came up the driveway, and then dismissed them as unimportant. There were four sand-coloured army trucks drawn up in a line behind the house, with Third Brigade troopers in full battle-kit grouped around them. Craig could sense their excitement, like hounds being whipped in for the hunt.

Peter Fungabera's office had been turned into operational headquarters. Two camp tables had been set up facing the huge relief map on the wall. At the first table were seated three junior officers. There was a radio apparatus on the second table, and Timon Nbebi was leaning over the operator's shoulder, speaking into the microphone in low rippling Shona that Craig could not follow, breaking off abruptly to give an order to the black sergeant at the map, who immediately moved one of the coloured markers to a new position.

Peter Fungabera greeted Craig and Sally-Anne perfunctorily and waved them to stools, then went on speaking into the telephone. When he hung up he explained quickly, 'We know the location of three of the dumps – one is at a *shamba* in the Chimanimani mountains, it's mostly leopard-skins and some ivory. The second is at a trading-post near Chiredzi in the south – that's mostly ivory. And the third is coming from the north. We think that it's being held at Tuti Mission Station. It's the biggest and most valuable shipment, ivory and rhino horn.'

He broke off as Captain Nbebi handed him a note, read it swiftly and said, 'Good, move two platoons up the north road as far as Karoi,' and then turned back to Craig.

'The operation is code-named "Bada", that is Shona for "leopard". Our suspect will be referred to as Bada during the entire operation.' Craig nodded. 'We have just heard that Bada has left Harare. He is in his official Mercedes with a driver and two bodyguards – all three of them Matabele, of course.'

'Which way?' Sally-Anne asked quickly.

'At this stage, he seems to be heading north, but it's still too early to be sure.'

'To meet the big shipment—' there was the light of battle in Sally-Anne's eyes, and Craig could feel his own excitement tickling the hairs at the back of his neck.

'We must believe that is so,' Peter agreed. 'Now let me explain our disposition if Bada moves north. The shipments from Chimanimani and Chiredzi will be allowed through unhindered as far as the airport. They will be seized as soon as they arrive, and the drivers, together with the reception committee, arrested, to be used as witnesses later. Of course, their progress will be under surveillance at

168

all times from the moment the trucks are loaded. The owners of the two warehouses will be arrested as soon as the trucks leave and are clear of the area.'

Both Craig and Sally-Anne were listening intently, as Peter went on, 'If Bada moves either east or south, we will switch the focus of the operation to that sector. However, we had anticipated that as the most valuable shipment was in the north, that's where he will go – if, of course, he goes at all. It looks as though we were right. As soon as we are certain, then we can move ourselves.'

'How are you planning to catch them?' Sally-Anne demanded.

'It will be very much a matter of opportunity, and what we will do depends necessarily on Bada's actions. We have to try and make a physical connection between him and the consignment. We will watch both the vehicle carrying the contraband and his Mercedes, and as soon as they come together, we will pounce—' Peter Fungabera emphasized this act of pouncing by slapping his leather-covered swagger-stick into the palm of his hand with a crack like a pistol shot, and Craig found that he was already so keyed up that he started nervously and then grinned sheepishly at Sally-Anne.

The radio set crackled and the side-band hummed, then a disembodied voice spoke in Shona, and Captain Nbebi acknowledged curtly, and glanced across at Peter.

'It's confirmed, sir. Bada is moving north on the Karoi road at speed.'

'All right, Captain, we can go up to condition three,' Peter ordered, and strapped on the webbing belt with his holstered sidearm. 'Do you have anything from the surveillance teams on the Tuti road?'

Captain Nbebi called three times into the microphone, and was answered almost immediately. The reply to his question was brief.

'Negative at this time, General,' he reported to Peter.

'It's still too early.' Peter adjusted his burgundy-red beret to a rakish angle, and the silver leopard's head glinted over his right eye. 'But we can begin moving into our forward positions now.' He led the way through the french doors onto the veranda.

The helicopter crew saw him, quickly dropped their cigarettes, ground them out and vaulted up into the hatch. Peter Fungabera climbed up into the fuselage and the starter-motor whined and the rotors began to spin overhead.

As they settled down on the bench seats and clinched their waist-belts, Craig asked impulsively the question that had been troubling him, but he asked it in a voice low enough not to be heard by the others in the rising bellow of the main engine.

'Peter, this is a full-scale military operation, almost a crusade. Why not merely hand it over to the police?'

'Since they fired their white officers, the police have become a bunch of heavy-handed bunglers—' then Peter gave him a rake-hell smile ' – and after all, old boy, they are my rhino also.'

The helicopter lifted off with a gut-sliding swoop, and its nose rotated onto a northerly heading. Keeping low, hugging the contours, it bore away, and the rush of air through the open hatch made further conversation impossible.

They kept well to the west of the main northern road, not risking a sighting by the occupants of the Mercedes. An hour later, as the helicopter hovered and then began its descent to the small military fort at Karoi, Craig glanced at his wrist-watch. It was after four o'clock.

Peter Fungabera saw the gesture and nodded. 'It looks as though it's going to be a night operation,' he agreed.

The village of Karoi had once been a centre for the white-owned ranches in the area, but now it was a single street of shabby trading-stores, a service station, a post office and a small police station. The military base was a little beyond the town, still heavily fortified from the days of the bush war with a barbed-wire surround and sloped walls of sandbags twenty feet thick.

The local commandant, a young black 2nd lieutenant, was clearly overawed by the importance of his visitor, and saluted theatrically every time Peter Fungabera spoke.

'Get this idiot out of my sight,' Peter snarled at Captain Nbebi, as he took over the command post. 'And get me the latest report on Bada's position.'

'Bada passed through Sinoia twenty-three minutes ago.' Captain Nbebi looked up from the radio set.

'Right. Do we have an accurate description of the vehicle?'

'It's a dark blue Mercedes 280 SE with a ministerial pennant on the bonnet. Registration PL 674. No motor-cycle outriders, nor other escort vehicle. Four occupants.'

'Make sure that all units have that description – and repeat once more that there is to be no shooting. Bada is to be taken unharmed. Harm him and we could well have another Matabele rebellion on our hands. Nobody is to fire at him or his vehicle, even to save their own lives. Make that clear. Any man who disobeys will have to face me personally.'

Nbebi called each unit individually, repeated Peter's orders and waited while they were acknowledged. Then they waited impatiently, drinking tea from chipped enamel mugs and watching the radio set.

It crackled abruptly to life and Timon Nbebi sprang to it.

'We have located the truck,' he translated triumphantly. 'It's a green five-ton Ford with a canvas canopy. A driver and a passenger in the cab. Heavily laden, well down on the suspension and using extra low gear on the inclines. It crossed the drift on the Sanyati river ten minutes ago, heading from the direction of Tuti Mission towards the road junction twenty-five miles north of here.'

'So, Bada and the truck are on a course to intercept each other,' said Peter Fungabera softly, and there was the hunter's gleam in his eyes.

Now the radio set was the focus of all their attention, each time it came alive all their eyes instantly swivelled to it.

The reports came in regularly, tracing the swift progress of the Mercedes northwards towards them and that of the lumbering truck, grinding slowly down the dusty rutted secondary road from the opposite direction. In the periods between each report, they sat in silence, sipping the strong over-sweetened tea and munching sandwiches of coarse brown bread and canned bully beef.

Peter Fungabera ate little. He had tilted back his chair and placed his feet on the commandant's desk. He tapped the swagger-stick against the lacings of his rubber-soled jungle boots with a monotonous rhythm that began to irritate Craig. Suddenly Craig found himself craving for a cigarette again, the first time in months, and he stood up and began to pace the small office restlessly.

Timon Nbebi acknowledged another report and when he replaced the microphone, translated from the Shona, 'The Mercedes has reached the village. They have stopped at the service station to refill with gasoline.'

Tungata Zebiwe was only a few hundred yards from where they sat. Craig found the knowledge disconcerting. Up to now, it had been more an intellectual exercise than an actual life-and-death chase. He had ceased to think of Tungata as a man, he was merely 'Bada', the quarry, to be outguessed and hunted into the trap. Now suddenly he remembered him as a man, a friend, an extraordinary human being, and he was once more torn between his residual loyalty of friendship and his desire to see a criminal brought to justice.

The command post was suddenly claustrophobic, and he went out into the tiny yard enclosed by high thick walls and sandbags. The sun had set, and the brief African twilight purpled the sky overhead. He stood staring up at it. There was a light footstep beside him and he glanced down.

'Don't be too unhappy,' Sally-Anne pleaded softly. He was touched by her concern.

'You don't have to go,' she went on. 'You could stay here.'

He shook his head. 'I want to be sure – I want to see it for myself,' he said. 'But I'll not hate it any less.'

'I know,' she said. 'I respect you for that.'

He looked down on her upturned face and knew that she wanted him to kiss her. The moment for which he had waited so long and so patiently had arrived. She was ready for him at last, her need as great as his.

Gently he touched her cheek with his fingertips, and her eyelids fluttered half-closed. She swayed towards him, and he realized that he loved her. The knowledge took his breath away for a moment. He felt an almost religious awe.

'Sally-Anne,' he whispered, and the door of the command post crashed open and Peter Fungabera strode out into the yard.

'We are moving out,' he snapped, and they drew apart. Craig saw her shake herself lightly as though waking from sleep and her eyes came back into focus.

Side by side, they followed Peter and Timon to the open Land-Rover at the gate of the fort.

The evening was chill after the heat of the day, and the wind clawed at them, for the windscreen had been strapped down on the Land-Rover's bonnet.

Timon Nbebi drove with Peter Fungabera in the passenger seat. Craig and Sally-Anne were crowded into the back seat with the radio operator. Timon drove cautiously with parking lights only burning, and the two open army trucks packed with Third Brigade troopers in full battle-gear kept close behind them.

The Mercedes was less than half a mile ahead. Occasionally they could see the glow of its tail-lights as it climbed the road up one of the heavily wooded hills.

Peter Fungabera checked the odometer. 'We've come twenty-three miles. The turn-off to the Sanyati and Tuti is only two miles ahead.' He tapped Timon on the shoulder with the swagger-stick. 'Pull over. Call the unit at the junction.'

Craig found himself shivering as much from excitement as the cold. With the engine still running, Timon called ahead to the road-junction where the forward observation team was concealed.

'Ah! That's it!' Timon could not keep the elation from his voice. 'Bada has turned off the main road, General. The target truck has stopped and is parked two miles from the crossroads. It has to be a pre-arranged meeting, sir.'

'Get going,' Peter Fungabera ordered. 'Follow them!'

Now Timon Nbebi drove fast, using the glow of his parking lights to hold the verge of the road.

'There's the turning!' Peter snapped, as the unmade road showed dusty pale out of the dark.

Timon slowed and swung onto it. A sergeant of the Third Brigade stepped out of the darkness of the encroaching bush. He jumped up onto the footboard and managed to salute with his free hand.

'They passed here a minute ago, General,' he blurted. 'The truck is just ahead. We have set up a road-block behind it and we will block here as soon as you are passed, sir. We have them bottled up.'

'Carry on, Sergeant,' Peter nodded, then turned to Timon Nbebi. 'The road drops steeply down from here to the drift. Have the trucks cut their engines as soon as we are rolling. We'll coast down.'

The silence was eerie after the growl of heavy engines. The only sound was the squeak of the Land-Rover's suspension, the crunch of the tyres over gravel, and the rustle of the wind around their ears.

The twists in the rough track sprang at them out of the night with unnerving speed, and Timon Nbebi wrenched the wheel through them as they careered down the first drop of the great escarpment. The two trucks were guided by their tail-lights. They made monstrous black shapes looming out of the darkness close behind. Sally-Anne reached out for Craig's hand as they were thrown together into the turns, and she hung on to it tightly all the way down.

'There they are!' Peter Fungabera snarled abruptly, his voice roughened with excitement.

Below them they saw the headlights of the Mercedes flickering beyond the trees. They were closing up swiftly. For a few seconds the headlights were blanketed by another turn in the winding road, and then they burst out again – two long beams burning the pale dust surface of the track, to be answered suddenly by another glaring pair of head-lights facing in the opposite direction, even at this range, blindingly white. The second pair of headlights flashed three times, obviously a recognition signal, and immediately the Mercedes slowed.

'We've got them,' Peter Fungabera exulted, and switched off the parking lights.

Below them a canopied truck was trundling slowly from the verge where it had been parked in darkness, into the middle of the road. Its headlights flooded the Mercedes which pulled to a halt. Two men climbed out of the Mercedes and crossed to the cab of the truck. One of them carried a rifle. They spoke to the driver through the open window.

The Land-Rover raced silently in complete darkness towards the brightly lit tableau in the valley below. Sally-Anne was clinging to Craig's hand with startling strength.

In the road below, one of the men began to walk back towards the rear of the parked truck, and then paused and looked up the dark road towards the racing Land-Rover. They were so close now that even over the engine noise of the Mercedes and truck, he must have heard the crunch of tyres.

Peter Fungabera switched on the headlights of the Land-Rover. They blazed out with stunning brilliance and at the same moment he lifted an electronic bull-horn to his mouth.

'Do not move!' his magnified voice bellowed into the night, and came crashing back in echoes from the close-pressed hills. 'Do not attempt to escape!'

The two men whirled and dived back towards the Mercedes. Timon Nbebi started the engine with a roar and the Land-Rover jerked forward.

'Stay where you are! Drop your weapons!'

The men hesitated, then the armed one threw down his rifle and they both raised their hands in surrender, blinking into the dazzle of headlights.

Timon Nbebi swung the Land-Rover in front of the Mercedes, blocking it. Then he jumped down and ran to the open window and pointed his Uzi submachine-gun into the interior.

'Out!' he shouted. 'Everybody out!'

Behind them the two trucks came to a squealing halt, clouds of dust boiling out from under their double rear wheels. Armed troopers swarmed out of them, rushing forward to club down the two unarmed men onto the gravel of the road. They surrounded the Mercedes, tearing open the doors and dragging out the driver and another man from the back seat.

There was no mistaking the tall, wide-shouldered figure. The headlights floodlit his dark, craggy features and exaggerated the rocky strength of his lantern jaw. Tungata Zebiwe shrugged off the grip of his captors, and glared about him, forcing them to fall back involuntarily.

'Back, you yapping jackals! Do you dare touch me?'

He was dressed in dark slacks and a white shirt. His cropped head was round and black as a cannon ball.

'Do you know who I am?' he demanded. 'You'll wish your twenty-five fathers had taught you better manners.'

His arrogant assurance drove them back another pace, and they looked towards the Land-Rover. Peter Fungabera stepped out of the darkness behind the headlights, and Tungata Zebiwe recognized him instantly.

'You!' he growled. 'Of course, the chief butcher.'

'Open the truck,' Peter Fungabera ordered, without taking his eyes off the other man. They stared at each other with such terrible hatred, that it rendered insignificant everything else around them. It was an elemental confrontation, seeming to embody all the savagery of a continent, two powerful men stripped of any vestige of civilized restraint, their antagonism so strong as to be barely supportable to them.

Craig had jumped down from the Land-Rover and started forward, but now he stopped beside the Mercedes in astonishment. He had not expected anything remotely like this. This almost tangible hatred was not a thing of that moment, it seemed that the two of them would launch themselves at each other like embattled animals, tearing with bare hands at each other's throats. This was a passion of deep roots, a mutual rage based on a monumental foundation of long-standing hostility.

From the back of the captured truck the troopers were

hurling out bales and crates. One of the crates burst open as it hit the road, and long yellow shafts of ivory glowed like amber in the headlights. A trooper hooked open one of the bales and pulled out handfuls of precious fur, the golden dappled skin of leopard, the thick red pelts of lynx.

'That's it!' Peter Fungabera's voice was choking with triumph and loathing and vindictive gloating. 'Seize the Matabele dog!'

'Whatever this is will rebound on your own head,' Tungata growled at him, 'you son of a Shona whore!'

'Take him!' Peter urged his men, but they hesitated, held at bay by the invisible aura of power that emanated from this tall imperial figure.

In the pause, Sally-Anne jumped down from the Land-Rover, and started towards the treasure of fur and ivory lying in the road. For a second she screened Tungata Zebiwe from his captors, and he moved with a blur of speed, like the strike of an adder, almost too fast to follow with the eye.

He seized Sally-Anne's arm, twisted and lifted her off her feet, holding her as a shield in front of him as he ducked low and scooped up the discarded rifle from the dust at his feet. He had chosen the moment perfectly. They were all crowded in upon each other. The troopers pressed so closely that none of them could fire without hitting one of their own.

Tungata's back was protected by the Land-Rover, his front by Sally-Anne's body.

'Don't shoot!' Peter Fungabera bellowed at his men. 'I want the Matabele bastard for myself.'

Tungata swung the barrel of the rifle up under Sally-Anne's armpit, holding it by the pistol grip single-handed, and he aimed at Peter Fungabera, as he fell back towards the Land-Rover, dragging Sally-Anne with him. The Land-Rover's engine was still running.

'You'll not escape,' Peter Fungabera gloated. 'The road is blocked, I have a hundred men. I've got you, at last.'

Tungata slipped the rate-of-fire selector across with his thumb and dropped his aim to Peter Fungabera's belly. Craig was standing diagonally behind his left shoulder, he saw the slight deflection of the rifle barrel at the instant before Tungata fired. Craig realized that he had deliberately aimed an inch to one side of Peter's hip. The clattering roar of automatic fire was deafening, and the group of men leapt apart as they went for cover.

The rifle rode up high in Tungata's single-handed grip. Bullets smashed into the parked truck, leaving dark rents through the bodywork, each surrounded by a halo of bright bare metal. Peter Fungabera hurled himself aside, spinning away along the truck body to fall flat in the road and wriggle frantically behind the truck wheels.

Gunsmoke and dust shrouded the blazing headlights, and troopers scattered, blanketing each other's field of fire, while in the chaos, Tungata lifted Sally-Anne bodily and threw her into the passenger-seat of the Land-Rover. In the same movement, he vaulted up into the driver's seat, threw the vehicle into gear and the engine roared as it leapt forward.

'Don't shoot!' Peter Fungabera shouted again, there was a desperate urgency in his voice. 'I want him alive!'

A trooper jumped in front of the Land-Rover, in a futile attempt to stop it. The impact sounded like a lump of bread-dough dropped on the kneading board, as the bonnet hit him squarely in the chest and he fell. There was a series of jolting bumps as he was dragged under the chassis, then he rolled out into the road and the Land-Rover was boring away up the dark hill.

Without conscious thought, Craig jerked open the driver's door of the abandoned ministerial Mercedes and slipped into the seat. He locked the wheel into a hard

180-degree turn and gunned her into it. The Mercedes' tail crabbed around, tyres spinning and he hit the high earth bank a glancing blow with the right front wing that swung her nose through the last few degrees of the turn. Craig lifted his foot off the accelerator, met the skid, centred the wheel, and then trod down hard. The Mercedes shot forward, and through the open window he heard Peter Fungabera shout, 'Craig! Wait!'

He ignored the call, and concentrated on the first sharp bend of the escarpment road as it flashed up at him. The Mercedes' steering was deceptively light, he almost over-steered and the off-wheels hammered over the rough verge. Then he was through the bend and ahead the red tail-lights of the Land-Rover were almost obscured in their own boiling white dust cloud.

Craig dropped the automatic transmission to sports mode, the engine shrieked and the needle of the rev-counter spun up into the red sector above 5000, and she arrowed up the hill, gaining swiftly on the Land-Rover.

It was swallowed by the next turn, and the dust blinded Craig so that he was forced to lift his right foot and grope through the turn, again he almost missed it and his rear wheels tore at the steep drop, inches from disaster before he took her through.

He was getting the feel of the machine, and four hundred yards ahead he had a brief glimpse of the Land-Rover through the dust. His headlights spotlit Sally-Anne. She was half-twisted over the side, trying to climb out and throw herself from the fleeing vehicle, but Tungata shot out a long arm and caught her shoulder, plucking her back and forcing her down into the seat.

The scarf flew off her head, winging up like a nightbird to be lost in the darkness, and her thick dark hair broke out and tangled about her head and face. Then dust obscured the Land-Rover again – and Craig felt his anger hit him in the chest with a force that made him choke. In that moment, he hated Tungata Zebiwe as he had never hated another human being in his life before. He took the next bend cleanly, tracking neatly through and pouring on full power again at the moment he was clear.

The Land-Rover was three hundred yards ahead, the gap shrinking at the rush of the Mercedes, then Craig was braking for the next twist of the road and when he came out the Land-Rover was much closer. Sally-Anne was craning around, looking back at him. Her face was white, almost luminous, in the headlights, her hair danced in a glossy tide around it, seeming at moments almost to smother her, and then the next bend snatched her away. Craig followed them into it, meeting the brake of the tail as she floated in the floury dust and then as he came through he saw the road-block ahead.

There was a three-ton army truck parked squarely across the road, and the gaps between it and the bank had been filled with recently felled thorn trees. The entwined branches formed a solid mattress and the heavy trunks had been chained together. Craig saw the steel links glinting in the headlights. That barrier would stop a bulldozer.

Five troopers stood before the barrier, waving their rifles in an urgent command to the Land-Rover to halt. That they hadn't already opened fire made Craig hope that Peter Fungabera had reached them on the radio, yet he felt a nauseating rush of anxiety when he saw how vulnerable Sally-Anne was in the open vehicle. He imagined a volley of automatic fire tearing into that lovely young body and face.

'Please don't shoot,' he whispered, and pressed so hard on the accelerator that the cup of his artificial leg bit painfully into his stump. The nose of the Mercedes was fifty feet from the Land-Rover's tail and gaining.

A hundred yards from the solid barrier across the road was a low place in the right-hand bank. Tungata swerved into it and the ugly blunt-nosed vehicle flew up it, all four wheels clawing as it went over the top and tore like a combine-harvester into the high yellow stand of elephant grass beyond.

Craig knew he could not follow him. The low-slung Mercedes would tear her guts out on the bank. He raced past it, and then hit the brakes as the road-block loomed up and filled his windshield. The Mercedes broadsided to a dead stop in a storm of its own dust and Craig threw his weight on the door and tumbled out into the road.

He caught his balance and scrambled up the right-hand bank. The Land-Rover was twenty yards away, engine roaring in low gear, crashing and bouncing over the broken ground, mowing down the dense yellow grass whose stems were thick as a man's little finger and taller than his head, weaving between the forest trees, its speed reduced by the terrain to that of a running man. Craig saw that Tungata would succeed in detouring around the road-block, and he ran to head off the Land-Rover. Anger and fear for Sally-Anne seemed to guide his feet, he stumbled only once on the rough footing.

Tungata Zebiwe saw him coming and lifted the rifle one-handed, aiming over the bonnet of the jolting, roaring Land-Rover, but Sally-Anne threw herself across the weapon, clinging to it with both arms, her weight forcing the barrel down and Tungata could not take his other hand from the wheel as it kicked and whipped in his grip. They were past the road-block now, and Craig was losing ground to them; realizing with a slide in his chest that he could not catch them, he floundered along behind the roaring vehicle.

Sally-Anne and Tungata were struggling confusedly together, until the big black man tore his arm free and, using the hand as a blade, chopped her brutally under the ear. She slumped face forward onto the dashboard, and Tungata swung the wheel over. The vehicle swerved, giving Craig a few precious yards' advantage, and then it seemed to hover for an instant on the high bank beyond the road-block before it leapt over the edge and dropped into the roadway with a clangour of metal and spinning tyres.

Craig used the last of his reserves of strength and determination and raced forward to reach the place on the bank an instant after it had disappeared.

Ten feet below him, the Land-Rover was miraculously still the right way up, and Tungata, badly shaken, his mouth bleeding from impact with the steering-wheel, was struggling for control.

Craig did not hesitate. He launched himself out over the bank, and the drop sucked his breath away. The Land-Rover was accelerating away, and he dropped half over the tail-gate. He felt his ribs crunch on metal, his breath whistled in his throat as it was driven from his lungs, and his vision starred for an instant – but he found a grip on the radio set and hung on blindly.

He felt the Land-Rover surging forward under him, and heard Sally-Anne whimpering with pain and terror. The sound steeled him, his vision cleared. He was hanging over the back of the tail-gate, his feet dangling and dragging.

Behind him the army truck was swinging out of the road-block, engine thundering and headlights glaring in pursuit, while just ahead the main-road T-junction was coming up with a rush as the Land-Rover built up to her top speed again.

Craig braced himself for the turn, but even so when it came his upper arms were almost torn from their shoulder sockets, as Tungata took the left fork on two wheels. Now he was heading north. Of course, the Zambian border was only a hundred miles ahead. The road went down into the great escarpment, and there was no human settlement in that tsetse-fly-infested, heat-baked wilderness before the border post and the bridge over the Zambezi at Chirundu. With a hostage it was just possible he could reach it. If

Craig gave up, he could reach it – or get himself and Sally-Anne killed in the attempt.

By inches Craig dragged himself back into the Land-Rover. Sally-Anne was crumpled down in the seat, her head lolling from side to side with each jerk and sway of the vehicle, and Tungata was tall and heavy-shouldered beside her, his white shirt gleaming in the reflected glare of the headlights.

Craig released his grip with one hand and made a grab for the back of the seat to pull himself on board. Instantly the Land-Rover swerved violently and in that same instant he saw the glint of Tungata's eyes in the rear-view mirror. He had been watching Craig, waiting to catch him off-balance and throw him.

The centrifugal force rolled Craig over and out over the side of the vehicle. He had a hold with his left hand only, and the muscles and tendons crackled with the strain as his full weight was thrown on it. He gasped with the agony as it tore up his arm into his chest, but he held on, hanging overboard with the steel edge catching him in his injured ribs again.

Tungata swerved a second time, running his wheels over the verge, and Craig saw the bank rushing at him in the headlights. Tungata was attempting to wipe him off the Land-Rover on the bank, trying to shred him to pieces between shaly rock and sharp metal. Craig screamed involuntarily with the effort as he jack-knifed his knees up and over. There was a rushing din of metal and stone as the Land-Rover brushed the bank. Something struck his leg a blow that jarred him to his hip and he heard the straps part as his leg was torn away. If it had been flesh and bone he would have been fatally maimed. Instead, as the Land-Rover swung back onto the road he used the momentum to roll across the back seat and whip his free arm around Tungata's neck from behind.

It was a strangle-hold and as he threw all his strength

into it, he felt the give of Tungata's larynx in the crook of his elbow, and the loaded feel of the vertebrae, like the tension of a dry twig on the point of snapping. He wanted to kill him, he wanted to tear his head off his body, but he could not anchor himself to apply those last few ounces of pressure.

Tungata lifted both hands off the wheel, tearing at Craig's wrist and elbow, making a glottal, cawing sound, and the untended steering-wheel spun wildly. The Land-Rover charged off the road, plunged over the unprotected verge onto the steep rocky slope, and with a rending screech of metal crashed end over end.

Craig's grip was torn open and he was flung clear. He hit hard earth, cartwheeled, and lay for a second, his ears humming and his body crushed and helpless until he rallied and pulled himself to his knees.

The Land-Rover lay on its back. The headlights still blazed, and thirty paces down the slope, full in their beam, lay Sally-Anne. She looked like a little girl asleep. Her eyes closed and he mouth relaxed, the lips very red against her pallor, but from her hairline a thin dark serpent of blood crawled down across her pale brow.

He started to crawl towards her, when another figure rose out of the intervening darkness, a great, dark, wide-shouldered figure. Tungata was clearly stunned, staggering in a half-circle, clutching his injured throat. At the sight of him Craig went berserk with grief and rage.

He hurled himself at Tungata and they came together, chest to chest. Long ago, as friends, they had often wrestled, but Craig had forgotten the sheer bull strength of the man. His muscles were hard and resilient and black as the cured rubber of a transcontinental truck tyre, and, one-legged, Craig was unbalanced. Dazed as he was, Tungata heaved him off his foot.

As he went down, Craig kept his grip and despite his own strength, Tungata could not break it. They went down together, and Craig used his stump, driving up with the hard rubbery pad at the end of it, using the swing of it and Tungata's own falling weight to slog into Tungata's lower body.

Tungata grunted and the strength went out of him. Craig rolled out from under him, reared back onto his shoulders, and used all his body to launch himself forward again to hit with the stump. It sounded like an axe swung double-handed against a tree trunk, and it caught Tungata in the middle of his chest, right over the heart.

Tungata dropped over backwards and lay still. Craig crawled to him and reached for his unprotected throat with both hands. He felt the ropes of muscle framing the sharp hard lump of the thyroid cartilage and he drove his thumbs deeply into it, and, at the feel of ebbing life under his hands, his rage fell away – he found he could not kill him. He opened his hands and drew away, shaking and gasping.

He left Tungata lying crumpled on the rocky earth and crawled to where Sally-Anne lay. He picked her up and sat with her in his lap, cradling her head against his shoulder, desolated by the slack and lifeless feel of her body. With one hand he wiped away the trickle of blood before it reached her eyes.

Above them on the road the following truck pulled up with a metallic squeal of brakes and armed men came swarming down the slope, baying like a pack of hounds at the kill. In his arms like a child waking from sleep, Sally-Anne stirred and mumbled softly.

She was alive, still alive – and he whispered to her, 'My darling, oh my darling, I love you so!'

Four of Sally-Anne's ribs were cracked, her right ankle was badly sprained, and there was serious bruising and swelling on her neck from the blow she had received. However, the cut in her scalp was superficial and the X-rays showed no damage to the skull. Nevertheless, she was held for observation in the private ward that Peter Fungabera had secured for her in the overcrowded public hospital.

It was here that Abel Khori, the public prosecutor assigned to the Tungata Zebiwe case, visited her. Mr Khori was a distinguished-looking Shona who had been called to the London bar and still affected the dress of Lincoln's Inn Fields, together with a penchant for learned, if irrelevant, Latin phrases.

'I am visiting you to clarify in my own mind certain points in the statement that you have already made to the police. For it would be highly improper of me to influence in any way the evidence that you will give,' Khori explained.

He showed Craig and Sally-Anne the reports of spontaneous Matabele demonstrations for Tungata's release, which had been swiftly broken up by the police and units of the Third Brigade, and which the Shona editor of the *Herald* had relegated to the middle pages.

'We must always bear in mind that this man is *ipso jure* accused of a criminal act, and he should not be allowed to become a tribal martyr. You see the dangers. The sooner we can have the entire business settled *mutatis mutandis*, the better for everybody.'

Craig and Sally-Anne were at first astonished and then made uneasy at the despatch with which Tungata Zebiwe was to be brought to trial. Despite the fact that the rolls were filled for seven months ahead, his case was given a date in the Supreme Court ten days hence.

'We cannot *nudis verbis* keep a man of his stature in gaol for seven months,' the prosecutor explained, 'and to grant him bail and allow him liberty to inflame his followers would be suicidal folly.'

Apart from the trial, there were other lesser matters to occupy both Craig and Sally-Anne. Her Cessna was due for its thousand-hour check and 'certificate of air-worthiness'. There were no facilities for this in Zimbabwe, and they had to arrange for a fellow pilot to fly the machine down to Johannesburg for her. 'I will feel like a bird with its wings clipped,' she complained.

'I know the feeling,' Craig grinned ruefully, and banged his crutch on the floor.

'Oh, I'm sorry, Craig.'

'No, don't be. Somehow I no longer mind talking about my missing pin. Not with you, anyway.'

'When will it be back?'

'Morgan Oxford sent it out in the diplomatic bag and Henry Pickering has promised to chase up the technicians at Hopkins Orthopaedic – I should have it back for the trial.'

The trial. Everything seemed to come back to the trial, even the running of King's Lynn and the final preparations for the opening of the lodges at Zambezi Waters could not seduce Craig away from Sally-Anne's bedside and the preparations for the trial. He was fortunate to have Hans Groenewald at King's Lynn and Peter Younghusband, the young Kenyan manager and guide whom Sally-Anne had chosen, had arrived to take over the daily running of Zambezi Waters. Though he spoke to these two every day on either telephone or radio, Craig stayed on in Harare close to Sally-Anne.

Craig's leg arrived back the day before Sally-Anne's discharge from hospital. He pulled up his trouser-cuff to show it to her.

'Straightened, panel-beaten, lubricated and thoroughly reconditioned,' he boasted. 'How's your head?'

'The same as your leg,' she laughed. 'Although the

doctors have warned me off bouncing on it again for at least the next few weeks.'

She was using a cane for her ankle, and her chest was still strapped when he carried her bag down to the Land-Rover the following morning.

'Ribs hurting?' He saw her wince as she climbed into the vehicle.

'As long as nobody squeezes them, I'll pull through.'

'No squeezing. Is that a rule?' he asked.

'I guess—' she paused and regarded him for a moment before she lowered her eyes and murmured demurely, 'but then rules are for fools, and for the guidance of wise men.'

And Craig was considerably heartened.

N umber Two Court of the Mashonaland division of the Supreme Court of the Republic of Zimbabwe still retained all the trappings of British justice.

The elevated bench with the coat of arms of Zimbabwe above the judge's seat dominated the courtroom; the tiers of oaken benches faced it, and the witness box and the dock were set on either hand. The prosecutors, the assessors and the attorneys charged with the defence wore long black robes, while the judge was splendid in scarlet. Only the colour of the faces had changed, their blackness accentuated by the tight snowy curls of their wigs and the starched white swallow-tail collars.

The courtroom was packed, and when the standing room at the back was filled, the ushers closed the doors, leaving the crowd overflowing into the passages beyond. The crowds were orderly and grave, almost all of them Matabele who had made the long bus journey across the country from Matabeleland, many of them wearing the rosettes of the **ZAPU** party. Only when the accused was led into the dock was there a stir and murmur, and at the rear of the court a black woman dressed in **ZAPU** colours cried hysterically 'Bayete, Nkosi Nkulu!' and gave the clenched-fist salute.

The guards seized her immediately and hustled her out through the doors. Tungata Zebiwe stood in the dock and watched impassively, by his sheer presence belittling every other person in the room. Even the judge, Mr Justice Domashawa, a tall, emaciated Mashona, with a delicately bridged atypical Egyptian nose and small, bright, birdlike eyes, although vested in all the authority of his scarlet robes, seemed ordinary in comparison. However, Mr Justice Domashawa had a formidable reputation, and the prosecutor had rejoiced in his selection when he told Craig and Sally-Anne of it.

'Oh, he is indeed *persona grata* and now it is very much *in gremio legis*, we will see justice done, never fear.'

While the country had still been Rhodesia, the British jury system had been abandoned. The judge would reach a verdict with the assistance of the two black-robed assessors who sat with him on the bench. Both these assessors were Shona: one was an expert on wildlife conservation, and the other a senior magistrate. The judge could call upon their expert advice if he so wished, but the final verdict would be his alone.

Now he settled his robes around him, the way an ostrich shakes out its feathers as it settles on the nest, and he fixed Tungata Zebiwe with his bright dark eyes while the clerk of the court read out the charge sheet in English.

There were eight main charges: dealing in and exporting the products of scheduled wild animals, abducting and holding a hostage, assault with a deadly weapon, assault with intent to do grievous bodily harm, attempted murder, violently resisting arrest, theft of a motor vehicle, and malicious damage to state property. There were also twelve lesser charges.

'By God,' Craig whispered to Sally-Anne, 'they are throwing the bricks from the walls at him.'

'And the tiles off the floor,' she agreed. 'Good for them, I'd love to see the bastard swing.'

'Sorry, my dear, none of them are capital charges.' And yet all through the prosecution's opening address, Craig was overcome by a sense of almost Grecian tragedy, in which an heroic figure was surrounded and brought low by lesser, meaner men.

Despite his feelings, Craig was aware that Abel Khori was doing a good businesslike job of laying out his case in his opening address, even displaying restraint in his use of Latin maxims. The first of a long list of prosecution witnesses was General Peter Fungabera. Resplendent in full dress, he took the oath and stood straight-backed and martial with his swagger-stick held loosely in one hand. His testimony was given without equivocation, so direct and impressive that the judge nodded his approval from time to time as he made his notes.

The Central Committee of the ZAPU party had briefed a London barrister for the defence, but even Mr Joseph Petal QC could not shake General Fungabera and very soon realized the futility of the effort, so he retired to wait for more vulnerable prey.

The next witness was the driver of the truck containing the contraband. He was an ex-ZIPRA guerrilla, recently released from one of the rehabilitation centres and his testimony was given in the vernacular and translated into English by the court interpreter.

'Had you ever met the accused before the night you were arrested?' Abel Khori demanded of him after establishing his identity.

'Yes. I was with him in the fighting.'

'Did you see him again after the war?'

'Yes.'

'Will you tell the court when that was?'

'Last year in the dry season.'

'Before you were placed in the rehabilitation centre?'

'Yes, before that.'

'Where did you meet Minister Tungata Zebiwe?'

'In the valley, near the great river.'

'Will you tell the court about that meeting?'

'We were hunting elephant – for the ivory.'

'How did you hunt them?'

'We used tribesmen, Batonka tribesmen, and a helicopter, to drive them into the old minefield.'

'I object to this line of questioning, my lord.' Mr Petal QC jumped up. 'This has nothing to do with the charges.'

'It has reference to the first charge,' Abel Khori insisted.

'Your objection is overruled, Mr Petal. Please continue, Mr Prosecutor.'

'How many elephant did you kill?'

'Many, many elephant.'

'Can you estimate how many?'

'Perhaps two hundred elephant, I am not sure.'

'And you state that the Minister Tungata Zebiwe was there?'

'He came after the elephant had been killed. He came to count the ivory and take it away in his helicopter—'

'What helicopter?'

'A government helicopter.'

'I object, your lordship, the point is irrelevant.'

'Objection overruled, Mr Petal, please continue.'

When his turn came for cross-examination, Mr Joseph Petal went into the attack immediately.

'I put it to you that you were never a member of Minister Tungata Zebiwe's resistance fighters. That you never, in fact, met the minister until that night on the Karoi road—'

'I object, your lordship,' Abel Khori shouted indignantly. 'The defence is trying to discredit the witness in the knowledge that no records of patriotic soldiers exist and that the witness cannot, therefore, prove his gallant service to the cause.'

'Objection sustained. Mr Petal, please confine your questions to the matter in hand and do not bully the witness.'

'Very well, your lordship.' Mr Petal was rosy-faced with frustration as he turned back to the witness. 'Can you tell the judge when you were released from the rehabilitation centre?'

'I forget. I cannot remember.'

'Was it a long time or a short time before your arrest?'

'A short time,' the witness replied sulkily, looking down at his hands in his lap.

'Were you not released from the prison camp on the condition that you drove the truck that night, and that you agreed to give evidence—'

'My lord!' shrieked Abel Khori, and the judge's voice was as shrill and indignant.

'Mr Petal, you will not refer to state rehabilitation centres as prison camps.'

'As your lordship pleases.' Mr Petal continued, 'Were you made any promises when you were released from the rehabilitation centre?'

'No.' The witness looked about him unhappily.

'Were you visited in the centre, two days before your release, by a Captain Timon Nbebi of the Third Brigade?'

'No.'

'Did you have any visitors in the camp?'

'No! No!'

'No visitors at all, are you sure?'

'The witness has already answered that question,' the judge stopped him, and Mr Petal sighed theatrically, and threw up his hands.

'No further questions, my lord.'

'Do you intend calling any further witnesses, Mr Khori?'

Craig knew that the next witness should have been

Timon Nbebi, but unaccountably Abel Khori passed over him and called instead the trooper who had been knocked down by the Land-Rover. Craig felt an uneasy little chill of doubt at the change in the prosecution's tactics. Did the prosecutor want to protect Captain Nbebi from cross-examination? Did he want to prevent Mr Petal from pursuing the question of a visit by Timon Nbebi to the rehabilitation centre? If this was so, the implications were unthinkable, so Craig forced himself to put his doubts aside.

The necessity for all questions and replies to be translated made the entire court process long-drawn-out and tedious, so it was only on the third day that Craig was called to the witness stand.

After Craig had taken the oath, and before Abel Khori had begun his examination, he glanced towards the dock. Tungata Zebiwe was watching him intently and as their eyes locked, Tungata made a sign with his right hand.

In the old days when they had worked together as rangers in the Game Department, Craig and Tungata had developed this sign language to a high degree. During the dangerous work of closing in on a breeding herd to begin the bloody elephant culls during which it had been their duty to destroy surplus animals that were over-populating the reserves, or when they were stalking a marauding cattle-killing pride of lions, they had communicated silently and swiftly with this private language.

Now Tungata gave him the clenched fist, his powerful black fingers closing over the clear pink of his palm in the sign that said 'Beware! Extreme danger.'

The last time Tungata had given him that sign, he had had only microseconds to turn and meet the charge of the enraged lung-wounded lioness as she came grunting in bloody pink explosive gasps of breath out of heavy brush cover, launching herself like a golden thunderbolt upon him, so that even though the bullet from his .458 magnum had smashed through her heart, her momentum had hurled Craig off his feet.

Now Tungata's sign made his nerves tingle and the hair on his forearms rise, at the memory of danger past and the promise of danger present. Was it a threat – or a warning, Craig wondered, staring at Tungata. He could not be certain, for Tungata was now expressionless and unmoving. Craig gave him the signal, 'Query? I do not understand,' but Tungata ignored it, and Craig abruptly realized that he had missed Abel Khori's opening question.

'I'm sorry – will you repeat that?'

Swiftly Abel Khori led him through his questions.

'Did you see the driver of the truck make any signal as the Mercedes approached?'

'Yes, he flashed his lights.'

'And what was the response?'

'The Mercedes stopped and two of the occupants left the vehicle and went to speak with the driver of the truck.'

'In your opinion, was this a pre-arranged meeting?'

'Objection, your lordship, the witness cannot know that.'

'Sustained. The witness will disregard the question.'

'We come now to your gallant rescue of Miss Jay from the evil clutches of the accused.'

'Objection – the word "evil".'

'You will discontinue the use of the adjective "evil".'

'As your lordship pleases.'

After that hand-signal, and during the rest of Craig's testimony, Tungata Zebiwe sat immovable as a figure carved in the granite of Matabeleland, with his chin sunk in his chest, but his eyes never left Craig's face.

As Mr Petal rose to cross-examine, he moved for the

first time, leaning forward to rumble a few terse words. Mr Petal seemed to protest, but Tungata made a commanding gesture.

'No questions, your lordship,' Mr Petal acquiesced, and sank back in his seat, freeing Craig to leave the witness box without harassment.

Sally-Anne was the last of the prosecution witnesses and, after Peter Fungabera, perhaps the most telling.

She was still limping with her sprained ankle, so that Abel Khori hurried forward to help her into the witness box. The dark shadow of the bruise on her neck was the only blemish on her skin, and she gave her evidence without hesitation in a clear pleasing voice.

'When the accused seized you, what were your feelings?'

'I was in fear of my life.'

'You say the accused struck you. Where did the blow land?'

'Here on my neck – you can see the bruise.'

'You state that the accused aimed the stolen rifle at Mr Mellow. What was your reaction?

'And will you tell the court whether you sustained any other injuries.'

Abel Khori made the most of such a lovely witness, and very wisely, Mr Petal once again declined to cross-examine. The prosecution closed its case on the evening of the third day, leaving Craig troubled and depressed.

He and Sally-Anne ate at her favourite steakhouse, and even a bottle of good Cape wine did not cheer him.

'That business about the driver never having met Tungata before, and being released only on a promise to drive the truck—'

'You didn't believe that?' Sally-Anne scoffed. 'Even the judge made no secret of how far-fetched he thought that was.'

After he dropped her at her apartment, Craig walked alone through the deserted streets, feeling lonely and betrayed – though he could not find a logical reason for the feeling.

M r Joseph Petal QC opened his defence by calling Tungata Zebiwe's chauffeur.

He was a heavily built Matabele, although young, already running to fat, with a round face that should have been jovial and smiling, but was now troubled and clouded. His head had been freshly shaved, and he never looked at Tungata once during his time on the witness stand.

'On the night of your arrest, what orders did Minister Zebiwe give you?'

'Nothing. He told me nothing.'

Mr Petal looked genuinely puzzled and consulted his notes.

'Did he not tell you where to drive? Did you not know where you were going?'

'He said "Go straight", "Turn left here," "Turn right here",' the driver muttered, 'I did not know where we were going.'

Obviously Mr Petal was not expecting this reply.

'Did Minister Zebiwe not order you to drive to Tuti Mission?'

'Objection, your lordship.'

'Do not lead the witness, Mr Petal.'

Mr Joseph Petal was clearly thinking on his feet. He shuffled his papers, glanced at Tungata Zebiwe, who sat completely impassive, and then switched his line of questioning.

'Since the night of your arrest, where have you been?'

'In prison.'

'Did you have any visitors?'

'My wife came.'

197

'No others?'

'No.' The chauffeur ducked his head defensively.

'What are those marks on your head? Were you beaten?'

For the first time Craig noticed the dark lumps on the chauffeur's shaven pate.

'Your lordship, I object most strenuously,' Abel Khori cried plaintively.

'Mr Petal, what is the purpose of this line of questioning?' Mr Justice Domashawa demanded ominously.

'My lord, I am trying to find why the witness's evidence conflicts with his previous statement to the police.'

Mr Petal struggled to obtain a clear reply from the sulky and uncooperative witness, and finally gave up with a gesture of resignation.

'No further questions, your lordship.' And Abel Khori rose smiling to cross-examine.

'So the truck flashed its lights at you?'

'Yes.'

'And what happened then?'

'I do not understand.'

'Did anybody in the Mercedes say or do anything when you saw the truck?'

'My lord—' Mr Petal began.

'I think that is a fair question – the witness will answer.'

The chauffeur frowned with the effort of recall, and then mumbled, 'Comrade Minister Zebiwe said, "There it is – pull over and stop."'

'"There it is"!' Abel Khori repeated slowly and clearly. '"Pull over and stop"! That is what the accused said when he saw the truck, is that correct?'

'Yes. He said it.'

'No further questions, your lordship.'

'Call Sarah Tandiwe Nyoni.' Mr Joseph Petal introduced his surprise witness, and Abel Khori frowned and conferred agitatedly with his two assistant prosecutors. One of them rose, bowed to the bench and hurriedly left the court.

Sarah Tandiwe Nyoni entered the witness stand and took the oath in perfect English. Her voice was melodious and sweet, her manner as reserved and shy as the day that Craig and Sally-Anne had first met her at Tuti Mission. She wore a lime-green cotton dress with a white collar and simple low-heeled white shoes. Her hair was elaborately braided in traditional style, and the moment she finished reading the oath, she turned her soft gaze onto Tungata Zebiwe in the dock. He neither smiled nor altered his expression, but his right hand, resting on the railing of the dock, moved slightly, and Craig realized that he was using the secret sign-language to the girl.

'Courage!' said that signal. 'I am with you!' And the girl took visible strength and confidence from it. She lifted her chin and faced Mr Petal squarely.

'Please state your name.'

'I am Sarah Tandiwe Nyoni,' she replied. *Tandiwe Nyoni*, her Matabele name, meant 'Beloved Bird' and Craig translated softly to Sally-Anne.

'It suits her perfectly,' she whispered back.

'What is your profession?'

'I am the headmistress of Tuti State Primary School.'

'Will you tell the court your qualifications.'

Joseph Petal established swiftly that she was an educated and responsible young woman. Then he went on:

'Do you know the accused, Tungata Zebiwe?'

She looked at Tungata again before answering, and her face seemed to glow. 'I do, oh yes, I do,' she whispered huskily.

'Please speak up, my dear.'

'I know him.'

'Did he ever visit you at Tuti Mission Station?'

'Yes,' she nodded.

'How often?'

'The Comrade Minister is an important and busy man, I am a school-teacher—'

Tungata made a small gesture of denial with his right hand. She saw it and a little smile formed on her perfectly sculptured lips.

'He came as often as he could, but not as often as I would have wished.'

'Were you expecting him on the night in question?'

'I was.'

'Why?'

'We had spoken together, on the telephone, the previous morning. He promised me he would come. He said he would drive up, and arrive before midnight.' The smile faded from her lips, and her eyes grew dark and desolate. 'I waited until daylight – but he did not come.'

'As far as you know was there any particular reason that he was going to visit you that weekend?'

'Yes.' Sarah's cheeks darkened, and Sally-Anne was fascinated. She had never seen a black girl blush before. 'Yes, he said he wished to speak to my father. I had arranged the meeting.'

'Thank you, my dear,' said Joseph Petal gently.

During Mr Petal's examination, the prosecutor's assistant had slipped back into his seat and handed Abel Khori a handwritten sheet of notes. Abel Khori was holding these in his hand as he rose to cross-examine.

'Miss Nyoni, can you tell the court the meaning of the Sindebele word, *Isifebi*?'

Tungata Zebiwe growled softly and began to rise, but the police guard laid a hand on his shoulder to restrain him.

'It means a harlot,' Sarah answered quietly.

'Does it not also mean an unmarried woman who lives with a man—'

'My lord!' Joseph Petal's plea was belated but outraged, and Mr Justice Domashawa sustained it.

'Miss Nyoni,' Abel Khori tried again. 'Do you love the accused? Please speak up. We cannot hear you.'

This time Sarah's voice was firm, almost defiant. 'I do.'

'Would you do anything for him?'

'I would.'

'Would you lie to save him?'

'I object, your lordship.' Joseph Petal leapt to his feet.

'And I withdraw the question.' Abel Khori forestalled the judge's intervention. 'Let me rather put it to you, Miss Nyoni, that the accused had asked you to provide a warehouse at your school where illegal ivory and leopard-skins could be stored!'

'No.' Sarah shook her head. 'He never would—'

'And that he had asked you to supervise the loading of those tusks into a truck, and the despatch of the truck—'

'No! No!' she cried.

'When you spoke to him on the telephone, did he not order you to prepare a shipment of—'

'No! He is a good man,' Sarah sobbed. 'A great and good man. He would never have done that.'

'No further questions, your lordship.' Looking very pleased with himself, Abel Khori sat down and his assistant leaned over to whisper his congratulations.

'I call the accused, the Minister Tungata Zebiwe, to the stand.'

That was a risky move on Mr Petal's part. Even as a layman, Craig could see that Abel Khori had shown himself to be a hardy scrapper.

Joseph Petal began by establishing Tungata's position in the community, his services to the revolution, his frugal life-style.

'Do you own any fixed property?'

'I own a house in Harare.'

'Will you tell the court how much you paid for it?'

'Fourteen thousand dollars.'

'That is not a great deal to pay for a house, is it?'

'It is not a great deal of house.' Tungata's reply was deadpan, and even the judge smiled.

'A motor-car?'

'I have a ministerial vehicle at my disposal.'

'Foreign bank accounts?'

'None.'

'Wives?'

'None—' he glanced in the direction of Sarah Nyoni who sat in the back row of the gallery ' – yet,' he finished.

'Common-law wives? Other women?'

'My elderly aunt lives in my home. She supervises my household.'

'Coming now to the night in question. Can you tell the court why you were on the Karoi road?'

'I was on my way to Tuti Mission Station.'

'For what reason?'

'To visit Miss Nyoni – and to speak to her father on a personal matter.'

'Your visit had been arranged?'

'Yes, in a telephone conversation with Miss Nyoni.'

'You have visited her before – on more than one occasion?'

'That is so.'

'What accommodation did you use on those occasions?'

'There was a thatched *indlu* set aside for my use.'

'A hut? With a sleeping-mat and open fire?'

'Yes.'

'You did not find such lodgings beneath you?'

'On the contrary, I enjoy the opportunity of returning to the traditional ways of my people.'

'Did anyone share these lodgings with you?'

'My driver and my bodyguards.'

'Miss Nyoni – did she visit you in these lodgings?'

'That would have been contrary to our custom and tribal law.'

'The prosecutor used the word *isifebi* – what do you make of that?'

'He might aptly apply that word to women of his acquaintance. I know nobody whom it might fit.'

Again the judge smiled, and the prosecutor's assistant nudged Abel Khori playfully.

'Now, Mr Minister, was anybody else aware of your intention of visiting Tuti Mission?'

'I made no secret of my intention. I wrote it down in my desk-diary.'

'Do you have that diary?'

'No. I requested my secretary to hand it over to the defence. It is, however, missing from my desk.'

'I see. When you ordered your chauffeur to prepare the car, did you inform him of your destination?'

'I did.'

'He says you did not.'

'Then his memory is at fault – or has been affected.' Tungata shrugged.

'Very well. Now, on the night that you were driving on the road between Karoi and Tuti Mission, did you encounter any other vehicle?'

'Yes. There was a truck parked in darkness, off the road, but facing in our direction.'

'Will you tell the court what transpired then?'

'The truck-driver switched on his lights, and then flicked them three times. At the same time he drove forward into the road.'

'In such a way as to force your car to halt?'

'That is correct.'

'What did you do then?'

'I said to my driver, "Pull over – but be careful. This could be an ambush."'

'You were not expecting to meet the truck then?'

'I was not.'

'Did you say, "There it is! Pull over!"?'

'I did not.'

'What did you mean by the words: "This could be an ambush"?'

'Recently, many vehicles have been attacked by armed bandits, *shufta*, especially on lonely roads at night.'

'So what were your feelings?'

'I was anticipating trouble.'

'What happened then?'

'Two of my bodyguards left the Mercedes, and went to speak to the driver of the truck.'

'From where you were seated in the Mercedes, could you see the truck-driver?'

'Yes. He was a complete stranger to me. I had never seen him before.'

'What was your reaction to this?'

'I was by this time extremely wary.'

'Then what happened?'

'Suddenly there were other headlights on the road behind us. A voice on a bull-horn ordering my men to surrender and throw down their arms. My Mercedes was surrounded by armed men and I was forcibly dragged from it.'

'Did you recognize any of these men?'

'Yes. When I was pulled from the Mercedes, I recognized General Fungabera.'

'Did this allay your suspicions?'

'On the contrary, I was now convinced that I was in danger of my life.'

'Why was that, Mr Minister?'

'General Fungabera commands a brigade which is

notorious for its ruthless acts against prominent Matabele—'

'I object, your lordship – the Third Brigade is a unit of
the regular army of the state, and General Fungabera a
well-known and respected officer,' Abel Khori cried.

'The prosecution is totally justified in its objection.' The
judge was suddenly trembling with anger. 'I cannot allow
the accused to use this courtroom to attack a prominent
soldier and his gallant men. I cannot allow the accused to
stand before me and disseminate tribal hatreds and preju-
dices. Be warned – I will not hesitate to find you guilty of
gross contempt if you continue in this vein.'

Joseph Petal took fully thirty seconds to let his witness
recover from this tirade.

'You say you felt that your life was in danger?'

'Yes,' said Tungata quietly.

'You were strung up and on edge?'

'Yes.'

'Did you see the soldiers unloading ivory and furs from
the truck?'

'I did.'

'What was your reaction?'

'I believed that these would somehow, I was not certain
how, but I believed they would incriminate me, and be
used as an excuse to kill me.'

'I object, your lordship,' Abel Khori called out.

'I will not warn the accused again,' Mr Justice Domashawa promised threateningly.

'What happened then?'

'Miss Jay left the vehicle in which she was travelling
and she came near me. The soldiers were distracted. I
believed that this would be my last chance. I took hold of
Miss Jay to prevent the soldiers firing and attempted to
escape in the Land-Rover.'

'Thank you, Mr Minister.' Mr Joseph Petal turned to the
judge. 'My lord, my witness has had a tiring examination.

May I suggest that the court rise until tomorrow morning to allow him a chance to recover?'

Abel Khori was instantly up on his feet, lusting for blood.

'It is barely noon yet, and the accused has been on the stand for less than thirty minutes, and his counsel has dealt with him *recte et suaviter*. For a trained and hardened soldier, that is a mere bagatelle *per se*.' Abel Khori, in his agitation, lapsed into Latin.

'We will continue, Mr Petal,' said the judge, and Joseph Petal shrugged.

'Your witness, Mr Khori.'

Abel Khori was in his element, becoming lyrical and poetic. 'You testified that you were in fear of your life – but I put it to you that you were attacked by guilt, that you were in deadly fear of retribution, that you were terrified by the prospect of facing the exemplary process of this very people's court, of facing the wrath of that learned and just scarlet-clad figure you now see before you.'

'No.'

'That it was nothing more than craven guilty conscience that made you embark on a series of heinous and callous criminal actions—'

'No. That is not so.'

'When you seized the lovely Miss Jay, did you not use excessive physical force to twist her young and tender limbs? Did you not rain brutal blows upon her?'

'I struck her once to prevent her hurling herself from the speeding vehicle and injuring herself seriously.'

'Did you not aim a deadly weapon – to wit, a military assault rifle – which you knew to be loaded, at the person of General Peter Fungabera?'

'I threatened him with the rifle – yes, that is true.'

'And then you fired deliberately at his nether regions – to wit, his abdomen?'

'I did not fire at Fungabera. I aimed to miss him.'

'I put it to you that you tried to murder the general, and only his marvellous reflexes saved him from your attack.'

'If I had tried to kill him,' said Tungata softly, 'he would be dead.'

'When you stole the Land-Rover, did you realize that it was state property?

'Did you aim the rifle at Mr Craig Mellow? And were you only prevented from murdering him by Miss Jay's brave intervention?'

For almost another hour Abel Khori flew at the impassive figure in the dock, extracting from him a series of damning admissions, so that when at last Abel Khori sat down, preening like a victorious game cock, Craig judged that Mr Joseph Petal had paid in heavy coin for any small advantage he might have gained by placing his client on the witness stand.

However, Mr Petal's closing address was finely pitched to incite sympathy, and to explain and justify Tungata Zebiwe's actions on that night, without flouting the judge's patriotic or tribal instincts in the process.

'I will reserve my judgment until tomorrow,' Mr Justice Domashawa announced, and the court rose, the spectators humming with excited comment as they streamed out into the passage.

Over dinner Sally-Anne admitted, 'For the first time in this whole business, I felt sorry when Sarah went on the stand – she is such a sweet child.'

'Child? I guess she is a year or two older than you,' Craig chuckled, 'that makes you a babe in arms.'

She ignored his levity and went on seriously, 'She so obviously believes in him that for a moment or two even I began to doubt what I knew – then, of course, Abel Khori brought me back to earth.'

M r Justice Domashawa read out his judgment in his precise, old-maidish voice that somehow did not suit the gravity of the subject. Firstly, he covered the events that were common cause between prosecution and defence, and then went on, 'The defence has based its case on two main pillars. The first of these is the testimony of Miss Sarah Nyoni that the accused was on his way to what, for want of a better word, we are led to believe was a love-tryst, and that his meeting with the truck was a coincidence or contrived in some unexplained manner by persons unknown.

'Now Miss Nyoni impressed this court as being a naive and unworldly young lady, and by her admission is completely under the influence of the accused. The court has had, perforce, to consider the prosecution's postulation that Miss Nyoni might even have been, in fact, so influenced by the accused as to consent to act as an accomplice in arranging the consignment of contraband.

'In view of the foregoing, the court has rejected the testimony of Miss Nyoni as potentially biased and unreliable –

'The second pillar of the defence's case rests on the premise that the life of the accused was threatened, or that he believed it to be threatened, by the arresting officers, and in this belief embarked on a series of unreasoned and unreasoning acts of self-protection.

'General Peter Fungabera is an officer of impeccable reputation, a high official of the state. The Third Brigade is an elite unit of the state's regular army, its members, although battle-hardened veterans, are disciplined and trained soldiers.

'The court, therefore, categorically rejects the accused's contention that either General Fungabera or his men could have, even in the remotest possibility, constituted a threat to his safety, let alone his life. The court also rejects the contention that the accused *believed* this to be the case.

'Accordingly, I come to the first charge. Namely, that of trading or dealing in the products of scheduled wild animals. I find the accused guilty as charged and I sentence him to the maximum penalty under the law. Twelve years at hard labour.

'On the second charge of abducting and holding a hostage, I find the accused guilty as charged and I sentence him to ten years at hard labour.

'On the third charge of assault with a deadly weapon, I find the accused guilty and sentence him to six years at hard labour –

'— Assault with intent to do grievous bodily harm – six years at hard labour.

'— Attempted murder – six years at hard labour –

'— I order that these sentences run consecutively and that no part of them be suspended—'

Even Abel Khori's head jerked up at that. The sentences totalled forty years. With full remission for good behaviour, Tungata could still expect to serve over thirty years, the rest of his useful life.

At the back of the court a black woman shrieked in Sindebele, 'Baba! The father! They are taking our father from us!' Others took up the cry. 'Father of the people! Our father is dead to us.'

A man began to sing in a soaring baritone voice.

'Why do you weep, widows of Shangani . . .
Why do you weep, little sons of the Moles,
When your fathers did the king's bidding?'

It was one of the ancient fighting songs of the impis of King Lobengula, and the singer was a man in his prime with a strong intelligent face and a short-cropped, spade-shaped beard barely speckled with grey. As he sang, the tears ran down his cheeks into his beard. In another time he might have been an induna of one of the royal impis.

His song was taken up by the men around him, and Mr Justice Domashawa came to his feet in a fury.

'If there is not silence this instant, I will have the court cleared and the offenders charged with contempt,' he shouted over the singing, but it was five minutes more of pandemonium before the ushers could restore order.

Through it all, Tungata Zebiwe stood quietly in the dock, with just the barest hint of a mocking smile on his lips. When at last it was over, but before his guards led him away, he gazed across the courtroom at Craig Mellow and he made a last hand-signal. They had only used it playfully before, perhaps after a hard-contested bout of wrestling or some other friendly competition. Now Tungata used it in deadly earnest. The sign meant: 'We are equal – the score is levelled,' and Craig understood completely. Craig had lost his leg and Tungata had lost his freedom. They were equal.

He wanted to call out to the man who had once been his friend that it was a sorry bargain, not of his choosing, but Tungata had turned away. His warders were trying to lead him out of the dock, but Tungata pulled back, his head turning as he searched for someone else in the crowded court.

Sarah Nyoni climbed up onto her bench, and over the heads of the crowd she reached out both hands towards him. Now Tungata made his last hand signal to her. Craig read it clearly. 'Take cover!' Tungata ordered her. 'Hide yourself. You are in danger.'

By the altered expression on her face, Craig saw that the girl had understood the command, and then the warders were dragging Tungata Zebiwe down the stairs that led to the prison cells below ground.

Craig Mellow shoved his way through the singing, lamenting crowds of Matabele who overflowed the buildings of the Supreme Court and disrupted the lunch-hour traffic in the broad causeway that it fronted. He dragged Sally-Anne by her wrist and brusquely shouldered aside the press photographers who tried to block his way.

In the car park he boosted Sally-Anne into the front seat of the Land-Rover, and ran around to the driver's side, threatening with a raised fist the last and most persistent photographer in his path. He drove directly to her apartment and halted at the front door. He did not turn off the engine.

'And now?' Sally-Anne asked.

'I don't understand the question,' he snapped.

'Hey!' she said. 'I'm your friend – remember me?'

'I'm sorry.' He slumped over the wheel. 'I feel rotten – plain bloody rotten.'

She did not reply, but her eyes were full of compassion for him.

'Forty years,' he whispered. 'I never expected that. If only I'd known—'

'There was nothing you could do then, or now.'

He balled his fist and hammered it on the steering-wheel. 'The poor bastard – forty years!'

'Are you coming up?' she asked softly, but he shook his head.

'I have to get back to King's Lynn. I've neglected everything while this awful bloody business has been going on.'

'You're going right now?' She was startled.

'Yes.'

'Alone?' she asked, and he nodded.

'I want to be alone.'

'So you can torture yourself.' Her voice firmed. 'And I'll be damned if I'll allow that. I'm coming with you. Wait! I

211

am going to throw some things in a bag – you needn't even kill the engine, I'll be that quick.'

She was five minutes, and then ran back down the stairs lugging her rucksack and her camera bag. She slung them into the back of the Land-Rover.

'Okay, let's go.'

They spoke very little on the long journey, but soon Craig was thankful to have her beside him, grateful for her smile when he glanced at her, for the touch of her hand on his when she sensed the black mood too strong upon him, and for her undemanding silence.

They drove up the hills of King's Lynn in the dusk. Joseph had seen them from afar, and was waiting on the front veranda.

'I see you, Nkosazana.' From their first meeting Joseph had taken an instant liking to Sally-Anne. Already she was his 'little mistress' and his welcoming grin kept breaking through his solemn dignity as he ordered his servants to unload her meagre luggage.

'I run bath for you – very hot.'

'That will be marvellous, Joseph.'

After her bath she came back to the veranda and Craig went to the drinks table and mixed a whisky for her the way she liked it, and another one for himself that was mainly Scotch and very little soda.

'Here's to Judge Domashawa,' he lifted his glass ironically, 'and to Mashona justice. All forty years of it.'

Sally-Anne refused wine at dinner despite his protest. 'Baron Rothschild would be frightfully affronted. His very best stuff. My last bottle, smuggled in personally.' Craig's gaiety was forced.

After dinner he lifted the brandy decanter and as he was about to pour, she said, 'Craig, please don't get drunk.'

He paused with the decanter over the snifter and studied her face.

'No,' she shook her head. 'I'm not being bossy – I'm being entirely selfish. Tonight I want you sober.'

He set down the decanter, pushed back his chair and came around the table to her. She stood up to meet him.

He paused in front of her. 'Oh, my darling, I've waited so long.'

'I know,' she whispered. 'Me too.'

He took her carefully into his arms, something precious and fragile, and felt her changing slowly. She seemed to soften, and her body became malleable, shaping itself to his own, so he could feel her against him from knees to firm young bosom, the heat of her soaking quickly through their thin clothing.

He bowed his head as she lifted her chin and their mouths came together. Her lips were cool and dry, but almost immediately he felt the heat rising in them and they parted, moist and sweet as a sun-warmed fig freshly plucked and splitting open with its ripe juices.

He looked into her eyes as he kissed her, and marvelled at the colours and the patterns that formed a nimbus around her pupils, green shot through with golden arrowheads, and then her eyelids fluttered down over them, and her long crisp lashes interlocked. He closed his own eyes, and the earth seemed to tilt and swing under him, he rode it easily, holding her to him, but not trying yet to explore her body, content with the wonder of her mouth, and the velvet feel of her tongue against his.

Joseph opened the door from the kitchen, and stood for a moment with the coffee tray in his hands, and then he smiled smugly and drew back, closing the door behind him. Neither of them had heard him come or go. When she took her mouth away, Craig felt deprived and cheated, and reached for it again. She laid her fingers across his lips, restraining him for a moment, and her whisper was so husky that she had to clear her throat and start again.

'Let's go to your bedroom, darling,' she said.

There was one awkward moment when he sat naked on the edge of the bed to remove his leg, but she knelt quickly in front of him, naked also, pushing his hands away and undid the straps herself. Then she bowed her head and kissed the neat hard pad of flesh at the extremity of his leg.

'Thank you,' he said. 'I'm glad you could do that.'

'It's you,' she said, 'and part of you,' and she kissed it again, and then ran her lips gently up to his knee and beyond.

He woke before she did, and lay with his eyes closed, surprised at the sense of wonder that possessed him, not knowing why, until suddenly he remembered and joy came upon him, and he opened his eyes and rolled his head, for an instant terrified that she would not be there – but she was.

She had thrown her pillow off the bed, and kicked the sheet aside. She was curled up like a baby, with her knees almost under her chin. The dawn light, filtered by the curtains, cast pearly highlights on her skin, and shaded the dips and hollows of her body. Her hair was loose, covering her face and undulating to each long slow breath she drew.

He lay very still so as not to disturb her and gloated over her, wanting to reach out, but denying himself, so as to make the ache of wanting more poignant, waiting for it to become unbearable. She must have sensed his attention, for she stirred and straightened out her legs, rolled over onto her back and arched in a slow voluptuous cat-like stretch.

He leaned across and with one finger lifted the shiny dark hair off her face. Her eyes swivelled towards him, came into focus, and she stared at him in cosmic astonishment. Then she crinkled her nose in a roguish grin.

'Hey, mister,' she whispered, 'you are something pretty damned special. Now I'm sorry I waited so long.'

And she reached out both brown arms towards him.

214

Craig, however, did not share her regrets. He knew it had been perfectly timed – even a day earlier would have been too soon. Later, he told her so as they lay clinging to each other, glued lightly together with their own perspiration.

'We learned to like each other first, that was the way I wanted it to be.'

'You're right,' she said, and drew back a little to look at his face so that her breasts made a delightfully obscene little sucking sound as they came unstuck from his chest. 'I do like you, I really do.'

'And I—' he started, but hastily she covered his lips with her fingertips.

'Not yet, Craig darling,' she pleaded. 'I don't want to hear that – not yet.'

'When?' he demanded.

'Soon, I think—' And then with more certainty. 'Yes,' she said, 'soon, and then I'll be able to say it back to you.'

The great estate of King's Lynn seemed to have waited as they had waited for this to happen again.

Long ago it had been hewn from the wilderness. The love of another man and woman had been the main inspiration in the building of it, and over the decades since then it had taken the love of the men and women who followed that first pair to sustain and cherish it. They and the generations who had followed them lay now in the walled cemetery on the kopje behind the homestead, but while they had lived, King's Lynn had flourished. Just as it had sickened when it fell into the hands of uncaring foreigners in a far land, had been stripped and desecrated and deprived of the vital ingredient of love.

Even when Craig rebuilt the house and restocked the pastures, that vital element had been lacking still. Now at last love burgeoned on King's Lynn, and their joy in each other seemed to radiate out from the homestead on the hill and permeate the entire estate, breathing life and the fecund promise of more life into the land.

The Matabele recognized it immediately. When Craig and Sally-Anne in the battered Land-Rover rode the red dust tracks that linked the huge paddocks, the Matabele women straightened up from the wooden mortars in which they were pounding maize, or turned stiff-necked under the enormous burden of firewood balanced upon their heads to call a greeting and watch them with a fond and knowing gaze. Old Joseph said nothing, but made up the bed in Craig's room with four pillows, put flowers on the table at the side of the bed that Sally-Anne had chosen, and placed four of his special biscuits on the early morning tea-tray when he brought it in to them each dawn.

For three days Sally-Anne restrained herself, and then one morning sitting up in bed, sipping tea, she told Craig, 'As curtains, those make fine dish rags.' She pointed a half-eaten biscuit at the cheap unbleached calico that he had tacked over the windows.

'Can you do better?' Craig asked with concealed cunning, and she walked straight into the trap. Once she was involved in choosing curtains, she was immediately involved in everything else. From designing furniture for Joseph's relative, the celebrated carpenter, to build, to laying out the new vegetable garden and replanting the rose bushes and shrubs that had died of neglect.

Then Joseph entered the conspiracy by bringing her the proposed dinner menu for the evening. 'Should it be roast tonight, Nkosazana, or chicken curry?'

'Nkosi Craig likes tripe,' Sally-Anne had made this discovery during casual discussion. 'Can you do tripe and onions?'

Joseph beamed. 'The old governor-general before the war, whenever he come to Kingi Lingi I make him tripe

216

and onions, Nkosazana. He tell me "Very good, Joseph, best in world!"'

'Okay, Joseph, tonight we'll have your "best-in-world tripe and onions",' she laughed, and only when Joseph formally handed over to her the pantry keys did she realize what a serious pronouncement that had been.

She was there at midnight when the first new calf was born on King's Lynn, a difficult birthing with the calf's head twisted back so that Craig had to soap his arm and thrust it up into the mother to free it while Shadrach and Hans Groenewald held the head and Sally-Anne held the lantern high to light the work.

When at last it came in a slippery rush, it was a heifer, pale beige and wobbly on its long ungainly legs. As soon as it began to nurse from its mother's udder, they could leave it to Shadrach and go home to bed.

'That was one of the most marvellous experiences of my life, darling. Who taught you to do that?'

'Bawu, my grandfather.' He held her close to him in the dark bedroom. 'You didn't feel sick?'

'I loved it, birth fascinates me.'

'Like Henry the Eighth, I prefer it in the abstract,' he chuckled.

'You rude boy,' she whispered. 'But aren't you too tired?'

'Are you?'

'No,' she admitted. 'I can't truthfully say that I am.'

She made one or two half-hearted attempts to break out and leave.

'I had a telegram today, the "C. of A." on the Cessna is complete, and I should go down to Johannesburg to collect her.'

'If you can wait two or three weeks or so, I'll come down with you. They are having a terrible drought in the south and stock prices are rock bottom. We could fly around the big ranches together and pick up a few bargains.'

So she let it pass, and the days telescoped into each other, filled for both of them with love and work – work on the photographic book, on the new novel, on collating her field research material for the Wildlife Trust, on the final preparations for the opening of Zambezi Waters, and on the daily running and embellishing of King's Lynn.

With each week that passed, her will to resist the spell that Craig and King's Lynn were weaving about her weakened, the exigencies of her previous life faded, until one day she caught herself referring to the house on the hill as 'home' and was only slightly shocked at herself.

A week later a registered letter was forwarded from her address in Harare. It was a formal application form for the renewal of her research grant from the Wildlife Trust. Instead of filling it in and returning it immediately, she slipped it into her camera bag.

'I'll do it tomorrow,' she promised herself, but deep in herself realized she had reached a crossroads in her life. The prospect of flying about Africa alone with her only possessions a change of clothes and a camera, sleeping where she lay down and bathing when she could, was no longer as attractive as it had always been to her.

That night at dinner she looked around the huge almost bare dining-room, the new curtains its only glory, and touched the refectory table of Rhodesian teak that, under her guidance, Joseph's relative had fashioned and she anticipated the patina of use and care it would soon acquire. Then she looked past the burning candles to the man who sat opposite her and she was afraid and strangely elated. She knew she had made the decision.

They took their coffee onto the veranda and listened to the cicadas' whining in the jacaranda trees, and the squeak of the flying bats hunting below a yellow moon.

She snuggled against his shoulder and said, 'Craig, darling, it's time to tell you. I do love you – so very dearly.'

C raig wanted to rush into Bulawayo and take the magistrate's court by storm, but she restrained him laughingly.

'My God, you crazy man, it isn't like buying a pound of cheese. You can't just up and get married, just like that.'

'Why not? Lots of people do.'

'I don't,' she said firmly. 'I want it to be done properly.' She did some counting on her fingers and pencilling on the calendar at the back of her notebook, and then decided, 'February 16th.'

'That's four months away,' Craig groaned, but his protests were ridden down ruthlessly.

Joseph, on the other hand, was in full accord with Sally-Anne's plans for a formal wedding.

'You get married on Kingi Lingi, Nkosikazi.'

It was a statement rather than a question, and Sally-Anne's Sindebele was now good enough to recognize that she had been promoted from 'little mistress' to 'great lady'.

'How many people?' Joseph demanded. 'Two hundred, three hundred?'

'I doubt we can raise that many,' Sally-Anne demurred.

'When Nkosana Roly get married Kingi Lingi, we have four hundred, even Nkosi Smithy he come!'

'Joseph,' she scolded him, 'you really are a frightful old snob, you know!'

F or Craig the pervading unhappiness that he had felt at Tungata's sentence slowly dissipated, swamped by all the excitement and activity at King's Lynn. In a few months he had all but put it from his mind, only at odd and unexpected moments his memory of his one-time friend barbed him. To the rest of the world, Tungata Zebiwe might have never existed. After the extravagant coverage by press and television of his trial, it seemed that a curtain of silence was drawn over him like a shroud.

Then abruptly, once again the name Tungata Zebiwe was blazed from every television screen and bannered on every front page across the entire continent.

Craig and Sally-Anne sat in front of the television set, appalled and disbelieving, as they listened to the first reports. When they ended, and the programme changed to a weather report, Craig stood up and crossed to the set. He switched it off and came back to her side, moving like a man who was still in deep shock from some terrible accident.

The two of them sat in silence in the darkened room, until Sally-Anne reached for his hand. She squeezed it hard, but her shudder was involuntary, it racked her whole body.

'Those poor little girls – they were babies. Can you imagine their terror?'

'I knew the Goodwins. They were fine people. They always treated their black people well,' Craig muttered.

'This proves – as nothing else possibly could – that they were right to lock him away like a dangerous animal.' Her horror was beginning to turn to anger.

'I can't see what they could possibly hope to gain by this—' Craig was still shaking his head incredulously, and Sally-Anne burst out.

'The whole country, the whole world must see them for what they are. Bloodthirsty, inhuman—' her voice cracked and became a sob. 'Those babies – oh Christ in heaven, I hate him. I wish him dead.'

'They used his name – that doesn't mean Tungata ordered it, condoned it, or even knew about it.' Craig tried to sound convincing.

'I hate him,' she whispered. 'I hate him for it.'

'It's madness. All they can possibly achieve is to bring

220

Shona troops sweeping through Matabeleland like the wrath of all the gods.'

'The little one was only five years old.' In her outrage and sorrow, Sally-Anne was repeating herself.

'Nigel Goodwin was a good man – I knew him quite well, we were in the same special police unit during the war, I liked him.' Craig went to the drinks table and poured two whiskies. 'Please God, don't let it all start again. All the awfulness and cruelty and horror – please God, spare us that.'

Although Nigel Goodwin was almost forty years of age, he had one of those beefy pink faces unaffected by the African sun that made him look like a lad. His wife, Helen, was a thin, dark-haired girl, her plainness alleviated by her patent good nature and her sparkly, toffee-brown eyes.

The two girls were weekly boarders at the convent in Bulawayo. At eight years, Alice Goodwin had ginger hair and gingery freckles and, like her father, she was plump and pink. Stephanie, the baby, was five, really too young for boarding-school. However, because she had an elder sister at the convent, the Reverend Mother made an exception in her case. She was the pretty one, small and dark and chirpy as a little bird with her mother's bright eyes.

Each Friday morning, Nigel and Helen Goodwin drove in seventy-eight miles from the ranch to town. At one o'clock they picked up the girls from the convent, had lunch at the Selbourne Hotel, sharing a bottle of wine, and then spent the afternoon shopping. Helen restocked her groceries, chose material to make into dresses for herself and the girls, and then, while the girls went to watch a matinée at the local cinema, had her hair washed, cut and set, the one extravagance of her simple existence.

Nigel was on the committee of the Matabele Farmers' Union, and spent an hour or two at the Union's offices in leisurely discussion with the secretary and those other members who were in town for the day. Then he strolled down the wide sun-scorched streets, his slouch hat pushed back on his head, hands in pockets, puffing happily on a black briar, greeting friends and acquaintances both white and black, stopping every few yards for a word or a chat.

When he arrived back where he had left the Toyota truck outside the Farmers' Co-operative, his Matabele headman, Josiah, and two labourers were waiting for him. They loaded the purchases of fencing and tools and spare parts and cattle medicines and other odds and ends into the truck, and as they finished, Helen and the girls arrived for the journey home.

'Excuse me, Miss,' Nigel accosted his wife, 'have you seen Mrs Goodwin anywhere?' It was his little weekly joke, and Helen giggled delightedly and preened her new hairdo.

For the girls he had a bag of liquorice allsorts. His wife protested, 'Sweets are so bad for their teeth, dear,' and Nigel winked at the girls and agreed, 'I know, but just this once won't kill them.'

Stephanie, because she was the baby, rode in the truck cab between her parents, while Alice went in the back with Josiah and the other Matabele.

'Wrap up, dear, it will be dark before we get home,' Helen cautioned her.

The first sixty-two miles were on the main road, and then they turned off on the farm track, and Josiah jumped down to open the wire gate and let them through.

'Home again,' said Nigel contentedly, as he drove onto his own land. He always said that and Helen smiled and reached across to lay her hand on his leg.

'It's nice to be home, dear,' she agreed.

The abrupt African night fell over them, and Nigel switched on the headlights. They picked up the eyes of the cattle in little bright points of light, fat contented beasts, the smell of their dung sharp and ammoniacal on the cool night air.

'Getting dry,' Nigel grunted. 'Need some rain.'

'Yes, dear.' Helen picked little Stephanie onto her lap, and the child cuddled sleepily against her shoulder.

'There we are,' Nigel murmured. 'Cooky has lit the lamps.'

He had been promising himself an electric generator for the last ten years, but there was always something else more important, so they were still on gas and paraffin. The lights of the homestead flickered a welcome at them between the stems of the acacia trees.

Nigel parked the truck beside the back veranda and cut the engine and headlights. Helen climbed down carrying Stephanie. The child was asleep now with her thumb in her mouth, and her skinny bare legs dangling.

Nigel went to the back of the truck and lifted Alice down.

'*Longile*, Josiah, you can go off now. We will unload the truck tomorrow morning,' he told his men. 'Sleep well!'

Holding Alice's hand, he followed his wife to the veranda, but before they reached it the dazzling beam of a powerful flashlight struck them and the family stopped in a small compact group.

'Who is it?' Nigel demanded irritably, shielding his eyes from the beam with one hand, still holding Alice's hand with the other.

His eyes adjusted and he could see beyond the flashlight, and suddenly he felt sick with fear for his wife and his babies. There were three black men, dressed in blue denim jeans and jackets. Each of them carried an AK 47 rifle. The rifles were pointed at the family group. Nigel glanced behind him quickly. There were other strangers, he was not sure how many. They had come out of the night, and under their guns Josiah and his two labourers were huddled fearfully.

Nigel thought of the steel gun safe in his office at the end of the veranda. Then he remembered that it was empty. At the end of the war, one of the first acts of the new black government had been to force the white farmers to hand in all their weapons. It didn't really matter, he realized. He could never have reached the safe, anyway.

'Who are they, Daddy?' Alice asked, her voice was small with fear. Of course she knew. She was old enough to remember the war days.

'Be brave, my darlings,' Nigel said to all of them, and Helen drew closer to his bulk, still holding baby Stephanie in her arms.

The muzzle of a rifle was thrust into Nigel's back. His hands were pulled behind him, and his wrists bound together. They used galvanized wire. It cut into his flesh. Then they took Stephanie from her mother's arms, and set her down. Her legs were unsteady from sleep and she blinked like an owlet in the flashlight beam, still sucking her thumb. They wired Helen's hands behind her back. She whimpered once as the wire cut in and then bit down on her lip. Two of them took the wire to the children.

'They are babies,' Nigel said in Sindebele. 'Please do not tie them, please do not hurt them.'

'Be silent, white jackal,' one of them replied in the same language and went down on one knee behind Stephanie.

'It's sore, Daddy,' she began to cry. 'He's hurting me. Make him stop.'

'You must be brave,' Nigel repeated, stupidly and inadequately, hating himself. 'You're a big girl now.'

The other man went to Alice.

'I won't cry,' she promised. 'I'll be brave, Daddy.'

'That's my own sweet girl,' he said, and the man tied her.

'Walk!' commanded the one with the flashlight, who was clearly the leader of the group, and with the barrel of his automatic rifle prodded the children up the back steps onto the kitchen veranda.

Stephanie tripped and sprawled. With her hands tied behind her she could not regain her feet. She wriggled helplessly.

'You bastards,' whispered Nigel. 'Oh, you filthy bastards.'

One of them took a handful of the child's hair and lifted her to her feet. She stumbled, weeping hysterically, to where her sister stood against the veranda wall.

'Don't be a baby, Stephy,' Alice told her. 'It's just a game.' But her voice quavered with her own terror, and her eyes in the lamplight were huge and brimming with tears.

They lined up Nigel and Helen beside the girls, and the flashlight played back and forth into each face in turn, blinding them so they could not see what was happening out in the yard.

'Why are you doing this?' Nigel asked. 'The war is over – we have done you no harm.'

There was no reply at all, just a beam of brilliant light moving across their pale faces, and the sound of Stephanie weeping, a racking piteous sobbing. Then there was the murmur of other voices in the darkness, many subdued frightened voices, women and children and men.

'They have brought our people to watch,' said Helen softly. 'It's just like the war days. It's going to be an execution.' She spoke so the girls could not hear her. Nigel could think of nothing to say. He knew she was right.

'I wish I had told you how much I love you, more often,' he said.

'That's all right,' she whispered. 'I knew all along.'

They could make out a throng of Matabele from the farm village now, a dark mass of them beyond the glaring torch, and then the voice of the leader was raised in Sindebele.

'These are the white jackals that feed upon the land of the Matabele. These are the white offal that are in league with the Mashona killers, the eaters-of-dirt in Harare, the sworn enemies of the children of Lobengula—'

The orator was working himself up into the killing frenzy. Already Nigel could see that the other men guarding them were beginning to sway and hum, losing themselves in that berserker passion where no reason exists. The Matabele had a name for it, 'the divine madness'. When old Mzilikazi had been king, one million human beings had died from this divine madness.

'These white lickers of Mashona faces are the traitors who delivered Tungata Zebiwe, the father of our people, to the death camps of the Mashona,' screamed the leader.

'I embrace you, my darlings,' Nigel Goodwin whispered.

Helen had never heard him say anything so tender before, and it was that, not fear, that made her begin to weep. She tried to force back the tears, but they ran down and dripped from her chin.

'What must we do with them?' howled the leader.

'Kill them!' cried one of his own men, but the massed farm Matabele were silent in the darkness.

'What must we do with them?' the question was repeated.

This time the leader leapt down from the veranda and shouted it into the faces of the farm people, still they were silent.

'What must we do with them?' Again the question, and this time the sound of blows, the rubbery slap of a rifle-barrel against black flesh.

'What must we do with them?' The same question for the fourth time.

'Kill them!' An uncertain terrified response, and more blows.

'Kill them!' The cry was taken up.

'Kill them!'

'*Abantwana kamina!*' A woman's voice, Nigel recognized it as that of fat old Martha, the girls' nanny. 'My babies,' she cried, but then her voice was lost in the rising chorus. 'Kill them! Kill them!' as the divine madness spread.

Two men, both denim-clad, stepped into the torch light. They seized Nigel by his arms and turned him to face the wall, before forcing him to his knees.

The leader handed the flashlight to one of his men and he took the pistol from the belt of his jeans, and pulled back the slide forcing a round into the chamber. The breech made a sharp snapping rattle. He put the muzzle of the pistol to the back of Nigel's head and fired a single shot. Nigel was thrown forward onto his face. The contents of his skull were dashed against the white wall, and then began to run down it in a jelly-like stream to the floor.

His feet were still kicking and dancing as they forced Helen down to her knees facing the wall beside her husband's corpse.

'Mummy!' screamed Alice as the next pistol bullet tore out through her mother's forehead and her skull collapsed inwards. Alice's pathetic little show of courage was over. Her legs gave way, and she crumpled to the veranda floor. With a soft spluttery sound her bowels voided involuntarily.

The leader stepped up to her. Her forehead was almost touching the floor. Her gingery curls had parted, exposing the back of her neck. The leader extended his right arm full length, and touched the muzzle of the pistol to the tender white skin at the nape. His arm jerked to the recoil and the shot was muffled to a jarring thud. Blue tendrils of gunsmoke spiralled upwards in the beam of the flashlight.

Little Stephanie was the only one who struggled, until the leader clubbed her with the barrel of the pistol. Even then she wriggled and kicked, lying on the veranda floor in the spreading puddle of her sister's blood. The leader placed his foot between her shoulder blades to hold her still for the shot. The bullet came out through Stephanie's temple just in front of her right ear, and it gouged a hole not much larger than a thimble in the concrete of the veranda floor. The hole filled swiftly with the child's blood.

The leader stooped and dipped his forefinger into the cup of dark blood, and with it wrote on the white veranda wall in large erratic letters, 'TUNGATA ZEBIWE LIVES.'

Then he jumped down off the veranda and, like a leopard, padded silently away into the night. His men followed him in Indian file at an easy swinging trot.

'I give you my solemn promise,' said the prime minister, 'these so-called dissidents will be destroyed, completely destroyed.'

His eyes behind the lenses of his spectacles had a steely, blind look. The poor quality of the television projection added haloes of ghost silhouettes to his head, but did not diminish his anger that seemed to spill over from the set and flood the living-room of King's Lynn.

'I've never seen him like that,' said Craig.

'He's usually such a cold fish,' Sally-Anne agreed.

'I have ordered the army and the police force to move in to hunt down and apprehend the perpetrators of this terrible outrage. We will find them, and their supporters, and they will feel the full force of the people's anger. We will not endure these dissidents.'

'Good for him,' Sally-Anne nodded. 'I can't say I've ever liked him very much – until now.'

'Darling, don't be too happy about it,' Craig cautioned her. 'Remember this is Africa, not America or Britain. This land has a different temper. Words have a different meaning here – words like "apprehend" and "hunt down".'

'Craig, I know that your sympathy is always with the Matabele, but this time surely—'

'All right,' he held up one hand in agreement, 'I admit it. The Matabele are special, my family has always lived with them, we've beaten and exploited them, we've fought them and slaughtered them – and been slaughtered by them in return. Yet, also, we have cherished and honoured them and come to know them and, yes, to love them. I don't know the Mashona. They are secretive and cold, clever and tricky. I can't speak their language, and I don't trust them. That's why I choose to live in Matabeleland.'

'You are saying the Matebele are saints – that they are incapable of committing an atrocity like this?' She was getting irritable with him now, her tone sharpening, and he was quick to placate her.

'Good God, no! They are as cruel as any other tribe in Africa, and a hell of a lot more warlike than most. In the old days when they raided a foreign tribe, they used to toss the infants in the air and catch them on the points of their assegais, and throw the old women in the watch-fires and laugh to see them burn. Cruelty has a different value in Africa. If you live here you have to understand that from the beginning.'

He paused and smiled. 'Once I was discussing political philosophy with a Matabele, an ex-guerrilla, and I explained the concept of democracy. His reply was, "That might work in your country, but it doesn't work here. It doesn't work here." Don't you see? That's the crux. Africa makes and keeps her own rules, and I lay you a million dollars to a pinch of elephant dung that we're going to see a few pretty things in the weeks ahead that you wouldn't see in Pennsylvania or Dorset! When Mugabe says "destroy", he doesn't mean "take into custody and process under the laws of evidence". He's an African and he means precisely that – destroy!'

That was on the Wednesday, and when Friday came round it was market day at King's Lynn, the day to go into Bulawayo for shopping and socializing. Craig and Sally-Anne left early on that Friday morning. The new five-ton truck followed them, filled with Matabele from the ranch, taking advantage of the free ride into town for the day. They were dressed in their best, and singing with excitement.

Craig and Sally-Anne came up against the road-block just before they reached the crossroads at Thabas Indunas. The traffic was backed up for a hundred yards, and Craig could see that most of the vehicles were being turned back.

'Hold on!' he told Sally-Anne, left her in the Land-Rover and jogged up to the head of the line of parked vehicles.

The road-block was not a casual temporary affair. There were heavy machine-guns in sandbagged emplacements on both sides of the highway, and light machine-guns set back in depth beyond it to cover a breakthrough by a speeding vehicle.

The actual barricade was of drums filled with concrete and spiked metal plates to puncture pneumatic tyres, and the guards were from the Third Brigade in their distinctive burgundy berets and silver cap-badges. Their striped camouflage battle-jackets gave them the tigerish air of jungle cats.

'What is happening, Sergeant?' Craig asked one of them.

'The road is closed, mambo,' the man told him politely. 'Only military permit-holders allowed to pass.'

'I have to get into town.'

'Not today,' the man shook his head. 'Bulawayo is not a good place to be today.'

As if to confirm this, there was a faint popping sound from the direction of the town. It sounded like green twigs in a fire, and the hair on Craig's forearms lifted instinctively. He knew that sound so well, and it brought nightmarish memories from the war days crowding back. It was the sound of distant automatic rifle-fire.

'Go back home, mambo,' said the sergeant in a kindly tone. 'This is not your *indaba* any more.'

Suddenly Craig was very anxious to get the truckload of his people safely back to King's Lynn.

He ran back to the Land-Rover, and swung it out of the line of parked vehicles in a hard 180-degree turn.

'What is it, Craig?'

'I think it has started,' he told her grimly, and thrust the accelerator flat to the floorboards.

They met the King's Lynn truck barrélling merrily along towards them, the women singing and clapping, their dresses fluttering brightly in the wind. Craig flagged them down, and jumped up onto the running-board. Shadrach, in the cast-off grey suit that Craig had given him, was sitting up in his place of honour beside the driver.

'Turn around,' Craig ordered. 'Go back to Kingi Lingi. There is big trouble. Nobody must leave Kingi Lingi until it is over.'

'Is it the Mashona soldiers?'

'Yes,' Craig told him. 'The Third Brigade.'

'Jackals and sons of dung-eating jackals,' said Shadrach, and spat out of the open window.

'To say that thousands of innocent persons have been killed by the state security forces is a non-sense—' The Zimbabwean minister of justice looked like a successful stockbroker in his dark suit and white shirt. He smiled blandly out of the television screen, his face shining with a light sheen of sweat from the brute arc lamps which only enhanced the coaly blackness of his skin. 'One or two civilians have been killed in the crossfire between the security forces and the outlaw Matebele dissidents – but thousands! Ha, ha, ha!' he chuckled jovially. 'If thousands have been killed, then I wish somebody would show me the bodies – I know nothing about them.'

'Well,' Craig switched it off. 'That's all you are going to get from Harare.' He checked his wrist-watch. 'Almost eight o'clock, let's see what the BBC has to say.'

During the rule of the Smith regime, with its draconian censorship, every thinking man in central Africa had made sure he had access to a short-wave radio receiver. It was still a good rule to follow. Craig's set was a Yaesu Musen, and he got the Africa service of the BBC on 2171 kilohertz.

'The Zimbabwe government has expelled all foreign journalists from Matabeleland. The British High Commission has called upon the prime minister of Zimbabwe to express Her Majesty's government's deep concern at the reports of atrocities being committed by security forces—'

Craig switched to Radio South Africa, and it came through sharp and clear ' – the arrival of hundreds of illegal refugees across the northern border from Zimbabwe. The refugees are all members of the Matabele tribe. A spokes-man for one group described a massacre of villagers and civilians that he had witnessed. "They are killing every-body," he said. "The women and the children, even the chickens and the goats." Another refugee said, "Do not send us back. The soldiers will kill us."'

Craig searched the bands and found the Voice of America.

'The leader of the ZAPU party, the Matabele faction of Zimbabwe, Mr Joshua Nkomo, has arrived in the neighbouring state of Botswana after fleeing the country. "They shot my driver dead," he told our regional reporter. "Mugabe wants me dead. He's out to get me."

'With the recent imprisonment and detention of all other prominent members of the ZAPU party, Mr Nkomo's departure from Zimbabwe leaves the Matabele people without a leader or a spokesman.

'In the meantime, the government of Mr Robert Mugabe has placed a total news blackout over the western part of the country, all foreign journalists have been expelled, and a request by the international Red Cross to send in observers has been refused.'

'It's all so familiar,' Craig muttered. 'I even have the same sick feeling in the bottom of my stomach as I listen to it.'

The Monday was Sally-Anne's birthday. After breakfast, they drove across to Queen's Lynn together to fetch her present. Craig had left it in the care of Mrs Groenewald, the overseer's wife, to preserve the secrecy and surprise.

'Oh, Craig, it's beautiful.'

'Now you have two of us to keep you at King's Lynn,' he told her.

Sally-Anne lifted the honey-coloured puppy in both hands and kissed his wet nose, and the puppy licked her back.

'He's a Rhodesian lion dog,' Craig told her, 'or now I suppose you'd call him a Zimbabwean lion dog.'

The puppy's skin was too big for him. It hung down in wrinkles over his forehead that gave him a worried frown. His back was crested in the distinctive ridge of his breed.

'Look at his paws!' Sally-Anne cried. 'He's going to be a monster. What shall I call him?'

Craig declared a public holiday to mark the occasion of Sally-Anne's birth. They took the puppy and a picnic lunch down to the main dam below the homestead, and lay on a rug under the trees at the water's edge, and tried to find a name for the puppy. Sally-Anne vetoed Craig's suggested 'Dog'.

The black-faced weaver birds fluttered and shrieked and hung upside-down from the basket-shaped nests above their heads, and Joseph had put a cold bottle of white wine in the basket. The puppy chased grasshoppers until he collapsed exhausted on the rug beside Sally-Anne. They finished the wine, and when they made love on the rug, Sally-Anne whispered seriously, 'Shh! Don't wake the puppy!'

They drove back up the hills and Sally-Anne said suddenly, 'We haven't spoken about the troubles all day.'

'Don't let's spoil our record.'

'I'm going to call him Buster.'

'Why?'

'The first puppy I was ever given I called Buster.'

They gave Buster his supper in the bowl labelled 'Dog' Craig had bought for him, and then made a bed in an empty wine crate near the Aga stove. They were both happily tired and that evening left the book and the photographs and went to bed immediately after their own meal.

C raig woke to the sound of gun-fire. His residual war reflexes hurled him from the bed before he was fully awake. It was automatic rifle-fire, short bursts, very close, he noted instinctively, short bursts meant good, trained riflemen. They were down by the farm village, or the workshop. He judged the distance.

He found his leg and clinched the strap, fully awake now, and his first thought was for Sally-Anne. Keeping low, beneath the sill level of the windows, he rolled back to the bed and dragged her down beside him.

She was naked, and muzzy with sleep.

'What is it?'

'Here,' he whipped her gown off the foot of the bed. 'Get dressed, but keep down.'

While she shrugged into the gown, he was trying to marshal his thoughts. There were no weapons in the house, except the kitchen knives and a small hand axe for chopping firewood on the back veranda. There was no sandbagged fall-back position, no defensive perimeter of wire and floodlights, no radio transmitter – none of even the most elementary defences with which every farm homestead had once been provided.

Another burst of rifle-fire, and somebody screamed – a woman – the faint scream abruptly cut off.

'What's happening? Who are they?' Sally-Anne's voice was level and crisp. She was awake and unafraid. He felt a little lift of pride for her. 'Are they dissidents?'

'I don't know, but we aren't going to wait around to find out,' he told her grimly.

He glanced up at the new highly inflammable thatch overhead. Their best chance was to get out of the house and into the bush. To do that, they needed a diversion.

'Stay here,' he ordered. 'Get your shoes on and be ready to run. I'll be back in a minute.'

He rolled under the window to the wall, and came to his feet. The bedroom door was unlocked and he darted into the passage. He wasted ten seconds on the telephone – he knew they would have cut the wires, and that was confirmed immediately by the dead echoless void in the earpiece. He dropped it dangling on the cord and ran through to the kitchens.

There was only one diversion he could think of – light. He hit the remote-control switch of the diesel generator, and there was the faint ripple of sound from the engine room across the yard and the overhead bulbs glowed yellow and then flared into full brilliance. He tore open the fuse box above the control-board, tripped out the house-lights, and then switched on the veranda and front garden lights. That would leave the back of the house in darkness. They would make their break that way, he decided, and it would have to be quick. The attackers hadn't hit the house yet, but they could only be seconds away.

He ran back out of the kitchen, paused at the door of the lounge, and glanced through it to check the lighting in the front garden and veranda. The lawns were a peculiarly lush green in the artificial light, the jacaranda trees domed over them like the roof of a cathedral. The firing had ceased, but down near the labourers' village a woman was keening, that doleful sound of African mourning. It made his skin creep.

Craig knew that they would be coming up the hill already, and he was turning away to go back to Sally-Anne when he caught the flicker of movement at the edge of the light and he narrowed his eyes and tried to identify it. To know who was attacking would give him some small advantage, but he was wasting precious seconds.

The movement was a running man, coming up towards the house. A black man, naked – no, he was wearing a loin-cloth. Not really running, but staggering and weaving drunkenly. In the veranda lights half his body glinted as though it had been freshly oiled, and then Craig realized that it was blood. The man was painted with his own blood, and it was falling in scattered drops from him like water from the coat of a retriever when it comes ashore with the duck in its jaws.

Then a more intense shock of horror. Craig realized that it was old Shadrach, and unthinkingly went to help him. He kicked open the french doors of the lounge, went out onto the veranda at a run, and vaulted the low half-wall. He caught Shadrach in his arms just as he was about to fall, and lifted him off his feet. He was surprised at how light was the old man's body. Craig carried him at a single bound onto the veranda and crouched with him below the low wall.

Shadrach had been hit in the upper arm, just above the elbow. The bone had shattered, and the limb hung by a ribbon of flesh. Shadrach held it to his breast like a nursing infant.

'They are coming,' he gasped at Craig. 'You must run. They are killing our people, they will kill you also.'

It was miraculous that the old man could speak, let alone move and run with such a wound. Crouching below the wall he ripped a strip of cotton from his loin-cloth with his teeth and started to bind it around his own arm above the wound. Craig pushed his hand away and tied the knot for him.

'You must run, little master,' and before Craig could prevent him, the old man rolled to his feet and disappeared into the darkness beyond the floodlights.

'He risked his life to warn me.' Craig looked after him for a second, and then roused himself and, doubled over, ran back into the house.

Sally-Anne was where he had left her, crouched below the window. Light fell through it in a yellow square, and he saw that she had tied back her hair and pulled on a T-shirt and shorts, and was lacing her soft, leather, training shoes.

'Good girl.' He knelt beside her. 'Let's go.'

'Buster,' she replied. 'My puppy!'

'For God's sake!'

'We can't leave him!' She had that stubborn look that he had already come to know so well.

'I'll carry you if I have to,' he warned fiercely, and raising himself quickly he risked a last glance over the window-sill.

The lawns and gardens were still brightly lit. There were the dark shapes of men coming up from the valley, armed men in disciplined extended order. For a moment he could not believe what he was seeing, and then he sagged with relief.

'Oh, thank you, God!' he whispered. He found that reaction had set in already. He felt weak and shivery, and he took Sally-Anne in his arms and hugged her.

'It's all right now,' he told her. 'It's going to be all right.'

'What has happened?'

'The security forces have arrived,' he said. He had recognized the burgundy-coloured berets and silver cap-badges of the men closing in across the lawns. 'The Third Brigade is here – we will be all right now.'

They went out onto the front veranda to greet their rescuers, Sally-Anne carrying the yellow puppy in her arms, and Craig with his arm about her shoulders.

'I am very glad to see you and your men, Sergeant,' Craig greeted the non-commissioned officer who led the advancing line of troopers.

'Please go inside.' The sergeant made a gesture with his rifle, imperative if not directly threatening. He was a tall man, with long sinewy limbs, his expression was cold and neutral, and Craig felt his relief shrink. Something was wrong. The line of troopers had closed like a net around the homestead, while skirmishers came forward in pairs, covering each other, the classical tactics of the street fighter, and they went swiftly into the house, breaking through windows and side doors, sweeping the interior.

There was a crash of breaking glass at the rear of the house. It was a destructive search.

'What's going on, Sergeant?' Craig's anger resurfaced, and this time the tall sergeant's gesture was unmistakably hostile.

Craig and Sally-Anne backed off before him into the dining-room and stood in the centre of the room beside the teak refectory table, facing the threatening rifle, Craig holding her protectively.

Two troopers slipped in through the front door, and reported to the sergeant in a gabble of Shona that Craig could not follow. The sergeant acknowledged with a nod and gave them an order. They spread out obediently along the wall, their weapons turned unmistakably onto the dishevelled couple in the centre of the room.

'Where are the lights?' the sergeant asked, and when Craig told him, he went to the switch and white light flooded the room.

'What is going on here, Sergeant?' Craig repeated, angry and uncertain and starting to be afraid for Sally-Anne again.

The sergeant ignored the question, and strode to the door. He called to one of the troopers on the lawn, and the man came at a run. He carried a portable radio transmitter strapped on his back, with the scorpion-tail aerial sticking up over his shoulder. The sergeant spoke softly into the handset of the radio and then came back into the room.

They waited now in an unmoving tableau. To Craig it seemed like an hour passed in silence, but it was less than five minutes before the sergeant cocked his head slightly, listening. Craig heard it, the beat of an engine, in a different tempo from that of the diesel generator. It firmed, and Craig knew that it was a Land-Rover.

It came up the driveway, headlights swept the windows, brakes squeaked and gravel crunched. The engine was cut, doors banged and then there were the footsteps of a group of men crossing the veranda.

General Peter Fungabera led his staff in through the french doors. He wore his beret pulled down over one eye and a matching silk scarf at his throat. Except for the pistol in its webbing holster at his side, he was armed only with the leather-covered swagger-stick.

Behind him Captain Nbebi was tall and round-shouldered, his eyes inscrutable behind the steel-rimmed spectacles. He carried a leather map-case in his hand, and a machine pistol on a sling over his shoulder.

'Peter!' Craig's relief was tempered by wariness. It was all too contrived, too controlled, too menacing. 'Some of my people have been killed. My induna is out there somewhere, badly wounded.'

'There have been many enemy casualties,' Peter Fungabera nodded.

'Enemy?' Craig was puzzled.

'Dissidents,' Peter nodded again. 'Matabele dissidents.'

'Dissidents?' Craig stared at him. 'Shadrach a dissident? That's crazy – he's a simple, uneducated cattleman, and doesn't give a damn for politics—'

'Things are often not what they seem.' Peter Fungabera pulled back the chair at the head of the long table and placed one foot on it, leaning an elbow on his knee. Timon Nbebi placed the leather map-case on the table in front of him and stood back, in a position of guard behind his shoulder, holding the machine pistol by the grip.

'Will somebody please tell me what in the hell is happening here, Peter?' Craig was exasperated and nervous. 'Somebody attacked my village – they've killed some of my people. God alone knows how many – why don't you get after them?'

'The shooting is over,' Peter Fungabera told him. 'We have cleaned out the vipers' nest of traitors that you were breeding on this colonial-style estate of yours.'

'What on earth are you talking about?' Craig was now truly flustered. 'You cannot be serious!'

'Serious?' Peter smiled easily. He straightened up and placed both feet back on the floor. He walked across to face them. 'A puppy,' he was still smiling. 'How adorable.'

He took Buster from Sally-Anne's arms before she realized his intentions. He strolled back to the head of the table, fondling the little animal, scratching behind its ear. It was still half-asleep and it made little whimpering sounds, nuzzling against him, instinctively searching for its mother's teat.

'Serious?' Peter repeated the original question. 'I want to impress upon you just how serious I am.'

He dropped the puppy onto the stone-flagged floor. It fell on its back, and lay stunned. He placed his boot upon its chest and crushed it with his full weight. The puppy screamed once only as its chest collapsed.

'That is how serious I am.' He was no longer smiling. 'Your lives are as valuable to me as this animal was.'

Sally-Anne made a small moaning sound and turned away, burying her face in Craig's chest. She heaved with nausea, and Craig could feel her fighting to control it. Peter Fungabera kicked the soft yellow corpse into the fireplace and sat down.

'We have wasted enough time on the theatricals,' he said, and opened the leather map-case, spreading the documents on the table in front of him.

'Mr Mellow, you have been acting as an *agent provocateur* in the pay of the notorious American CIA—'

'That's a bloody lie!' Craig shouted, and Peter ignored the outburst.

'Your local control was the American agent Morgan Oxford at the United States Embassy, while your central control and paymaster was a certain Henry Pickering, who masquerades as a senior official of the World Bank in New York. He recruited both you and Miss Jay—'

'That's not true!'

'Your remuneration was sixty thousand dollars per annum, and your mission was to set up a centre of subversion in Matabeleland, which was financed by CIA monies channelled to you in the form of a loan from a CIA-controlled subsidiary of the World Bank – the sum allocated was five million dollars.'

'Christ, Peter, that's nonsense, and you know it.'

'During the rest of this interrogation, you will address me as either "Sir" or "General Fungabera", is that clear to you?' He turned away to listen as there was sudden activity outside the french doors. It sounded like the arrival of a convoy of light trucks, from which more troops were disembarking with orders being called in Shona. Through the glass doors, Craig saw a dozen troopers carrying heavy crates up onto the veranda.

Peter Fungabera glanced enquiringly at Timon Nbebi, who nodded in confirmation of the unspoken question.

'Right!' Peter Fungabera turned back to face Craig. 'We can continue. You opened negotiations with known Matebele traitors, using your fluent knowledge of the language and the character of these intractable people—'

'You can't name one, because there aren't any.'

Peter Fungabera nodded to Timon Nbebi. He shouted an order.

A man was led into the room between two troopers. He was barefooted, dressed only in ragged khaki shorts, and was emaciated to the point where his head appeared grotesquely huge. His pate was shaven and covered with lumps and fresh scabs, his ribs latticed with the scars of beatings – probably the wicked hippo-hide whips called sjamboks had been used on him.

'Do you know this white man?' Peter Fungabera demanded of him. The man stared at Craig. His eyes had an opaque dullness, as though they had been sprinkled with dust.

'I've never seen him—' Craig started, and then broke off as he recognized him. It was Comrade Dollar, the youngest and most truculent of the men from Zambezi Waters.

'Yes?' Peter Fungabera invited, smiling again. 'What were you about to say, Mr Mellow?'

'I want to see somebody from the British High Commission,' Craig said, 'and Miss Jay would like to make a telephone call to the United States Embassy.'

'Of course,' Peter Fungabera nodded. 'All in good time, but first we must complete what we have already begun.' He swung back to Comrade Dollar. 'Do you know the white man?'

Comrade Dollar nodded. 'He gave us money.'

'Take him away,' Peter Fungabera ordered. 'Care for him well, and give him something to eat. Now, Mr Mellow, do you still deny any contact with the subversives?' He did not wait for a reply, but went on smoothly, 'You built up an arsenal of weapons on this estate to be used against the elected people's government in a *coup d'état* which would place a pro-American dictator—'

'No,' Craig said quietly. 'I have no weapons.'

Peter Fungabera sighed. 'Your denials are pointless – and tiresome.' Then to the tall Shona sergeant, 'Bring the two of them.'

He led the way onto the wide veranda, to where his men had stacked the crates.

'Open them,' he commanded, and his men knocked back the clips and lifted the lids.

Craig recognized the weapons that were packed into them. They were American Armalite 5.56 mm AR 18 automatic rifles. Six to the case, and brand-new, still in their factory grease.

'These are nothing to do with me.' Craig was at last able to deny it with vehemence.

'You are testing my patience.' Peter Fungabera turned to Timon Nbebi. 'Fetch the other white man.'

Hans Groenewald, Craig's overseer, was dragged from the cab of one of the parked trucks, and led to the veranda. His hands were manacled behind his back, and he was terrified. His broad tanned face seemed to have deflated into heavy wrinkles and folds of loose skin like a diseased bloodhound, and his dark suntan had faded to the colour of creamed coffee. His eyes were bloodshot and rheumy, like those of a drunkard.

'You stored these weapons in the tractor sheds on this ranch?' Peter Fungabera asked, and Groenewald's reply was inaudible.

'Speak up, man.'

'Yes I stored them, sir.'

'On whose orders?'

Groenewald looked piteously at Craig, and suddenly Craig's heart was sheathed in ice, and the cold spread down into his belly and his loins.

'Whose orders?' Peter Fungabera repeated patiently.

'Mr Mellow's orders, sir.'

'Take him away.'

As the guards led him back to the truck, Groenewald's head was screwed around, his eyes still on Craig's face, his expression harrowed. Suddenly he shouted, 'I'm sorry, Mr Mellow, I've got a wife and kids—'

One of the guards swung the butt of his rifle into Groenewald's stomach, just below the ribs. Groenewald gasped, and doubled over. He would have fallen but they seized his arms and swung him up into the cab. The driver of the truck started the engine and the big machine roared away down the hill.

Peter Fungabera led them back into the dining-room and resumed his seat at the head of the table. While he rearranged and studied the papers from the map-case, he ignored Craig and Sally-Anne. They were forced to stand against the opposite wall, a trooper on each side of them, and the silence stretched out. Even though Craig realized this silence was deliberate, he wanted to break it, to shout out his innocence, to protest against the web of lies and half-truths and distortions in which they were being slowly enmeshed.

Beside him Sally-Anne stood upright, gripping her own hands at waist level to prevent them trembling. Her face had a sick greenish hue, under a light sheen of sweat, and she kept turning her eyes towards the fireplace where the puppy's crushed carcass lay like a discarded toy.

At last Peter Fungabera pushed the papers aside and rocked back in his chair, tapping lightly on the table-top with his swagger-stick.

'A hanging matter,' he said, 'a capital offence for both you and Miss Jay—'

'It has nothing to do with her.' Craig put a protective arm around her shoulders.

'Women's lower organs are less able to withstand the downward shock of the hangman's drop,' Peter Fungabera remarked. 'The effect can be quite bizarre – or at least, so I am told.' It conjured up an image that sickened Craig, saliva of nausea flooded his mouth. He swallowed it down and could not speak.

'Fortunately, it need not come to that. The choice will be yours.'

Peter rolled the swagger-stick lightly between his fingers. Craig found himself staring fixedly at Peter's hands. The palms and insides of his long powerful fingers were a soft delicate pink.

'I believe that you are the dupes of your imperialistic masters.' Peter smiled again. 'I'm going to let you go.'

Both their heads jerked up, and they watched his face.

'Yes, you look disbelieving, but I mean it. Personally I have grown quite fond of both of you. To have you hanged would give me no special pleasure. Both of you possess artistic talents which it would be wasteful to terminate, and from now on you will be unable to do any further harm.'

Still they were silent, beginning to hope, and yet fearful, sensing that it was all part of a cruel cat's game.

'I am prepared to make you an offer. If you make a clean breast of it, a full and unreserved confession, I will have you escorted to the border, with your travel documents and any readily portable possessions and items of value you choose. I will have you set free, to go and trouble me and my people no more.'

He waited, smiling, and the swagger-stick went tap tap tap on the table-top, like a dripping faucet. It distracted Craig. He found himself unable to think clearly. It had all happened too swiftly. Peter Fungabera had kept him off balance, shifting and changing his attack. He had to have time to pull himself together, and to begin thinking clearly and logically again.

'A confession?' he blurted. 'What kind of confession? One of your exhibitions – before a people's court? A public humiliation?'

'No, I don't think we need go that far,' Peter Fungabera assured him. 'I will need only a written statement from you, an account of your crimes and the machinations of your masters. The confession will be properly witnessed, and then you will be escorted to the border and set at liberty. All very straightforward, simple and, if I may be allowed to say so, very civilized and humane.'

'You will, of course, prepare my confession for me to sign?' Craig asked bitterly, and Peter Fungabera chuckled.

'How very perceptive of you.' He selected one of the documents from the pile in front of him. 'Here it is. You need only fill in the date and sign it.'

Even Craig was surprised at that.

'You've had it typed already?'

Nobody replied, and Captain Nbebi brought the document to him.

'Please read it, Mr Mellow,' he invited.

There were three typewritten foolscap sheets, much of them filled with denunciations of his 'imperialistic masters' and the hysterical cant of the extreme left. But in this mish mash, like plums in a stodgy pudding, were the hard facts of which Craig stood accused.

He read through it slowly, trying to force his numbed brain to function clearly, but it was all somehow dreamlike and unreal, seeming not really to affect him personally – until he read the words that jerked him fully conscious again. The words were so familiar, so well remembered, and they burned like concentrated acid into the core of his being.

'I fully admit that by my actions I have proved myself to be *an enemy of the state and the people of Zimbabwe.*'

It was the exact wording used in another document he had signed, and suddenly he was able to see the design behind it all.

'King's Lynn,' he whispered, and he looked up from the typewritten confession at Peter Fungabera. 'That's what it's all about. You are after King's Lynn!'

There was silence, except for the tap of the swagger-stick on the table-top. Peter Fungabera did not miss a beat with it, and he was still smiling.

'You had it all worked out from the very beginning. The surety for my loan – you wrote in that clause.'

The numbness and lethargy sloughed away, and Craig felt his anger rising again within him. He threw the confession on the floor. Captain Nbebi retrieved it, and stood with it held awkwardly in both hands. Craig found himself shaking with rage. He took a step forward towards the elegant figure seated before him, his hands reaching out involuntarily, but the tall Shona sergeant barred his way with the barrel of his rifle held across Craig's chest.

'You bloody swine!' Craig hissed at Peter, and there was a little white froth of saliva on his lower lip. 'I want the police, I want the protection of the law.'

'Mr Mellow,' Peter Fungabera replied evenly, 'in Matabeleland, I am the law. It is my protection that you are being offered.'

'I won't do it. I won't sign that piece of dung. I will go to hell first.'

'That might be arranged,' Peter Fungabera mused softly, and then persuasively, 'I really do urge you to put aside these histrionics and bow to the inevitable. Sign the paper and we can dispense with any further nastiness.'

Crude words crowded to Craig's lips, and with an effort he resisted using them, not wanting to degrade himself in front of them.

'No,' he said instead. 'I'll never sign that thing. You'll have to kill me first.'

'I give you one last chance to change your mind.'

'No. Never!'

Peter Fungabera swivelled in his chair towards the tall sergeant.

'I give you the woman,' he said. 'You first and then your men, one at a time until they have all had their turn. Here, in this room, on this table.'

'Christ, you aren't human,' Craig blurted, and tried to hold Sally-Anne, but the troopers seized him from behind and hurled him back against the wall. One of them pinned him there with the point of a bayonet against his throat.

The other twisted Sally-Anne's wrist up between her shoulder blades and held her in front of the sergeant. She began to struggle wildly, but the trooper lifted her until just the toes of her running shoes touched the stone-flagged floor, and her face contorted with pain.

The sergeant was expressionless, neither leering nor making any obscene gesture. He took the front of Sally-Anne's T-shirt in both hands, and tore it open from neck to waist. Her breasts swung out. They were very white and tender-looking, their pink tips seemed sensitive and vulnerable.

'I have one hundred and fifty men,' Peter Fungabera remarked. 'It will be some time before they have all finished.'

The sergeant hooked his thumbs into the waistband of her shorts and yanked them down. He let them fall in a tangle around her ankles. Craig strained forward, but the point of the bayonet pierced the skin at his throat. A few drops of blood dribbled down his shirt-front. Sally-Anne tried to cover the dark triangular mound of her pudenda with her free hand. It was a pathetically ineffectual gesture.

'I know how fiercely even a so-called white liberal like you resents the thought of black flesh penetrating his woman.' Peter Fungabera's tone was almost conversational. 'It will be interesting to see just how many times you will allow it to happen.'

The sergeant and the trooper lifted Sally-Anne between them and laid her on her back on the refectory table. The sergeant freed the silk shorts that bound her ankles but left the running shoes on her feet, and the tatters of her shirt around her upper body.

Expertly they pulled her knees up against her chest and then forced them down, tucking them under her armpits. They must have done this often before. She was helpless, doubled over, wide open and completely defenceless. Every man in the room was staring into her body's secret depths. The sergeant began to unbuckle his webbing belt with his free hand.

'Craig!' Sally-Anne screamed, and Craig's body bucked involuntarily as though to the stroke of a whip.

'I'll sign it,' he whispered. 'Just let her go, and I'll sign it.'

Peter Fungabera gave an order in Shona, and immediately they released Sally-Anne. The trooper stood back and the sergeant helped her to her feet. Politely, he handed her back her shorts, and she hopped on one foot, sobbing softly and trembling, as she pulled them on.

Then she rushed to Craig and threw both her arms about him. She could not speak, but she choked and gulped down her tears. Her body shook wildly and Craig held her close and made incoherent soothing noises to her.

'The sooner you sign, the sooner you can go.'

Craig went to the table, still holding Sally-Anne in the curve of his left arm.

Captain Nbebi handed him a pen and he initialled the two top sheets of the confession, and signed the last one in full. Both Captain Nbebi and Peter Fungabera witnessed his signature, and then Peter said, 'One last formality. I want both you and Miss Jay to be examined by the regimental doctor for any signs of ill-treatment or undue coercion.'

'God damn you, hasn't she had enough?'

'Humour me, please, my dear fellow.'

The doctor must have been waiting in one of the trucks outside. He was a small dapper Shona and his manner was brisk and businesslike.

'You may examine the woman in the bedroom, Doctor. In particular, please satisfy yourself that she has not been forcibly penetrated,' Peter Fungabera instructed him, and then as they left the dining-room, he turned to Craig. 'In the meantime, you may open the safe in your office and take out your passport and whatever other documents you may need for the journey.'

Two troopers escorted Craig to his office at the far end of the veranda, and waited while he struck the combination of the safe. He took out his passport, the wallet containing his credit cards and World Bank badge, three folders of American Express travellers' cheques, and the bundle of manuscript for the new novel. He stuffed them into a British Airways flight bag and went back to the dining-room.

Sally-Anne and the doctor came back from the bed-room. She had changed into a blue cashmere jersey, shirt and jeans, and she had controlled her hysteria to an occasional gulping sob, though she was still shivering in little convulsive fits. She dragged her camera bag and under one arm carried the art folder of photographs and text for their book.

'Your turn,' Peter Fungabera invited Craig to follow the doctor, and when he returned Sally-Anne was seated in the back seat of a Land-Rover parked in front of the veranda. Captain Nbebi was beside her, and there were two armed troopers in the back of the vehicle. The seat beside the driver was empty for Craig.

Peter Fungabera was waiting on the veranda. 'Goodbye, Craig,' he said, and Craig stared at him, trying to project the full venom he felt for him.

'You didn't really believe that I would allow you to rebuild your family's empire, did you?' Peter asked without rancour. 'We fought too hard to destroy that world.'

As the Land-Rover drove down the hills in the night, Craig turned and looked back. Peter Fungabera still stood on the lighted veranda, and somehow his tall figure was transformed. He looked as though he belonged there, like a conqueror who has taken possession, like the *patron* of the grand estate. Craig watched him until the trees hid him, and only then did the leaven of his true hatred begin to rise within him.

T he headlights of the Land-Rover swung across the signboard:

King's Lynn Afrikander Stud
Proprietor: Craig Mellow

It seemed to mock him, then they were past it and rattling across the steel cattle-grid. They left the soil of King's Lynn and Craig's dreams behind them, and swung westwards. The lugged tyres began their monotonous hum as they hit the black top of the main road, and still nobody in the Land-Rover spoke.

Captain Nbebi opened the map-case that he was holding on his knees and took out a bottle of fiery locally made cane spirits. He passed the bottle over the front seat to Craig. Craig waved it brusquely aside, but Timon Nbebi insisted, and Craig took it with ill grace. He unscrewed the cap, and swallowed a mouthful, then exhaled the fumes noisily. It brought tears to his eyes, but immediately the fireball in his belly spread out through his blood, giving him comfort. He took another swig and passed the bottle back to Sally-Anne. She shook her head.

'Drink it,' Craig ordered, and meekly she obeyed. She had stopped weeping, but the fits of shivering still persisted. The spirits made her cough and choke, but she got them down, and they steadied her.

'Thank you.' She handed the bottle back to Timon Nbebi, and the politeness from a woman who had been so recently degraded and humiliated was embarrassing to all of them.

They reached the first road-block on the outskirts of the town of Bulawayo, and Craig checked his wrist-watch. It was seven minutes to three in the morning. There were no other vehicles waiting at the barrier, and two troopers stepped out from behind the barricade and came to each side of the Land-Rover. Timon Nbebi slid back his window and spoke quietly to one of them, offering his pass at the same time. The trooper examined it briefly in the beam of his flashlight, then handed it back. He saluted, and the barrier lifted. They drove through.

Bulawayo was silent and devoid of life, only very few of the windows were lit. A traffic-light flashed green and amber and red, and the driver stopped obediently, although the streets were completely deserted. The engine throbbed in idle and then above it, far off and faint, came the popping sound of automatic rifle-fire.

Craig was watching Timon Nbebi's face in the rear-view mirror, and saw him wince slightly at the sound of gunfire. Then the light changed and they drove on, taking the south road through the suburbs. On the edge of the town there were two more road-blocks and then the open road.

They ran southwards in the night, with the whine of the tyres and the buffet of the wind against the cab. The glow from the dashboard gave their faces a sickly greenish hue and once or twice the radio in the back crackled and gabbled distorted Shona. Craig recognized Peter Funga-bera's voice on one of the transmissions, but he must have been calling another unit, for Timon Nbebi made no effort to reply and they drove on in silence. The monotonous hum of engine and tyres and the warmth of the cab lulled Craig, and in a reaction from anger and fear he found himself dozing.

He awoke with a start as Timon Nbebi spoke for the first time, and the beat of the Land-Rover's engine altered. It was dawn's first light. He could see the silhouette of the tree-tops against the paling lemon sky. The Land-Rover slowed and then swung off the main tarmac road onto a dirt track. Immediately the mushroom smell of talcum dust permeated the cab.

'Where are we?' Craig demanded. 'Why are we leaving the road?'

253

Timon Nbebi spoke to the driver and he pulled to the side of the track and stopped.

'You will please step out,' Timon ordered, and as Craig did so, Timon was waiting for him, seeming to help him down – but instead he took Craig's arm, turned it slightly, and before Craig could react to the icy touch of steel on his skin, Timon had handcuffed both his wrists. It had been so unexpected and so expertly done that for seconds Craig stood bewildered with his manacled hands thrust out in front of him, staring at them. Then he shouted, 'Christ, what is this?'

By then Timon Nbebi had handcuffed Sally-Anne as quickly and efficiently, and ignoring Craig's outburst, was talking quietly to his driver and the two troopers. It was too quick for Craig to follow, although he caught the Shona words 'kill' and 'hide'. One of the troopers seemed to protest and Timon leaned through the open door of the Land-Rover and lifted the microphone of the radio. He gave a call sign, repeated three times, and after a short wait was patched through to Peter Fungabera. Craig recognized the general's voice despite the VHF distortion. There was a brief exchange, and when Timon Nbebi hung the microphone, the trooper was no longer protesting. Clearly Timon Nbebi's orders had been endorsed.

'We will go on,' Timon reverted to English, and Craig was roughly hustled back into the front seat. The change in their treatment was ominous.

The driver threaded the Land-Rover deeper and deeper into the thorn veld, and the morning light strengthened. Outside the cab, the dawn bird chorus was in full voice. Craig recognized the high clear duet of a pair of collared barbets in an acacia tree beside the track. A brown hare was trapped in the beam of the headlights and lolloped ahead of them with his long pink ears flapping. Then the sky began to burn with the stupendous colours of the African dawn and the driver switched off the headlights.

'Craig, darling. They are going to kill us, aren't they?' Sally-Anne asked quietly. Her voice was clear and firm now. She had conquered her hysteria and was in control of herself again. She spoke as though they were alone.

'I'm sorry.' Craig could find nothing else to say. 'I should have known that Peter Fungabera would never let us go.'

'There is nothing you could have done. Even if you *had* known.'

'They'll bury us in some remote place and our disappearance will be blamed on the Matabele dissidents,' Craig said, and Timon Nbebi sat silent and impassive, neither admitting nor denying the accusation.

The road forked, the left-hand track barely discernible, and Timon Nbebi indicated it. The driver slowed further and changed to a lower gear. They bumped along it for another twenty minutes. By then it was fully light, the promise of sunrise flaming the tiptops of the acacia.

Timon Nbebi gave another order and the driver turned off the track and drove blindly through the waist-high grass, skirting the edge of a grey granite kopje, until they were entirely screened from even the rudimentary bush track that they had been following. Another short order, and the driver stopped and switched off the engine.

The silence closed in on them, enhancing their sense of isolation and remoteness.

'No one will ever find us here,' Sally-Anne said quietly, and Craig could find no word of comfort for her.

'You will remain where you are,' Timon Nbebi ordered.

'Don't you feel anything for what you are going to do?' Sally-Anne asked him, and he turned his head to her. Behind the steel-rimmed spectacles his eyes were perhaps shaded with misery and regret, but his mouth was set hard. He did not reply to her question, and after a moment turned from her and alighted. He gave orders in Shona, and the troopers racked their weapons in the back of the

Land-Rover while the driver climbed up onto the roofrack and brought down three folding trenching-tools.

Timon Nbebi reached through the window and took the keys out of the Land-Rover's engine, then he led his men a short distance away and with the toe of his boot marked out two oblongs on the sandy grey earth. The three Shonas shucked off their webbing and battle-jackets, and began to dig out the graves. They went down swiftly in the loose soil. Timon Nbebi stood aside watching them. He lit a cigarette and the grey smoke spiralled straight up in the still, cool dawn.

'I am going to try to get one of the rifles,' Craig whispered. The weapons were in the back of the vehicle. He would have to crawl over the backs of both seats, then reach the rifles which were standing upright in the racks. He would have to open the clip on the rack, load the weapon, change the rate-of-fire selector and aim through the back window – all with his hands manacled.

'You won't make it,' Sally-Anne whispered.

'Probably not,' he agreed grimly, 'but can you think of anything else? When I say "Go", I want you to throw yourself flat on the floor.'

Craig wriggled around in the seat, his leg hampering him, catching by the ankle on the lever of the four-wheel-drive selector. He kicked it free and gathered himself. He took a slow breath, and glanced out of the rear window at the little group of grave-diggers.

'Listen,' he told her urgently. 'I love you. I have never loved anyone the way I love you.'

'I love you, too, my darling,' she whispered back.

'Be brave!' he said.

'Good luck!' She was crouching down, and he almost made his move, but at that moment Timon Nbebi turned towards the Land-Rover. He saw Craig twisted around in the seat, and Sally-Anne down below the sill. He frowned and came back to the vehicle with quick businesslike strides. At the open window he paused and spoke softly in English.

'Don't do it, Mr Mellow. We are all of us in great danger. Our only chance is for you to remain still and not to interfere or make any unexpected move.' He took the ignition keys from his pocket, and with his other hand loosened the flap of the webbing pistol-holster on his belt. He kept on talking softly, 'I have effectively disarmed my men, and their attention is on their work. When I enter the Land-Rover, do not hamper me or try to attack me. I am in as great a danger as you are. You must trust me. Do you understand?'

'Yes,' Craig nodded. Christ! Do I have any choice, he thought.

Timon opened the driver's door of the Land-Rover, and slid in under the wheel. He glanced once at the three soldiers who were by now waist-deep in the two graves, then Timon slipped the key into the ignition and turned it.

The engine turned over loudly, and the three soldiers looked up, puzzled. The starter-motor whirred and churned, and the engine would not fire. One of the troopers shouted, and jumped out of the grave. His chest was snaked with sweat and powdered with grey dust. He started towards the stranded Land-Rover. Timon Nbebi pumped the accelerator, and kept turning the engine. He had a desperate, terrified look on his face.

'You'll flood her,' Craig told him. 'Take your foot off!'

The trooper broke into a run towards them. He was shouting angry questions, and the starter went on – Whirr! Whirr! Whirr! – with Timon frozen to the wheel.

The running trooper was almost alongside, and now the others, slower and less alert, began to follow him. They were shouting also, one of them swinging his trenching-tool menacingly.

'Lock the door!' Craig shouted urgently, and Timon

pushed down the handle into the lock position just as the trooper threw his weight on it. He heaved at the outside handle with all his weight, and then darted to the rear door and before Sally-Anne could lock it, jerked it open. He reached in and caught Sally-Anne by the upper arm and began dragging her from the open door.

Craig was still hunched around in the front seat and now he lifted both manacled hands high and brought them down on the trooper's shaven head. The sharp steel edge of the cuffs cut down to the bone of the skull, and the man collapsed half in and half out of the open door.

Craig hit him again, in the centre of the forehead, and had a brief glimpse of white bone in the bottom of the wound before quick bright blood obscured it. The other two soldiers were only paces away, baying like wolfhounds and armed with their spades.

At that moment the engine of the Land-Rover fired and roared into life. Timon Nbebi hit the gear-lever, and with a clash of metal it engaged and the Land-Rover shot forward. Craig was thrown over the seat half on top of Sally-Anne, and the bleeding trooper was caught by his dangling legs in a thorn bush and ripped out through the rear door.

The Land-Rover swerved and bucked over the rough ground, with the two screeching black soldiers running behind it, and the open door flapping and banging wildly. Then Timon Nbebi straightened the wheel and changed gear. The Land-Rover accelerated away, crashing over rock and fallen branches, and the pursuing troopers fell back. One of them hurled his spade despairingly after them. It shattered the rear window, and broken glass spilled over the rear of the cab.

Timon Nbebi picked up their own incoming tracks through the high grass, and at last they were going faster than a man could run. The two troopers gave up and stood panting in the tracks, their shouts of recrimination and anger dwindled and then were lost. Timon reached the bush track at the point that they had left it, and turned onto it, picking up speed.

'Give me your hands,' he ordered, and when Craig offered his manacled hands, Timon unlocked the cuffs. 'Here!' he gave Craig the key. 'Do the same for Miss Jay.'

She rubbed her wrists. 'My God, Craig, I truly thought that was the end of the line.'

'A close-run thing,' Timon Nbebi agreed, with all his attention on the track. 'Napoleon said that, I think.' And then, before Craig could correct him, 'Please to arm yourself with one of the rifles, Mr Mellow, and place the other beside me.'

Sally-Anne passed the short, ugly weapons over to the front seat. The Third Brigade was the only unit of the regular army still armed with AK 47s, a legacy from their North Korean instructors.

'Do you know how to use it, Mr Mellow?' Timon Nbebi asked.

'I was an armourer in the Rhodesian Police.'

'Of course, how stupid of me.'

Swiftly Craig checked the curved 'banana' magazine and then reloaded the chamber. The weapon was new and well cared for. The weight of it in Craig's hands changed his whole personality. Minutes before, he had been mere flotsam on the stream, swept along by events over which he had no control, confused and uncertain and afraid – but now he was armed. Now he could fight back, now he could protect his woman and himself, now he could shape events rather than be shaped by them. It was the primeval, atavistic instinct of primitive man, and Craig revelled in it. He reached over the seat and took Sally-Anne's hand. He squeezed it briefly, and fervently she returned the pressure.

'Now we have a fighting chance, at least.' The new

tone of his voice reached her. Her spirits lifted a little, and she gave him the first smile he had seen that night. He freed his hand, found the bottle of cane spirit in the cubby-hole, and passed it to her. After she had drunk, he gave it to Timon Nbebi.

'All right, Captain, what the hell is going on here?'

Timon gasped at the sting of the liquor and his voice was roughened by it as he replied.

'You were perfectly correct, Mr Mellow, my orders from General Fungabera were to take you and Miss Jay into the bush and execute you. And you were also correct in guessing that your disappearance would be blamed on the Matabele dissidents.'

'Well, why didn't you obey your orders?'

Before replying, Timon handed the bottle back to Craig, and then glanced over his shoulder at Sally-Anne.

'I am sorry that I had to go through the preparations for your execution, without being able to reassure you, but my men speak English. I had to make it look real. It galled me, for I didn't want to inflict more on you, after what you have already suffered.'

'Captain Nbebi, I forgive you everything and I love you for what you are doing, but why, in God's name, are you doing it?' Sally-Anne demanded.

'What I am about to tell you, I have never told a living soul before. You see, my mother was a full-blooded Matabele. She died when I was very young, but I remember her well and honour that memory.' He did not look at them, but concentrated on the track ahead. 'I was raised as a Shona by my father, but I have always been aware of my Matabele blood. They are my people, and I can no longer stomach what is being done to them. I am certain that General Fungabera has become aware of my feelings, though I doubt that he knows about my mother, but he knows that I have reached the end of my usefulness to him. Recently there have been small signs of it. I have lived too close to the man-eating leopard for too long not to know its moods. After I had buried you, there would have been something for me also, an unmarked grave – or Fungabera's puppies.'

Timon used the Sindebele, *amawundhla ka Fungabera*, and Craig was startled. Sarah Nyoni, the schoolteacher at Tuti Mission, had used the same phrase.

'I have heard that expression before – I do not understand it.'

'Hyena,' Timon explained. 'Those who die or are executed at the rehabilitation centres are taken into the bush and laid out for the hyena. The hyena leaves nothing, not a chip of bone nor a tuft of hair.'

'Oh God,' said Sally-Anne in a small voice. 'We were at Tuti. We heard the brutes, but didn't understand. How many have gone that way?'

Timon Nbebi said, 'I can only guess – many thousands.'

'It's scarcely believable.'

'General Fungabera's hatred for the Matabele is a kind of madness, an obsession. He is planning to wipe them out. First it was their leaders, accused of treason – falsely accused, like Tungata Zebiwe—'

'Oh no!' Sally-Anne said miserably. 'I can't bear it – was Zebiwe innocent?'

'I'm sorry, Miss Jay,' Timon Nbebi confirmed it. 'Fungabera had to be very careful when he tackled Zebiwe. He knew if he seized him for his political activities, he would have the entire Matabele tribe in revolt. You and Mr Mellow provided him with the perfect opportunity – a non-political crime. A crime of greed.'

'I'm being stupid,' said Sally-Anne. 'If Zebiwe wasn't the master poacher, was there ever a poacher? And if there was – who was it?'

'General Fungabera himself,' said Timon Nbebi simply.

'Are you sure?' Craig was incredulous.

'I was personally in charge of many of the shipments of animal contraband that left the country.'

'But that night on the Karoi road?'

'That was easily arranged. The general knew that sooner or later Zebiwe would be going to Tuti Mission again. Zebiwe's secretary informed us of the exact time and date. We arranged for the truck loaded with contraband, driven by a Matabele detainee we had bribed, to be waiting for him on the Tuti road. Of course, we had not anticipated Tungata Zebiwe's violent reaction – that was merely a bonus for us.'

Timon drove as fast as the track would allow, while Sally-Anne and Craig hunched down in their seats, their artificial elation at their escape rapidly giving way to fatigue and shock.

'Where are we heading?' Craig asked.

'Botswana border.'

That was the landlocked state to the south and west which had become an established staging post for political fugitives from its neighbours.

'On our way I hope you will have a chance to see what is really happening to my people. No one else will bear witness. General Fungabera has sealed off the whole of south-western Matabeleland. No journalists are allowed in, no clergymen, no Red Cross—'

He slowed for an area where ant bears had dug their holes in the track, burrowing for the nests of termites, and then he accelerated again.

'The pass I have from General Fungabera will take us a little further, but not as far as the border. We will have to use side roads and back roads until we can find a crossing place. Very soon General Fungabera will learn of my defection, and we will be hunted by the whole of the Third Brigade. We must make as much distance as we can before that happens.'

They reached the main fork in the track and Timon stopped, but kept the motor running. He took a large-scale map from his leather map-case and studied it attentively.

'We are just south of the railway line. This is the road to Empandeni Mission Station. If we can get through there before the alarm goes out for us, then we can try for the border between Madaba and Matsumi. The Botswana police run a regular patrol along the fence.'

'Let's get on with it.' Craig was impatient and becoming fearful, the comfort of the weapon across his lap beginning to fade. Timon folded the map and drove on.

'Can I ask you some more questions?' Sally-Anne spoke after a few minutes.

'I will try to answer,' Timon agreed.

'The murder of the Goodwins, and the other white families in Matabeleland – were those atrocities ordered by Tungata Zebiwe? Is he responsible for those gruesome murders?'

'No, no, Miss Jay. Zebiwe has been trying desperately to control those killers. I believe that he was on his way to Tuti Mission for just such a reason – to meet with the radical Matabele elements and try to reason with them.'

'But the writing in blood, "Tungata Zebiwe Lives"?'

Now Timon Nbebi was silent, his face contorted as though he fought some inner battle, and they waited for him to speak. At last he sighed explosively, and his voice had changed.

'Miss Jay, please try to understand my position, before you judge me for what I am about to tell you. General Fungabera is a persuasive man. I was carried along by his promises of glory and reward. Then suddenly I had gone too far and I was not able to turn back. I think the English expression is "riding the tiger". I was forced to move on from one bad deed to another even worse.' He paused, and then, in a rush, 'Miss Jay, I personally recruited the killers of the Goodwin family from the rehabilitation centre. I

263

told them where to go, what to do – and what to write on the wall. I supplied their weapons, and arranged for them to be driven to the area in transport of the Third Brigade.'

There was silence again, broken only by the throb of the Land-Rover engine, and Timon Nbebi had to break it, speaking as though words were an opiate for his guilt.

'They were Matabele, veterans, war-hard men, men who would do anything for the return of their personal liberty, the chance to carry weapons again. They did not hesitate.'

'And Fungabera ordered it?' Craig asked.

'Of course. It was his excuse to begin the purge of the Matabele. Now perhaps you understand why I am fleeing with you. I could not continue along this path.'

'The other murders – the killing of Senator Savage and his family?' Sally-Anne asked.

'General Fungabera did not have to order those,' Timon shook his head. 'Those were copy-cat murders. The bush is still full of wild men from the war. They hide their weapons and come into the towns, some even have regular jobs, but at the weekend or on a public holiday, they return to the bush, dig up their rifles and go on the rampage. They are not political dissidents, they are armed bandits and the white families are the juiciest, softest targets, rich and helpless, deprived of their weapons by Mugabe's government so they cannot defend themselves.'

'And it all plays right into Peter Fungabera's hands. Any bandit is labelled a political dissident, any grisly robbery an excuse to continue the purge, held up to the world as proof of the savagery and intractability of the Matabele tribe,' Craig continued for him.

'That is correct, Mr Mellow.'

'And he has already murdered Tungata Zebiwe—' Craig felt old and tired with regret and guilt for his old comrade ' – you can be sure of that!'

'No, Mr Mellow.' Timon shook his head. 'I do not

believe that Zebiwe is dead. I believe General Fungabera wants him alive. He has some plans for him.'

'What plans?' Craig demanded.

'I do not know for certain, but I believe Peter Fungabera is dealing with the Russians.'

'The Russians?' Craig showed his disbelief.

'He has had secret meetings with a stranger, a foreigner, a man who I believe is an important member of Russian intelligence.'

'Are you sure, Timon?'

'I have seen the man with my own eyes.'

Craig thought about that for a few seconds, and then reverted to his original question.

'Okay, leave the Russians for the moment – where is Tungata Zebiwe? Where is Fungabera holding him?'

'Again, I do not know, I'm sorry, Mr Mellow.'

'If he is alive, then may the Lord have mercy on his soul,' Craig whispered.

He could imagine what Tungata must be suffering. He was silent for a few minutes and then he changed the line of questioning.

'General Fungabera has seized my property for himself, not for the state? I am correct in believing that?'

'The general wanted that land very badly. He spoke of it often.'

'How? I mean, even quasi-legally, how will he work it?'

'It is very simple,' Timon explained. 'You are an admitted enemy of the state. Your property is forfeited. It will be confiscated to the state. The Land Bank will repudiate the suretyship for your loan under the release clause which you signed. The custodian of enemy property will put up your shares of Rholands Company for sale by private tender. General Fungabera's tender will be accepted – his brother-in-law is custodian of enemy property. The tender price will be greatly advantageous to the general.'

265

'I bet,' said Craig bitterly.

'But why should he go to such lengths?' Sally-Anne demanded. 'He must be a millionaire many times over. Surely he has enough already?'

'Miss Jay. For some men there is no such thing as enough.'

'He cannot hope to get away with it, surely?'

'Who is there to prevent him doing so, Miss Jay?' And when she did not reply, Timon went on, 'Africa is going back to where it was before the white man intruded. There is only one criterion for a ruler here and that is strength. We Africans do not trust anything else. Fungabera is strong, as Tungata Zebiwe was once strong.' Timon glanced at his wrist-watch. 'But we must eat. I think we will have a long day ahead of us.'

He pulled off the track, and drove the Land-Rover into a patch of second-growth scrub. He climbed onto the bonnet and arranged branches to cover the vehicle, hiding it from detection from the air, and then opened the case of emergency rations from the locker under the passenger seat. There was water in the tank under the floorboards.

Craig filled a metal canteen with sand and soaked the sand with gasoline from the reserve tank. It made a smokeless burner on which to brew tea. They ate the unappetizing cold rations with little conversation.

Once Timon turned up the volume on the radio to listen to a transmission, then shook his head.

'Nothing to do with us.' He came back to squat beside Craig.

'How far to the border, do you reckon?' Craig asked with a mouth full of cold, sticky bully beef.

'Forty miles, or a little more.'

The radio crackled to life again, and Timon jumped up, and stooped over it attentively.

'There is a unit of the Third Brigade just a few miles ahead of us,' he reported. 'They are at the mission station at Empandeni. There has been action against dissidents, but they had dealt with them and they are moving out. Perhaps this way. We must be careful.'

'I will check that we are hidden from the road.' Craig stood up. 'Sally-Anne, douse the fire! Captain, cover me!'

He picked up the AK 47 and ran back to the track. Critically he examined the patch of scrub that concealed the Land-Rover and then brushed over his own tracks and those of the vehicle with a leafy twig, and carefully straightened the grass that the Land-Rover had flattened where it left the road. It wasn't perfect, but it would bear a cursory examination from a speeding vehicle, he thought, and then there was a faint vibration on the windless air. He listened. The sound of truck motors, strengthening. Craig ran back to the Land-Rover and climbed into the front seat beside Timon.

'Put your rifle back in the rack,' Timon said, and when Craig hesitated, 'Please do as I say, Mr Mellow. If they find us, it will be useless to fight. I will have to try and talk our way through. I couldn't explain if you were armed.'

Reluctantly Craig passed the weapon back to Sally-Anne. She racked it and Craig was left feeling naked and vulnerable. He clenched his fists in his lap. The sound of motors grew swiftly, and then over them the voices of men singing. The song grew louder, and despite his tension Craig felt the hair prickle on the nape of his neck to the peculiar beauty of African voices raised in song.

'Third Brigade,' Timon said. 'That is the "Song of the Rain Winds", the praise song of the regiment.'

Neither of them replied, and Timon hummed the tune to himself, and then began to sing softly. He had a startlingly true and thrilling voice.

'When the nation burns, the rain winds bring relief,
When the cattle are drought-stricken, the rain winds
    lift them up,

When your children cry with thirst, the rain winds
　　slake them,
We are the winds that bring the rain,
We are the good winds of the nation.'

Timon translated from the Shona for their benefit, and
now Craig could see the grey dust of the trucks smoking up
above the scrub, and the singing was close and clear.

There was a flash of reflected sunlight off metal, and
then through the foliage Craig caught quick glimpses of
the passing convoy. There were three trucks, painted a dull
sand colour, and the backs were crowded with soldiers in
battle camouflage and bush hats, their weapons held ready
at the high port position. On the cab of the last truck rode
an officer, the only one of them wearing the red beret and
silver cap-badge. He looked directly at Craig, and seemed
very close, the screen of foliage suddenly very sparse. Craig
shrank back in his seat.

Then, thankfully, the convoy was past, the rumble of
engines and the singing dwindling, the pale dust settling.

Timon Nbebi exhaled a long breath. 'There will be
others,' he cautioned, and, with his fingers on the ignition
key, waited until the silence was complete once again.
Then he started the Land-Rover, reversed out of the scrub
and turned back onto the track.

He swung the Land-Rover in the opposite direction
from the convoy, and they drove over the rugged tracks
that the trucks had imprinted deeply into the sandy earth.
They drove for another twenty minutes before Timon
ducked down abruptly in his seat, to peer up at the sky
through the windshield.

'Smoke,' he said. 'Empandeni is just ahead. Will you
have your camera ready, Miss Jay? I believe the Third
Brigade will have left something for you.'

They came to the maize fields that surrounded the
mission village. The maize stalks had dried, the cobs in

their yellow sheaths were beginning to droop heavily, ready for the harvest. There had been women working in the fields. One of them lay beside the track. She had been shot in the back as she ran, the bullet had exited between her breasts. The unweaned child that she carried on her back had been bayoneted, many times. The flies rose up in a blue hum as they passed and then settled again.

Nobody spoke. Sally-Anne reached into her camera-bag and brought out her Nikon. She was bloodless grey under her freckles.

The other women lay further from the road, mere bundles of gay cloth, heavily stained. There were possibly fifty huts in the village, all of them were burning, the thatched roofs torching up to the clear blue morning sky. They had thrown most of the corpses into the burning huts, leaving black puddles drying where they had fallen and drag marks in the dust. The smell of seared flesh was very strong, it coated the roofs of their mouths like congealed pork fat. Craig's stomach heaved, and he covered his mouth and nose with his hand.

'These are dissidents?' Sally-Anne whispered. Her lips were icy white. The motor drive of her Nikon whirred as she shot through the open window.

They had killed the chickens, the loose feathers rolled on the light breeze, like the stuffing from a burst pillow.

'Stop!' Sally-Anne ordered.

'It is dangerous to stay,' said Timon.

'Stop,' Sally-Anne repeated.

She left the door open, and went among the huts. Working swiftly, changing roll after roll of film with practised nimble fingers, while her white lips trembled and her eyes behind the lens were huge with horror.

'We must move on,' said Timon.

'Wait.' Sally-Anne moved quickly forward, doing her job like the professional she was. She moved behind a group of huts. The smell of burning flesh nauseated Craig, and the heat from the fires came at him in great furnace gusts as the breeze veered.

Sally-Anne screamed and the two men jumped from the Land-Rover and ran, cocking their rifles, diverging to give each other covering fire, Craig finding his old training returning instinctively. He came around the side of a hut.

Sally-Anne stood in the open, no longer able to use her camera. A naked black woman lay at her feet. The woman's upper body was that of a comely, healthy young woman, below her navel she was a pink skinless monstrosity. She had dragged herself back out of the fire into which they had thrown her. There were places on her lower body where the burning was not deep, here the flesh was piebald pink and weeping lymph. Then in other places the bone was exposed; her hip-bone, charred black as charcoal, protruded obscenely from the scorched meat of her pelvic area. The lining of her stomach had burned through and her entrails bulged from the opening. Miraculously, she was still alive. Her fingers raked the dust with a repetitive, mechanical movement. Her mouth opened and closed convulsively, making no sound, and her eyes were wide open, aware and suffering.

'Go back to the Land-Rover, please, Miss Jay,' Timon Nbebi said. 'There is nothing you can do to help her.'

Sally-Anne stood stiffly, unable to move. Craig put his arms around her shoulders and turned her away. He led her back towards the Land-Rover.

At the corner of the burning hut Craig glanced back. Timon Nbebi had moved up close to the maimed woman, he stood over her with the AK 47 held ready on his hip, his whole attention was focused upon her and his face was almost as riven with suffering as was the woman's.

Craig took Sally-Anne around the hut. Behind them there was the whip-crack of a single shot, muted by the crackle of flames all around them. Sally-Anne stumbled and then caught her balance. When they reached the

Land-Rover, Sally-Anne leaned against the cab and doubled over slowly. She vomited in the dust and then straightened up and wiped her mouth with the back of her hand.

Craig took the bottle of cane spirit from the cubby hole. There was an inch of the clear liquor remaining. He gave it to Sally-Anne and she drank it like water. Craig took the empty bottle back from her, and then abruptly and savagely hurled it into the burning hut.

Timon Nbebi came around the hut. Wordlessly he climbed behind the steering-wheel and Craig helped Sally-Anne into the rear seat. They drove slowly through the rest of the village, their heads turning from side to side as each fresh horror was revealed.

As they passed the little church of red brick, the roof collapsed in upon itself, and the wooden cross on the spire was swallowed in a belch of sparks and flames and blue smoke. In the bright sunlight the flames were almost colourless.

T imon Nbebi used the radio the way a navigator uses an echo sounder to find the channel through shoal water.

The Third Brigade road-blocks and ambushes were reporting over the VHF net to their area headquarters, giving their positions as part of their routine reports, and Timon pin-pointed them on his map.

Twice they avoided road-blocks by taking side-tracks and cattle paths, groping forward carefully through the acacia forest. Twice more they came to small villages, mere cattle stations, homes of two or three Matabele families. The Third Brigade had preceded them, and the crows and vultures had followed, picking at the partially roasted carcasses in the warm ashes of the burned-out huts.

They kept moving westwards, when the tracks allowed. At each prominence that afforded a view ahead, Timon parked in cover and Craig climbed to the crest to scout ahead. In every direction he looked, the towering blue of the sky above the wide horizon was marred by standing columns of smoke from burning villages. Westwards still they crawled, and the terrain changed swiftly as they approached the edge of the Kalahari Desert. There were fewer and still fewer features. The land levelled into a grey, monotonous plain, burning endlessly under the high merciless sun. The trees became stunted, their branches heat-tortured as the limbs of cripples. This was a land able to support only the most rudimentary human needs, the beginning of the great wilderness. Still they edged westwards into it.

The sun made its noon and slid down the sky, and they had made good a mere thirty miles since dawn. Still at least another twenty miles to reach the border, Craig estimated from the map, and all three of them were exhausted from the unremitting strain and the heat in the unlined metal cab.

In the middle of the afternoon, they stopped again for a few minutes. Craig brewed tea, Sally-Anne went behind a low clump of thorn scrub nearby and squatted out of view, while Timon hunched over the radio.

'There are no more villages ahead,' Timon said as he retuned the set. 'I think we are clear, but I have never been further than this. I am not sure what to expect.'

'I worked here with Tungata when we were in the Game Department. That was back in '72. We followed a pride of cattle-killing lions nearly a hundred miles across the border. It's bad country – no surface water, soft going with salt-pans and—' he broke off as Timon signalled him urgently to silence.

Timon had picked up another voice on the radio. It was more authoritative, more cutting than the reports of the platoon he had been monitoring. Clearly it was demanding priority and clearing the net for an urgent flash. Timon Nbebi stiffened, and exclaimed under his breath.

'What is it?' Craig could not contain his forebodings, but Timon held up a hand for silence and listened to the long staccato transmission that followed in Shona. When the carrier beam of the radio went mute, he looked up at them.

'A patrol has picked up the three men we marooned this morning. That was an alert to all units. General Fungabera has given top priority to our recapture. Two spotter aircraft have been diverted to this area. They should be overhead very soon. The general has calculated our position with great accuracy, he has ordered the punitive units to the east of us to abandon their missions and to move in this direction immediately. He has guessed that we are trying to reach the border south of Plumtree and the railway-line. He is rushing two platoons down from the main border-post at Plumtree to block us.' He paused, took off his spectacles and polished the lenses on the tail of his silk cravat. Without his spectacles, he was as myopic as an owl in daylight.

'General Fungabera has given the "leopard" code to all units—' He paused again, and then almost apologetically explained, 'The "leopard" code is the "kill on sight" order, which is rather bad news, I'm afraid.'

Craig snatched the map and unrolled it on the bonnet. Sally-Anne came back and stood close behind them.

'We are here,' he said, and Timon nodded agreement. 'This is the only track from here on, and it angles northwards about west-north-west,' Craig muttered to himself. 'The patrol from Plumtree must come down it to meet us, and the punitive groups must come up it behind us.'

Again Timon nodded. 'This time they won't drive past us. They'll be on the lookout.'

The radio came alive again and Timon darted back to

273

it. His expression became even more lugubrious as he listened.

'The punitive unit behind us has picked up the tracks of the Land-Rover. They are not far behind and they are coming up fast,' he reported. 'They have contacted the patrol on the road ahead of us. We are boxed in. I don't know what to do, Mr Mellow. They'll be here in a few minutes.' And he looked appealingly at Craig.

'All right.' Craig took control quite naturally. 'We'll go for the border cross-country.'

'But you said that is bad country—' Timon began.

'Put her into four-wheel drive and get going,' Craig snapped. 'I'll ride on the roofrack to guide you. Sally-Anne, take the front seat.'

Perched on the roofrack, the AK 47 slung over one shoulder, Craig took a sight with the hand-bearing compass from Timon's map-case, made a rough calculation of the magnetic deflection, and called down to Timon.

'Right, turn right – that's it. Hold that course.' He was lined up on the white glare of a small salt-pan a few miles ahead, and the surface under them seemed firm and reasonably fast. The Land-Rover accelerated away, barging through the low thorn scrub, weaving only when they came to coarser thorn or one of the stunted trees. Craig called corrections after every deviation.

They were making twenty-five miles an hour, and it was clear as far as the horizon. The pursuing trucks, heavy and cumbersome, couldn't outrun them, Craig was sure, and the border was less than an hour ahead, darkness not far off. That cup of tea had cheered him, and Craig felt his spirits lift.

'All right, you bastards, come and get us!' he challenged the unseen enemy and laughed into the wind. He had forgotten the way adrenalin buzzed in the blood when danger was close. Once he had thrived on the feel of it, and the addiction was still there, he realized.

He swivelled and looked back, and saw it immediately – like a little willy-willy, the dust devils that dance on the desert in the hot stillness of midday, but this dust cloud was moving with purpose, and it was exactly where he had expected to find it, due east of them and coming fast down the road they had just left.

'I have one patrol in sight,' he leaned out and shouted down to the open driver's window. 'They are about five miles behind.'

Then he looked back again, and grimaced at their own dust cloud thrown up by the four-wheel drive. It followed them like a bridal train and hung for minutes after they had passed, a long pale smear above the scrub. They could hardly miss it. He was watching the dust when he should have been looking ahead. The ant-bear hole was screened from the driver's view by the pale desert grass. They hit it at twenty-five miles an hour, and it stopped them dead.

Craig was hurled forward off the roof, flying out over the bonnet to hit the earth with his elbows and his knees and the side of his face. He lay in the dust, stunned and hurting. Then he rolled into a sitting position and spat muddy blood from his mouth. He checked his teeth with his tongue, and they were all firm. There was no skin on his elbows, and blood seeped through the knees of his jeans. He fumbled at the strap of his leg and it was intact. He dragged himself to his feet.

The Land-Rover was down heavily on her left front, chassis deep in the hole. He limped to the passenger side, cursing his own inattention, and jerked the door open. The windscreen was cracked and starred where Sally-Anne's head had hit, and she was slumped forward in the seat.

'Oh God!' he whispered, and lifted her head gently. There was a lump the size of a blue acorn over her eye, but when he touched her cheek, her vision focused and she looked at him.

'Are you hurt badly?'

She struggled upright. 'You are bleeding,' she mumbled, like a drunk.

'It's a graze,' he reassured her, and squeezed her arm, looking across her at Timon.

His mouth had struck the steering-wheel, his upper lip was cut through and one of his incisors had broken off at the gum. His mouth was full of blood, and he staunched it with the silk scarf.

'Get her in reverse,' Craig ordered him, and pulled Sally-Anne from the cab to lighten the vehicle. She staggered a few paces and flopped down on her backside, still groggy and confused from the head blow.

The engine had stalled, and it baulked at the starter while Craig fretted and watched the dust cloud behind them. It was no longer distant, and it was coming on fast. At last the engine caught, stuttered and then roared as Timon trod too heavily on the pedal. He let out the clutch with a bang, and all four wheels spun wildly.

'Easy, man, you'll break a halfshaft,' Craig snarled at him.

Timon tried again, more gently, but again the wheels spun, blowing out dust behind them, and the vehicle rocked crazily but remained bogged down.

'Stop it!' Craig pounded Timon's shoulder to make him obey. The spinning wheels in the soft earth were digging the Land-Rover into its own grave. Craig dropped on his belly and peered under the chassis. The left front wheel had dropped into the hole, and was turning in air; the weight of the vehicle rested on the blades of the front suspension.

'Trenching-tool,' Craig called to Timon.

'We left them,' Timon reminded him, and Craig went at the earth on the rim of the hole with his bare hands.

'Find something to dig with!' He kept on digging frantically.

Timon hunted in the back locker and brought him the jack handle and a broad-bladed panga. Craig attacked the edge of the hole with them, grunting and panting, his own sweat stinging the open graze on his cheek.

The radio jabbered. 'They have found the spot where we left the road,' Timon translated.

'Christ!' Craig sobbed with effort, that was less than two miles back.

'Can I help you?' Timon was lisping through the gap in his teeth.

Craig did not bother to reply. There was only room for one man at a time to work under the chassis. The earth crumbled and the Land-Rover subsided a few inches, and then the free tyre found purchase in the bottom of the hole. Craig turned his attention to the sharp edge of the hole, cutting it away in a ramp so that it would not block the wheel.

'Sally-Anne, you get behind the steering-wheel.' He spoke jerkily between each blow with the panga. 'Timon and I will try to lift the front.' He crawled out from under the body, and wasted a second to look back. The dust of the pursuit was clearly visible from ground level. 'Come on, Timon.'

They stood shoulder to shoulder in front of the radiator, and bent their knees to get a good grip on the front fender. Sally-Anne sat behind the dust-smeared windscreen. The lump on her forehead looked like a huge, blue, blood-sucking tick clinging to her pale skin. She stared at Craig through the glass, her eyes and her expression desperate.

'Hit it!' Craig grunted and they straightened together, lifting with their knees and all the strength of their bodies. Craig felt the front end come up a few inches on the suspension and he nodded at Sally-Anne. She let out the clutch and the engine blustered, the wheel spun, and she jerked back and then stuck fast, blocking on the edge of the hole.

'Rest!' Craig grunted, and they slumped gasping over the bonnet.

Craig saw the dust of the pursuit was so close that he expected the trucks to appear beneath it as he watched.

'Okay, we'll bounce her,' he told Timon. 'Hit it! One! Two! Three!'

While Sally-Anne raced the engine, they flung their weight on the fender in a short regular rhythm. 'One! Two! Three!' Craig gasped, and the vehicle started surging and bouncing wildly against the rim of the hole.

'Keep her going!'

Dust boiled around them, and the voice on the radio yelped exultantly like a lead hound taking the scent. They had seen the dust.

'Keep it up!'

Craig found strength and reserves that he had never known were there. His teeth ground together, his breath whined in his throat, his face swelled dark angry red, and his vision starred and filled with shooting light. Still he heaved, and knew that the sinew and muscle in his back was tearing, his spine felt as though it was crushing – and suddenly the Land-Rover's wheels bounced over the rim and it shot backwards, clear and free.

Deprived of support, Craig fell on his knees, and thought he did not have the strength to rise again.

'Craig! Hurry!' Sally-Anne yelled at him. 'Get in!'

With another vast effort, he heaved himself upright, and staggered to the moving Land-Rover. He dragged himself up onto the bonnet, and Sally-Anne accelerated away; for long seconds Craig clung to the bonnet, as strength oozed back into his limbs. He crawled up onto the roofrack, and peered over the back of the cab.

There was only one truck behind them, a five-ton Toyota painted the familiar sand colour. Through the shimmer of heat mirage, it appeared monstrous, seeming to float towards them, disembodied from the earth. Craig blinked the sweat out of his eyes. How close was it? Hard to tell over level ground and through the mirage.

His vision cleared, and he saw that the ungainly black superstructure above the Toyota's cab was a heavy machine-gun on a ring mount with the gunner's head behind it. It looked at this distance to be the modified Goryunov Stankovy, a nasty weapon.

'Sweet Jesus!' he whispered, as for the first time he became aware of the Land-Rover's altered motion. She was vibrating and shaking brutally, and there was the shrill protest of metal bearing on metal from the left front end where she had hit – and the speed was down, way down.

Craig leaned out and yelled into the driver's window.

'Speed up!'

'She's busted up front.' Sally-Anne stuck her head out of the window. 'Any faster and she'll tear herself to pieces.'

Craig looked back. The truck was closing, not rapidly, but inexorably. He saw the gunner on the cab roof traverse his weapon slightly.

'Go for it, Sally-Anne!' he shouted. 'Take a chance of it holding. They've got a heavy machine-gun and they're coming into range.'

The Land-Rover lumbered forward, and now there was a heavy clattering combined with the whine of metal. The vibration chattered Craig's teeth, and he looked back. They were holding the truck off – and then he saw the pursuing vehicle judder to the recoil of the heavy weapon on the cab.

No sound of gunfire yet, Craig watched with an academic interest. Abruptly dust fountained close down their left flank, jumping six feet into the heated air in a diaphanous curtain, appearing ethereal and harmless, but the sound of passing shot spranged viciously like a copper telegraph wire hit with an iron bar.

'Turn left!' Craig yelled. Always turn towards the fall of shot. The gunner will be correcting the opposite way, and the dust will help obscure his aim.

The next burst fell right and very wide.

'Turn right!' Craig shouted.

'Shoot back at them!' Sally-Anne stuck her head out again. She was obviously recovering from the head knock, and getting fighting mad.

'I'm giving the orders,' he told her. 'You keep driving.'

The next burst was wide again, a hundred feet out.

'Turn left!'

Their weaving was confusing the gunner's aim, and their dust obscuring the range, but it was costing them ground. The truck was gaining on them again.

The salt-pan was close ahead, hundreds of bare acres shimmering silver in the path of the sun. Craig narrowed his eyes against the glare, and picked up the tracks where a small herd of zebra had crossed the smooth surface. Their hooves had broken through the salt crust into the yellow mush beneath. It would bog any vehicle that attempted that deceptively inviting crossing.

'Angle to miss the right edge of the pan – left! More! More! Okay, hold that,' he shouted.

There was a narrow horn of salt-pan extending out towards them, perhaps he could tempt the pursuit to take the cut across it. He stared back over their own dust cloud and said, 'Shit!' softly.

The truck commander was too canny to try to cut across the horn. He was following them around, and a burst of machine-gun fire fell all around them. Three rounds crashed into the metal of the cab, leaving jagged craters rimmed with shiny metal where the camouflage paint flaked off.

'Are you okay?'

'Okay!' Sally-Anne called back, but the tone of her voice was no longer so cocky. 'Craig, I can't keep her going. I've got my foot flat and she is slowing down. Something is binding up!'

Now Craig could smell red-hot metal from the damaged front end.

'Timon, hand me up a rifle!'

They were still well out of range of the AK 47, but the burst he fired made him feel less helpless, even though he could not even mark the fall of his bullets. They roared around the horn of the salt-pan, in the stink of hot metal and dust, and Craig looked ahead while he reloaded the rifle.

How far to the border now? Ten miles perhaps? But would a punitive patrol of the Third Brigade, given the 'leopard' code, stop at an international border? The Israelis and South Africans had long ago set a precedent for 'hot pursuit' into neutral territory. He knew they would follow them to the death.

The Land-Rover lurched rhythmically now to her unbalanced suspension and for the first time Craig knew that they weren't going to make it. The realization made him angry. He fired the second magazine in short-spaced bursts, and at the third burst the Toyota swerved sharply and stopped in a billow of its own dust.

'I got him!' he bellowed exultantly.

'Way to go!' Sally-Anne shouted back. 'Geronimo!'

'Well done, Mr Mellow, jolly well done.'

The truck stood massively immobile while the wreaths of dust subsided around it.

'Eat that!' Craig howled. 'Stick that up your rear end, you sons of porcupines!' And he emptied the rifle at the distant vehicle.

Men were swarming around the cab of the truck like black ants around the carcass of a beetle, and the Land-Rover limped away from them gamely.

'Oh, no,' Craig groaned.

The silhouette of the truck altered as it turned back

towards them, once again dust rose in a feathery tail behind it.

'They are coming on!'

Perhaps he had fluked a hit on the driver, but whatever damage he had inflicted, it was not permanent. It had stopped them for less than two minutes and now, if anything, the truck was coming on faster than before. As if to emphasize that fact, another burst of heavy machine-gun fire hit the Land-Rover with a crash.

In the cab, somebody screamed, and the sound was shrill and feminine. Craig went cold, not daring to ask, clinging to the roofrack, frozen with dread.

'Timon's been hit.' Sally-Anne's voice – and Craig's heart raced with relief.

'How bad?'

'Bad. He's bleeding all over.'

'We can't stop. Keep going.'

Craig looked desperately ahead, and there was a great nothingness stretched before him. Even the stunted trees had disappeared. It was flat and featureless, the reflection from the white pans turned the sky milky pale and smudged the horizon so that there was no clear dividing line between earth and air, nothing to hold the eye.

Craig dropped his gaze, and shouted, 'Stop!'

To enforce the order he stamped on the roof of the cab with all his strength. Sally-Anne reacted instantly, and locked the brakes. The crippled Land-Rover skidded broadside, and came up short.

The cause of Craig's urgency was an apparently innocuous little yellow ball of fur, not as big as a football. It hopped in front of the vehicle, on long kangaroo back legs, totally out of proportion to the rest of its body, and then abruptly disappeared into the earth.

'Spring hare!' Craig called. 'A huge colony, right across our front.'

'Kangaroo rats!' Sally-Anne leaned out of the window, the engine idling, turning her face up to his for guidance.

They had been fortunate. The spring hare was almost entirely nocturnal, the single animal outside the burrows was an exceptional warning in daylight. Only now, under close scrutiny, could Craig make out the extent of the colony. There were tens of thousands of burrows, the entrances inconspicuous little mounds of loose earth, but Craig knew that the sandy soil beneath them would be honeycombed with the interlinking burrows, the entire area undermined to a depth of four feet or so.

That ground would not bear the weight of a mounted man, let alone the Land-Rover. With the engine idling, Craig could clearly hear the roar of the truck behind them, and machine-gun fire whiplashed over them, so close that Craig ducked instinctively.

'Turn left!' he shouted. 'Back towards the pan.'

They turned at right-angles across the front of the approaching truck, machine-gun fire goading them on, Timon's groans reaching Craig above the engine beat. He closed his ears to them.

'There is no way through!' Sally-Anne called. The spring-hare burrows were everywhere.

'Keep going,' Craig answered her. The truck had swung to cut them off, closing very swiftly now.

'There!' Craig cried with relief. As he had guessed, the spring-hare colony stopped short of the salt-pan's edge, avoiding the brackish seepage from the pan. There was a narrow bridge through, and Craig guided Sally-Anne into it. Within five hundred paces they were over the bridge with the ground firm ahead. Sally-Anne pushed the Land-Rover to its limit, directly away from the pursuit.

'No! No!' Craig called. 'Turn right, hard right.' She hesitated. 'Do it, damn you!' And suddenly she saw what he intended, and she spun the steering-wheel, running back in the opposite direction across the front of the approaching truck.

Immediately the truck turned to head them off again, turning away from the pan, and from the bridge of firm ground through the subterranean maze of burrows. It was so close that they could see the heads of the troopers in the open back, catch the colour of a burgundy-red beret and the bright spark of a silver cap-badge, hear the fierce, bloodthirsty yells, see an AK 47 rifle brandished triumphantly.

Machine-gun fire ploughed up the earth ten feet ahead of the Land-Rover and they tore into the standing dust.

Craig was blazing away with the AK 47, trying to keep the driver's attention off the ground ahead of the truck.

'Please! Please, let it happen,' he pleaded as he changed the magazine on the hot rifle. And the gods were listening. The truck went into the undermined ground at full bore.

It was like an elephant running into a pitfall. The earth opened and swallowed her down, and as she went in she toppled to one side hurling the load of armed men out of the back. When the dust rolled aside, she was half buried, lying on her side. Human bodies were strewn around her, some of them beginning to drag themselves upright, others lying where they had been thrown.

'That's it!' Craig shouted down. 'They'll need a bull-dozer to get out of that.'

'Craig!' she called back. 'Timon is in a bad way. Can't you help him?'

'Stop for a second.'

Craig dropped off the roof, and scrambled into the back seat, and immediately Sally-Anne drove on.

Timon was lying sprawled half off the seat, his head thrown back and pillowed against the door. He had lost his glasses. His breathing gargled in his throat, and the back of his battle-jacket was a soggy mess of blood. Craig eased him cautiously back in the seat and unzipped his jacket.

He was appalled. The bullet must have come in through the metal cab, and been deformed by the impact into a primitive dum-dum. It had torn a hole the size of a demi-tasse coffee cup in Timon's back. There was no exit wound. The bullet was still in there.

There was a first-aid box clamped to the dashboard. Craig took out two field dressings, stripped the wrappers and wadded them over the wound. Hampered by the Land-Rover's erratic and violent motion, he strapped them tightly.

'How is he?' Sally-Anne took her eyes off the ground ahead for a moment.

'He's going to be okay,' Craig said for Timon's benefit, but to Sally-Anne he shook his head and mouthed a silent denial.

Timon was a dead man. It was merely a matter of an hour or two. Nobody could survive a wound like that. The smell of hot metal in the cab was suffocating.

'I can't breathe,' Timon whispered, and sawed for breath.

Craig had hoped he was unconscious, but Timon's eyes were focusing on his face. Craig knocked out the Perspex pane of the window above Timon's head with his fist, to give him more air.

'My glasses,' Timon said. 'I can't see.'

Craig found the steel-rimmed spectacles on the floor between the seats, and placed them on the bridge of his nose, hooking the side frames over his ears.

'Thank you, Mr Mellow.' Incredibly, Timon smiled. 'It doesn't look as though I'll be coming with you, after all.'

Craig was surprised by the strength of his own regret. He gripped Timon's shoulder firmly, hoping that physical contact might comfort him a little.

'The truck?' Timon asked.

'We knocked it out.'

'Good for you, sir.'

As he spoke, the cab filled with the smell of burning rubber and oil.

'We're on fire!' Sally-Anne cried, and Craig whipped around in the seat.

The front end of the Land-Rover was burning, red hot metal from the damaged bearing had ignited the grease and rubber of the front tyre. Almost immediately the bearing seized up completely, and although the engine roared vainly, they ground to a halt. The slipping clutch burned out, more smoke spewing out from under the chassis.

'Switch off!' Craig ordered and banged open the door, grabbing the fire-extinguisher from its rack on the door-post.

He sprayed a white cloud of powder over the burning front end, snuffing out the flames almost instantly, and then unhitched and lifted the bonnet, scalding his fingers on hot metal. He sprayed the engine compartment to prevent a resurgence of the fire, and then stood back.

'Well,' he said with finality. 'This bus isn't going anywhere any more!'

The silence after the engine roar and the gunfire was overpowering. The pinking of cooling metal from the body of the Land-Rover sounded loud as cymbals. Craig walked to the rear of the cab and looked back. The bogged truck was out of sight behind them in the heat haze. The silence buzzed in his ears and the loneliness of the desert bore down upon him with a physical weight and substance, seeming to slow his movements and his thinking.

His mouth felt chalky dry from the adrenalin hangover.

'Water!' He went quickly to the reserve tank under the seat, unscrewed the cap and checked the level.

'At least twenty-five litres.'

There was an aluminium canteen hanging beside the AK 47 in the rack, left by one of the grave-diggers. Craig topped it up from the tank, and then took it to Timon.

Timon drank gratefully, gulping and choking in his haste to swallow. Then he lay back panting. Craig passed the canteen to Sally-Anne and then drank himself. Timon seemed a little easier, and Craig checked the dressings. The bleeding was staunched for the moment.

'The first rule of desert survival,' Craig reminded himself, 'stay with the vehicle.'

But it didn't apply here. The vehicle would draw the pursuit like a beacon. Timon had mentioned spotter aircraft. On this open plain they would see the Land-Rover from thirty miles. Then there was the second patrol coming down from the Plumtree border-post. They would be here in a few hours.

They couldn't stay. They had to go on. He looked down at Timon, and understanding flashed between them.

'You'll have to leave me,' Timon whispered.

Craig could not hold his eyes, or reply. Instead he climbed on to the roof again and looked back.

Their tracks showed very clearly on the soft earth, filled with shadows by the lowering angle of the sun. He followed them with the eye towards the hazy horizon, and then started with alarm.

Something moved on the very edge of his vision. For long seconds he hoped it was a trick of light. Then it swelled up again, like a wriggling caterpillar, floated free of earth on a lake of mirage, changed shape once more, anchored itself to earth again and became a line of armed men, running in Indian file, coming in on their tracks. The men of the Third Brigade had not abandoned the chase. They were coming on foot, trotting steadily across the plain. Craig had worked with crack black troops before, he knew that they could keep up that pace for a day and a night.

He jumped down and found Timon's binoculars in the cubby beside the driver's seat.

'There is a foot patrol following us,' he told them.

'How many?' Timon asked.

On the roof he focused the binoculars. 'Eight of them – they took casualties when the truck overturned.'

He looked back at the sun. It was reddening and losing its heat, sinking into the ground haze. Two hours to sunset, he guessed.

'If you move me into a good place, I'll give you delaying fire,' Timon told him. And as Craig hesitated, 'Don't waste time arguing, Mr Mellow.'

'Sally-Anne, refill the canteen,' Craig ordered. 'Take the chocolate and high-protein slabs from the emergency rations. Take the map and the compass and these binoculars.'

He was surveying the fields of fire around the stranded vehicle. No advantage to be wrung from that flat terrain. The only strong point was the Land-Rover itself. He knocked the drain plug out of the bottom of the gasoline tank and let the remaining fuel run into the sandy soil, to prevent a lucky shot torching the vehicle and Timon with it. Swiftly he built a rudimentary screen around the back wheels, placing the spare wheels and the steel toolbox to cover Timon's flanks when they started to enfilade him.

He helped Timon out of the back seat and laid him belly down behind the rear wheels. The bleeding started again, soaking the dressing, and Timon was grey as ash and sweating in bright little bubbles across his upper lip. Craig placed one of the AK 47s in his hands and arranged a seat cushion as an aiming rest in front of him. The box of spare magazines he set at Timon's right hand, five hundred rounds.

'I'll last until dark,' Timon promised in a croak. 'But leave me one grenade.'

They all knew what that was for. Timon did not want to be taken alive. At the very end he would hold the grenade to his own chest and blow it away.

Craig took the remaining five grenades and packed them into one of the rucksacks. He placed the British Airways bag that contained his papers and the book manuscript on top of them. From the toolbox he took a roll of light gauze wire and a pair of side cutters; from the ammunition box, six spare magazines for the AK 47. He divided the contents of the first-aid box, leaving two field dressings, a blister pack of pain-killers and a disposable syringe of morphine for Timon. The rest he tipped into his rucksack.

He glanced quickly around the interior of the Land-Rover. Was there anything else he might need? A rolled plastic groundsheet in camouflage design lay on the floor-boards. He stuffed that into the bag, and hefted it. That was all he could afford to carry. He looked across at Sally-Anne. She had the canteen slung on one shoulder, and the second rucksack on the other. She had rolled the portfolio of photographs and crammed them into the rucksack. She was very pale and the lump on her forehead seemed to have swelled even larger.

'Right?' Craig asked.

'Okay.'

He squatted beside Timon. 'Goodbye, Captain,' he said.

'Goodbye, Mr Mellow.'

Craig took his hand and looked into his eyes. He saw no fear there, and he wondered again at the equanimity with which the African can accept death. He had seen it often.

'Thank you, Timon – for everything,' he said.

'*Hamba gashle*,' said Timon gently. 'Go in peace.'

'*Shala gashle*,' Craig returned the traditional response. 'Stay in peace.'

He stood up and Sally-Anne knelt in his place.

'You are a good man, Timon,' she said, 'and a brave one.'

Timon unfastened the flap of his holster and drew the pistol. It was a Chinese copy of the Tokarev type 51. He reversed it, and handed it to her, butt first. He said nothing, and after a moment she took it from him.

'Thank you, Timon.'

They all knew that, like the grenade, it was for the very end – the easier way out. Sally-Anne pushed the weapon into the belt of her jeans, and then impulsively stooped and kissed Timon.

'Thank you,' she said again, and stood up quickly and turned away.

Craig led her away at a trot. He looked back every few yards, keeping the vehicle directly between them and the approaching patrol. If they suspected that two of them had left the vehicle, they would simply leave half their men to attack it, and circle back onto the spoor again with the rest of the force.

Thirty-five minutes later they heard the first burst of automatic fire. Craig stopped to listen. The Land-Rover was just a little black pimple in the distance, with the dusk darkening and drooping down over it. The first burst was answered by a storm of gunfire, many weapons firing together furiously.

'He's a good soldier,' Craig said. 'He would have made sure of that first shot. There aren't eight of them any more. I'd bet on that.'

With surprise he saw that the tears were running down her cheeks, turning to muddy brown in the dust that coated her skin.

'It's not the dying,' Craig told her quietly, 'but the manner of it.'

She flared at him angrily. 'Keep that literary Hemingway crap to yourself, buster! It's not you that's doing the dying.'

And then, contrite immediately, 'I'm sorry, darling, my head hurts and I liked him so much.'

The sound of gunfire became fainter as they trotted on, until it was just a whisper like footsteps in dry brush far behind them.

'Craig!' Sally-Anne called, and he turned. She had fallen back twenty paces behind him and her distress was apparent. As soon as he stopped, she sank down and put her head between her knees.

'I'll be all right in a moment. It's just my head.'

Craig split open a blister pack of pain-killers from the first-aid box. He made her take two of them and swallow them with a mouthful of water from the canteen. The lump on her forehead frightened him. He put his arm around her and held her tightly.

'Oh, that feels good.' She slumped against him.

On the silence of the desert dusk came the distant woof of an explosion, muted by distance, and Sally-Anne stiffened.

'What's that?'

'Hand grenade,' he told her, and checked his wrist-watch. 'It's over, but he gave us a start of fifty-five minutes. Bless you, Timon, and God speed you.'

'We mustn't waste it,' she told him determinedly and pulled herself to her feet. She looked back. 'Poor Timon,' she said, and then set off again.

It would take them only minutes to discover that there was but one man defending the Land-Rover. They would find the outgoing tracks almost immediately, and they would follow. Craig wondered how many Timon had taken out and how many there were left.

'We'll find out soon enough,' he told himself, and the night came down with the swiftness of a theatre fire-curtain.

New moon three days past, and the only light was from the stars. Orion stood tall on one hand, and the great cross blazed on the other. Through the dry desert air their brilliance was marvellous, and the milky way smeared the heavens like the phosphorescence from a firefly crushed between a child's fingers. The sky was magnificent, but when Craig looked back he saw that it gave enough light to pick out their footprints.

'Rest!' he told Sally-Anne, and she stretched out full-length on the ground. With the bayonet from the AK 47 he chopped a bunch of scrub, wired it together and fastened the wire to the back of his belt.

'Lead!' he told her, saving energy with economy of words. She went ahead of him, no longer at a trot, and he dragged the bunch of dry scrub behind him. It swept the earth, and when he checked again, their footprints had dissolved.

Within the first mile the weight of the scrub dragging like an anchor from his belt was beginning to take its toll on his strength. He leaned forward against it. Three times in the next hour Sally-Anne asked for water. He grudged it to her. Never drink on the first thirst, one of the first survival laws. If you do, it will become insatiable, but she was sick and hurting from the head injury, and he did not have the heart to deny her. He did not drink himself. Tomorrow, if they lived through it, would be a burning hell of thirst. He took the canteen from her, to remove temptation.

A little before midnight, he untied the wire from his belt; the dragging weight of the scrub thorn brush was too much for him, and if the Shona were still on their spoor, it would not serve much further purpose. Instead, he lifted the rucksack from Sally-Anne's back and slung it over his own shoulder.

'I can manage it,' she protested, although she was reeling like a drunkard. She had not complained once, although her face in the starlight was silver as the saltpan they were crossing.

He tried to think of something to comfort her.

'We must have crossed the border hours ago,' he said.

'Does that mean we are safe?' she whispered, and he could not bring himself to lie. She shivered.

The night wind cut through their thin clothing. He unfolded the nylon groundsheet and spread it over her shoulders, then he took her weight on his arm and led her on.

A mile further on they reached the far edge of the saltpan, and he knew she could go no further that night. There was a crusty bank eighteen inches high, and then firm ground again.

'We'll stop here.' She sagged to the ground and he covered her with the groundsheet.

'Can I have a drink?'

'No. Not until morning.'

The water canteen was light, sloshing more than half-empty as he lowered the pack.

He cut a pile of scrub to break the wind and keep it off her head, and then pulled off her jogging shoes, massaging her feet and examining them by touch.

'Oh, that stings.' Her left heel was rubbed raw. He lifted it to his mouth and licked the abrasion clean, saving water. Then he dripped Mercurochrome on it and strapped it with a band-aid from the first-aid kit. He changed her socks from foot to foot, and then laced up her shoes again.

'You're so gentle,' she murmured, as he slipped under the groundsheet and took her in his arms, 'and so warm.'

'I love you,' he said. 'Go to sleep.'

She sighed and snuggled, and he thought she was asleep until she said softly, 'Craig, I'm so sorry about King's Lynn.'

Then, at last, she did sleep, her breathing swelling deeply and evenly against his chest. He eased out from under the groundsheet and left her undisturbed. He went to sit on the low bank with the AK 47 across his knees, keeping the open pan under surveillance, waiting for them to come.

While he kept the watch, he thought about what Sally-Anne had said. He thought about King's Lynn. He thought of his herds of great red beasts, and the homestead on the hill. He thought about the men and the women who had lived there and bred their families there. He thought about the dreams he had fashioned from their lives and how he had planned to do with this woman what they had done.

My woman. He went back to where she lay and knelt over her to listen to her breathing, and he thought about her spread naked and open on the long table under the cruel scrutiny of many eyes.

He went back to wait at the edge of the pan and he thought about Tungata Zebiwe, and remembered the laughter and comradeship they had shared. He saw again the hand-signal from the dock as they led Tungata away.

'We are equal – the score is levelled,' and he shook his head.

He thought about once being a millionaire, and the millions he now owed. From a man of substance he had been reduced in a single stroke to something worse than a pauper. He did not even own the bundle of paper in the British Airways bag. The manuscript would be forfeit, his creditors would take that also. He had nothing, nothing except this woman and his rage.

Then the image of General Peter Fungabera's face filled his imagination – smooth as hot chocolate, handsome as mortal sin, as powerful and as evil as Lucifer – and his rage grew within him, until it threatened to consume him.

He sat through the long night without sleep, hating with all the strength of his being. Every hour he went back to where Sally-Anne slept and squatted beside her. Once he adjusted the groundsheet over her, another time he touched the lump on her forehead lightly with his fingertips and she whimpered in her sleep, then he went back to his vigil.

Once he saw dark shapes out on the pan, and his stomach turned over queasily, but when he put Timon's binoculars on them, he saw they were pale-coloured gemsbok, huge desert gazelle, large as horses, the diamond-patterned face masks that gave them their name showing clearly in the starlight. They passed silently up-wind of where he sat and merged into the night.

Orion hunted down the sky and faded at dawn's first glimmering. It was time to go on, but he lingered, reluctant to put Sally-Anne to the terrors and the trials that day would bring, giving her just those last few minutes of oblivion.

Then he saw them, and his guts and his loins filled with the molten lead of despair. They were still far out across the pan, a darkness too large to be one of the desert animals, a darkness that moved steadily towards him. The scrub brush that he had dragged must have been effective to delay them so long. But once he had abandoned it, they would have come on swiftly down the deeply trodden spoor.

Then his despair changed shape. If it had to come, it might as well be now, he thought, this was as good a place as any to make their last stand. The Shona must come across the open pan, and he had the slight advantage afforded by the bank and the sparse cover of knee-high scrub, but little time in which to exploit them.

He ran back to where he had left his rucksack, keeping doubled over so as to show no silhouette against the lightening sky. He stuffed the five grenades down the front of his shirt, snatched up the roll of wire and the side cutters, and hurried back to the edge of the bank.

He peered out at the advancing patrol. They were in single file because the pan was so open, but he guessed they would spread out into a skirmishing line as soon as they reached the bank, adopting the classic arrowhead running formation that would give them overlapping cover, and prevent them being enfiladed by ambush.

Craig began to place his fragmentation grenades on that assumption. He sited them along the top of the bank, that slight elevation would spread the blast out a little more.

He wired each grenade securely to the stem of a bush, twenty paces apart, and then used a haywire twist to secure a single strand to each of the split pins that held down the firing-handles. Then he led the strands back one at a time to where Sally-Anne slept and secured them to the flap of his rucksack.

He was down on his knees now, for the light was coming up strongly and the patrol was closer each minute. He readied the fifth and last grenade, and this time wriggled back on his belly. The strands of wire were spread out fanlike from where he lay behind the screen of cut brush. He checked the load of the AK 47 and placed the spare magazines at his right hand.

It was time to wake her. He kissed her softly on the lips, and she wrinkled her nose and made little mewing sounds, then she opened her eyes and love dawned green in them for an instant, to be replaced by dismay as she remembered their circumstances. She started to sit up, but he held her down with an arm over her chest.

'They are here,' he warned her. 'I'm going to fight.'

She nodded.

'Have you got Timon's pistol?'

She nodded again, groping for it in the waistband of her jeans.

'You do know how to use it?'

'Yes.'

'Keep one bullet for the end.'

She stared at him.

'Promise you won't hesitate.'

'I promise,' she whispered.

He lifted his head slowly. The patrol was four hundred yards out from the edge of the pan, and as he had guessed, they were already spreading into the arrowhead hunting formation.

As they separated from a single amorphous blot in the poor light, he was able to count them. Five! His spirits dropped again sharply. Timon had not done as well as he had hoped for. He had culled out only three of the original pursuit. Five was too many for Craig. Even with all the advantages of surprise and concealment, it was just too many.

'Keep your face down,' he whispered. 'It can shine like a mirror.' Obediently she dropped it into the crook of her arm. He pulled up his shirt to cover his own mouth and nose, and watched them come on.

Oh God, they are good, he thought. Look at them move! They have been going all night, and they are still as sharp and wary as lynx. The point was a tall Shona who moved like a reed in the wind. He carried his AK 47 low on the right hip, and he was charged with a deadly intensity of concentration. Once the light of coming dawn caught his eyes and they flashed like distant cannon-fire in the blackness of his face. Craig recognized him as the main man.

His drags, two on each side of him, were sombre, stocky figures, full of dark menace and yet subservient to the man who led. They reacted like puppets to the hand-signals that the tall Shona gave them. They came on silently towards the edge of the pan, and Craig arranged the wires across the palm of his left hand and ran them out between his fingers.

Fifty paces from the bank the Shona stopped them with a cut-out signal, and the line froze. The Shona's head turned slowly from side to side as he surveyed the low bank and the scrub beyond it. He took five paces forward, stepping lightly, and stopped again. His head turned once more, back and forth – and then back again. He had seen something. Craig instinctively held his breath as the seconds drew out.

Then the Shona moved again. He swivelled and picked out his flanks, marking them with a stab of his forefinger, and then a pumped fist. Their formation changed into a reversed arrowhead – the Shona had adopted the traditional fighting formation of the Nguni tribes, the 'bull's horns' that King Chaka had used to such terrible effect, and now the horns were moving to invade Craig's position.

Craig felt a surge of relief at his own foresight in spreading the grenades so widely. The two flank men would walk almost on top of his outside grenades. He sorted the wires in his hand, taking up the slack, and watching the flank men come on. He wished it had been the tall Shona, the danger man, but he had not moved again. He was still way back out of blast range, watching and directing the flanking movement.

The man on the right reached the bank, and gingerly stepped up onto it, but the man on the left was still ten paces out on the pan.

'Together,' Craig whispered. 'I've got to take them together.'

The man on the bank must have almost brushed the hidden grenade with his knee as Craig let him overrun it. The man on the left reached the bank, there was a bloody bandage around his head, Timon's work. The grenade would be at about the level of his navel. Craig heaved with all his weight on the two outside wires, and heard the firing handles fly off the grenades with a metallic Twang! Twang!

Three seconds delay on the primers, and the Shona were reacting with trained reflexes. The man on the bank dropped from sight, but Craig judged he was too close to the grenade to survive. The three others out on the pan

298

went down also, firing as they dropped, rolling sideways as they hit the crust, firing again, raking the top of the bank.

Only the trooper out on the left, the wounded man, perhaps slowed by his injury, stayed on his feet those fatal seconds. The grenade exploded with the brilliance of a flashbulb, and the man was hit by fragmenting shrapnel. He was lifted off his feet as the blast tore into his belly. On the right the other grenade burst in brief thunder, and Craig heard the taut, drumlike sound of shrapnel slapping into flesh.

Two of the bastards, he thought, and tried for the tall Shona, but his aim was through scrub and over the lip of the bank, and the Shona was rolling. Craig's first burst kicked white salt inches short, but on line, his second burst was a touch left, and the Shona fired back and kept rolling.

One of the other troopers jumped up and charged the bank, jinking like a quarter-back with the ball, and Craig swung onto him. He hit him cleanly with a full burst, starting at the level of his crotch and pulling up across his belly and chest. The AK 47 was notorious for the way she rode up in automatic and Craig had compensated for it. The trooper dropped his rifle, and spun around sharply, fell onto his knees and then toppled forward on his face like a Muslim at prayer.

The tall Shona was up, coming in, shouting an order, the second man followed him, twenty paces behind. Craig switched his aim back to him exultantly. He couldn't miss now. The AK 47 kicked once, and then snapped on an empty chamber. The Shona kept on coming, untouched.

Craig was not as quick on the reload as he had once been; just that micro-second too late he swung back onto the Shona, and as he squeezed the trigger, the man dropped out of sight, below the rim of the bank, and Craig's burst flew high and harmless.

Craig swore, and swung left onto the last trooper who was just five paces from the safety of the bank. It was snap shooting, but a single lucky bullet out of the long burst hit him in the mouth, and snapped his head back like a heavy punch. The burgundy-red beret, glowing like a pretty bird in the dawn light, flew high in the air, and the trooper collapsed.

Four out of five in the first ten seconds, it was more than Craig could possibly have hoped for, but the fifth man, the danger man, was alive down there below the bank – and he must have marked Craig's muzzle flashes. He had Craig pinpointed.

'Keep under the sheet,' Craig ordered Sally-Anne, and pulled the wires on the other three grenades. The explosions were almost simultaneous, a thunderous roll like the broadside of a man-of-war, and in the dust and flame, Craig moved.

He went forward and right, thirty running paces, doubled over, with the reloaded AK in his hand, and he dived forward and rolled and then waited, belly down, covering the spot below the bank where the Shona had disappeared, but darting quick glances left and right.

The light was better, the dawn coming up fast, and the Shona moved. He came up over the bank, a brief silhouette against the white pan, quick as a mamba but where Craig had not expected him. He must have elbow-walked under the bank, and he was way out on Craig's left.

Craig swung the AK onto him, but held his fire, that quick chance wasn't good enough to betray his new position, and the Shona disappeared into the low brush fifty paces away. Craig crawled forward to intercept, slowly as an earthworm, making no noise, raising no dust, and listening and staring with all his being. Long seconds drew out, slow as treacle, and Craig inched forward, knowing that the Shona must be working towards where he had left Sally-Anne.

Then Sally-Anne screamed. The sound raked his nerve ends like an emery wheel, and out of the brush they rose together, Sally-Anne fighting and clawing like a cat and the Shona holding her by the hair, down on his knees, but holding her easily, turning with her to frustrate any chance of a shot.

Craig charged. It was not a conscious decision. He found himself on his feet, hurling forward, swinging the AK 47 like a club. The Shona saw him, released Sally-Anne and she staggered backwards and fell. The Shona ducked under the swinging rifle, and hit Craig in the ribs with his shoulder as he came off his knees. The rifle flew from Craig's hands, and he grappled, holding desperately as he fought to regain the breath that had been driven out of him. The Shona, realizing that his rifle was useless in hand-to-hand contact, let it fall, and used both arms.

Craig knew in that first moment of contact that the Shona was simply too strong for him. He had height and weight and he was trained to the hardness of black anthracite. He whipped a long arm around the back of Craig's neck, but Craig, instead of resisting, put all his own weight into the direction of the Shona's pull. It took him by surprise, and they cartwheeled. As he went over, Craig kicked out with the metal leg – but he didn't connect cleanly.

The Shona twisted and struck back at him. Craig smothered it and they locked, chest to chest, rolling first one on top, then the other, flattening the coarse scrub, their breathing hissing into each other's face. The Shona snapped like a wolf at Craig's face with his square white teeth. If he got a grip, he would bite off Craig's nose or rip his cheek away. Craig had seen it done before in beerhall brawls.

Instead of pulling his head back, Craig butted forward with his forehead, and hit him in the mouth. One of the Shona's incisors snapped off at the gum and his mouth glutted with blood. Craig reared back to butt him again, but the Shona shifted over him and suddenly he had the trench knife out of its scabbard on his belt. Craig grabbed his wrist desperately, only just smothering the stab.

They rolled and the Shona came out on top, straddling Craig, the knife in his right hand probing with the bright silver point for Craig's throat and face. Craig got both hands to it, one on the Shona's wrist, the other into the crook of his elbow, but he couldn't hold him. The knife point descended slowly towards him, and the Shona kicked his legs and locked one between Craig's, pinning him like a lover.

Down came the knife, and behind it, the Shona's face, swollen with effort, his broken tooth pink with blood, blood running from his chin and dripping into Craig's upturned face, his eyes mottled with tiny brown veins, bulging from their sockets – and the knife came down.

Craig put all his strength against him. The knife point checked for a second, then moved down to touch Craig's skin in the notch where his collar-bones met. It stung like a hypodermic needle as it pierced the skin. With a sense of horror, Craig felt the Shona's body gathering for the final thrust that would force the silver steel through his larynx – and he knew that he could not prevent it.

Miraculously, the Shona's head changed shape, distorting like a rubber Hallowe'en mask, collapsing upon itself, the contents of the skull bursting in a liquid fountain from his temple – and the sound of a shot dinned in on Craig's eardrums. The strength went out of the Shona's body and he rolled off and flopped on the ground like a fresh-caught catfish.

Craig sat up. Sally-Anne was only feet away, kneeling facing him, the Tokarev pistol held double-handed, the barrel still pointing skywards where the recoil had thrown it. She must have placed the muzzle against the Shona's temple before she fired.

'I killed him,' she breathed gustily and her eyes were filled with horror.

'Thank God for it!' Craig gasped, using the collar of his shirt to dry the nick on his throat.

'I've never killed anything before,' Sally-Anne whispered. 'Not even a rabbit nor a fish – nothing.'

She dropped the pistol and started to dry-wash her hands, scrubbing one with the other, staring at the Shona's corpse. Craig crawled to her, and took her in his arms. She was shaking wildly.

'Take me away,' she pleaded. 'Please, Craig. I can smell the blood, take me away from here.'

'Yes. Yes.' He helped her to her feet, and in a frenzy of haste rolled the groundsheet and buckled the straps of the rucksacks.

'This way.' Burdened by both packs and the rifle, Craig led her away from the killing ground towards the west.

They had been going for almost three hours and had stopped for the first sparing drink, before Craig realized his terrible oversight. *The water bottles!* In his panickly haste, he had forgotten to take the water bottles from the dead Shona.

He looked back longingly. Even if he left Sally-Anne here and went back alone, it would cost him four hours, and the Third Brigade patrols would surely be coming up. He weighed the water bottle in his hand, a quarter full: barely enough to see out this day, even if they laid up now and waited for nightfall and the cool, not nearly enough if they kept going – and they had to keep going.

The decision was made for him. The sound of a single-engined aircraft throbbing down from the north. Bitterly he stared up into the pale desert sky, feeling the helplessness of the rabbit below the towering falcon.

'Spotter plane,' he said, and listened to the beat of the engine. It receded for a while, and then grew stronger again.

'They are flying a grid search.'

As he spoke, he saw it. It was closer than he had

thought, and much lower. He forced Sally-Anne down with a hand on her shoulder, and spread the cape over her, glancing back as he did so. It was coming on swiftly, a low-winged, single-engined monoplane. It altered course slightly, heading directly towards him. He dropped down beside Sally-Anne and crawled under the groundsheet beside her.

The engine roared louder. The pilot had spotted them. Craig lifted a corner of the groundsheet and looked out.

'Piper Lance,' said Sally-Anne softly.

It carried Zimbabwe Air Force roundels, and incongruously the pilot was a white man, but there was a black man in the right-hand seat, and he wore the dreaded burgundy-red beret and silver cap-badge. They both stared down expressionlessly as the Piper made a steep turn, with one wingtip pointed like a knife directly at where Craig lay. The black officer was holding the radio microphone to his lips. The wings of the Piper levelled and she came out of her turn, heading back the way she had come. The throb of the engine receded and was lost in the desert silence.

Craig pulled Sally-Anne to her feet.

'Can you go on?'

She nodded, pushing back the sweat-damp wisp of hair from her forehead. Her lips were flaking, and the lower one had cracked through. A drop of blood sat on it like a tiny ruby.

'We must be well inside Botswana, the border road can't be far ahead. If we can find a Botswana police patrol—'

The road was single width, two continuous ruts running north and south, jinking now and then to avoid a spring-hare colony or a soft pan. It was patrolled regularly by the Botswana police on anti-poaching and prevention of alleged entry duties.

Craig and Sally-Anne reached the road in the middle of the afternoon. By this time Craig had discarded the rifle and ammunition, and stripped the pack of all but essentials. He had even considered for a while burying his manuscript for later retrieval. It weighed eight pounds, but Sally-Anne had dissuaded him in a hoarse whisper.

The water bottle was empty. They had had their last drink, a blood-warm mouthful each, just before noon. Their speed was reduced to little more than a mile an hour. Craig was no longer sweating. He could feel his tongue beginning to swell and his throat closing as the heat sucked the moisture out of him.

They reached the road. Craig's gaze was fastened grimly on the heat-smudged horizon ahead, all his being concentrated on lifting one foot and placing it ahead of the other. They crossed the road without seeing it, and kept going on into the desert. They were not the first to walk past the chance of succour and go on to death by thirst and exposure. They staggered onwards for two hours more before Craig stopped.

'We should have reached the road by now,' he whispered, and checked the compass heading again. 'The compass must be wrong! North isn't there.' He was confused and doubting. 'Damaged the bloody thing. We are too far south,' he decided, and began the first aimless circle of the lost and totally disorientated, the graveyard spiral that precedes death in the desert.

An hour before sunset Craig stumbled over a dried brown vine growing in the grey soil. It bore only a single green fruit the size of an orange. He knelt and plucked it as reverently as if it had been the Cullinan diamond.

Mumbling to himself through cracked and bleeding lips, he split the fruit carefully with the bayonet. It was warm as living flesh from the sun.

'Gemsbok melon,' he explained to Sally-Anne as she sat and watched him with dull, uncomprehending eyes.

He used the point of the bayonet to mash the white flesh of the melon, and then held the half shell to Sally-Anne's mouth. Her throat pumped in the effort of swallowing the clear warm juice, and she closed her eyes in ecstasy as it spread over her swollen tongue.

Working with extreme care, Craig wrung a quarter of a cupful of liquid from the fruit and fed it to her. His own throat ached and contracted at the smell of the liquid as he made her drink. She seemed to recharge with strength before his eyes, and when the last drop had passed between her lips, she suddenly realized what he had done.

'You?' she whispered.

He took the hard rind and the squeezed-out pith, and sucked on them.

'Sorry.' She was distraught at her own thoughtlessness, but he shook his head.

'Cool soon. Night.'

He helped her up, and they stumbled onwards.

Time telescoped in Craig's mind. He looked at the sunset and thought it was the dawn.

'Wrong.' He took the compass and hurled it from him. It did not fly very far. 'Wrong – wrong way.' He turned, and led Sally-Anne back.

Craig's head filled with shadows and dark shapes, some were faceless and terrifying and he shouted soundlessly at them to drive them away. Some he recognized. Ashe Levy rode past on the back of a huge shaggy hyena, he was brandishing Craig's new manuscript, and his gold-rimmed spectacles glinted blindly in the sunset.

'Can't make a paperback sale,' he gloated. 'Nobody

wants it, baby, you're finished. One-book man, Craig baby – that's you.'

Then Craig realized that it was not his manuscript, but the winelist from the Four Seasons.

'Shall we try the Corton Charlemagne?' Ashe taunted Craig. 'Or a magnum of the Widow?'

'Only witch-doctors ride hyena,' Craig yelled back, no sound issuing from his desiccated throat. 'Always knew you were—'

Ashe hooted with malicious laughter, spurred the hyena into a gallop and threw the manuscript in the air. The white pages fluttered to the earth like roosting egrets, and when Craig went down on his knees to gather them, they turned to handfuls of dust and Craig found he could not rise. Sally-Anne was down beside him and as they clung to each other, the night came down upon them.

When he woke it was morning, and he could not rouse Sally-Anne. Her breathing snored and sawed through her nose and open mouth.

On his knees he dug the hole for a solar still. Though the soil was soft and friable, it went slowly. Laboriously, still on his knees, he gathered an armful of the scattered desert vegetation. It seemed there was no moisture in the woody growth when he chopped it finely with the bayonet, and laid it in the bottom of his hole.

He cut the top off the empty aluminium water bottle, and placed the cup this formed in the centre of the hole. It required enormous concentration to perform even these simple tasks. He spread the plastic groundsheet over the hole, and anchored the edges with heaped earth. In the centre of the sheet he gently laid a single round of ammunition, so that it was directly above the aluminium cup.

Then he crawled back to Sally-Anne and sat over her so that his shadow kept the sun off her face.

'It's going to be all right,' he told her. 'We'll find the road soon. We must be close—'

He did not realize that no sound came from his throat, and that she would not have been able to hear him even if it had.

'That little turd Ashe is a liar. I'll finish the book, you'll see. I'll pay off what I owe. We'll get a movie deal – I'll buy King's Lynn. It will be all right. Don't worry, my darling.'

He waited out the baking heat of the morning, containing his impatience, and at noon by his wrist-watch he opened the still. The sun beating down on the plastic sheet had raised the temperature in the covered hole close to the boiling point. Evaporation from the chopped plants had condensed on the under-side of the plastic sheet and run down it towards the sag of the bullet. From there it had dripped into the aluminium cup.

He had collected half a pint. He took it up between both hands, shaking so violently that he almost spilled it. He took a small sip and held it in his mouth. It was hot, but it tasted like honey and he had to use all his self-control to prevent himself swallowing.

He leaned forward and placed his mouth over Sally-Anne's blackened and bleeding lips. Gently he injected the liquid between them.

'Drink, my sweet, drink it up.' He found he was giggling stupidly as he watched her swallow painfully.

A few drops at a time he passed the precious fluid from his own mouth into hers and she swallowed each sip more easily. He kept the last mouthful for himself and let it trickle down his throat. It went to his head like strong drink and he sat grinning stupidly through fat, scaly black lips, his face swollen and sun-baked purple red, the abrasions on his cheek covered with a crusty weeping scab, and his bloodshot eyes gummed up with dried mucus.

He rebuilt the still and lay down beside Sally-Anne. He

covered his face from the sun with the tail torn from his shirt and whispered, 'All right – find help – soon. Don't worry – my love—'

But he knew that this was their last day. He could not keep her alive for another. Tomorrow they would die. It would be either the sun or the men of the Third Brigade – but tomorrow they would die.

At sunset the still gave them another half cup of distilled water, and after they had drunk it, they fell into a heavy, deathlike sleep in each other's arms.

Something woke Craig, and for a moment he thought it was the night wind in the scrub. With difficulty he pushed himself into a sitting position, and cocked his head to listen, not sure whether he was still hallucinating or whether he was truly hearing that soft rise and fall of sound. It must be nearly dawn, he realized, the horizon was a crisp dark line beneath the velvet drape of the sky.

Then abruptly the sound firmed, and he recognized it. The distinctive beat of a four-cylinder Land-Rover engine. The Third Brigade had not abandoned the hunt. They were coming on relentlessly, like hyenas with the reek of blood in their nostrils.

He saw a pair of headlights, far out across the desert, their pale beams swinging and tilting as the vehicle covered the rough ground. He groped for the AK 47. He could not find it. Ashe Levy must have stolen it, he thought bitterly, taken it off with him on the hyena. 'I never did trust the son-of-a-bitch.'

Craig stared hopelessly at the approaching headlights. In their beams danced a little pixie-like figure, a diminutive yellow mannikin. 'Puck,' he thought. 'Fairies. I never believed in fairies. Don't say that – when you do, one dies.

Don't want to kill fairies. I believe in them.' His mind was going, fantasy mixed with flashes of lucidity.

Suddenly he recognized that the little half-naked yellow mannikin was a Bushman, one of the pygmy desert race. A Bushman tracker, the Third Brigade were using a Bushman tracker to hunt them down. Only a Bushman could have run on their spoor all night, tracking by the headlights of the Land-Rover.

The headlights flashed over them, like a stage spotlight, and Craig lifted his hand to shade his eyes. The light was so bright that it hurt. He had the bayonet in his other hand behind his back.

I'll get one of them, he told himself. *I'll take one of them*.

The Land-Rover stopped only a few paces away. The little Bushman tracker was standing near them, clicking and clucking in his strange birdlike language. Craig heard the door of the Land-Rover open behind the blinding lights, and a man came towards them. Craig recognized him instantly. *General Peter Fungabera* – he seemed as tall as a giant in the back lighting of the headlights as he strode towards where Craig huddled on the desert floor.

Thank you, God, Craig prayed, *thank you for sending him to me before I died*, and he gripped the bayonet. *In the throat*, he told himself, *as he stoops over me*. He marshalled all his remaining strength, and General Peter Fungabera stooped towards him. *Now!* Craig made the effort. *Drive the point into his throat!* But nothing happened. His limbs would not respond. He was finished. There was nothing left.

'I have to inform you that you are under arrest for illegal entry into the Republic of Botswana, sir,' said General Fungabera – but he had changed his voice. He was using a deep, gentle, caring voice, in heavily accented English.

He won't fool me, Craig thought, *the tricky bastard*, and he saw that Peter Fungabera was wearing the uniform of a sergeant of Botswana police.

'You are lucky.' He went down on one knee. 'We found

where you were crossing the road.' He was holding a felt-covered water bottle to Craig's mouth. 'We have been following you, since three o'clock yesterday.'

Cool, sweet water gushed into Craig's mouth and ran down his chin. He let the bayonet drop and grabbed for the bottle with both hands. He wanted to gulp it all down at once, he wanted to drown in it. It was so marvellous that his eyes flooded with tears.

Through the tears he saw the Botswana police crest on the open door of the Land-Rover.

'Who?' he stared at Peter Fungabera, but he had never seen this face before. It was a broad, flat-nosed face, puckered now with worry and concern, like that of a friendly bulldog.

'Who?' he croaked.

'Please not to talk, we must get you and the lady to hospital at Francistown pretty bloody quickly. Plenty people die in desert – you goddamned lucky.'

'You aren't General Fungabera?' he whispered. 'Who are you?'

'Botswana police, border patrol. Sergeant Simon Mafekeng at your honour's service, sir.'

As a boy, before the great patriotic war, Colonel Nikolai Bukharin had accompanied his father on the wolf hunts, hunting the packs that terrorized their remote village in the high Urals during the long harsh winter months.

Those expeditions into the vast gloomy Taiga forest had nurtured in him a deep passion for the hunt. He enjoyed the solitude of wild places and the primeval joy of pitting all his senses against a dangerous animal. Eyesight, hearing, smell, and the other extraordinary sense of the born hunter that enabled him to anticipate the twists and evasions of his quarry – all these the colonel still possessed in full strength, despite his sixty-two years. Together with a memory for facts and faces that was almost computerlike, they had enabled him to excel at his work, had seen him elevated to the head of his department of the Seventh commissariat where he had hunted professionally the most dangerous game of all – man.

When he hunted boar and bear on the great estates reserved for the recreations of high officers of the GRU and KGB, he had alarmed his comrades and the game-keepers by scorning to fire from the prepared hides and by going on foot alone into the thickest cover. The thrill of great physical danger had satisfied some deep need in him.

When the assignment on which he was now engaged had been channelled through to his office on the second floor of the central headquarters on Dzerzhinsky Square, he had recognized its importance immediately, and taken control of it personally. With careful cultivation, that first potential was gradually being realized, and when the time had come for Colonel Bukharin at last to meet his subject face to face on the ground over which they would manoeuvre, he had chosen the cover which best suited his tastes.

Russians, especially Russians of high rank, were objects of hostile suspicion in the new republic of Zimbabwe. During the *chimurenga*, the war of independence, Russia had chosen the wrong horse and given her support to Joshua Nkomo's ZIPRA – the Matabele revolutionary wing. As far as the government in Harare was concerned, the Russians were the new colonialist enemy, while it was China and North Korea who were the true friends of the revolution.

For these reasons, Colonel Nikolai Bukharin had entered Zimbabwe on a Finnish passport, bearing a false name. He spoke Finnish fluently, as he did five other languages, including English. He needed a cover under which he could freely leave the city of Harare, where his every move would be watched over, and go out into the unpopulated wilderness where he could meet his subject without fear of surveillance.

Although many of the other African republics under pressure from the World Bank and the International Monetary Fund had banned big-game hunting, Zimbabwe still licensed professional hunters to operate their elaborate safaris in the designated 'controlled hunting areas'. These were large earners of foreign exchange for the embattled economy.

It amused the colonel to pose as a prosperous timber merchant from Helsinki, and to indulge his own love of the hunt in this decadent manner reserved almost exclusively for the financial aristocrats of the capitalist system.

Of course, the budget that had been allocated for this operation could not stand such extravagance. However, General Peter Fungabera, the subject of the operation, was a wealthy and ambitious man. He had made no difficulties when Colonel Bukharin had suggested that they use a big-game hunting safari as a cover for their meeting, and that General Fungabera should be allowed the honour of acting as host and of paying the thousand dollars *der diem* that the safari cost.

Standing in the centre of the small clearing now, Colonel Bukharin looked at his man. The Russian had deliberately wounded the bull. Nikolai Bukharin was a fine shot with pistol, rifle and shotgun, and the range had been thirty yards. If he had chosen, he could have placed a bullet in either of the bull's eyes, in the very centre of the bright black pupil. Instead he had shot the animal through the belly, a hand's width behind the lungs so as not to impair its wind, but not far enough back to damage the hindquarters and so slow it down in the charge.

It was a marvellous bull, with a mountainous boss of black horn that would stretch fifty inches or more around the curve from point to point. A fifty-inch bull was a trophy few could match, and as he had drawn first blood it would belong to the colonel no matter who delivered the *coup de grâce*. He was smiling at Peter Fungabera as he poured vodka into the silver cup of his hip-flask.

'*Na Zdorovye!*' he saluted Peter, and tossed it down without blinking, refilled the silver cup and offered it to him.

Peter was dressed in starched and crisply ironed fatigues with his name tag on the breast, and a khaki silk scarf at his throat, but he was bare-headed with no insignia to sparkle in the sunlight and alarm the game.

He accepted the silver cup and looked over the rim at the Russian. He was as tall as Peter, but even slimmer, erect as a man thirty years younger. His eyes were a peculiarly pale, cruel blue. His face was riven with the scars of war and of other ancient conflicts, so that it was a miniature lunar landscape. His skull was shaven, the fine stubble of hair that covered it was silver and sparkled in the sunlight like glass fibres.

Peter Fungabera enjoyed this man. He enjoyed the aura of power that he wore like an emperor's cloak. He enjoyed the innate cruelty of him that was almost African, and which Peter understood perfectly. He enjoyed his devious-ness, the layering of lies and truths and half-truths, so that they became indistinguishable. He was excited by the sense of danger that exuded from him so powerfully that it had almost an odour of its own. 'We are the same breed,' Peter thought, as he lifted the silver cup and returned the salute. He drank down the pungent spirit at one swallow. Then, breathing carefully so as not to show the smallest sign of distress, he handed back the cup.

'You drink like a man,' Nikolai Bukharin admitted. 'Let us see if you hunt like one.'

Peter had guessed correctly. It had been a test: the vodka and the buffalo bull, both of them. He shrugged to show his indifference, and the Russian beckoned to the professional hunter who stood respectfully out of earshot.

The hunter was a Zimbabwe-born white man, in his late thirties, dressed for the part in wide-brimmed hat and khaki gilet with heavy-calibre cartridges in the loops across his breast. He had a thick curly dark beard and an extremely unhappy expression on his face, as befits a man who is about to follow a gun-shot buffalo bull into dense riverine bush.

'General Fungabera will take the .458,' Colonel Bukharin said, and the hunter nodded miserably. How had this strange old bastard managed to make a muck-up of a sitting shot like that? He had been shooting like a Bisley champion up to now. Christ, but that bush looked really nasty. The hunter suppressed a shiver and snapped his fingers for the number two gunbearer to bring up the heavy rifle.

'You will wait here with the bearers,' said the Russian quietly.

'Sir!' the hunter protested quickly. 'I can't let you go in alone. I'd lose my licence. It's just not on—'

'Enough,' said Colonel Bukharin.

'But, sir, you don't understand—'

'I said, enough!' The Russian never raised his voice, but those pale eyes silenced the younger man completely. He found suddenly that he was more afraid of this man than of losing his licence, or of the wounded bull in the bush ahead. He subsided and stepped back thankfully.

The Russian took the .458 from the gunbearer, shot the bolt back to check that it was loaded with soft-tipped bullets, and then handed it to Peter Fungabera. Peter took it from him, smiling slightly, hefted it, then handed it back to the gunbearer. Colonel Bukharin raised one silver eyebrow and smiled also. The smile was mockery shaded with contempt.

Peter spoke sharply in Shona to the bearer, 'Eh he, mambo!'

The man ran, and snatched another weapon from one of the other back bearers. He brought it back to Peter, clapping softly to show his respect.

Peter weighed this new weapon in his hands. It was a short-shafted stabbing assegai. The handle was of hardwood bound with copper wire. The blade was almost two feet long and four inches broad. Carefully Peter shaved the hairs off the back of his thumb with the edge of the silver blade, then, deliberately, he shrugged off his jacket and stripped his trousers and jungle boots.

Dressed only in a pair of olive-green shorts and carrying the stabbing assegai, he said, 'This is the African way, Colonel.' The Russian was no longer smiling. 'But I do not expect a man of your years to hunt the same way.' Peter excused him courteously. 'You may use your rifle again.'

The Russian nodded, conceding the exchange. He had lost that one, but now let's see if this black *mujik* can make good his boast. Bukharin looked down at the spoor. The great hoof prints were the size of soup plates, and the thin watery gouts of blood were tinged with greenish-yellow dung from the ruptured bowels.

'I will track,' he said. 'You will watch for the break.'

They moved off easily, with the Russian five paces ahead, stooped attentively to the blood spoor, and Peter Fungabera drifting behind him, the assegai held underhand, and his dark eyes covering the bush ahead with a steady rhythmic sweep, trained eyes not expecting to see the whole animal, searching for the little things, perhaps the shine of a wet muzzle or the drooping curve of a great horn.

Within twenty paces the bush closed in around them. It was sultry green as a hothouse, dank vegetation pressing breathlessly around them. The air stank of the rotting leaf mould that deadened their footfalls. The silence was oppressive, so that the drag of a thorny branch across the Russian's leather leggings sounded loud as a truck engine.

He was sweating; perspiration soaked his shirt in a dark patch between the shoulder-blades and sparkled like dewdrops on the back of his neck. Peter could hear his breathing, deep and harsh, but knew instinctively that it was not fear that worked in the Russian, but the pervading excitement of the hunter.

Peter Fungabera did not share it. There was a coldness in him where his own fear should have been. He had trained himself to that during the *chimurenga*. This was a necessary task, this thing with the assegai. It was to impress the Russian only, and with all fear and feeling anaesthetized by the coldness, Peter Fungabera prepared himself. He felt his muscles charging, felt the tension build in his sinews and nerves until he was like an arrow, notched against the curve of the long-bow.

With his eyes he swept the bush directly in the run of the spoor only lightly, and concentrated his main attention on the flanks. This beast that they were hunting was the most cunning of all the dangerous game of Africa, except perhaps the leopard. But it was possessed of the brute strength of a hundred leopards. The lion will growl before he charges, the elephant will turn under the punishment of heavy bullets in the chest, but the Cape buffalo comes in silence, and only one thing will stop his charge – and that is death.

A big, metallic-blue fly settled on Peter Fungabera's lip and crawled into his nostril. So complete was his concentration that he did not feel it, or brush it away. He watched the flanks, he concentrated the very essence of his being on the flanks.

The Russian checked, examining the change in the spoor, the plant of solid hooves, the puddle of loose bloody dung. This was where the bull had stood, after his first wild run. Peter Fungabera could imagine him, standing massive and black, with his nose held high, looking back towards the hunters with the spreading agony in his guts and liquid

317

faeces from his torn intestines beginning to ooze uncontrollably down his quarters. Here he had stood and listened and heard their voices, and the hatred and anger had begun to seethe in him. Here the killing rage had begun. He had dropped his head, and gone on, humping his back against the agony in his bowels, sustained by the rage within him.

The Russian glanced back at Peter, and they did not have to speak. In unison they moved forward.

The bull was acting on an atavistic memory: everything he did had been done countless times before by his ancestors. From that first wild gallop as he received the bullet, the stop to listen and peer back, the gathering of great muscles, and now the more sedate trot, angling to present his haunches to the fitful breeze so that the scent of the hunters would be borne down to him, great armoured head swinging from side to side as he began the search for the ambush point, it was all part of a pattern.

The bull crossed a narrow clearing ten paces across, forced his head into the wall of glossy green leaves on the far side, leaving it smeared with fresh bright blood, and went on another fifty yards. Then he turned sharply aside, and started back in a wide circle. Now he moved with deliberate stealth, insinuating his bulk gently through the intertwined creeper and branch a single pace at a time – until he came back to the clearing again.

Here he stopped, hidden on the far edge of the clearing, covering from the side his own bloody tracks across the narrow opening, his body screened entirely by dense growth, and a terrible stillness settled upon him. He let the stinging flies feast on his open wound without shuddering his skin or swinging his tail. He did not twitch either of his large, cup-shaped ears but strained them forward. Not even his eyes blinked as he peered back along the blood spoor and waited for the hunters to come.

The Russian stepped lightly into the clearing, his gaze

darting ahead to where blood-painted branches hung on the far side and a huge body had forced its way through into the forest beyond. He started forward quietly. Peter Fungabera followed him, watching the flanks, moving like a dancer, his body glowing with a light sheen of sweat, the flat, hard muscle in his chest and arms changing shape at his slightest movement.

He saw the bull's eye. It caught the light like a new coin, and Peter froze. He snapped the fingers of his left hand, and the Russian froze with him. Peter Fungabera stared at the bull buffalo's eye, not quite sure what he was seeing, but knowing that it was in the right place – thirty yards out on the left. If the bull had doubled, that was where he would be.

Peter blinked his eyes, and suddenly the image cleared. He was no longer focused only on the eye, and so he could see the curve of one horn held so still that it could have been a branch. He saw the crenellations of the boss meeting above the bull's eye, and now he looked into the eye itself – and it was like a glimpse into hell.

The bull charged. The forest burst open before his rush, branches crackled and broke, the leaves shook and fluttered as though struck by a hurricane and the bull came out into the clearing. He came out crabbing sideways, a deceptive but characteristic feint that had lulled many a hunter until the sudden direct lunge at the end.

He came fast. It seemed impossible that any beast so enormous could move so fast. He was broad and tall as a granite kopje, his back and shoulder crusted with dried mud from the wallow, and there were obscene silvery bald patches on his shoulders and neck, criss-crossed with the long-healed scars of thorn and lions' claws.

From his open jaws drooled silver ropes of saliva, and tears had tracked wet lines down his hairy cheeks. A man could barely have encompassed that neck with both arms, or matched the spread of those horns with arms extended.

In the skin folds of his throat hung bunches of blue ticks like ripe grapes, and the rank bovine smell of him was choking in the hothouse of the forest.

He came on, majestic in his killing rage, and Peter Fungabera went out to meet him. He passed in front of the Russian just as Colonel Bukharin swung up the stubby heavy-calibre rifle, screening the shot, forcing him to throw the barrel up towards the sky. Peter moved like a dark forest wraith, crossing the bull at the opposite angle to his crabbing charge, taking him off balance so that the bull hooked at him like a boxer punching as he moves away, not timing the swing of horns, not sighting true, and Peter swayed away from it with his upper body only, letting the curved point hiss past his ribs by the breadth of a hand and then swaying back as the bull's head was flung high at the finish of the stroke.

In that instant the bull was open, from his reaching chin to the soft folds of skin between his forelegs, and Peter Fungabera put the full weight of his body and all the momentum of his run behind the silver blade.

The bull ran onto the point. It went into him with the sucking sound of a foot in mud, and the blade was swallowed by living flesh. It went in until the fingers of Peter's right hand on the shaft followed the blade into the wound and spurting blood drenched him to the shoulder. Peter released his grip on the assegai, and pirouetted away, spinning clear while the bull bucked stiff-legged against the long steel in his chest cavity. He tried to follow Peter round, but came up short and stood with his thick stubby forelegs braced, staring at the naked man with a glaze spreading over his eyes.

Peter Fungabera posed before him, with both arms lifted gracefully. 'Ha, earth-shaker!' he called in Shona. 'Ha, you sky thunder!'

The bull made two plunging strides forward and something burst inside him. Blood erupted in a double gush from his flaring nostrils. He opened his jaws and bellowed, and blood shot up his throat in a frothing bright cascade and drenched his chest. The great bull reeled, fighting to keep his balance.

'Die, spawn of the black gods!' Peter taunted. 'Feel the steel of a future king – and die!'

The bull went down. The earth jumped beneath their feet as the weight of him struck.

Peter Fungabera stepped up to the huge bossed head in which the smouldering eyes were fading. He went down on one knee and, with his cupped hands, scooped up the rich hot blood as it streamed from the bull's gaping mouth, and he lifted his hands to his mouth and drank the blood like wine. It streamed down his arms and dribbled from his chin, and Peter laughed, a sound that made even the Russian's vinegary blood chill.

'I have drunk your living blood, oh great bull. Now your strength is mine!' he shouted, as the bull arched his back in the final spasm of death.

Peter Fungabera had showered and changed into mess kit. His trousers were black with a burgundy watered-silk side stripe. His short bumfreezer jacket was in the regiment's same distinctive burgundy-red with black silk lapels. His white shirt was starch-fronted and wing-collared with a black bow-tie and he wore a double row of miniature decorations.

The camp servants had set a table under the spread branches of a mhoba-hoba tree, on the edge of an open vlei of short lush green grass, out of sight and earshot of the main camp. On the table was a bottle of Chivas Regal whisky and another of vodka, a bucket of ice and two crystal glasses.

Colonel Nikolai Bukharin sat opposite Peter. His long

loose cotton shirt hung outside his baggy Cossack pants and was belted at the waist. His feet were thrust into boots of soft glove-leather. He leaned forward and filled the glasses, and then passed one to Peter.

This time there was no flamboyant tossing back of liquor. They drank slowly, watching the African sky turn mauve and smouldering gold. The silence was the companionable accord of two men who have risked their lives together and have each found the other worthy, a comrade to die with, or an adversary to fight to the death.

At last Colonel Bukharin placed his glass back on the table with a click.

'And so, my friend, tell me what you want,' he invited.

'I want this land,' said Peter Fungabera simply.

'All of it?' the colonel asked.

'All of it.'

'Not just Zimbabwe?'

'Not just Zimbabwe.'

'And we are to help you take it?'

'Yes.'

'In exchange?'

'My friendship.'

'Your friendship unto death?' the colonel suggested drily. 'Or until you have what you want and find a new friend?'

Peter smiled. They spoke the same language, they understood each other.

'What tangible signs of this eternal friendship will you give us?' the Russian insisted.

'A poor little country like mine,' Peter shrugged, 'a few strategic minerals – nickel, chrome, titanium, beryllium – a few ounces of gold.'

The Russian nodded sagely. 'They will be useful to us.'

'Then, once I am the Monomatapa of Zimbabwe, my eyes will become restless, naturally—'

'Naturally.' The Russian watched his eyes. He did not like black men, this racist bigotry was a common Russian trait, he did not like their colour nor their smell – but this one!

'My eyes might turn southwards,' Peter Fungabera said softly. Ha! Colonel Bukharin hid his glee behind a doleful expression. This one is different!

'The direction in which your own eyes have been focused all along,' Peter went on, and the Russian could have chortled.

'What will you see in the south, Comrade General?'

'I will see a people enslaved and ripe for emancipation.'

'And what else?'

'I will see the gold of the Witwatersrand and the Free State fields, I will see the diamonds of Kimberley, the uranium, the platinum, the silver, the copper – in short, I will see one of the great treasure houses of this earth.'

'Yes?' the Russian probed with delight. This one is quick, this one has brains, and this one has the courage that it would take.

'I will see a base that divides the western world, a base that controls both the south Atlantic and the Indian oceans, that sits upon the oil lines between the Gulf and Europe, between the Gulf and the Americas.'

The Russian held up a hand. 'Where will these thoughts lead you?'

'It will be my duty to see this land to the south elevated to its true place in the community of nations, in the tutelage of and under the protection of that greatest of all lovers of freedom, the Union of Soviet Socialist Republics.'

The Russian nodded, still watching his eyes. Yes, this black man had seen the design behind it all. The south was the grand prize, but to win it they needed to take it in the strangler's grasp. To the east they already had Mozambique, to the west Angola was theirs and Namibia would soon be also. They needed only the north to isolate the prize. The north was Zimbabwe, like the strangler's thumb on the windpipe, and this man could deliver it to them.

Colonel Bukharin sat forward in his canvas camp-chair and became businesslike and brisk.

'Opportunity?'

'Economic chaos, and intertribal warfare, the break-down of central government.' Peter Fungabera counted them off on his fingers.

'The present government is meeting you more than halfway in creating its own economic breakdown,' the Russian observed, 'and you are already doing fine work in fanning tribal hatreds.'

'Thank you, comrade.'

'However, the peasants must begin to starve a little before they become manageable—'

'I am pushing in the Cabinet for the nationalization of the white-owned farms and ranches. Without the white farmers I can produce you a goodly measure of starvation,' Peter Fungabera smiled.

'I hear you have already made a start. I congratulate you on the recent acquisition of your own estate, King's Lynn? That is the name is it not?'

'You are well informed, Colonel.'

'I take pains to ensure that I am. But when the moment comes to seize the reins of state, what kind of man will the people look to?'

'A strong man,' Peter answered without hesitation. 'One whose ruthlessness has been demonstrated.'

'As yours was during the *chimurenga*, and more recently in Matabeleland.'

'A man of charisma and presence, a man well known to the people.'

'The women sing your praises in the streets of Harare, not a single day passes without your image on the television screens or your name on the front page of the newspapers.'

'A man with force behind him.'

'The Third Brigade,' the Russian nodded, 'and the blessing of the people of the USSR. However,' he paused significantly, 'two questions need answers, Comrade General.'

'Yes?'

'The first is a mundane and distasteful question to raise between men such as you and I – money. My paymasters become restless. Our expenses have begun to exceed by a considerable amount the shipments of ivory and animal products that you have sent us—' He held up his hand again to forestall argument. It was an old man's hand, dappled with withered dark spots and criss-crossed with prominent blue veins. 'I know that we should do these things merely for the love of freedom, that money is a capitalist obscenity, but nothing is perfect in this world. In short, Comrade General, you are reaching the limits that Moscow has set on your credit.'

'I understand,' Peter Fungabera nodded. 'What is your second question?'

'The Matabele tribe. They are a warlike and difficult people. I know that you have been forced to stir up enmity, to cause dissension and strife and to bring upon the present government the disapproval of the Western powers by your campaign in Matabeleland. But what happens afterwards? How do you control them once you yourself have seized power?'

'I answer both questions with a single name,' Peter Fungabera replied.

'The name?'

'Tungata Zebiwe.'

'Ha! Yes! Tungata Zebiwe. The Matabele leader. You had him put away. I presumed that by now he had been liquidated.'

'I am holding him in great secrecy and safety at one of my rehabilitation centres near here.'

'Explain.'

'Firstly, the money.'

'From what we know, Tungata Zebiwe is not a rich man,' the Russian demurred.

'He has the key to a fortune which might easily exceed two hundred million US dollars.'

The Russian raised a silver eyebrow in the gesture of disbelief that Peter was coming to know well, and which was beginning to irritate him.

'Diamonds,' he said.

'The mother country is one of the world's largest producers.' The Russian spread his hands disparagingly.

'Not industrial rubbish, not black boart, but gem stones of the first water, large stones, huge stones, some of the finest ever mined anywhere.'

The Russian looked thoughtful. 'If it is true—'

'It is true! But I will not explain further. Not yet.'

'Very well. At least I can hold out some sort of promise to the money-sucking leeches in our treasury department? And the second question. The Matabele? You cannot plan to obliterate them, man, woman and child?'

Peter Fungabera shook his head regretfully. 'No. Though it would be the better way, America and Britain would not allow it. No, my answer is Tungata Zebiwe again. When I take over the country, he will reappear – it will be almost miraculous. He will come back from the dead. The Matabele tribe will go wild with joy and relief. They will follow him, they will dote upon him, and I will make him my vice-president.'

'He hates you. You destroyed him. If you ever free him, he will seek to revenge that.'

'No,' Peter shook his head. 'I will send him to you. You have special clinics for difficult cases, do you not? Institutes where a mentally sick man can be treated with drugs – and other techniques to make him rational and reasonable once more?'

This time the Russian actually began to chortle, and he poured himself another vodka, shaking with silent laughter. When he looked up at Peter, there was respect in those pale eyes for the first time.

'I drink to you, Monomatapa of Zimbabwe, may you reign a thousand years!'

He set down his glass and turned to stare down the long open vlei to the distant waterhole. A herd of zebra had come down to drink. They were nervous and skittish, for the lions lie in ambush at the water. At last they waded in, knee-deep and in a single rank, dipped their lips to touch the surface in unison. They formed an overlapping frieze of identical heads like an infinity of mirror images until the old stallion sentinel snorted in nervous alarm and the pattern exploded in foaming water and wildly galloping forms.

'The treatment of which you speak is drastic.' Colonel Bukharin watched the zebra herd tear away into the forest. 'Some patients do not survive it. Those that do are—' he searched for the word ' – altered.'

'Their minds are destroyed.' Peter said it for him.

'In plain terms – yes,' the colonel nodded.

'I need his body, not his brain. I need a puppet, not a human being.'

'We can arrange that. When will you send him to us?'

'The diamonds first,' Peter replied.

'Of course, the diamonds first. How long will that take?'

Peter shrugged. 'Not long.'

'When you are ready I will send a doctor to you, with the appropriate medications. We can bring this Tungata Zebiwe out on the same route as the ivory: Air Zimbabwe to Dar-es-Salaam and one of our freighters from there to Odessa.'

'Agreed.'

'You say that he is being held near here? I would like to see him.'

'Is it wise?'

'Indulge me, please!' From Colonel Bukharin it was an order rather than a request.

Tungata Zebiwe stood in the flat white glare of the noonday sun. He stood facing a whitewashed wall that caught the sun's rays and flung them back like a huge mirror. He had stood there since before the rise of the sun, when the frost had crusted the sparse brown grass at the edge of the parade ground.

Tungata was stark naked, as were the two men that flanked him. All three of them were so thin that every rib showed clearly, and the crests of their spines stood out like the beads of a rosary down the centre of their backs. Tungata had his eyes closed to slits to keep out the glare of sunlight off the wall, but he concentrated on a mark in the plaster to counter the effects of giddy vertigo which had already toppled the men on each side of him more than once. Only heavy lashing by the guards had forced them to their feet again. They were still swaying and reeling as they stood.

'Courage, my brothers,' Tungata whispered in Sindebele. 'Do not let the Shona dogs see you beaten.'

He was determined not to collapse, and he stared at the dimple in the wall. It was the mark of a bullet strike, painted over with limewash. They limewashed the wall after every execution – they were meticulous about it.

'*Amanzi*,' husked the man on his right, 'water!'

'Do not think of it,' Tungata ordered him. 'Do not speak of it, or it will drive you mad.'

The heat came off the wall in waves that struck with physical weight.

'I am blind,' whispered the second man. 'I cannot see.'

The white glare had seared his eyeballs like snow-blindness.

'There is nothing to see but the hideous faces of Shona apes,' Tungata told him. 'Be thankful for your blindness, friend.'

Suddenly from behind them brusque orders were shouted in Shona and then came the tramp of feet from across the parade ground.

'They are coming,' whispered the blinded Matabele, and Tungata Zebiwe felt a vast regret arising within him.

Yes, they were coming at last. This time for him.

During every day of the long weeks of his imprisonment, he had heard the tramp of the firing-squad crossing the parade ground at noon. This time it was for him. He did not fear death, but he was saddened by it. He was sad that he had not been able to help his people in their terrible distress, he was saddened that he would never see again his woman, and that she would never bear him the son for whom he longed. He was sad that his life which had promised so much would end before it had delivered up its fruits, and he thought suddenly of a day long ago when he had stood at his grandfather's side and looked out over the maize fields that had been scythed by a brief and furious hail-storm.

'All that work for nothing, what a waste!' his grandfather had murmured, and Tungata repeated his words softly to himself as rude hands turned him and hustled him to the wooden stake set in the ground before the wall.

They tied his wrists to the stake and he opened his eyes fully. His relief from the glare of the wall was soured by the sight of the rank of armed men who faced him.

They brought the two other naked Matabele from the wall. The blind one fell to his knees, weak with exposure and terror, and his bowels voided involuntarily. The guards laughed and exclaimed with disgust.

329

'Stand up!' Tungata ordered him harshly. 'Die on your feet like a true son of Mashobane!'

The man struggled back to his feet.

'Walk to the stake,' Tungata ordered. 'It is a little to your left.'

The man went, groping blindly, and found the stake. They bound him to it.

There were eight men in the firing-squad and the commander was a captain in the Third Brigade. He went slowly down the rank of executioners, taking each rifle and checking the load. He made little jokes in Shona that Tungata could not follow, and his men laughed. Their laughter had an unrestrained quality, like men who had taken alcohol or drugs. They had done this work before, and enjoyed it. Tungata had known many men like them during the war; violence and blood had become their addictions.

The captain came back to the head of the rank, and from his breast-pocket took a sheet of typescript which was grubby and dog-eared from much handling. He read from it, stumbling over the words and mispronouncing them like a schoolboy, his English only barely intelligible.

'You have been condemned as enemies of the state and the people,' he read. 'You have been declared incorrigible. Your death warrant has been approved by the vice-president of the Republic of Zimbabwe—'

Tungata Zebiwe lifted his chin and began to sing. His voice soared, deep and beautiful, drowning out the thin tones of the Shona captain:

'The Moles are beneath the earth,
"Are they dead?" asked the daughters of Mashobane.'

He sang the ancient fighting song of the Matabele, and at the end of the first verse he snarled at the two condemned men who flanked him.

'Sing! Let the Shona jackals hear the Matabele lion growl.'

And they sang with him:

> 'Like the black mamba from under a stone
> We milked death with a fang of silver steel—'

Facing them, the captain gave an order, and as one man the squad advanced a right foot and lifted their rifles. Tungata sang on, staring into their eyes, defying them, and the men beside him fed on his courage and their voices firmed. A second order and the rifles were levelled. The eyes of the executioners peered over the sights, and the three naked Matabele sang on in the sunlight.

Now, marvellously, there was the sound of other voices, distant voices, lifted in the war song. They came from the prison huts beyond the parade ground. Hundreds of imprisoned Matabele were singing with them, sharing the moment of their deaths, giving them strength and comfort.

The Shona captain lifted his right hand, and in the last instants of his life Tungata's sadness fell away to be replaced by a soaring pride. *These are men*, he thought, *with or without me they will resist the tyrant.*

The captain brought his hand down sharply, as he bellowed the command. 'Fire!'

The volley was simultaneous. The line of executioners swayed to the sharp recoil of rifles – and the blast dinned in on Tungata's eardrums so that he flinched involuntarily.

He heard the vicious slap of bullets into living flesh, and from the corners of his vision saw the men beside him jerk as though from the blows of invisible sledgehammers, and then fall forward against their bonds. The song was cut off abruptly on their lips. Yet the song still poured from Tungata's throat and he stood erect.

The riflemen lowered their weapons, laughing and nudging each other as though at some grand joke. From the prison huts the war song had changed to the dismal ululation of mourning, and now at last Tungata's voice dried and he faltered into silence.

He turned his head and looked at the men beside him. They had shared the volley between them, and their torsos were riddled with shot. Already the flies were swarming to the wounds.

Now suddenly Tungata's knees began to buckle, and he felt his sphincter loosening. He fought his body, hating its weakness. Gradually, he brought it under control.

The Shona captain came to stand in front of him and said in English, 'Good joke, hey? Heavy, man, heavy!' and grinned delightedly. Then he turned and shouted, 'Bring water, quickly!'

A trooper brought an enamel dish, brimming with clear water, and the captain took it from him. Tungata could smell the water. It is said that the little Bushmen can smell water at a distance of many miles, but he had not truly believed it until now. The water smelled sweet as a freshly sliced honeydew melon, and his throat convulsed in a spasmodic swallowing reflex. He could not take his eyes off the dish.

The captain lifted the dish with both hands to his own lips and took a mouthful, then he rinsed his mouth and gargled with it noisily. He spat the mouthful and grinned at Tungata, then held the dish up before his face. Slowly and deliberately he tipped the dish and the water spilled into the dust at Tungata's feet. It splashed his legs to the knees. Each drop felt cold as ice chips and every cell of Tungata's body craved for it with a strength that was almost madness. The captain inverted the dish and let the last drops fall.

'Heavy, man!' he repeated mindlessly, and turned to shout an order at his men. They doubled away across the parade ground, leaving Tungata alone with the dead and the flies.

They came for him at sunset. When they cut his wrist bonds, he groaned involuntarily at the agonizing rush of fresh blood into his swollen hands, and fell to his knees. His legs could not support him. They had to half-carry him to his hut.

The room was bare, except for an uncovered toilet bucket in the corner and two bowls in the centre of the baked-mud floor. One dish contained a pint of water, the other a handful of stiff white maize cake. The cake was heavily oversalted. On the morrow, he would pay for eating it in the heavy coin of thirst, but he had to have strength.

He drank half the water and set the rest aside for the morning, and then he stretched out on the bare floor. Residual heat beat down on him from the corrugated iron roof, but by morning he knew he would be shivering with cold. He ached in every joint of his body, and his head pounded with the effects of the sun and the glare until he thought his skull would pop like a ripe cream of tartar pod on a baobab tree.

Outside in the darkness beyond the wire, the hyena packs disputed the feast that had been laid for them. Their cries and howls were a lunatic bedlam of greed, punctuated by the crunch of bone in great jaws.

Despite it all, Tungata slept, and woke to the tramp of feet and shouted orders in the dawn. Swiftly he gulped down the remains of the water to fortify himself, and then squatted over the bucket. His body had so nearly played him false the day before. He would not let it happen today.

The door was flung open.

'Out, you Matabele dog! Out of your stinking kennel!'

They marched him back to the wall. There were three other naked Matabele facing it already. Irrelevantly he noticed that they had limewashed the wall. They were very conscientious about that. He stood with his face two feet from the pristine white surface and steeled himself for the day ahead.

They shot the three other prisoners at noon. This time Tungata could not lead them in the singing. He tried, but his throat closed up on him. By the middle of the afternoon, his vision was breaking up into patches of darkness and stabbing white light. However, every time his legs collapsed and he fell forward against his bound wrists, the pain in his shoulder sockets as his arms twisted upwards revived him.

The thirst was unspeakable.

The patches of darkness in his head became deeper and lasted longer, the pain could no longer revive him completely. Out of one of the dark areas a voice spoke.

'My dear fellow,' said the voice. 'This is all terribly distasteful to me.'

The voice of Peter Fungabera drove away the darkness and gave Tungata new strength. He struggled upright, lifted his head and forced his vision to clear. He looked at Peter Fungabera's face and his hatred came to arm him. He cherished his hatred as a life-giving force.

Peter Fungabera was in fatigues and beret. He carried his swagger-stick in his right hand. At his side was a white man whom Tungata had never seen before. He was tall and slim and old. His head was freshly shaven, his skin ruined with cicatrices and his eyes were a strange pale shade of blue that Tungata found as repulsive and chilling as the stare of a cobra. He was watching Tungata with clinical interest, devoid of pity or other human sentiment.

'I regret that you are not seeing Comrade Minister Zebiwe at his best,' Peter told the white man. 'He has lost a great deal of weight, but not here—'

With the tip of the swagger-stick, Peter Fungabera lifted the heavy black bunch of Tungata's naked genitalia.

'Have you ever seen anything like that?' he asked, using the swagger-stick with the same dexterity as a chopstick. Bound to the stake, Tungata could not pull away. It was

334

the ultimate degradation, this arrogant mauling and examination of his private parts.

'Enough for three ordinary men,' Peter estimated with mock admiration, and Tungata glared at him wordlessly.

The Russian made an impatient gesture and Peter nodded.

'You are right. We are wasting time.'

He glanced at his wrist-watch and then turned to the captain who was close by, waiting with his squad.

'Bring the prisoner up to the fort.'

They had to carry Tungata.

Peter Fungabera's quarters in the blockhouse on the central rock kopje were spartanly furnished, but the dirt floor had been freshly swept and sprinkled with water. He and the Russian sat on one side of the trestle-table that served as a desk. There was a wooden bench on the opposite side, facing them.

The guards helped Tungata to the bench. He pushed their hands away and sat upright, glaring silently at the two men opposite him. Peter said something to the captain in Shona, and they brought a cheap grey blanket and draped it over Tungata's shoulders. Another order, and the captain carried in a tray on which stood a bottle of vodka and another of whisky, two glasses, an ice-bucket and a pitcher of water.

Tungata did not look at the water. It took all his self-control, but he kept his eyes on Peter Fungabera's face.

'Now, this is much more civilized,' Peter said. 'The Comrade Minister Zebiwe speaks no Shona, only the primitive Sindebele dialect, so we will use the language common to all of us – English.'

He poured vodka and whisky and as the ice clinked into

the glasses Tungata winced, but kept his gaze fixed on Peter Fungabera.

'This is a briefing,' Peter explained. 'Our guest,' he indicated the old white man, 'is a student of African history. He has read, and remembered, everything ever written about this country. While you, my dear Tungata, are a sprig of the house of Kumalo, the old robber chiefs of the Matabele, who for a hundred years raided and terrorized the legitimate owners of this land, the Mashona people. Therefore both of you might already know something of what I am about to relate. If that is so, I beg your indulgence.' He sipped his whisky, and neither of the other two moved or spoke.

'We must go back a hundred and fifty years,' said Peter, 'to when a young field commander of the Zulu King Chaka, a man who was the king's favourite, failed to render up to Chaka the spoils of war. This man's name was Mzilikazi, son of Mashobane of the Kumalo subtribe of Zulu, and he was to become the first Matabele. In passing, it is interesting to note that he set a precedent for the tribe which he was to found. Firstly, he was a master of rapine and plunder, a famous killer. Then he was a thief. He stole from his own sovereign. He failed to render to Chaka the king's share of the spoils. Then Mzilikazi was a coward, for when Chaka sent for him to face retribution, he fled.' Peter smiled at Tungata. 'Killer, thief and coward – that was Mzilikazi, father of the Matabele, and that description fits every member of the tribe from then until the present day. Killer! Thief! Coward!' He repeated the insults with relish, and Tungata watched his face with eyes that glowed.

'So this paragon of manly virtues, taking with him his regiment of renegade Zulu warriors, fled northwards. He fell upon the weaker tribes in his path, and took their herds and their young women. This was the *umfecane*, the great killing. It is said that one million defenceless souls perished under the Matabele assegais. Certainly Mzilikazi left behind him an empty land, a land of bleached skulls and burned-out villages.

'He blazed this path of destruction across the continent until he met, coming from the south-west, a foe more bloodthirsty, more avaricious even than he, the white men, the Boers. They shot down Mzilikazi's vaunted killers like rabid dogs. So Mzilikazi, the coward, ran again. Northwards again.'

Peter gently agitated the ice cubes in his glass, a soft tinkling that made Tungata blink, but he did not look down at the glass.

'Bold Mzilikazi crossed the Limpopo river and found a pleasant land of sweet grass and clear waters. It was inhabited by a gentle, pastoral people, descendants of a race who had built great cities of stone, a comely people whom Mzilikazi contemptuously named the "eaters of dirt" and referred to as his cattle. He treated them like cattle, killing them for sport, or husbanding them to provide his indolent warriors with slaves. The young women of Mashona, if they were nubile, were mounted for pleasure and used as breeding-stock to provide more warriors for his murderous impis – but then you know all this.'

'The broad facts, yes,' the old white man nodded. 'But not your interpretation of them. Which proves that history is merely propaganda written by the victors.'

Peter laughed. 'I hadn't heard it put that way before. However, it's true. Now, we, the Shona, are the ultimate victors, so it is our right to redraft history.'

'Go on,' the white man invited. 'I find this instructive.'

'Very well. In the year 1868, as white men measure time, Mzilikazi, this great fat debauched and diseased killer, died. It is amusing to recall that his followers kept his corpse fifty-six days in the heat of Matabeleland before committing it to burial, so he stank in death as powerfully

337

as he did in life. Another endearing Matabele trait.' He waited for Tungata to protest, and when he did not, went on.

'One of his sons succeeded him, Lobengula, "the one who drives like the wind", as fat and devious and blood-thirsty as his illustrious father. However, at almost the same time as he took the chieftainship of the Matabele, two seeds were sown that would soon grow into great creeping vines that would choke and finally bring the fat bull of Kumalo crashing to earth.' He paused for effect, like a practised storyteller, and then held up one finger. 'Firstly, far to the south of his plundered domains, the white men had found on a desolate kopje in the veld, a little shiny pebble, and secondly from a dismal island far to the north, a sickly young white man embarked on a ship, seeking clean dry air for his weak lungs.

'The kopje was soon dug away by the white ants, and became a hole a mile across and four hundred feet deep. The white men called it Kimberley, after the foreign secretary in England who condoned its theft from the local tribes.

'The sickly white man was named Cecil John Rhodes, and he proved to be even more devious and cunning and unprincipled than any Matabele king. He simply ate up the other white men who had discovered the kopje of shiny stones. He bullied and bribed and cheated and wheedled until he owned it all. He became the richest man in the world.

'However, the winning of these shiny pebbles called for enormous amounts of physical labour by tens of thousands of men. Whenever there is hard work to be done, where does the white man in Africa look?' Peter chuckled and left his rhetorical question unanswered.

'Cecil Rhodes offered simple food, a cheap gun and a few coins for three years of a black man's life. The black men, unsophisticated and naive, accepted those wages, and made their master a multi-millionaire many times over.

'Amongst the black men who came to Kimberley were the young *amadoda* of the Matabele. They had been sent by Lobengula – have I mentioned that Lobengula was a thief? His instruction to his young men was to steal the shiny pebbles and bring them back to him. Tens of thousands of Matabele made the long journey southwards to the diamond diggings and they brought back diamonds.

'The diamonds they picked were the largest and the brightest, the ones that showed up most clearly in the washing and processing. How many diamonds? One Matabele whom the white police caught had swallowed 348 carats of diamonds worth £3000 in the coin of those days – say £300,000 in today's terms. Another had slit open his thigh and pouched in his own flesh a single diamond that weighed 200 carats.' Peter shrugged. 'Who can say what its present value might have been? Perhaps £2,000,000.'

The old white man who had been aloof, even disinterested, during the first part of this recital, was now leaning forward intently, his head twisted to watch Peter Fungabera's lips.

'Those were the few that the white police caught, but there were thousands upon thousands of Matabele diamond-smugglers who were never caught. Remember, in the early days of the diggings, there was virtually no control over the black labourers, they came and went as the fancy moved them. So some stayed a week before drifting away, others worked a full three-year contract before leaving, but when they went, the shiny pebbles went with them – in their hair, in the heels of their new boots, in their mouths, in their bellies, stuffed up their anuses or in the vaginas of their women – the diamonds went out in thousands upon thousands of carats.

'Of course, it could not last. Rhodes introduced the

compound system. The labourers were locked up in barbed-wire compounds for the full three years of their contract. Before they left they were stripped naked, and placed in special quarantine huts for ten days, during which time their heads and pudenda were shaved, and their bodies minutely examined by the white doctors, their rear ends were thoroughly probed and any recently healed scars sounded, and if necessary, reopened with a surgeon's scalpel.

'They were given massive doses of castor oil, and finely meshed screens were placed under the latrines so that their droppings could be washed and processed as though they were the blue earth of the diggings. However, the Matabele were crafty thieves, and they still found ways to get the stones out of the compounds. The river of diamonds had been reduced to a trickle, but the trickle went northwards still to Lobengula.

'Again you ask, how many? We can only guess. There was a Matabele named Bazo, the Axe, who left Kimberley with a belt of diamonds around his waist. You have heard of Bazo, son of Gandang, my dear Tungata. He was your great-grandfather. He became a notorious Matabele induna, and slew hundreds of defenceless Mashona during his depredations. The belt of diamonds that he laid before Lobengula, so legend tells us, weighed the equivalent of ten ostrich eggs. As a single ostrich egg has the same capacity as two dozen domestic hens' eggs, and even allowing for legend's exaggerations, we come to a figure in excess of five million pounds sterling in today's inflated currency.

'Another source tells us that Lobengula had five pots full of first-water diamonds. That is five gallons of diamonds, enough to rock the monopoly of De Beers' central diamond-selling organization.

'Yet another verbal history talks of the ritual *khombisile* that Lobengula held for his indunas, his tribal counsellors.

Khombisile is the Sindebele word for a showing, or putting on display,' Peter explained to the white man, and then went on. 'In the privacy of his great hut, the king would strip naked and his wives would anoint his bloated body with thick beef grease. Then they would stick diamonds onto the grease, until his entire body was covered in a mosaic of precious stones, a living sculpture covered with a hundred million pounds' worth of diamonds.

'So that is the answer to your question, gentlemen. Lobengula probably had more diamonds than have ever been assembled in one place at one time, other than in the vaults of De Beers' central selling organization in London.

'While this was happening, Rhodes, the richest man in the world, sitting in Kimberley and obsessed with the concept of empire, looked northwards and dreamed. Such was the strength of his obsession that he began to speak of "my north". In the end, he took it as he had done the diamond diggings of Kimberley – a little at a time. He sent his envoys to negotiate with Lobengula a concession to prospect and exploit the minerals of his domains, which included the land of the Mashona.

'From the white queen in England, Rhodes obtained approval for the formation of a Royal Charter Company, and then he sent a private army of hard and ruthless men to occupy these concessions. Lobengula had not expected anything like this. A few men digging little holes, yes, but not an army of brutal adventurers.

'Firstly, Lobengula protested to no avail. The white men pressed him harder and harder, until they forced him to a fatal error of judgement. Lobengula, feeling his very existence threatened, assembled his impis in a warlike display.

'This was the provocation for which Rhodes and his henchmen had worked and planned. They fell upon Lobengula in a savage and merciless campaign. They machine-gunned his famous impis, and shattered the Matabele nation. Then they galloped to Lobengula's kraal at

GuBulawayo. However, Lobengula, that wily thief and coward, had already fled northwards, taking with him his wives, his herds, what remained of his fighting impis – and his diamonds.

'A small force of white men pursued him for part of the way, until they ran into a Matabele ambush and were slaughtered to a man. More white men would have followed Lobengula, but the rains came and turned the veld to mud and the rivers to torrents. So Lobengula escaped with his treasure. He wandered on northwards without a goal, until the will to go on deserted him.

'In a wild and lonely place, he called Gandang, his half-brother, to him. He entrusted to him the care of the nation, and, coward to the very end, ordered his witch-doctor to prepare a poisonous potion and drank it down.

'Gandang sat his body upright in a cave. Around his body he placed all Lobengula's possessions: his assegais and regimental plumes and furs, his sleeping-mat and head-stool, his guns and knives and beer-pots – and his diamonds. Lobengula's corpse was wrapped in a sitting position in the green skin of a leopard and at his feet were placed the five gallon beer-pots of diamonds. Then the entrance to the cave was carefully sealed and disguised, and Gandang led the Matabele nation back to become the slaves of Rhodes and his Royal Charter Company.

'You ask when this occurred? It was in the rainy season of the year 1894. Not long ago – barely ninety years ago.

'You ask where? The answer is – very close to where we now sit. Probably within twenty miles of us. Lobengula travelled directly northwards from GuBulawayo and had almost reached the Zambezi river before he despaired and committed suicide.

'You ask if any living man knows the exact location of the treasure cave? The answer is yes!'

Peter Fungabera stopped, and then exclaimed, 'Oh, *do* forgive me, my dear Tungata, I have neglected to offer you any refreshment.' He called for another glass, and when it came, filled it with water and ice and, with his own hands, carried it to Tungata.

Tungata held the glass in both hands and drank with careful control, a sip at a time.

'Now, where was I?' Peter Fungabera returned to his chair behind the desk.

'You were telling us about the cave,' the white man with the pale eyes could not resist.

'Ah, yes, of course. Well, it seems that before Lobengula died, he charged this half-brother of his, Gandang, with the guardianship of the diamonds. He is supposed to have told him, "There will come a day when my people will need these diamonds. You and your son and his sons will keep this treasure until that day."

'So the secret was passed on in the Kumalo family, the so-called royal family of the Matabele. When a chosen son reached his manhood he was taken by his father or his grandfather on a pilgrimage.'

Tungata was so reduced by his ordeal that he felt weak and feverish, his mind floated and the iced water in his empty stomach seemed to drug him, so that fantasy became mixed with reality, and the memory of his own pilgrimage to Lobengula's tomb was so vivid that he seemed to be reliving it as he listened to Peter Fungabera's voice.

It had been during his first year as an undergraduate at the University of Rhodesia. He had gone home to spend the long vacation with his grandfather. Gideon Kumalo was the assistant headmaster at Khami Mission School, just outside the town of Bulawayo.

'I have a great treat for you,' the old man had greeted him, smiling through the thick lenses of his spectacles. He still had a little of his eyesight left, though within the following five years he would lose the last vestiges of it.

'We are going on a journey together, Vundla.' It was the old man's pet name for him. *Vundla*, the hare, the clever lively animal always beloved by the Africans. The slaves had taken him with them in legend to America in the form of Brer Rabbit.

The two of them took the bus northwards, changing half a dozen times at lonely trading-stores or remote crossroads, sometimes waiting for forty-eight hours at a stop, when their connection was delayed. However, the delay did not rankle. They made a picnic of it, sitting at night round their camp-fire and talking.

What marvellous stories old grandfather Gideon could tell. Fables and legends and tribal histories, but it was the histories that fascinated Tungata. He could hear them repeated fifty times without tiring of them: the story of Mzilikazi's exodus from Zululand, and the *umfecane*, the war with the Boers, and the crossing of the Limpopo river. He could recite the names of the glorious impis and the men who had commanded them, the campaigns they had waged and the battle honours they had won.

Most especially, he learned from the old man the history of the 'Moles who burrowed under a mountain', the impi that had been founded and commanded by his great-grandfather, Bazo the Axe. He learned to sing the war songs and the praise songs of the Moles, and he dreamed that in a perfect world he would himself have commanded the Moles one day, wearing the regimental head-band of mole-skin and the furs and the feathers.

So the pair, the greybeard with failing eyesight and the stripling, travelled together for five leisurely companion-ship-filled days, until at the old man's request, the rackety, dusty old bus set them down on a rutted dirt track in the forest.

'Mark this spot well, Vundla,' Gideon instructed. 'Here, the water-course with the fall of rock, and the kopje over there shaped like a sleeping lion – this is the starting point.'

344

They set off northwards through the forest, following a succession of landmarks that the old man made him recite in the form of a rhyming poem. Tungata found he could still recite it without hesitation:

'The beginning is the lion that sleeps, follow his gaze to the crossing place of the elephant—'

It was another three days' travel at Gideon's reduced pace before he toiled up the steep hillside with Tungata handing him over the worst places, and they stood before the tomb of Lobengula at last.

Tungata remembered kneeling before the tomb, sucking blood from the self-inflicted cut on his wrist and spitting the blood on the rocks that blocked the entrance and repeating after his grandfather the terrible oath of secrecy and guardianship. Of course neither the old man nor the oath had mentioned diamonds or treasure. Tungata had merely sworn to guard the secret of the tomb, passing it to his chosen son, until the day when 'The children of Mashobane cry out for succour, and the stones are burst open to free the spirit of Lobengula, and it shall come forth like fire – Lobengula's fire!'

After the ceremony the old man had lain down in the shade of the *ficus* tree that grew beside the entrance, and, exhausted by the long journey, had slept until nightfall. Tungata had remained awake, examining the tomb and the area around it. He had found certain signs that had led him to a conclusion that he did not confide to his grandfather, not then nor during the journey homewards. He had not wanted to alarm and disturb Gideon, his love for him was too great and protective.

Peter Fungabera's voice intruded on his reverie, jerking him back to the present.

'In fact, we are privileged to have with us at this very

moment an illustrious member of the Kumalo clan, and the present guardian of the old robber's tomb, the honourable Comrade Minister Tungata Zebiwe.'

The white man's pale, cruel eyes riveted him, and Tungata stiffened on the hard wooden bench. Tungata tried his voice, and found that even the small quantity of water that he had taken had eased his throat. His voice was deep and measured, only slightly ragged at the edges.

'You delude yourself, Fungabera.' He made the name into an insult, but Peter's smile never slipped. 'I know nothing of this nonsense that you have dreamed up, and even if I did—' Tungata did not have to finish the sentence.

'You will find my patience inexhaustible,' Peter promised him. 'The diamonds have lain there ninety years. A few more weeks will not spoil them. I have brought with me a doctor to supervise your treatment. We will find just how much you can bear before your Matabele courage fails you. On the other hand, you have the option at any time to make an end to this unpleasantness. You can elect to take us to Lobengula's burial site, and immediately after you have done so, I will arrange to have you flown out of the country to any destination of your choice—' Peter paused before adding the final sweetener to his proposition ' – and with you will go the young woman who so gallantly defended you in the courtroom, Sarah Nyoni.'

This time there was a flash of emotion behind the contemptuous mask of Tungata's features.

'Oh yes,' Peter nodded. 'We have her safely taken care of.'

'Your lies need no denial. If you had her, you would have used her already.' Tungata forced himself to believe that Sarah would have obeyed him. She had read and understood the hand-sign that he had flashed to her across the courtroom as he was being led away. 'Take cover! Hide yourself. You are in danger!' he had ordered her and she had acknowledged and agreed. She was safe, he had to believe that, it was all he had to believe in.

'We shall see,' Peter Fungabera promised.

'Not that it matters.' Tungata had to try and protect her, now that it was clear that the Shona were hunting for Sarah. 'She is a mere woman – do what you will to her. It will mean little to me.'

Fungabera raised his voice. 'Captain!' The guard commander came immediately. 'Take the prisoner back to his quarters. His treatment will be ordered and supervised by the doctor. Do you understand?'

When they were alone, Colonel Bukharin said quietly, 'He will not be easy. He has physical strength and something else beyond that. Some men simply will not bend, even under the most extreme coercion.'

'It may take a little time, but in the end—'

'I am not so certain,' Bukharin sighed morosely. 'Do you indeed have the woman you spoke of, this Sarah Nyoni?'

Peter hesitated. 'Not yet. She has disappeared, but again, it's only a matter of time. She cannot hide for ever.'

'Time,' Colonel Bukharin repeated. 'Yes, there is a time for everything, but your time is passing. This thing must be done soon, or not at all.'

'Days only, not weeks,' Peter promised, but his voice had become thin and Colonel Bukharin, the consummate hunter of men, sensed his advantage.

'This Zebiwe is a hard man, I am not sure he will respond to the treatment at our clinic. I do not like this business of a diamond treasure. It smacks too much of a story for young boys. And I do not like the fact that you have let this Matabele woman elude you. This whole business begins to depress me.'

'You are unduly pessimistic – everything is going well. I need just a little time to prove it to you.'

'You already know that I cannot remain here much longer, I must return to Moscow. And what must I tell them there – that you are digging for treasure?' Bukharin threw up both hands. 'They will believe that I am turning senile.'

'A month,' Peter Fungabera said. 'I need another month.'

'Today is the tenth. You have until the last day of the month to deliver both money and the man to us.'

'That is cutting it too fine,' Peter protested.

'On the first of next month, I will return. If on that date you cannot deliver, I will recommend to my superiors that this entire project be aborted.'

The adder was almost six feet long and seemed as gross as a pregnant sow. It was coiled upon itself in a corner of the mesh cage, and the patterning of its scales was in soft purples and golds, in russet and madder, all the colours of autumn enclosed in perfect diamonds each of which was outlined in the black of mourning.

However, the colours and patterns were not sufficiently spectacular to divert attention from the creature's hideous head. It was the size of a poisonous gourd, but shaped like the ace of spades, flattening and tapering to the snout with its nostril slits. The adder's eyes were bright as beads of polished jet and its tongue was bifurcated and feathery light as it slipped in and out between the grinning lips.

'I can claim no credit for this,' said Peter Fungabera. 'The good doctor is responsible for this little entertainment.' He smiled at Tungata. 'It is many days since last we spoke, and frankly, your time is up. So is mine. I must have your agreement today or else it does not matter. After today you are expendable, Comrade Zebiwe.'

Tungata was strapped to a sturdy chair of red Rhodesian teak. The mesh cage stood on the table before him.

'You were once in the Game Department,' Peter Fungabera went on. 'So you will recognize this reptile as *bitis gabonica*, the Gaboon adder. It is one of the most venomous of African snakes, its toxicity exceeded only by the mamba. However, its sting is more agonizing than either mamba or cobra. It is said that the pain drives men mad before they die.'

He touched the cage with the tip of his swagger-stick, and the adder struck at him. The coils propelled the monstrous head across the cage in a liquid blur of movement, half its gross body aerialized by the power of the strike; the jaws gaped to expose the butter-yellow lining of the throat, and the long recurved fangs were gleaming white as polished porcelain, as it crashed into the wire mesh with a force that shook the table. Even Peter Fungabera jumped back involuntarily, and then chuckled apologetically.

'I cannot stand snakes,' he explained. 'They make my flesh crawl. What about you, Comrade Minister?'

'Whatever you are planning, it is a bluff,' Tungata answered. His voice was weaker now. Since their last meeting, he had spent many days at the wall in the sun. His body seemed to have shrunk until it was too small for his head. His skin had a grey tone, and looked dusty and dry. 'You cannot afford to let that thing sting me. I expect you have removed the poison sacs.'

'Doctor.' Peter Fungabera turned to the regimental doctor who sat at the far end of the table. He rose immediately and left the room.

'We were quite fortunate to find a specimen of the Gaboon,' Peter Fungabera went on conversationally. 'They are really rather rare, as you know.'

The doctor returned. He now wore thick gloves that reached to his elbows, and carried a large striped bushrat the size of a kitten. The rat squealed piercingly and struggled in his gloved hands. Gingerly the doctor opened

349

the door in the top of the mesh cage, dropped the rat through it and immediately snapped the sprung door closed. The furry little animal scampered around the cage, testing the mesh walls with its nose and whiskers until suddenly it saw the adder in the corner. It leaped high and landed on stiff legs and then retreated into the opposite corner and crouched there, staring across the cage.

The adder began to uncoil, its scales glowing with an unearthly loveliness as it slid silently over the sanded floor towards the cornered rat. An unnatural stillness overcame the small animal. Its nose no longer twitched and wriggled. It sank down on its belly, fluffed out its fur and watched with mesmeric fascination as repulsive death slid inexorably towards it.

Two feet from the rat the adder stopped, its neck arched into a taut 'S' and then, so swiftly that the eye could not record it, it struck.

The rat was hurled back against the mesh, and immediately the adder withdrew, its coils flowing back upon itself. Now there were tiny droplets of blood on the rat's russet fur, and its body began to pulsate rapidly. The limbs twitched and jumped without coordination and then, abruptly, it squealed, a shrill cry of unbearable agony, and rolled over on its back in the final convulsion of death.

The doctor lifted the carcass out of the cage with a pair of wooden tongs and carried it from the room.

'Of course,' said Peter Fungabera. 'You have many times the body mass of that rodent. With you it would take much longer.'

The doctor had returned and with him were the guard captain and two troopers.

'As I said, the doctor has designed the apparatus. I think he has done excellent work, given the limited materials and shortage of time.'

They lifted Tungata's chair and placed him closer to

the cage. One of the troopers carried another smaller mesh cage. It was shaped like an oversized fencing helmet, and it fitted over Tungata's head, closing snugly around his throat. From the front of the encompassing helmet protruded a mesh tube that resembled the thickened and shortened trunk of a deformed elephant.

The two troopers stood behind Tungata's chair and forced him forward until the open tube of mesh aligned with the door of the adder's cage. Dexterously the Shona doctor clipped the tube of Tungata's helmet and the cage together.

'When the door of the cage is raised, you and the Gaboon will be sharing the same living space.' Tungata stared down the mesh tube to the door at its extremity. 'But we can stop this at any time you say the word.'

'Your father was a dung-eating Shona hyena,' said Tungata softly.

'We will induce the adder to leave its cage and join you in yours by applying heat to the far wall. I do advise you to be sensible, Comrade. Take us to old Lobengula's tomb.'

'The king's tomb is sacred—' Tungata broke off. He was weaker than he had realized. It had slipped out. Up to now he had stubbornly denied the existence of the tomb.

'Good,' said Peter happily. 'At least we have now agreed that there is a tomb. Now agree to take us there, and this will all end. A safe flight to another land, for you and the woman—'

'I spit on you, Fungabera, and I spit on the diseased whore that was your mother.'

'Open the cage,' ordered Fungabera.

It rattled up in its runners – and Tungata stared down the tube as though down the barrel of a rifle. The adder was coiled on the far side of the cage, staring back at him with those bright black eyes.

'There is still time, Comrade.'

Tungata did not trust his voice to speak again. He steeled himself, and stared into the adder's eyes, trying to dominate it.

'Proceed,' said Peter, and one of the troopers placed a small charcoal brazier on the table. Tungata could feel the heat from it even where he sat. Slowly the soldier pushed the glowing stove closer to the far mesh of the cage, and the adder hissed explosively and uncoiled its body. To escape the heat, it began to slither towards the opening of the mesh tube.

'Quickly, Comrade,' Peter urged him. 'Say you will do it. There are only seconds left. I can still close the door.'

Tungata felt the sweat prickle as it burst out on his forehead and slid down his naked back. He wanted to shout a curse at Peter Fungabera, to consign him to a fate as horrid as this, but his pulse was pounding in his own ears, deafening him.

The adder hesitated at the mouth of the tube, reluctant to enter.

'There is still time,' Peter whispered. 'You do not deserve such a loathsome death – say it? Say you will do it!'

Tungata had not realized how huge the adder was. Its eyes were only eighteen inches from his, and it hissed again as loudly as a punctured truck tyre, a vast exhalation of air that dinned in his eardrums. The trooper pushed the glowing charcoal brazier hard up against the mesh, and the adder thrust its head into the opening of the tube and its belly scales made a dry rasping sound against the wire.

'It's not too late yet.' Peter Fungabera unbuckled the flap of his holster and drew his pistol. He placed the muzzle against the wire, only inches from the adder's head. 'Say the word, and I will blow its head off.'

'Damn you to your own stinking Shona hell,' whispered Tungata. He could smell the adder now, not a strong odour, a faint mousy sweetness tinged with corruption. It nauseated him. He felt vomit rise and scald the back of his throat. He swallowed it down and began to struggle against the straps that held him. The cage shook with his efforts, but the two troopers held his shoulders, and the great adder, alarmed by his movements, hissed again and arched its neck into the 'S' of the strike.

Tungata stopped struggling and forced himself to remain still. He could feel his sweat pouring down his body, trickling coldly down his flanks and puddling under him on the seat of his chair.

Gradually the adder uncocked its neck, and crept forward towards his face. Six inches from his eyes, and Tungata sat still as a statue in his own sweat and loathing and horror. It was so close now that he could not focus on it. It was merely a blur that filled all his vision – and then the adder shot out its tongue and explored his face with feather-light strokes of the black forked tongue.

Every nerve in Tungata's body was screwed up to snapping point, and his weakened body was overdosed with adrenalin so that he felt he was suffocating. He had to cling to consciousness with all his remaining strength or he would have slipped over the edge into the black void of oblivion.

The adder moved on slowly. He could feel the cool slippery touch of coils across his cheek, under his ear, around the back of his neck, and then, in a final orgasm of horror, he realized that the huge reptile was throwing coil after coil of its body about his head, enveloping him, covering his mouth and his nose. He dared not scream nor move, and the seconds drew out.

'He likes you,' Peter Fungabera's voice had thickened with excitement and anticipation. 'He's settling down with you.'

Tungata swivelled his eyes and Peter was on the periphery of his field of vision, blurred by the fine mesh of the cage.

'We can't have that,' Peter gloated, and Tungata saw his hand reach out towards the charcoal brazier. For the first time Tungata noticed that a thin steel rod, like a poker, had been thrust into the burning charcoal. When Peter drew it out, the tip glowed red hot.

'This is your absolutely final chance to agree,' he said. 'When I touch the creature with this, it will go crazy.'

He waited for a reply. 'You cannot speak, of course. If you agree, just blink your eyes rapidly.'

Tungata stared fixedly at him through the mesh, trying to convey to him the universe of hatred that he experienced.

'Ah well, we tried,' said Peter Fungabera. 'Now you have only yourself to blame.'

He slipped the point of the glowing poker through the mesh and touched the adder with it. There was a sharp hiss of searing flesh, a tiny puff of stinking smoke and the adder went berserk.

Tungata felt the coils enfold his head, pumping and swelling, and then the great body whipped and slashed, filling the confined space of the cage with crazy uncoordinated convulsions. The cage banged and jarred and clattered, and Tungata lost control, he heard himself screaming, as terror engulfed him.

Then the snake's head filled his vision. Its jaws flared open, and its bright yellow throat gaped at him, as it struck into his face. The force of the strike stunned him. It hit him in the cheek below the eye, a heavy punch that jarred him so his teeth clashed together and he bit through his own tongue. Blood filled his mouth and he felt the long curved fangs snag into his flesh like fishhooks tugging and jerking, as they spurted jets of deadly toxin into his flesh – and then, mercifully, darkness took him and Tungata slumped unconscious against the straps that held him.

'Y**ou've killed him, you bloody idiot!' Peter Fungabera's voice was shrill and petulant with panic.
'No, no.' The doctor was working quickly.
With the help of the troopers, he pulled the mesh helmet
off Tungata's head. One of the troopers hurled the maimed
adder against the wall and then crushed its head under the
butt of an AK 47. 'No. He's passed out, that's all. He was
weak from the wall.'

Between them they lifted Tungata and carried him to
the camp-bed against the far wall. With exaggerated care
they laid him on it, and swiftly the doctor checked his
pulse.

'He's all right.' He filled a disposable syringe from a glass
ampoule, and shot it into Tungata's sweat-slicked upper
arm. 'I've given him a stimulant – ah, there!' The doctor's
relief was obvious. 'There! He is coming round already.'

The doctor swabbed the deep punctures in Tungata's
cheek from which watery lymph was oozing.

'There is always risk of infection from these bites,' the
doctor explained anxiously. 'I will inject an antibiotic.'

Tungata moaned and muttered, and then began to
struggle weakly. The troopers restrained him, until he came
fully conscious and then they helped him into a sitting
position. His eyes focused with difficulty on Peter Fungabera, and his confusion was obvious.

'Welcome back to the land of the living, Comrade.'
Peter's voice was once more smooth and richly modulated.
'You are now one of the privileged few who have had a
glimpse of the beyond.'

The doctor still fussed over him, but Tungata's eyes
never left Peter Fungabera's face.

'You do not understand,' Peter said, 'and nobody can
blame you for that. You see, the good doctor *had* removed
the creature's poison sacs, as you suggested he might have.'

Tungata shook his head, unable to speak.

'The rat!' Peter spoke for him. 'Yes, of course, the rat.

355

That was rather clever. Whilst he was out of the room the doctor gave it a little injection. He had tested the dosage on other rodents to get the correct delay. You were right, my dear Tungata, we aren't ready to let you go just yet. Maybe next time, or the time after that – you will never know for certain. Then of course, we might miscalculate. There might, for instance, have been a little residual toxin in that adder's fangs—' Peter shrugged. 'It's all very delicate – this time, next time – who knows? How long can you keep it up, Comrade, before your mind snaps?'

'I can keep it up as long as you can,' Tungata whispered huskily. 'I give you my oath on that.'

'Now, now, no rash promises,' Peter scolded him mildly. 'The next little production that I am planning involves my puppies – you have heard Fungabera's puppies, every night you have heard them. I am not sure how we can control them. It will be interesting – you could easily lose an arm or a foot – it only takes one snap of those jaws.' Peter played with his swagger-stick, rolling it between his fingers. 'The choice is yours, and of course it only takes one word from you to end it all.' Peter held up one hand. 'No, please don't tax yourself. There is no need to give an answer now. We'll let you have another few days at the wall to recuperate from this ordeal, and then—'

Tungata had lost track of time. He could not remember how many days he had spent at the wall, how many men he had seen executed, how many nights he had lain and listened to the hyena.

He found it difficult to think further ahead than the next bowl of water. The doctor had judged the amount required to keep him alive with precision. Thirst was a torment that never ceased, not even when he slept, for his nightmares now were filled with images of water – lakes and running streams which he could not reach, rain that fell all around him and did not touch him, and raging, intolerable thirst.

Added to the thirst, Peter Fungabera's threat of delivering him to the hyena pack festered in his imagination and became more potent for every day that it was delayed. Water and hyena – they were beginning to drive him beyond the borders of sanity. He knew that he could not hold out much longer, and he wondered confusedly why he had held out this long. He had to keep reminding himself that Lobengula's tomb was all that was keeping him alive. While he had the secret, they could not kill him. He did not entertain for even a moment the hope that Peter Fungabera would keep his promise of sending him to safety once he led them to the tomb.

He had to stay alive, it was his duty. As long as he lived, there was still hope, however faint, of delivery. He knew that with his death his people would sink deeper into the tyrant's coils. He was their hope of salvation. It was his duty to them to live, even though death would now be a blessing and a release, he could not die. He must live on.

He waited in the icy darkness of pre-dawn, his body too stiff and weak to rise. This day they would have to carry him to the wall, or to whatever they had planned for him. He hated that thought. He hated to show such weakness in front of them.

He heard the camp beginning to stir. The march of the guards, the orders shouted with needless violence, the sound of blows and the cries of a prisoner in the adjoining cell being dragged to the execution wall.

Now soon they would come for him. He reached out for the water bowl and his disappointment hit him in a cold gust as he remembered that the previous evening he had not been able to control himself. The bowl was empty. He crouched over it and licked the enamel like a dog, in case a drop remained of the precious fluid. It was dry.

357

The bolts shot back and the door was flung open. The day had begun. Tungata tried to rise. He lurched up onto his knees. A guard entered and placed a large dark object on the threshold and then quietly withdrew. The door was bolted again and Tungata was left alone.

This had never happened before. Tungata was stupefied and uncomprehending. He crouched in the darkness and waited for something more to happen, but nothing did. He heard the other prisoners being led away, and then silence beyond the door of his cell.

The light began to strengthen and cautiously he examined the object that had been left by the guard. It was a plastic bucket, and in the dawn light the contents shimmered.

Water. A full gallon of water. He crawled to it and examined it, not yet beginning to hope. Once before, they had tricked him. They had doctored his water bowl and he had gulped down a mouthful before he realized that it was heavily laced with salt and bitter alum. The thirst that followed had driven him delirious and shaking as though in malarial crisis.

Gingerly he dipped his forefinger into the liquid in the bucket and tasted a drop. It was sweet, clean water. He made a little whining sound in his throat, and scooped the empty bowl full of the precious fluid. He tilted back his head and poured the water down his throat. He drank with a terrible desperation, expecting that at any moment the door would crash open and a guard would kick the bucket over. He drank until his empty belly bulged, and pangs of colic stabbed through it. Then he rested for a few minutes, feeling the fluid flowing into his desiccated tissues, feeling them recharge with strength, and then he drank again, and rested and drank again. After three hours he urinated copiously in the toilet bucket for the first time in as long as he could remember.

When they finally came for him at noon, he could stand up unaided and curse them with fluency and artistry.

They led him towards the execution wall, and he felt almost cheerful. With his belly sloshing with water, he knew he could resist them for ever. The execution stake had no terror for him any longer. He had stood there too long and too often. He welcomed it as a part of the routine which he understood. He had reached the point where he feared only the unknown.

Halfway across the parade ground he realized that something was different. They had built a new structure facing the wall. A neatly thatched sun-shelter. Under the shelter two chairs were set and a table had been laid for lunch.

Seated at the table was the dreadfully familiar figure of Peter Fungabera. Tungata had not seen him for days, and his new-found courage faltered, weakness came back over him. He felt a rubbery give to his knees and he stumbled. What had they planned for today? If only he knew, he could meet it. The uncertainty was the one truly unbearable torture.

Peter Fungabera was lunching and he did not even look up as Tungata was led past the thatched shelter. Peter ate with his fingers in the African manner, taking the stiff white maize cake and moulding it into bite-sized balls, pressing a depression into it with his thumb and then filling it with a sauce of stewed greens and salted kapenta fish from Lake Kariba. The smell of the food flooded Tungata's mouth with saliva, but he trudged on towards the wall and the execution stake.

There was only one other victim today, he noticed, narrowing his eyes against the glare. He was already strapped to one of the stakes. Then, with a small shock of surprise, Tungata realized that it was a woman.

She was naked – a young woman. Her skin had a soft velvety sheen in the sunlight, like polished amber. Her body was graciously formed, her breasts symmetrical and firm, their aureolas were the colour of ripe mulberries, the nipples upturned and out-thrust. Her legs were long and willowy, the bare feet small and neat. Bound as she was, she could not cover herself. Tungata sensed her shame at her naked sex, nestled dark and fluffy in the juncture of her thighs like a tiny animal with separate life. He averted his eyes, looked up at her face – and at last he despaired.

It was all over. The guards released his arms, and he tottered towards the young woman at the stake. Though her eyes were huge and dark with terror and shame, her first words were for him. She whispered softly in Sindebele, 'My lord, what have they done to you?'

'Sarah.' He wanted to reach over and touch her dear and lovely face, but he would not do so under the lewd gaze of his guards.

'How did they find you?' He felt very old and frail. It was all over.

'I did as you commanded,' she told him in soft apology. 'I went into the hills, but then a message reached me – one of my children from the school was dying – dysentery and no doctor. I could not ignore the call.'

'Of course, it was a lie,' he guessed flatly.

'It was a lie,' she admitted. 'The Shona soldiers were waiting for me. Forgive me, lord.'

'It does not matter any longer,' he answered.

'Not for me, lord,' she pleaded. 'Do not do anything for me. I am a daughter of Mashobane. I can bear anything these Shona animals can do to me.'

He shook his head sadly, and at last reached out and touched her lips with the tips of his fingers. His hand was trembling like that of a drunkard. She kissed his fingers. He dropped his hand and, turning, trudged wearily back to the thatched shelter. The soldiers made no effort to prevent him.

Peter Fungabera looked up as he approached and motioned to the empty canvas chair. Tungata sat down and his body slumped.

360

'First,' Tungata said, 'the woman must be untied and clothed.'

Peter gave the order. They covered her and led her away to one of the hutments.

'My lord—' she strained back against their grip, her face turned piteously to him.

'She must not be ill-treated in any way.'

'She has not been,' Peter said. 'She will not be, unless you make it necessary.'

He pushed a bowl of maize cake towards Tungata. He ignored it.

'She must be taken out of the country and delivered to a representative of the international Red Cross in Francistown.'

'There is a light aircraft waiting at Tuti airfield. Eat, Comrade, we must have you strong and well.'

'When she is safe, she will speak to me – radio or telephone – and give me a code-word that I will arrange with her before she leaves.'

'Agreed.' He poured hot sweet tea for Tungata.

'We will be left alone together to agree on the code.'

'You may speak to her, of course,' Peter nodded. 'But in the middle of this parade ground. None of my men will be closer than a hundred yards to you, but there will be a machine-gun trained upon you at all times. I will allow you precisely five minutes with the woman.'

'I have failed you,' Sarah said, and Tungata had forgotten how beautiful she was. His whole being ached with longing for her.

'No,' he told her, 'it was inevitable. There is no blame to you. It was for duty, not for yourself that you came out of hiding.'

'My lord, what can I do now?'

361

'Listen,' he said, and spoke quietly and quickly. 'Some of my trusted people have escaped from the scourge of Fungabera's Third Brigade – you must find them. I believe they are in Botswana.' He gave her the names and she repeated them faithfully. 'Tell them—' She memorized all that he told her, and repeated it to him perfectly.

From the corner of his eye Tungata saw the guards at the edge of the parade ground start towards where they stood alone in the centre. Their five minutes together was up.

'When you are safe, they will allow us to speak on the radio. To let me know that all is well, you will repeat to me, "Your beautiful bird has flown high and swiftly". Repeat it.'

'Oh my lord,' she choked.

'Repeat it!'

She obeyed, and then flung herself into his arms. She clung to him, and he to her.

'Will I ever see you again?'

'No,' he told her. 'You must forget me.'

'Never!' she cried. 'Not if I live to be an old woman – never, my lord.'

The guards dragged them apart. A Land-Rover drove out onto the parade ground. They hustled Sarah into it.

The last he saw of her was her face in the rear window, looking back at him – her beautiful beloved face.

On the third day, they came to fetch Tungata from his cell and take him up to Peter Fungabera's command post on the central kopje.

'The woman is ready to speak to you. You will converse only in English. Your conversation will be recorded.' Peter indicated the transistor tape deck beside the radio apparatus. 'If you do attempt to slip in any Sindebele message, it will be translated later.'

'The code we have arranged is in Sindebele,' Tungata told him. 'She will have to repeat it.'

'Very well. That is acceptable, but nothing else.' He looked Tungata over critically. 'I am delighted to see you looking so well again, Comrade, a little good food and rest have worked wonders.'

Tungata wore faded suntans, but they were freshly laundered and pressed. He was still gaunt and wasted, but his skin had lost the dusty grey look and his eyes were clear and bright. The swelling of the adder bite on his cheek had abated, and the scab covering it looked dry and healthy.

Peter Fungabera nodded to the guard captain and he passed the radio microphone to Tungata and pressed the 'record' button on the tape deck.

'This is Tungata Zebiwe.'

'My lord, this is Sarah.' Her voice was scratchy and distorted by static, but he would have known it anywhere. The ache of longing filled his chest.

'Are you safe?'

'I am in Francistown. The Red Cross are caring for me.'

'Do you have a message?'

She replied in Sindebele. 'Your beautiful bird has flown high and swiftly.' Then she added, 'I have met others here. Do not despair.'

'That is good – I want you to—'

Peter Fungabera reached across and took the microphone from his hand. 'Excuse me, Comrade, but I am paying for the call.' He held the microphone to his lips and depressed the transmit button. 'Transmission ends,' he said, and broke the connection.

He tossed the microphone casually to the guard captain. 'Have the tape translated – by one of the Matabele trusties – and bring me a copy immediately.' Then he turned back to Tungata.

'Your little holiday is over, Comrade, now you and I have work to do. Shall we go?'

How long would he be able to draw out the search for Lobengula's grave, Tungata wondered. For every hour he could gain would have value – another hour of life, another hour of hope.

'It is almost twenty years since my grandfather took me to visit the site. My memory is unclear—'

'Your memory is as brilliant as that sun up there,' Peter told him. 'You are renowned for your ability to remember places and faces and names, Comrade, you forget that I have heard you speak in the Assembly, without notes. Besides which, you will have a helicopter to ferry you directly to the site.'

'That will not work. The first time I went was on foot. I must go back the same way. I would not recognize the landmarks from the air.'

So they went back along the dirt roads that Tungata and old Gideon had bussed over so many years before, and Tungata genuinely could not find the starting place – the fall of rocks in the old river course and the kopje shaped like an elephant's head. They spent three days searching, with Peter Fungabera becoming more and more short-tempered and disbelieving, before they stopped at the tiny village and trading-store that was the last reference point that Tungata could remember.

'Hau! The old road. Yes, the bridge was washed away many years ago. It was never used again. Now the new road goes so and so—'

They found the overgrown track at last and four hours later reached the dry river-bed. The old bridge had collapsed into a heap of shattered concrete already overgrown with lianas, but the rock wall upstream was exactly as

Tungata had remembered it and he experienced a pang of nostalgia. Suddenly old Gideon seemed very close to him, so much so that he glanced around and made a small sign with his right hand to appease the ancestral spirits and whispered, 'Forgive me, Baba, that I am going to betray the oath.'

Strangely the presence that he sensed was benign and fondly indulgent, as Old Gideon had always been. 'The path lies this way.' They left the Land-Rover at the broken bridge and continued on foot.

Tungata led with two armed troopers at his back. He set an easy pace, that chafed Peter Fungabera who followed behind the guards. As they went, Tungata could allow his imagination to wander freely. He seemed to be part of the exodus of the Matabele people of almost a hundred years before, an embodiment of Gandang, his great-great-grand-father, faithful and loyal to the end. He felt again the despair of a defeated people and the terror of the hard-riding white pursuit that might appear at any instant from the forest behind them, with their chattering three-legged machine-guns. He seemed to hear the lament of the women and the small children, the lowing of herds as they faltered and fell in this hard and bitter country.

When the last of the draught oxen were dead, Gandang had ordered the warriors of his famous Inyati regiment into the traces of the king's remaining wagon. Tungata imagined the king, obese and diseased and doomed, sitting up on the rocking wagon box staring into the forbidding north, a man caught up in the millstones of history and destiny and crushed between them.

'And now the final betrayal,' Tungata thought, bitterly. 'I am leading these Shona animals to disturb his rest once again.'

Three times, deliberately, he took the wrong path, drawing it out to the very limit of Peter Fungabera's patience. The third time, Peter Fungabera ordered him stripped naked and his wrists and ankles bound together, then he had stood over him with a cured hippo-hide whip, the vicious kiboko that the Arab slave-traders had introduced to Africa, and he thrashed Tungata like a dog until his blood dripped into the sandy grey earth.

It was the shame and humiliation of the beating rather than the pain that had made Tungata turn back and pick up his landmarks again. When he reached the hill at last, it appeared ahead of them with all the suddenness that Tungata recalled so vividly from his first visit.

They had been following a deep gorge of black rock, polished by the roaring torrential spates of the millennia. The depths were studded with stagnant green pools in which giant whiskered catfish stirred the scummy surface as they rose to feed, and lovely swallow-tailed butterflies floated in the heated air above, gems of scarlet and iridescent blue.

They came around a bend in the gorge, clambering over boulders the size and the colour of elephants, and abruptly the surrounding cliffs opened and the forest fell back. Before them, like a vast monument to dwarf the pyramids of the pharaohs, the hill of Lobengula rose into the sky.

The cliffs were sheer and daubed with lichens of twenty different shades of yellow and ochre and malachite. There was a breeding colony of vultures in the upper ledges, the parent birds sailing gracefully out over the heated void, tipping their wings in the rising thermals as they banked and spiralled.

'There it is,' Tungata murmured. '*Thabas Nkosi*, the hill of the king.'

The natural pathway to the summit followed a fault in the rock face where limestone overlaid the country rock. At places it was steep and daunting and the troopers, weighted with packs and weapons, glanced nervously over the drop and hugged the inner wall of rock as they edged upwards, but Peter Fungabera and Tungata climbed easily and sure-footed over even the worse places, leaving the escort far below.

'I could throw him over the edge,' Tungata thought, 'if I can take him unawares.' He glanced back and Peter was ten paces below him. He had the Tokarev pistol in his right hand and he smiled like a mamba.

'No,' he warned, and they understood each other without further words. For the moment Tungata put away the thought of vengeance and went on upwards. He turned a corner in the rock and they came out onto the crown of the hill, five hundred feet above the dark gorge.

Standing a little apart, both of them sweating lightly in the white sunlight, they looked down into the deep wide valley of the Zambezi. On the edge of their vision, the wide waters of the man-made lake of Kariba glinted softly through the haze of heat and blue smoke from the first bush-fires of the dry season. The troopers came off the path with transparent relief, and Peter Fungabera looked expectantly at Tungata.

'We are ready to go on, Comrade.'

'There is not much further to go,' Tungata answered him.

Over the crest of the cliff the rock formation had eroded and broken up into buttress and tumbled ramparts, the trees that had found purchase in the cracks and crevices had intertwined their root systems over the rock-face like mating serpents, while their stems were thickened and deformed by the severe conditions of heat and drought.

Tungata led them through the broken rock and tortured forest, into the mouth of a ravine. At the head of the ravine grew an ancient *ficus Natalensis*, the strangler fig tree, its fleshy limbs of blotched yellow loaded with bunches of bitter fruit. As they approached it a flock of brown parrots, green wings flagged with bright yellow, that had been feasting on the wild figs, exploded into flight. At the base of the *ficus* tree, the cliff was segmented, and the roots had found the cracks and forced them apart.

Tungata stood before the cliff and Peter Fungabera, suppressing an exclamation of impatience, glanced at him and saw his lips were moving silently, in a prayer or entreaty. Peter Fungabera began to examine the cliff-face more carefully, and realized with rising excitement that the cracks in the rock were too regular to be natural.

'Here!' he shouted to his troopers, and when they hurried forward, he pointed out one of the blocks in the face, and they set to work on it with bayonets and bare hands.

Within fifteen minutes of sweaty labour, they had worked the block free, and it was now clear that the face was in reality a wall of carefully fitted masonry. In the depths of the aperture left by the block, they could make out a second wall of masonry.

'Bring the prisoner,' Peter ordered. 'He will work in the front rank.'

By the time it was too dark to go on, they had opened an aperture just wide enough for two men to work shoulder to shoulder in the outer wall, and had begun on the inner wall. In the forefront, Tungata was able to confirm what he had guessed on his first visit to the tomb so long ago – the signs that he had noticed then and concealed from old grandfather Gideon were even more apparent on the inner wall of the tomb. They helped salve his conscience and ease the pain of oath-breaking.

Reluctantly Peter Fungabera called a halt on the work for the night. Tungata's hands were raw from contact with the rough blocks and he had lost a fingernail where it had been trapped and torn off in a slide of masonry. He was handcuffed to one of the Third Brigade troopers for the night, but even this could not keep him from dreamless exhaustion-drugged sleep. Peter Fungabera had to kick both him and his guard awake the next morning.

It was still dark and they ate their meagre rations of cold maize cake and sweet tea in silence. They had barely gulped it down before Peter Fungabera ordered them back to the masonry wall.

Tungata's torn hands were clumsy and stiff. Peter Fungabera stood behind him in the opening and when he faltered slashed him with the kiboko around the ribs, in the soft and sensitive flesh below the armpit. Tungata growled like a wounded lion and lifted a hundredweight block out of the wall.

The sun cleared the crown of the hill, and its golden rays illuminated the cliff-face. With a branch of dead wood, Tungata and one of the Shona troopers levered up another lump of rock, and as it began to move, there was a rumble and a harsh grating and the inner wall collapsed towards them. They jumped clear and stood coughing in the swirl of dust, peering into the aperture that they had made.

The air from the cave stank like a drunkard's mouth, stale and sour, and the darkness beyond was forbidding and menacing.

'You first,' Peter Fungabera ordered, and Tungata hesitated. He was overcome with a superstitious awe. He was an educated and sophisticated man, but beneath that, he was African. The spirits of his tribe and his ancestors guarded this place. He looked at Peter Fungabera and knew that he was experiencing the same dread of the supernatural, even though he was armed with a flashlight, whose batteries he had conserved zealously for this moment.

'Move!' Fungabera ordered. His harsh tone could not disguise his disquiet, and Tungata, to shame him, stepped cautiously over the rock fall into the cave.

He stood for a while until his eyes adjusted to the gloom

and he could make out the configuration of the cave. The floor beneath his feet was smooth and worn, but it sloped downwards at a steep angle. Obviously this cave had been the lair of animals and the home of primitive man for tens of thousands of years before it became the tomb of a king.

Peter Fungabera, standing behind Tungata, played the beam of his flashlight over walls and roof. The roof was crusted with the soot of ancient cooking-fires, and the smooth walls were rich with the art of the little yellow Bushmen who had lived here. There were depictions of the wild game that they had hunted and observed so minutely: herds of black buffalo, and tall, dappled giraffe, rhinoceros and horned antelope in glowing colours, all delightfully caricatured. With them the pygmy artist had drawn his own people, sticklike figures with buttocks as pronounced as a camel's hump and imperial erections to boast of their manhood. Armed with bows, they pursued the herds across the rock wall.

Peter Fungabera flicked the torch beam over this splendid gallery and then held it steady into the inner recesses of the cave where the throat narrowed and the rocky passage turned upon itself and was shrouded in darkness and mysterious shadow far below them.

'Forward!' he ordered, and Tungata moved cautiously down the sloping floor of the chamber.

They reached the throat of the cave and were forced to stoop under the low roof. Tungata turned the corner of the rocky passage and went on for fifty paces before he stopped short.

He had come out into a capacious cavern with a domed roof twenty feet above their heads. The floor was level, but cluttered with rock fallen from above. Peter Fungabera flashed his beam around the cavern. Against the far wall was a ledge the height of a man's shoulder and he held the beam on a jumble of objects that were stacked upon it.

For a moment Tungata was puzzled, and then he

recognized the shape of a wagon wheel of a design from a hundred years before, a wheel taller than the oxen that drew it; then he made out the wagon bed and the frames. The vehicle had been broken down into its separate parts and carried up to the cave.

'Lobengula's wagon,' he whispered. 'His most cherished possession, the one his warriors pulled when the oxen failed—'

Peter Fungabera prodded him with the barrel of the Tokarev and they picked their way forward through the litter of fallen rock.

There were rifles, stacked like wheat-sheaves, old Lee-Enfields, part of the payment that Cecil Rhodes had made to Lobengula for his concessions. Rifles and a hundred gold sovereigns every month – the price of a land and a nation sold into slavery, Tungata recalled bitterly. There were other objects piled upon the ledge, salt-bags of leather, stools and knives, beads and ornaments and snuff-horns and broad-bladed assegais.

Peter Fungabera exclaimed with avarice and impatience. 'Hurry. We must find his corpse, the diamonds will be with the body.'

Bones! They gleamed in the torchlight. A pile of them below the ledge.

A skull! It grinned mirthlessly up at them, a cap of matted wool still covering the pate.

'That's him!' cried Peter jubilantly. 'There is the old devil.' He dropped to his knees beside the skeleton.

Tungata stood aloof. After the first pang of alarm, he had realized that it was the skeleton of a small and elderly man, not much larger than a child, with teeth missing in the front upper jaw. Lobengula had been a big man with fine flashing teeth. Everyone who had met him in life had commented on his smile. This skeleton was still decked in the gruesome paraphernalia of the witch-doctor's trade: beads and shells and bones, plugged duiker-horns of

371

medicine and skulls of reptiles belted about the bony waist. Even Peter recognized his mistake, and he jumped to his feet.

'This isn't him!' he cried anxiously. 'They must have sacrificed his witch-doctor and placed him here as a guardian.' He was playing the torch wildly about the cave.

'Where is he?' he demanded. 'You must know. They must have told you.'

Tungata remained silent. Above the skeleton of the witch-doctor, the ledge jutted out, rather like a large pulpit of rock. The king's possessions were laid out neatly around this prominence, the human sacrifice laid below it. The entire focus of the cavern was on this spot. It was the logical and natural position in which to place the king's corpse. Peter Fungabera sensed that also and slowly turned the beam back to it.

The rock pulpit was empty.

'He isn't here,' Peter whispered, his voice tense with disappointment and frustration. 'Lobengula's body is gone!'

The signs that Tungata had noticed at the outer wall, the place where the masonry wall had been opened and resealed with less meticulous workmanship, had led him to the correct conclusion. The old king's tomb had obviously been robbed many years previously. The corpse had long ago been spirited away and the tomb resealed to hide the traces of this desecration.

Peter Fungabera clambered up onto the rock pulpit, and searched it frantically on his hands and knees. Standing back impassively, Tungata marvelled at how ludicrous greed could render even such a dangerous and impressive man as Peter Fungabera. He was muttering incoherently to himself as he strained the dusty detritus from the floor through his hooked fingers.

'Look! Look here!' He held up a small dark object, and Tungata stepped closer. In the torchlight he recognized that it was a shard from a clay pot, a piece of the rim decorated in the traditional diamond pattern used on the Matabele beer-pots.

'A beer-pot.' Peter turned it in his hands. 'One of the diamond pots – broken!' He dropped the fragment and scratched in the dirt, stirring up a soft cloud of dust that undulated in the torch beam.

'Here!' He had found something else. Something smaller. He held it up between thumb and forefinger. It was the size of a small walnut. He turned the torch beam full upon it, and immediately the light was shattered into the rainbow hues of the spectrum. Shafts of coloured light were reflected into Peter Fungabera's face, like sunlight off water.

'Diamond,' he breathed with religious awe, turning it slowly in his fingers so that it shot out arrows and blades of light.

It was an uncut stone, Tungata realized, but the crystal had formed in such symmetry and each plane was so perfect as to catch and reflect even the meagre beam of the torch.

'How beautiful!' Peter murmured, bringing it closer still to his face.

This diamond was a perfect natural octahedron and its colour, even in artificial light, was clear as snowmelt in a mountain stream.

'Beautiful,' Peter Fungabera repeated, and then gradually his face lost its dreamy, gloating expression.

'Only one!' he whispered. 'A single stone dropped in haste, when there should have been five beer-pots brimming with diamonds.'

His eyes swivelled from the diamond to Tungata. The torch was held low, and it cast weird shadows across his face, giving him a demoniacal look.

'You knew,' he accused. 'I sensed all along you were holding something back. You knew the diamonds had been taken, and you knew where.'

Tungata shook his head in denial, but Peter Fungabera

was working himself into a fury. His features contorted, his mouth worked soundlessly and a thin white froth coated his lips.

'You knew!'

He launched himself from the ledge with all the fury of a wounded leopard.

'You'll tell me!' he shrieked. 'In the end you'll tell me.'

He hit Tungata in the face with the barrel of the Tokarev.

'Tell me!' he screamed. 'Tell me where they are!' And the steel thudded into Tungata's face as he struck again and again.

'Tell me where the diamonds are!'

The barrel crunched against Tungata's cheekbone, splitting the flesh, and he fell to his knees. Peter Fungabera pulled himself away, and braced himself against the rock ledge to contain his own fury.

'No,' he told himself. 'That is too easy. He's going to suffer—'

He folded his own arms tightly across his chest to restrain himself from attacking Tungata again.

'In the end you will tell me – you will plead with me to allow you to take me to the diamonds. You'll plead with me to kill you—'

'Babes in the fornicating woods,' said Morgan Oxford. 'That's what you two are! By God, you have dropped us in this cesspool as well, right up to the eyebrows.'

Morgan Oxford had flown down from Harare as soon as he had heard that a Botswana border patrol had brought Craig and Sally-Anne in from the desert.

'Both the American ambassador and the Brits have had notes from Mugabe. The Brits are hopping up and down and frothing at the mouth also. They know nothing about you, Craig, and you are a British subject. I gather that they'd like to lock you up in the tower and chop your head off.'

Morgan stood at the foot of Sally-Anne's hospital bed. He had declined the chair that Craig offered him.

'As for you, missy, the ambassador has asked me to inform you that he would like to see you on the next plane back to the States.'

'He can't order me to do that.' Sally-Anne stopped his flow of bitter recriminations. 'This isn't Soviet Russia, and I'm a free citizen.'

'You won't be for long. No, by God, not if Mugabe gets his hands on you! Murder, armed insurrection and a few other charges—'

'Those are all a frame-up!'

'You and your boyfriend here left a pile of warm bodies behind you like empty beer cans at a labour-day picnic. Mugabe has started extradition proceedings with the Botswana government—'

'We are political refugees,' Sally-Anne flared.

'Bonny and Clyde, sweetheart, that's the way the Zimbabweans are telling it.'

'Sally-Anne!' Craig intervened mildly. 'You are not supposed to get yourself excited—'

'Excited!' cried Sally-Anne. 'We've been robbed and beaten, threatened with rape and a firing squad – and now the official representative of the United States of America, the country of which I happen to be a citizen, barges in here and calls us criminals.'

'I'm not calling you anything,' Morgan denied flatly. 'I'm just warning you to get your cute little ass out of Africa and all the way home to mommy.'

'He calls us criminals, and then patronizes me with his male chauvinistic—'

'Throttle back, Sally-Anne.' Morgan Oxford held up one hand wearily. 'Let's start again. You are in big trouble – we are in big trouble. We've got to work something out.'

'Now will you sit down?' Craig pushed the empty chair towards him and Morgan slumped into it and lit a Chesterfield.

'How are you, anyway?' he asked.

'I thought you'd never ask, sweetheart,' Sally-Anne snapped tersely.

'She was badly desiccated. They suspected renal failure, but they've had her on a drip and liquids for three days. She is okay that end. They were also worried about the crack on her head but the X-rays are negative, thank God. It was only a mild concussion. They have promised to discharge her tomorrow morning.'

'So she's fit to travel?'

'I thought your concern was too touching—'

'Look, Sally-Anne, this is Africa. If the Zimbabweans get hold of you, there will be nothing we can do to help. It's for your own good. You've got to get out. The ambassador—'

'Screw the ambassador,' said Sally-Anne with relish, 'and screw you, Morgan Oxford.'

'I can't speak for His Excellency,' Morgan grinned for the first time, 'but for myself, when can we begin?' And even Sally-Anne laughed.

Craig took advantage of the softening of attitudes.

'Morgan, you can rely on me to see she does the right thing—'

Immediately Sally-Anne puffed up in the high bed, preparatory to fending off another chauvinistic onslaught, but Craig gave her a tiny frown and shake of the head and she subsided reluctantly. Morgan turned on Craig instead.

'As for you, Craig. How the hell did they find out you were working for the agency?' Morgan demanded.

376

'Was I?' Craig looked stunned. 'If I was, nobody told me.'

'Who the hell do you think Henry Pickering is anyway – Santa Claus?'

'Henry, he is a vice-president of the World Bank!'

'Babes,' moaned Morgan, 'babes in the tupping woods.' He braced up. 'Well, anyway, that is over. Your contract is terminated. If there was anything sooner than immediately, that would be the date of termination.'

'I sent Henry a full report three days ago—'

'Yeah!' Morgan nodded resignedly. 'About Peter Fungabera being the Moscow candidate. Peter is a Shona, the Ruskies would never touch him. Just so you put it out of your head, General Fungabera is a Russian-hater from way back and we have a very good relationship with Peter Fungabera – very good indeed. Enough said.'

'For God's sake, Morgan. Then he is playing a double game. I had it from his own aide. Captain Timon Nbebi!'

'Who is now conveniently dead,' Morgan reminded him. 'If it makes you feel better, we've put your report into the computer – with a D-minus credibility rating. Henry Pickering sends you his sincere thanks.'

Sally-Anne cut in, 'Morgan, you have seen my photographs of the burned villages, the dead children, the devastation caused by the Third Brigade—'

'Like the man said, eggs to make omelettes,' Morgan interrupted. 'Naturally we don't like the violence, but Fungabera is anti-Russian. The Matabele are pro-Russian. We have to support the anti-communist regimes, even if we don't like some of their methods – there are women and kids taking a beating in El Salvador. So does that mean that we must stop aid to that country? Must we back out of any situation where our people aren't sticking precisely to the rules of the Geneva Convention? Grow up, Sally-Anne, this is the real world.'

There was silence in the tiny ward, except for the pinking of the galvanized iron roof as it expanded in the noon heat. On the parched brown lawn beyond the window, the walking patients were dressed in a uniform of pink bathrobes stamped across the back with the initials of the Botswana Health Department.

'That's all you came to tell us?' Sally-Anne asked at last.

'Isn't it enough?' Morgan stubbed out his cigarette and stood up. 'There is one other thing, Craig. Henry Pickering asked me to tell you that the Land Bank of Zimbabwe has repudiated its suretyship for your loan. Their grounds are that you have been officially declared an enemy of the people. Henry Pickering asked me to tell you they will be looking to you for repayment of capital and interest. Does this make sense to you?'

'Unfortunately,' Craig nodded glumly.

'He said he would try to work something out with you when you reach New York, but in the meantime they have been forced to freeze all your bank accounts and serve your publishers with a restraining order to withhold all future royalty payments.'

'That figures.'

'Sorry, Craig. It sounds real tough.' Morgan held out his hand. 'I liked your book, I really did, and I liked you. I'm just sorry it all had to end this way.'

Craig walked with him as far as the green Ford with diplomatic registration plates that Morgan Oxford was driving.

'Will you do me one last favour?'

'If I can.' Morgan looked suspicious.

'Can you see that a package is delivered to my publisher in New York?' And when Morgan's suspicions were unabated, 'It's only the final pages of my new manuscript, I give you my word.'

'Okay, then,' said Morgan Oxford dubiously. 'I'll see he gets it.'

Craig fetched the British Airways bag from the hired Land-Rover at the far end of the car park. 'Look after it,' he pleaded. 'It's my heart's blood and my hope of salvation.'

He watched the green Ford drive away and went back into the hospital building.

'What was all that about the banks and loans?' Sally-Anne asked as he entered her ward.

'It means that when I asked you to marry me I was a millionaire.' Craig came back to sit on the edge of her bed. 'Now I'm just about as broke as anybody who has no assets and owes a couple of million bucks can be.'

'You've got the new book. Ashe Levy says it's a winner.'

'Darling, if I wrote a bestseller every year for the rest of my life, I would just about keep level with the interest payments on what I owe to Henry Pickering and his banks.'

She stared at him.

'So what I am trying to say is this – my original offer is up for review, you've got a chance to change your mind. You don't *have* to marry me.'

'Craig,' she said. 'Lock the door and pull the shutters.'

'You've got to be joking – not here, not now! It's probably a serious offence in this country, illicit cohabitation or something.'

'Listen, mister, when you are wanted for murder and armed insurrection, a little bit of illicit nip and tuck with your future husband, even if he is a pauper, sits lightly on the conscience.'

Craig picked Sally-Anne up from the hospital the following morning. She wore the same jeans, shirt and trainers as she had when she was admitted.

'Sister had them washed and mended—' she stopped as she saw the Land-Rover. 'What's this? I thought we were broke.'

'The computer hasn't had the happy news yet, they are still honouring my American Express card.'

'Is that kosher?'

'When you owe five big Ms, lady, another couple of hundred bucks sits pretty lightly on the conscience.' He grinned at her as he turned the ignition key and when the engine fired, said cheerfully, 'Eat your heart out, Mr Hertz.'

'You're taking it very well, Craig.' She slid across the seat closer to him.

'We are both alive – that is cause for fireworks and general rejoicing. As for the money – well, I don't think I was truly cut out to be a millionaire. When I've got money I spend all my time worrying about losing it. It saps my energy. Now that I've lost it, I feel free again in a funny sort of way.'

'You're happy to have lost everything you ever owned?' She turned sideways in the seat to look at him. 'Even for you, that's cuckoo!'

'I'm not happy, no,' he denied the charge. 'What I truly regret is losing King's Lynn and Zambezi Waters. We could have made something wonderful out of them, you and I. I regret that very much – and I regret Tungata Zebiwe.'

'Yes. We destroyed him.' Both of them were sobered and saddened. 'If there was only something we could do for him.'

'Not a damned thing.' Craig shook his head. 'Despite Timon's assurances, we don't know that he is still alive, and even if he is, we don't have the faintest idea where he is, or how to find him.'

They rattled across the railway lines and into the main street of Francistown.

'"Jewel of the north",' said Craig. 'Population two thousand, main industry consumption of alcoholic beverage, reason for existing uncertain.'

He parked outside the single hotel. 'As you can see,

total population now in permanent residence in the public bar.'

However, the young Botswana receptionist was pretty and efficient.

'Mr Mellow, there is a lady waiting to see you,' she called, as Craig entered the lobby. Craig did not recognize his visitor, not until Sally-Anne ran forward to embrace her.

'Sarah!' she cried. 'How did you get here? How did you find us?'

Craig's room had two single beds with a dressing-table between them, a threadbare imitation Persian rug on the shiny red-painted cement floor and a single wooden chair. The two girls sat on one bed, with their legs curled up under them in that double-jointed feminine attitude.

'They told me at the Red Cross that you had been found in the desert and brought in by the police, Miss Jay.'

'My name is Sally-Anne, Sarah.'

Sarah smiled softly in acknowledgement. 'I wasn't sure if you would want to see me again, not after the trial. But then my friends here told me how you had been ill-treated by Fungabera's soldiers. I thought you might have realized that I was right all along, that Tungata Zebiwe was not a criminal, and that he needs friends now.'

She turned towards Craig. 'He was your friend, Mr Mellow. He told me about you. He spoke of you with respect and great feeling. He was afraid for you, when he heard that you had returned to Zimbabwe. He realized that you wanted to take up your family land in Matabeleland, and he knew there were going to be terrible troubles and that you would be caught up in them. He said that you were too gentle for the hard times that were coming. He called you "Pupho", the dreamer, the gentle dreamer, but he said that you were also stubborn and obstinate. He wanted to save you from being hurt again. He said, "Last

381

time he lost his leg – this time he could lose his life. To be his friend, I must make myself his enemy. I must drive him out of Zimbabwe."'

Craig sat in the straight-backed wooden chair and remembered his stormy meeting with Tungata when he had come to him for assistance in acquiring King's Lynn. Had it been an act, then? Even now he found that hard to believe. Tungata's passion had been so real, his fury so convincing.

'I am sorry, Mr Mellow. These are very rude things that I am saying about you. I am telling you only what Tungata said. He was your friend. He still is your friend.'

'It doesn't really matter any more, what he thought of me,' Craig murmured. 'Sam is probably dead by now.'

'No!' For the first time Sarah raised her voice, her tone vehement, almost angry. 'No, do not say that, never say that! He is alive. I have seen and spoken to him. They can never kill a man like that!'

The chair creaked under Craig as he leaned forward eagerly. 'You have seen him? When?'

'Two weeks ago.'

'Where? Where was he?'

'Tuti – at the camp.'

'Sam alive!' Craig changed as he said it. The despondent slump of his shoulders squared out, he held his head at a more alert angle and his eyes were brighter, more eager. He wasn't really looking at Sarah. He was looking at the wall above her head, trying to marshal the torrent of emotions and ideas that came at him, so he did not see that Sarah was weeping.

It was Sally-Anne who put a protective and comforting arm about her, and Sarah sobbed. 'Oh, my lord Tungata. The things they have done to him. They have starved and beaten him. He is like a village cur, all bones and scars. He walks like a very old man, only his eyes are still proud.'

Sally-Anne hugged her wordlessly. Craig jumped up

from the chair and began to pace. The room was so small, he crossed it in four strides, turned and came back. Sally-Anne dug in her pocket and found a crumpled tissue for Sarah.

'When will the Cessna be ready?' Craig asked, without pausing in his stride. His artificial leg made a tiny click each time he swung it forward.

'It's been ready since last week. I told you, didn't I?' Sally-Anne replied distractedly, fussing over Sarah.

'What is her all-up capacity?'

'The Cessna? I've had six adults in her, but that was a squeeze. She's licensed for—' Sally-Anne stopped. Slowly her head turned from Sarah towards him and she stared at him in total disbelief.

'In the love of all that's holy, Craig, are you out of your mind?'

'Range fully loaded?' Craig ignored the question.

'Twelve hundred nautical miles, throttle setting for maximum endurance – but you can't be serious.'

'Okay.' Craig was thinking aloud. 'I can get a couple of drums in the Land-Rover. You can land and refuel on a pan right on the border – I know a spot near Panda Matenga, five hundred kilometres north of here. That is the closest point of entry—'

'Craig, do you know what they'd do if they caught us?' Sally-Anne's voice was husky with shock.

Sarah had the tissue over her nose, but her eyes swivelled between the two of them as they spoke.

'Weapons,' Craig muttered. 'We'd need arms. Morgan Oxford? No, damn it, he's written us off.'

'Guns?' Sarah's voice was muffled by tears and tissue.

'Guns and grenades,' Craig agreed. 'Explosives, whatever we can get.'

'I can get guns. Some of our people have escaped. They are here in Botswana. They had guns hidden in the bush from the war.'

'What kind?' Craig demanded.

'Banana guns and hand grenades.'

'AKs,' Craig rejoiced. 'Sarah, you are a star.'

'Just the two of us?' Sally-Anne paled as she realized that he truly meant it. 'Two of us, against the entire Third Brigade – is that what you are thinking about?'

'No, I'm coming with you.' Sarah put aside the tissue. 'There will be three of us.'

'Three of us, great!' said Sally-Anne. 'Three of us – bloody marvellous!'

Craig came back and stood in front of them.

'Number one: we are going to draw up a map of Tuti camp. We are going to put down every detail we can remember.'

He started pacing again, unable to stand still.

'Number two: we meet with Sarah's friends and see how much help they can give us. Number three: Sally-Anne takes the commercial flight down to Johannesburg and brings back the Cessna – how long will that take?'

'I can be back in three days.' Colour was coming back into Sally-Anne's cheeks. 'That's if I decide to go!'

'Okay! Fine!' Craig rubbed his hands together. 'Now we can start on the map.'

Craig ordered sandwiches and a bottle of wine to be sent to the room and they worked through until 2 a.m. when Sarah left them with a promise to return at breakfast time. Craig folded the map carefully and then he and Sally-Anne climbed into one of the narrow beds together, but they were so keyed up that neither of them could sleep.

'Sam was trying to protect me,' Craig marvelled. 'He was doing it for me, all along.'

'Tell me about him,' Sally-Anne whispered and she lay against his chest and listened to him talk of their friendship. When at last he fell silent, she asked softly, 'So you are serious about this thing?'

'Deadly serious, but will you do it with me?'

'It's crazy,' she said. 'It's plain dumb – but let's do it then.'

The sooty black smoke from the beacon fires of oil rags that Craig had set climbed straight up in two columns into the clear desert sky. Craig and Sarah stood together on the bonnet of the Land-Rover, staring into the south. This was the dry wild land of north-eastern Botswana. The Zimbabwe border was thirty kilometres east of them, the flat arid plain between pimpled with camel-thorn trees and blotched with the leprous white saltpans.

The mirage shimmered and tricked the eye so that the stunted trees on the far side of the pan seemed to swim and change shape like dark amoeba under a microscope. A spinning dust devil jumped up from the white pan surface, and swirled and swayed sinuously as a belly dancer, rising two hundred feet into the hot air until it collapsed again as suddenly as it had risen.

The sound of the Cessna engine rose and fell and rose again on the heat-flawed air. 'There!' Sarah pointed out the mosquito speck, low on the horizon.

Craig made a last anxious appraisal of his makeshift landing-strip. He had lit the beacon fires at each end of it as soon as they had picked up the first throb of the Cessna's motor. He had driven the Land-Rover back and forth between the beacons to mark the hard crust at the edge of the pan. Fifty metres out, the surface was treacherously soft.

Now he looked back at the approaching aircraft. Sally-Anne was banking low over the baobab trees, lining up with the strip he had set out for her. She made a prudent precautionary pass along it, her head twisted in the cockpit

385

window as she examined it, then she came around again and touched down lightly, and taxied towards the Land-Rover.

'You were gone for ever.' Craig seized her as she jumped down from the cockpit.

'Three days,' she protested with her feet off the ground.

'That's for ever,' he said and kissed her.

He set her down but kept one arm around her as he led her to the Land-Rover. After she had greeted Sarah, Craig introduced her to the two Matabele who were squatting in the shade of the Land-Rover.

They rose courteously to meet her.

'This is Jonas, and this is Aaron. They led us to the arms cache and they are giving us all the help they can.'

They were reserved and unsmiling young men with old eyes that had seen unspeakable things, but they were willing and quick.

They pumped the Avgas from the forty-four-gallon drums on the back of the Land-Rover directly into the Cessna's wing tanks, while Craig stripped out the seats from the rear of the cockpit to reduce weight and give them cargo space.

Then they began loading. Sally-Anne weighed each item of cargo on the spring balance that she had bought for the purpose, and entered it on her loading table. The ammunition was the heaviest part of the load. They had eight thousand rounds of 7.62 mm ball Ps. Craig had broken bulk and repacked it in black plastic garbage-bags to save weight and space. It had been buried for years and many of the rounds were so corroded as to be useless. However, Craig had hand-sorted it, and test-fired a few rounds from each case without a single misfire.

Most of the rifles had also been corroded and Craig had worked through the nights by gas lantern, stripping and cannibalizing until he had twenty-five good weapons. There were also five Tokarev pistols and two cases of fragmentation grenades which seemed in better condition than the rifles. Craig had set off one grenade from each case, popping them down an ant-bear hole to a satisfactory crump and cloud of dust. That had left forty-eight from the original fifty. Craig packed them in five cheap canvas haversacks that he had bought from a general dealer in Francistown.

The rest of the equipment he had also purchased in Francistown. Wire-cutters and bolt-cutters, nylon rope, pangas that Jonas and Aaron sharpened to razor edges, flashlights and extra batteries, canteens and water bottles and a dozen or so other items which might prove useful. Sarah had been appointed medical orderly and had made up a first-aid kit with items purchased at the Francistown pharmacy. The food rations were spartan. Raw maize meal packed in five-kilo plastic bags, the best nourishment-to-weight ratio available, and a few bags of coarse salt.

'Okay, that's it,' Sally-Anne called a halt to the loading. 'Another ounce and we won't get off the ground. The rest of it will have to wait for the second trip.'

When darkness fell, they sat around the camp-fire and gorged on the steaks and fresh fruit that Sally-Anne had brought with her from Johannesburg.

'Eat hearty, my children,' she encouraged them. 'It could be a long time.'

Afterwards Craig and Sally-Anne carried their blankets away from the fire, out of earshot of the others, and they lay naked in the warm, desert air and made love under the silver sickle of the moon, both of them poignantly aware that it might be for the last time.

They ate breakfast in the dark, after the moon had set and before the first glimmering of the dawn. They left Jonas and Aaron to guard the Land-Rover and help with loading and refuelling for the second trip and Sally-Anne taxied out to the end of the strip when it was just light enough to make out the tracks.

387

Even in the cool of night it took the overloaded Cessna for ever to unstick, and they climbed away slowly towards the glow of the sunrise.

'Zimbabwe border,' Sally-Anne murmured. 'And I still can't believe what we are doing.'

Craig was perched up beside her on the bags of ammunition, while Sarah was curled up like a salted anchovy on top of the load behind them.

Sally-Anne banked slightly as she picked up her landmarks from the map on her lap. She had laid out a course to cross the railway line fifteen miles south of the coal-mining town of Wankie, and then to cross the main road a few miles beyond, avoiding all human habitation. The terrain below them changed swiftly, the desert falling away and becoming densely forested with open glades of golden grass. There were some high fair-weather cumulus clouds in the north, otherwise the sky was clear. Craig squinted ahead down the track of the rising sun.

'There is the railway.'

Sally-Anne closed the throttle and they descended sharply. Fifty feet above the tree-tops they roared over the deserted railway tracks, and minutes later crossed the main road. They had a glimpse of a truck crawling along the blue-grey tarmac ribbon, but they crossed behind it and were visible to it for only seconds. Sally-Anne pulled a face.

'Let's hope they make nothing of us – there must be quite a bit of light aircraft traffic around here.' She glanced at her wrist-watch. 'Expected time of arrival, forty minutes.'

'All right,' Craig said. 'Let's go over it one more time. You drop Sarah and me, then clear out again as quickly as possible. Back to the pan. Reload and refuel. Two days from now you come back. If there is a smoke-signal, you land. No signal and you head back to the pan. Give it two more days and then the last trip. If there is no smoke-signal on the second trip, that's it. You head out and don't come back.'

She reached out and took his hand. 'Craig, don't even say it. Please, darling, come back to me.'

They held hands for the rest of the trip, except for the brief moments when she needed both for the controls.

'There it is!'

The Chizarira river was a dark green python across the vast brown land, and there was a glint of water through the trees.

'Zambezi Waters – just up there.'

They were keeping well clear of the camps that they had built with so much loving labour, but both of them stared longingly upstream to where the dreaming blue hills studded the line of the horizon.

Sally-Anne dropped lower and still lower until she was shaving the tree-tops, and then she turned slowly back in a wide circle, keeping the hills between them and the buildings on Zambezi Waters.

'There it is,' Craig called, and pointed out under the port wingtip, and they had a glimpse of white beads at the edge of the trees.

'They are still there!' The bones of Craig's poached rhinoceros had been picked over by the scavengers and bleached by the sun.

Sally-Anne ran her landing-check, and then lined up for the narrow strip of grassland along the head of the gorge where she had landed before.

'Just pray the warthog and ant-bear haven't been digging around,' she murmured, and the overloaded Cessna wallowed sluggishly and the stall warning bleeped and flashed intermittently at the reduced power setting.

Sally-Anne dropped in steeply over the tree-tops and touched down with a jarring thud. The Cessna pitched and bounced over the rough ground, but maximum safe braking and the coarse grass wrapping the undercarriage pulled them up quickly, and Sally-Anne let out her breath.

'Thank you, Lord.'

They offloaded with frenzied haste, piling everything in a heap and spreading over it the green nylon nets designed for shading young plants from the sun that Craig had found in Francistown.

Then Sally-Anne and Craig looked at each other miserably.

'Oh God, I hate this,' she said.

'Me too – so go! Go quickly, damn it.'

They kissed and she broke away and ran back to the cockpit. She taxied to the end of the clearing, flattening the grass, and then came back at full throttle in her own tracks. The lightened aircraft leapt into the air, and the last he saw of her was her pale face in the side window turning back towards him, and then the tree-tops cut them off from each other.

Craig waited until the last vibration of the engine died away and the silence of the bush closed in again. Then he picked up the rifle and haversack and slung them over his shoulders. He looked at Sarah. She wore denims and blue canvas shoes. She carried the food bag and water bottles, with a Tokarev holstered on her belt.

'Ready?'

She nodded, fell in behind him, and stayed with the forcing pace he set. They reached the kopje in the early part of the afternoon, and from the summit Craig looked towards the camps of Zambezi Waters on the river.

This would be the dangerous part now, but he lit the signal fire and then, taking Sarah with him, moved out and set up an ambush on the approach path, just in case the smoke signal brought unwanted visitors.

He and Sarah lay up in good cover, and neither of them moved nor spoke for three hours. Only their eyes were busy, sweeping the slopes below and above and the bush all around.

Even so, they were taken unawares. The voice was a harsh, raw whisper in Sindebele, close – very close by.

'Ha! Kuphela. So you have brought my money.' Comrade Lookout's scarred visage peered at them. He had crept up to within ten paces without alerting them. 'I thought you had forgotten us.'

'No money for you – but hard and dangerous work,' Craig told him.

There were three men with Comrade Lookout, lean, wolflike men. They extinguished the signal fire and then spread back into the bush in an extended scouting order, that would cover their march.

'We must go,' Comrade Lookout explained. 'Here in the open the Shona *kanka* press us like hunting dogs. Since we last met, we have lost many good men. Comrade Dollar has been taken by them.'

'Yes.' Craig remembered him, beaten and bedraggled, giving evidence against him on that terrible night at King's Lynn.

They marched until two hours after darkness, northwards into the bad and broken land along the escarpment of the great river. The way was cleared for them and guarded by the scouts who were always invisible in the forest ahead. Only their bird calls guided and reassured them.

They came at last to the guerrilla camp. There were women at the small smokeless cooking-fires and one of them ran to embrace Sarah as soon as she recognized her.

'She is my aunt's youngest daughter,' Sarah explained. She and Craig spoke only Sindebele to each other now.

The camp was an uncomfortable and joyless place, a series of rude caves, hacked out of the steep bank of a dried water-course and screened by the overhang of the trees. It had a temporary air about it. There were no luxuries and no items of equipment that could not be packed within minutes and carried on a man's back. The guerrilla women were as unsmiling as their men.

'We do not stay at one place,' Comrade Lookout explained. 'The *kanka* see the signs from the air if we do. Even though we never walk the same way, not even to the latrines, in a short time our feet form pathways and that is what they look for. We must move again soon.'

The women brought them food and Craig realized how hungry and tired he was, but before he ate he opened his pack and gave them the cartons of cigarettes he had carried in. For the first time he saw these embittered men smile as they passed a single butt around the circle.

'How many men in your group?'

'Twenty-six.' Comrade Lookout puffed on the cigarette and passed it on. 'But there is another group nearby.'

Twenty-six was enough, Craig brooded. If they could exploit the element of surprise, it would be just enough.

They ate with their fingers from the communal pot and then Comrade Lookout allowed them to share another cigarette.

'Now, Kuphela, you said you had work for us.'

'The Comrade Minister Tungata Zebiwe is the prisoner of the Shona.'

'This is a terrible thing. It is a stab in the heart of the Matabele people – but even here in the bush we have known of this for many months. Did you come to tell us something that all the world knows?'

'They are holding him alive at Tuti.'

'Tuti. Hau!' Comrade Lookout exclaimed violently and every man spoke at once.

'How do you know this?'

'We heard he was killed—'

'This is old women's talk—'

Craig called across to where the women sat apart.

'Sarah!' She came to them.

'You know this woman?' Craig asked.

'She is my wife's cousin.'

'She is the teacher at the mission.'

'She is one of us.'

'Tell them,' Craig ordered her.

They listened in attentive silence, while Sarah related her last meeting with Tungata, their eyes glittering in the firelight, and when she had finished, they were silent. Sarah rose quietly and went back to the other women, and Comrade Lookout turned to one of his men.

'Speak!' he invited.

The one chosen to give his opinion first was the youngest, the most junior. The others would speak in their ascending order of seniority. It was the ancient order of council and it would take time. Craig composed himself to patience, this was the tempo of Africa.

After midnight Comrade Lookout summed up for them. 'We know the woman. She is trustworthy and we believe what she tells us. Comrade Tungata is our father. His blood is the blood of kings, and the stinking Shona hold him. On this we are all agreed.' He paused. 'But there are some who would try to wrest him from the Shona child-rapers, and others who say we are too few, and that we have only one rifle between two men, and only five bullets for each rifle. So we are divided.' He looked at Craig. 'What do you say, Kuphela?'

'I say that I have brought you eight thousand rounds of ammunition and twenty-five rifles and fifty grenades,' said Craig. 'I say that Comrade Tungata is my friend and my brother. I say that if there are only women and cowards here and no men to go with me, then I will go alone with this woman, Sarah, who has the heart of a warrior, and I will find men somewhere else.'

Comrade Lookout's face puckered up with affront, pulled out of true by the scar, and his tone was reproachful.

'Let there be no more talk of women and cowards, Kuphela. Let there be no more talking at all. Let us rather go to Tuti and do this thing that must be done. That is what I say.'

They lit the smoke signal as soon as they heard the Cessna, and extinguished it immediately Sally-Anne flashed her landing lights to acknowledge. Comrade Lookout's guerrillas had cut the grass in the clearing with pangas and filled in the holes and rough spots, so Sally-Anne's landing was confident and neat.

The guerrillas unloaded the rest of the ammunition and the weapons in disciplined silence, but they could not conceal their grins of delight as they handed down the bags of ammunition and the haversacks of grenades, for these were the tools of their trade. The loads disappeared swiftly into the forest. Within fifteen minutes Craig and Sally-Anne were left alone under the wing of the empty Cessna.

'Do you know what I prayed for?' Sally-Anne asked. 'I prayed that you wouldn't be able to find the gang, and if you did, that they would refuse to go with you, and that you had been forced to abort and had to come back with me.'

'You aren't very good at praying, are you?'

'I don't know. I'm going to get in a lot of practice in the next few days.'

'Five days,' Craig corrected her. 'You come in again on Tuesday morning.'

'Yes,' she nodded. 'I will take off in the dark, and be over Tuti airfield at sunrise – that's at 05.22 hours.'

'But you are not to land until I signal that we have secured the strip. Now, for the love of God, don't run yourself short of fuel to get back to the pan. If we don't show up, don't stay on hoping.'

'I will have three hours' safe endurance over Tuti. That means you will have until 08.30 hours to get there.'

'If we don't make it by then, we aren't going to make it. It's time for you to go now, my love.'

'I know,' Sally-Anne said, and made no move.

'I have to go,' he said.

'I don't know how I'm going to live through the next few days, sitting out there in the desert, not knowing a thing, just living with my fears and imagination.'

He took her in his arms and found she was trembling.

'I'm so very afraid for you,' she whispered against his throat.

'See you Tuesday morning,' he told her. 'Without fail.'

'Without fail!' she agreed, and then her voice quavered. 'Come back to me, Craig. I don't want to live without you. Promise me you'll come back.'

'I promise.' He kissed her.

'There now, I feel much better.' She gave him that cheeky grin of hers, but it was all soft around the edges.

She climbed up into the cockpit and started the engine.

'I love you.' Her lips formed the words that the engine drowned, and she swung the Cessna round with a burst of throttle and did not look back.

It was only sixty miles on the map and from the front seat of an aircraft it had not looked like hard going. On the ground it was different.

They were crossing the grain of the land; the watershed dropped away from their right to their left, towards the escarpment of the Zambezi valley. They were forced to follow the switchback of hills and the intervening valleys so they were never on level ground.

The guerrillas had hidden their own women in a safe place, and only reluctantly consented to Sarah accompanying the raiding party, but she carried a full load and kept up with the hard pace that Comrade Lookout set for them.

The ironstone hills soaked up the heat of the sun and bounced it back at them, as they toiled up the steep hillsides and dropped again into the next valley. The descents were as taxing as the climbs, the heavy loads jarring their spines and straining the backs of their legs and their Achilles tendons. The old elephant trails that they were following were littered with round pebbles washed out by the rains that rolled under foot like ball-bearings and made each pace fraught with danger.

One of the guerrillas fell, and his ankle swelled up so that they could not get his boot back on his foot. They distributed his load amongst them and left him to find his own way back to where they had left the women.

The tiny mopani bees plagued them during the day, clouding around their mouths and nostrils and eyes in their persistent search for moisture, and in the nights the mosquitoes from the stagnant pools in the valleys took over from them. At one stage of the trek they passed through the edge of the fly-belt, and the silent, light-footed tsetse-flies joined the torment, settling so softly that the victim was unaware until a red-hot needle stabbed into the soft flesh at the back of the ear, or under the armpit.

Always there was danger of attack. Every few miles either the scouts out ahead or the rear-guard dragging the trail behind them would signal an alert, and they would be forced to dive into cover and wait with finger on trigger until the all-clear signal was passed down the line.

It was slow and gruelling and nerve-racking – two full days' marching from freezing dawn through burning noon into darkness again, to reach Sarah's father's village. Vusamanzi was his name and he was a senior magician, soothsayer and rainmaker of the Matabele tribe. Like all his kind, he lived in isolation, with only his wives and immediate family around him. However great their respect for them, ordinary mortals avoided the practitioners of the dark arts; they came to them only for divination or treatment, paid the goat or beast that was the fee, and hurried thankfully away again.

Vusamanzi's village was some miles north of Tuti Mission Station. It was a prosperous little community on a hilltop, with many wives and goats and chickens and fields of maize in the valley.

The guerrillas lay up in the forest below the kopje, and they sent Sarah in to make certain all was safe and to warn the villagers of their presence. Sarah returned within an hour, and Craig and Comrade Lookout went back to the village with her.

Vusamanzi had earned his name, 'Raise the Waters', from his reputed ability to control the Zambezi and its tributaries. As a much younger man he had sent a great flood to wash away the village of a lesser chief who had cheated him of his fees, and since then a number of others who had displeased him had drowned mysteriously at fords or bathing holes. It was said that at Vusamanzi's behest the surface of a quiet pool would leap up suddenly in a hissing wave as the marked victim approached to drink or bathe or cross, and he would be sucked in. No living man had actually witnessed this terrible phenomenon – but nevertheless, Vusamanzi, the magician, did not have much trouble with bad debts from his patients and clients.

Vusamanzi's hair was a cap of pure white and he wore a small beard, also white, dressed out to a spade shape in the fashion of the Zulus. Sarah must have been a child of his old age, but she had inherited her fine looks from him, for he was handsome and dignified. He had put aside his regalia. He wore only a simple loin-cloth and his body was straight and lean, and his voice, when he greeted Craig courteously, was deep and steady.

Clearly Sarah revered him, for she took the beer-pot from one of his junior wives and knelt to offer it to him herself. In her turn, Sarah obviously had a special place in the old man's affections, for he smiled at her fondly, and when she sat at his feet, he fondled her head casually as he listened attentively to what Craig had to tell him. Then he sent her to help his wives to prepare food and beer and take it down to the guerrillas hidden in the valley before he turned back to Craig.

'The man you call Tungata Zebiwe, the Seeker after Justice, was born Samson Kumalo. He is in direct line of succession from Mzilikazi, the first king and father of our people. He is the one upon whom the prophecies of the ancients descend. On the night he was taken by the Shona soldiers, I had sent for him to appraise him of his responsibility and to make him privy to the secrets of the kings. If he is still alive, as my daughter tells us he is, then it is the duty of every Matabele to do all in his power to seek his freedom. The future of our people rests with him. How can I assist you? You have only to ask.'

'You have already helped us with food,' Craig thanked him. 'Now we need information.'

'Ask, Kuphela. Anything that I can tell you, I will.'

'The road between Tuti Mission and the camp of the soldiers passes close to this place. Is that correct?'

'Beyond those hills,' the old man pointed.

'Sarah tells me that every week the trucks come along this road on the same day, taking food to the soldiers and the prisoners at the camp.'

'That is so. Every week, on the Monday late in the afternoon, the trucks pass here loaded with bags of maize and other stores. They return empty the following morning.'

'How many trucks?'

'Two or, rarely, three.'

'How many soldiers to guard them?'

'Two in front beside the driver, three or four more in the back. One stands on the roof with a big gun that shoots fast.' A heavy machine-gun, Craig translated for himself. 'The soldiers are very watchful and alert and the trucks drive fast.'

'They came last Monday, as usual?' Craig asked.

'As usual,' Vusamanzi nodded his cap of shiny white wool. He must believe then that the routine was still in operation, Craig decided, and bet everything on it.

'How far is it to the mission station from here?' he asked.

'From there to there.' The witch-doctor swept his arm through a segment of the sky, about four hours of the sun's passage. Reckoned as the pace of a man on foot, that was approximately fifteen miles.

'And from here to the camp of the soldiers?' Craig went on.

Vusamanzi shrugged. 'The same distance.'

'Good.' Craig unrolled his map, they were equidistant between the two points. That gave him a fairly accurate fix. He began calculating times and distances and scribbling them in the margin of the map.

'We have a day to wait.' Craig looked up at last. 'The men will rest and ready themselves.'

'My women will feed them,' Vusamanzi agreed.

'Then on Monday I will need some of your people to help me.'

'There are only women here,' the old man demurred.

'I need women – young women, comely women,' Craig told him.

The next morning, leaving before dawn, Craig and Comrade Lookout, taking a runner with them, reconnoitred the stretch of road that lay just beyond the line of low hills. It was as Craig remembered it, a crude track into which heavy trucks had ground deep ruts, but the Third Brigade had cleared the brush on both sides to reduce the risk of ambush.

A little before noon they reached the spot where Peter Fungabera had stopped during their first drive to Tuti, the causeway where the road crossed the timber bridge across the green river, and where they had eaten that lunch of baked maize cobs.

Craig found that his memory was accurate. The approaches to the bridge, firstly down the steep slope of the valley and then across the narrow earthen causeway, must force the supply convoy to slow down and engage low gear. It was the perfect spot for an ambush, and Craig sent the runner back to Vusamanzi's village to bring up the rest of the force. While they waited, Craig and Comrade Lookout went over their plans and adapted them to the actual terrain.

The main attack would take place at the bridge, but if that failed, they must have a back-up plan to prevent the convoy getting through. As soon as the main force of guerrillas arrived, Craig sent Comrade Lookout with five men along the road beyond the bridge. Out of sight from the bridge, they felled a large mhoba-hoba tree so that it fell across the track, as an effective road-block. Comrade

Lookout would command here, while Craig coordinated the attack at the bridge.

'Which are the men who speak Shona?' Craig demanded.

'This one speaks it like a Shona, this one not as well.'

'They are to be kept out of any fighting. We cannot risk losing them,' Craig ordered. 'We will need them for the camp.'

'I will hold them in my hand,' Comrade Lookout agreed.

'Now the women.'

Sarah had chosen three of her half-sisters from the village, ranging in age from sixteen to eighteen years.

They were the prettiest of the old witch-doctor's multitudinous daughters, and when Craig explained their role to them, they giggled and hung their heads, and covered their mouths with their hands and went through all the other motions of modesty and maidenly shyness. But they were obviously relishing the adventure hugely, nothing so exciting and titillating had happened to them in all their young lives.

'Do they understand?' Craig asked Sarah. 'It will be dangerous – they must do exactly as they are told.'

'I will be with them,' Sarah assured him. 'All the time – tonight as well, especially tonight.' This last was for the benefit of the girls. Sarah had been fully aware of mutual ogling between her sisters and the young guerrillas. She shooed them away, still giggling, to the rough shelter of thorn branches that she had made them build for themselves, and settled herself across the entrance.

'The thorns are sharp enough to keep out a man-eating lion, Kuphela,' she had told Craig, 'but I do not know about a buck with an itchy spear and a maid determined to scratch it for him. I will have little sleep tonight.'

In the end, Craig spent a sleepless night as well. He had the dreams again, those terrible dreams that had almost driven him mad during his long slow convalescence from

401

the minefield and the loss of his leg. He was trapped in them, unable to escape back into consciousness, until Sarah shook him awake, and when he came awake, he was shaking so violently that his teeth chattered and sweat had soaked his shirt as though he had stood under a warm shower.

Sarah understood. Compassionately, she sat beside him and held his hand until the tremors stilled, and then they talked the night away, keeping their voices to a whisper so as not to disturb the camp. They talked of Tungata and Sally-Anne, and what each of them wanted from life and their chances of getting it.

'When I am married to the Comrade Minister, I will be able to speak for all the women of Matabele. Too long they have been treated like chattels by their men. Even now I, a trained nursing sister and teacher, must eat at the women's fire. After this, there will be another campaign to wage. A fight to win for the women of my tribe their rightful place and to have their true worth recognized.'

Craig found his respect for Sarah beginning to match his liking. She was, he realized, a fitting woman for a man like Tungata Zebiwe. While they talked, he managed to subdue his fear for the morrow, and the night passed so swiftly that he was surprised when he checked his wrist-watch.

'Four o'clock. Time to move,' he whispered. 'Thank you, Sarah. I am not a brave man. I needed your help.'

She rose to her feet with a lithe movement and for a moment stood looking down at him. 'You do yourself injustice. I think you are a very brave man,' she said softly and went to rouse her sisters.

The sun was high, and Craig lay in the cleft between two black water-polished boulders on the far bank of the stream. The AK 47 was propped in front of him, covering the causeway and the far banks on each side of the timber bridge. He had paced out the ranges. It was one hundred and twenty yards from where he lay to the end of the handrail. Off a dead rest, he could throw in a six-inch group at that range.

'Please let it not be necessary,' he thought, and once more ran a restless eye over his stake-out. There were four guerrillas under the bridge, stripped to the waist. Although their rifles were propped against the bridge supports close at hand, they were armed with the five-foot elephant bows. Craig had been dubious of these weapons until he had watched a demonstration. The bows were of hard, elastic wood, bound with strips of green kudu hide which had been allowed to dry and shrink on the shaft until they were hard as iron. The bowstring was of braided sinew, almost as tough as monofilament nylon. Even with all his strength, Craig had been unable to draw one of the bows to his full reach. The pull must have been well over one hundred pounds. To draw it required calloused fingertips and specially developed muscle in chest and arm.

The arrowheads were barbless mild steel, honed to a needle-point for penetration, and one of the guerrillas had stood off thirty paces and sunk one of these arrows twenty inches into the fleshy fibrous trunk of a baobab tree. They had been forced to cut it free with an axe. The same arrow would have flown right through an adult human being, from breast to backbone with hardly a check, or pierced the chest cavity of a full-grown bull elephant from side to side.

So there were now four bowmen under the bridge, and ten other men crouching in knee-deep water below the bank. Only the tops of their heads showed, and they were screened from anyone on the far side by the sharp drop-off of the bank, and the growth of fluffy-topped reeds.

The engine beat of the approaching trucks altered, as they changed gear on the up-slope before cresting and dropping down this side to the causeway and the bridge. Craig had walked down that slope himself looking for give-away signs, all his old training in the Rhodesian police coming back to him, looking for litter or disturbed vegetation, for the shine of metal, for footprints on the white sand-banks of the river or the verge of the road, and he had found no give-away signs.

'We must do it now,' said Sarah. She and her sisters were squatting behind the rock at his side. She was right – it was too late to alter anything, to make any other arrangements. They were committed.

'Go,' he told her and she stood up and let the denim shirt slip off her shoulders and drop to the sand. Quickly her younger sisters followed her example, letting drop their loin-cloths as they stood.

All four of them were naked, except for the tiny beaded aprons suspended from their waists by a string of beads. The aprons hung down over their *mons pubis* but bounced up revealingly with every movement as they ran down to the water's edge. Their plump young buttocks were bared, swelling enticingly below the hour-glass nip of their waists.

'Laugh!' Craig called after them. 'Play games.'

They were totally unashamed of their nudity. In the rural areas the beaded apron was still the traditional casual dress of the unsophisticated unmarried Matabele girl. Even Sarah had worn it until she had gone in to the town to begin her schooling.

They splashed each other. The water sparkled on their glossy dark skins, and their laughter had an excited, breathless quality that must attract any man. Yet, Craig saw that his guerrillas were unaffected. They had not even turned their heads to watch. They were professionals at work, all their attention focused on the dangerous job in hand.

The lead truck crested the far rise. It was a five-ton Toyota, similar to the one that had pursued them across the Botswana border. It was painted the same sandy colour. There was a trooper behind the ring-mounted heavy machine-gun on the cab. A second truck, heavily laden and armed, came over the rise behind it.

'Not a third. Please, only two,' Craig breathed, and cuddled the butt of the AK 47 into his shoulder. The barrel was festooned with dried grass to disguise its shape, and his own face and hands were thickly smeared with black clay from the river-bank.

There were only two trucks. They came trundling out onto the causeway and Sarah and her sisters stood knee-deep in the green waters below the handrail of the bridge and waved to them. The lead truck slowed, and the girls swung their hips, shrieked with provocative laughter and joggled their wet and shiny breasts.

There were two men in the cab of the lead truck. One was a subaltern, Craig could make out his cap-badge and the glitter of his shoulder pips even through the dusty windscreen. He was grinning and his teeth were almost as bright as his badges. He spoke to the driver and, with a squeal of brakes, the lead truck pulled up on the threshold of the bridge. The second truck was forced to pull up behind it.

The young officer opened the door and stood on the running board. The troopers in the back of the truck and the heavy machine-gunner craned forward, grinning and calling ribald comment. The girls, following Sarah's example, sank down coyly to cover their lower bodies and answered the suggestions and comments with dissembling coyness. Some of the troopers in the second truck, not to be out-done, jumped down and came forward to join the fun.

One of the older girls made a slyly obscene gesture with thumb and forefinger and there was an appreciative bellow of raunchy masculine laughter from the bank. The young officer replied with an even more specific gesture, and the rest of his troopers left the trucks and crowded up behind him. Only the two heavy machine-gunners were still at their posts.

Craig darted a glance at the underside of the bridge. On their bellies the bowmen were wriggling up the far side of the bank, keeping the timber baulks of the bridge between them and the bunch of troopers.

In the river Sarah stood up. She had loosened the string of her apron, and now carried the minuscule garment in her hand, swinging it with artful provocation. She waded towards the men on the bank, with the water swirling around her thighs, and the laughter choked off as they stared at her. She walked slowly, the pull of water exaggerating the churning movement of her pelvis. She was sleek and beautiful as a wet otter, the sunlight on her body gave it a plastic sheen, an unearthly glow, and even from where he lay, Craig could feel the jocular mood of the men watching her thicken with lust, and begin to steam with the stirring of sexual fury.

Sarah paused below them, cupped her hands under her breasts and lifted them, pointing her nipples up at them. Now they were totally concentrated upon her, even the machine-gunners high up on the ring mounts of the trucks were rapt and enchanted.

Behind them the four bowmen had slid up under the lee of the causeway. They were not more than ten paces from the side of the leading truck as they came up onto their knees in unison and drew. The bows arched, their right hands came back to touch their lips, wet muscle bulged in their backs as they sighted along the shafts, and then one after the other they let their arrows fly.

There was no sound, not even the softest fluting, but

406

one of the machine-gunners slid gently forward and hung over the side of the cab with head and arms dangling. The other arched his back, his mouth wide open but no sound coming from it, and tried to reach back over his own shoulder to the shaft that stood stiffly out between his shoulder-blades. Another arrow hit him, a hand's breadth lower, and he convulsed in agony and dropped from view.

The bowmen changed their target and the silent arrows flew into the bunch of troopers on the river-bank -- and a man screamed. In the same instant the guerrillas hiding below the bank burst from the water, and went up through the reeds, just as the troopers whirled to face the bowmen. The naked guerrillas took them from behind, and this time Craig heard the explosive grunts as they swung the long-bladed pangas, like a tennis-player hitting a hard forehand volley. A panga blade cleaved through the subaltern's burgundy-red beret and split his skull to the chin.

Sarah whirled and raced back, gathering the other girls. One of the younger ones was screaming as they floundered over the submerged sandbanks.

There was a single shot, and then all the troopers were down, scattered along the edge of the bank, but the guerrillas were still working over them, swinging and chopping and hacking.

'Sarah,' Craig called to her as she reached the bank. 'Get the girls back into the bush!' She snatched up her shirt, and pushed her sisters ahead of her, shepherding them away.

Carrying the AK, Craig ran across the bridge. The guerrillas were already stripping and looting the dead men. They worked with the dexterity of much practice, wrist-watches first and then the contents of pockets and webbing pouches.

'Was anyone hit?' Craig demanded. That single shot had worried him, but there were no casualties. Craig gave them two minutes to finish with the corpses, and then sent a patrol back to the crest to cover them against surprise. He turned back to the dead Shona. 'Bury them!' They had prepared the mass grave the previous afternoon, and they dragged the naked bodies away.

There was blood down the side of one truck where the machine-gunner had hung. 'Wash that off!' One of the guerrillas dipped a canteen of water from the river. 'And wash off those uniforms.' They would dry out in an hour or less.

Sarah returned before the burial party had finished. She was fully dressed again.

'I have sent the girls back to the village, they know the country well. They will be safe.'

'You did well,' Craig told her and climbed into the cab of the leading truck. The keys were in the ignition.

The burial party returned from out of the thick bush, and Craig called in his pickets. The guerrilla detailed to drive the second truck started it, and then the rest of them climbed aboard. The two trucks crossed the bridge and growled up the far slope. The entire operation had taken less than thirty-five minutes. They reached the felled mhoba-hoba tree and Comrade Lookout stepped into the track and directed them off the road. Craig parked in thick cover, and immediately a gang of guerrillas covered both vehicles with cut branches, and another gang began unloading the cargo, and clearing the road-block.

There were two-hundred-pound sacks of maize meal, cases of canned meat, blankets, medicines, cigarettes, ammunition, soap, sugar, salt – all of it priceless to the guerrillas. It was all carried away, and Craig knew it would be hidden and retrieved later whenever the opportunity occurred. There were a dozen kit bags containing the dead troopers' personal gear, a treasure trove of Third Brigade uniforms, even two of the famous burgundy berets. While the guerrillas dressed in these uniforms, Craig checked the time. It was a little after five o'clock.

Craig had noted that the radio operator at Tuti camp started the generator and made his routine report at seven o'clock every evening. He checked the radio in the leading truck. It had a fifteen-amp output, more than enough to reach Tuti camp, but not sufficient power to reach Harare headquarters. That was good.

He called Comrade Lookout and Sarah to the cab and they went over their notes. Sally-Anne would be over Tuti airstrip at 5.20 a.m. tomorrow morning, and she could stay in the circuit until 8.30 a.m. Craig allowed three hours for the journey from Tuti camp back to the airstrip at the mission station – that would take into account any minor delays or mishaps. Ideally they should leave the camp at 2.30 a.m., but not later than 5 a.m.

That meant they should time their arrival at the gates of the camp for midnight, or close to it. Two and a half hours to secure the position, refuel the trucks from the storage tank, release the prisoners, find Tungata and start back.

'All right,' Craig said, 'I want each group to go over their duties. First you, Sarah—'

'I take my two with the bolt-cutters, and we go straight to Number One hutment—' He had given her two men. Tungata might be so weak as to be unable to walk unassisted. Number One hutment was set a little apart from the others behind its own wire and was obviously used as the highest security cell. Sarah had seen them lead Tungata from it to their last meeting on the parade ground.

'When we find him, we bring him back to the assembly point at the main gate. If he can walk on his own I will leave my two men to open the other cells and release the prisoners.'

'Good.' She had it perfectly.

'Now the second group.'

'Five men for the perimeter guard towers—' Comrade Lookout went through his instructions.

'That's it then.' Craig stood up. 'But it all depends on one thing. I've said this fifty times already, but I'm going to say it again. We must get the radio before they can transmit. We have about five minutes from the first shot to do it, two minutes for the operator to realize what is happening, two minutes to start the electric generator and run up to full power, another minute to make his contact with Harare headquarters and pass the warning. If that happens, we are all dead men.' He checked his watch. 'Five minutes past seven – we can make the call now. Where is your man who speaks Shona?'

Carefully Craig coached the man in what he had to say, and was relieved to find him quick-witted.

'I tell them that the convoy is delayed on the road. One of the trucks has broken down, but it will be repaired. We will arrive much later than usual, in the night,' he repeated.

'That's it.'

'If they begin asking questions, I reply, "Your message not understood. Your transmission breaking up and unreadable." I repeat, "Arriving late", and then I sign off.'

Craig stood by anxiously while the guerrilla made the radio transmission, listening to the unintelligible bursts of Shona from the operator at Tuti camp, but he was unable to detect any trace of suspicion or alarm in the static-distorted voice.

The guerrilla imposter signed off and handed the microphone back to Craig. 'He says it is understood. They expect us in the night.'

'Good. Now we can eat and rest.'

However, Craig could not eat. His stomach was queasy with tension for the night ahead and from reaction to the ghastly violence at the bridge. Those pangas, wielded with pent-up hatred, had inflicted hideous mutilation. Many times during the long bush war he had witnessed death in some of its most unlovely forms, but had never become accustomed to it, it still made him sick to the guts.

'There is too much moon,' Craig thought as he peered out from under the canvas canopy of the leading truck. It was only four days from full and it rode so high and so bright as to cast hard-edged shadows on the earth. The truck lurched and jolted over the rough tracks and dust filtered up and clogged his throat.

He had not dared to ride in the cab, not even with his face blackened. A sharp eye would have picked him out readily. Comrade Lookout sat up beside the driver, dressed in the subaltern's spare uniform complete with beret and shoulder-flashes. Beside him was the Shona-speaker wearing the second beret. The heavy machine-guns were loaded and cocked, each served by a picked man, and eight others dressed in looted uniforms rode up on the coachwork in plain view, while the remainder crouched with Craig under the canvas canopy.

'So far, everything is going well,' Sarah murmured.

'So far,' Craig agreed. 'But I prefer bad starts and happy endings—'

There were three taps on the cab, beside Craig's head. That was Comrade Lookout's signal that the camp was in sight.

'Well, one way or the other, here we go.' Craig twisted round to peer through the peep-hole he had cut in the canvas hood.

He could make out the watchtowers of the camp, looking like oil-rigs against the moon-bright sky, and there was a glint of barbed-wire. Then quite suddenly the sky lit up. The floodlights on their poles around the perimeter of the camp glowed and then bloomed with stark white light. The entire compound was illuminated with noon-day brilliance.

'The generator,' Craig groaned. 'Oh, Christ, they've started the generator to welcome us in.'

Craig had made his first mistake. He had planned for everything to happen in darkness, with only the truck headlights to dazzle and confuse the camp guards. And yet, he now realized how logical and obvious it was for the guards to light up the camp to check the arrival of the convoy and to facilitate the unloading.

They were committed already. They could only ride on into the glare of floodlights, and Craig was helpless, pinned by the lights beneath the canopy, not even able to communicate with Comrade Lookout in the cab in front of him. Bitterly reviling himself for not having planned for this contingency, he kept his eye to the peep-hole.

The guards were not opening the gates, there was the sandbagged machine-gun emplacement to one side of the guard house, and Craig could see the barrel of the weapon traversing slowly to keep them covered as they approached. The guard was turning out, four troopers and a non-commissioned officer, falling in outside the guardroom.

The sergeant stepped in front of the leading truck as it drove up to the gate and held up one hand. As the truck pulled up he came round to the offside window, asked a question in Shona, and the bereted guerrilla answered him easily. But immediately the sergeant's tone altered, clearly the reply had been incorrect. His voice rose, became hectoring and strident. He was outside Craig's limited circle of vision, but Craig saw the armed guard react. They began to unsling their rifles, started to spread out to cover the truck, the bluff was over before it had begun.

Craig tapped the leg of the uniformed guerrilla standing above him. It was the signal, and the guerrilla lobbed the grenade that he was holding in his right hand with the pin already drawn. It went up in a high, lazy parabola and dropped neatly into the machine-gun emplacement.

At the same instant, Craig said quietly to the man on either side of him, 'Kill them.'

They thrust the muzzles of their AKs through the firing slits in the canopy and the range was less than ten paces. The volley ripped into the unprepared guards before they could bring up their weapons. The sergeant raced back towards the guard-room door, but Comrade Lookout leaned out of the cab with the Tokarev pistol in a stiff-armed double grip and shot him twice in the back.

As the sergeant sprawled, the grenade burst behind the sandbags, and the barrel of the heavy machine-gun swivelled aimlessly towards the sky as the hidden gunner was torn by flying shrapnel.

'Drive!' Craig stuck his head and shoulders through the slit in the canopy, and yelled at the driver through the open window of the cab. 'Smash through the gate!'

The powerful diesel of the Toyota bellowed, and the truck surged forward. There was a rending crash, and the vehicle bucked and shuddered, checked for an instant, and then roared into the brightly lit compound, dragging a tangle of barbed-wire and shattered gate-timbers behind it.

Craig scrambled up beside the machine-gunner on the cab.

'On the left—' He directed his fire at the barrack room of adobe and thatch beside the gate. The machine-gunner fired a long burst into the knot of half-naked troopers as they spilled out of the front door.

'Guard tower on the right.'

They were receiving fire from the two guards in the tower. It hissed and cracked around their heads like the lash of a stock whip. The machine-gunner traversed and elevated, and the belted ammunition fed into the clattering breech and empty cases poured in a glittering stream from the ejector slide. Splinters of timber and glass flew from the walls and windows of the tower, and the two guards were picked up and flung backwards by the solid strike of shot.

'Number One hutment just ahead,' Craig warned Sarah with a shout. She and her two men were crouched at the tailboard, and as the Toyota slowed, they jumped over and hit the ground running. Sarah carried the bolt-cutters and the two guerrillas ran ahead of her, jinking and dodging and firing from the hip.

Craig slid over the side of the truck, onto the running-board and clung to the cab.

'Drive for the kopje,' he shouted at the driver. 'We have to take the radio!'

The fortified kopje lay directly ahead, but they had to cross the wide, brightly lit parade ground, with the white-washed wall at the far end, to reach the foot of the kopje.

Craig glanced backwards. Sarah and her team had reached the hutment and were working on the wire with the bolt-cutters. Even as he watched, they completed their opening and broke through, disappearing into the building.

He looked for the second truck. It was roaring around the perimeter, just inside the wire, taking on each guard tower as they came to it, and pouring suppressing fire into it with the heavy machine-gun. They had knocked out four towers already, only two more to go.

The bright flash of bursting grenades dragged his attention to the barracks abutting the main prison hutment. The second truck had dropped a group of guerrillas to attack these barracks. Craig could see them crouched below the sills of the barracks, popping grenades through the windows, and then, as they exploded, darting forward, bright as moths in the floodlights, towards the main prison hutment.

In the first few minutes they had taken control of the entire camp. They had knocked out the towers, devastated the guard house and both barrack blocks – it was all theirs. He felt a surge of triumph, and then he looked ahead across the parade ground to the kopje. *Everything but the kopje*, and as he thought it, a line of white tracer stretched out towards him from the sandbagged upper slopes of the rocky hillock. It looked like a string of bright white fire-beads, at first coming quite slowly but accelerating miraculously as they closed, and suddenly there was flying dust and the shriek of ricochets all around them and the jarring crashing of shot into the metal body of the racing truck.

The truck swerved wildly, and Craig screamed at the driver as he clung desperately to the projecting rear-view mirror.

'Keep going – we have to get the radio!'

The driver wrestled with the wrenching, bucking steering-wheel, and the nose of the truck swung back towards the kopje just as the second burst of machine-gun fire hit it. The windscreen exploded in flying diamond chips, and the driver was hurled against the door of the cab, his chest shot half-away. The truck slowed as his foot slipped from the accelerator pedal.

Craig hit the handle and yanked the door open. The driver's body slid out of the seat and tumbled overside. Craig swung himself into his place and jammed his foot flat on the accelerator. The truck lunged forward again.

Beside Craig, Comrade Lookout was firing his AK through the gaping hole where the windscreen had been shot away, and overhead the heavy machine-gun returned the fire from the kopje with a fluttering ear-numbing clatter. The streams of opposing tracer fire seemed to meet and mingle in the air above the bare earth of the parade ground, and then Craig saw something else.

From one of the embrasures in the sandbagged walls at the foot of the hill, a black blob, the size of a pineapple, flew towards them on a tiny tail of flame. He knew instantly what it was, but he didn't even have time to shout a warning as the RPG-7 rocket missile hit them.

It hit low into the front end of the truck, that was all that saved them – the main blast was absorbed by the solid engine block, but nevertheless, it tore the front end off the truck and stopped it as though it had run into an ironstone cliff. The Toyota somersaulted over its ruined front wheel assembly, hurling Craig out of the open cab door.

Craig crawled up onto his knees, and the machine-gun on the hill traversed back towards him. A stream of bullets showered him with chunks of hard, dried clay from the surface of the parade ground and he fell flat again.

There were stunned and wounded guerrillas scattered around the wrecked Toyota, one man was trapped under it, his legs and pelvis crushed by the steel side and he was screaming like a rabbit in a wire snare.

'Come on,' Craig shouted in Sindebele. 'Get to the wall – the wall – run for the wall.'

He jumped up and started to run. The whitewashed execution wall was off to their right-hand side, seventy yards away, and a handful of men heard him and ran with him.

The machine-gun came hunting back, the whip-crack of passing shot around his head made Craig reel like a drunkard, but he steadied himself – and the man just ahead of him went down, both legs shot from under him. As Craig passed him, he rolled on his back and threw his AK up at Craig.

'Here, Kuphela, take it. I am dead.'

Craig snatched the rifle from the air without missing a step.

'You are a man,' he called to the downed guerrilla, and sprinted on. Ahead of him, Comrade Lookout reached the shelter of the wall, but the machine-gunner on the kopje traversed back towards Craig, kicking up curtains of dust and lumps of clay as the stream of bullets reached out for him.

Craig went for the corner of the wall feet first, sliding like a baseball player for home base, and shot flew close around him. He kept rolling until he hit the wall and lay in a tangle of limbs, fighting for breath. Only Comrade Lookout and two others had made it to the wall – the rest of them were dead in the truck or lying broken and crumpled on the open ground between.

'We have to get that gun,' he gasped, and Comrade Lookout gave him a twisted grin.

'Go to it, Kuphela – we will watch you with great interest.'

Another RPG rocket missile slammed into the wall, deafening them and covering them with a fine haze of white dust.

Craig rolled on his side and checked the AK 47. It had a full magazine. Comrade Lookout passed him another full magazine from the haversack on his shoulder, and Craig had the Tokarev pistol on his belt and two remaining grenades buttoned into his breast pockets.

He darted another quick glance around the corner of the wall and instantly a burst of machine-gun fire kicked and jarred into the brickwork around his head. He rolled back. It was only a hundred yards or so to the foot of the kopje, but it could as well have been a hundred miles. They were pinned helplessly, and the gunner up there on the hill commanded the entire compound. Nobody could move under the floodlights without drawing instant fire or a rocket from the RPG launcher.

Craig looked anxiously for the second truck, but sensibly the driver must have parked it behind one of the buildings as soon as the RPG opened up. There was no sign of any of the other guerrillas, they were all under cover, but they had taken more casualties than they could afford.

'It can't end like this—' Craig was consumed by his own sense of frustration and helplessness. 'We've got to get that gun!'

The gun up on the hill, without a target, fell silent – and then suddenly in the silence Craig heard the singing begin, low at first, just a few voices, but swelling and growing strong:

'Why do you weep, widows of Shangani
When the three-legged guns laugh so loudly?'

Then the ancient fighting chant crashed into the silence, flung out by hundreds of throats.

'Why do you weep, little sons of the Moles,
When your fathers did the king's bidding?'

And then from the prison huts they came, a motley army of naked figures, some of them staggering with weakness, others running strongly, carrying stones and bricks, and poles torn from the roofs of their prison. A few, a very few, had picked up the weapons of the dead guards, but all of them were singing with wild defiance as they charged the hill and the machine-gun.

'Oh, Christ!' whispered Craig. 'It's going to be a massacre.'

In the front rank of the throng brandishing an AK 47 came a tall gaunt figure, looking like a skeletal caricature of death itself, and the army of starvelings and gaol-sweepings rallied to him. Even altered as he was, Craig would have recognized Tungata Zebiwe anywhere this side of hell.

'Sam, go back!' he shouted, using the name by which he had known his friend, but Tungata came on heedlessly, and beside Craig Comrade Lookout said phlegmatically, 'They will draw fire, that will be our chance.'

'Yes, be ready,' Craig answered. Lookout was right. They must not let them die in vain and, as he spoke, the machine-gun opened up.

'Wait!' Craig grabbed Comrade Lookout's arm. 'He must change belts soon.' And while he waited for the gun to fire away its first belt, he watched the terrible havoc it was playing amongst the throng of released prisoners.

The stream of tracer seemed to wash them away like a fire hose, but as the front rank fell, so the men behind raced forward into the gaps, and still Tungata Zebiwe was coming on, outdistancing his fellows, firing the AK as he ran – and the gunner on the hilltop singled him out and swung the machine-gun onto him so that he was wreathed in smoking dust, still miraculously untouched as the machine-gun abruptly fell silent.

'Gun empty!' Craig shouted. 'Go! Go! Go!'

They launched themselves, like sprinters off the blocks, and the open ground seemed to stretch ahead of Craig to the ends of the earth.

Another rocket missile howled over their heads, and Craig ducked on the run, but it was high, aimed in panic. It flew across the parade ground and it hit the silver bulk fuel storage tank next to the guard barracks. The fuel went up with a vast whooshing detonation. The flames shot up two hundred feet in the air, and Craig felt the hot breath of the blast sweep over him, but he kept running and firing.

He had been losing ground steadily to Comrade Lookout and the other guerrillas, his bad leg hampering him in the race for the hill, but while he ran he was counting in his head. A good man might need ten seconds to change ammunition boxes and reload the machine-gun. Since leaving the sheltering wall seven seconds had passed – eight, nine, ten – it must come now! And there were still twenty paces to cover.

Comrade Lookout reached the sandbagged fortifications and shinned up and over.

Then something hit Craig a crushing hammer-blow and he was thrown violently to the ground as bullets flew all around him. He rolled over and came up again running, but the gunner had seen him go down and swung the machine-gun away, back to the charging mob of released prisoners.

Hit but unharmed, Craig ran on as strongly as before, and he realized that he had taken it in the leg, the artificial leg. He wanted to laugh, it was so ridiculous and he was so terrified.

'You can only do that to me once,' he thought, and

suddenly he had reached the foot of the kopje. He jumped up, found a hold on the top of the sandbag parapet with one hand, and heaved himself up and over. He dropped onto the narrow, deserted firing platform on the other side.

'The radio,' he fixed his will upon it, 'got to get the radio.' And he jumped down into the communication trench and ran down it to the bend in the passage. There was the sound of a scuffle, and a cry ahead of him, and as he came around the corner, Comrade Lookout was straightening up from the body of the Third Brigade trooper who had been manning the RPG.

'Go for the gun,' Craig ordered him. 'I'll take the radio room.'

Craig climbed up the sandbagged passageway, passing the dugout where he had been quartered on his last visit.

'Now, first on the left—' He dived into the opening, brushing aside the curtain of hessian, and he heard the radio operator in his dugout at the end of the passage shouting frantically. Craig hurled himself down the narrow passage, and paused in the doorway.

Too late. His stomach turned over in a despairing convulsion. The radio operator, dressed only in a vest and underpants, was hunched over the radio set on the bench by the far wall of the dugout. He was holding the microphone to his mouth with both hands, shouting his warning into it in English, repeating it for the third time, and, as Craig hesitated, the acknowledgement boomed from the speaker, also spoken in clear English.

'Message received and understood,' said the voice of the operator at Brigade headquarters in Harare. 'Hold on! We will reinforce you immediately—'

Craig fired a long burst of the AK, and his bullets smashed into the radio, shattering the housing and ripping the wiring out of it in a glittering tangle. The unarmed radio operator dropped the microphone and cowered

420

against the sandbag wall, staring at Craig, blubbering with terror. Craig swung the AK onto him, but could not force himself to fire.

Instead, the burst of automatic fire came from the passageway behind Craig, startling him, and then for an instant the operator was pinned to the wall by striking bullets and he slid down into a huddle on the floor.

'You always were too soft, Pupho,' said the deep voice beside Craig and he turned and looked up at the gaunt naked figure that towered over him, into the scarred and desiccated visage, into the dark, hawk-fierce eyes.

'Sam!' Craig said weakly. 'By God, it's good to see you again.'

T he first truck had its entire front section wrecked by the RPG while the rear wheels of the second truck had been destroyed by heavy machine-gun fire. The fuel tanks of both vehicles were registering empty.

As briefly as he could, Craig explained to Tungata the plans for getting out of the country.

'Eight o'clock is the deadline. If we don't make it back to the airstrip by then, the only way out will be on foot.'

'It's thirty miles to the airstrip,' Tungata mused. 'There is no other vehicle here. Fungabera took the Land-Rover when he left two days ago.'

'I can pull the rear wheels out of the wrecked truck – but fuel! Sam, we need fuel.'

They both looked towards the blazing tank. The flames were still towering into the night sky and clouds of dense, black smoke rolled across the parade ground. In the light of the flames, the dead men lay in windrows where the machine-gun had scythed them down, but there were no surviving prison guards either. They had been torn to pieces and beaten to bloody pulp by their prisoners. How many dead, Craig wondered, and shied away from the answer, for every death was his direct responsibility.

Tungata was watching him. He was now dressed in random items of clothing gleaned from the lockers of the barrack room, most of it too small for his huge frame, and the prison stench still hung around him like a cloak.

'You were always like this,' Tungata told him softly, 'after an unpleasant task. I remember the elephant culls – you would not eat for days afterwards.'

'I'll drain the one tank into the other,' said Craig quickly. He had forgotten how perceptive Tungata was. He had recognized Craig's remorse. 'And I will get them started on changing the wheels. But, you must find fuel for us, Sam. You must!' Craig turned and limped towards the nearest truck, thankful to be able to evade Tungata's scrutiny.

Comrade Lookout was waiting for him. 'We lost fourteen men, Kuphela,' he said.

'I am sorry.' *God! How inadequate.*

'They had to die one day,' the guerrilla shrugged. 'What do we do now?'

There were heavy wheel-wrenches in the toolboxes of the trucks, and enough men to lift the rear end bodily and chock it with timber baulks while they worked. Craig supervised the swopping of rear axle and wheels, while at the same time he rolled up his trouser leg and stripped off his leg. The machine-gun bullet had ripped through his aluminium shin, leaving a ragged exit hole in the calf, but the articulated ankle was undamaged. He tapped the sharp petals of torn metal down neatly with a hammer from the toolbox, and strapped the leg back in place. 'Now, you just hold together a little longer,' he told it firmly, gave the leg an affectionate pat and took the wheel-wrench away from Comrade Lookout who had already cross-threaded two of the nuts on the rear wheel of the truck.

An hour later Tungata came striding up to where Craig and his gang were lowering the truck's body onto its cannibalized rear axle. Craig was black to the elbows with thick grease. Sarah hurried to keep up with Tungata. Next to him she seemed slim and girlish, despite the rifle she carried.

'No fuel,' Tungata said. 'We've searched the camp.'

'I reckon we have fifteen litres.' Craig straightened up and wiped the sweat off his face with his shirt-sleeve. It left a smear of grease down his cheek. 'That might take us twenty miles. If we are lucky.' He checked his watch. 'Three o'clock – where did the time go? Sally-Anne will be overhead in just over two hours. We aren't going to make it—'

'Craig, Sarah has told me what you have done, the risks, the planning, all of it—' Tungata said quietly.

'We haven't got time for that now, Sam.'

'No,' he agreed. 'I must speak to my people, then we can go.'

The prisoners who had survived the slaughter on the parade ground gathered around him as Tungata stood on the bonnet of the truck. Their faces were upturned towards him, lit by the harsh glare of the floodlights.

'I must leave you,' Tungata told them, and they groaned, 'but my spirit stays with you, it remains with you until the day that I return. And I swear to you on the beard of my father and by the milk that I drank from my mother's breast, that I shall return to you.'

'Baba!' they called to him. 'You are our father.'

'The Shona *kanka* will be here very soon. You must go into the bush, carry with you all weapons and food you can find and go with these men.' Tungata pointed to the little group of guerrillas around Comrade Lookout. 'They will lead you to a safe place, and you will wait until I return in strength to lead you to what is rightfully yours.' Tungata held his arms extended in blessing. 'Go in peace, my friends!'

They reached up to touch him, some of them weeping like children. Then, in little groups, they began to drift away towards the gate of the compound and the darkness beyond.

Comrade Lookout was the last to go. He came to Craig and smiled that cold white wolfish smile.

'Though you were in the forefront of the fighting, you did not kill a single Shona – not here nor at the bridge,' he said. 'Why is that, Kuphela?'

'I leave the killing to you,' Craig told him. 'You are better at it than I am.'

'You are a strange man, oh writer of books – but we are grateful to you. If I live that long I will boast to my grandchildren of the things we did together this day.'

'Goodbye, my friend,' said Craig, and held out his hand, and when they shook hands it was with the double grip of palm and wrist and palm, a salute of deep significance. Then Comrade Lookout turned and loped away, carrying his rifle at the trail and the night swallowed him. The three of them, Craig, Tungata and Sarah, stood by the cab of the truck and the loneliness held them mute.

Craig spoke first. 'Sam, you heard the radio operator speaking to his headquarters. You know that Fungabera will have already sent in reinforcements. Are there any troopers between here and Harare?'

'I do not think so,' Tungata shook his head. 'A few men at Karoi, but not a large enough force to respond to an attack like this.'

'All right – let's say that it took them an hour to assemble and despatch a force. It will take them another five hours to reach Tuti—' he looked at Tungata for confirmation, and he nodded.

'They will hit the mission at approximately six – and Sally-Anne should be overhead at five. It will be close, especially if we have to make the last few miles on foot – let's get moving.'

While the others climbed up into the cab, Craig took a last look around the devastated compound. The flames had died down, but smoke drifted over the deserted hutments and across the parade ground where the dead men lay. The scene was still brightly lit by the floodlights.

'The lights—' Craig said aloud. There was something about the lights that worried him. The generator? Yes, that was it – something about the generator that he must think of.

'That's it!' he whispered aloud, and jumped up into the cab. 'Sam, the generator—'

He started the motor, and put the truck into a roaring turn. The engine room was at the back of the hill, part of the central complex protected by sandbags and by the fortifications on the high ground above it. Craig parked the truck close to the steps that led down into the power house, and he ran down and burst into it.

The generator was a twenty-five-kilowatt Lister, a big squat green machine, and its fuel tank was bolted on steel brackets to the wall above it. Craig tapped the side of the tank and it gave back a reassuring dull tone.

'Full!' Craig breathed. 'Forty glorious gallons, at least!'

The road twisted like a dying python and the truck, her fuel-tank brimming, was unwieldy and stiff on the turns. Craig had to wrench the wheel into them with both arms. The uphills were steep and the speed bled away to a walking pace as Craig changed down through the gears. Then they roared down the far side, too fast for safety, the empty truck bouncing them about unmercifully as they hit the deep ruts.

Craig almost missed the causeway at the bridge, and they lurched out over the drop with the edge crumbling away under the big double back wheels before he swerved back and they went lumbering over the narrow timber bridge.

'Time?' he asked, and Sarah checked her watch in the dashboard lights.

'Four fifty-three.'

Craig glanced away from the bright tunnel of the headlights and for the first time he could see the silhouette of the tree-tops against the lightening sky. At the top of the slope he pulled into the verge and switched on the radio set. He searched the channels slowly, listening for military traffic, but there was only the buzz of static.

'If they are in range, they are keeping mum.' He switched off the set and pulled out into the track again, marvelling at the swiftness of the African dawn. Below them in the valley, the landscape was emerging out of the fleeing night, the great, dark, forested plain leading from the foot of the hills down to the mission station stretched below them.

'Ten miles,' said Tungata.

'Another half an hour,' Craig replied and sent the Toyota bellowing down the last hills. Before they reached the bottom, it was light enough for him to switch off the headlights. 'No point drawing attention to ourselves.'

Suddenly he sat up straighter, alarmed by the change in the engine note of the truck; it was harsher and louder.

'Oh God, not that, not now,' he whispered, and then realized that he was hearing the sound not of the Toyota, but of another motor outside the cab. It was growing louder, closer, more compelling. He rolled down the side window and stuck his head out into the cool rush of the wind.

Sally-Anne's Cessna was roaring down from behind them, only fifty feet above the road, sparkling blue and silver in the first rays of the sun.

Craig let out a whoop of joy and waved wildly.

Swiftly the Cessna overhauled them and drew level. Sally-Anne's beloved face looked down at him from the cockpit. She had a pink scarf around her head, and those thick dark eyebrows framed her eyes. She was laughing, as she recognized Craig, and she waved and mouthed at him, 'Go for it!' Then she was roaring past, climbing, waggling the wings of the Cessna from side to side, heading for the airstrip.

They burst out of the forest, racing through the maize fields that surrounded the tiny mission village. The tin roofs of the church and the schoolhouse glittered in the sunrise. From the huts beside the road, a few sleepy villagers, yawning and scratching, came out to watch them pass through.

Craig slowed the truck, and Sarah shouted through the window, 'Soldiers coming! Big trouble! Warn everybody! Go into the bush! Hide!'

Craig had not thought that far ahead. The retaliation of the Third Brigade on the local population would be horrific. He accelerated through the village and the airstrip was a kilometre ahead, the tattered windsock undulating on its pole at the far end. The Cessna was circling low overhead. Craig saw Sally-Anne lower her undercarriage and start her turn onto final approach for the landing.

'Look!' said Tungata harshly, and another aircraft came roaring in, from their left-hand side, low and fast, another much larger, twin-engined machine. Craig recognized it immediately.

It was an old Dakota transport, a veteran of the desert war in north Africa, and the bush war in Rhodesia. It was sprayed with non-reflective anti-missile grey paint and it was now decorated with the Zimbabwe Air Force roundels. The main hatch just abaft the wing root was open, and there were men poised in the opening. They were dressed in camouflage jump smocks and helmets. The bulky bundles of their parachutes dangled below their buttocks. Two of them were in the hatchway, but others crowded up close behind them.

'Paras!' shouted Craig, and the Dakota banked steeply towards them and passed them so low that the blast from the propellers churned the tops of the standing maize in the field beside them. As the aircraft flashed past them, Craig and Tungata simultaneously recognized one of the men in the hatchway.

'Fungabera!' Tungata snapped. 'It's him!'

As he said it, Tungata threw open the door at his side and clambered up the outside of the cab to reach the ring-mounted machine-gun. Despite his size and weakness, he was so quick that he reached the gun and swung it and got off a long burst before the Dakota was out of range. Tracer flew under the Dakota's port wing, close enough to alarm the pilot, and make him throw the aircraft into a tight climbing turn.

'They are climbing up to drop altitude!' Craig shouted.

Surely Fungabera had seen and recognized the blue and silver Cessna. He would have realized that it was the escape plane and that the truck was heading for a rendez-vous at the airstrip. His paratroopers could be more swiftly deployed by dropping, than by landing the Dakota. He was going to drop in and seize the airstrip with his paras before the Cessna could take off again. A thousand feet was safe drop altitude, but these were crack troopers. The Dakota levelled out on its drop run, five hundred feet, Craig estimated, and they were going to make the drop down the length of the airstrip.

The Cessna was just coming in over the fence at the far end of the strip. As Craig glanced back at her Sally-Anne touched down and then taxied at speed down the strip towards the racing Toyota.

Above the airstrip the tiny figure of a man fell clear of the lumbering Dakota and the green silk parachute flared open almost instantly. He was followed in rapid succession by a string of other paras, and the sky was filled with a forest of sinister mushrooms, poisonous green and swaying gently in the light morning breeze, but sinking towards the parched brown turf of the airstrip.

The Cessna reached the end of the strip and swung around sharply in a 180-degree turn. Only then did Craig realize that Sally-Anne had been far-seeing enough to assess the danger and urgency, and that she had landed with the wind behind her, accepting the hazard of the higher approach speed and the longer roll-out in order to be able immediately to turn back into the wind for her take-off which would be with a full load, and under attack from the paras.

On the cab, Tungata was firing up into the sky, measured controlled bursts, hoping more to intimidate the descending paras than to inflict casualties. A man dangling on swinging parachute-shrouds makes an almost impossible target.

Sally-Anne was leaning out of the open cockpit door, shouting and waving them on, already she was running up her engine to full power, holding the Cessna on the wheel brakes. They bumped over the verge of the runway and Craig swung the Toyota into a brake-squealing skid, parking so as to screen and protect the aircraft and themselves while they made the transfer.

'Get out,' he yelled at Sarah, and she jumped down and ran to the aircraft. Sally-Anne grabbed her arm and helped her swing up and tumble into the back seat.

On the cab, Tungata fired a last burst with the heavy machine-gun. The first three paras were down, their green parachutes rolling softly in front of the light breeze, and Tungata's bullets kicked dust amongst them. Craig saw one of the paras fall and drag away loose and lifeless on his shrouds. Craig grabbed the AK 47 and the bag of spare ammunition and shouted, 'Let's go, Sam. Let's go!'

They ran to the Cessna, and Tungata, weak and sick, fell at the steps, and Craig had to drag him to his feet and shove him up.

Sally-Anne let go the brakes before Tungata was aboard, and Craig ran beside the Cessna as it gathered speed. Tungata fell into the back seat beside Sarah, and Craig jumped up and got a hold. Though he was hampered by the AK rifle and bag, he dragged himself into the front seat beside Sally-Anne.

'Get the door closed!' Sally-Anne screamed, without looking at him, all her attention on the strip ahead. The dangling seat-belt was jammed in the door and Craig wrestled with it as they built up to rotation speed. Craig managed to extricate the strap and slam the door closed. When he looked up, he saw paratroopers sprinting forward from the edge of the strip to intercept the Cessna.

It did not need the shiny general's star on the front of his helmet to identify Peter Fungabera. The set of his shoulders, the way he carried his head, and the fluid catlike grace of his run were all distinctive. His men were spread out behind him – they were almost directly ahead of the Cessna, only four or five hundred paces ahead.

Sally-Anne rotated and the Cessna lifted its nose, bounced lightly and became airborne. Peter Fungabera and his line of paratroopers disappeared from view under the nose and engine section as the Cessna climbed away, but the aircraft would have to pass directly over the top of their heads at little more than a few hundred feet.

'Oh mother!' Sally-Anne spoke in almost conversational tones. 'This is it!' And as she said it, the instrument panel in front of Craig exploded, covering him with fine chips of glass like sugar crystals. Hydraulic fluid sprayed over the front of his shirt.

Machine-gun fire came in through the floor of the cabin and tore out through the thin metal roof so that the interior was filled with a gale of swirling wind as the slipstream found the holes.

In the back seat, Sarah cried out, and the body of the machine was racked and jarred by the storm of AK 47 bullets. Craig felt the seat under him jump as bullets smacked into the metal frame. Jagged punctures appeared miraculously in the wing roots just outside his window.

Sally-Anne shoved the control wheel forward and the Cessna dived back towards the airstrip again with a gut-swooping rush, ducking under the maelstrom of machine-gun fire and giving them a moment's respite. The brown earth came up at them, and Sally-Anne caught the Cessna's suicidal dive and held it off, but the wheels hit the surface and they bounced wildly thirty feet back into the air. Craig saw two paratroopers dive to the side as the plane raced towards them.

The wild dive towards the earth had pushed their speed way up, so that Sally-Anne could instantly throw the Cessna into a maximum rate turn, the port wingtip brushing the earth. Her face was contorted and the muscle stood proud in her forearms with the effort of holding the Cessna's nose up in the turn and preventing her from going in. Ahead of them on the left-hand side of the airstrip, only a hundred yards or so from the verge, stood a single tree with dense, wide-spread branches. It was a marula, ninety feet tall.

Sally-Anne levelled out for an instant and flew for the marula, her wingtip almost touched its outermost branches, and immediately she threw the Cessna into an opposite turn, neatly placing the tree between them and the line of paratroopers on the airstrip behind them.

She kept at ground level, her undercarriage brushing the tops of the maize plants in the open fields, glancing up in the rear-view mirror above her head to keep the marula tree exactly behind the Cessna's tail, blanketing the paratroopers' field of fire.

431

'Where is the Dakota?' Craig asked, raising his voice above the rush of wind through the cabin.

'It's going in to land,' Tungata called, and, twisting in his seat, Craig had a glimpse of the big grey machine going in low over the tree-tops behind them, lined up for the airstrip.

'I can't get the undercarriage up.' Sally-Anne was thumbing the rocker switch but the three green eyes of the undercarriage warning light still glared at her from the console. 'We have damage there, it's stuck.'

The forest beyond the open fields rushed towards them and as she eased back on the control wheel to lift the Cessna over the tree-tops, a hydraulic lead burst under the shot-ruptured engine housing and hydraulic fluid sprayed in viscous sheets over the windscreen.

'Can't see!' Sally-Anne cried, and pulled open her side window, flying by reference to the horizon under her wing-tip.

'We've got no instruments,' Craig checked the shattered panel. 'Airspeed's gone, rate of climb, artificial horizon, altimeter, gyro compass—'

'The undercarriage—' Sally-Anne interrupted him. 'Too much drag, it will cut down our range – we'll never make it back!'

She was still climbing, but gradually starting to come around onto her course, using the compass in its glass oil-bath above her head, when the engine stuttered, almost cut – and then surged again in full power.

Quickly Sally-Anne adjusted pitch and power-settings.

'That sounded like fuel starvation,' she whispered. 'They must have hit a fuel line.' She switched the fuel-tank selector cock from 'starboard' to 'both' and then glanced up at Craig and grinned. 'Hi there! I missed you something awful.'

'Me too.' He reached across and squeezed her thigh.

'Time check.' Businesslike again.

'05.17 hours,' Craig told her and looked overside. The brown snake of the Tuti road was angling away towards the north, and they were crossing the first line of hills – Vusamanzi's village would be out there a few miles beyond the road.

The engine missed again, and Sally-Anne's expression was taut with apprehension.

'Time?' she demanded again.

'05.27,' Craig told her.

'We will be out of sight of the airstrip by now. Out of earshot too.'

'Fungabera won't know where we are, where we are heading.'

'They've got a helicopter gunship at Victoria Falls.' Tungata leaned forward over the seats. 'If they guess that we are heading for Botswana, they will send it down to intercept.'

'We can outrun a helicopter,' Craig guessed.

'Not with our undercarriage down,' Sally-Anne contradicted him, and without another warning, the engine cut out completely.

It was suddenly eerily quiet, just the whistle of the wind through the bullet-holes in the fuselage, the propeller windmilling softly for a few seconds longer, and then with a jerk stopping dead and pointing skywards like a headsman's blade.

'Well,' Sally-Anne said softly, 'it's all immaterial now. Engine out. We are going in.' And then briskly she began her preparations for a forced landing as the Cessna started to sink gently away towards the broken hilly and forested land beneath them. She pulled on full flap to slow their airspeed.

'Seat-belts, everybody,' she said. 'Shoulder-straps also.'

She was switching off the fuel-tanks, the master switches, shutting down to prevent fire on impact.

'Can you see an opening?' she asked Craig, peering hopelessly through the smeared windscreen.

'Nothing.' The forest was a dark green mattress below them.

'I will try to pick two big trees and knock our wings off between them – that will take the speed off us. But it's still going to be a daddy of a hit,' she said, as she struggled with the panel of her side-window.

'I can knock it out for you,' Tungata offered.

'Good,' Sally-Anne accepted.

Tungata leaned over and with three blows of his bunched fist smashed the Perspex sheet out of its frame. Sally-Anne thrust her head out, slitting her eyes against the wind.

The earth came up towards them, faster and faster, the hills seemed to grow in size, beginning to tower above them as Sally-Anne made a gentle gliding turn into a narrow valley. She had no air-speed indicator, so she was flying by the seat of her pants, holding up the nose to bleed off speed. Through the hazy smear of the windshield Craig saw the loom of trees.

'Doors unlocked and open!' Sally-Anne ordered. 'Keep your straps fastened until we stop rolling, then get out as fast as you can, and run like a pack of long thin dogs!'

She pulled up the nose, the Cessna stalled and the nose dropped again like a stone, but she had judged it to a micro-second, for before it could drop through the horizontal, she hit the trees. The wings were plucked out of the Cessna, and they were hurled against their shoulder-straps with a force that grazed away the skin and bruised their flesh. But even though the impact took most of their speed off, the dismembered carcass of the aircraft went slithering and banging into the forest. They were slammed from side to side and shaken in their seats, the fuselage slewing violently and wrapping sideways around the base of another tree and coming, at last, to rest.

'Out!' yelled Sally-Anne. 'I can smell gas! Get out and run!'

The open doors had been ripped away from their hinges, and they flung off their seat-belts and tumbled out onto the rocky ground, and they ran.

Craig caught up with Sally-Anne. The scarf had come off her head and her long dark tresses streamed behind her. He reached out and put an arm around her shoulders, guided her towards the lip of a dry ravine and they leaped into it and crouched panting on the sandy bottom, clinging to each other.

'Is she going to flame out?' Sally-Anne gasped.

'Wait for it.' He held her, and they tensed themselves for the whooshing detonation of leaking gasoline, and the explosion of the main tanks.

Nothing happened, and the silence of the bush settled over them, so they spoke in awed whispers.

'You fly like an angel,' he said.

'An angel with broken wings.'

They waited another minute.

'By the way,' he whispered, 'what the hell is a long thin dog?'

'A greyhound,' she giggled with reaction from fear. 'A dachshund is a long short dog.' And he found he was giggling with her as they hugged each other.

'Take a look.' She was still laughing nervously. They stood up cautiously, and peered over the rim of the ravine. The fuselage was crashed and the metal skin of the Cessna had crumpled like aluminium foil, but there was no fire. They climbed out of the ravine.

'Sam!' Craig called. 'Sarah!'

The two of them stood up from where they had taken cover at the foot of the rocky side of the valley.

'Are you all right?'

All four of them were shaken and bruised, Sarah had a

bloodied nose and a scratch on her cheek, but none of them had been seriously hurt.

'What the hell do we do now?' Craig asked, and they stood in a huddle and looked at each other helplessly.

They ransacked the shattered carcass of the Cessna – the toolbox, the first-aid kit, the survival kit with the flashlight, a five-litre aluminium water bottle, thermal blankets and malt tablets, the pistol, the AK 47 rifle and ammunition, the map-case, and Craig unscrewed the compass from the roof of the cabin. Then they worked for an hour trying to hide all traces of the crash from a searching aircraft. Between them Tungata and Craig dragged the severed wing sections into the ravine and covered them with dried brush. They could not move the fuselage and engine section, but they heaped more branches and brush over it.

Twice while they worked, they heard the sound of an aircraft in the distance. The resonant throb of twin engines was unmistakable.

'The Dakota,' Sally-Anne said.

'They are searching for us.'

'They can't know that we are down,' Sally-Anne protested.

'No, not for certain, but they must know that we took a real beating,' Craig pointed out. 'They must realize that there is a good chance that we are down. They will probably send in foot patrols to scout the area, and question the villagers.'

'The sooner we get out of here—'

'Which way?'

'May I suggest something?' Sarah joined the discussion deferentially. 'We need food and a guide. I think I can lead us from here to my father's village. He will hide us until we have decided what we are going to do, until we are ready to go.'

Craig looked at Tungata.

'Makes sense – any objections, Sam? Okay, let's do it.'

Before they left the site of the crash, Craig took Sally-Anne aside.

'Do you feel sad? It was a beautiful aircraft.'

'I don't get sentimental over machinery.' She shook her head. 'Once it was a great little kite, but it's buggered and bent now. I save my sentiments for things that are more cuddly,' and she squeezed his hand. 'Time to move on, darling.'

Craig carried the rifle and pointed for them, keeping half a mile ahead and marking the trail. Tungata, lacking stamina, took the drag, with the two girls in the centre.

That evening they dug for water in a dry river-bed and sucked a malt tablet before they rolled into the thermal foil survival blankets. The girls took the first two sentry goes, while Tungata and Craig spun a coin for the more arduous later watches.

Early the next morning, Craig cut a well-used footpath, and when Sarah came up she recognized it immediately. Two hours later they were in the cultivated valley below Vusamanzi's hilltop village and while the rest of the party took cover in the standing maize, Sarah climbed up to find her father. When she returned an hour later the old witch-doctor was with her.

He came directly to Tungata and went down on his arthritically swollen knees before him, and he took one of Tungata's feet and placed it upon his silver pate. 'Son of kings, I see you,' he greeted him. 'Sprig of great Mzilikazi, branch of mighty Kumalo, I am your slave.'

'Stand up, old man,' Tungata lifted him up, and used the respectful term *kehla*, honoured elder.

'Forgive me that I do not offer refreshment,' Vusamanzi apologized, 'but it is not safe here. The Shona soldiers are everywhere. I must lead you to a safe place, and then you can rest and refresh yourselves. Follow me.'

He set off at a remarkable pace on his skinny old legs, and they had to lengthen their stride to hold him in view. They walked for two hours by Craig's wrist-watch, the last hour through dense thorn thicket and broken rocky ground. There was no defined footpath, and the heated hush of the bush and the claustrophobic crowding in of the hills was enervating and oppressive.

'I do not like this place,' Tungata told Craig softly. 'There are no birds, no animals, there is a feeling here of evil – no, not evil, but of mystery and of menace.'

Craig looked about him. The rocks had the blasted look of slag from the iron furnace and the trees were deformed and crooked, black as charcoal against the sun and leprous silver when the sun's rays struck them full on. Their branches were bearded with trailing lichens, the sickly green of chlorine gas. And Tungata was correct, there were no bird sounds, no rustles of small animals in the undergrowth. Suddenly Craig felt chilled and he shivered in the sunlight.

'You feel it also,' said Tungata, and as he spoke the old man disappeared abruptly, as though he had been swallowed by the black and blasted rock. Craig hurried forward, suppressing a shudder of superstitious dread. He reached the spot where Vusamanzi had disappeared and looked around, but there was no sign of the old man.

'This way.' Vusamanzi's voice was a sepulchral echo. 'Beyond the turn of the rock.'

The cliff was folded back upon itself, a narrow concealed cleft, just wide enough for a man to squeeze through. Craig stepped round the corner and paused to let his eyes adjust to the poor light.

Vusamanzi had taken a cheap storm lantern from a shelf in the rock above his head and was filling the base with

438

paraffin from the bottle he had carried in his pouch. He struck a match and held it to the wick.

'Come,' he invited, and led them into the passageway.

'These hills are riddled with caves and secret passages,' Sarah explained. 'They are all dolomite formations.'

A hundred and fifty yards further on, the passage opened into a large chamber. Soft natural light filtered in through an opening in the domed roof high above their heads. Vusamanzi extinguished the lantern and set it down on a ledge to one side of a hearth, man-made from blocks of limestone. The rock above the hearth was blackened with soot, and there was a pile of old ash upon the floor. Beside it was a neat stack of firewood.

'This is a sacred place,' Vusamanzi told them. 'It is here that the apprentice magicians live during the training period. It was here, as a young man, that I served under my own father, and learned the ancient prophecies and the magical arts.' He gestured to them to sit down, and all of them slumped thankfully to the rocky floor. 'You will be safe here. The soldiers will not find you. In a week or a month, when they grow weary of searching for you, it will be safe for you to leave. Then we will find a man to guide you.'

'It's spooky,' Sally-Anne whispered, when Craig translated this for her.

'Some of my women are following us with food. They will come every second day while you are here, with food and news.'

Two of Sarah's half-sisters arrived at the cavern before darkness fell. They carried heavy bundles balanced upon their heads, and they set about preparing a meal immediately. Their laughter and merry chatter, the flicker of the flames on the hearth, the smell of woodsmoke and food cooking, partially dispelled the oppressive atmosphere of the cavern.

'You must eat with the women,' Craig explained to Sally-Anne. 'It's the custom. The old man will be very unhappy—'

'He looks such an old dear, but underneath he turns out to be just another male chauvinist pig,' she protested.

The three men passed the beer-pot around their circle, and ate from the communal bowl in the centre and the old man spoke to Tungata between mouthfuls.

'The spirits prevented our first meeting, Nkosi. We waited for you to come that night, but the Shona had taken you. It was a time of sorrow for all of us, but now the spirits have relented, they have delivered you from the Shona and brought us together at last.' Vusamanzi looked at Craig. 'There are things of great portent that you and I must discuss – tribal matters.'

'You say that the spirits have arranged my escape from the Shona,' Tungata replied. 'It may be so – but if it is, then this white man is their agent. He and his woman have risked their very lives to free me.'

'Still, he is a white man,' said the old man delicately.

'His family has lived in this land for a hundred years – and he is my brother,' said Tungata simply.

'You vouch for him, Nkosi?' the old man persisted.

'Speak, old man,' Tungata assured him. 'We are all friends, here.'

The magician sighed and shuffled and took another handful of food. 'As my lord wishes,' he agreed at last, and then abruptly, 'You are the guardian of the old king's tomb, are you not?'

Tungata's dark eyes hooded in the firelight.

'What do you know of these things, old man?' he countered.

'I know that the sons of the house of Kumalo, when they reach manhood, are taken to the tomb of the king and made to swear the oath of guardianship.'

Tungata nodded reluctantly. 'This may be so.'

'Do you know the prophecy?' the old man demanded.

And Tungata nodded and said, 'That when the tribe is sorely in need, the spirit of the old king will come forth to give them succour.'

'The spirit of Lobengula will come forth as a fire,' the old man corrected him.

'Yes,' Tungata agreed. 'Lobengula's fire.'

'And there is more, much more – do you know the rest of it, son of Kumalo?'

'Tell it to me, old father.'

'The prophecy goes on thus: *The leopard cub will first break an oath, then break his chains. The leopard cub will first fly like an eagle, then swim like a fish. When these things have come to pass, the fire of Lobengula will be freed from the dark places and come forth to succour and save his people.*'

They were all silent, considering this conundrum.

'The leopard skin is the prerogative of the house of Kumalo,' Vusamanzi reminded them. 'Thus the leopard cub of the prophecy would be a descendant of the royal house.'

Tungata grunted non-committally.

'I do not know that you have broken an oath,' the old man went on, 'but you have broken the chains with which the Shona bound you.'

'Eh-heh!' Tungata nodded, his face closed and impassive.

'You escaped from Tuti in an *indeki*, flying like an eagle indeed,' the old man pointed out, and again Tungata nodded, but in English he murmured to Craig, 'The beauty of these ancient prophecies is that they can be moulded to fit nearly any circumstance. They gain a little or lose a little with each repetition, depending on the mood and the motives of the seer at the time.' Then he reverted smoothly to Sindebele. 'You are wise, old man, and well versed in magic, but tell us what of the swimming of the fish? I must warn you that I am not able to swim, and that

441

the only one thing I truly fear is death by drowning. You must seek another fish.'

Vusamanzi wiped the grease off his chin and looked smug.

'There is something else I must tell you,' Tungata went on. 'I have entered Lobengula's tomb. It is empty. The body of Lobengula has gone. The prophecy has been voided long, long ago.'

The old magician showed no distress at Tungata's words. Instead he sat back on his heels and unscrewed the stopper of the snuff-horn that hung around his neck.

'If you have entered the king's tomb, then you have broken your oath to defend it intact,' he pointed out with a wicked twinkle of his eyes. 'The oath-breaking of the prophecy – could that be it?' He did not wait for a reply but poured red snuff into the palm of his hand and drew it up each nostril. He sneezed ecstatically with tears running down his withered old cheeks.

'If you broke your oath, Nkosi, it was beyond your powers to prevent it. The spirits of your ancestors drove you to it and you are without blame. But, now let me explain the empty tomb.' He paused and then seemed to take off at a tangent. 'Have either of you heard of a man who lived long ago, a man they called Taka-Taka?' They both nodded.

'On the maternal side Taka-Taka was the great-grand-father of Pupho here.' Tungata nodded at Craig. 'Taka-Taka was a famous white soldier in the old days of Lobengula. He fought against the king's impis, Taka-Taka is the sound that his machine-guns made when the warriors of the Matabele went against him.'

'Old Sir Ralph Ballantyne,' Craig agreed. 'One of Rhodes' righthand men, and the first prime minister of Rhodesia.' He changed back into Sindebele. 'Taka-Taka lies buried in the Matopos Hills close by the grave of Lodzi, of Cecil Rhodes himself.'

'That is the one.' Vusamanzi wiped the snuff from his upper lip, and the tears from his cheeks with his thumb. 'Taka-Taka, the soldier and the robber of the sacred places of the tribe. It was he who stole the stone birds from the ruined city of Great Zimbabwe. It was he also that came into these very hills to desecrate the tomb of Lobengula, and to steal the fire-stones that hold the spirit of the king.'

Now both Craig and Tungata leaned forward attentively. 'I have read the book that Taka-Taka wrote describing his life—' old Sir Ralph's handwritten diaries were part of Craig's personal treasure that he had left at King's Lynn when Peter Fungabera had driven him out. 'I have read the very words of Taka-Taka, and he does not tell of reaching Lobengula's tomb. And what are these fire-stones you speak of?'

The old man held up a restraining hand. 'You go too swiftly, Pupho,' he admonished Craig. 'Let the son of Kumalo explain these mysteries to us. Have you heard of the fire-stones, Tungata Zebiwe, who was once Samson Kumalo?'

'I have heard something of them,' Tungata agreed cautiously. 'I have heard that there was a huge treasure in diamonds, diamonds collected by Lobengula's *amadoda* from the white man Lodzi's mines in the south—'

Craig started to interrupt, but Tungata silenced him. 'I will explain later,' he promised, and turned back to the old magician.

'What you heard is the truth,' Vusamanzi assured him. 'There are five beer-pots filled with the fire-stones.'

'And they were stolen by Sir Ralph, by Taka-Taka?' Craig anticipated.

Vusamanzi looked severe. 'You should go to the women's fire, Pupho, for you chatter like one of them.'

Craig smothered his smile, and sat back suitably chastened while Vusamanzi rearranged his skin cloak before going on.

443

'When Lobengula was put to earth and his tomb sealed by his half-brother and loyal induna, a man named Gandang—'

'Who was my great-great-grandfather,' Tungata murmured.

'Who was your great-great-grandfather,' the old man agreed. 'Gandang placed all the king's treasures with him in the tomb, and then led the vanquished tribe of Matabele back. He went back to treat with Lodzi and this man Taka-Taka, and the tribe went in to the white man's bondage. But one man stayed in these hills, he was a famous magician named Insutsha, the arrow. He stayed to guard the king's tomb, and he built a village near the tomb, and took wives and bred sons. Insutsha, the arrow, was my grandfather—' they made small movements of surprise, and Vusamanzi looked complacent. 'Yes, do you see how the spirits work? It is all planned and predestined – the three of us are bound by our history and our bloodlines, Gandang and Taka-Taka and Insutsha. The spirits have brought us, their descendants, together in their marvellous fashion.'

'Sally-Anne is right – it's bloody spooky,' said Craig, and Vusamanzi frowned at his gauche use of a foreign language.

'This Taka-Taka, as I have hinted already, was a famous rogue, with a nose like a hyena and an appetite like a vulture.' Vusamanzi gave this summation with relish and glanced significantly at Craig.

'Got it!' Craig smiled inwardly, but kept a solemn expression.

'He learned the legend of the five pots of fire-stones, and he went amongst the survivors of Gandang's impi, the men who had been present at the time of the king's death, and he spoke sweet and gentle words and offered gifts of cattle and gold coins – and he found a traitor, a dog of a dog who was not fit to be called Matabele. I will not speak

444

the name of this piece of offal, but I spit on his unmarked and dishonoured grave.' Vusamanzi's spittle hit the embers of the fire with a spluttering hiss.

'This dog agreed to lead Taka-Taka to the king's burial place. But before he could do so, there was a great war between the white men, and Taka-Taka went north and fought against the German induna called Hamba-Hamba, "the one-who-marches-here-and-there-and-is-never-caught".'

'Von Lettow-Vorbeck,' Craig translated, 'the German commander in East Africa during the 1914–1918 war.' And Tungata nodded agreement. 'When the war was over Taka-Taka returned and he called the Matabele traitor, and they came into these hills with the dog of a dog leading them – four white men with Taka-Taka as their chief – and they searched for the tomb. They searched for twenty-eight days, for the traitor did not remember the exact location and the tomb was cunningly concealed. However, with his hyena nose Taka-Taka smelled it out at last, and he opened the royal tomb, and he found wagons and guns, but the king's body and the five beer-pots for which he hungered so violently were gone!'

'This I have already seen and told you,' Tungata said. It was an anti-climax and Tungata turned one palm up in a gesture of resignation, and Craig shrugged, but Vusamanzi went on resolutely.

'They say that Taka-Taka's rage was like the first great storms of the rains. They say he roared like a man-eating lion and that his face went red and then purple and finally black.' Vusamanzi chortled with glee. 'They say he took his hat from his own head and threw it on the ground, then he took his gun and wanted to shoot the Matabele guide, but his white companions restrained him. So he tied the dog to a tree and beat him with a kiboko until he could see his ribs sticking out of the meat of his back, then he took back the gold coins and cattle with which he had bribed him, then he beat him again and finally, still squealing like a bull elephant in musk, Taka-Taka went away and never came back to these hills.'

'It is a good tale,' Tungata agreed. 'And I will tell it to my children.' He stretched and yawned. 'Now it grows late.'

'The tale is not yet told,' said Vusamanzi primly, and placed a hand on Tungata's shoulder to prevent him from rising.

'There is more?'

'There is indeed. We must go back a little, for when Taka-Taka and his companions and the traitor dog first arrived in these hills to begin the search, my grandfather Insutsha grew immediately suspicious. Everybody knew of Taka-Taka. They knew he did nothing without purpose. So Insutsha sent three of his prettiest young wives to where Taka-Taka was camped, bearing small gifts of eggs and sour milk, and Taka-Taka answered the girls' questions and said that he had come into these hills to hunt rhinoceros.' Vusamanzi paused, glanced at Craig, and elaborated, 'Taka-Taka was also a renowned liar. However, the prettiest of the wives waited for the traitor dog of a Matabele at the bathing-pool of the river. Under the water she touched that thing of which it is said, the harder it becomes, the softer becomes the brain of the man who wields it and the faster it waggles that fast waggles his tongue. With the girl's hand on his man spear, the Matabele traitor spilled out boasts and promises of cattle and gold coins, and the pretty wife ran back to my grandfather's village.'

Vusamanzi had all their attention again, and he clearly relished it.

'My grandfather was thrown into terrible consternation. Taka-Taka had come to desecrate and rob the king's tomb. Insutsha fasted and sat vigil, he threw the bones and stared into the water-divining vessel, and finally he called his four apprentice witch-doctors to him. One of the apprentices was my own father. They went in the full moon and opened the king's tomb and made sacrifice to placate the king's ghost, and then, with reverence, they bore him away, and they resealed the empty tomb. They took the king's body to a safe place and deposited it there, with the beer-pots of bright stones – although my father told me that in their haste one of the beer-pots was overturned and broken, and that they gathered up the fallen stones and placed them in a zebra-skin bag, leaving the broken shards in the tomb.'

'Both the apprentices and Taka-Taka overlooked one of the diamonds,' Tungata said softly. 'We found the clay shards and a single diamond where they had left it.'

'Now you may go to sleep – if you are still weary, Nkosi.' Vusamanzi gave his permission with a gleam in his rheumy old eyes. 'What? You want to hear more? There is nothing else to tell. The tale is finished.'

'Where did they take the king's body?' Tungata asked. 'Do you know the place, my wise and revered old father?'

Vusamanzi grinned. 'It is indeed an unexpected pleasure to find respect and honour for age in the young people of this new age, but to answer your question, son of Kumalo: I do know where the king's body is. The secret was passed to me by my father.'

'Can you lead me to the place?'

'Did I not tell you that this place in which we now sit is sacred? It is sacred for good reason.'

'My God!'

'Here!' both Craig and Tungata exclaimed together, and Vusamanzi cackled happily and hugged his bony old knees, well pleased with their reaction.

'In the morning I will take you to view the site of the king's grave,' he promised, 'but now my throat is dry with too much talking. Pass the beer-pot to an old man.'

W hen Craig woke, the first morning light was diffusing through the hole in the roof of the cavern, milky and blued by the smoke from the cooking-fire where the girls were busy preparing the morning meal.

While they breakfasted, and with Vusamanzi's reluctant permission, Craig related in English the outlines of the tale of Lobengula's reburial to Sarah and Sally-Anne. They were both enthralled, and immediately on fire to join the expedition.

'It is a difficult place to reach,' the old man huffed, 'and it is not for the eyes of mere womenfolk.' But Sarah smiled her sweetest, stroked the old man's head and whispered in his ear, and finally, after a further show of gruff severity, he relented.

Under Vusamanzi's direction, the men made a few simple preparations for the expedition. In one of the ancillary branches of the cavern beneath a flat stone was a hidey-hole containing another kerosene lantern, two native axes and three large coils of good-quality nylon rope – which the old man clearly prized highly.

'We liberated this fine rope from the army of Smithy during the bush war,' he boasted.

'One great blow for freedom,' Craig murmured, and Sally-Anne frowned him to silence.

They set off down one of the branches of the cavern, Vusamanzi leading and carrying one of the lanterns followed by Tungata with one of the rope coils, the girls in the centre, and Craig with a second coil of rope and the other lantern in the rear.

Vusamanzi strode along the passage as it narrowed and twisted. When the passage forked, he did not hesitate. Craig opened his clasp-knife and marked the wall of the right-hand fork, and then hurried to catch up with the rest of the party.

The system of tunnels and caves was a three-dimensional

maze. Water and seepage had mined the limestone of the hills until it was as perforated as Gruyère cheese. In some places they scrambled down rock scree, and at one point they climbed a rough, natural staircase of limestone. Craig blazed every twist and turn of the way. The air was cold and dank and musky with the smell of guano. Occasionally there was a flurry of shadowy wings around their heads, and the shrill squeal of disturbed bats echoed down the passageways.

After twenty minutes they came to an almost vertical drop of glossy smooth limestone, so deep that the lantern glow did not reach the depths. Under Vusamanzi's direction, they secured the end of one coil of nylon rope to a pillar of limestone, and one at a time slid down fifty feet to the next stage. This was a vertical fault in the rock formation, where two geological bodies had shifted slightly and formed an open crack in the depths of the earth. It was so narrow that he could touch either wall, and in the lantern light Craig could just make out the bright eyes of the bats hanging inverted from the rocky roof above them.

Uncoiling the second rope Vusamanzi cautiously climbed down the treacherous floor of the crack. The crack widened as it descended, and the roof receded into the gloom above their heads. It reminded Craig of the great gallery in the heart of Cheops' pyramid, a fearsome cleft through living rock, dangerously steep, so they had to steady themselves with the rope at every pace. They had almost reached the limit of the rope, when Vusamanzi halted and stood tall on a tilted slab, lit by his own lantern, looking like a black Moses descended from the mountain.

'What is it?' Craig called.

'Come on down!' Tungata ordered, and Craig scrambled down the last slope and found Vusamanzi and the others perched on the rock slab peering over the ledge into the still surface of a subterranean lake.

'Now what?' Sally-Anne asked, her voice muted with awe of this deep and secret place.

The lake had filled the limestone shaft. Across the surface, a hundred and fifty feet away, the roof of the shaft dipped into it at the same angle as the floor on which they stood.

Craig used the flashlight that they had salvaged from the wrecked Cessna for the first time. He shone it into the water that had stood undisturbed through the ages so that all sediment had settled out of it, leaving it clear as a trout stream. They could see the inclined floor of the gallery sinking away at the same angle into the depths. Craig switched off the flashlight, conserving the batteries.

'Well, Sam.' Craig put one hand on his shoulder. 'Here's your big chance to swim like a fish.' Tungata's chuckle was brief and insincere, and they both looked at Vusamanzi.

'Where now, revered father?'

'When Taka-Taka came to these hills and my grandfather and my father saved the king's body from defilement, there had been seven long terrible years of drought scorching the land. The level of the water in this shaft was much lower than it is now. Down there,' Vusamanzi pointed into the limpid depths, 'there is another branch in the rock. In that place they laid Lobengula's body. In the many years since then, good and plentiful rains have blessed the land, and each year the level of these waters has risen. The first time I visited this place, brought here by my father, the waters were below that pointed rock—'

Briefly Craig switched on the flashlight and in its beam the splintered limestone lay thirty feet or more below the surface.

'But even then the king's grave was far below the surface.'

'So you have never seen the grave with your own eyes?' Craig demanded.

'Never,' Vusamanzi agreed. 'But my father described it to me.'

Craig knelt at the edge of the lake and put his hand into the water. It was so cold that he shivered and jerked his hand out. He dried it on his shirt, and when he looked up, Tungata was watching him with a quizzical expression.

'Now you just hold on there, my beloved Matabele brother,' Craig said vehemently. 'I know exactly what that look means – and you can forget all about it.'

'I cannot swim, Pupho my friend.'

'Forget it,' Craig advised him.

'We will tie one of the ropes around you. You can come to no harm.'

'You know where you can put your ropes.'

'The torch is waterproof, it will shine underwater,' Tungata went on with equanimity.

'Christ!' Craig said bitterly. 'African rule number one: when all else fails, look around for the nearest white face.'

'Do you remember how you swam across the Limpopo river for a ridiculous wager, a case of beer?' Tungata asked sweetly.

'That day I was drunk, now I'm sober.' Craig looked at Sally-Anne for support and was disappointed.

'Not you also!'

'There are crocs in the Limpopo, no crocs here,' she pointed out.

Slowly Craig began to unbutton his shirt, and Tungata smiled and began readying the rope. They all watched with interest while Craig unstrapped his leg and laid it carefully aside. He stood one-legged in his underpants at the edge of the pool while Tungata fastened the end of the rope around his waist.

'Pupho,' Tungata said quietly, 'you will need dry clothes afterwards. Why do you wish to wet these?'

'Sarah,' Craig explained and glanced at her.

'She is Matabele. Nudity does not offend us.'

'Leave him his secrets,' Sarah smiled, 'though I have none from him.' And Craig remembered her nakedness in the water below the bridge. He sat on the edge of the rock slab and pulled off his underpants, tossing them on top of the heap of his clothing. Neither of the girls averted their eyes, and he slid into the water, gasping at the cold. He paddled out gently into the centre of the pool and trod water.

'Time me,' he called back to them. 'Give me a double tug on the rope every sixty seconds. At three minutes, pull me up regardless, okay?'

'Okay.' Tungata had the coils of rope between his feet, ready to feed out.

Craig hung in the water and began to hyperventilate, pumping his lungs like a bellows, purging them of carbon dioxide. It was a dangerous trick, an inexperienced diver could black out from oxygen starvation before the build-up of CO_2 triggered the urge to breathe again. He grabbed a full lung and flipped his leg and lower body above the surface in a duck dive, and went down cleanly into the cold clear water.

Without a glass face-plate, his vision was grossly distorted, but he held the flashlight beam on the sharp pinnacle of limestone thirty feet below and went down swiftly, the pressure popping and squeaking in his ears.

He reached it and gave himself a push off from the rock. He was going down more readily now as the water pressure compressed the air in his lungs and reduced his buoyancy. The steep rocky floor of the pool flew in a myopic blur past his face, and he rolled on his side and scanned the walls of gleaming limestone on each side for an opening.

There was a double tug on the rope around his waist: one minute gone, and he saw the entrance to the tomb below him. It was an almost circular opening in the left-hand wall of the main gallery, and it reminded Craig of the empty eye-socket in a human skull.

He sank down towards it and put out a hand to brace himself on the limestone sill above the opening. The mouth of the tomb was wide enough for a man to stoop through. He ran his hand over the walls and they were polished by running water and silky with a coating of slime. Craig guessed that this was a drain-hole from the earth's surface carved out of the limestone by the filtering of rain waters over the millennia.

He was suddenly afraid. There was something forbidding and threatening about this dark entrance. He glanced back towards the surface. He could see the faint reflected glow of old Vusamanzi's lantern forty feet above him, and the icy water sapped his vitality and courage. He wanted to thrash wildly back towards the surface, and he felt the first involuntary pumping of his lungs.

Something tugged at his waist, and for an instant he teetered on the edge of wild panic before he realized it was the signal. Two minutes – almost his limit.

He forced himself forward into the entrance of the tomb. It angled gently upwards again, round as a sewer pipe. Craig swam for twenty feet flashing the torch beam ahead of him, but the water was turning murky and dark as he stirred up the sediment from the floor.

Abruptly the passage ended and he ran his hand over rough rock. His lungs were beginning to pump in earnest and there was a singing in his ears, his vision was clouded with swirling sediment and the beginnings of dizzy vertigo, but he forced himself to stay on and examine the end of the tunnel from side to side and top to bottom, running his free hand over it.

Quickly he realized that he was feeling a wall of limestone masonry, packed carefully into place to block off the tunnel, and his spirits plunged. The old witch-doctors had once again sealed Lobengula's tomb, and in the brief seconds he had left, he realized that they had made a thorough job of it.

His searching fingers touched something with a smooth metallic feel lying at the foot of the wall. He took it up and turned away from the wall, shoving himself down the passage, with panic and the need for air rising in him. He reached the main gallery again, still carrying the metallic object in one hand.

High above him, the lantern glowed and he swam upwards, with his senses beginning to flutter like a candle flame in the wind; darkness and stars of light played before his eyes as his brain starved and he felt the first deadly lethargy turning his hands and his foot to lead.

With a jerk, the rope around his waist came tight, and he felt himself being drawn swiftly upwards. Three minutes, and Tungata was pulling him out. The lantern light spun dizzily overhead as he windmilled on the end of the rope, and he could not prevent himself, he tried to breathe and freezing water shot down his throat and went into his lungs, stinging like the cut of a razor.

He exploded out through the surface, and Tungata was waist-deep, hauling double-handed on the life-line. The instant he broke through, Tungata seized him, a thick muscled arm around his chest, and he dragged Craig to the edge.

The two girls were ready to grab his wrists and help him up onto the slab. Craig collapsed on his side, doubled up like a foetus, coughing and heaving the water from his lungs and shaking violently with cold.

Sally-Anne rolled him onto his stomach and bore down on his back with both hands. Water and vomit shot up his throat, but his breathing gradually eased and at last he sat up wiping his mouth. Sally-Anne had stripped off her own shirt and was chafing him vigorously with it. In the lantern light his body was dappled blue with cold and he was still shivering uncontrollably.

'How do you feel?' Sarah asked.

'Bloody marvellous,' he gasped. 'Nothing like a bracing dip.'

'He's all right,' Tungata assured them, 'as soon as he starts snarling, he's all right.'

Craig cupped his hands over the chimney of the lantern for warmth and gradually his shivering eased. Sarah leaned across to Tungata, and with a wicked smile directed at Craig's naked lower body, whispered something.

'Right on!' Tungata chuckled, imitating a black American accent. 'And what's more, these honkys ain't got no rhythm neither.'

Craig quickly reached for his underpants, and Sally-Anne rushed loyally to his defence. 'You're not seeing him at his best, that water is freezing.'

Craig's hands were stained red-brown with rust, they marked his underpants and he remembered the metal object he had found at the wall of the tomb. It lay where he had dropped it at the edge of the slab.

'Part of a trek chain,' he said, as he picked it up. 'From an ox wagon.'

Vusamanzi had been squatting silently on one side, at the edge of the lantern light. Now he spoke. 'That chain was from the king's wagon. My grandfather used it to lower the king's body down the shaft.'

'So you have found the king's grave?' Tungata asked. This mundane little scrap of metal was for all of them the proof that changed fantasy to factual reality.

'I think so,' Craig began strapping on his leg, 'but we will never know for certain.' They all watched his face and waited. Craig suffered another paroxysm of coughing, then his breathing settled and he went on, 'There is a passage, just as Vusamanzi described. It is about another fifteen feet below that pinnacle and it goes off to the left, a round opening with a shaft that rises sharply. About twenty feet from the entrance, the shaft has been blocked with masonry, big blocks and lumps of limestone, packed closely together. There is no way of telling how thick the wall is, but one thing is certain, it is going to take a lot of work to get through it. I had about twenty seconds' endurance at the face, not long enough to prise out even a single block. Without diving apparatus, nobody is going to get past that seal.'

Sally-Anne was shrugging on her damp shirt over her white bra, but she stopped and stared at him challengingly. 'We can't just give up, Craig darling, we can't just walk away and never know. It would eat me up not knowing – a mystery like that! I'd never be happy, never again as long as I lived.'

'I'm open to suggestions,' Craig agreed sarcastically. 'Anybody got a scuba tucked in their back pocket? How about paying Vusamanzi a goat and he can make the water jump aside, shades of Moses and the Red Sea.'

'Don't be flippant,' said Sally-Anne.

'Come on somebody, be intelligent and inventive – what? No takers? Okay, then let's get back to where there is a fire and a little sunlight.'

Craig dropped the rusted piece of chain back into the pool.

'Sleep well, Lobengula, "the one who drives like the wind", keep your fire-stones beside you, and *shala gashle*, stay in peace!'

The climb back up through the maze of passages and interleading caverns was a dismal and silent procession, although Craig checked and remarked each turn and juncture as he passed it.

When they reached the main cavern again, it took only a few minutes to blow the embers on the hearth to flames and boil a canteen of water.

The strong, oversweetened tea warmed away the last of Craig's chills and heartened them all.

'I must return to the village,' Vusamanzi told them. 'If the Shona soldiers come and do not find me, they will become suspicious – they will begin to bully and torture my women. I must be there to protect them, for even the Shona fear my magic.' He gathered up his pouch and cloak and his ornately carved staff. 'You must remain in the cavern at all times. To leave it is to risk discovery by the soldiers. You have food and water and firewood and blankets and paraffin for the lanterns, there is no need for you to go out. My women will come to you the day after tomorrow with food and news of the Shona.' He went to kneel before Tungata. 'Stay in peace, great prince of Kumalo. My heart tells me that you are the leopard-cub of the prophecy, and that you will find a way to free the spirit of Lobengula.'

'Perhaps I will return here one day with the special machines that are necessary to reach the king's resting place.'

'Perhaps,' Vusamanzi agreed. 'I will make sacrifice and consult the spirits. They might condescend to show me the way.' At the entrance of the cave he paused and saluted them. 'When it is safe, I shall return. Stay in peace, my children.' And then he was gone.

'Something tells me it's going to be a long, hard time,' said Craig, 'and not the most attractive place to pass it.'

They were all active and restlessly intelligent people, and the confinement began to irk almost immediately.

Tacitly they divided the cavern, a communal area around the hearth and a private area at either end for each couple. The seepage of water down the rock face when collected in a clay pot was sufficient for all their needs, including ablutions, and there was a vertical pothole shaft in one of the passages which served as a natural latrine. But there was nothing to read and – a lack that Craig felt keenly – no writing material. To alleviate the boredom, Sarah began teaching Sally-Anne Sindebele, and her progress was so rapid that she could soon follow ordinary conversation and respond to it fairly fluently.

Tungata recovered rapidly during those days of enforced inactivity. His gaunt frame filled out, the scabs on his face and body healed rapidly, and he regained his vitality. It was often Tungata who led the long rambling discussions at the fireside, and that irrepressible sense of humour that Craig remembered so well from the old days began to break through the sombre moods that had at first overwhelmed him.

When Sally-Anne made a disparaging remark about the neighbouring South African state and its apartheid policies, Tungata contradicted her with mock severity.

'No, no, Pendula—' Tungata had given her the Matabele name of 'the one who always answers back' ' – no, Pendula, rather than condemn them, we black Africans should give thanks for them every time we pray! For they can bring a hundred tribes together with a single rallying cry. It is only necessary for one of us to stand up and shout, "Racist Apartheid Boers!" and all the others stop beating each other over the head and for a moment we become a band of brothers.'

Sally-Anne clapped her hands. 'I'd love to hear you make that speech at the next meeting of the Organization for African Unity!'

Tungata chuckled at her, they were becoming good

friends. 'Another thing we have to be grateful for—' he went on.

'Tell me more,' she incited him.

'Those tribes down there are some of the fightingest niggers in Africa,' Tungata obeyed. 'Zulus and Xhosas and Tswanas. We have got our hands full with the Shona. Imagine if that lot were turned loose on us also. No, from now on my motto is going to be "Kiss an Afrikaner every day"!'

'Don't encourage him,' Sarah pleaded with Sally-Anne. 'One day he is going to talk like this in front of people who will take him seriously.'

At other times Tungata relapsed back into those intense and dark moods. 'It is like Northern Ireland or Palestine, only a hundred times bigger and more complex. This conflict between ourselves and the Shona is a microcosm of the entire problem of Africa.'

'Do you see a solution?' Sally-Anne demanded.

'Only a radical and difficult one,' he told her. 'You see, the European powers in their nineteenth-century scramble for Africa divided the continent up amongst themselves with no thought for tribal boundaries, and it is an entrenched article of the Organization for African Unity that these boundaries are sacrosanct. One possible solution would be to overturn the article and repartition the continent along tribal boundaries, but after the terrible experience of partitioning India and Pakistan, no rational person would support that view. The only other solution seems to me to be a form of federal government, based loosely on the American system, with the state divided into tribal provinces possessing autonomy in their own affairs.'

Their talk ranged across time, and for the entertainment and instruction of the two girls, both Craig and Tungata related the history of this land between the Limpopo and

Zambezi rivers, with each of them concentrating on the role played by their own nations and families in the discovery and occupation and the strife that had torn it.

Twice on successive days their talk at the hearth was interrupted by sounds from the world outside the cavern – the unmistakable whistling, clattering roar of a helicopter rotor hammering through the air in coarse pitch setting, and they fell silent and looked up at the roof of stone above them until the sound faded. Then the talk would turn to their chances of escape from the forces that pursued and hunted them so relentlessly.

Every second day the women came from Vusamanzi's village, travelling in the darkness of pre-dawn to elude the eyes in the sky above them. They brought food and news.

The Third Brigade troopers had come to the village, surrounding it first and then storming in and ransacking the huts. They had cuffed one of the young girls and they had shouted threats and badgered the old man, but Vusamanzi had faced them down with dignity and in the end his formidable reputation for magic had protected them. The soldiers had left without stealing much of value, without burning a single hut or killing more than a few chickens – but they had promised to return.

However, a massive manhunt was still in progress over the entire area. On foot and from the helicopters the Shona scoured the forest and hills during the hours of daylight and hundreds of the escapees from the camp had already been recaptured. The girls had seen them being transported in heavy trucks, naked and chained together.

As far as Vusamanzi knew, the Shona had not yet discovered the wrecked Cessna, but it was still extremely dangerous, and Vusamanzi had ordered the girls to impress upon them they must remain in the cavern. He would come to them in person when he judged it safe to do so.

This news depressed them all and it took all Craig's best storytelling and clowning to lighten the mood in the cavern. He turned their attention back to their perennially favourite topic, the tomb of Lobengula and the vast fortune they liked to believe it contained. They had already discussed in detail the equipment that would be needed to enable a team of divers to open the tomb and reach the burial area, and now Sally-Anne asked Tungata, 'Tell us, Sam, *if* there were a treasure, and *if* you could reach it, and *if* it were as rich as we hope, how would you use it?'

'I think it would have to be treated as belonging to the Matabele people. It would have to be placed in trust and used for their benefit, firstly to procure for them a better political dispensation. To be pragmatic, a negotiator with that sort of financial clout behind him would find it easier to get the attention of the British Foreign Office and the American State Department. He could prevail upon them to intervene. The government in Harare would have to take them seriously, options which are at present closed to us would become accessible.'

'After that, it would finance all sorts of social programmes – education, health, the forwarding of women's rights,' Sarah said, for the moment her timidity put aside.

'You would use it to make land-purchases to add to the existing tribal trustlands,' Craig added, 'financial assistance to the peasant farmers, aid for tractors and machinery, blood-stock improvement programmes.'

'Craig,' Sally-Anne laid her hand on his good leg, 'isn't there *any* way at all to reach the burial chamber? Couldn't you try another dive?'

'My precious girl, for the hundredth time, let me explain that I could probably move a single rock with each dive, and twenty dives would kill me.'

'Oh God, it's so frustrating!' Sally-Anne jumped up and began pacing up and down between them and the fire. 'I feel so helpless. If we don't do something, I'm going to go mad. I feel as though I am suffocating – I need a good breath of oxygen. Can't we just go outside for a few minutes?' And then immediately, she answered herself. 'That just isn't on, I know. Forgive me. I'm being silly.' She looked at her wrist-watch. 'My God, I've lost all track of time, do you realize it's after midnight already?'

Craig and Sally-Anne lay on their mattress of cut grass and tanned skins, holding each other close and whispering with their lips touching each other's ears so as not to disturb the other pair at their end of the cavern.

'I am ashamed of my part in having him imprisoned. He is such a marvellous man, darling, sometimes I feel so humble when I listen to him.'

'He might just make it to greatness,' Craig agreed.

'Coming back here to free him may be the most important thing that you and I ever do in our lives.'

'If we get away with it,' Craig qualified.

'There must be some justice in this naughty world.'

'It's a nice thought.'

'Kiss me goodnight, Craig.'

Craig loved to listen to her sleeping, the gentle sound of her breathing, and to feel the total relaxation of her body against his, with only the occasional little snuggling movement in his arms, but tonight he could not follow her into sleep.

Something was snagged in his subconscious like a burr in his sock, and the longer he lay, the fiercer became its irritation. Something somebody had said that evening, he figured it that far, but every time it started to rise to the surface of his mind, he tried too hard and it sank away again. At last he resorted to the old trick of emptying his mind, imagining a wastepaper-basket, and as each unbidden thought came, he tore it in half, crumpled it, and dropped it into the imaginary basket.

'Christ!' he said loudly, and sat bolt upright. Sally-Anne was jolted awake and came up beside him, pushing the hair out of her eyes, and mumbling drowsily.

'What is it?' Tungata called across the cavern.

462

'Oxygen!' cried Craig. Sally-Anne had said, 'I am suffocating – I need a good breath of oxygen.'

'I don't understand,' Sally-Anne mumbled, still more asleep than awake.

'Darling, wake up! Come on!' He shook her gently. 'Oxygen! The Cessna is equipped for high-altitude flight, isn't it?'

'Oh sweet heavens,' she stared at him. 'Why didn't we think of it before?'

'Life-jackets – do you have them?'

'Yes. When I was doing the flamingo survey over Lake Tanganyika, I had to have them installed. They are under the seat cushions.'

'And the oxygen system, is it a recycling circuit?'

'Yes.'

'Pupho!' Tungata had lit the lantern and carried it across to them with Sarah naked and unsteady on her feet trailing behind him like a sleepy puppy. 'Tell us, Pupho, what is happening?'

'Sam, you beauty,' Craig grinned at him, as he reached for his pants. 'You and I are going for a little walk.'

'Now?'

'Now, while it is still dark.'

There was enough moon to light their way as far as Vusamanzi's village. They bypassed the hilltop, not wanting to alarm the old man. A village dog yapped at them, but they found the footpath and hurried along it.

Morning found them still on the footpath.

Twice they were forced to take cover. The first time was when they almost ran head-on into a patrol of camouflage-clad Shona troopers. Tungata, who was on point, warned Craig with the hand-signal for dire danger. They lay in a thick yellow stand of elephant grass beside the path and watched them go padding silently past. Afterwards, Craig found that his heart was racing and his hands shaking.

'I'm getting too old for this,' he whispered.

'Me too,' Tungata agreed.

The second time they were warned by the whacking beat of helicopter rotors, and they dived into the ravine beside the path. The ungainly machine dragon-flyed down the far crest of the valley, with a machine-gunner in the fuselage port and the helmeted heads of an assault squad popping up behind him like poisonous green toadstools. The helicopter passed swiftly and did not return.

They overran the spot where they had originally intersected the footpath, and had to back-track for almost a mile, so it was late afternoon when they approached the wreck site.

They closed in with elaborate caution, circling the area and casting for ingoing spoor, checking with infinite patience that the wreck had not been discovered and staked-out. Finally, when they walked up, they discovered that it was undisturbed and exactly as they had left it.

Tungata climbed back up the side of the valley, and stood guard with the AK 47, while Craig began stripping the equipment they had come for. The four inflatable life-jackets were under the seats, as Sally-Anne had told him. They were of excellent quality, impregnated nylon, each with a carbon dioxide cartridge for inflation and a non-return valve on the mouthpiece for topping up. Attached to the bosom cushions were a whistle and – blessings upon the manufacturer – a light globe powered by a long-life battery. Under the pilot seat was – a thousand more blessings – a repair kit for the jackets, with scissors and scraper and two tubes of epoxy cement.

The steel oxygen bottles were bolted into a rack behind the rear bulkhead of the passenger compartment. There were three of them, each of two-litre capacity. From them flexible plastic tubing carried along behind the panelling to each seat, and terminated in a face-mask with two built-in valves. The user inhaled pure oxygen and exhaled a mixture of unused oxygen, water vapour and carbon dioxide. This was passed through the exit valve and ran through the two metal canisters under the floorboards. The first canister contained silica gel which removed the water vapour, the second canister was packed with soda lime which removed the carbon dioxide, and the purified oxygen was cycled back to the face-masks. When the pressure of pure oxygen in the system fell to that of ambient atmosphere, it was automatically supplemented from the three steel bottles. The flexible tubing was fitted with top-quality aluminium couplings, T-pieces and bends, all of the bayonet-fitting type.

Working as carefully as time would permit, Craig stripped out the system and then converted the heavy-duty canvas seat-covers into carry bags. He packed the salvaged equipment into them, making up two heavy bundles.

It was dark by the time that he whistled Tungata down from the hillside. Each of them shouldered a bundle and they started back.

When they intersected the footpath, they spent nearly half an hour sweeping their tracks, and hiding any sign of their detour from the path.

'You think it will hold good in daylight?' Craig said doubtfully. 'We don't want to signpost the wreck.'

'It's the best we can do.'

They stepped it out on the path, pushing hard, and despite their heavy, uncomfortable packs, they shaved an hour off their return time and reached the cavern just after dawn.

Sally-Anne said nothing when Craig stepped into the cavern. She merely stood up from the fire, came to him and pressed her face against his chest. Sarah bobbed the traditional curtsey to Tungata and brought him the beer-pot, letting him refresh himself before bothering him with greetings. Only after he had drunk did she kneel beside him, clap her hands softly and whisper in Sindebele, 'I see you, my lord, but dimly, for my eyes are filled with tears of joy!'

The Shona sergeant had been on foot patrol for thirty-three hours without rest. The previous morning they had made a brief and indecisive contact with a small band of the escapees they were hunting, an exchange of fire that had lasted less than three minutes, then the Matabele guerrillas had pulled out and splintered into four groups. The sergeant had gone after one group with five men, followed them until dark and then lost them on the rocky rim of the Zambezi valley. He was bringing in his patrol now for re-supply and new orders.

Despite the long patrol and the trauma of a good contact and hot pursuit, the sergeant was still vigilant and alert. There was an elastic spring in his stride, his head turned restlessly from side to side as he moved down the footpath, and the whites of his eyes under the brim of his jungle hat showed clear and sharp.

Suddenly he gave the urgent hand signal for deployment, and as he changed the AK 47 from one hip to the other to cover his left flank and dropped into cover, he heard his men spread and go down behind, covering him and backing him. They lay in the elephant grass beside the track, searching and waiting while the sergeant examined the small sign that had alerted him. It was a bunch of long grass on the opposite side of the path: the stems had been broken and then lifted carefully to try to disguise the break, but they had sagged slightly again. It was the type of sign a man might make when leaving the path to set up an ambush beside it.

The sergeant lay for two minutes, and when there was no hostile fire, he doubled forward ten paces and then went flat again, rolling twice to throw off an enemy's aim, and he waited two minutes longer.

Still no fire – and he came up cautiously, and went forward to the damaged clump of grass. It was man sign: a small band of men had left the path here or joined it, and they had swept their spoor. A man only took this much trouble if he was anticipating pursuit. The sergeant whistled up his tracker and put him to the spoor.

The tracker worked out from the path, casting ahead, and within minutes he reported, 'Two men, wearing boots. One of them walks with a slight favour to his left leg. They were headed down the valley.' He touched one of the footprints in a sandy patch. An ant-lion had built its tiny cone-shaped trap in the toe of the spoor, giving the tracker an accurate timing.

'Six to eight hours,' said the tracker, 'during the night. They went on the path, but we cannot follow them, their spoor has been covered by others.'

'If we cannot find where they are going, then we will see where they came from,' said the sergeant. 'Backtrack them!'

Three hours later, the sergeant walked up to the wreck of the Cessna.

C raig slept for a few hours and then by the light of the paraffin lantern began modifying the oxygen equipment for use underwater. The central part of his primitive oxygen rebreathing set was the bag. For this he used one of the inflatable life-jackets. Oxygen from the steel bottle was introduced into the bag through the one-way valve of the mouthpiece, the connection made with a length of flexible tubing.

As he worked, Craig explained, 'At a depth of forty feet underwater, the pressure will be greater than two atmospheres – you remember your high school physics: thirty-three feet of water equals one atmosphere, plus the pressure of the air above it – two atmospheres, right?'

His interested audience of three made affirmative sounds.

'Right! So for me to be able to breathe freely, the oxygen has to be fed into my lungs at the same pressure as the surrounding water – the oxygen in the bag is under the same ambient pressure as I am, *et voilà!*'

'My old daddy always used to say, it's brains what counts!' Sally-Anne applauded him.

'The chemicals in these two canisters remove the water vapour and carbon dioxide from the air that I exhale, and the purified oxygen goes back into the bag via this tube, and I breathe it again.'

He was sealing the new connections to the bag with epoxy cement from the repair kit.

'As I use up the oxygen in the bag, I keep topping it up with fresh oxygen from the steel bottle strapped on my back. Like this—' he cracked the tap of the black-and-white-coded bottle and there was an adder hiss of escaping gas.

'There are a few problems, of course—' Craig began work on altering the shape of the face-mask to give him a watertight fit.

'Such as?' Sally-Anne asked.

'Buoyancy,' Craig answered. 'As I use up the oxygen in the bag I will become less buoyant, and the steel bottle will pull me down like a stone. When I top up the bag I'll tend to shoot up like a balloon.'

'How will you beat that?'

'I will weight myself with rocks to get down to the tomb entrance, and once I'm there, I'll rope myself down to stay there.'

Craig was making up a back-pack on which were suspended the two canisters and the oxygen bottle. Carefully he positioned the steel bottles so that he could reach the tap over his shoulder.

'However, buoyancy isn't the big problem,' he said.

'You've got more?' Sally-Anne demanded.

'As many as you ask for,' Craig grinned. 'But did you know that pure oxygen breathed for an extended period at more than two atmospheres absolute, that is at any depth below thirty-three feet, becomes a deadly gas, as lethal as the carbon monoxide in the exhaust fumes of an automobile?'

'What can you do about that?'

'Not much,' Craig admitted. 'Except limit the duration of each dive, and monitor my own reactions very carefully while I am working at the wall of the tomb.'

'Can't you work out how much safe time you will have before it starts to poison—'

Craig interrupted. 'No, the formula would be too complicated and there are too many variables to calculate, from my body mass to the exact water depth. Then there is a cumulative effect of the poisoning. Each successive dive will become more risky.'

'Oh my God, darling.' Sally-Anne stared at him.

'We will keep the dives short, and we will work out a series of signals,' Craig reassured her. 'You will give me a rope signal from the surface every minute, and if I don't reply or if my reply is not immediate and decisive, you will haul me out. The poisoning is insidious but gradual, it will affect my reactions to the signal before I go out completely. It gives us a little leeway.'

He set the bulky equipment carefully aside, close to the fire, so that the warmth would hasten the setting of the epoxy cement.

'As soon as the joints are sealed, we can test it, and then go for the bank.'

'How long?'

'It's twenty-four-hour epoxy.'

'So long?'

'Rest will increase my resistance to the effects of oxygen poisoning.'

T he forest was too dense to allow the helicopter to alight. It hovered above the tree-tops, and the flight engineer on the winch lowered General Peter Fungabera into a hole in the mat of dark green vegetation below them.

Peter turned slowly on the thin steel cable, and the down-draught from the rotors fluttered his camouflage battle-smock about his torso. Six feet above the earth, he slipped out of the padded sling and dropped clear, landing neatly as a cat. He returned the salute of the Shona sergeant who was waiting for him, cleared the drop area quickly and looked up as the next man was lowered from the hovering helicopter.

Colonel Bukharin was also dressed in camouflage and jump helmet. His scarred face seemed impervious to the tropical sun, it was bloodless and almost as pale as those cold arctic eyes. He shrugged off the helping hands of the Shona sergeant and strode on up the valley. Peter Fungabera fell in beside him and neither man spoke until they reached the crumpled and shattered fuselage of the Cessna.

'There is no doubt?' Bukharin asked.

'The registration, ZS-KYA. You must remember I have flown in this aircraft,' Peter Fungabera replied, as he went

470

down on one knee to examine the belly of the fuselage. 'If further proof is needed,' he touched the neat puncture in the metal skin, 'machine-gun fire from directly below.'

'No corpses?'

'No.' Peter Fungabera straightened up, and leaned into the cockpit. 'No blood, no indication that any of the occupants was injured. And the wreck has been stripped.'

'It could easily have been looted by local tribesmen.'

'Perhaps,' Peter agreed. 'But I don't think so. The trackers have examined the sign, and this is their recon-struction. After the crash twelve days ago, four people left the site, two of them women, and one of the men with an unbalanced gait. Then within the last thirty-six hours, two men returned to the wreck. They are certain it was the same two – the boot prints match, and one of them has the same favour to his left leg.'

Bukharin nodded.

'On the second visit the wreck was stripped of much loose equipment. The two men left the area carrying heavy packs and joined the footpath that crossed the head of the valley about six miles from here. There the tracks have been confused and covered by other traffic.'

'I see,' Bukharin was watching him. 'Now tell me your other conclusions.'

'There are two black and two white persons. With my own eyes I saw them at Tuti airstrip. The one black is undoubtedly Minister Tungata Zebiwe – I recognized him.'

'Wishful thinking? He is your one last hope of making good our bargain.'

'I would know that man anywhere.'

'Even from an aircraft?'

'Even then.'

'Go on,' Bukharin invited.

'The other black person I did not recognize. Nor did I get a good enough view to positively identify either of the whites, but the pilot is almost certainly an American

471

woman named Jay. Although the aircraft belongs to the World Wildlife Trust, she had the use of it. The other white is probably her lover, a British writer of sensational fiction, who has an artificial leg, accounting for the unbalanced tracks. These three are unimportant and expendable. The only one of importance is Zebiwe. And now we know that he is still alive.'

'We also know that he has eluded you, my dear General,' Bukharin pointed out.

'I do not think he will continue to do so much longer.' Peter Fungabera turned to the sergeant who was standing attentively behind him. 'You have done well. Very well, so far.'

'Mambo!'

'I believe that this Matabele dog and his white friends are being hidden and fed by the local people.'

'Mambo!'

'We will question them.'

'Mambo!'

'We will start with the nearest village, which is it?'

'The village of Vusamanzi lies beyond this valley and the next.'

'You will move in and surround it. Nobody must leave or escape, not a goat, not a child.'

'Mambo!'

'When you have secured the village, I will come to supervise the interrogation.'

Craig and Tungata made three climbs down to Lobengula's pool at the foot of the grand gallery, carrying the makeshift diving gear, the spare oxygen bottles, the underwater lamps that Craig had made up with the batteries and globes scavenged from the life-jackets, firewood and fur blankets to warm Craig after each dive, and provisions to avoid the necessity of climbing back to the upper cavern for meals.

After discussion it was agreed that the two girls would take turns at remaining in the upper cavern, to meet the messengers from Vusamanzi's village and to carry down a warning to the others in the event of a Shona patrol stumbling on the entrance.

Before testing the diving equipment, Craig and Tungata made a careful survey of the route down to the pool, choosing the positions on which they would fall back if they were ever forced to defend the inner recesses of the cave system against a Shona attack. Although neither of them mentioned it, they were both acutely aware that there was no final position, no ultimate escape hole from the mountain depths, and that any defence must end at the icy waters of the pool.

Tungata made the only open acknowledgement of this when, in plain sight of the other three, he took four 7.62 bullets for the Tokarev pistol, wrapped them in a scrap of goat-skin, and wedged them in a crack in the limestone wall beside the pool. The two girls watched him with sickly fascination, and though Craig made a show of checking his breathing equipment, they all understood. This was the final assurance against torture and slow mutilation, one bullet for each of them.

'Okay!' Craig's voice was overloud for the silence of the gallery. 'I'm going to see how efficiently this contraption is going to drown me.'

Tungata lifted the set and Craig knelt and slipped his head through the yoke of the life-jacket. Sally-Anne and Sarah settled the bottle and canisters on his back, and then strapped them in place with strips of canvas cut from the seat covers. Craig checked the knots. If the set ever failed, he must be able to jettison it in a hurry.

At last he hopped into the pool, shuddered at the cold as he fitted the mask over his mouth and nose, secured the strap behind his head and half-filled his chest bag with oxygen. He gave the three on the bank a thumbs-up sign, and lowered himself below the surface.

As he had anticipated, buoyancy was his first problem. The pull of the bag on his chest rolled him onto his back like a dead fish, and with the thrust of his one leg, he was unable to right himself. He paddled back to the slab, and began the irksome business of experimenting with rock weights to adjust his attitude in the water. In the end he found that the only way to do it was to hold an excessively heavy stone and let it draw him down head-first. However, as soon as he released the stone, he was borne irresistibly upwards.

'At least the joints are watertight,' he told them when he surfaced again. 'And I'm getting oxygen. There is a lot of water leaking in around the edges of the mask, but I can purge that in the usual way.' He demonstrated the trick of holding the mask at the top and forcing the accumulated water out of the bottom with a sharp exhalation of breath.

'When are you going to go for the wall?'

'I guess I'm as ready now as I'll ever be,' Craig admitted reluctantly.

'You must understand that I wish to be as a father to you,' Peter Fungabera smiled gently. 'I look upon you as my children.'

'I can understand this Shona chattering as little as I can the barking of baboons from the hilltops,' Vusamanzi replied courteously, and Peter Fungabera made a gesture of irritation as he turned to his sergeant.

'Where is that translator?'

'He will be here very soon, mambo.'

Tapping his swagger-stick against his thigh, Peter Fungabera walked slowly down the ragged rank of villagers that his troopers had gathered in from their hoeing on the maize fields and had flushed from the huts. Apart from the old man, they were all women and children. Some of the women were as ancient as the witch-doctor, with white woolly pates and wizened dugs hanging to their waists, others were still capable of child-bearing with fat infants strapped to their backs, or standing naked at their knees; snot had dried white around the toddlers' nostrils and flies crawled unnoticed on their lips and at the corners of their eyes, and they stared up at Peter as he passed with fathomless eyes. There were still younger women with firm full breasts and glossy skin, pre-pubescent girls and uncircumcised boys. Peter Fungabera smiled kindly at them, but they stared back at him without expression.

'My Matabele puppies, we will hear you yap a little before this day is done,' he promised softly, and turned at the end of the line. He walked back slowly to where the Russian waited in the shade of one of the huts.

'You will get nothing out of the old one.' Bukharin took the ebony cigarette-holder from between his teeth and coughed softly, covering his mouth with his hand. 'He is dried up, beyond pain, beyond suffering. Look at his eyes. Fanatic.'

'I agree, these *sangoma* are capable of self-hypnosis, he will be impervious to pain.' Peter Fungabera shot back the cuff of his battle-smock and glanced impatiently at his watch. 'Where is that translator?'

It was another hour before the Matabele trusty from the rehabilitation centre was hustled up the path from the valley. He fell on his knees before Peter Fungabera, blubbering and holding up his manacled hands.

'Get up!' Then, to the sergeant, 'Remove his manacles. Bring the old man here.'

Vusamanzi was led into the centre of the village square.

'Tell him I am his father,' Fungabera ordered.

'Mambo, he replies that his father was a man, not a hyena.'

'Tell him that although I cherish him and all his people, I am displeased with him.'

'Mambo, he replies that if he has made Your Honour unhappy, then he is well content.'

'Tell him he has lied to my men.'

'Mambo, he hopes for the opportunity to do so again.'

'Tell him that I know he is protecting and feeding four enemies of the state.'

'Mambo, he suggests that Your Honour is demented. There are no hidden enemies of the state.'

'Very well. Now address all these people. Repeat that I wish to know where the traitors are hidden. Tell them that if they lead me to them, then nobody in the village will come to any harm.'

The translator stood before the silent rank of women and children, and made a long and passionate plea, but when he ended, they stared back at him stolidly. One of the infants began to scream petulantly, and its mother swung it under her arm and pressed her swollen nipple into its tiny mouth. There was silence again.

'Sergeant!' Peter Fungabera gave terse orders, and Vusamanzi's hands were snatched behind his back and bound at the wrists. One of the troopers fashioned a hangman's noose in a length of nylon rope and tossed the free end of the rope over one of the main supports of an elevated maize bin at the edge of the square. They stood Vusamanzi under the maize bin and dropped the noose over his head.

'Now tell his people that when any one of them agrees to lead us to the traitors, this punishment will end immediately.'

The translator raised his voice, but he had not finished before Vusamanzi called over him in a firm voice, 'My curse upon any of you who speak to this Shona pig. I command silence upon you, no matter what is done – he who breaks it will be visited by me from beyond the grave. I, Vusamanzi, master of the waters, command this thing!'

'Do it!' Peter Fungabera ordered, and the sergeant inched in the slack of the rope. The noose closed around the old man's neck, and gradually he was forced up onto his tiptoes.

'Enough!' Peter Fungabera ordered and they secured the free end of the rope.

'Now, let them come forward and speak.'

The translator moved down the rank of women, urging them and finally pleading unashamedly, but Vusamanzi glared at his women fiercely, unable to speak but still commanding them with all his will.

'Break one of his feet,' ordered Peter Fungabera, and the sergeant faced the old man and, with a dozen blows, using the butt of his rifle like a maize stamp, he crushed Vusamanzi's left foot. As the women heard the brittle old bones snap like kindling for the hearth, they began to wail and ululate.

'Speak!' Peter Fungabera commanded.

Vusamanzi stood on one leg, his neck twisted to one side at the pull of the rope. His damaged foot began to swell, like a balloon being inflated, to three times its natural size, the skin stretched black and shiny as an over-ripe fruit on the point of splitting open.

'Speak!' Peter Fungabera ordered the second time, and the mourning cries of the women drowned him out.

'Break his other foot!' he nodded to the sergeant.

As the rifle-butt shattered the complex of small bones in Vusamanzi's right foot, he fell sideways against the rope, and the sergeant stepped back, grinning at the contortions of the old man as he tried frantically to relieve the pressure of the rope by taking his weight on his mutilated feet.

All the women were screaming now, and the children's cries swelled the anguished chorus. One of the old women, the senior wife, broke the line and ran forward with both thin arms outstretched towards her husband of fifty years.

'Leave her!' Peter Fungabera ordered the guards who would have restrained her. They stepped aside.

The frail old woman reached her husband and tried to lift him, crying out her love and her compassion, but she did not have the strength even for Vusamanzi's emaciated body. She succeeded only in relieving the pressure on his larynx enough to prolong the agonies of his strangulation. The old man's mouth was open, hunting for air, and white froth coated his lips. He was making a harsh, cawing sound, and the old wife's antics were ludicrous.

'Listen to the Matabele rooster crow, and his ancient hen cackle!' Peter Fungabera smiled, and his troopers guffawed delightedly.

It took a long time, but when at last Vusamanzi hung still and silent with his face twisted up to the sky, his wife sank to the earth at his feet and rocked her body rhythmically as she began the keen of mourning.

Peter Fungabera walked back to the Russian, and Bukharin lit another cigarette and murmured, 'Crude – and ineffective.'

'There was never any chance with the old fool. We had to get him out of the way, and set the mood.' Peter dabbed at his chin and forehead with the tail of his scarf. 'It was effective, Colonel, just look at the faces of the women.'

He tucked the scarf back into the neck of his smock and strolled back to the women.

'Ask them where the enemies of the state are hidden.' But as the translator began to speak, the old woman sprang to her feet and rushed back to face them.

'You saw your lord die without speaking,' she screeched. 'You heard his command. You know that he will return!'

Peter Fungabera altered the grip on his swagger-stick and with little apparent effort drove the point of it up under the old woman's ribs. She screamed and collapsed.

478

Her spleen, enlarged by endemic malarial infection, had ruptured at the blow.

'Get rid of her,' Peter ordered, and one of the troopers seized her ankles and dragged her away behind the huts.

'Ask them where the enemies of the state are hidden.'

Peter walked slowly along the rank, looking into their faces, evaluating the degree of terror that he saw in each pair of black Matabele eyes. He took his time over the selection, coming back at last to the youngest mother, barely more than a child herself, her infant strapped upon her back with a strip of patterned blue cloth.

He stood in front of her and stared her down, then, when he judged the moment, he reached out and took her wrist. He led her gently to the centre of the open square, where the remains of the watch-fire still burned.

He kicked the smouldering ends of the logs together, and, still holding the girl, waited until they burst into flames again. Then he twisted the girl's arm, forcing her to her knees. Slowly silence fell over the other women, and they watched with deadly fascination.

Peter Fungabera loosened the blue cloth and lifted the infant off the girl's back. It was a boy. A chubby infant, with skin the colour of wild honey, his little pot-belly was gorged with his mother's milk, and there were creases of fat like bracelets, at his wrists and ankles. Peter tossed him up lightly and as he fell seized one ankle. The child shrieked with shocked outrage, dangling upside down from Peter's fist.

'Where are the enemies of the state hidden?'

The child's face was swelling and darkening with blood.

'She says she does not know.'

Peter Fungabera lifted the child high above the flames.

'Where are the enemies of the state?'

Each time he repeated the question he lowered the infant a few inches.

'She says she does not know.'

Suddenly Peter lowered the little wriggling body into the very heart of the flames, and the child squealed with a totally new sound. Peter lifted it clear of the flames after a second and dangled it in front of its mother's face. The flames had frizzled away the child's eyelashes and the tight little criss-curls from its scalp.

'Tell her that I will roast this little piglet slowly and then I will force her to eat it.'

The girl tried to snatch her child back, but he kept it just beyond her reach. The girl started screaming a single phrase, repeating it over and over again, and the other women sighed and covered their faces.

'She says she will lead you to them.'

Peter Fungabera dropped the infant into her arms and strolled back to the Russian. Colonel Bukharin inclined his head slightly in grudging admiration.

Forty feet down Craig hung suspended before the wall of the tomb. He had anchored his waist strap to a lump of limestone, and by the feeble yellow light of the lamp from one of the life-jackets was carefully examining the masonry for a weak point of entry. Using his hands to supplement his water-distorted vision, he found that there was no break or aperture, but that the foot of the wall was composed of much larger lumps of limestone than the top. Probably the availability of large rocks within easy portability of the tomb had been exhausted as the work progressed and the old witch-doctor and his apprentices had fallen back on smaller material, and yet the smallest was larger than a man's head.

Craig seized one of these and struggled to dislodge it. His hands had been softened by the water, and a tiny puff of blood clouded the water as his skin split on the sharp edge of the stone, but there was no pain for the cold had numbed him.

Almost immediately the bloodstain in the water was obscured by a darker shadow as the dirt and debris that had lain so long undisturbed swirled into suspension at his efforts. Within seconds he was totally blinded as the water was filthied, and he switched off the lamp to conserve the battery. Small particles of dirt irritated his eyes, and he closed them tightly, working only by sense of touch.

There are degrees of darkness, but this was total. It was a darkness that seemed to have physical weight and it crushed down upon him, emphasizing the hundreds of feet of solid rock and water above him. The oxygen he drew into his mouth had a flat chemical taste, and every few breaths a spurt of water would find its way around the ill-fitting seal of his mask and he choked upon it, forcing himself not to cough, for a coughing fit might dislodge the mask entirely.

The cold was like a terminal disease, sapping and destroying him, affecting his judgement and reactions, making it more and more difficult to guard against the onset of oxygen poisoning, and each signal on the rope from the surface seemed to be an eternity after the last. But he worked at the wall with a grim determination, beginning to hate the long-dead ancestors of Vusamanzi for their thoroughness in building it.

By the time his half-hour shift finally ended, he had pulled down a pile of rock from the head of the wall and had tunnelled a hole three or four feet into the masonry just wide enough to accommodate his upper body with its bulky oxygen equipment strapped to it, but there was still no indication as to just how much thicker the wall was.

He cleared the rock he had dislodged, kicking it down the incline of the chute and letting it fall away into the depths of the grand gallery. Then, with soaring relief, he untied the anchor rope and slid down after it and began the long ascent to the surface of the pool.

Tungata helped him clamber out of the water onto the slab, for he was weak as a child and the equipment on his back weighed him down. Tungata pulled the set off over his head, while Sarah poured a mug of black tea and ladled sticky brown sugar into it.

'Sally-Anne?' he asked.

'Pendula is standing guard in the upper cavern,' Tungata answered.

Craig cupped his hands around the mug, and edged closer to the smoky little fire, shaking with the cold.

'I have started a small hole in the top of the wall and gone into it about three feet, but there is no way of guessing how thick it is or how many more dives it will need to get through it.' He sipped the tea. 'One thing we have overlooked: I will need something to carry the goodies, if we find them.' Craig crossed his fingers and Sarah made her own sign to ward off misfortune. 'The beer-pots are obviously brittle – old Insutsha broke one – and they will be awkward to carry. We will have to use the bags I made from the canvas seat covers. When Sarah goes up to relieve Pendula, she must send them down.'

As the numbness of cold was dispelled by the fire and hot tea, so the pain in his head began. Craig knew that it was the effect of breathing high-pressure oxygen, the first symptom of poisoning. It was like a high-grade migraine, crushing in on his brain so that he wanted to moan aloud. He fumbled three pain-killers from the first-aid kit and washed them down with hot tea.

Then he sat in a dejected huddle and waited for them to take effect. He was dreading his return to the wall so strongly that it sickened his stomach and corroded his will. He found that he was looking for an excuse to postpone the next dive, anything to avoid that terrible cold and the suffocating press of dark waters upon him.

Tungata was watching him silently across the fire, and Craig slipped the fur cape off his shoulders and handed the empty mug back to Sarah. He stood up. The headache had degraded to a dull throb behind his eyes.

'Let's go,' he said, and Tungata laid a hand on his upper arm and squeezed it before he stooped to lift the oxygen set over Craig's head.

Craig quailed at this new contact with the icy water, but he forced himself into it, and the stone he held weighted him swiftly into the depths. In his imagination the entrance to the tomb no longer resembled an eyeless socket, but rather the toothless maw of some horrible creature from African mythology, gaping open to ingest him.

He entered it and swam up the inclined shaft, and anchored himself before the untidy hole he had burrowed into the wall. The sediment had settled, and in the glow of his lamp the shadows and shapes of rock crowded in upon him, and he wrestled with another attack of claustrophobia, anticipating the clouds of filth which would soon render him blind. He reached out and the rock was brutally rough on his torn hands. He prised a lump of limestone free, and a small slide of the surrounding stones sent sediment billowing around his head. He switched off his lamp and began the cold blind work again.

The rope signals at his waist were his only contact with reality and finite time – somehow they helped him to control his mounting terror of the cold and darkness. Twenty minutes, and his headache was breaking through the drugs with which he had subdued it. It felt as though a blunt nail was being driven with hammer blows into his temple, and as though the iron point was cutting in behind his eyes.

'I can't last another ten minutes,' he thought. 'I'm going up now.' He began to turn away from the wall and then just managed to prevent himself.

'Five minutes,' he promised himself. 'Just five minutes more.'

He forced his upper body into the opening, and the steel oxygen cylinder struck a rock and rang like a bell. He groped around the edges of a triangular-shaped rock that had been frustrating his efforts for the past few minutes. Once again he wished for a short jemmy bar to get into that crack and break it open. His fingers ached as he used them instead, getting them in under the rock, and then he wedged himself against the sides of the hole and began to jerk at it, slowly exerting more strength with each heave, until his back was bunched with muscle and his belly ached with the effort.

Something moved and he heard rock grate on rock. He heaved again and the crack closed on his fingers and he screamed with pain into his mask. But the pain of his crushed fingertips unlocked reserves of strength he had not yet tapped. He flung all of this against the rock and it rolled, his fingers came free and there was a rumbling, clanking roar of falling sliding stone blocks.

He lay in the hole and hugged his injured fingers to his chest, whimpering into his mask, half-drowning in the water that flooded in when he screamed.

'I'm going up now,' he decided. 'That's it. I've had enough.' He began to wriggle out of the aperture, gingerly putting out one hand to push himself backwards. He felt nothing. In front of him, his hand was waving around in the open. He lay still, the water sloshing in his mask, trying to make a decision. Somehow he knew that if he pulled out now and surfaced, he would not be able to force himself to enter the pool again.

Once again he groped ahead, and when he touched nothing, he inched forward and reached out again. His anchor-line held him and he slipped the knot, crept forward a little further and the pack on his back jammed up under the stone roof. He rolled half onto his side, and

484

was able to free it. Still he could touch nothing ahead of him. He was through the wall, and a sudden superstitious dread seized him.

He pulled back and the pack hit the roof again, and this time it jammed solidly. He was stuck fast, and immediately he began to fight to be free. His breathing hunted, beating the mechanical efficiency of the valves in his mask so that he could get no more oxygen and as he starved, his heart began to race and the pulse in his ears deafened him.

He could not go backwards, and he kicked with his one good leg, and with his stump got a purchase against smooth rock. He pushed forward with both legs – and, in a sudden rush similar to the moment of childbirth, he slid forward through the hole in the wall of the tomb into the space beyond.

He groped wildly about him and one hand hit the smooth wall of the shaft at his side, but now he was free of his anchor and the buoyancy of the bag on his chest bore him helplessly upwards. He threw up both hands to prevent his head striking the roof of the shaft, and to grab a handhold. Under his numb fingertips the rock was slippery as soaped glass, and as he ascended, so the oxygen in the bag expanded with the release of pressure and he went up more swiftly, only the signal rope at his waist slowing his headlong upward rush. As he struggled to stabilize himself, the excess oxygen poured out of the sides of the mask, and panic at last rode him completely. He was swirled aloft in total terrifying darkness.

Suddenly he burst out through the surface and lay on his back bobbing around like a cork. He tore the mask off his face and took a lungful of air. It was clean, but faintly tainted with the smell of bat guano. He lay on the surface and sucked it down gratefully.

The rope tugged rapidly at his waist. Six tugs repeated. It was the code question from Tungata. 'Are you all right?' His uncontrolled ascent must have ripped rope off the coil that lay between Tungata's feet and thoroughly alarmed him. Craig signalled back to reassure him and fumbled with the switch of his lamp.

The dim glow of light was dazzling to his eyes that had been blinded so long and they smarted from the irritation of the muddied waters. He blinked around him.

The passage had come up at a sharply increased angle from the masonry wall, until it was now a vertical shaft. The old witch-doctors had been forced to chip niches in the walls and build in a ladder of rough-hewn timber to enable them to make the ascent. The poles of the ladder were secured with bark rope and were latticed up the open shaft above Craig's head, but the light of his lantern was too feeble to illuminate the top of the steep shaft. The ladder disappeared into the gloom.

Craig paddled to the side and steadied himself with a handhold on the primitive wooden ladder while he assembled his thoughts and figured out the lay of the shaft and its probable shape. He realized that by returning to water level, he must have ascended forty feet after his access through the wall. He must have travelled an approximately U-shaped journey – the first leg was down the grand gallery, the bottom of the U was along the shaft to the wall, and the last leg was up the steeper branch of the shaft to return to water level again.

He tested the timber ladderwork, and though it creaked and sagged a little, it bore his weight. He would have to jettison the diving-gear and leave it floating in the shaft while he climbed up the rickety ladder, but first he must rest and regain full control of himself. He put both hands to his head and squeezed his temples, the pain was scarcely bearable.

At that moment, the rope at his waist jerked taut – three tugs, repeated. The urgent recall – the signal for mortal danger – something was desperately wrong, and Tungata was sending a warning and a plea for help.

Craig crammed the mask back onto his face and signalled, 'Pull me up!'

The rope came taut and he was drawn swiftly below the surface.

The young Matabele mother was allowed to keep her infant strapped to her back, but she was manacled by her wrist to the wrist of the Third Brigade sergeant.

Peter Fungabera was tempted to use the helicopter to speed the pursuit and recapture of the fugitives, but finally he made the decision to go in on foot, silently. He knew the quality of the men he was hunting. The beat of a helicopter would alert them and give them a chance to slip away into the bush once again. For the same reasons of stealth, he kept the advance party small and manageable – twenty picked men, and he briefed each of them individually.

'We must take this Matabele alive. Even if your own life is the exchange, I want him alive!'

The helicopter would be called in by radio as soon as they had good contact, and another three hundred men could be rushed up to seal off the area.

The small force moved swiftly. The girl was dragged along by the big Shona sergeant, and, weeping with shame at her own treachery, she pointed out the twists and forks of the barely distinguishable path.

'The villagers have been feeding and supplying them,' Peter murmured to the Russian. 'This path has been used regularly.'

'Bad place for an ambush.' Bukharin glanced up at the slopes of the valley that overlooked the path. 'They may have elements of the escapees with them.'

'An ambush will mean a contact – I pray for it,' Peter

told him softly. And once again the Russian felt satisfaction at his choice of man. This one had the heart for the task. Now it needed only a small change in the fortunes of war and his masters in Moscow would have their foothold in central Africa.

Once they had it, of course, this man Fungabera would need careful watching. He was not just another gorilla to be manipulated with a heavy pressure on the puppet strings. This one had depths which had not yet been fathomed, and it would be Bukharin's task to undertake this exploration. It would require subtlety and finesse. He looked forward to the work, he would enjoy it just as he was enjoying the present chase.

He swung easily along the track behind Peter Fungabera, pacing him without having to exert himself fully, and there was that delicious tightness in his guts and the stretching of the nerves, the heightening of all the senses – that special rapture of the manhunt.

Only he knew that the hunt would not end with the taking of the Matabele. After that there would be other quarry, as elusive and as prized. He studied the back of the man who strode ahead of him, delighting in the way he moved, in the long elastic strides, in the way he held his head upon the corded neck, in the staining of sweat through the camouflage cloth – yes, even in the odour of him, the feral smell of Africa.

Bukharin smiled. What a set of trophies to crown his long and distinguished career, the Matabele, the Shona and the land.

These mental preoccupations had in no way distracted Bukharin's physical senses. He was fully aware that the valley was narrowing down upon them, of the increased steepness of the slopes above and the peculiar stunted and deformed nature of the forest. He reached forward to touch Peter's shoulder, to draw his attention to the change in the geological formation of the cliff beside them, the contact of dolomite on country rock, when abruptly the Matabele woman began to shriek. Her voice echoed shrilly off the cliffs and repeated through the surrounding forest, shattering the hot and brooding silences of this strangely haunted valley. Her screams were unintelligible, but the warning they carried was unmistakable.

Peter Fungabera took two swift strides up behind her, reached over her shoulder and cupped his hand under her chin; he placed his other forearm at the base of her neck and with a clean jerk pulled her head back against it. The girl's neck broke with an audible snap, and her screams were cut off as abruptly as they had begun.

As her lifeless body dropped, Peter spun and urgently signalled his troopers. They reacted instantly, diving off the path and circling swiftly out ahead in the hooking movement of encirclement.

When they were in position, Peter glanced back at the Russian and nodded. Bukharin moved up silently beside him, and they went forward together, weapons held ready, quickly and warily.

The faint track led them to the base of the cliff, and then disappeared into a narrow vertical cleft in the rock. Peter and Bukharin darted forward and flattened themselves against the cliff on each side of the opening.

'The burrow of the Matabele fox,' Peter gloated quietly. 'I have him now!'

'The Shona are here!' The scream came from the entrance of the cavern, muted by the fold of the rock and the screening brush. 'The Shona have come for you! Run! The Shona—' a woman's voice cut off suddenly.

Sarah sprang up from the fire, overturning the three-legged iron cooking-pot, and she fled across the cavern, snatching up the lantern as she went, racing into the maze of passages.

From the head of the steep natural staircase into the grand gallery she screamed her warning down towards the pool, 'The Shona are here, my lord! They have discovered us!' And the echoes magnified the terror and urgency of her voice.

'I am coming to you!' Tungata boomed back up the gallery, and he came bounding up the shaft into the light of her lantern. He climbed the stone staircase, swinging himself up on the rope, and placed an arm around her shoulders.

'Where are they?'

'At the entrance – there was a voice, one of our women calling a warning – I could hear the fear in her and then it was cut off. I think she has been killed.'

'Go down to the pool. Help Pendula to bring Pupho up.'

'My lord, there is no escape for us, is there?'

'We will fight,' he said. 'And in fighting we may find a way. Go now, Pupho will tell you what to do.'

Carrying the AK 47 at the trail, Tungata disappeared into the passage leading upwards towards the main cavern. Sarah scrambled down the rock rampway, in her haste falling the last few feet, barking her knees.

'Pendula!' she called, desperate for the comfort of human contact.

'Here, Sarah. Help me.'

When she reached the slab at the bottom of the gallery, Sally-Anne was waist-deep at the edge of the pool, straining on the rope.

'Help me, it's stuck!'

Sarah jumped down beside her, and grabbed the tail of the rope.

'The Shona have found us.' She heaved on the rope.

'Yes. We heard you.'

'What shall we do, Pendula?'

'Let's get Craig out of here first. He will think of something.'

Suddenly the rope gave, as forty feet below Craig managed to force himself through the narrow opening in the wall, and the two girls hauled him upwards hand over hand.

Oxygen bubbles burst in a seething rash on the surface of the pool, and they saw Craig coming up through the gin-clear water, the masking transforming him into some grotesque sea monster. He reached the surface and ripped the mask off his head, snorting and coughing at the fresh air.

'What is it?' he choked as he splashed to the edge of the rock slab.

'The Shona are here.' Both girls together, in English and Sindebele.

'Oh God!' Craig collapsed weakly onto the slab. 'Oh God!'

'What shall we do, Craig?' They were both staring at him piteously, and the cold and the pain in his head seemed to paralyse him.

Abruptly the air around their heads reverberated as though they were within the sounding body of a kettle-drum beaten at a furious tempo.

'Gunfire!' Craig whispered, covering his ears to protect them. 'Sam has made contact.'

'How long can he hold them?'

'Depends if they use grenades, or gas—' he left it hanging and straightened up, shivering violently. He stared back at them. They seemed to sense his despair, and looked away.

'Where is the pistol?' Sarah asked fearfully, glancing up at the twist of goat-skin in the crack of the rock wall.

'No,' Craig snapped. 'Not that.' He reached out and caught her arm. He pulled himself together, shaking off despair as he shook the water from his hair.

'Have you ever used an aqualung?' he demanded of Sally-Anne. She shook her head.

'Well, now is as good a time—'

'I couldn't go in there!' Fearfully Sally-Anne stared into the pool.

'You can do anything you have to do,' he snarled at her. 'Listen, I have found another branch of the shaft that comes up above surface. It will take three or four minutes—'

'No,' Sally-Anne cringed away from him.

'I'll take you through first,' he said. 'Then I will come back for Sarah.'

'I would rather die here, Pupho,' the black girl whispered.

'Then you'll get your wish.'

Craig was already changing the oxygen bottle, screwing on one of the fresh cylinders, and he turned his attention back to Sally-Anne.

'You put your arms around me and breathe slowly and easily. Hold each breath as long as you can, then let it out carefully. The hole in the wall is narrow, but you are smaller than I am, you'll make it easily.'

He lifted the oxygen set over her head and lowered it onto her shoulders. 'I will go through first, and pull you behind me. Once we are through it is straight up. As we go up just remember to exhale as the oxygen in your lungs expands again or you will pop like a paper bag. Come on.'

'Craig, I'm afraid.'

'Never thought I'd hear you say that.'

Waist-deep in the pool he fitted the mask over the lower half of her face.

'Don't fight it,' he told her. 'Keep your eyes closed and relax. I will tow you. Don't struggle, for God's sake, don't struggle.'

She nodded at him, gagged by the mask, and again the

492

gallery echoed to the deafening roar of automatic rifle-fire from above.

'Closer,' Craig muttered. 'Sam is being driven back.' Then he called to Sarah on the slab above them.

'Give me my leg!' Sarah handed it down to him. He strapped it to his belt. 'While I'm away, pack all the food you can find into the canvas bags. The spare lamps and batteries also – I'll be back for you inside ten minutes.'

He began to hyperventilate, holding to his chest the boulder that would weigh them down. He gestured to Sally-Anne and she waded up behind him and put her arms around him under his armpits.

'Take a good breath and play dead,' he ordered, and filled his own lungs for the last time. He fell forward with Sally-Anne clinging to his back and they dropped together down towards the tomb entrance.

Halfway down Craig heard the click of the valves in her mask, and felt Sally-Anne's chest subside and swell as she breathed, and he tensed for her coughing fit. There wasn't one.

They reached the entrance and he dropped the stone and drew her up to the wall. Gently he disentangled her hands, trying to make his movements calm and unhurried. He backed into the aperture, holding both her hands, and pulled her in after him. Unencumbered by the oxygen gear he slid through easily.

He heard her breathe again. 'Good girl!' he applauded silently. 'Good brave girl!'

For a moment her gear jammed in the aperture, but he reached forward and freed it, then eased her towards him. She was through. Thank you, God, she was through.

Now up! They were accelerating, pressure squeaking in his ears. He prodded her sharply in the ribs, and heard the rush of bubbles as she released the expanding oxygen from her lungs.

'Clever girl.' He squeezed her hand, and she squeezed back.

The ascent took so long that he began to fear he had lost his way, and taken a false branch of the tunnel, and then suddenly they broke out through the surface and he pumped for air.

Gasping, he reached across and switched on her lamp.

'You're not good,' he panted. 'You are simply bloody marvellous!'

He towed her to the foot of the ladder and began stripping off her oxygen gear.

'Get up the ladder, out of the water,' he grunted. 'Here, strap my leg to the rung. I'll be back soonest.'

He did not waste time on the difficult task of donning the gear while treading water, instead he tucked the canisters under his arm.

He had no stone to weight himself down – so he depressed the valve and emptied the oxygen bag. The set was now negatively buoyant, starting to pull him under. He could not use oxygen so he would have to free-dive again. He hung onto a rung of the ladderwork while he pumped his lungs with air, and then duck-dived.

At the wall he slid backwards through the opening and pulled the empty set after him. With the bag deflated, it came through readily enough. At the entrance to the grand gallery, he opened the tap of the oxygen cylinder. Gas hissed into the bag, swelling it, and immediately it was buoyant again. It drew Craig rapidly up to the surface of the pool.

Sarah was perched on the edge of the slab, but she had the canvas bags packed and ready.

'Come on!' Craig gasped.

'Pupho, I cannot.'

'Get your little black arse down here!' he rasped hoarsely.

'Here, take the bags, I will stay.'

Craig reached up and caught her ankle. He yanked her off the slab, and she splashed into the water and clung to him.

'Do you know what the Shona will do to you?' Roughly he pulled the yoke of the set over her head, and there was another burst of machine-gun fire above them, the ricochets wailing off the upper walls of the gallery.

Craig pressed the mask over her face.

'Breathe!' he ordered. She sucked air through the mask.

'Do you see how easy it is?'

She nodded.

'Here, hold the mask on your face with both hands. Breathe slowly and easily. I will carry you – lie still. Do not move!' She nodded again. He strapped the canvas bags to his waist and picked up the weight stone. He began hyperventilating.

From above them came the pocking report of a grenade-launcher, something clattered down the gallery and the entire cavern was lit by the fierce blue glare of a phosphorus flare.

With a rock tucked under one arm, and Sarah under the other, Craig ducked below the surface. Halfway down he felt Sarah try to breathe and immediately he knew they were in trouble. She took water, and began choking and wheezing into her mask. Her body convulsed against him, and she began writhing and struggling. He held her with difficulty; she was surprisingly strong and her hard slim body twisted in his arms.

They reached the entrance to the shaft, and as Craig let the weight fall, their buoyancy altered drastically. Sarah whirled on top of him, and drove her elbow into his face. The blow stunned him and for a moment he relaxed his grip. She broke away from him, starting to rise rapidly, kicking and windmilling.

He reached up and just managed to grip her ankle. Anchoring himself on the sill of the entrance, he hauled her down again and in the lamp glow saw that she had torn the mask off her face. It was snaking wildly about her head on its hose.

He dragged her bodily towards the wall, and she clawed at him and kicked him in the lower belly, but he raised his knees to protect his groin and swung her bodily around. Holding her from behind, he dragged her to the hole, and she fought him with the maniacal strength of terror and panic. He got her halfway through the wall before the hose caught in a crack in the rock, anchoring them.

While he struggled to free it, Sarah began to weaken, her movements became spasmodic and uncoordinated. She was drowning.

Craig got both his hands on the hose, and a foothold on the rock of the wall. He pulled with all the strength of his arms and his body – and the hose ripped out of the oxygen bag. The gas escaped through the rent in a roar of silver bubbles, but Sarah was free.

He pulled her out of the hole and started pedalling upwards, his one leg only just pushing them against the weight of the purged oxygen set and the drag of the canvas food-bags at his waist.

Craig's struggles to subdue Sarah had burned up his own oxygen reserves. His lungs were on fire, and his chest spasmed violently. He kept on pedalling. Sarah was quiescent in his arms, and he felt that despite all his efforts they were no longer moving, that they were hanging in the black depths, both of them drowning slowly. Gradually the urge to breathe passed, and it all ceased to be worth further effort. It was much easier just to relax and let it happen. Slowly he became aware of a mild pain. Through his indifference he wondered vaguely about that, but it was only when his head broke surface that he realized that someone had him by the hair.

Even in his half-drowned state, he realized that Sally-Anne must have seen the lamp glow below the surface and recognized their predicament. She had dived down to them, seized Craig by the hair and dragged him up to the surface.

As he struggled for breath, he realized also that he still had his grip on Sarah's arm. The black girl was floating face-down on the surface beside him.

'Help me!' he choked on his own breath. 'Get her out!'

Between them, they stripped the damaged oxygen set off her and lifted the unconscious girl onto the first rung of the ladderwork above the water, where Sally-Anne cradled her face-down over her lap. Sarah hung there like a drowned black kitten.

Craig put his finger into her mouth, making sure that her tongue was clear, and then pressed the finger down into her throat to trigger the retching reflex. Sarah spewed up a mixture of water and vomit, and began to make small unco-ordinated twitching movements.

Hanging in the water beside her, Craig splashed the vomit off her lips and then covered her mouth with his own, forcing his breath down into her lungs while Sally-Anne cradled the limp body as best she could on the awkward perch.

'She's breathing again.'

Craig lifted his mouth off Sarah's. He felt sick and dizzy and weak from his own near-drowning.

'The diving set is buggered,' he whispered, 'the hose is torn out.' He groped around for it, but it had sunk into the shaft.

'Sam,' he whispered. 'I've got to go back for Sam.'

'Darling, you can't – you've done enough. You'll kill yourself.'

'Sam,' he repeated. 'Got to get Sam.'

Clumsily he untied the straps of the canvas food-bags and hung them beside his leg on the ladder. He clung to the ladder, breathing as deeply as his aching lungs would allow. Sarah was coughing and wheezing, but trying to sit up. Sally-Anne lifted her and held her on her lap like a child.

'Craig, darling, come back safely,' she pleaded.

'Too right,' he agreed, allowing himself the indulgence of another half-dozen breaths of air, before he pushed himself off the ladder and the cold waters closed around his head again.

The underwater section of the grand gallery, even down as deep as the mouth of the shaft, was lit by the phosphorus flares, and as Craig ascended, so the intensity of the light increased to a crackling electric blue like the glare of brute arc-lamps.

As he broke through the surface of the pool, he found that the upper gallery was filled with the swirling smoke of the burning flares. He gasped for air and immediately pain shot down his throat into his chest and his eyes burned and smarted so that he could barely see.

'Tear gas,' he realized. The Shona were gassing the cavern.

Craig saw Tungata was in the water, crouched waist-deep behind the slab of rock. He had torn a strip from his shirt, wet it and bound it over his mouth and nose, but his eyes were red and running with tears.

'The whole cavern is swarming with troopers,' he told Craig, his voice muffled by the wet cloth, and he stopped as a stentorian disembodied voice echoed down the gallery, its English distorted by an electronic megaphone.

'If you surrender immediately, you will not be harmed.'

As if to punctuate this announcement, there was the 'pock' of a grenade-launcher and another tear-gas canister came flying down the gallery, bouncing off the limestone floor like a football, belching out white clouds of the irritant gas.

'They are down the staircase already, I couldn't stop them.' Tungata bobbed up from behind the edge of the slab and fired a short burst up the gallery. His bullets cracked and whined from the rock, and then the AK went silent and he ducked down.

'The last magazine,' he grunted and dropped the empty rifle into the water. He groped for the pistol on his belt.

'Come on, Sam,' Craig gasped. 'There is a way through beyond this pool.'

'I can't swim.' Tungata was checking the pistol, slapping the magazine into the butt and jerking back the slide to load.

'I got Sarah through.' Craig was trying to breathe through the searing clouds of gas. 'I'll get you through.'

Tungata looked up at him.

'Trust me, Sam.'

'Sarah is safe?'

'I promise you, she is.'

Tungata hesitated, fighting his fear of the waters.

'You can't let them take you,' Craig told him. 'You owe it to Sarah and to your people.'

Perhaps Craig had discovered the only appeal that would move him. Tungata pushed the pistol back into his belt.

'Tell me what to do,' he said.

It was impossible to hyperventilate in the gas-laden atmosphere.

'Get what air you can, and hold it. Hold it, force yourself not to breathe again,' Craig wheezed. The tear gas was ripping his lungs and he could feel the cold and deadly spread of lethargy like liquid in his veins. It was going to be a long, hard road home.

'Here!' Tungata pulled him down. 'Fresh air!' There was still a pocket of clean air trapped below the angle of the slab. Craig drank it in greedily.

He took Tungata's hands and placed them on the canvas belt. 'Hold on!' he ordered, and when Tungata nodded, he pulled one last long breath, and they ducked under together. They went down fast.

When they reached the wall there was no bulky oxygen set to encumber them, and Craig pulled Tungata through with what remained of his strength. But he was slowing and weakening drastically, once again losing the urge to breathe, a symptom of anoxia, of oxygen starvation.

They were through the wall, but he could not think what to do next. He was confused and disorientated, his brain playing tricks with him. He found he was giggling weakly, precious air bubbling out between his lips. The glow of the lamp turned a marvellous emerald green, and then split into prisms of rainbow light. It was beautiful, and he examined it drunkenly, starting to roll onto his back. It was so peaceful and beautiful, just like that fall into oblivion after an injection of pentathol. The air trickled out of his mouth and the bubbles were bright as precious stones. He watched them rise upwards.

'Upwards!' he thought groggily. 'Got to go up!' and he kicked lazily, pushing weakly upwards.

Immediately there was a powerful heave on his waist-belt, and he saw Tungata's legs driving like the pistons of a steam locomotive in the lamplight. He watched them with the weighty concentration of a drunkard, but slowly they faded out into blackness. His last thought was, 'If this is dying, then it's better than its publicity,' and he let himself go into it with a weary fatalism.

He woke to pain, and he tried to force himself back into that comforting womb darkness of death, but there were hands bullying and pummelling him, and the rough-barked timber rungs of the ladder cutting into his flesh. Then he was aware that his lungs burned and his eyes felt as though they were swimming in concentrated acid. His nerve ends flared up, so that he could feel every aching muscle and the sting of every scratch and abrasion on his skin.

Then he heard the voice. He tried to shut it out.

'Craig! Craig darling, wake up!' And the painful slap of

a wet hand against his cheek. He rolled his head away from it.

'He's coming round!'

They were like drowning rats at the bottom of a well, clinging half-submerged to the rickety ladderwork, all of them shivering with the cold.

The two girls were perched on the lower rung, Craig was strapped to the main upright with a loop of canvas under his armpits, and Tungata, in the water beside him, was holding his head, preventing it from flopping forward.

With an effort Craig peered around at their anxious faces and then he grinned weakly at Tungata. 'Sam, you said you couldn't swim – well, you could have fooled me!'

'We can't stay here.' Sally-Anne's teeth chattered in her head.

'There is only one way—' they all looked up the gloomy shaft above them.

Craig's head still felt wobbly on his neck, but he pushed Tungata's hand away, and forced himself to begin examining the condition of the timberwork.

It had been built sixty years ago. The bark rope that had been used by the old witch-doctors to bind the joints together had rotted, and now hung in brittle strings like the shavings from the floor of a carpentry shop. The entire structure seemed to have sagged to one side, unless the original builder's eye had not been straight enough to erect a plumb-line.

'Do you think it will hold us all?' Sarah voiced the question.

Craig found it difficult to think, he saw it all through a fine mesh of nausea and bone-weariness.

'One at a time,' he mumbled, 'lightest ones first. You Sally-Anne, then Sarah—' he reached up and untied his

501

leg from the rung. 'Take the rope up with you. When you get to the top, pull up the bags and the lamps.'

Obediently Sally-Anne coiled the rope over her shoulder, and began to climb up the ladder.

She went swiftly, lightly, but the ladderwork creaked and swayed under her. As she went upwards, her lamp chased the shadows ahead of her up the shaft. She drew away until only the lamp glow marked her position, then even that disappeared abruptly.

'Sally-Anne!'

'All right!' Her voice came echoing down the shaft. 'There is a platform here.'

'How big?'

'Big enough – I'm sending down the rope.'

It came snaking down to them, and Tungata secured the bags to the end.

'Haul away!'

The bundle went jerkily up the shaft, swinging on the rope.

'Okay, send Sarah.'

Sarah climbed out of sight, and they heard the whisper of the girls' voices high above. Then, 'Okay – next!'

'Go, Sam!'

'You are lighter than I am.'

'Oh for Chrissake, just do it!'

Tungata climbed powerfully, but the timberwork shook under his weight. One of the rungs broke free, and fell away beneath his feet.

'Look out below!'

Craig ducked under the surface, and the pole hit the water above him with a heavy splash.

Tungata clambered out of sight, and his voice came back, 'Carefully, Pupho! The ladder is breaking up!'

Craig pulled himself out of the water, and sitting on the bottom rung strapped on his leg.

'God, that feels good.' He patted it affectionately, and gave a few trial kicks.

'I'm coming up,' he called.

He had not reached the halfway point when he felt the structure move under him and he flung himself upwards too violently.

One of the poles broke with a report like a musket shot, and the entire structure lurched sideways. Craig grabbed the side frame, just as three or four cross-rungs broke away under him and fell, hitting the water below with a resounding series of splashes. His legs were dangling in space, and every time he kicked for a foothold, he felt the timberwork sag dangerously.

'Pupho!'

'I'm stuck. I can't move or the whole bloody thing will come down.'

'Wait!'

A few seconds of silence and then Tungata's voice again. 'Here's the rope. There is a loop in the end.'

It dropped six feet from him.

'Swing it left a little, Sam.'

The loop swung towards him.

'A little more! Lower, a little lower!' It dangled within reach.

'Hold hard!'

Craig made a lunge at it and got his arm through the loop.

'I'm coming on!'

He released his hold on the side frame and swung free. He was too weak to climb.

'Pull me up!'

Slowly he was drawn upwards, and even in that dangerously exposed position, Craig appreciated the strength that it needed to lift a full-grown man this way. Without Tungata, he would never have made it.

He saw the glow of the lamp reflected off the walls of the shaft and getting closer, and then Sally-Anne's head peering over the edge of the platform at him.

'Not far now. Hold on!'

He came level with the edge of the rock platform, and there was Tungata braced against the far wall, a loop of the rope over his back and shoulder, hauling double-handed on the rope with the cords standing out in his throat and his mouth open, grunting with the effort. Craig hooked his elbow over the edge and then as Tungata heaved again he kicked wildly and wriggled over the edge on his belly.

It was many minutes before he could sit up and take an interest in his surroundings again. The four of them were huddled, shivering and sodden, on a canted platform of water-worn limestone, just large enough to accommodate them.

Above them, the vertical shaft continued upwards, disappearing into darkness, the walls smooth and unscalable. The ladderwork built by the old witch-doctors reached only as high as this platform. In the silence, Craig could hear the drip of water somewhere up there in the darkness and the squeak of bats disturbed by their voices and movements. Sally-Anne held the lamp high, but they could not make out the top of the shaft.

Craig looked about the ledge. It was about eight feet wide, and then in the far wall he saw the entrance to a subsidiary branch of the tunnel, much lower and narrower than the main shaft, cutting into the rock on the horizontal.

'That looks like the only way to go,' Sally-Anne whispered. 'That's where the old witch-doctors were headed.'

Nobody replied. They were all exhausted by the climb and chilled to the bone.

'We should keep going!' Sally-Anne insisted, and Craig roused himself.

'Leave the bags and rope here.' His voice was still hoarse and scratchy from the tear gas and he coughed painfully. 'We can come back for them when we need them.'

He did not trust himself to stand. He felt weak and unsteady and the black drop of the shaft was close at his side. He crawled on hands and knees to the opening in the far wall.

'Give me the lamp.' Sally-Anne handed it to him and he crawled into the low entrance.

There was a passage beyond. After fifty feet the roof lifted so that he could rise into a crouch and, steadying himself against the wall with his free hand, go on a little faster. The others were following him. Another hundred feet, and he stooped through a last low natural doorway of stone and then stood to his full height. He looked about him with swiftly rising wonder. The others coming out of the opening behind him jostled him, but he hardly noticed it. He was so enraptured by his new surroundings.

They stood in a group, close together, as if to draw comfort and courage from each other, and they stared. Their heads revolved slowly, craning upwards and from side to side.

'My God, it's beautiful,' whispered Sally-Anne. She took the lamp from Craig's hand and lifted it high.

They had entered a cavern of lights, a cavern of crystal. Over countless ages the sugary crystalline calcium had been deposited by water seepage over the tall vaulted ceiling and down the walls. It had dripped onto the floor and solidified.

It had crafted marvellous sculptures in glittering iridescent light. On the walls there were traceries, like ancient Venetian lace, so delicate that the lamplight shone through them as though through precious porcelain. There were cornices and pillars of monolithic splendour joining the high roof to the floor, there were suspended marvels of rainbow colours shaped like the wings of angels in flight. Huge spiked stalactites hung as menacingly as the burnished sword of Damocles, or as the white teeth in the upper jaw of a man-eating shark. Others suggested gigantic chandeliers, or the pipes of a celestial organ, while from the floor the stalagmites rose in serried ranks, platoons and squadrons of fantastic shapes, hooded monks dressed in cassocks of mother-of-pearl, wolves and hunchbacks, heroes in gleaming armour, ballerinas and hobgoblins, graceful and grotesque, but all burning with a million tiny crystalline sparks in the lamplight.

Still in a small group, hesitantly, a step at a time, they moved forward down the length of the cavern, picking their way through the gallery of tall stalagmitic statues and stumbling over the daggerlike points of limestone that had broken off the ceiling and littered the floor like ancient arrowheads.

Craig stopped again, and the others pressed up so closely to him that they were all touching.

The centre of the cavern was open. The floor had been swept of fallen debris, and in the open space human hands had built, from gleaming limestone, a square platform, a stage – or a pagan altar. On the altar, with legs drawn up against his chest, clad in the golden and dappled skin of a leopard, sat the body of a man.

'Lobengula.' Tungata sank down on one knee. 'The one who drives like the wind.'

Lobengula's hands were clasped over his knees, and they were mummified, black and shrunken. His fingernails had continued growing after death. They were long and curved, like the claws of a predatory beast. Lobengula must once have worn a tall headgear of feathers and fur, but it had fallen from his head and now lay on the altar beside him.

The heron feathers were still blue and crisp, as though plucked that very day.

Perhaps by design, but more likely by chance, the sitting corpse had been placed directly beneath one of the seepages from the roof. Even as they stood before the altar, another droplet fell from high above and, with a soft tap, burst upon the old king's forehead, and then snaked down over his face like slow tears. Millions upon millions of drops must have fallen upon him, and each drop had laid down its deposit of shining calcium on the mummified head.

Lobengula was being transformed into stone, already his scalp was covered with a translucent helmet, like the tallow from a guttering candle. It had run down and filled his eye-cavities with the pearly deposit, it had lined his withered lips and built up the line of his jaw. Lobengula's perfect white teeth grinned out of his stone mask at them.

The effect was unearthly and terrifying. Sarah whimpered with superstitious dread and clutched at Sally-Anne who returned her grip as fervently. Craig played the lamp beam over that dreadful head and then slowly lowered it.

On the rock altar in front of Lobengula had been placed five dark objects. Four beer-pots, hand-moulded from clay with a stylized diamond pattern inscribed around each wide throat, and the mouth of each pot had been sealed with the membrane from the bladder of a goat. The fifth object was a bag, made from the skin of an unborn zebra foetus, the seams stitched with animal sinew.

'Sam, you—' Craig started, and his voice cracked. He cleared his throat, and started again. 'You are his descendant. You are the only one who should touch anything here.'

Tungata was still down on one knee, and he did not reply. He was staring at the old king's transformed head, and his lips moved as he prayed silently. Was he addressing the Christian God, Craig wondered, or the spirits of his ancestors?

Sally-Anne's teeth chattered spasmodically, the only sound in the cavern, and Craig placed his arms around the two girls. They pressed against him gratefully, both of them shivering with the cold and with awe.

Slowly Tungata rose to his feet and stepped forward to the stone altar. 'I see you, great Lobengula,' he spoke aloud. 'I, Samson Kumalo, of your totem and of your blood, greet you across the years!' He was using his tribal name again, claiming his lineage as he went on in a low but steady voice. 'If I am the leopard cub of your prophecy, then I ask your blessing, oh king. But if I am not that cub, then strike my desecrating hand and wither it as it touches the treasures of the house of Mashobane.'

He reached out slowly and placed his right hand on one of the black clay pots.

Craig found that he was holding his breath, waiting for he was not sure what, perhaps for a voice to speak from the king's long-dead throat, or for one of the great stalactites to crash down from the roof, or for a bolt of lightning to blast them all.

The silence drew out, and then Tungata placed his other hand on the beer-pot, and slowly lifted it in a salute to the corpse of the king.

There was a sharp crack and the brittle baked clay split. The bottom fell out of the pot, and from it gushed a torrent of glittering light that paled and rendered insipid the crystalline coating of the great cavern. Diamonds rattled and bounced on the altar stone, tumbling and slithering over each other, piled in a pyramid, and lay smouldering like live coals in the lamplight.

'I cannot believe these are diamonds,' Sally-Anne whispered. 'They look like pebbles, pretty, shiny pebbles, but pebbles.'

They had poured the contents of all four pots and of the zebra-skin bag into the canvas food-bag, and leaving the empty clay pots at the feet of the old king's corpse, they retreated from Lobengula's presence to the end of the crystal cavern nearest the entrance passage.

'Well, first thing,' Craig observed, 'legend was wrong. Those pots weren't a gallon each, more like a pint.'

'Still, five pints of diamonds is better than a poke in the eye with a rhino horn,' Tungata countered.

They had salvaged a dozen poles from the top section of the ladderwork in the shaft and built a small fire on the cavern floor. As they squatted in a circle around the pile of stones, their damp clothing steamed in the warmth from the flames.

'If they are diamonds,' Sally-Anne was still sceptical.

'They *are* diamonds,' Craig declared flatly, 'every single one of them. Watch this!'

Craig selected one of the stones, a crystal with a knife edge to one of its facets. He drew the edge across the lens of the lamp. It made a shrill squeal that set their teeth on edge, but it gouged a deep white scratch in the glass.

'That's proof! That's a diamond!'

'So big!' Sarah picked out the smallest she could find. 'Even the smallest is bigger than the top joint of my finger.' She compared them.

'The old Matabele labourers picked only those large enough to show up in the first wash of gravel,' Craig explained. 'And remember that they will lose sixty per cent or more of their mass in the cutting and polishing. That one will probably end up no bigger than a green pea.'

'The colours,' Tungata murmured, 'so many different colours.'

Some were translucent lemon-coloured, others dark

509

amber or cognac, with all shades in between, while again there were those that were untinted, clear as snow-melt in a mountain stream, with frosted facets that reflected the flames of the smoky little fire.

'Just look at this one.'

The stone Sally-Anne held up was the deep purplish blue of the Mozambique current when the tropic midday sun probes its depths.

'And this.' Another as bright as the blood from a spurting artery.

'And this.' Limpid green, impossibly beautiful, changing with each flicker of the light.

Sally-Anne laid out a row of the coloured stones on the cavern floor in front of her.

'So pretty,' she said. She was grading them, the yellows and golds and ambers in one row, the pinks and reds in another.

'The diamond can take any of the primary colours. It seems to take pleasure in imitating the colours proper to other gems. John Mandeville, the fourteenth-century traveller, wrote that.' Craig spread his hands to the blaze. 'And it can crystallize to any shape from a perfect square to octahedron or dodecahedron.'

'Blimey, mate,' Sally-Anne mocked him, 'what's an octahedron, pray?'

'Two pyramids with triangular sides and a common base.'

'Wow! And a dodecahedron?' she challenged.

'Two rhombs of lozenge shape with common facets.'

'How come you know so much?'

'I wrote a book – remember?' Craig smiled back. 'Half the book was about Rhodes and Kimberley and diamonds.'

'Enough already,' she capitulated.

'Not nearly enough,' Craig shook his head. 'I can go on. The diamond is the most perfect reflector of light, only chromate of lead refracts more light, only chrysolite disperses it more. But the diamond's combined powers of reflection, refraction and dispersion are unmatched.'

'Stop!' ordered Sally-Anne, but her expression was still interested, and he went on.

'It's brilliance is undecaying, though the ancients did not have the trick of cutting it to reveal its true splendour. For that reason, the Romans treasured pearls more highly and even the first Hindu artisans only rubbed up the natural facets of the Kohinoor. They would have been appalled to know that modern cutters reduced the bulk of that stone from over seven hundred carats to a hundred and six.'

'How big is seven hundred carats?' Sarah wanted to know.

Craig selected a stone from the ranks that Sally-Anne had set out. It was the size of a golf ball.

'That is probably three hundred carats – it might cut to a paragon, that is a first-water diamond over a hundred carats. Then men will give it a name, like the Great Mogul or the Orloff or the Shah, and legends will be woven around it.'

'Lobengula's Fire,' Sarah hazarded.

'Good!' Craig nodded. 'A good name for it. Lobengula's Fire!'

'How much?' Tungata wanted to know. 'What is the value of this pile of pretty stones?'

'God knows,' Craig shrugged. 'Some of them are rubbish—' He picked out a huge amorphous lump of dark grey colour, in which the black specks and fleckings of its imperfections were obvious to the naked eye and the flaws and fracture lines cut through its interior like soft silver leaves. 'This is industrial quality, it will be used for machine tools and the cutting edges in the head of an oil drill, but some of the others – the only answer is that they are worth as much as a rich man will pay. It would be impossible to sell them all at one time, the market could not absorb them. Each stone would require a special buyer and involve a major financial transaction.'

'How much, Pupho?' Tungata insisted. 'What is the least or the most?'

'I truly don't know, I could not even hazard.' Craig picked out another large stone, its imperfect facets frosted and stippled to hide the true fire in its depths. 'Highly skilled technicians will work on this for weeks, perhaps months, charting its grain and discovering its flaws. They will polish a window on it, so they can microscopically examine its interior. Then, when they had decided how to "make" the stone, a master cutter with nerves of steel will cleave it along the flaw line with a tool like a butcher's cleaver. A false hammer stroke and the stone could explode into worthless chips. They say the master cutter who cleaved the Cullinan diamond fainted with relief when he hit a clean stroke and the diamond split perfectly.' Craig juggled the big diamond thoughtfully. 'If this stone "makes" perfectly, and if its colour is graded "D", it could be worth, say, a million dollars.'

'A million dollars! For one stone!' Sarah exclaimed.

'Perhaps more,' Craig nodded. 'Perhaps much more.'

'If one stone is worth that,' Sally-Anne lifted a cupped double handful of diamonds and let them trickle slowly through her fingers, 'how much will this hoard be worth?'

'As little as a hundred million, as much as five hundred million,' Craig guessed quietly, and those impossible sums seemed to depress them all, rather than render them delirious with joy.

Sally-Anne dropped the last few stones, as though they had burned her fingers, and she hugged her own arms and shivered. Her damp hair hung in lank strands down her face and the firelight underscored her eyes with shadow. They all of them looked exhausted and bedraggled.

'Then as we sit here,' said Tungata, 'we are probably as

rich as any man living – and I would give it all for one glimpse of sunlight and one taste of freedom.'

'Pupho, talk to us,' Sarah pleaded. 'Tell us stories.'

'Yes,' Sally-Anne joined in. 'That's your business. Tell us about diamonds. Help us forget the rest. Tell us a story.'

'All right,' Craig agreed, and while Tungata fed the fire with splinters of wood, he thought for a moment. 'Did you know that Kohinoor means "Mountain of Light" and that Baber, the Conqueror, set its value at half the daily expense of the entire known world? You would think there could be no other gem like it, but it was only one of the great jewels assembled in Delhi. That city outstripped imperial Rome or vainglorious Babylon in its treasures. The other great jewels of Delhi had marvellous names also. Listen to these: the Sea of Light, the Crown of the Moon, the Great Mogul—'

Craig ransacked his memory for stories to keep them from dwelling on the hopelessness of their position, from the despair of truly realizing that they were entombed alive deep in the earth.

He told them of the faithful servant whom de Sancy entrusted with the great Sancy diamond, when he sent it to Henry of Navarre to add to the crown jewels of France. 'Thieves learned of his journey, and they waylaid the poor man in the forest. They cut him down and searched his clothing and his corpse. When they could not find the diamond, they buried him hastily and fled. Years afterwards, Monsieur de Sancy found the grave in the forest, and ordered the servant's decomposed body to be gutted. The legendary diamond was found in his stomach.'

'Ghastly,' Sally-Anne shuddered.

'Perhaps,' Craig agreed with her. 'But every noble diamond has a sanguine history. Emperors and rajahs and sultans have intrigued and mounted campaigns for them, others have used starvation or boiling oil or hot irons to prick out eyes, women have used poison or prostituted themselves, palaces have been looted and temples have been profaned. Each stone seems to have left a comet's train of blood and savagery behind it. And yet none of these terrible deeds and misfortunes ever seemed to discourage those who lusted for them. Indeed when Shah-Shuja stood before Runjeet Singh, "The Lion of the Punjab", starved to a skeleton and with his wives and family broken and mutilated by the tortures that had at last forced him to give up the Great Mogul, the man who had once been his dearest friend, gloating over the huge stone in his fist, asked, "Tell me, Shah-Shuja, what price do you put upon it?"

'Even then Shah-Shuja, broken and vanquished, knowing himself at the very threshold of ignoble death, could still answer, "It is the price of fortune. For the Great Mogul has always been the bosom talisman of those who have triumphed mightily."'

Tungata grunted as the tale ended, and prodded the pile of treasure in the firelight before him with a spurning finger. 'I wish one of these could bring us just a little of that good fortune.'

And Craig had run out of stories, his throat had closed painfully from cold and talking and the searing tear gas, and none of the others could think of anything to say to cheer them. They ate the unappetizing scorched maize cakes in silence and then lay down as close to the fire as they could get. Craig lay and listened to the others sleeping, but despite his fatigue, his brain spun in circles, chasing its tail and keeping him awake.

The only way out of the cavern was back through the subterranean lake and up the grand gallery, but how long would the Shona guard that exit? How long could they last out here? There was food for a day or two, water seepage from the cavern roof would give them drink, but the batteries of the two lamps were failing, the light they gave was turning yellow and dull, the timber from the ladder might feed the fire for a few days more, and then – the cold and the darkness. How long before it drove them crazy? How long before they were forced to attempt that terrible swim back through the shaft into the arms of the waiting troopers at the—

Craig's broodings were violently interrupted. The rock on which he lay shuddered and jumped under him, and he scrambled to his hands and knees.

From the shadows of the cavern roof one of the great stalactities, twenty tons of gleaming limestone, snapped off like a ripe fruit in a high wind, and crashed to the floor barely ten paces from where they lay. It filled the cavern with billows of limestone dust. Sarah awoke screaming with terror, and Tungata was thrashing around him and shouting as he came up from deep sleep.

The earth tremor lasted for seconds only, and then the stillness, the utter silence of the earth's depths, fell over them again and they looked into each other's frightened faces across the smouldering fire.

'What the hell was that?' Sally-Anne asked, and Craig was reluctant to answer. He looked to Tungata.

'The Shona—' Tungata said softly ' – I think they have dynamited the grand gallery. They have sealed us off.'

'Oh my God.' Slowly Sally-Anne covered her mouth with both hands.

'Buried alive.' Sarah said it for them.

The shaft was just over 160 feet deep from the edge of the platform to water level. Tungata plumbed it with the nylon rope before Craig began the descent. It was deep enough to kill or maim anybody who slipped and fell into the chasm.

They secured the end of the rope to one of the poles

wedged like an anchor in the opening of the tunnel that led to the crystal cavern, and Craig abseiled down the rope to the water at the bottom of the shaft once more. Gingerly he committed his weight to the rickety remains of the ladderwork as he neared the surface of the water and then lowered himself into the water.

Craig made one dive. It was enough to confirm their worst fears. The tunnel leading into the grand gallery was blocked by a heavy fall of rock. He could not even penetrate as far as the remains of the wall built by the witch-doctors. It was sealed off with loose rock that had fallen from the roof, and it was dangerously unstable. His groping hands brought down another avalanche of rumbling rolling rock all around him.

He backed out of the tunnel, and fled thankfully back to the surface. He clung to the timber ladderwork, panting wildly from the terror of almost being pinned in the tunnel.

'Pupho, are you all right?'

'Okay!' Craig yelled back up the shaft. 'But you were right. The tunnel has been dynamited. There is no way out!'

When he climbed back to the platform, they were waiting for him. Their expressions were grim and taut in the firelight.

'What are we going to do?' Sally-Anne asked.

'The first thing to do is to explore the cavern minutely.' Craig was still gasping from the swim and the climb. 'Every corner and nook, every opening and branch of every tunnel. We will work in pairs. Sam and Sarah, start working from the left – use the lamps with care, save the batteries.'

Three hours later by Craig's Rolex, they met back at the fire. The lanterns were giving out only a feeble yellow glow by now, the batteries drained and on the point of failing.

'We found one tunnel at the back of the altar,' Craig

reported. 'It looked good for quite a way, but then it pinched out completely. And you? Anything?' Craig was cleaning a scrape on Sally-Anne's knee where she had fallen on the treacherous footing. 'Nothing,' Tungata admitted. Craig bound the knee with a strip torn from the tail of Sally-Anne's shirt. 'We found a couple of likely leads, but they all petered out.'

'What do we do now?'

'We will eat a little and then rest. We have got to try and sleep. We will need to keep our strength up.' Craig realized it was an evasion even as he said it, but surprisingly, he did sleep.

When he awoke, Sally-Anne was cuddled against his chest, and she coughed in her sleep. It was a rough phlegmy sound. The cold and damp was affecting them all, but the sleep had refreshed Craig and given him strength. Although his own throat and chest were still painful from the gas, they seemed to have eased a little and he felt more cheerful. He lay back against the rock wall, careful not to disturb Sally-Anne. Tungata was snoring across the fire, but then he grunted and rolled over and was silent.

The only sound in the cavern now was the drip of water from the seepages in the roof, and then, very faintly, another sound, a whispering, so low that it might have been merely the echoes of silence in his own ears. Craig lay and concentrated his hearing. The sound annoyed him, niggled at his mind as he tried to place it.

'Of course,' he recognized it, 'bats!'

He remembered hearing it more clearly when he had first reached the platform. He lay and thought about it for a while and then gently eased Sally-Anne's head off his shoulder. She made a soft gurgling in her throat, rolled over and subsided again.

Craig took one of the lanterns, and went back into the tunnel that led to the platform and the shaft. He flashed the lantern only once or twice, conserving what was left in the batteries, and in darkness he stood on the platform with his back against the rock wall and listened with all his being.

There were long periods of silence, broken only by the musical pinging of water drips on rock, and then suddenly a soft chorus of squeaks that echoed down the chimney of the shaft, then silence again.

Craig flicked on the lantern, and the time was five o'clock. He was not certain if it was morning or evening, but if the bats were roosting up there, then it must still be daylight in the outside world. He squatted down and waited an hour, at intervals checking the slow passage of time, and then there was a new outburst of far-off bat sounds, no longer the occasional sleepy squeaks, but an excited chorus, many thousands of the tiny rodents coming awake for the nocturnal hunt.

The chorus dwindled swiftly into silence, and Craig checked his watch again. Six-thirty-five. He could imagine somewhere up above the airborne horde pouring out of the mouth of a cave into the darkening evening sky, like smoke from a chimney pot.

He moved carefully to the edge of the platform, steadied himself on the side wall and leaned out over the drop very cautiously, keeping a handhold. He twisted his head to look up the shaft, holding the lantern out to the full stretch of his arm. The feeble yellow light seemed only to emphasize the blackness above him.

The shaft was semicircular in plan, about ten feet across to the far wall. He gave up on trying to penetrate the upper darkness and concentrated on studying the rock of the shaft wall opposite him, prodigally using up the battery of the lamp.

It was smooth as glass, honed by the water that had bored it open. No hold or niche, nothing, except— He strained out over the drop for an extra inch. There was a darker mark on the rock just at the very edge of his vision, directly opposite him, and well above the level of his head. Was it a stratum of colour, or was it a crack? He could not be sure, and the light was fading. It could even be a trick of shadow and light.

'Pupho,' Tungata's voice spoke behind him and he pulled back. 'What is it?'

'I think this is the only way open to the surface.' Craig switched off the lantern to save it.

'Up that chimney?' Tungata's voice was incredulous in the darkness. 'Nobody could get up there.'

'The bats – they are roosting up there somewhere.'

'Bats have wings,' Tungata reminded him, and then after a while, 'How high up there?'

'I don't know, but I think there may be a crack or a ledge on the other side. Shine the other lamp, its battery is stronger.'

They both leaned out and stared across.

'What do you think?'

'There is something there, I think.'

'If I could get across to it!' Craig switched off again.

'How?'

'I don't know, let me think.'

They sat with their backs against the wall, their shoulders just touching.

After a while Tungata murmured, 'Craig, if we ever get out of here – the diamonds. You will be entitled to a share—'

'Do shut up, Sam. I'm thinking.' Then, after many minutes, 'Sam, the poles, the longest pole in the ladder – do you think it would reach across to the other side?'

They built a second fire on the ledge, and it lit the shaft with an uncertain wavering light. Once again Craig went down the rope, onto the remains of the timber ladder, and this time he examined each pole in the structure. Most of them had been axed to shorter lengths, probably to make it easier to carry them down through the tunnels and passages from the surface, but the side frames were in longer pieces. The longest of these was not much thicker than Craig's wrist, but the bark was the peculiar pale colour that gave it the African name of 'the elephant tusk tree'. Its common English name was 'leadwood', one of the toughest, most resilent woods of the veld.

Moving along it, measuring it with the span of his arms, Craig reckoned this pole was almost sixteen feet long. He secured the end of the rope to the upper end of the pole, shouting up to the platform to explain what he was doing, and then he used his clasp-knife from the kit to cut the bark rope holding the pole into the ladderwork. There was the terrifying moment when the pole finally broke free and hung on the rope, swinging like a pendulum, and the entire structure, deprived of its king-pin, began to break up and slide down the shaft.

Craig hauled himself up the rope and flung himself thankfully onto the platform, and when he had recovered his breath, the pole was still dangling down the shaft on the end of the rope, although the rest of the ladderwork had collapsed into the water at the bottom.

'That was the easy part,' Craig warned them grimly.

With Tungata and himself providing the brute strength, and the two girls coiling and guiding the rope, they worked the pole up an inch at a time until the tip of it appeared above the level of the platform. They anchored it, and Craig lay on his belly and used the free end of the rope to lasso the bottom end of the pole. Now they had it secured at both ends and could begin working it up and across.

After an hour of grunting and heaving, and coaxing, they had one end of the pole resting against the wall of the shaft opposite them, and the other end thrust back into the tunnel behind them.

'We have got to lift the far end,' Craig explained while they rested, 'and try and get it into that crack on the far wall – if it is a crack.'

Twice they nearly lost the pole as it rolled out of their grip and almost fell into the well below, but each time they just held it on the rope and then began the heart-breaking task all over again.

It was after midnight by Craig's Rolex before they at last had the tip of the pole worked up the far wall to the height of the dark mark only just visible in the beam of the lamp.

'Just an inch to the right,' Craig grunted, and they rolled it gently, felt the pole slide in their hands, and then with a small bump the tip of it lodged in the crack in the wall opposite them and both Craig and Tungata sagged onto their knees and hugged each other in weary congratulations.

Sarah fed the fire with fresh wood and in the flare of light they reviewed their work. They now had a bridge across the shaft, rising from the platform on which they stood at a fairly steep angle, the rear end jammed solidly against the wall behind them, and the far end wedged in the narrow crack in the opposite wall.

'Somebody has to cross that.' Sally-Anne's voice was small and unsteady.

'And what happens on the other side?' Sarah asked.

'We'll find out when we get there,' Craig promised them.

'Let me go,' Tungata said quietly to Craig.

'Have you ever done any rock climbing?' Tungata shook his head. 'Well, that answers that,' Craig told him with finality. 'Now we'll take two hours' rest – try to sleep.'

However, none of them could sleep, and Craig roused them before the two hours were up. He explained to Tungata how to set himself up firmly as anchorman, sitting flat with both feet braced, the rope around his waist and up over his back and shoulder.

'Don't give me too much slack, but don't cramp me,' Craig explained. 'If I fall I'll shout "I'm off!", then jam the rope like this and hold with everything you've got, okay?'

He hung one of the lanterns over his shoulder with a strip of canvas as a sling and then, with both the girls sitting on the end of the pole to hold it firmly, Craig straddled it and began working out along it with both feet dangling into the void. The loop of rope hung behind him as Tungata fed it out.

Within a few feet Craig found that the upward angle was too steep, and he had to lie flat along the pole with his ankles hooked over it, and push himself upwards with his legs. He moved quickly out of the firelight, and the black emptiness below him was mesmeric and compelling. He did not look down. The pole flexed under the weight of each of his movements and he heard the far tip of it grating against the rock above him, but at last his fingertips touched the cold limestone of the shaft wall.

He groped anxiously for the crack, and felt a little lift of his spirits as his fingers made out the shape of it. It ran vertically up the shaft, the outside lips about three inches apart, just enough to accommodate the end of the pole, then it narrowed quickly as it went deeper.

'It's a crack all right!' he called back. 'And I'm going to have a shot at it.'

'Be careful, Craig.'

'Christ!' he thought. 'What a stupid bloody thing to say.'

He reached up to a comfortable stretch of his left arm and thrust his hand, with the fingers folded into a loose fist, as deeply as it would go into the crack. Then he bunched his fist, and as it changed shape it swelled and jammed firmly in the crack and he could put his weight on it.

He pulled himself into a sitting position on the pole bridge, drew one knee up to his chest and with his free hand reached down and locked the clip on his artificial ankle. The ankle was now rigid.

He took a full breath, and said softly, 'Okay, here we go.'

He reached up with his free hand, pushed it into the crack and made another 'jam hold' with his right fist. He used the strength of both arms to pull himself up onto his knees, balancing on the pole.

He relaxed the lower hand and it slipped easily out of the crack. He reached up as high as he could and thrust it into the crack and expanded his fist again. He pulled himself upright, and he was standing on the pole facing the wall.

He stepped up with his artificial foot, turning it so the toe went into the crack as deeply as the instep and then when he straightened his leg the toe twisted and bit into both sides of the rock crack. He stepped up, leaving the pole below him.

'Good old tin toes,' he grunted. His good leg and foot could not have borne the weight, not without specialized climbing boots to protect and strengthen them.

He reached up and took a jam hold with each hand, and lifted himself by the strength of his arms alone. As soon as the weight came off his leg, he twisted the foot, slipped it out of the crack and pulled up his knee to make another toe-hold eighteen inches higher. Suspended alternately on his arms and then on his one leg, he pushed upwards, and the rope slithered up after him.

He was now right out of the firelight and into the darkness. He had only his sense of touch to guide him, and the dark drop seemed to suck at his heels, as he hung out backwards from the sheer wall. He was counting each step upwards, reckoning each at eighteen inches, and he had gone up forty feet when the crack started to widen. He had to reach deeper into it each time to make a jam, and in consequence each of his steps became shorter and placed more strain on his arms and leg.

Forced contact with the stone had abraded the skin off his knuckles, making every successive hold more agonizing, and the unaccustomed exercise was cramping the muscles on the inside of his thigh and groin into knots of fire.

He couldn't go on much longer. He had to rest. He found himself pulling in against the wall, pressing himself to it, touching the cold limestone with his forehead like a worshipper. *To lie against the wall is to die*, that is the first law of the rock climber. It is the attitude of defeat and despair. Craig knew it, and yet he could do nothing to prevent it.

He found he was sobbing. He took one fist out of the crack, and flapped it with loose fingers, forcing blood back into it, and then he held it to his mouth and licked the broken skin. He changed hands, whimpering as fresh blood flowed back into the cramped hand.

'Pupho, why have you stopped?' The rope was no longer paying out. They were anxious.

'Craig, don't give up, darling. Don't give up.' Sally-Anne had sensed his despair. There was that something in her voice that gave him new strength.

Gradually he pushed himself outwards, hanging back from the wall, coming into balance again, his weight on the leg, and he reached up, one hand at a time, left and right, hold hard, pull up the leg, step up – and again, and then the whole hellish torturous thing again, and yet again. Another ten feet, twenty feet – he was counting in the darkness.

Reach up with the right hand and – and – nothing. Open space.

Frantically he groped for the crack – nothing. Then his hand struck rock out to one side, the crack had opened wide into a deep V-shaped niche, wide enough for a man to force his whole body into it.

'Thank you, God, oh thank you, thank you—' Craig dragged himself up into it, wedging his hips and shoulders, and hugging his damaged hands to his chest.

'Craig!' Tungata's shout rang up the shaft.

'I'm all right,' Craig called back. 'I've found a niche. I'm resting. Give me five.'

He knew he couldn't wait too long, or his hands would stiffen and become useless. He kept flexing them as he rested.

'Okay!' he called down. 'Going up again.'

He pushed himself upwards with the palms of his hands on each side of the cleft, facing outwards into the total darkness of the shaft.

Swiftly the cleft opened, and became a wide, deep chimney so that he could no longer reach across it with his arms. He had to turn sideways, wedge his shoulders on one side of it, and walk up the other side with his feet, wriggling his shoulders and pushing up with his palms on the stone under him a few inches at a time. It went quickly, until abruptly the chimney ended. It closed to a crack so narrow that reaching upwards he could not even fit his finger into it.

He reached around the top of the chimney out onto the wall of the shaft. He groped as high as he could reach and there was no hold or irregularity in the smooth limestone above him.

'End of the road!' he whispered, and suddenly every muscle in his body began to shriek in silent spasms of pain, and he felt crushed under a load of weariness. He did not have the energy for that long dangerous retreat back down the chimney, and he did not have the strength to keep himself wedged awkwardly in the rocky cleft.

Then abruptly a bat squeaked shrilly above him. It was so close and clear that he almost relaxed his grip with shock. He caught himself, and though his legs juddered under the strain, he worked his way sideways to the outermost edge of the chimney. The bat squeaked again, and was answered by a hundred others. It must be dawn already, the bats were returning to their roosts somewhere up there.

Craig balanced himself, so that he had his outside hand free. He groped for the lantern on its strip of canvas around his neck, and held it out into the open shaft. Then he twisted his head, and wriggled even further outwards until he was holding with only the point of one shoulder, and his head was protruding around the sharp corner of the chimney into the open shaft.

He switched on the lantern. Instantly there was a hubbub of alarmed bats – their terrified shrills and the flutter of their wings – and three feet above Craig's head, impossibly out of reach, there was a window in the rock wall, from which the sounds reverberated as though from the brass throat of a trumpet. He reached for it, but his fingers were twelve inches short of the sill.

As he yearned upwards, so the yellow glow of the lantern faded away. For some seconds the filaments still burned redly in their tiny glass ampoule and then they too died, and the darkness rushed back to engulf Craig, and he retreated into the chimney.

In frustration he hurled the useless lantern from him, and it clattered against the rock as it fell, each rattle becoming fainter until seconds later there was a distant splash as it hit the water far below.

'Craig!'

'Okay, I dropped the light.'

He heard the bitterness and despondency in his own voice, but in darkness he tried once more to reach the window above him. His fingernails scratched futilely on the stone, and he gave up and began slipping back down the chimney. In the V-shaped niche where the crack and chimney met, he wedged himself again.

'What is happening, Craig?'

'It doesn't go,' he called down. 'There is no way out. We are finished, unless—' he broke off.

'What is it? Unless what?'

'Unless one of the girls will come up and help me.'

There was silence in the darkness below him.

'I'll come,' Tungata broke the silence.

'No good. You are too heavy. I couldn't hold you.'

Silence again, and then Sally-Anne said, 'Tell me what to do.'

'Tie on to the end of the rope. Use a bowline knot.'

'Okay.'

'All right, come out across the pole. I'll be holding you.'

Peering down he could see her silhouetted against the glow of the fire, as she worked her way across. He took up the slack in the rope carefully, ready to jam it if she fell.

'I'm across.'

'Can you find the crack?'

'Yes.'

'I'm going to pull you up. You must help me by pushing with your toes in the crack.'

'Okay.'

'Go!'

He felt her full weight come on the rope, and it bit into his shoulder.

'Push up!' he ordered, and as he felt the load lighten, he grabbed the slack.

'Push!' She came up another four inches.

'Push!' It seemed to go on and on, and then she screamed and the rope burned out in a hard, heavy run across his shoulder. He was almost jerked out of his niche.

He fought it, jamming hard, feeling the skin smear off his palms on the harsh nylon until he stopped it. Sally-Anne was still screaming, and the rope pendulumed back and forth as she swung sideways along the wall.

'Shut up!' he roared at her. 'Get a hold of yourself.'

She stopped screaming, and gradually her swings became shorter.

'I lost my footing.' Her voice was almost a sob.

'Can you find the crack again?'

'Yes.'

'All right, tell me when you are ready.'

'Ready!'

'Push up!'

He thought it would never end, and then he felt her hand touch his leg.

'You made it,' he whispered. 'You marvellous bloody female.'

He made a space for her in the chimney below him and he helped her into it. He showed her how to wedge herself securely, and then he held her shoulder, squeezing hard.

'I can't go any further.' Her first words after she recovered.

'That was the worst, the rest is easy.'

He wouldn't tell her about the window – not yet.

'Listen to the bats,' he cheered her instead. 'The surface must be close, very close. Think of that first glimpse of sunlight, that first breath of sweet dry air.'

'I'm ready to go on,' she said at last, and he led her up the chimney.

As soon as it was wide enough to cross over, he made her climb ahead of him so that he could place her feet with his hands, and help her to push upwards when the chimney became too wide for her to be able to exert her full strength.

'Craig. Craig! It's closed. It has pinched in. It's a dead end.'

Her panic was just below the surface and he could feel she was shaking as she choked down her sobs.

'Stop it,' he snapped. 'Just one more effort. Just one, I promise you.'

He waited for her to quieten, then he went on, 'There is a window in the wall just above your head, just around the corner of the chimney. Only a foot or two—'

'I won't be able to reach it.'

'Yes! Yes, you will. I'm going to make a bridge for you with my body. You will stand on my stomach, you'll reach it easily. Do you hear me? Sally-Anne, answer me.'

'No.' Very small and faint. 'I can't do it.'

'Then none of us are going anywhere,' he said sharply. 'It's the only way out. You do it or we rot here. Do you hear me?'

He worked up close beneath her, so that her sagging buttocks were pressed into his belly. Then he braced with all his strength, pressing with both legs into one side of the chimney and with his shoulders into the other, forming a human bridge beneath her.

'Slowly let go,' he whispered. 'Sit on my stomach.'

'Craig, I'm too heavy.'

'Do it, damn you. Do it!'

Her weight came onto him, and the pain was too much to bear. His sinews and muscles were tearing, his vision filled with flashing lights.

'Now straighten up,' he blurted.

She came up onto her knees; her knee-caps bit into his flesh like crucifixion nails.

'Stand!' he groaned. 'Quickly!'

She tottered on the unsteady platform of his body as she came upright.

'Reach up! High as you can!'

'Craig, there is a hole up here!'

'Can you get into it?'

No reply. She shifted her stance on him, and he cried aloud with the effort of holding her.

She bounced, and then her weight was gone. He heard her feet scrabbling against the shaft and the brush of the rope as she dragged herself upwards and it followed her like a monkey's tail.

'Craig, it's a shelf – a cave!'

'Find somewhere to tie your end of the rope.'

A minute, and another – he couldn't hold out, his limbs were numb, his shoulders were—

'I've tied it! It's safe.'

He tugged on the rope and it came up firm and secure. He took a loop around his wrist and let his feet go. He swung out of the chimney and dangled into the open shaft.

He pulled himself up the rope, hand over hand, and then he tumbled over the sill into the stone window, and Sally-Anne hugged him to her bosom. Too far gone to speak, he clung to her like a child to its mother.

'What is happening up there?' Tungata could not contain his impatience.

'We have found another lead,' Craig called back. 'It must be open to the surface somewhere, there are bats.'

'What must we do?'

'I am going to drop the rope. There will be a loop in it. Sarah first. She will have to cross the pole and get into the loop. The two of us will be able to pull her up.' It was a long message to shout. 'Do you understand?'

'Yes. I'll make her do it.'

Craig tied a loop in the end of the rope, and then, in complete darkness, crawled back to the anchor point that Sally-Anne had chosen. He ran his hands over it. It was a pinnacle of rock, twelve feet back from the ledge and her knot was good. He went back and dropped the looped end down into the shaft. He lay on his stomach and peered down into the echoing darkness. The fire glow was far below, a dull furnace redness. He could hear the whisper of their voices.

'What's keeping you?' he demanded.

Then he saw the dark shape, only just visible in the firelight, moving out across the pole bridge. It was too big to be one person, and then he realized that both Tungata and Sarah were on the pole together. Tungata was coaxing her across, riding out backwards and drawing her after him.

They moved out of sight, directly below the window.

'Pupho, swing the rope to the left.'

Craig obeyed, and felt the tug on it as Tungata grabbed the swinging loop.

'All right, Sarah is in the loop.'

'Explain to her that she must walk up the rock as we pull her.'

Sally-Anne sat directly behind Craig, the rope running over his shoulder to her. Craig had his feet braced against the side wall.

'Pull!' he ordered, and quickly she picked up the rhythm of it. Sarah was small and slim, but it was a long haul and Craig's hands were raw. It was five minutes of hard work before they dragged her over the sill and the three of them rested together.

'All right, Sam. We are ready for you now.' He dropped the loop into the shaft.

There were three of them on the rope now, sitting one behind the other, but Tungata was a big, heavy man. Craig could hear the girls whimpering and sobbing with the effort.

'Sam, can you jam yourself into the chimney?' Craig gasped. 'Give us a rest?'

He felt the weight go off the rope, and the three of them lay in a heap and rested.

'All right, let's go again.'

Tungata seemed even heavier now, but finally he came tumbling into the window, and none of them could talk for a while.

Craig was the first to find his voice. 'Oh, shit, we forgot the diamonds! We left the bloody diamonds.'

There was a click and a yellow glow of light as Tungata switched on the second lantern that he had brought up with him. They all blinked owlishly at each other, and Tungata chuckled hoarsely.

'Why do you think I was so heavy?'

He held the canvas bag in his lap, and as he patted it, the diamonds crunched together with a sound like a squirrel chewing nuts.

'Hero!' Craig grunted with relief. 'But switch off, there are only a few minutes' life left in that battery.'

They used the lantern in flashes. The first flash showed them that the rock window opened into a low-roofed cave, so wide that they could not make out the side walls. The roof was coated with a furry mass of bats. Their eyes were a myriad pinpricks of reflected light and their naked faces were pink and hideous as they stared down at them, hanging upside down.

The floor of the cave was carpeted with their droppings. The reeking guano had filled every irregularity, and the floor was level and soft underfoot, deadening their footfalls as they went forward in a group, holding hands to keep contact in the darkness.

Tungata led them, flashing the lantern every few minutes to check the floor ahead and to reorientate himself. Craig was in the rear with the coiled rope looped over his shoulder. Gradually the floor started to slope upwards under them and the roof hung lower.

'Wait,' said Sally-Anne. 'Don't switch on the light again.'

'What is it?'

'Ahead – up the slope. Is it my imagination?'

There are degrees of darkness. Craig stared into the blackness ahead, and slowly out of it emerged a faint nimbus, a lessening of the utter blackness.

'Light,' he whispered. 'There is light up there.'

They started forward, bumping into each other in their

haste, running and pushing, laughing as the light strength-ened and they could make out each other's shapes, the laughter becoming wild hysteria. The light turned to a golden glory ahead and they fought their way up the soft yielding slope of guano towards it.

Gradually the roof pressed down onto them, forcing them to their knees, and then onto their bellies, and the light was a thin horizontal blade that blinded them with its brilliance. They clawed their way towards the light, stirring the guano dust so that it coated their faces and choked them, but they whooped and shouted hysterically through it.

Craig saw that Sarah was weeping unashamedly, tears shining on her face. Tungata was bellowing with wild laughter, and Craig flung himself forward and grabbed his ankles just as he reached the low slitted entrance of the cave.

'Wait, Sam. Be careful.'

Tungata tried to kick his hands away and crawl on, but Craig held him.

'Shona! There are Shona out there.'

That name halted and silenced them. They lay just within the threshold of the cavern, and their euphoria evaporated.

'Craig and I will go ahead to scout the lay of the land.' Tungata groped in the guano and passed a rock the size of a baseball back to Craig. 'It's the best weapon I have. You two girls will stay here until we call you, okay?'

Craig took a double handful of the guano and blackened his face and limbs with it. Then he slipped the coil of rope off his shoulder, and crawled up beside Tungata. He was content to let Tungata take control now. In the cavern, Craig had been the leader, but out there was Tungata's world. In the bush Tungata was a leopard man.

They crawled up the last few feet to the entrance. It was a low horizontal slit in the rock, less than eighteen inches high and screened by golden elephant grass growing just beyond the threshold. It was facing east for the early morning sunshine was blazing into their faces. They lay for a while, letting their eyes adjust to its glare after those days of darkness.

Then Tungata slid forward like a black mamba, barely moving the tall grass as he went through it.

Craig gave him a count of fifty and then followed him. He came out on a hillside with the stratum of limestone forming buttresses across it, over which grew the stunted desiccated brush and wiry elephant grass. They were just below the summit, and the slope dropped away steeply below them into the heavily forested valley. Already the morning sun was hot and Craig revelled in it.

Tungata was lying below him, and he gave Craig the hand-signal, 'Cover my left side.'

Craig moved carefully into position, walking on his elbows and dragging his legs.

'Search!' Tungata gave him the peremptory signal, and they lay for fully ten minutes scrutinizing the ground below, above and on both sides, covering every inch, every bush and rock and field.

'All clear,' Craig signalled, and Tungata began to move along the contour of the slope towards the shoulder of the hill. Craig kept behind and above him, covering him.

A bird came towards them, a black and white bird with a disproportionately large yellow beak, a huge, semitically curved yellow bill that gave it its common name of hornbill, and its nickname of Yiddish canary. Its flight was characteristically erratic and swooping, and it settled on a low bush just ahead and below Tungata – but almost immediately it let out a harsh squawk of alarm and hurled itself into the air again, swooping away down the hillside.

'Danger!' Tungata made the urgent hand-signal, and they froze.

Craig stared at the clump of rock and grass and bush

from which the hornbill had fled, trying to discover what had alarmed it.

Something moved, a tiny stirring, and it was so close that Craig clearly heard the flare of a match being struck and lit. A feather of ethereal smoke drifted from the clump of brush and prickled his nostrils with the stink of tobacco burning. Then he made out the shape of a steel battle-helmet, covered with camouflage net. It moved away as the man wearing it drew again on his cigarette.

Now Craig saw the whole picture. In his camouflage smock, the man was lying behind a light machine-gun on a tripod, the barrel of the weapon was bound with streamers of hessian to disguise its stark outline.

'How many?' Tungata signalled the question, and then Craig saw the second man. He was sitting with his back to the base of the low thorn tree. The shadow of the branches over his head blended perfectly with the tiger stripes of his camouflage. He was a big man, bare-headed, with a sergeant's chevrons on his arm, and an Uzi machine-gun laid beside him.

Craig was about to signal, 'Two,' when the man slipped a soft pack of cigarettes out of his breast-pocket and held it out. A third man who had been lying flat on his back in the shade, sat up and accepted the pack. He tapped out a cigarette and then tossed the pack to a fourth man, who rolled onto his elbow to catch it, revealing himself for the first time.

'Four!' Craig signalled.

It was a machine-gun post, perfectly sited on the shoulder of the hill to cover the slopes below. Peter Fungabera had obviously anticipated the existence of boltholes from the main cavern. The hills must all be staked out with nests of machine-guns. It was mere fortune that had brought them out above this post. The gunner was facing downhill, his mates were stretched out, relaxed and bored from days of unrewarded vigil.

'Move into attack position,' Tungata signalled.

'Query?' Craig flicked his thumb. 'Four! Query?' Craig questioned the odds.

'Go right!' Tungata signalled, and then enforced the order with the clenched fist. 'Imperative!'

Craig felt his blood charging with adrenalin, the heat of it spreading down his limbs, his mouth drying out. He clutched the round stone in his right hand.

They were so close that he could see the wet spit on the tip of the cigarette as the machine-gunner took it from his lips. The nest was littered with their rubbish: paper wrappers and empty food cans and cigarette butts. Their weapons were laid carelessly aside. The man lying on his back had covered his eyes with his elbow and the burning cigarette stuck up like a candle from his lips. The sergeant against the tree was whittling a piece of wood with his trench-knife. The third had unbuttoned his smock and was minutely searching his own chest hair for body vermin. Only the man behind the gun was alert.

Tungata was sliding into position beside Craig.

'Ready?' He raised his hand and glanced at Craig.

'Affirmative.'

Tungata's hand came down, the order to execute.

Craig went in, rolling over the edge of the nest, and he hit the man with the trench-knife. He hit him in the temple with the stone, and he knew instantly that it was too hard. He felt bone break in the man's head.

The sergeant sagged forward without a sound, and at the same instant Craig heard a soft scuffle and grunt behind him as Tungata took on the machine-gunner. Craig did not even glance around. He snatched up the Uzi machine-gun and cocked it.

The searcher after body vermin looked up and his jaw sagged open as Craig thrust the muzzle into his face, pressing the circle of steel against his cheek and glaring into his eyes, dominating him, compelling silence.

Tungata had picked up the sergeant's fallen trench-knife and now he dropped onto the reclining trooper, driving one knee into his diaphragm, forcing all the air from his lungs in a single explosive sigh, and then pressing the point of the knife into the soft flesh below his ear. Still on his back, the man's face swelled and contorted, as he struggled to refill his lungs.

'If any man cries out,' Tungata whispered, 'I will cut off his testicles and stick them in his mouth.'

It had all taken less than five seconds.

Tungata knelt beside the sergeant whom Craig had stoned, and felt for the pulse in his throat. After a few seconds he shook his head, and began stripping the corpse of its battle-smock. He shrugged into it. It was too small for him, binding across the chest.

'Take the gunner's uniform,' he ordered, while he took the Uzi from Craig and covered the two prisoners with it.

The machine-gunner's neck was broken. Tungata had jerked back his helmet and the strap had caught under his chin. The dead man's camouflage smock stank of rancid stale sweat and tobacco smoke, but it fitted Craig well enough. The steel helmet was too big, it came down to his eyes, but covered his long straight hair.

Tungata thrust his face close to those of the prisoners.

'Drag the bodies of these Shona dogs with you.'

Craig and Tungata covered them while they pulled the two naked dead men, feet first, through the grass to the cave entrance and then rolled them down the slope into the dark interior.

The two girls were shocked and silenced.

'Strip!' Tungata ordered the prisoners. When they were in their army issue shorts, Tungata ordered Craig, 'Tie them!'

Craig gestured them to lie on their stomachs, and using the nylon rope bound their wrists at the small of the back, then pulled up their legs and bound wrists to ankles. It was a hogtie that left them helpless. Then he pulled the stockings off their feet and stuffed them into their mouths and tied the gags in place.

While he was working, Tungata was dressing the girls in the discarded battle-dress. It was many sizes too large, but they folded back the cuffs at wrists and ankles and belted the trousers in a bunch around their waists.

'Black your face, Pendula,' Tungata ordered, and she smeared herself. 'Hands also. Now cover your hair.' He pulled a beret out of a pocket of his purloined smock, and tossed it to her.

'Come on.' Tungata picked up the canvas bag of diamonds and started back up the slope. He led them back to the abandoned machine-gun nest.

Tungata tipped up a field pack, emptying it out onto the ground, and then shoved the bag of diamonds into the pack and rebuckled it. He slung the pack onto his back.

Craig had been ransacking the other equipment. He passed two grenades to Tungata and stuffed two more into his own pockets. He found a Tokarev pistol for Sarah, and gave another Uzi to Sally-Anne. There was an AK 47 for himself, with five spare magazines. Tungata kept the second Uzi. Craig added a water bottle to his load. He broke open an emergency pack of chocolate and they all stuffed their mouths as they prepared to leave. It tasted so good that Craig's eyes watered.

'I'll take the point.' Tungata spoke through a sticky mouthful of chocolate. 'We'll try and get down into the valley, under cover of the trees.'

They kept just under the shoulder of the hill, going directly down the slope, taking the chance that the open slope to their right was clear.

They were just above the tree line when they heard the helicopter. It was coming up the valley. It was still behind the shoulder of the hill, but coming on fast.

'Hit the ground!' Craig ordered, and slammed Sally-

Anne between the shoulder-blades with the flat of his hand. They went down and pushed their faces to the earth, but the beat of the rotors changed, altering to coarse pitch and now the sound was stationary, just out of their line of sight behind the fold of rocky hillside.

'It's landing,' Sally-Anne said, and the engine noise died away.

'She's down.' Sally-Anne cocked her head. 'She's landed. There! He has cut the motor.'

Into the silence they could hear, very faintly, orders being shouted.

'Pupho, come up here,' Tungata ordered. 'You two, wait.'

Craig and Tungata crawled up to the shoulder of the hill and very slowly raised their heads to look over the crest.

Below them, a quarter of a mile down the valley, there was a small level clearing at the edge of the forest. The grass had been flattened and there was an open-sided canvas sun shelter at the edge of the trees on the far side of the clearing. The helicopter stood in the centre of the clearing, and the pilot was climbing down from the fuselage port. There were uniformed troopers of the Third Brigade under the trees near the tent, and in the tent they could make out three or four other men sitting at a table.

'Advanced headquarters,' Craig murmured.

'This is the valley that we entered, the main cave is just below us.'

'You are right.' Craig had not recognized the ground from this direction and height.

'Looks as though they are pulling out,' Tungata pointed into the trees. A platoon of camouflaged troopers was moving back down the valley in Indian file.

'They probably waited for forty-eight hours or so after dynamiting the grand gallery, now they must have given us up for dead and buried.'

'How many?' Tungata asked.

'I can see,' Craig screwed up his eyes, 'twenty at least, not counting those in the tent. There will be others staking out the hills, of course.'

Tungata drew back from the skyline and beckoned to Sally-Anne. She crawled up beside him.

'What do you make of that machine?' He pointed at the helicopter.

'It's a Super Frelon,' she replied without hesitation.

'Can you fly it?'

'I can fly anything.'

'Damn it, Sally-Anne, don't be clever,' Craig whispered irritably. 'Have you ever flown one of those?'

'Not a Super Frelon, but I have five hundred hours on helicopters.'

'How long would it take you to start up and get moving, once you are in the cockpit?'

Now she hesitated. 'Two or three minutes.'

'Too long.' Craig shook his head.

'What if we can pull the guards away from the clearing while Pendula starts up?' Tungata asked.

'That might work,' Craig agreed.

'This is it then.' Tungata set it out quickly. 'I will track up to the head of the valley. You take the girls down to the edge of the clearing. Got it?'

Craig nodded.

'Forty-five minutes from now,' Tungata checked his wrist-watch, 'nine-thirty exactly, I will start throwing grenades and firing with the AK. That should pull most of the Shona away from the clearing. As soon as the shooting starts, you head for the helicopter. When I hear the helicopter lift off, I'll run out on the open slope, there!' He pointed up the valley. 'Just below that rock sheet. The Shona will not have reached me by that time – you can make the pick-up from there.'

'Let's do it.' Craig passed Tungata the AK 47 and the

spare magazines. 'I'll keep the Uzi and one grenade.' He took the submachine-gun from Tungata.

'Take the diamonds also.' Tungata shrugged out of the straps of the back pack and pushed it across to Craig.

'See you later.' Craig slapped his shoulder, and Tungata slid away down the slope.

Craig led the two girls straight down along the spine of the hill, keeping in the scrub and broken rock. It was a relief to reach the tree-line, and discover a ravine that angled back along the edge of the clearing. They crept down it, Craig cautiously lifting his head above the bank to check their progress every few hundred feet.

'This is as close as we can get to the helicopter,' he whispered and the girls sank down, resting below the lip of the bank. Craig slipped out of the heavy pack and had another look over the bank.

The helicopter stood out in the open, a hundred and fifty paces away. The pilot was squatting beside the landing-gear in the shade cast by the fuselage. The Super Frelon was a bulky, blunt-nosed machine, painted dull sage green. Craig sank down again beside Sally-Anne.

'What range does it have?' Craig asked in a whisper.

'Not certain,' Sally-Anne whispered back. 'With full tanks about six hundred miles, I'd guess.'

'Pray for full tanks.' Craig glanced at his Rolex. 'Ten minutes.' From his pocket he handed them each another slab of chocolate.

Sally-Anne's sweat had streaked the blackening on her cheeks. Craig mixed dirt and water from the bottle into a muddy paste and repaired her make-up. Then she did the same to him.

'Two minutes.' Craig checked the time, and glanced over the bank.

The helicopter pilot stood up and stretched, then he climbed back into the Super Frelon.

'Something is happening,' Craig murmured.

The helicopter partially obscured his view of the tent across the clearing, but he could see that there was activity over there as well.

A small group was leaving the tent. The guards were saluting and strutting about importantly, and then suddenly the rotors of the helicopter turned and the starter motor whirred noisily. Blue smoke fired from the exhaust vents and with a roar the main engine of the Super Frelon came to life.

A pair of officers left the group in front of the tent and started across the clearing, heading for the helicopter.

'We have got trouble,' Craig muttered grimly, 'they are pulling out.' And then he started, 'That's Peter Fungabera!'

Peter was wearing the burgundy beret with silver leopard-head cap-badge, the bright rows of decoration ribbons on his chest, and the scarf in the opening of his battle-smock. Under one arm was tucked his swagger-stick. While he walked, he was in deep discussion with a tall, elderly white man whom Craig had never seen before.

The white man wore a plain khaki safari jacket. His head was bare. His hair was cropped to the scalp and his skin had a peculiarly repulsive pasty white texture. He carried a black leather attaché case which was locked to his wrist with a steel chain. He cocked his head to listen to Peter Fungabera's impassioned discourse as they walked towards the waiting helicopter.

Halfway between the tent and the helicopter, the two of them came to a stop, and argued animatedly. The white man was gesticulating vehemently with his free hand. He was close enough now for Craig to notice that his eyes were so pale that they gave him the sightless stare of a marble bust. His skin was pocked with ancient scars, yet he was very much the dominating figure of the pair. His manner was brusque, almost contemptuous, as though he now regarded Peter Fungabera as superfluous, unworthy of his serious attention. Peter Fungabera, on the other hand, had the shattered look of a survivor of an aircrash. He appeared confused. His voice was raised so that Craig could hear its pleading tone, if not the actual words. This was hardly the man that Craig had known.

The white man made a gesture of dismissal and, turning away from Peter Fungabera, started once more towards the helicopter.

At that moment there was the crumping detonation of an exploding grenade and the two men in the clearing turned quickly to look up the valley in the direction from which the explosion had sounded. Now there was a burst of automatic AK 47 fire from the same direction and immediately the urgent shout of orders around the tent. Troopers began doubling along the edge of the clearing, heading up the valley.

Another burst of automatic fire, and the attention of every man was focused in that direction. Hastily, Craig pulled the pack onto his back.

'Come on!' he snapped. 'You know what to do!' The three of them scrambled out of the ravine and moved out into the clearing.

'Don't hurry,' Craig cautioned them softly. They kept in a compact group, moving quickly but purposefully over the open ground towards Fungabera and his companion.

Craig took the grenade from his pocket and with his teeth drew the pin. He held the grenade in his left hand. In his right he carried the Uzi, loaded and cocked and with rapid-fire selected. They were within five paces before Peter Fungabera glanced around and his astonishment was almost comical as he recognized Craig, even under his mud mask.

'At this range I can cut you in half,' Craig warned him, lifting the Uzi to the level of Peter's belly. 'This grenade is armed. If I drop it, it will blow us all to hell.' He had to shout above the sound of the helicopter's engine.

The white man spun to face him, and his pale arctic eyes were savage.

'Go for the pilot,' Craig ordered the girls and they ran to the fuselage port of the helicopter.

'Now, both of you,' Craig told the two men, 'walk to the helicopter. Don't hurry, don't shout.'

Craig followed three paces behind them. Before they reached the helicopter, the pilot appeared in the open port, both his hands high above his head, and Sarah behind him with the Tokarev pistol in his back.

'Get out!' Craig ordered, and with obvious relief, the pilot jumped down to the ground.

'Tell them that General Fungabera is a hostage,' Craig said. 'Any attack will endanger him. Do you understand?'

'Yes,' the pilot nodded.

'Now walk back to that tent. Walk slowly. Don't run. Don't shout.'

The pilot set off gratefully, but as soon as he was clear, he broke into a trot.

'Get in!' Craig gestured to the port with the Uzi, but Peter Fungabera glared at him and his head sank down menacingly on his wide shoulders.

'Don't do it.' Craig backed off a pace, for there was an air of desperation about Peter Fungabera, the reckless quality of a man with nothing more to lose.

'Move!' Craig ordered. 'Get up that ladder!' and Peter Fungabera charged at him. Almost as though he were courting death, he ran straight onto the muzzle of the Uzi. However, Craig was poised to meet him. He brought up the weapon and crashed the barrel across the side of Peter Fungabera's head with a force that dropped him onto his knees.

As Peter went down, Craig swung the Uzi back on to the white man, anticipating any move he might make.

'Help him up the ladder,' he ordered, and although the white man was encumbered by the black attaché case chained to his wrist, the menace of the Uzi was persuasive and he stooped over Peter Fungabera and lifted him to his feet. Still stunned by the blow, Peter reeled in the man's grasp. He was mumbling dazedly.

'It doesn't matter now, it's all over anyway.'

'Shut up, you fool,' the white man hissed at him.

'Get him into the helicopter.' Craig prodded the Uzi into the white man's back, and the pair started towards the ladder.

'Keep the gun on them, Sarah,' Craig called and glanced over his shoulder. The helicopter pilot had almost reached the edge of the clearing. 'Hurry it up,' Craig snarled at them, and the white man shoved Peter Fungabera through the port and clambered up after him, with the black case dangling on its chain from his wrist.

Craig jumped up into the body of the helicopter.

'Over there!' he ordered his two prisoners to the bench seat. 'Strap yourselves in!' Then to Sarah, 'Tell Pendula to get going!'

The helicopter lifted off and rose swiftly out of the clearing, and Craig tossed the grenade out of the open port. It dropped away and exploded in the forest far below. Craig hoped the explosion would heighten the confusion down there.

Craig stood behind Peter Fungabera with the Uzi pressed to the nape of his neck, while with his free hand he reached over and pulled the Tokarev pistol from the holster on Peter's hip. He thrust it into his own pocket, then he backed off and buckled on the engineer's safety straps at the doorway. As Sarah clambered down from the cockpit, he ordered her, 'Cover them both!' and he leaned out of the port and peered ahead.

Almost immediately, he saw Tungata. He was already out of the trees, just below the rock slope, waving both hands over his head, brandishing the AK 47.

'Hold on! I'm going down for the pick-up,' Sally-Anne's

voice squealed from the two-way speaker above Craig's head.

The big helicopter dropped swiftly down towards where Tungata was waiting, and Sally-Anne steadied the machine and hovered above his head.

All around Tungata the grass was blown flat by the down-draught and Tungata's stolen battle-smock rippled and whipped about his body. He threw the AK 47 aside and looked up at Craig. The helicopter sank down the last few feet, and Craig leaned out of the hatch and made an arm for him. Tungata jumped and they locked arms at the elbows and Craig swung him aboard.

'Okay!' he yelled up at the speaker. 'Go for it!' And they went bounding up into the sky so swiftly that Craig's knees buckled.

At a little over a thousand feet, Sally-Anne went straight and level and turned onto a westerly heading.

Tungata turned to the figures on the bench seat and checked. He stared at Peter Fungabera ferociously, but Peter slumped, still dazed and beaten, on the bench seat.

'Where did you find them, Pupho?' Tungata asked huskily.

'They are a little present for you, Sam.' Craig handed him the Uzi submachine-gun. 'It's loaded and cocked. Can I leave you to look after this pair of beauties?'

'It will afford me the greatest of pleasure.' Tungata turned the gun on the two men sitting side by side on the bench seat.

'I'm going to see how Pendula is making out.' Craig began to turn away, but something in the way the captive white man was holding himself alerted him, and he turned back quickly. The white prisoner had used the confusion to unlock the steel cuff from his wrist, and now he hurled the black attaché case across the hold towards the open port.

In a reflex action, Craig threw himself to one side, like

546

a basket-ball player intercepting a pass, and he got a hand to the flying case, deflecting it aside so that it missed the open doorway and clattered against the bulkhead. He dived for it and hugged it to his chest.

'This must be a very interesting piece of goods,' he observed mildly, as he stood up. 'I'd watch that one, Sam, he is as tricky as he is beautiful,' he advised.

Lugging the case, Craig made his way forward and clambered up into the raised cockpit. He dropped into the co-pilot's seat next to Sally-Anne, and shrugged out of the pack that contained the diamonds. He wedged it securely beside the seat.

'So you *can* fly this damned thing, after all, bird lady!'

She grinned at him, her teeth very white in her blackened face.

'I'm heading back towards the pan where we left the Land-Rover.'

'Good thinking – how's the fuel?'

'One tank full, the other three quarters – we have plenty in hand.'

Craig placed the attaché case in his lap and checked the locks. They were combinations.

'How long to the border?' he asked.

'We are making 170 knots, less than two hours – better than walking home, isn't it?'

'My oath!' Craig grinned back at her.

With his clasp-knife he ripped out the combination locks and opened the lid of the attaché case. On top there were two spare shirts and a ball of socks, a bottle of Russian vodka half full, a cheap wallet containing four passports, Finnish, Swedish, East German and Russian, airline tickets for Aeroflot.

'Well-travelled gentleman!' Craig unscrewed the top of the vodka bottle and took a swig. 'Brrr!' he said. 'That's the real stuff!' He passed the bottle to Sally-Anne and lifted the shirts. Under them were three green-covered folders, they were stamped with Cyrillic lettering and black hammer and sickle crests.

'Russian, by God! The man is a Bolshie!'

He opened the top folder and his interest quickened. 'It's typed in English!' He read the top page, and became gradually immersed in the contents. He did not even look up when Sally-Anne asked, 'What's it say?'

He skimmed through the first file and then the other two. Twenty-five minutes later he looked up with a stunned bemused expression and stared unseeingly through the windshield.

'I can hardly believe it,' he shook his head. 'They were so damned sure of themselves. They even typed it out in clear English for Peter Fungabera's benefit. No attempt at concealing it. They didn't even bother to use code names.'

'What is it?' Sally-Anne glanced sideways at him.

'It just boggles the mind.' He took another mouthful of vodka. 'Sam has got to read these!'

He stood up and balancing against the lurch of the helicopter, he dropped down into the hold and hurried back to Tungata.

Tungata and Sarah sat opposite the two hostages. Tungata had used the spare seat-belts to truss them securely at wrist and ankles. Peter Fungabera seemed to have recovered a little, and he and Tungata were glaring at each other, arguing with the acrimony and deadly concentration of mortal enemies.

'Cool that!' Craig dropped onto the bench beside Tungata.

'Give me the Uzi.' Craig took it from him. 'Now read what is in here!' He placed the attaché case on Tungata's lap.

'Delighted to meet you, Colonel Bukharin,' Craig said pleasantly. 'You must be happy to be missing the Moscow winter?' He pointed the Uzi at his belly.

'I am a senior member of the diplomatic corps of the United Soviet—'

'Yes, Colonel, I have read your visiting card.' Craig indicated the files. 'On the other hand I, Colonel, am a desperate fugitive quite capable of doing you a serious injury if you don't shut up.'

Then he turned to Peter Fungabera. 'I do hope you are looking after King's Lynn properly, remembering to wipe your feet and all that?'

'You escaped me once, Mr Mellow,' Peter Fungabera said softly. 'I don't make the same mistakes twice.'

And despite the gun in his hands and the fact that Peter was trussed up like a sacrificial goat, Craig felt a chilly little breeze of fear down his spine and he could not go on holding the smouldering gaze of hatred with which Peter Fungabera fixed him. He glanced sideways at Tungata.

He was skimming quickly through the green files, and as he read his expression changed from disbelief to outrage.

'Do you know what this is, Pupho?'

'It's a blueprint for bloody revolution,' Craig nodded, 'written out in plain English, obviously for the benefit of Peter Fungabera.'

'Everything – they cover everything. Look at this. The lists of those to be executed – they spell out the names – and those who can be relied on to collaborate. They have even prepared the radio and television announcements for the day of the coup!'

'Page twenty-five,' Craig suggested. 'Check that.'

Tungata turned to it. 'Me—' he read on. 'Sent to a clinic in Europe, mind-bending treatment, the mindless traitor, to lead the Matabele peoples into perpetual slavery—'

'Yes, Sam, you were the pivot on which the whole operation turned. When Fungabera lost you in the cavern

– when he dynamited the grand gallery – he admitted defeat. Just look at him now.'

However, Tungata was no longer listening. He dumped the attaché case and its contents back on Craig's lap and leaned forward until his face was a foot from Fungabera's. He thrust forward that craggy lantern jaw and slowly his eyeballs glazed over with the reddish sheen of rage.

'You would sell this land and all its peoples into a new slavery, into an imperialism that would make the rule of Smith's regime appear benign and altruistic by comparison? You would condemn your own tribe, and mine and all the others – madness—' In his rage, Tungata was becoming incoherent. 'A rabid dog, crazy with the lust for power.'

Suddenly he roared, involuntarily giving vent to his anguish and hatred and outrage. He hurled himself at Peter Fungabera and seized the wide nylon strap that bound him. With the other hand he unclipped the huge Shona's seat-belt and jerked him off the bench. With the strength of a wounded buffalo bull, he swung him bodily across the hold towards the square open port in the fuselage.

'Mad dog!' he roared, and before Craig could move, he had thrust Peter Fungabera backwards through the opening.

Craig tossed the Uzi to Sarah and sprang to Tungata's side. Tungata had been dragged to his knees by the weight of Peter Fungabera's body and he was clinging with one arm to the jamb of the doorway. With the other hand he still had a grip on the strap around Peter's chest.

Peter Fungabera dangled outboard. His hands were strapped helpless, his neck twisted back so that he stared up into Tungata's face above him. The fierce brown hills of Africa lay two thousand feet below him, the black stone crests bared like the teeth of a man-eating shark.

'Sam, wait!' Craig screamed above the wind-roar and the deafening beat of the engine.

'Die, you treacherous murderous—' Tungata roared, down into Peter Fungabera's upturned face.

Craig had never seen such naked terror as that in Peter Fungabera's dark eyes. His mouth was wide open and the wind blew his spittle over his lips in silver strings, but no sound came from his throat.

'Wait, Sam,' Craig screamed, 'don't kill him. He is the only one who can clear you, can clear all of us. If you kill him you'll never be able to live in Zimbabwe again—'

Tungata rolled his head sideways and stared at Craig.

'Our only chance to clear ourselves!'

The red glaze of rage began to fade from Tungata's eyes, but the muscles stood out in his arms from the effort of holding Peter Fungabera's body against the whip and buffet of the wind.

'Help me!' he grated, and in one movement Craig snatched the safety-belt, pulling it off the inertia reel, and buckled it around his own waist. He dropped belly-down on the deck, hooked his ankles around the base of the bench and reached down and out to get a double grip on the nylon strap. Between them they lifted Peter Fungabera back into the port, and his legs were so rubbery with terror that they could not bear his weight when he tried to stand.

Tungata hurled him backwards across the cabin, and Peter hit the rear bulkhead. He slid down it and rolled onto his side, pulling up his knees into the foetal position, and under the crushing weight of defeat and capitulation he moaned quietly and covered his head with both arms.

Craig climbed unsteadily up into the cockpit, and sank into the co-pilot's seat.

'What the hell is happening?' Sally-Anne demanded.

'Nothing serious. I only just managed to stop Sam killing Peter Fungabera.'

'Why did you bother?' Sally-Anne raised her voice above the clatter of the rotors overhead. 'I'd love a shot at that swine myself.'

'Darling, can you get a radio connection to the United States Embassy in Harare?'

She thought about it. 'Not from this aircraft.'

'Give them the registration of the Cessna, I'll lay odds it hasn't been reported missing yet.'

'I'll have to go through Johannesburg approach, they're the only station with sufficient range.'

'I don't care how – just get Morgan Oxford on the blower.'

Johannesburg approach radio responded promptly to Sally-Anne's call and accepted her call-sign with equanimity.

'Report your position, Kilo Yankee Alpha.'

'Northern Botswana—' Sally-Anne anticipated by an hour's flying time, *'en route* Francistown to Maun.'

'What is the number you wish to connect in Harare?'

'Person-to-person with the cultural attaché, Morgan Oxford, at the United States Embassy. I'm sorry, I don't know the number.'

'Hold on.' And in less than a minute Morgan Oxford spoke through the static.

'Oxford here. Who is this?'

Sally-Anne passed the microphone to Craig and he held it to his lips and depressed the transmit button.

'Morgan, it's Craig, Craig Mellow.'

'Holy shit!' Morgan's voice became strident. 'Where the hell are you? All hell is breaking out. Where is Sally-Anne?'

'Morgan, listen. This is deadly serious. How would you like to interrogate a full colonel of Russian intelligence, complete with his files of planned Russian aggression in and destabilization of the southern half of the African continent?'

There was nothing but the hum of static for many seconds and then Morgan said, 'Wait ten!'

The wait seemed much longer than ten seconds, and then Morgan came back.

'Don't say anything else. Just give me a rendezvous point.'

'These are map references—'

Craig read off the map coordinates that Sally-Anne had scribbled down for him. 'There is an emergency landing-strip there. I will light a signal fire. How long for you to get there?'

'Wait ten!' This time it was shorter. 'Dawn tomorrow.'

'Understood,' Craig acknowledged. 'We will be waiting.'

'Over and out.' He handed the microphone back to Sally-Anne.

'Border crossing in forty-three minutes,' she told him. 'That mud pack suits you. I'm beginning to think it's an improvement.'

'And you, beautiful, are a racing certainty for the cover of *Vogue*!'

She blew the hair off her nose and stuck her tongue out at him.

They crossed the border between Zimbabwe and Northern Botswana and seventeen minutes later they saw the hired Land-Rover standing exactly where they had left it on the edge of the wide white salt-pan.

'My God, Sarah's buddies are still there – that's constancy for you.' Craig made out the two tiny figures standing beside the vehicle. 'We'd better warn them, or when they see the government markings they are going to start shooting.'

Sarah called down to the waiting Matabele through the 'sky-shout' loudhailer as they approached, reassuring them, and Craig saw them lower their rifles as the Super Frelon sank lower. He could make out the beatific grins on the upturned faces of the two young Matabele.

Jonas had shot a springbuck that morning, so there was a feast of broiled venison steaks and salted maize cakes that evening, and afterwards they drew lots for guard duty over the two prisoners.

They first heard the drone of an approaching aircraft when it was still pearly half-light the next morning, and Craig drove out onto the pan in the Land-Rover to light the smudge fires. It came in from the south, an enormous Lockheed cargo plane with US Air Force markings. Sally-Anne recognized it. 'That is the NASA machine based at Johannesburg to monitor the shuttle programme.'

'They are really taking us seriously,' Craig murmured, as the Lockheed lowered itself to earth.

'It has amazing short take-off and landing capability,' Sally-Anne told him. 'Just watch.'

The gigantic aircraft pulled up in the same distance that the Cessna had used. The nose section opened like the bill of a pelican and five men came down the ramp, led by Morgan Oxford.

'Like five sardines from a can,' Craig observed, as they went forward to greet them. The visitors all wore tropical suits, white shirts with button-down collars and neckties and they all moved with athletes' balance and awareness.

'Sally-Anne. Craig.' Morgan Oxford shook hands briefly, and then acknowledged Tungata. 'Of course, I know you, Mr Minister, these are my colleagues.' He did not introduce them, but went straight on, 'Are these the subjects?'

The two young Matabele brought the prisoners forward at gunpoint.

'Son of a gun!' Morgan Oxford exclaimed. 'That's General Fungabera – Craig, are you out of your mind?'

'Read what is in here.' Craig proffered the attaché case. 'And then you tell me.'

'Wait here, please.' Morgan accepted the case.

Jonas and Aaron led the two captives towards the aircraft and the Americans came forward to receive them.

Peter Fungabera was still bound at the wrists with the nylon straps from the helicopter. He seemed to have shrunk in physical stature, he was no longer an impressive debonair figure. The cloak of defeat weighed him down. His skin had a grey tone and he did not lift his eyes as he came level with Tungata Zebiwe.

It was Tungata who reached out and seized his jaw in one hand, pressing his fingers into his cheeks, forcing his mouth open and twisting his head up so he could look into his face. For long seconds he stared into Peter Fungabera's eyes, and then contemptuously he pushed him away, so that Peter staggered and might have fallen had not one of the Americans steadied him.

'At the bottom of nearly every bully and tyrant lurks a coward,' Tungata said in that deep rumbling voice. 'You did right when you stopped me killing him, Pupho, a clean drop from the sky is too good for the likes of him. He goes now to a juster fate. Take him out of my sight, for he sickens me to the gut.'

Peter Fungabera and the Russian were led into the interior of the Lockheed, and Craig and his party settled down to wait. It was a long wait. They sat in the shade thrown by the Land-Rover and chatted in a desultory distracted fashion, breaking off every now and then as the squawk and warble from the radio in the Lockheed carried to where they sat.

'They're talking to Washington,' Craig guessed, 'via satellite.'

It was after ten o'clock before Morgan came down the ramp again, accompanied by one of his colleagues.

'This is Colonel Smith,' he told them and the way he said it, he didn't mean to be taken literally. 'We have appraised the items you have delivered to us, and we conclude, at this stage, anyway, that they are genuine.'

'That's very generous of you,' Craig dead-panned.

'Minister Tungata Zebiwe, we would be very grateful if you could spare us a deal of your valuable time. There are persons in Washington very anxious to talk to you. It will be to our mutual benefit, I assure you.'

'I would like this young lady to accompany me.' Tungata indicated Sarah.

'Yes, of course.' Morgan turned to Craig and Sally-Anne. 'In your case it's not an invitation, it's an order – you're coming with us.'

'What about the helicopter, and the Land-Rover?' Craig asked.

'Don't worry about them. Arrangements will be made to have them returned to their rightful owners.'

Three weeks later, at the United Nations building, a file was handed to the head of the Zimbabwe delegation. It contained excerpts from the three green files, and transcripts of the debriefing of General Peter Fungabera by persons unnamed. The file was rushed to Harare, and as a direct result an urgent request was made by the Zimbabwe government for the repatriation of General Fungabera. Two senior inspectors of the Zimbabwe police Special Branch flew to New York to escort the general home.

When the Pan Am flight landed at Harare, General Fungabera descended the boarding staircase from the first-class section of the Boeing handcuffed to one of the police inspectors. There was a closed van waiting on the tarmac.

There was no media coverage of his return.

He was driven directly to Harare central prison, where sixteen days later he died in one of the interrogation cells. His face, when his corpse was spirited out of the rear entrance to the main prison block, was so altered as to be unrecognizable.

A little after midnight that same night, a ministerial black Mercedes went off the road at speed on a lonely stretch of country road outside the city and burst into flames. There was one occupant. By his dental bridgework, the charred body was identified as that of General Peter Fungabera, and five days later he was buried with full military honours in 'Heroes' Acre', the cemetery for the patriots of the *Chimurenga* on the hills overlooking Harare.

On Christmas Day at ten o'clock in the morning, Colonel Bukharin left his escort of American military police at the allied guardhouse at Checkpoint Charlie and set out across the few hundred yards to the East Berlin side of the frontier.

Bukharin wore an American military-issue greatcoat over his safari clothes, and a knitted fisherman's cap on his bald head.

Halfway across, he passed a middle-aged man in a cheap suit coming in the opposite direction. The man might once have been plump, for his skin seemed too large for his skull and it had the grey, lifeless tone of long captivity.

They glanced at each other incuriously as they passed.

'A life for a life,' thought Bukharin, and suddenly he felt very tired. He walked at last with an old man's short hobbled gait over the icy tarmac.

There was a black sedan waiting for him beyond the frontier buildings. There were two men in the back seat and one of them climbed out as Bukharin approached. He wore a long civilian raincoat and a wide-brimmed hat in the style much favoured by the KGB.

'Bukharin?' he asked. His tone was neutral but his eyes were cold and relentless.

When Bukharin nodded, he jerked his head curtly. Bukharin slid into the rear seat and the man followed him in and slammed the door. The interior was overheated and smelled of garlic, last night's vodka, and unwashed socks.

The sedan pulled away and Bukharin lay back and closed his eyes. It was going to be bad, he thought, it might even be worse than he had anticipated.

Henry Pickering hosted the luncheon in the private dining suite of the World Bank overlooking Central Park.

Sarah and Sally-Anne had not seen each other for almost five months, and they embraced like sisters and then went into a huddle in a corner of the private lounge, trying to catch up with each other's news in the first thirty seconds, ignoring everybody else.

Tungata and Craig were more restrained.

'I feel so guilty, Pupho – five months. It was too long.'

'I know how they have kept you busy,' Craig forgave him. 'And I have been jumping about myself. Last time I saw you was in Washington—'

'Nearly a month of talks with the American State Department,' Tungata nodded, 'and then here in New York with the Zimbabwe ambassador and the World Bank. There is so much to tell, that I don't know where to begin.'

'All right, as a start,' Henry Pickering suggested, 'tell him about the dispensation that you prised out of the Zimbabwe government.'

'That's a good start,' Tungata agreed. 'First of all, my conviction and sentence under the poaching charge have been set aside—'

'Sam, that's the very least they could do—'

'That's for starters,' Tungata smiled and clasped his arm. 'That confession that you signed for Fungabera has been declared void, as it was obtained under duress. The order declaring you an enemy of the state and people has been rescinded, the sale of Rholands' shares to Peter Fungabera has been declared null and void. King's Lynn and Zambezi Waters revert to you.'

Craig stared at him wordlessly as he went on, 'The prime minister has accepted that all the acts of violence committed by either of us were acts of self-defence, everything from your killing of the Third Brigade troopers who were pursuing you on the Botswana border to the theft of the Super Frelon helicopter, and he has issued a full pardon—'

Craig merely shook his head.

'Then the Third Brigade has been withdrawn from Matabeleland. It has been disbanded and integrated into the regular army, the pogrom against my people has been called off, and independent observers have been allowed into the Matabele tribal areas to "monitor the peace".'

'That's the best news yet, Sam.'

'Still more – still more,' Tungata assured him. 'My Zimbabwe citizenship and passport have been returned to me. I am allowed to return home, with the assurance that there will be no check placed on my political activities. The government is to consider a referendum on instituting a form of federal autonomy for the Matabele people, and, in return, I am to use all my influence to convince the armed dissidents to come in from the bush and surrender their weapons under general amnesty.'

'It's all that you have been working towards – congratulations, Sam, I really mean that.'

'Only with your help.' Tungata turned to Henry Pick-ering. 'Can I tell him about Lobengula's Fire!'

'Wait!' Henry Pickering took both their arms and turned them towards the dining-room. 'Let's start lunch first.'

The dining-room was panelled in light oak, a perfect frame for the set of five Remington paintings of the old west that decorated three walls. The fourth wall was an enormous picture window that looked out across the city and Central Park. The curtains were open.

From the head of the table Henry smiled down at Craig. 'I thought we had better pull out all the stops,' and he showed Craig the wine label.

'Wow! The '61.'

'Well, it's not every day that I entertain the current number one best-selling author—'

'Yes, isn't it wonderful!' Sally-Anne cut in. 'Craig was number one in the *New York Times* the very first week of publication!'

'What about the TV deal?' Tungata asked.

'It's not signed yet,' Craig demurred.

'But my information is that it soon will be,' said Henry, as he filled the wine-glasses. 'Ladies and gentlemen, I give you the toast: Craig Mellow's latest opus, and its long ride at the top.'

They drank, laughing and festive, and Craig protested with his glass untouched. 'Come on! Give me a toast that I can drink as well.'

'Here it is!' Henry Pickering held up his glass again. 'Lobengula's Fire! Now you can tell him.'

'If those two women will stop chattering for ten seconds—'

'Not fair!' Sally-Anne protested. 'We never chatter, we seriously debate.'

Tungata smiled at her as he went on, 'As you know, Henry arranged for Lobengula's diamonds to be placed in safe-keeping and for them to be appraised. Harry Winston's top men have vetted them and come up with an estimate—'

'Tell us!' Sally-Anne called. 'How much?'

'As you know the diamond market is in a very serious depression at the moment – stones selling for seventy thousand dollars two years ago are fetching only twenty thousand—'

'Come on, Sam, don't tease us!'

'All right, Winston's have valued the collection at six hundred million dollars—'

Everybody spoke at once and it took a while for Tungata to regain the floor.

'As we all agreed from the beginning, the diamonds are to be placed in a trust fund, and I am going to ask Craig to be one of the trustees.'

'I accept.'

'However, fourteen of the stones have already been sold. I authorized the deal and the proceeds from it were five million dollars. The entire amount has been handed over to the World Bank in complete discharge of capital and interest on the loan made to Craig.' Tungata drew an envelope from his inside pocket. 'Here is the receipt, Pupho, your share of Lobengula's Fire. You are free and clear of all debt now. King's Lynn and Zambezi Waters are yours.'

Craig turned the envelope between his fingers, staring at Tungata, struck dumb, and Tungata's smile faded as he leaned towards him and spoke seriously. 'In return, there is one thing I would ask from you, Pupho.'

'Ask it,' said Craig. 'Anything.'

'Your promise that you will return to Africa. We need men like you to help stave off these new dark ages that threaten to overwhelm the land we both love.'

Craig reached across the table and took Sally-Anne's hand.

'You tell him,' he said.

'Yes, Sam, we are coming home with you,' she said softly. 'That's a promise.'

S ally-Anne and Craig drove up the hills of King's Lynn in the old Land-Rover. The late afternoon had turned the grasslands to cloth-of-gold, and the trees on the crest of the hills wove delicate lacework against the high serene blue of the African summer sky.

They were waiting for them on the lawns under the jacaranda trees – all the house servants and herders from King's Lynn. When Craig embraced Shadrach, the old man's empty sleeve flapped against his skinny chest.

'Do not worry, Nkosi, I can work better with one arm than any of these puppies can with two.'

'I will make you a bargain,' Craig suggested, so that all could hear. 'I will lend you an arm, if you will lend me a leg.' And Shadrach laughed until the tears dripped onto his shirt and his newest and youngest wife had to lead him away.

Joseph waited on the wide veranda, aloof from the common throng, resplendent in snowy white *kanza* and with the tall chef's cap on his head.

'I see you, Nkosikazi,' he greeted Sally-Anne gravely, as she reached the top of the stairs, but he could not disguise the sparkle of pleasure in his eyes.

'I see you also, Joseph. And I have decided we will have two hundred guests at the wedding,' she answered him in fluent Sindebele, and Joseph covered his mouth with both hands in astonishment, the first time she had ever seen him off balance.

'Hau!' he said, and then turned to his underlings.

'Now we have a truly great lady at Kingi Lingi who understands all your monkey chatter,' he told them sternly. 'So woe unto any of you who lie or cheat or steal!'

Craig and Sally-Anne stood at the top of the stairs, holding hands while the people of King's Lynn sang the song that welcomes the traveller home after a long and dangerous journey, and when it was ended, Craig looked down at her.

'Welcome home, my darling,' he said.

And while the women ululated and danced so that the heads of the infants strapped to their backs jerked like little black puppets and the men roared approval, Craig kissed her on the mouth.

WHEN THE
LION FEEDS

This book is for
Elfreda and Herbert James Smith
with love

– I –
Natal

A single wild pheasant flew up the side of the hill almost brushing the tips of the grass in its flight. It drooped its wings and hung its legs as it reached the crest and then dropped into cover. Two boys and a dog followed it up from the valley: the dog led, with his tongue flopping pink from the corner of his mouth, and the twins ran shoulder to shoulder behind him. Both of them were sweating in dark patches through their khaki shirts, for the African sun still had heat although it stood half-mast down the sky.

The dog hit the scent of the bird and it stopped him quivering: for a second he stood sucking it up through his nostrils, and then he started to quarter. He worked fast, back and forth, swinging at the end of each tack, his head down and only his back and his busy tail showing above the dry brown grass. The twins came up behind him. They were gasping for breath for it had been a hard pull up the curve of the hill.

'Keep out to the side, you'll get in my way,' Sean panted at his brother and Garrick moved to obey. Sean was his senior by four inches in height and twenty pounds in weight: this gave him the right to command. Sean transferred his attention back to the dog.

'Put him up, Tinker. Seek him up, boy.'

Tinker's tail acknowledged Sean's instructions, but he held his nose to the ground. The twins followed him, tensed for the bird to rise. They carried their throwing sticks ready and moved forward a stealthy pace at a time, fighting to control their breathing. Tinker found the bird crouched flat in the grass; he jumped forward giving tongue for the first time, and the bird rose. It came up fast on noisy wings, whirling out of the grass.

Sean threw; his kerrie whipped past it. The pheasant swung away from the stick, clawing at the air with frantic wings and Garrick threw. His kerrie cartwheeled up, hissing, until it smacked into the pheasant's fat brown body. The bird toppled, feathers flurried from it and it fell. They went after it. The pheasant scurried broken-winged through the grass ahead of them, and they shouted with excitement as they chased it. Sean got a hand to it. He broke its neck and stood laughing, holding the warm brown body in his hands, and waited for Garrick to reach him.

'Ring-a-ding-a-doody, Garry, you sure gave that one a beauty!'

Tinker jumped up to smell the bird and Sean stooped and held it so he could get his nose against it. Tinker snuffled it, then tried to take it in his mouth, but Sean pushed his head away and tossed the bird to Garrick. Garrick hung it with the others on his belt.

'How far do you reckon that was – fifty feet?' Garrick asked.

'Not as much as that,' Sean gave his opinion. 'More like thirty.'

'I reckon it was at least fifty. I reckon it was farther than any you've hit today.' Success had made Garrick bold. The smile faded from Sean's face.

'Yeah?' he asked.

'Yeah!' said Garrick. Sean pushed the hair off his forehead with the back of his hand, his hair was black and soft and it kept falling into his eyes.

'What about that one down by the river? That was twice as far.'

'Yeah?' asked Garrick.

'Yeah!' said Sean truculently.

'Well, if you're so good, how did you miss this one – hey? You threw first. How come you missed, hey?'

Sean's already flushed face darkened and Garrick realized suddenly that he had gone too far. He took a step backwards.

'You'd like to bet?' demanded Sean. It was not quite clear to Garrick on what Sean wished to bet, but from past experience he knew that whatever it was the issue would be settled by single combat. Garrick seldom won bets from Sean.

'It's too late. We'd better be getting home. Pa will clobber us if we're late for dinner.' Sean hesitated and Garrick turned, ran back to pick up his kerrie then set off in the direction of home. Sean trotted after him, caught up with him and passed him. Sean always led. Having proved conclusively his superior prowess with the throwing sticks Sean was prepared to be forgiving. Over his shoulder he asked, 'What colour do you reckon Gypsy's foal will be?'

Garrick accepted the peace-offering with relief and they fell into a friendly discussion of this and a dozen other equally important subjects. They kept running: except for an hour, when they had stopped in a shady place by the river to roast and eat a couple of their pheasants, they had run all day.

Up here on the plateau it was grassland that rose and fell beneath them as they climbed the low round hills and dropped into the valleys. The grass around them moved with the wind: waist-high grass, soft dry grass the colour of ripe wheat. Behind them and on each side the grassland rolled away to the full range of the eye, but suddenly in front of them was the escarpment. The land cascaded down into it, steeply at first then gradually levelling out to become the Tugela flats. The Tugela river was twenty miles away across the flats, but today there was a haze in the air so they could not see that far. Beyond the river, stretched far to the north and a hundred miles east to the sea, was Zululand. The river was the border. The steep side of the escarpment was cut by vertical gulleys and in the gulleys grew dense, olive-green bush.

Below them, two miles out on the flats, was the homestead of Theunis Kraal. The house was a big one, Dutch-gabled and smoothly thatched with combed grass. There were horses in the small paddock: many horses, for the twins' father was a wealthy man. Smoke from the cooking fires blued the air over the servants' quarters and the sound of someone chopping wood carried faintly up to them.

Sean stopped on the rim of the escarpment and sat down in the grass. He took hold of one of his grimy bare feet and twisted it up into his lap. There was hole in the ball of his heel from which he had pulled a thorn earlier in the day and now it was plugged with dirt. Garrick sat down next to him.

'Man, is that going to hurt when Ma puts iodine on it!' gloated Garrick. 'She'll have to use a needle to get the dirt out. I bet you yell – I bet you yell your head off!'

Sean ignored him. He picked a stalk of grass and started probing it into the wound. Garrick watched with interest. Twins could scarcely have been less alike. Sean was already taking on the shape of a man: his shoulders were thickening, and there was hard muscle forming in his puppy fat. His colouring was vivid: black hair, skin brown from the sun, lips and cheeks that glowed with the fresh young blood beneath their surface, and blue eyes, the dark indigo-blue of cloud shadow on mountain lake.

Garrick was slim, with the wrists and ankles of a girl. His hair was an undecided brown that grew wispy down the back of his neck, his skin was freckled, his nose and the rims of his pale blue eyes were pink with persistent hay fever. He was fast losing interest in Sean's surgery. He reached across and fiddled with one of Tinker's pendulous ears, and this broke the rhythm of the dog's panting; he gulped twice and the saliva dripped from the end of his tongue. Garrick lifted his head and looked down the slope. A little below where they were sitting was the head of one of the bushy gullies. Garrick caught his breath.

'Sean, look there – next to the bush!' His whisper trembled with excitement.

'What's it?' Sean looked up startled. Then he saw it.

'Hold Tinker.' Garrick grabbed the dog's collar and pulled his head around to prevent him seeing and giving chase. 'He's the biggest old inkonka in the world,' breathed Garrick. Sean was too absorbed to answer.

The bushbuck was picking its way warily out of the thick cover. A big ram, black with age; the spots on his haunches were faded like old chalk marks. His ears pricked up and his spiral horns held high, big as a pony, but stepping daintily, he came out into the open. He stopped and swung his head from side to side, searching for danger, then he trotted diagonally down the hill and disappeared into another of the gullies. For a moment after he had gone the twins were still, then they burst out together.

'Did you see him, hey – did you see them horns?'

'So close to the house and we never knew he was there—'

They scrambled to their feet jabbering at each other, and Tinker was infected with their excitement. He barked around them in a circle. After the first few moments of confusion Sean took control simply by raising his voice above the opposition.

'I bet he hides up in the gulley every day. I bet he stays there all day and comes out only at night. Let's go and have a look.'

Sean led the way down the slope.

On the fringe of the bush, in a small cave of vegetation that was dark and cool and carpeted with dead leaves, they found the ram's hiding-place. The ground was trampled by his hooves and scattered with his droppings and there was the mark of his body where he had lain. A few loose hairs, tipped with grey, were left on the bed of leaves. Sean knelt down and picked one up.

'How are we going to get him?'

'We could dig a hole and put sharpened sticks in it,' suggested Garrick eagerly.

'Who's going to dig it – you?' Sean asked.

'You could help.'

'It would have to be a pretty big hole,' said Sean doubtfully. There was silence while both of them considered the amount of labour involved in digging a trap. Neither of them mentioned the idea again.

'We could get the other kids from town and have a drive with kerries,' said Sean.

'How many hunts have we been on with them? Must be hundreds by now, and we haven't even bagged one lousy duiker – let alone a bushbuck.' Garrick hesitated and then went on. 'Besides, remember what that inkonka did to Frank Van Essen, hey? When it finished sticking him they had to push all his guts back into the hole in his stomach!'

'Are you scared?' asked Sean.

'I am not, so!' said Garrick indignantly, then quickly, 'Gee, it's almost dark. We'd better run.'

They went down the valley.

2

S ean lay in the darkness and stared across the room at the grey oblong of the window. There was a slice of moon in the sky outside. Sean could not sleep: he was thinking about the bushbuck. He heard his parents pass the door of the bedroom; his stepmother said something and his father laughed: Waite Courtney had a laugh as deep as distant thunder.

Sean heard the door of their room close and he sat up in bed. 'Garry.' No answer.

'Garry.' He picked up a boot and threw it; there was a grunt. 'Garry.'

'What you want?' Garrick's voice was sleepy and irritable.

'I was just thinking – tomorrow's Friday.'

'So?'

'Ma and Pa will be going into town. They'll be away all day. We could take the shotgun and go lay for that old inkonka.'

Garrick's bed creaked with alarm.

'You're mad!' Garrick could not keep the shock out of his voice. 'Pa would kill us if he caught us with the shotgun.' Even as he said it he knew he would have to find a stronger argument than that to dissuade his brother. Sean avoided punishment if possible, but a chance at a bushbuck ram was worth all his father's right arm could give. Garrick lay rigid in his bed, searching for words.

'Besides, Pa keeps the cartridges locked up.'

It was a good try, but Sean countered it.

'I know where there are two buckshots that he has forgotten about: they're in the big vase in the dining-room. They've been there over a month.'

Garrick was sweating. He could almost feel the sjambok

curling round his buttocks, and hear his father counting the strokes: eight, nine, ten.

'Please, Sean, let's think of something else . . .'

Across the room Sean settled back comfortably on his pillows. The decision had been made.

– 3 –

Waite Courtney handed his wife up into the front seat of the buggy. He patted her arm affectionately then walked around to the driver's side, pausing to fondle the horses and settle his hat down over his bald head. He was a big man, the buggy dipped under his weight as he climbed up into the seat. He gathered up the reins, then he turned and his eyes laughed over his great hooked nose at the twins standing together on the veranda.

'I would esteem it a favour if you two gentlemen could arrange to stay out of trouble for the few hours that your mother and I will be away.'

'Yes, Pa,' in dutiful chorus.

'Sean, if you get the urge to climb the big blue gum tree again then fight it, man, fight it.'

'All right, Pa.'

'Garrick, let us have no more experiments in the manufacture of gunpowder – agreed?'

'Yes, Pa.'

'And don't look so innocent. That really frightens the hell out of me!'

Waite touched the whip to the shiny round rumps in front of him and the buggy started forward, out along the road to Ladyburg.

'He didn't say anything about not taking the shotgun,'

whispered Sean virtuously. 'Now you go and see if all the servants are out of the way – if they see us, they'll kick up a fuss. Then come round to the bedroom window and I'll pass it out to you.'

Sean and Garrick argued all the way to the foot of the escarpment. Sean was carrying the shotgun across one shoulder, hanging onto the butt with both hands.

'It was my idea, wasn't it?' he demanded.

'But I saw the inkonka first,' protested Garrick. Garrick was bold again: with every yard put between him and the house his fear of reprisal faded.

'That doesn't count,' Sean informed him. 'I thought of the shotgun, so I do the shooting.'

'How come you always have the fun?' asked Garrick, and Sean was outraged at the question.

'When you found the hawk's nest by the river, I let you climb for it. Didn't I? When you found the baby duiker, I let you feed it. Didn't I?' he demanded.

'All right. So I saw the inkonka first, why don't you let me take the shot?'

Sean was silent in the face of such stubbornness, but his grip on the butt of the shotgun tightened. In order to win the argument Garrick would have to get it away from him – this Garrick knew and he started to sulk. Sean stopped among the trees at the foot of the escarpment and looked over his shoulder at his brother.

'Are you going to help – or must I do it alone?'

Garrick looked down at the ground and kicked at a twig. He sniffed wetly; his hayfever was always bad in the mornings.

'Well?' asked Sean.

'What do you want me to do?'

'Stay here and count to a thousand slowly. I'm going to circle up the slope and wait where the inkonka crossed

11

yesterday. When you finish counting come up the gulley. Start shouting when you are about halfway up. The inkonka will break the same way as yesterday – all right?'

Garrick nodded reluctantly.

'Did you bring Tinker's chain?'

Garrick pulled it from his pocket, and at the sight of it the dog backed away. Sean grabbed his collar, and Garrick slipped it on. Tinker laid his ears flat and looked at them reproachfully.

'Don't let him go. That old inkonka will rip him up. Now start counting,' said Sean and began climbing. He kept well out to the left of the gulley. The grass on the slope was slippery under his feet, the gun was heavy and there were sharp lumps of rock in the grass. He stubbed his toe and it started to bleed, but he kept on upwards. There was a dead tree on the edge of the bush that Sean had used to mark the bushbuck's hide. Sean climbed above it and stopped just below the crest of the slope where the moving grass would break up the silhouette of his head on the skyline. He was panting. He found a rock the size of a beer barrel to use as a rest for the gun, and he crouched behind it. He laid the stock of the gun on the rock, aimed back down the hill and traversed the barrels left and right to make sure his field of fire was clear. He imagined the bushbuck running in his sights and he felt excitement shiver along his forearms, across his shoulders and up the back of his neck.

'I won't lead on him – he'll be moving fairly slowly, trotting most probably. I'll go straight at his shoulders,' he whispered.

He opened the gun, took the two cartridges out of his shirt pocket, slid them into the breeches and snapped the gun closed. It took all the strength of both his hands to pull back the big fancy hammers, but he managed it and the gun was double-loaded and cocked. He laid it on the rock in front of him again and stared down the slope. On his left the gulley was a dark-green smear on the hillside, directly below him was open grass where the bushbuck would cross. He pushed impatiently at the hair on his forehead: it was damp with sweat and stayed up out of his eyes.

The minutes drifted by.

'What the hell is Garry doing? He's so stupid sometimes!' Sean muttered and almost in answer he heard Garrick shout below him. It was a small sound, far down the slope and muffled by the bush. Tinker barked once without enthusiasm; he was also sulking, he didn't like the chain. Sean waited with his forefinger on one trigger, staring down at the edge of the bush. Garrick shouted again – and the bushbuck broke from cover.

It came fast into the open with its nose up and its long horns held flat against its back. Sean moved his body sideways swinging the gun with its run, riding the pip of the foresight on its black shoulder. He fired the left barrel and the recoil threw him off balance; his ears hummed with the shot and the burnt powder smoke blew back into his face. He struggled to his feet still holding the gun. The bushbuck was down in the grass, bleating like a lamb and kicking as it died.

'I got him,' screamed Sean. 'I got him first shot! Garry, Garry! I got him, I got him!'

Tinker came pelting out of the bush dragging Garry behind him by the chain and, still screaming, Sean ran down to join them. A stone rolled under his foot and he fell. The shotgun flew out of his hand and the second barrel fired. The sound of the explosion was very loud.

When Sean scrambled onto his feet again Garrick was sitting in the grass whimpering – whimpering and staring at his leg. The blast of the shotgun had smashed into it and churned the flesh below the knee into tatters – bursting it open so the bone chips showed white in the wound and the blood pumped dark and strong and thick as custard.

'I didn't mean it . . . Oh God, Garry, I didn't mean it. I slipped. Honest, I slipped.' Sean was staring at the leg also. There was no colour in his face, his eyes were big and dark with horror. The blood pumped out onto the grass.

'Stop it bleeding! Sean, please stop it. Oh, it's sore! Oh! Sean, please stop it!'

Sean stumbled across to him. He wanted to vomit. He unbuckled his belt and strapped it round the leg, and the blood was warm and sticky on his hands. He used his sheathed knife to twist the belt tight. The pumping slowed and he twisted harder.

'Oh, Sean, it's sore! It's sore . . .' Garrick's face was waxy-white and he was starting to shiver as the cold hand of shock closed on him.

'I'll get Joseph,' Sean stammered. 'We'll come back quickly as we can. Oh, God, I'm sorry!' Sean jumped up and ran. He fell, rolled to his feet and kept running.

They came within an hour. Sean was leading three of the Zulu servants. Joseph, the cook, had brought a blanket. He wrapped Garrick and lifted him and Garrick fainted as his leg swung loosely. As they started back down the hill Sean looked out across the flats: there was a little puff of dust on the Ladyburg road. One of the grooms was riding to fetch Waite Courtney.

They were waiting on the veranda of the homestead when Waite Courtney came back to Theunis Kraal. Garrick was conscious again. He lay on the couch: his face was white and the blood had soaked through the blanket. There was blood on Joseph's uniform and blood had dried black on Sean's hands. Waite Courtney ran up onto the veranda; he stooped over Garrick and drew back the

14

blanket. For a second he stood staring at the leg and then very gently he covered it again.

Waite lifted Garrick and carried him down to the buggy. Joseph went with him and they settled Garrick on the back seat. Joseph held his body and Garrick's stepmother took the leg on her lap to stop it twisting. Waite Courtney climbed quickly into the driver's seat: he picked up the reins, then he turned his head and looked at Sean still standing on the veranda. He didn't speak, but his eyes were terrible – Sean could not meet them. Waite Courtney used the whip on the horses and drove them back along the road to Ladyburg: he drove furiously with the wind streaming his beard back from his face.

Sean watched them go. After they had disappeared among the trees he remained standing alone on the veranda; then suddenly he turned and ran back through the house. He ran out of the kitchen door and across the yard to the saddle-room, snatched a bridle down from the rack and ran to the paddock. He picked a bay mare and worked her into a corner of the fence until he could slip his arm around her neck. He forced the bit into her mouth, buckled the chin strap and swung up onto her bare back.

He kicked her into a run and put her to the gate, swaying back as her body heaved up under him and falling forward on her neck as she landed. He gathered himself and turned her head towards the Ladyburg road.

It was eight miles to town and the buggy reached it before Sean. He found it outside Doctor Van Rooyen's surgery: the horses were blowing hard, and their bodies were dark with sweat. Sean slid down off the mare's back; he went up the steps to the surgery door and quietly pushed it open. There was the sweet reek of chloroform in the room. Garrick lay on the table, Waite and his wife stood on each side of him, and the doctor was washing his hands in an

15

enamel basin against the far wall. Ada Courtney was crying silently, her face blurred with tears. They all looked at Sean standing in the doorway.

'Come here,' said Waite Courtney, his voice flat and expressionless. 'Come and stand here beside me. They're going to cut off your brother's leg and, by Christ, I'm going to make you watch every second of it!'

– 4 –

They brought Garrick back to Theunis Kraal in the night. Waite Courtney drove the buggy very slowly and carefully and Sean trailed a long way behind it. He was cold in his thin khaki shirt, and sick in the stomach with what he had seen. There were bruises on his upper arm where his father had held him and forced him to watch.

The servants had lanterns burning on the veranda. They were standing in the shadows, silent and anxious. As Waite carried the blanket-wrapped body up the front steps one of them called softly in the Zulu tongue. 'The leg?'

'It is gone,' Waite answered gruffly.

They sighed softly all together and the voice called again. 'He is well?'

'He is alive,' said Waite.

He carried Garrick through to the room that was set aside for guests and sickness. He stood in the centre of the floor holding the boy while his wife put fresh sheets on the bed; then he laid him down and covered him.

'Is there anything else we can do?' asked Ada.

'We can wait.'

Ada groped for her husband's hand. 'Please, God, let him live,' she whispered. 'He's so young.'

'It's Sean's fault!' Waite's anger flared up suddenly.

'Garry would never have done it on his own.' He tried to disengage Ada's hand.

'What are you going to do?' she asked.

'I'm going to beat him! I'm going to thrash the skin off him!'

'Don't, please don't.'

'What do you mean?'

'He's had enough. Didn't you see his face?'

Waite's shoulders sagged wearily and he sat down on the armchair beside the bed. Ada touched his cheek.

'I'll stay here with Garry. You go and try to get some sleep, my dear.'

'No,' Waite said. She sat down on the side of the chair and Waite put his arm around her waist. After a long while they slept, huddled together on the chair beside the bed.

– 5 –

The days that followed were bad. Garrick's mind escaped from the harness of sanity and ran wild into the hot land of delirium. He panted and twisted his fever-flushed face from side to side; he cried and whimpered in the big bed; the stump of his leg puffed up angrily and the stitches were drawn so tight it seemed they must tear out of the swollen flesh. The infection oozed yellow and foul-smelling onto the sheets.

Ada stayed by him all that time. She swabbed the sweat from his face and changed the dressings on his stump, she held the glass for him to drink and gentled him when he raved. Her eyes sunk darkly into their sockets with fatigue and worry, but she would not leave him. Waite could not bear it. He had the masculine dread of suffering that threatened to suffocate him if he stayed in the room: every half hour or so he came in and stood next to the bed and

17

then he turned away and went back to his restless wandering around the house. Ada could hear his heavy tramp along the corridors.

Sean stayed in the house also: he sat in the kitchen or at the far end of the veranda. No one would speak to him, not even the servants; they chased him when he tried to sneak into the bedroom to see Garrick. He was lonely with the desolate loneliness of the guilty – for Garry was going to die, he knew it by the evil silence that hung over Theunis Kraal. There was no chatter nor pot-clatter from the kitchens, no rich deep laughter from his father: even the dogs were subdued. Death was at Theunis Kraal. He could smell it on the soiled sheets that were brought through to the kitchen from Garrick's room; it was a musky smell, the smell of an animal. Sometimes he could almost see it: even in bright daylight sitting on the veranda he sensed it crouched near him like a shadow on the edge of his vision. It had no form as yet. It was a darkness, a coldness that was gradually building up around the house, gathering its strength until it could take his brother.

On the third day Waite Courtney came roaring out of Garrick's room. He ran through the house and out into the stable yard. 'Karlie. Where are you? Get a saddle onto Rooiberg. Hurry, man, hurry – damn you. He's dying, do you hear me, he's dying.'

Sean did not move from where he sat against the wall next to the back door. His arm tightened around Tinker's neck and the dog touched his cheek with a cold nose; he watched his father jump up onto the stallion's back and ride. The hooves beat away towards Ladyburg and when they were gone he stood up and slipped into the house: he listened outside Garrick's door and then he opened it quietly and went in. Ada turned towards him, her face was tired. She looked much older than her thirty-five years, but her black hair was drawn back behind her head into a neat

18

bun and her dress was fresh and clean. She was still a beautiful woman despite her exhaustion. There was a gentleness about her, a goodness that suffering and worry could not destroy. She held out her hand to Sean and he crossed and stood beside her chair and looked down at Garrick. Then he knew why his father had gone to fetch the doctor. Death was in the room – strong and icy cold hovered over the bed. Garrick lay very still: his face was yellow, his eyes were closed and his lips were cracked and dry.

All the loneliness and the guilt came swelling up into Sean's throat and choked him into sobs, sobs that forced him to his knees and he put his face into Ada's lap and cried. He cried for the last time in his life, he cried as a man cries – painfully, each sob tearing something inside him.

Waite Courtney came back from Ladyburg with the doctor. Once more Sean was driven out and the door closed. All night he heard them working in Garrick's room, the murmuring of their voices and the scuff of feet on the yellow wood floor. In the morning it was over. The fever was broken and Garrick was alive. Only just alive – his eyes were sunk into dark holes like those of a skull. His body and his mind were never to recover completely from that brutal pruning.

It was slow – a week before he was strong enough to feed himself. His first need was for his brother, before he was able to talk above a whisper it was, 'Where's Sean?'

And Sean, still chastened, sat with him for hours at a time. Then when Garrick slept Sean escaped from the room, and with a fishing-rod or his hunting sticks and Tinker barking behind him went into the veld. It was a measure of Sean's repentance that he allowed himself to be contained within the sick-room for such long periods. It chafed him like ropes on a young colt: no one would ever know what it cost him to sit quietly next to Garrick's bed while his body itched and burned with unexpended energy and his mind raced restlessly.

Then Sean had to go back to school. He left on a Monday morning while it was still dark. Garrick listened to the sounds of departure, the whicker of the horses outside on the driveway and Ada's voice reciting last minute instructions: 'I've put a bottle of cough mixture under your shirts, give it to Fräulein as soon as you unpack. Then she'll see that you take it at the first sign of a cold.'

'Yes, Ma.'

'There are six vests in the small case – use a new one every day.'

'Vests are sissy things.'

'You will do as you're told, young man.' Waite's voice, 'Hurry up with your porridge – we've got to get going if I'm to have you in town by seven o'clock.'

'Can I say goodbye to Garry?'

'You said goodbye last night – he'll still be asleep now.'

Garrick opened his mouth to call out, but he knew his voice would not carry. He lay quietly and listened to the chairs scraping back from the dining-room table, the procession of footsteps out onto the veranda, voices raised in farewells and at last the wheels of the buggy crunching gravel as they moved away down the drive. It was very quiet after Sean had left with his father.

After that the weekends were, for Garrick, the only bright spots in the colourless passage of time. He longed for them to come and each one was an eternity after the last – time passes slowly for the young and the sick. Ada and Waite knew a little of how he felt. They moved the centre of the household to his room: they brought two of the fat leather armchairs from the lounge and put them on each side of his bed and they spent the evenings there. Waite with his pipe in his mouth and a glass of brandy at his elbow, whittling at the wooden leg he was making and laughing his deep laugh, Ada with her knitting and the two of them trying to reach him. Perhaps it was this conscious effort that was the cause of their failure, or perhaps it is impossible to reach back down the years to a small boy. There is always that reserve, that barrier between the adult and the secret world of youth. Garrick laughed with them and they talked together, but it was not the same as having Sean there. During the day Ada had the running of a large household and there were fifteen thousand acres of land and two thousand head of cattle that needed Waite's attention. That was the loneliest time for Garrick. If it had not been for the books, he might not have been able to bear it. He read everything that Ada brought to him: Stevenson, Swift, Defoe, Dickens and even Shakespeare. Much of it he didn't understand, but he read hungrily and the opium of the printed word helped him through the long days until Sean came home each Friday.

When Sean came home it was like a big wind blowing through the house. Doors slammed, dogs barked, servants scolded and feet clattered up and down the passages. Most of the noise was Sean's, but not all of it. There were Sean's followers: youngsters from his class at the village school. They accepted Sean's authority as willingly as did Garrick, and it was not only Sean's fists that won this acceptance but also the laughter and the sense of excitement that went with him. They came out to Theunis Kraal in droves that summer, sometimes as many as three on one bare-backed pony: sitting like a row of sparrows on a fence rail. They came for the added attraction of Garry's stump. Sean was very proud of it.

'That's where the doc sewed it up,' pointing to the row of stitch marks along the pink fold of scar tissue.

'Can I touch it, man?'

'Not too hard or it'll burst open.' Garrick had never

received attention like this in his life before. He beamed round the circle of solemn, wide-eyed faces.

'It feels funny – sort of hot.'

'Was it sore?'

'How did he chop the bone – with an axe?'

'No.' Sean was the only one in a position to answer technical questions of this nature. 'With a saw. Just like a piece of wood.' He made the motions with his open hand.

But even this fascinating subject couldn't hold them for long and presently there would be a restlessness amongst them.

'Hey, Sean, Karl and I know where there's a nest of squawkers – you wanta have a look?' or 'Let's go and catch frogs,' and Garrick would cut in desperately.

'You can have a look at my stamp collection if you like. It's in the cupboard there.'

'Naw, we saw it last week. Let's go.'

This was when Ada, who had been listening to the conversation through the open kitchen door, brought in the food. Koeksusters fried in honey, chocolate cakes with peppermint icing, watermelon konfyt and half a dozen other delicacies. She knew they wouldn't leave until it was finished and she knew also that there'd be upset stomachs as it was, but that was preferable to Garrick lying alone and listening to the others riding off into the hills.

The weekends were short, gone in a breathless blur. Another long week began for Garrick. There were eight of them, eight dreary weeks before Doctor Van Rooyen agreed to let him sit out on the veranda during the day. Then suddenly the prospect of being well again became a reality for Garrick. The leg that Waite was making was nearly finished: he shaped a leather bucket to take the stump and fitted it to the wood with flat-headed copper nails; he worked carefully, moulding the leather and adjusting the straps that would hold it in place. Meanwhile, Garrick exercised along the veranda, hopping beside Ada with an arm around her shoulder, his jaws clenched with concentration and the freckles very prominent on his face that had been without the sun for so long. Twice a day Ada sat on a cushion in front of Garrick's chair and massaged the stump with methylated spirits to toughen it for its first contact with the stiff leather bucket.

'I bet old Sean'll be surprised, hey? When he sees me walking around.'

'Everyone will,' Ada agreed. She looked up from his leg and smiled.

'Can't I try it now? Then I can go out fishing with him when he comes on Saturday.'

'You mustn't expect too much, Garry, it's not going to be easy at first. You will have to learn to use it. Like riding a horse – you remember how often you fell off before you learned to ride.'

'But can I start now?'

Ada reached for the spirits bottle, poured a little into her cupped hand and spread it on the stump. 'We'll have to wait until Doctor Van Rooyen tells us you're ready. It won't be long now.'

It wasn't. After his next visit Doctor Van Rooyen spoke to Waite as they walked together to the doctor's trap.

'You can try him with the peg-leg – it'll give him something to work for. Don't let him overtire himself and watch the stump doesn't get rubbed raw. We don't want another infection.'

'Peg-leg.' Waite's mind echoed the ugly word as he watched the trap out of sight. 'Peg-leg': he clenched his fists at his sides, not wanting to turn and see the pathetically eager face behind him on the veranda.

23

'Are you sure that's comfortable?' Waite squatted in front of Garrick's chair adjusting the leg and Ada stood next to him.

'Yes, yes, let me try it now. Gee, old Sean will be surprised, hey? I'll be able to go back with him on Monday, won't I?' Garrick was trembling with eagerness.

'We'll see,' Waite grunted non-committally. He stood up and moved round beside the chair.

'Ada, my dear, take his other arm. Now listen, Garry, I want you to get the feel of it first. We'll help you up and you can just stand on it and get your balance. Do you understand?'

Garrick nodded vigorously.

'All right, then up you come.'

Garrick drew the leg towards him and the tip scraped across the wooden floor. They lifted him and he put his weight on it.

'Look at me – I'm standing on it. Hey, look I'm standing on it.' His face glowed. 'Let me walk, come on! Let me walk.'

Ada glanced at her husband and he nodded. Together they led Garrick forward. He stumbled twice but they held him. Klunk and klunk again the peg rang on the floor boards. Before they reached the end of the veranda Garrick had learned to lift the leg high as he swung it forward. They turned and he stumbled only once on the way back to the chair.

'That's fine, Garry, you're doing fine,' laughed Ada.

'You'll be on your own in no time,' Waite grinned with relief. He had hardly dared to hope it would be so easy, and Garrick fastened on his words. 'Let me stand on my own now.'

'Not this time, boy, you've done well enough for one day.'

'Oh, gee, Pa. Please. I won't try and walk, I'll just stand. You and Ma can be ready to catch me. Please, Pa, please.'

Waite hesitated and Ada added her entreaty. 'Let him, dear, he's done so well. It'll help build up his confidence.'

'Very well. But don't try to move,' Waite agreed. 'Are you ready, Garry? Let him go!' They took their hands off him cautiously. He teetered slightly and their hands darted back.

'I'm all right – leave me.' He grinned at them confidently and once more they released him. He stood straight and steady for a moment and then he looked down at the ground. The grin froze on his face. He was alone on a high mountain, his stomach turned giddily within him and he was afraid, desperately unreasonably afraid. He lurched violently and the first shriek tore from him before they could hold him. 'I'm falling. Take it off! Take it off!'

They sat him in the chair with one swift movement.

'Take it off! I'm going to fall!' The terrified screams racked Waite as he tore at the straps that held the leg.

'It's off, Garry, you're safe. I'm holding you.' Waite took him to his chest and held him, trying to quieten him with the strength of his arms and the security of his own big body, but Garrick's terrified struggling and his shrieks continued.

'Take him to the bedroom, get him inside.' Ada spoke urgently and Waite ran with him, still holding him against his chest.

Then for the first time Garrick found his hiding-place. At the moment when his terror became too great to bear he felt something move inside his head, fluttering behind his eyes like the wings of a moth. His vision greyed as though he was in a mist bank. The mist thickened and blotted out all sight and sound. It was warm in the mist –

warm and safe. No one could touch him here for it wrapped and protected him. He was safe.

'I think he's asleep,' Waite whispered to his wife, but there was a puzzled expression in his voice. He looked carefully at the boy's face and listened to his breathing.

'It happened so quickly though – it isn't natural. And yet – and yet he looks all right.'

'Do you think we should call the doctor?' Ada asked.

'No.' Waite shook his head. 'I'll just cover him up and stay with him until he wakes.'

He woke in the early evening, sat up and smiled at them as though nothing had happened. Relaxed and shyly cheerful, he ate a big supper and no one mentioned the leg. It was almost as though Garrick had forgotten about it.

– 7 –

Sean came home on the following Friday afternoon. He had a black eye – not a fresh one; it was already turning green round the edges of the bruise. Sean was very reticent on the subject of how he had obtained it. He brought with him also a clutch of flycatchers' eggs which he gave to Garrick, a live red-lipped snake in a cardboard box which Ada immediately condemned to death despite Sean's impassioned speech in its defence, and a bow carved from M'senga wood which was, in Sean's opinion, the best wood for a bow.

His arrival wrought the usual change in the household of Theunis Kraal – more noise, more movement and more laughter.

There was a huge roast for dinner that evening, with potatoes baked in their jackets. These were Sean's favourite foods and he ate like a hungry python.

'Don't put so much in your mouth,' Waite remonstrated

from the head of the table, but there was a fondness in his voice. It was hard not to show favouritism with his sons. Sean accepted the rebuke in the spirit it was given. 'Pa, Frikkie Oberholster's bitch had pups this week, six of them.'

'No,' said Ada firmly.

'Gee, Ma, just one.'

'You heard your mother, Sean.' Sean poured gravy over his meat, cut a potato in half and lifted one piece to his mouth. It had been worth a try. He hadn't really expected them to agree.

'What did you learn this week?' Ada asked. This was a nasty question. Sean had learned as much as was necessary to avoid trouble – no more.

'Oh, lots of things,' he replied airily and then to change the subject. 'Have you finished Garry's new leg yet, Pa?'

There was a silence. Garrick's face went expressionless and he dropped his eyes to his plate. Sean put the other half of the potato in his mouth and spoke around it.

'If you have, me and Garry can go fishing up at the falls tomorrow.'

'Don't talk with your mouth full,' snapped Waite with unnecessary violence. 'You've got the manners of a pig.'

'Sorry, Pa,' Sean muttered. The rest of the meal passed in uneasy silence and as soon as it finished Sean escaped to the bedroom. Garry went with him hopping along the passage with one hand on the wall to balance himself.

'What's Pa so mad about?' Sean demanded resentfully as soon as they were alone.

'I don't know.' Garrick sat on the bed. 'Sometimes he just gets mad for nothing – you know that.'

Sean pulled his shirt off over his head, screwed it into a ball and threw it against the far wall.

'You'd better pick it up, else there'll be trouble,' Garrick warned mildly. Sean dropped his pants and kicked them after the shirt. This show of defiance put him in a better mood. He walked across and stood naked in front of Garrick.

'Look,' he said with pride. 'Hairs!'

Garrick inspected them. Indisputably they were hairs.

'There aren't very many.' Garrick couldn't disguise the envy in his voice.

'Well, I bet I've got more than you have,' Sean challenged. 'Let's count them.'

But Garrick knew himself to be an outright loser; he slipped off the bed and hopped across the room. Steadying himself against the wall he stooped and picked up Sean's discarded clothing, he brought it back and dropped it in the soiled linen basket beside the door. Sean watched him and it reminded him of his unanswered question.

'Has Pa finished your leg yet, Garry?'

Garry turned slowly, he swallowed and nodded once, a quick jerky movement.

'What's it like? Have you tried it yet?'

The fear was on Garrick again. He twisted his face from side to side as though seeking an escape. There were footsteps in the passage outside the door. Sean dived at his bed and snatching up his nightgown pulled it over his head as he slid between the sheets. Garrick was still standing beside the clothes basket when Waite Courtney came into the room. 'Come on, Garry, what's holding you up?'

Garrick hurried across to his bed and Waite looked at Sean. Sean grinned at him with all the charm of his good looks and Waite's face softened into a grin also. 'Nice to have you home again, boy.' It was impossible to be angry with Sean for long.

He reached out and took a handful of Sean's thick black hair. 'Now I don't want to hear any talking in here after the lamp's out – do you understand?'

He tugged Sean's head from side to side gently, embarrassed by the strength of his feeling for his son.

28

The next morning Waite Courtney rode back to the homestead for his breakfast when the sun was high. One of the grooms took his horse and led it away to the paddock and Waite stood in front of the saddle room and looked around him. He looked at the neat white posts of the paddock, at the well-swept yard, at his house filled with fine furniture. It was a good feeling to be rich – especially when you knew what it was like to be poor. Fifteen thousand acres of good grassland, as many cattle as the land would carry, gold in the bank. Waite smiled and started across the yard.

He heard Ada singing in the dairy.

> 'How rides the farmer
> Sit, sit, so
> Sit, sit, so – tra la
> The Capetown girls say
> Kiss me quick
> Kiss me quick – tra la.'

She had a clear sweet voice and Waite's smile broadened – it was a good feeling to be rich and to be in love. He stopped at the door of the dairy; because of the thick stone walls and heavy thatch it was cool and dark in the room. Ada stood with her back to the door, her body moving in time to the song and the turning of the butter churn. Waite watched her a moment, then he walked up behind her and put his arms around her waist.

Startled, she turned within his arms and he kissed her on the mouth. 'Good morning, my pretty maid.'

She relaxed against him. 'Good morning, sir,' she said.

'What's for breakfast?'

'Ah, what a romantic fool I married!' She sighed, 'Come along, let's go and see.'

She took off her apron, hung it behind the door, patted her hair into place and held her hand out to him. They walked hand-in-hand across the yard and into the kitchen. Waite sniffed loudly.

'Smells all right. Where are the boys?'

Joseph understood English though he could not speak it. He looked up from the stove.

'Nkosi, they are on the front veranda.'

Joseph had the typical moon-round face of the Zulu, when he smiled his teeth were big and white against the black of his skin.

'They are playing with Nkosizana Garry's wooden leg.'

Waite's face flushed. 'How did they find it?'

'Nkosizana Sean asked me where it was and I told him you had put it in the linen cupboard.'

'You bloody fool!' roared Waite. He dropped Ada's hand and ran. As he reached the lounge he heard Sean shout and immediately there was the sound of someone falling heavily on the veranda. He stopped in the middle of the lounge floor; he couldn't bear to go out and face Garrick's terror. He felt sick with dread and with his anger at Sean.

Then he heard Sean laugh. 'Get off me, man, don't just lie there.'

And then, incredibly, Garrick's voice. 'Sorry, it caught in the floor boards.'

Waite walked across to the window and looked out onto the veranda. Sean and Garrick lay in a heap together near the far end. Sean was still laughing and on Garrick's face was a set nervous smile. Sean scrambled up. 'Come on. Get up.'

He gave Garrick his hand and dragged him to his feet. They stood clinging to each other, Garrick balancing

30

precariously on his peg. 'I bet if it was me I could just walk easy as anything,' said Sean.

'I bet you couldn't, it's jolly difficult.'

Sean let go of him and stood back with his arms spread ready to catch him. 'Come on.'

Sean walked backwards in front of him and Garrick followed unsteadily, his arms flapping out sideways as he struggled to keep his balance, his face rigid with concentration. He reached the end of the veranda and caught onto the rail with both hands. This time he joined in Sean's laughter.

Waite became aware that Ada was standing beside him; he glanced sideways at her and her lips formed the words 'come away'. She took his arm.

– 9 –

At the end of June 1876 Garrick went back to school with Sean. It was almost four months since the shooting. Waite drove them. The road to Ladyburg was through open forest, two parallel tracks with the grass growing in between – it brushed the bottom of the buggy. The horses trotted in the tracks, their hooves silent on the thick powder dust. At the top of the first rise Waite slowed the horses and turned in his seat to look back at the homestead. The early sun gave the whitewashed walls of Theunis Kraal an orange glow and the lawns around the house were brilliant green. Everywhere else the grass was dry in the early winter and the leaves of the trees were dry also. The sun was not yet high enough to rob the veld of its colour and light it only with the flat white glare of midday. The leaves were golden and russet and red-brown, the same red-brown as the bunches of Afrikander cattle that grazed among the trees. Behind it all was the back-drop of the escarpment, striped like a zebra with the green-black bush that grew in its gullies.

'Look, there's a hoopoe, Sean.'

'Yeah, I saw it long ago. That's a male.'

The bird flew up from in front of the horses: chocolate and black and white wings, its head crested like an Etruscan helmet.

'How do you know?' challenged Garrick.

''Cause of the white in its wings.'

'They've all got white in their wings.'

'They haven't – only the males.'

'Well, all the ones I've seen got white in their wings,' said Garrick dubiously.

'Perhaps you've never seen a female. They're jolly rare. They don't come out of their nests much.'

Waite Courtney smiled and turned back in his seat. 'Garry's right, Sean, you can't tell the difference by their feathers. The male's a little bigger, that's all.'

'I told you,' said Garrick, brave under his father's protection.

'You know everything,' muttered Sean sarcastically. 'I suppose you read it in all those books, hey?'

Garrick smiled complacently. 'Look, there's the train.'

It was coming down the escarpment, dragging a long grey plume of smoke behind it. Waite started the horses into a trot. They went down to the concrete bridge over the Baboon Stroom.

'I saw a yellow fish.'

'It was a stick, I saw it too.'

The river was the boundary of Waite's land. They crossed the bridge and went up the other side. In front of them was Ladyburg. The train was running into the town past the cattle sale pens; it whistled and shot a puff of steam high into the air.

32

The town was spread out, each house padded around by its orchard and garden. A thirty-six ox team could turn in any of the wide streets. The houses were burnt brick or whitewashed, thatched or with corrugated-iron roofs painted green or dull red. The square was in the centre and the spire of the church was the hub of Ladyburg. The school was on the far side of town.

Waite trotted the horses along Main Street. There were a few people on the side walks; they moved with early morning stiffness beneath the flamboyant trees that lined the street and every one of them called a greeting to Waite. He waved his whip at the men and lifted his hat to the women, but not high enough to expose the bald dome of his head. In the centre of town the shops were open, and standing on long thin legs in front of his bank was David Pye. He was dressed in black like an undertaker.

'Morning, Waite.'

'Morning, David,' called Waite a little too heartily. It was not six months since he had paid off the last mortgage on Theunis Kraal and the memory of debt was too fresh in his mind; he felt as embarrassed as a newly released prisoner meeting the prison governor on the street.

'Can you come in and see me after you've dropped off your boys?'

'Have the coffee ready,' agreed Waite. It was well known that no one was ever offered coffee when they called on David Pye. They went on down the street, turned left at the far end of Church Square, passed the courthouse and down the dip to the school hostel.

There were half a dozen Scotch carts and four-wheelers standing in the yard. Small boys and girls swarmed over them unloading their luggage. Their fathers stood in a group at one end of the yard – brown-faced men, with carefully brushed beards, uncomfortable in their suits which still showed the creases of long hanging. These men lived too far out for their children to make the daily journey into school. Their land sprawled down to the banks of the Tugela or across the plateau halfway to Pietermaritzburg.

Waite stopped the buggy, climbed down and loosened the harness on his horses and Sean jumped from the outside seat to the ground and ran to the nearest bunch of boys. Waite walked across to the men; their ranks opened for him, they smiled their welcomes and in turn reached for his right hand. Garrick sat alone on the front seat of the buggy, his leg stuck out stiffly in front of him and his shoulders hunched as though he were trying to hide.

After a while Waite glanced back over his shoulder. He saw Garrick sitting alone and he made as if to go to him, but stopped immediately. His eyes quested among the swirl of small bodies until they found Sean. 'Sean.'

Sean paused in the middle of an animated discussion. 'Yes, Pa.'

'Give Garry a hand with his case.'

'Aw, gee, Pa – I'm talking.'

'Sean!' Waite scowled with both face and voice.

'All right, I'm going.' Sean hesitated a moment longer and then went back to the buggy.

'Come on, Garry. Pass the cases down.'

Garrick roused himself and climbed awkwardly over the back of the seat. He handed the luggage down to Sean who stacked it beside the wheel, then turned to the group that had followed him across.

'Karl, you carry that. Dennis, take the brown bag. Don't drop it, man, it's got four bottles of jam in it.' Sean issued his instructions.

'Come on, Garry.'

They started off towards the hostel and Garrick climbed down from the buggy and limped quickly after them.

'You know what, Sean?' said Karl loudly. 'Pa let me start using his rifle.'

Sean stopped dead, and then more with hope than conviction, 'He did not!'

'He did,' Karl said happily. Garrick caught up with them and they all stared at Karl.

'How many shots did you have?' asked someone in an awed voice.

Karl nearly said, 'Six' but changed it quickly.

'Oh, lots – as many as I wanted.'

'You'll get gun-shy – my Pa says if you start too soon you'll never be a good shot.'

'I never missed once,' flashed Karl.

'Come on,' said Sean and started off once more – he had never been so jealous in his life. Karl hurried after him.

'I bet you've never shot with a rifle, Sean, I bet you haven't, hey?' Sean smiled mysteriously while he searched for some new topic; he could see that Karl was going to kick the subject to death.

From the veranda of the hostel a girl ran to meet him.

'It's Anna,' said Garrick.

She had long brown legs, skinny; her skirts fussed about them as she ran. Her hair was black, her face was small with a pointed chin. 'Hello, Sean.'

Sean grunted. She fell in beside him, skipping to keep pace with him.

'Did you have a nice holiday?'

Sean ignored her, always coming and trying to talk to him, even when his friends were watching.

'I've got a whole tin of shortbread, Sean. Would you like some?' There was a flash of interest in Sean's eyes; he half turned his head towards her, for Mrs Van Essen's shortbread was rightly famous throughout the district, but he caught himself and kept grimly on towards the hostel.

35

'Can I sit next to you in class this term, Sean?'

Sean turned furiously on her. 'No, you can't. Now go away – I'm busy.'

He went up the steps. Anna stood at the bottom; she looked as though she was going to cry and Garrick stopped shyly beside her.

'You can sit next to me if you like,' he said softly.

She glanced at him, looking down at his leg. The tears cleared and she giggled. She was pretty. She leaned towards him.

'Peg-leg,' she said and giggled again. Garrick blushed so vividly, and suddenly his eyes watered. Anna put both hands to her mouth and giggled through them, then she turned and ran to join her friends in front of the girls' section of the hostel. Still blushing, Garrick went up the steps after Sean; he steadied himself on the banisters.

Fräulein stood at the door of the boys' dormitory. Her steel-rimmed spectacles and the iron grey of her hair gave her face an exaggerated severity, but this was relieved by the smile with which she recognized Sean.

'Ah, my Sean, you have come.' What she actually said was, 'Ach, mein Sean, you haf gom.'

'Hello, Fräulein.' Sean gave her his number one very best smile.

'Again you have grown,' Fräulein measured him with her eyes. 'All the time you grow, already you are the biggest boy in the school.'

Sean watched her warily, ready to take evasive action if she attempted to embrace him as she did sometimes when she could no longer contain her feelings. Sean's blend of charm, good looks and arrogance had completely captured her Teutonic heart.

'Quickly, you must unpack. School is just now starting.' She turned her attention to her other charges and Sean, with relief, led his men through into the dormitory.

'Pa says that next weekend I can use his rifle for hunting, not just targets,' Karl steered the conversation back.

'Dennis, put Garry's case on his bed.' Sean pretended not to hear.

There were thirty beds arranged along the walls, each with a locker beside it. The room was as neat and cheerless as a prison or a school. At the far end a group of five or six boys sat talking. They looked up as Sean came in but no greetings were exchanged – they were the opposition.

Sean sat down on his bed and bounced experimentally. It was hard as a plank. Garrick's peg thumped as he walked down the dormitory and Ronny Pye, the leader of the opposition, whispered something to his friends and they all laughed, watching Garrick. Garrick blushed again and sat down quickly on his bed to hide his leg.

'I guess I'll shoot duiker first before Pa lets me shoot kudu or bushbuck,' Karl stated and Sean frowned.

'What's the new teacher like?' he asked.

'He looks all right,' one of the others answered. 'Jimmy and I saw him at the station yesterday.'

'He's thin and got a moustache.'

'He doesn't smile much.'

'I suppose next holiday Pa will take me shooting across the Tugela,' Karl said aggressively.

'I hope he's not too keen on spelling and things,' Sean declared. 'I hope he doesn't start all that decimal business again, like old Lizard did.'

There was a round of agreement and then Garrick made his first contribution. 'Decimals are easy.'

There was a silence while they all looked at him.

'I might even shoot a lion,' said Karl.

There was a single schoolroom to accommodate the youngest upwards of both sexes. Double desks; on the walls a few maps, a large set of multiplication tables and a picture of Queen Victoria. From the dais Mr Anthony Clark surveyed his new pupils. There was a hushed anticipation; one of the girls giggled nervously and Mr Clark's eyes sought the sound, but it stopped before he found it.

'It is my unfortunate duty to attempt your education,' he announced. He wasn't joking. Long ago his sense of vocation had been swamped by an intense dislike for the young: now he taught only for the salary.

'It is your no more pleasant duty to submit to this with all the fortitude you can muster,' he went on, looking with distaste at their shining faces.

'What's he saying?' whispered Sean without moving his lips.

'Shh,' said Garrick.

Mr Clark's eyes swivelled quickly and rested on Garrick. He walked slowly down the aisle between the desks and stopped beside him; he took a little of the hair that grew at Garrick's temple between his thumb and his forefinger and jerked it upwards. Garrick squeaked and Mr Clark returned slowly to his dais.

'We will now proceed. Standard Ones kindly open your spelling books at page one. Standard Twos turn to page fifteen . . .' He went on allocating their work.

'Did he hurt you?' breathed Sean. Garrick nodded almost imperceptibly and Sean conceived an immediate and intense hatred for the man. He stared at him.

Mr Clark was a little over thirty years old – thin, and his tight three-piece suit emphasized this fact. He had a pale face made sad by his drooping moustache, and his nose was upturned to such a degree that his nostrils were exposed; they pointed out of his face like the muzzle of a double-barrelled shotgun. He lifted his head from the list he held in his hand and aimed his nostrils straight at Sean. For a second they stared at each other.

'Trouble,' thought Mr Clark; he could pick them unerringly. 'Break him before he gets out of control.'

'You, boy, what's your name?'

Sean turned elaborately and looked over his shoulder. When he turned back there was a little colour in Mr Clark's cheeks. 'Stand up.'

'Who, me?'

'Yes, you.'

Sean stood.

'What's your name?'

'Courtney.'

'Sir!'

'Courtney, sir.'

They looked at each other. Mr Clark waited for Sean to drop his eyes but he didn't.

'Big trouble, much bigger than I thought,' he decided and said aloud, 'All right, sit down.'

There was an almost audible relaxation of tension in the room. Sean could sense the respect of the others around him; they were proud of the way he had carried it off. He felt a touch on his shoulder. It was Anna, the seat behind him was as close as she could sit to him. Ordinarily her presumption would have annoyed him, but now that small touch on his shoulder added to his glow of self-satisfaction.

An hour passed slowly for Sean. He drew a picture of a rifle in the margin of his spelling book then rubbed it out carefully; he watched Garrick for a while until his brother's absorption with his work irritated him.

'Swot,' he whispered, but Garrick ignored him.

Sean was bored. He shifted restlessly in his seat and looked at the back of Karl's neck – there was a ripe pimple on it. He picked up his ruler to prod it. Before he could do so Karl lifted his hand as if to scratch his shoulder but there was a scrap of paper between his fingers. Sean put down the ruler and surreptitiously reached for the note. He held it in his lap, on it was written one word.

'Mosquitoes.'

Sean grinned. Sean's imitation of a mosquito was one of the many reasons why the previous schoolmaster had resigned. For six months old Lizard had believed that there were mosquitoes in the room – then for the next six months he had known there were not. He had tried every ruse he could think of to catch the culprit, and in the end it had got him. Every time the monotonous hum began the tic in the corner of his mouth became more noticeable.

Now Sean cleared his throat and started to hum. Instantly the room was tense with suppressed laughter. Every head, including Sean's, was bent studiously over a book. Mr Clark's hand hesitated in writing on the black-board but then went on again evenly.

It was a clever imitation; by lowering and raising the volume Sean gave the effect of an insect moving about the room. A slight trembling at his throat was the only sign that he was responsible.

Mr Clark finished writing and turned to face the room. Sean did not make the mistake of stopping, he allowed the mosquito to fly a little longer before settling.

Mr Clark left his dais and walked down the row of desks furthest from Sean. Once or twice he paused to check the work of one of his pupils. He reached the back of the room and moved across to Sean's row. He stopped at Anna's desk.

'It is unnecessary to loop your L's like that,' he told her. 'Let me show you.' He took her pencil and wrote, 'You see what I mean. To show off when writing is as bad as showing off in your everyday behaviour.'

He handed her back her pencil and then pivoting on one foot he hit Sean a mighty crack across the side of the head with his open hand. Sean's head was knocked sideways and the sound of the blow was very loud in the quiet room.

'There was a mosquito sitting on your ear,' said Mr Clark.

– 11 –

In the following two years Sean and Garrick made the change from child to young manhood. It was like riding a strong current, being swept with speed along the river of life.

There were parts of the river that flowed steadily:

Ada was one of these. Always understanding, with the ability to give her understanding expression, unchanging in her love for her husband and the family she had taken as her own.

Waite was another. A little more grey in his hair but big as ever in body, laugh and fortune.

There were parts of the river that ran faster:

Garrick's reliance on Sean. He needed him more strongly each month that passed, for Sean was his shield. If Sean was not there to protect him when he was threatened, then he used his final refuge: he crawled back into himself, into the warm dark mists of his mind.

They went to steal peaches: the twins, Karl, Dennis and two others. There was a thick hedge around Mr Pye's orchard and the peaches that grew on the other side of it were as big as a man's fist. They were sweet as honey but tasted even sweeter when taken on the plunder account. You reached the orchard through a plantation of wattle trees.

'Don't take too many off one tree!' Sean ordered. 'Old Pye will notice it as sure as anything.'

They came to the hedge and Sean found the hole.

'Garry, you stay here and keep cats for us. If anyone comes give a whistle.' Garrick tried not to show his relief, he had no stomach for the expedition.

Sean went on. 'We'll pass the peaches out to you – and don't eat any until we're finished.'

'Why doesn't he come with us?' asked Karl.

''Cause he can't run, that's why. If he gets caught they'll know who the rest of us are for sure and we'll all get it.'

Karl was satisfied. Sean went down on his hands and knees and crawled into the hole in the hedge and one at a time the others followed him until Garrick was left alone.

He stood close to the hedge, drawing comfort from its protecting bulk. The minutes dragged by and Garrick fidgeted nervously – they were taking an awfully long time.

Suddenly there were voices, someone was coming through the plantation towards him. Panic beat up inside him and he shrank back into the hedge, trying to hide; the idea of giving a warning never even entered his head.

The voices were closer and then through the trees he recognized Ronny Pye: with him were two of his friends. Each of them was armed with a slingshot and they walked with their heads thrown back, searching the trees for birds.

For a time it seemed they would not notice Garrick in the hedge; but then, when they had almost passed, Ronny turned his head and saw him. They stared at each other, ten paces apart, Garrick crouched against the hedge and Ronny's expression of surprise slowly changing to one of cunning. He looked around quickly, to make sure that Sean was not there.

'It's old Hobble-dee-hoy,' he announced and his friends came back and stood on each side of him.

'What're you doing, Peg-leg?'

'Rats got your tongue, Peg-leg?'

'No, termites got his leg!' – laughter aimed to hurt.

'Talk to us, Peg-leg.' Ronny Pye had ears that stood out on each side of his head like a pair of fans. He was small for his age which made him vicious and his hair was ginger.

'Come on. Talk to us, Peg-leg.'

Garrick moistened his lips with his tongue, already there were tears in his eyes.

'Hey, Ronny, make him walk for us, like this.' One of the others gave a graphic imitation of Garrick's limp. Again laughter, louder now, more confident and they closed in on him. 'Show us how you walk.'

Garrick swung his head from side to side searching for an escape.

'Your brother's not here,' crowed Ronny. 'No good looking for him, Peg-leg.'

He caught a hold of Garrick's shirt and pulled him out of the hedge.

'Show us how you walk.'

Garrick plucked ineffectually at Ronny's hand.

'Leave me, I'll tell Sean. I'll tell Sean unless you leave me.'

'All right, I'll leave you,' agreed Ronny and with both hands shoved him in the chest. 'Don't come my way – go that way!' Garrick stumbled backwards.

One of the others was ready for him. 'Don't come my way – go that way!' and pushed him in the back. They formed a ring around him and kept him staggering between them.

'Go that way!'

43

'Go that way!'

The tears were streaked down his cheeks now. 'Please, please stop.'

'Please, please,' they mimicked him.

Then, with a rush of relief, Garrick felt the fluttering start behind his eyes – their faces dimmed, he hardly felt their hands upon him. He fell and his face hit the ground, but there was no pain. Two of them stooped over him to lift him, and there was dirt mixed with the tears on his cheeks.

Sean came through the hedge behind them; the front of his shirt bulged with peaches. For a second he crouched on his hands and knees while he took in what was happening, then he came out of his crouch at a run. Ronny heard him, dropped Garrick and turned.

'You've been pinching Pa's peaches,' he shouted. 'I'll tell—'

Sean's fist hit him on the nose and he sat down. Sean swung towards the other two but they were already running, he chased them a few paces and then came back for Ronny, but he was too late. Ronny was dodging away between the trees holding his face and his nose was bleeding onto his shirt.

'Are you all right, Garry?' Sean knelt beside him, trying to wipe the dirt off his face with a grubby handkerchief. Sean helped him to his feet, and Garrick stood swaying slightly with his eyes open but a remote and vacant smile on his lips.

There were landmarks along the course of the river. Some of them small as a pile of rocks in shallow water:

Waite Courtney looked at Sean across the breakfast table at Theunis Kraal. The fork-load of egg and grilled gammon stopped on the way to his mouth.

'Turn your face towards the window,' he commanded suspiciously. Sean obeyed. 'What the hell is that on your face?'

'What?' Sean ran his hand over his cheek.

'When did you last bath?'

'Don't be silly, my dear.' Ada touched his leg under the table. 'It isn't dirt – it's whiskers.'

'Whiskers, are they?' Waite peered closely at Sean and started to grin, he opened his mouth to speak and Ada knew instantly that he was going to make a joke – one of those ponderous jokes of his, as subtle as an enraged dinosaur, that would wound Sean deep in his half-formed manhood. Quickly she cut in, 'I think you should buy him a razor, don't you, Waite?'

Waite lost the thread of his joke, he grunted and put the egg into his mouth.

'I don't want to cut them,' said Sean and flushed scarlet.

'They'll grow quicker if you shave them a bit at first,' Ada told him.

Across the table from her Garrick fingered his jowls wistfully.

Some of the landmarks were big as headlands:

Waite fetched them from school at the beginning of the December holidays. In the confusion of loading their cases onto the buggy and shouting farewells to Fräulein and to their friends, some of whom they would not see for another six weeks, the twins did not notice that Waite was acting strangely.

It was only later when the horses were heading for home at twice their normal speed that Sean asked, 'What's the hurry, Pa?'

'You'll see,' said Waite, and both Garrick and Sean looked at him with sudden interest. It had been an idle

45

question of Sean's but Waite's answer had them immediately intrigued. Waite grinned at the bombardment of questions but he kept his answers vague. He was enjoying himself. By the time they reached Theunis Kraal the twins were in a frenzy of curiosity.

Waite pulled the horses up in front of the house and one of the grooms ran to take the reins. Ada was waiting on the veranda and Sean jumped down and ran up the steps to her. He kissed her quickly. 'What's happening?' he pleaded. 'Pa won't tell us but we know it's something.'

Garrick hurried up the steps also. 'Go on, tell us.' He caught hold of her arm and tugged it.

'I don't know what you're talking about,' Ada laughed. 'You'd better ask your father again.'

Waite climbed up after them, put one arm around Ada's waist and squeezed her.

'I don't know where they got this idea from,' said Waite, 'but why not tell them to go and have a look in their bedroom? They might as well have their Christmas presents a bit earlier this year.'

Sean beat Garrick to the lounge and was far in the lead by the time he reached the door of their bedroom.

'Wait for me,' called Garrick desperately. 'Please wait for me.'

Sean stopped in the doorway.

'Jesus Christ,' he whispered – they were the strongest words he knew. Garrick came up behind him and together they stared at the pair of leather cases that lay on the table in the middle of the room – long flat cases, heavy polished leather with the corners bound in brass.

'Rifles!' said Sean. He walked slowly to the table as though he were stalking the cases, expecting them at any moment to vanish.

'Look!' Sean reached out to touch with one finger the

46

gold lettering stamped into the lid of the nearest case. 'Our names on them even.'

He sprung the locks and lifted the lid. In a nest of green baize, perfumed with gun oil, glistened a poem in steel and wood.

'Jesus Christ,' said Sean again. Then he looked over his shoulder at Garrick. 'Aren't you going to open yours?'

Garrick limped up to the table trying to hide his disappointment: he had wanted a set of Dickens so badly.

In the river there were whirlpools:

The last week of the Christmas holidays and Garrick was in bed with one of his colds. Waite Courtney had gone to Pietermaritzburg for a meeting of the Beef Growers' Association and there was very little work to do on the farm that day. After Sean had dosed the sick cattle in the sanatorium paddock and ridden an inspection around the south section he returned to the homestead and spent an hour talking to the stableboys, then he drifted up to the house. Garry was asleep and Ada was in the dairy making butter. He asked for and got an early lunch from Joseph and ate it standing in the kitchen. While he ate he thought over the problem of how to fill the afternoon. He weighed the alternatives carefully. Take the rifle and try for duiker along the edge of the escarpment or ride to the pools above the White Falls and fish for eels. He was still undecided after he had finished eating so he crossed the yard and looked into the cool dimness of the dairy.

Ada smiled at him across the churn. 'Hello, Sean, I suppose you want your lunch.'

'Joseph gave it to me already, thanks, Ma.'

'Joseph has already given it to me,' Ada corrected mildly. Sean repeated it after her and sniffed the dairy smell – he liked the cheesy warmth of new butter and the tang of the cow dung smeared on the earth floor.

'What are you going to do this afternoon?'

'I came to ask you if you wanted venison or eels – I don't know if I want to go fishing or shooting.'

'Eels would be nice – we could jelly them and have them for dinner tomorrow when your father comes home.'

'I'll get you a bucket full.'

He saddled the pony, hung his tin of worms on the saddle and with his pole over his shoulder rode towards Ladyburg. He crossed the Baboon Stroom bridge and turned off the road to follow the stream up to the falls. As he skirted the wattle plantation below the Van Essens' place he realized he had made a mistake in picking this route. Anna, with her skirts held up to her knees, came pelting out from among the trees. Sean kicked the pony into a trot and looked straight ahead.

'Sean – hey, Sean.'

She was ahead of him, running to intercept him; there was no chance of evading her so he stopped the pony.

'Hello, Sean.' She was panting and her face was flushed.

'Hello,' he gruffed.

'Where are you going?'

'There and back to see how far it is.'

'You're going fishing – may I come with you?' She smiled appealingly. Her teeth were small and white.

'No, you talk too much; you'll frighten the fish.'

He started the pony.

'Please, I'll be quiet; honest I will.' She was running next to him.

'No.' He flicked the reins and pulled away from her. He rode for a hundred yards then looked round and she was still following with her black hair streaming out behind her. He stopped the pony and she caught up with him.

'I knew you'd stop,' she told him through her gasps.

'Will you go home? I don't want you following me.'

'I'll be quiet as anything – honest I will.'

He knew she'd follow him right up to the top of the escarpment and he gave in. 'All right, but if you say a word, just one single word, I'll send you home.'

'I promise – help me up, please.'

He dragged her onto the pony's rump and she sat sideways with her arms round his waist. They climbed the escarpment. The path ran close beside the White Falls and they could feel the spray blowing off them fine as mist. Anna kept her promise until she was sure they'd gone too far for Sean to send her back alone. She started talking again. When she wanted an answer from him, which wasn't very often, she squeezed his waist and Sean grunted. Sean knee-haltered the pony, and left him among the trees above the pools. He hid his saddle and bridle in an ant-bear hole and they walked down through the reeds to the water. Anna ran ahead of him and when he came out on to the sandbank she was throwing pebbles into the pool.

'Hey, stop that! You'll frighten the fish,' Sean shouted.

'Oh. I'm sorry. I forgot.'

She sat down and wriggled her bare toes into the sand. Sean baited his hook and lobbed it out into the green water – the current drifted his float in a wide circle under the far bank and they both watched it solemnly.

'It doesn't seem as though there are any fish here,' Anna said.

'You've got to be patient – you can't expect to catch one right away.'

Anna drew patterns in the sand with her toes and five minutes passed slowly. 'Sean—'

'Ssh!'

Another five minutes.

'Fishing's a silly old thing.'

'Nobody asked you to come,' Sean told her.

'It's hot here!' Sean didn't answer.

The high reed beds shut out any breeze and the white sand threw the sun's heat back at them. Anna stood up and wandered restlessly across the sand to the edge of the reeds. She picked a handful of the long spear-shaped leaves and plaited them together.

'I'm bored,' she announced.

'Well, go home then.'

'And I'm hot.'

Sean pulled his line in, inspected the worms and cast them out again. Anna stuck her tongue out at his back.

'Let's have a swim,' she suggested.

Sean ignored her. He stuck the butt of his rod into the sand, pulled his hat down to shield his eyes from the glare and leaned back on his elbows with his legs stretched out in front of him. He could hear the sand crunching as she moved and then there was another silence. He started to worry about what she was doing, but if he looked around it would be a show of weakness.

'Girls!' he thought bitterly.

There was the sound of running feet just behind him. He sat up quickly and started to turn. Her white body flashed past him and hit the water, with a smack like a rising trout. Sean jumped up. 'Hey, what're you doing?'

'I'm swimming,' laughed Anna, waist-deep in green water, with her hair slicked wetly down her shoulders and over her breasts. Sean looked at those breasts, white as the flesh of an apple and nippled in dark pink, almost red. Anna dropped onto her back and kicked the water white.

'*Voet sak*, little fishes! Scat, little fishes,' she gurgled.

'Hey, you mustn't do that,' Sean said half-heartedly. He wanted her to stand up again, those breasts gave him a strange tight feeling in his stomach, but Anna knelt with the water up to her chin. He could see them through the water. He wanted her to stand up.

'It's lovely! Why don't you come in?' She rolled on her stomach and ducked her head under the water; the twin ovals of her bottom broke the surface and Sean's stomach tightened again.

'Are you coming in?' she demanded, rubbing the water out of her eyes with both hands. Sean stood bewildered – within a few seconds his feelings towards her had undergone a major revolution. He wanted very much to be in the water with all those mysterious white bulges – but he was shy.

'You're scared! Come on, I give you guts to come in.' She teased him. The challenge pricked him.

'I'm not scared.'

'Well, come on then.'

He hesitated a few seconds longer, then he threw off his hat and unbuttoned his shirt. He turned his back on her while he dropped his pants then spun round and dived into the pool, thankful for the cover it gave him. His head came out and Anna pushed it under again. He groped and caught her legs, straightened up and threw her on her back. He dragged her towards the shallows, where the water wouldn't cover her. She was thrashing her arms to keep her head out and screaming delightedly. Sean's heels snagged a rock and he fell, letting go of her; before he could recover she had leapt on him and straddled his back. He could have thrown her off, but he liked the feel of her flesh on his – warm through the cool water, slippery with wetness. She picked up a handful of sand and rubbed it into his hair. Sean struggled gently. She threw her arms round his neck and he could feel the whole length of her body along his back. The tightness in his stomach moved up into his chest and he wanted to hold her. He rolled over and reached for her but she twisted out of his hands and dived back into the deep again. Sean splashed after her but she kept out of his reach, laughing at him.

At last they faced each other, still chin deep, and Sean was getting angry. He wanted to hold her. She saw the change of his mood and she waded to the bank, walked to his clothes and picked up his shirt. She dried her face on it, standing naked and unashamed – she had too many brothers for modesty. Sean watched the way her breasts changed shape as she lifted her arms, he looked at the lines of her body and saw that her once skinny legs had filled out; her thighs touched each other all the way up to the base of her belly and there she wore the dark triangular badge of woman-hood. She spread the shirt out on the sand and sat down upon it, then she looked at him.

'Are you coming out?'

He came out awkwardly, covering himself with his hands. Anna moved over on the shirt. 'You can sit down, if you like.'

He sat hurriedly and drew his knees up under his chin. He watched her from the corner of his eye. There were little goose-pimples round her nipples from the cold water. She was aware that he was watching her and she pulled back her shoulders, enjoying it. Sean felt bewildered again – she was so clearly in control now. Before she had been someone to growl at but now she was giving the orders and he was obeying.

'You've got hairs on your chest,' Anna said, turning to look at him. Sparse and silky though they were, Sean was glad that he had them. He straightened out his legs.

'And you're much bigger there than Frikkie.' Sean tried to pull up his knees again but she put her hand on his leg and stopped him.

'Can I touch you?'

Sean tried to speak but his throat had closed and no sound came through it. Anna did not wait for an answer.

'Oh, look! It's getting all cheeky – just like Caribou's.'

Caribou was Mr Van Essen's stallion.

'I always know when Pa is going to let Caribou service a mare, he tells me to go and visit Aunt Lettie. I just hide in the plantation. You can see the paddock jolly well from the plantation.'

Anna's hand was soft and restless, Sean could think of nothing else.

'Do you know that people service, just like horses do?' she asked.

Sean nodded, he had attended the biology classes conducted by Messrs Daffel and Company in the school latrines. They were quiet for a while, then Anna whispered.

'Sean, would you service me?'

'I don't know how,' croaked Sean.

'I bet horses don't either the first time, nor people for that matter,' Anna said. 'We could find out.'

They rode home in the early evening, Anna sitting up behind Sean, her arms tight round his waist and the side of her face pressed between his shoulders. He dropped her at the back of the plantation.

'I'll see you at school on Monday,' she said and turned to go.

'Anna—'

'Yes?'

'Is it still sore?'

'No,' and then, after a moment's thought, 'it feels nice.'

She turned and ran into the wattle trees.

Sean rode slowly home. He was empty inside; it was a sad feeling and it puzzled him.

'Where are the fish?' asked Ada.

'They weren't biting.'

'Not even one?'

Sean shook his head and crossed the kitchen.

'Sean.'

53

'Yes, Ma.'

'Is something wrong?'

'No' – quick denial – 'No, I'm fine.' He slipped into the passage.

Garrick was sitting up in bed. The skin around his nostrils was inflamed and chapped; he lowered the book he was reading and smiled at Sean as he came into the room. Sean went to his own bed and sat on it.

'Where have you been?' Garrick's voice was thick with cold.

'Up at the pools above the falls.'

'Fishing?'

Sean didn't answer, he leaned forward on the bed with his elbows on his knees. 'I met Anna, she came with me.'

Garrick's interest quickened at the mention of her name and he watched Sean's face. Sean still had that slightly puzzled expression.

'Garry,' he hesitated; he had to talk about it. 'Garry, I screwed Anna.'

Garrick drew in his breath with a small hiss. He went very pale, only his nose was still red and sore-looking.

'I mean,' Sean spoke slowly as though he were trying to explain it to himself, 'I mean really screwed her, just like we've talked about. Just like . . .' He made a helpless gesture with his hands, unable to find the words. Then he lay back on the bed.

'Did she let you?' Garrick's voice was almost a whisper.

'She asked me to,' Sean said. 'It was slippery – sort of warm and slippery.'

And then later, long after the lamp was out and they were both in bed, Sean heard Garrick's soft movements in the darkness. He listened for a while until he was certain.

'Garry!' He accused him loudly.

'I wasn't, I wasn't.'

'You know what Pa told us. Your teeth will fall out and you'll go mad.'

'I wasn't, I wasn't.' Garrick's voice was choked with his cold and his tears.

'I heard you,' said Sean.

'I was just scratching my leg. Honestly, honestly, I was.'

And at the end the river plunged over the last waterfall and swept them into the sea of manhood.

Mr Clark had not been able to break Sean. He had provoked instead a bitter contest in which he knew himself to be slowly losing ground, and now he was afraid of Sean. He no longer made Sean stand, for Sean was as tall as he was. The contest had been on for two years; they had explored each other's weaknesses and knew how to exploit them.

Mr Clark could not bear the sound of anyone sniffing; perhaps subconsciously he took it as mockery of his own deformed nose. Sean had a repertoire that varied from a barely audible connoisseur testing-the-bouquet-of-brandy sniff to a loud hawking in the back of his throat.

'Sorry, sir, I can't help it. I've got a bit of a cold.'

But then, to even the score, Mr Clark had realized that Sean was vulnerable through Garrick. Hurt Garrick even a little and you were inflicting almost unbearable agony on Sean.

It had been a bad week for Mr Clark. His liver, weakened by persistent bouts of malaria, had been troubling him. He had suffered with a bilious headache for three days now; there had been unpleasantness with the Town Council about the terms on which his contract was to be renewed; Sean had been in good sniffing form the day before and Mr Clark had had about as much as he was prepared to take.

He came into the schoolroom and took his place on the dais; he let his eyes move slowly over his pupils until they came to Sean.

'Just let him start,' thought Mr Clark. 'Just let him start today and I'll kill him.'

The seating had been rearranged in the last two years. Sean and Garrick had been separated and Garrick was now at the front of the room where Mr Clark could reach him easily. Sean was near the back.

'English Readers,' said Mr Clark. 'Standard Ones turn to page five. Standard Twos turn to—'

Garrick sniffed wetly, hayfever again.

Mr Clark shut his book with a snap.

'Damn you!' he said softly, and then, his voice rising, 'Damn you!' Now he was shaking with rage, the edges of his nostrils were white and flared open.

He came down from the dais to Garrick's desk. 'Damn you! Damn you – you bloody little cripple,' he screamed and hit Garrick across the face with his open hand. Garrick cupped both hands over his cheek and stared at him.

'You dirty little swine,' Mr Clark mouthed at him. 'Now you're starting it too.'

He caught a handful of Garrick's hair and pulled his head down so that his forehead hit the top of the desk. 'I'll teach you. By God, I'll teach you.'

'I'll show you.' Bump.

'I'll teach you.' Bump.

It took Sean that long to reach them. He grabbed Mr Clark's arm and pulled him backwards. 'Leave him alone! He didn't do anything!'

Mr Clark saw Sean's face in front of him – he was passed all reason – the face that had tormented him for two long years. He bunched his fist and lashed out at it.

Sean staggered back from the blow, the sting of it made

his eyes water. For a second he lay sprawled across one of the desks, watching Clark and then he growled.

The sound sobered Clark, he backed away but only two paces before Sean was on him. Hitting with both hands, grunting with each punch, Sean drove him against the blackboard. Clark tried to break away but Sean caught the collar of his shirt and dragged him back – the collar tore half loose in his hand and Sean hit him again. Clark slid down the wall until he was sitting against it and Sean stood panting over him.

'Get out,' said Clark. His teeth were stained pink by the blood in his mouth and a little of it spilled out onto his lips. His collar stood up at a jaunty angle under one ear.

There was no sound in the room except Sean's breathing.

'Get out,' said Clark again and the anger drained out of Sean, leaving him trembling with reaction. He walked to the door.

'You too,' Clark pointed at Garrick. 'Get out and don't come back!'

'Come on, Garry,' said Sean.

Garrick stood up from his desk and limped across to Sean and together they went out into the school yard.

'What are we going to do now?' There was a big red lump on Garrick's forehead.

'I suppose we'd better go home.'

'What about our things?' asked Garrick.

'We can't carry all that – we'll have to send for them later. Come on.'

They walked out through the town and along the road to the farm. They had almost reached the bridge on the Baboon Stroom before either of them spoke again.

'What do you reckon Pa will do?' asked Garrick. He was only putting into words the problem that had occupied them both since they left the school.

'Well, whatever he does, it was worth it.' Sean grinned. 'Did you see me clobber him, hey? Smackeroo – right in the chops.'

'You shouldn't have done it, Sean. Pa's going to kill us. Me too and I didn't do anything.'

'You sniffed,' Sean reminded him.

They reached the bridge and leaned over the parapet side by side to watch the water.

'How's your leg?' asked Sean.

'It's sore – I think we should rest a bit.'

'All right, if you say so,' Sean agreed.

There was a long silence, then, 'I wish you hadn't done it, Sean.'

'Well, wishing isn't going to help. Old Nose-Holes is as punched up as he'll ever be and all we can do is think of something to tell Pa.'

'He hit me,' said Garrick. 'He might have killed me.'

'Yes,' agreed Sean righteously, 'and he hit me too.'

They thought about it for a while.

'Perhaps we should just go away,' suggested Garrick.

'You mean without telling Pa?' The idea had attraction.

'Yeah, we could go to sea or something,' Garrick brightened.

'You'd get seasick, you even get sick in a train.'

Once more they applied their minds to the problem. Then Sean looked at Garrick, Garrick looked at Sean and as though by agreement they straightened up and started off once more for Theunis Kraal.

Ada was in front of the house. She had on a wide-brimmed straw hat that kept her face in shadow and over one arm she carried a basket of flowers. Busy with her garden, she didn't notice them until they were halfway across the lawn and when she did she stood motionless. She was steeling herself, trying to get her emotions under control; from experience she had learned to expect the worst from her stepsons and be thankful when it wasn't as bad as that.

As they came towards her they lost momentum and finally halted like a pair of clockwork toys running down.

'Hello,' said Ada.

'Hello,' they answered her together.

Garrick fumbled in his pocket, drew out a handkerchief and blew his nose. Sean stared up at the steep Dutch-gabled roof of Theunis Kraal as though he had never seen it before.

'Yes?' Ada kept her voice calm.

'Mr Clark said we were to go home,' announced Garrick.

'Why?' Ada's calm was starting to crack.

'Well—' Garrick glanced at Sean for support. Sean's attention was still riveted on the roof.

'Well . . . You see Sean sort of punched him in the head until he fell down. I didn't do anything.'

Ada moaned softly, 'Oh, no!' She took a deep breath. 'All right. Start at the beginning and give me the whole story.'

They told it in relays, a garbled rush of words, interrupting each other and arguing over the details. When they had finished Ada said, 'You better go to your room. Your father is working in the home section today and he'll be back for his lunch soon. I'll try and prepare him a little.'

The room had the cheery atmosphere of a condemned cell.

'How much do you reckon he'll give us?' asked Garrick.

'I reckon until he gets tired, then he'll rest and give us some more,' Sean answered.

They heard Waite's horse come into the yard. He said something to the stable boy and they heard him laugh; the kitchen door slammed and there was half a minute of suspense before they heard Waite roar. Garrick jumped nervously.

For another ten minutes they could hear Waite and Ada

talking in the kitchen, the alternate rumble and soothing murmur. Then the tap of Ada's feet along the passage and she came into the room.

'Your father wants to see you – he's in the study.'

Waite stood in front of the fireplace. His beard was powdered with dust and his forehead as corrugated as a ploughed land with the force of his scowl.

'Come in,' he bellowed when Sean knocked and they filed in and stood in front of him. Waite slapped his riding-whip against his leg and the dust puffed out of his breeches.

'Come here,' he said to Garrick and took a handful of his hair. He twisted Garrick's face up and looked at the bruise on his forehead.

'Hmm,' he said. He let go of Garrick's hair and it stood up in a tuft. He threw the riding-whip on the stinkwood desk.

'Come here,' he said to Sean. 'Hold out your hands – no, palms down.'

The skin on both hands was broken and one knuckle was swollen and puffy looking.

'Hmm,' he said again. He turned to the shelf beside the fireplace, took a pipe out of the rack and filled it from the stone jar of tobacco.

'You're a pair of bloody fools,' he said, 'but I'll take a chance and start you on five shillings a week all found. Go and get your lunch . . . we've got work to do this afternoon.'

They stared at him a moment in disbelief and then back towards the door.

'Sean.' Sean stopped, he knew it was too good to be true. 'Where did you hit him?'

'All over, Pa, anywhere I could reach.'

'That's no good,' Waite said. 'You must go for the side of his head – here,' he tapped the point of his jaw with his pipe, 'and keep your fists closed tight or you'll break every finger in your hands before you're much older.'

'Yes, Pa.'

The door closed softly behind him and Waite allowed himself to grin.

'They've had enough book learning anyway,' he said aloud and struck a match to his pipe; when it was drawing evenly he blew out smoke.

'Christ, I wish I could have watched it. That little penpusher will know better than to tangle with my boy again.'

– 12 –

Now Sean had a course along which to race. He was born to run and Waite Courtney led him out of the stall in which he had fretted and gave him his lead. Sean ran, unsure of the prize, unsure of the distance; yet he ran with joy, he ran with all his strength.

Before dawn, standing with his father and Garrick in the kitchen, drinking coffee with hands cupped around the mug, Sean felt excitement for each coming day.

'Sean, take Zama and N'duti with you and make sure there are no strays in the thick stuff along the river.'

'I'll only take one herdboy, Pa, you'll need N'duti at the dipping tank.'

'All right, then. Try and meet us back at the tank before midday, we've got to push through a thousand head today.'

Sean gulped the remains of his coffee and buttoned his jacket. 'I'll get going then.'

A groom held his horse at the kitchen door. Sean slid his rifle into the scabbard and went up into the saddle without putting his foot into the steel; he lifted a hand and grinned at Waite, then he swung the horse and rode across the yard. The morning was still dark and cold. Waite watched him from the doorway.

'So goddamned sure of himself,' thought Waite. Yet he had the son he had hoped for and he was proud.

'What you want me to do, Pa?' Garrick asked beside him.

'Well, there are those heifers in the sick paddock—'

Waite stopped. 'No. You'd better come with me, Garry.'

Sean worked in the early morning when the sunlight was tinted as a stage effect, all golden and gay, and the shadows were long and black. He worked in the midday sun and sweated in the heat; in the rain; in the mist that swirled down grey and damp from the plateau; in the short African twilight, and came home in the dark. He loved every minute of it.

He learned to know cattle. Not by name, for only the trek oxen were named, but by their size and colour and markings, so that by running his eye over one of the herds he knew which animals were missing.

'Zama, the old cow with the crooked horn. Where is she?'

'Nkosi,' no longer the diminutive Nkosizana – little lord.

'Nkosi, yesterday I took her to the sick paddock, she has the worm in her eye.'

He learned to recognize disease almost before it started. The way a beast moved and held its head. He learned the treatment for them. Screw worm – kerosene poured into the wound until the maggots fell out like a shower of rice. Ophthalmia – rinse the eye with permanganate. Anthrax and quarter-evil – a bullet and a bonfire for the carcass.

He delivered his first calf among the acacia trees on the bank of the Tugela; he did it alone with his sleeves rolled up above the elbows and the soapy feel of the slime on his hands. Afterwards, while the mother licked it and it

62

staggered at each stroke of the tongue, Sean felt a choking sensation in his throat.

All this was not enough to burn up his energy. He played while he worked.

Practising his horsemanship: swinging from the saddle and running beside his horse, up again and over the other side, standing on the saddle at full gallop and then opening his legs and smacking down on his backside – his feet finding the stirrups without groping.

Practising with his rifle until he could hit a running jackal at a hundred and fifty paces, cutting the fox-terrier-sized body in half with the heavy bullet.

Then there was much of Garrick's work to do also.

'I don't feel very well, Sean.'

'What's wrong?'

'My leg's sore, you know how it chafes if I ride too much.'

'Why don't you go home, then?'

'Pa says I've got to fix the fence round the Number Three dip tank.' Garrick leaned forward on his horse to rub his leg, giving a brave little smile.

'You fixed it last week,' Sean protested.

'Yes – but the wires sort of came loose again.' There was always a strange impermanency about any repairs that Garrick effected.

'Have you got the wire cutters?' and Garrick produced them with alacrity from his saddle bag.

'I'll do it,' said Sean.

'Hell, man, thanks a lot,' and then a second's hesitation. 'You won't tell Pa, will you?'

'No – you can't help it if your leg's sore,' and Garrick rode home, sneaked through to his bedroom and escaped with Jim Hawkins into the pages of *Treasure Island*.

From this work came a new emotion for Sean. When the rain brought the grass out in green and filled the shallow pans on the plateau with water it was no longer simply a sign that the birdnesting season had begun and that the fishing in the Baboon Stroom would improve – now it meant that they could take cattle up from the valley, it meant that there would be fat on the herds they drove into the sale pens at Ladyburg, it meant that another winter had ended and again the land was rich with life and the promise of life. This new emotion extended to the cattle also. It was a strong, almost savage feeling of possession.

It was in the late afternoon. Sean was sitting on his horse among trees, looking out across open vleiland at the small herd that was strung out before him. They were feeding, heads down, tails flicking lazily. Between Sean and the main body of cattle was a calf – it was three days old, still pale-beige in colour and unsure of its legs. It was trying them out, running clumsy circles in the short grass. From the herd a cow lowed and the calf stopped dead and stood with its legs splayed awkwardly under it and its ears up. Sean grinned and picked up the reins from his horse's neck; it was time to start back for the homestead.

At that moment he saw the lammergeyer: it had already begun its stoop at the calf, dropping big and dark brown from the sky, wings cocked back and its talons reaching for the strike. The wind rustled against it with the speed of its dive.

Sean sat paralysed and watched. The eagle hit the calf and Sean heard bone break, sharp as the snap of a dry stick, and then the calf was down in the grass struggling feebly with the eagle crouched on top of it.

For a second longer Sean sat, dazed with the speed at which it had happened. Then hatred came on him. It came with a violence that twisted his stomach. He hit his horse with his heels and it jumped forward. He drove it at the eagle and as he rode he screamed at it, a high-pitched formless sound, an animal expression of hate.

The eagle turned its head, looking at him sideways with one eye. It opened its great yellow beak and answered his scream, then it loosed its claws from the calf and launched itself into the air. Its wings flogged heavily and it moved low along the ground, gaining speed, lifting, drawing away from Sean.

Sean pulled his rifle from the scabbard and hauled his horse back onto its haunches. He threw himself out of the saddle and levered open the breech of the rifle.

The eagle was fifty yards ahead of him rising fast now. Sean slipped a cartridge into the breech, closed it and brought the rifle up in one continuous movement.

It was a difficult shot. Moving away from him and rising, the beat of its wings jerking its body. Sean fired. The rifle jumped back into his shoulder and the gunsmoke whipped away on the wind, so he could watch the bullet connect.

The eagle collapsed in the air. It burst like a pillow in a puff of feathers and fell with its six-feet-long wings fluttering limply. Before it hit the ground Sean was running.

It was dead when he reached it, but he reversed his rifle: holding it by the muzzle, he swung the butt down from above his head onto its body. At the third blow the butt of his rifle broke off, but he kept on hitting. He was sobbing with fury.

When he stopped and stood panting the sweat was running down his face and his body was trembling. The eagle was a squashy mess of broken flesh and feathers.

The calf was still alive. The rifle was jammed. Sean knelt beside it with tears of anger burning his eyes and killed it with his hunting-knife.

13

So strong was this new feeling that Sean could hate even Garrick. He did not hate for long, though. Sean's anger and his hatred were quick things, with flames like those of a fire in dry grass: hot and high but soon burnt out and afterwards the ashes dead with no smouldering.

Waite was away when it happened. For three consecutive years Waite Courtney had been nominated for the chairmanship of the Beef Growers' Association and each time he had stood down. He was human enough to want the prestige the office carried with it, but he was also sensible to the fact that his farm would suffer from his frequent absences. Sean and Garrick had been working for two years when the annual election of office bearers came around again.

The night before Waite left for the meeting in Pietermaritzburg he spoke to Ada. 'I had a letter from Bernard last week, my dear.' He was standing before the mirror in their bedroom trimming his beard. 'They insist that I stand for the chair this year.'

'Very wise of them,' said Ada. 'They'd have the best man if you did.'

Waite frowned with concentration as he snipped at his whiskers. She believed so unquestioningly in him that he seldom doubted himself. Now looking at his face in the mirror he wondered how much of his success was owed to Ada's backing.

'You can do it, Waite.' Not a challenge, not a question, but a calm statement of fact. When she said it he believed it.

He laid the scissors down on the chest of drawers and turned to her. She sat cross-legged on the bed in a white nightgown, her hair was down in a dark mass around her shoulders. 'I´ think Sean can look after things here,' she said, and then quickly, 'and of course Garry.'

'Sean's learning fast,' Waite agreed.

'Are you going to take the job?'

Waite hesitated. 'Yes,' he nodded and Ada smiled.

'Come here.' She held out her hands to him.

Sean drove Waite and Ada to the station at Ladyburg: at the last minute Waite had insisted that she go with him, for he wanted her to be there to share it with him.

Sean put their luggage into the coach and waited while they talked with the small group of cattlemen who were going up to the meeting. The whistle blew and the travellers scattered to their compartments. Ada kissed Sean and climbed up. Waite stayed a second longer on the platform.

'Sean, if you need any help go across to Mr Erasmus at Lion Kop. I'll be back on Thursday.'

'I won't need any help, Pa.'

Waite's mouth hardened. 'Then you must be God, he's the only one who never needs help,' Waite said harshly. 'Don't be a bloody fool – if you run into trouble ask Erasmus.'

He climbed up after Ada. The train jerked, gathered speed and ran out towards the escarpment. Sean watched it dwindle, then he walked back to the buggy. He was master of Theunis Kraal and he liked the feeling. The small crowd on the platform was dispersing and out of it came Anna.

'Hello, Sean.' She had on a green cotton dress that was faded with washing, her feet were bare. She smiled with her small white teeth and watched his face.

'Hello, Anna.'

'Aren't you going up to Pietermaritzburg?'

'No, I've got to look after the farm.'

'Oh!'

They waited in silence, uncomfortable before so many people. Sean coughed and scratched the side of his nose.

'Anna, come on. We've got to get home.' One of her brothers called from in front of the ticket office and Anna leaned towards Sean.

'Will I see you on Sunday?' she whispered.

'I'll come if I can. But I don't know – I've got to look after the farm.'

'Please try, Sean.' Her face was earnest. 'I'll be waiting for you, I'll take some lunch and wait all day. Please come, even if it's only for a little while.'

'All right, I'll come.'

'Promise?'

'Promise.'

She smiled with relief. 'I'll wait for you on the path above the waterfall.'

She turned and ran to join her family and Sean drove back to Theunis Kraal. Garrick was lying on his bed reading.

'I thought Pa told you to get on with the branding of those new cattle we bought on Wednesday.'

Garrick laid down his book and sat up. 'I told Zama to keep them in the kraal until you got back.'

'Pa told you to get on with it. You can't keep them there all day without feed or water.'

'I hate branding,' muttered Garrick. 'I hate it when they moo like that as you burn them, and I hate the stink of burning hair and skin – it gives me a headache.'

'Well someone's got to do it. I can't, I've got to go down and mix new dip into the tanks for tomorrow.' Sean was losing his temper. 'Hell, Garry, why are you always so damn helpless?'

'I can't help it, I can't help it if I've only got one leg.' Garrick was close to tears again. The reference to his leg had the desired effect – Sean's temper steadied instantly.

'I'm sorry.' Sean smiled his irresistible smile. 'I tell you what. I'll do the branding – you fix the tanks. Get the drums of dip loaded onto the Scotch cart, take a couple of the stable boys with you to help. Here are the keys of the storeroom.' He tossed the bunch onto the bed beside Garrick. 'You should be finished before dark.'

At the door he turned.

'Garry, don't forget to do all six tanks – not just the ones near the house.'

So Garrick loaded six drums of dip onto the Scotch cart and went off down the hill. He was home well before dark. The front of his breeches was stained with the dark, tarry chemical and some of it had soaked into the leather of his single riding-boot. As he came out of the kitchen into the passage Sean shouted from the study, 'Hey, Garry, did you finish them?'

Garrick was startled. Waite's study was a sacred place, the inner sanctum of Theunis Kraal. Even Ada knocked before going into it and the twins went there only to receive punishment. Garrick limped along the passage and pushed open the door.

Sean sat with his boots on top of the desk and his ankles neatly crossed. He leaned back in the swivel chair.

'Pa will kill you,' Garrick's voice was shaky.

'Pa's in Pietermaritzburg,' said Sean.

Garrick stood in the doorway and looked around the room. It was the first time he had really seen it. On every previous visit he had been too preoccupied with the violence to come and the only item in the room he had studied closely was the seat of the big leather easy chair as he bent over the arm of it and exposed his backside to the sjambok.

Now he looked at the room. The walls were panelled to the ceiling, the wood was dark yellow and polished. The ceiling was fancy plaster, in a pattern of oak leaves. A single lamp hung from the centre of it on a brass chain. You could walk into the fireplace of brown chipped stone and there were logs laid ready for the match.

Pipes and tobacco jar on the ledge beside the fireplace, guns in a rack along one wall, a bookcase of green and maroon leather bound volumes: encyclopaedias, dictionaries, books on travel and farming, but no fiction. There was an oil painting of Ada on the wall opposite the desk, the artist had captured a little of her serenity: she wore a white dress and carried her hat in her hand. A magnificent set of Cape buffalo horns above the fireplace dominated the room with their great crenellated bosses and wide sweep to the tips.

It was a man's room, with loose dog-hairs on the leopard-skin rugs, and the presence of the man strongly there – it even smelled of Waite. It was as distinctively his as the tweed coat and Terai hat that hung behind the door.

Next to where Sean sat the cabinet was open and a bottle of brandy stood on top of it. Sean had a goblet in his hand.

'You're drinking Pa's brandy,' Garrick accused.

'It's not bad.' Sean lifted the glass and inspected the liquid; he took a careful sip and held it in his mouth, preparing himself to swallow. Garrick watched him with awe and Sean tried not to blink as it went down his throat.

'Would you like some?'

Garrick shook his head and the fumes came up Sean's nose and his eyes ran.

'Pa will kill you!' said Garrick again.

'Sit down,' ordered Sean, his voice husky from the brandy. 'I want to work out a plan for the time Pa's away.'

Garrick advanced on the armchair, but before he reached it he changed his mind – the associations were too painful. He went to the sofa instead and sat on the edge.

'Tomorrow,' Sean held up one finger, 'we'll dip all the

cattle in the home section. I've told Zama to start bringing them early – you did do the tanks, didn't you?'

Garrick nodded and Sean went on.

'On Saturday,' Sean held up his second finger, 'we'll burn fire breaks along the top of the escarpment. The grass is dry as hell up there. You take one gang and start near the falls, I'll ride down to the other end, near Fredericks Kloof. On Sunday...' Sean said and then paused. On Sunday Anna.

'I want to go to church on Sunday,' said Garrick quickly.

'That's fine,' agreed Sean. 'You go to church.'

'Are you going to come?'

'No,' said Sean.

Garrick looked down at the leopard-skin rugs that covered the floor – he didn't try to persuade Sean for Anna would be at the service. Perhaps afterwards, if Sean wasn't there to distract her, he could drive her home in the buggy. He started a day dream and wasn't listening as Sean went on talking.

In the morning it was full daylight by the time Sean reached the dip tank. He pushed a small herd of stragglers before him and they came out through the trees and stirrup high grass into the wide area of trampled earth around the tank. Garrick had started running cattle through the dip and there were about ten head already in the draining kraal at the far end, standing wet and miserable, their bodies dark with dip.

Sean drove his herd through the gates of the entrance kraal into the solid pack of brown bodies that were already there. N'duti slid the bars of the gate back into place to hold them.

'I see you, Nkosi.'

'I see you, N'duti. Plenty of work today!'

'Plenty,' agreed N'duti, 'always plenty of work.'

Sean rode around the kraal and tied his horse beneath

one of the trees, then walked across to the tank. Garrick was standing by the parapet and leaning against one of the columns that supported the roof.

'Hello, Garry, how's it going?'

'Fine.'

Sean leaned over the parapet next to Garry. The tank was twenty feet long and eight wide, the surface of the liquid was below ground level. Around the tank was a low wall and over it a roof of thatch to prevent rain diluting the contents.

The herdboys drove the cattle up to the edge and each beast hesitated on the brink.

'E'yapi, E'yapi,' screamed the herdboys and the push of bodies behind it forced it to jump. If one was stubborn, Zama leaned over the railing of the kraal, grabbed its tail and bit it.

Each beast jumped with its nose held high and its forefeet gathered up under its chest; it disappeared completely under the oil black surface and came up again swimming frantically along the tank until its hooves touched the sloping bottom at the far end and it could lumber up into the draining kraal.

'Keep them moving, Zama,' shouted Sean.

Zama grinned at him and bit with big white teeth into a reluctant tail.

The ox was a heavy animal and it splashed a drop up onto Sean's cheek as he leaned over the wall. Sean did not bother to wipe it off, he went on watching.

'Well, if we don't get top prices for this lot at the next sale then the buyers don't know good cattle,' he said to Garry.

'They're all right,' agreed Garry.

'All right? They're the fattest oxen in the district.' Sean was about to enlarge on the theme, but suddenly he was aware of discomfort – the drop of dip was burning his cheek.

He wiped it off with his finger and held it to his nose; the smell of it stung his nostrils. For a second he stared at it stupidly and the spot on his cheek burned like fire.

He looked up quickly. The cattle in the draining kraal were milling restlessly and as he looked one of them staggered sideways and bumped against the railing.

'Zama!' shouted Sean, and the Zulu looked up. 'Stop them. For God's sake don't let any more through.'

There was another ox poised on the edge. Sean snatched off his hat and jumped up onto the wall, he beat the ox in the face with his hat trying to drive it back, but it sprang out into the tank. Sean caught hold of the railing and stepped into the space it had left on the edge of the tank.

'Stop them,' he shouted. 'Get the bars in, don't let any more through.'

He spread his arms across the entrance, holding onto the railing on each side, kicking at the faces of the cattle in front of him.

'Hurry, damn you, get the bars in,' he shouted. The oxen pressed towards him, a wall of horned heads. Pushed forward by those behind and held back by Sean they started to panic; one of them tried to jump over the railing. As it swung its head its horn raked Sean's chest, up across the ribs, ripping his shirt.

Behind him Sean felt the wooden bars being dropped into place, blocking the entrance to the tank, and then Zama's hands on his arm pulling him up out of the confusion of horns and hooves. Two of the herdboys helped him over the railing and Sean shrugged their hands off as soon as he was on the ground.

'Come on,' he ordered and ran to his horse.

'Nkosi, you are bleeding.'

Blood had splotched the front of Sean's shirt but he felt no pain. The cattle that had been through the dip were now in terrible distress. They charged about the kraal, bellowing pitifully; one of them fell and when it got to its feet again its legs were shaking so that it could barely stand.

'The river,' shouted Sean, 'get them down to the river. Try and wash it off. Zama, open the gate.'

The Baboon Stroom was a mile away. One of the oxen died before they could get them out of the kraal, another ten before they reached the river. They died in convulsions, with their bodies shuddering and their eyes turned back into their heads.

Sean drove those that remained down the bank into the river. The water was clear and as each beast went into it, the dip washed off in a dark brown cloud.

'Stand here, Zama. Don't let them come out.'

Sean swam his horse to the far bank and turned back the oxen that were trying to climb it.

'Nkosi – one is drowning,' called N'duti and Sean looked across the river. A young ox was in convulsions in the shallows: its head was under water and its feet thrashed the surface.

Sean slid off his horse and waded out to it. The water was up to his armpits. He tried to hold its head out and drag it to the bank.

'Help me, N'duti,' he shouted, and the Zulu came into the river. It was a hopeless task: each time the ox lunged it pulled them both under with it. By the time they got the ox to the bank it was dead.

Sean sat in the mud beside the body of the ox: he was exhausted and his lungs ached with the water he had breathed.

'Bring them out, Zama,' he gasped. The survivors were standing in the shallows or swimming in aimless circles. 'How many?' asked Sean. 'How many are dead?'

'Two more while you were in the water. Altogether thirteen, Nkosi.'

'Where's my horse?'

'It ran, and I let it go. It will be back at the house.'

Sean nodded.

'Bring them up to the sick paddock. We must watch them for a few days.'

Sean stood up and started walking back towards the dip tank. Garrick was gone, and the main herd was still in the kraal. Sean opened the gate and turned them loose. He felt better by then, and as his strength returned with it came his anger and his hatred. He started along the track towards the homestead. His boots squelched as he walked and he hated Garrick more strongly with each step. Garrick had mixed the dip. Garrick had killed his cattle and Sean hated him.

As Sean came up the slope below the house he saw Garrick standing in the yard. Garrick saw him also; he disappeared into the kitchen and Sean started to run. He went in through the kitchen door and nearly knocked down one of the servants.

'Garrick,' shouted Sean. 'Damn it – where are you?'

He searched the house; once quickly and then again thoroughly. Garrick was gone, but the window of their bedroom was open and there was a dusty boot print on the sill. Garrick had gone over it.

'You bloody coward,' howled Sean and scrambled out after him. He stood a second, with his head swinging from side to side and his fists opening and closing.

'I'll find out,' he howled again. 'I'll find you wherever you're hiding.'

He started across the yard towards the stables and halfway there he saw the door of the dairy was closed. When he tried it he found it was locked from inside. Sean backed away from it and then charged it with his shoulder – the lock burst and the door flew open. Sean skidded across the room and came up against the far wall. Garrick was trying to climb out of the window, but it was small and high up. Sean caught him by the seat of his pants and pulled him down.

'Whatcha do to the dip, hey? Whatcha do to it?' He shouted in Garrick's face.

'I didn't mean to. I didn't know it'd kill them.'

'Tell me what you did.' Sean had hold of the front of his shirt and was dragging him towards the door.

'I didn't do anything. Honest I didn't know.'

'I'm going to hammer you anyway, so you might as well tell me.'

'Please, Sean, I didn't know.'

Sean jammed Garrick against the doorway and held him there with his left hand – his right hand he drew back with the fist bunched.

'No, Sean. Please, no.'

And suddenly the anger was gone from Sean, his hands sank back to his sides.

'All right – just tell me what you did,' he said coldly. His anger was gone but not his hatred.

'I was tired and it was getting late and my leg was hurting,' whispered Garrick, 'and there were still four more tanks to do, and I knew you'd check that all the drums were empty, and it was so late . . . and . . .'

'And?'

'And so I emptied all the dip into the one tank . . . but I didn't know it would kill them, truly I didn't.'

Sean turned away from him and started walking slowly back towards the house. Garrick stumbled after him.

'I'm sorry, Sean, honest I'm sorry. I didn't know that . . .'

Sean walked ahead of him into the kitchen and slammed the door in his face. He went through into Waite's study. From the bookshelf he lifted down the heavy leather-covered stock register and carried it to the desk. He opened the book, picked up a pen and dipped it. For a moment he stared at the page and then in the 'deaths' column he wrote the number 13 and after it the words 'dip poisoning'. He pressed down so hard with the pen that the nib cut the paper.

It took Sean and the herdboys all the rest of that day and the next to bale out the tank, refill it with clean water and mix in fresh dip. He saw Garrick only at meals and they didn't speak.

The next day was Sunday. Garrick went into town early, for the church service started at eight o'clock. When he had gone Sean began his preparations. He shaved – leaning close to the mirror and handling the cut-throat gingerly, shaping his side burns and clearing the hair from the rest of his face until his skin was smooth and fresh-looking. Then he went through to the master-bedroom and helped himself to a generous portion of his father's brilliantine, taking care to screw the lid back on the bottle and replace it exactly as he had found it. He rubbed the brilliantine into his hair and sniffed its perfume appreciatively. He combed his hair over his forehead, parted it down the centre and polished it into a gloss with Waite's silver-backed brushes. Then a clean white shirt, breeches worn only once before, boots as shiny as his hair – and Sean was ready.

The clock on the mantelpiece in the lounge assured him that he was well ahead of time. To be exact, he was two hours early. Eight o'clock now: church didn't end until nine and it would be another hour before Anna could escape from under the eyes of her family and reach the rendezvous above the falls. He settled down to wait. He read the latest copy of the *Natal Farmer*. He had read it three times before for it was a month old, and now even the excellent article on 'Stomach parasites in Cattle and Sheep' had lost much of its punch. Sean's attention wandered – he thought about the day ahead and felt the familiar movement within his breeches. This necessitated a rearrangement for the breeches were tight fitting. Then fantasy palled; Sean was a doer not a thinker, and he went through to the kitchen to solicit a cup of coffee from Joseph. When he had finished it, there was still half an hour to go.

'The hell with it,' said Sean and shouted for his horse. He climbed the escarpment, letting his horse move diagonally up the slope and at the top he dismounted and let it blow. Today he could see the course of the Tugela river out across the plain – it was a belt of dark green. He could count the roofs of the houses in Ladyburg and the church spire, copper clad, shone in the sunlight like a beacon fire.

He mounted again and rode along the edge of the plateau until he reached the Baboon Stroom above the falls. He followed it back and forded it at a shallow place, lifting his feet up on the saddle in front of him to keep his boots dry. He off-saddled next to the pools and knee-haltered his horse, then he followed the path until it dropped over the edge of the plateau into the thick forest that surrounded the falls. It was cool and damp in the forest with moss growing on the trees, for the roof of leaves and creepers shut out the sun. There was a bottle-bird in the undergrowth.

'Glug, glug, glug,' it said, like water poured from a bottle, and its call was almost drowned in the ceaseless thunder of the falls.

Sean spread his handkerchief on a rock beside the path, sat down on it and waited. Within five minutes he was fidgeting impatiently – within half an hour he was grumbling aloud.

'I'll count to five hundred . . . If she hasn't come by then I'm not going to wait.'

He counted and when he reached the promised figure he stopped and peered anxiously down the path. There was no sign of Anna.

'I'm not going to sit here all day,' he announced and made no effort to stand up. A fat yellow caterpillar caught his eye; it was on the trunk of a tree farther down the slope. He picked up a pebble and threw it. It bounced off the tree an inch above the caterpillar.

'Close,' Sean encouraged himself and stooped for another stone. After a while he had exhausted the supply of pebbles around his feet and the caterpillar was still moving leisurely up the trunk. Sean was forced to go out on a foraging expedition for more pebbles. He came back with both hands full and once more took up his position on the rock. He piled the pebbles between his feet and reopened the bombardment. He aimed each throw with the utmost concentration and with his third pebble he hit squarely and the caterpillar popped in a spurt of green juice. Sean felt cheated. He looked around for a new target and instead found Anna standing beside him.

'Hello, Sean.' She had on a pink dress. She carried her shoes in one hand and a small basket in the other. 'I brought some lunch for us.'

'What took you so long?' Sean stood up and wiped his hands on his breeches. 'I thought you weren't coming.'

'I'm sorry – everything went wrong.'

There was an awkward pause and Anna flushed slightly as Sean looked at her. Then she turned and started up the path. 'Come on – I'll race you to the top.'

She ran fast on bare feet, holding her skirts up to her knees and she was out in the sunshine before Sean caught her. He put his arms around her from behind and they fell together into the grass beside the path. They lay holding each other, laughing and panting at the same time.

'The service went on and on – I thought it would never finish,' said Anna, 'and afterwards—'

Before she could finish Sean covered her mouth with his and immediately her arms came up around his neck. They kissed with the tension building up steadily between them until Anna was moaning softly and moving her body against

79

his. Sean released her mouth and moved his lips down across her cheek to her neck.

'Oh, Sean, it's been so long. It's been a whole week.'

'I know.'

'I've missed you so – I thought about you every day.'

Sean had his face pressed into her neck, he didn't answer.

'Did you miss me, Sean?'

'Hmm,' Sean murmured and lifted his mouth to take the lobe of her ear between his teeth.

'Did you think about me while you were working?'

'Hmm.'

'Tell me properly, Sean, say it properly.'

'I missed you, Anna, I thought about you all the time,' lied Sean and kissed her on the mouth. She clung to him and Sean's hand went down, right down to her knee and then up again under her clothes. Anna caught his wrist and held his hand away. 'No, Sean, just kiss me.'

Sean waited until her grip relaxed and then tried again, but this time she twisted away from him and sat up. 'Sometimes I think that's all you want to do.'

Sean felt his temper coming up, but he had the good sense to check it.

'That's not true, Anna. It's just that I haven't seen you for so long and I've missed you so much.'

She softened immediately and reached out to touch his cheek. 'Oh, Sean, I'm sorry. I don't mind really, it's just that – oh, I don't know.' She scrambled to her feet and picked up the basket. 'Come on, let's go on to the pools.'

They had a special place. It was walled in by the reeds and shaded by a big tree that grew on the bank above; the sand was washed clean and white. Sean spread his saddle blanket for them to sit on. They could hear the river, close by but hidden, and the reeds rustled and nodded their fluffy heads with each breath of the wind.

' – and I couldn't get rid of him,' Anna chattered as she knelt on the blanket and unpacked the basket. 'He just sat there and every time I said something he blushed and wriggled on his seat. In the end I just told him, "I'm sorry, Garry, I have to go!"'

Sean scowled. The mention of Garrick had reminded him of the dip; he hadn't forgiven him yet.

'And then when I got into the house I found that Pa and Frikkie were fighting. Ma was in tears and the other kids were locked in the bedroom.'

'Who won?' asked Sean with interest.

'They weren't really fighting – they were just shouting at each other. They were both drunk.'

Sean was always slightly shocked at Anna's casual reference to her family's drinking habits. Everybody knew about Mr Van Essen and his two eldest boys but Anna didn't have to talk about it. Once Sean had tried to correct her. 'You shouldn't say things like that about your Pa. You should respect him.'

And Anna had looked at him calmly and asked, 'Why?' which was a difficult question. But now she changed the subject.

'Do you want to eat yet?'

'No,' said Sean and reached for her. She fought back, shrieking demurely until Sean held her down and kissed her. Then she lay quietly, answering his kisses.

'If you stop me now I'm going to get mad,' whispered Sean and deliberately unfastened the top button of her dress. She watched his face with solemn eyes and her hands stayed on his shoulders until he had undone her blouse down to the waist and then with her fingers she traced the bold black curves of his eyebrows.

'No, Sean, I won't stop you. I want to as well, I want to as much as you do.'

There was so much to discover and each thing was

strange and wonderful and they were the first to find it. The way the muscles stood out down the side of his chest beneath his arms and yet left a place where she could see the outline of his ribs. The texture of her skin, smooth and white with the faint blue suggestion of veins beneath. The deep hollow down the centre of his back – pressing her fingers into it she could feel his spine. The down on her cheeks, so pale and fine he could see it only in the sunlight. The way their lips felt against each other and the tiny flutter of tongues between. The smell of their bodies, one milky warm and the other musky and vigorous. The hair that covered his chest and grew thicker under his arms, and hers: startlingly dark against white skin, a small silky nest of it. Each time there was something new to find and greet with soft sounds of delight.

Now, kneeling before her as she lay with her head thrown back and her arms half-raised to receive him, Sean suddenly bowed his head and touched her with his mouth. The taste of her was clean as the taste of the sea.

Her eyes flew open. 'Sean, no, you mustn't – oh no, you mustn't.' There were lips within lips and a bud as softly resilient as a tiny green grape. Sean found it with the tip of his tongue.

'Oh, Sean, you can't do that. Please, please, please.' And her hands were in the thick hair at the back of his head holding him there.

'I can't stand it any more, come over me . . . quickly, quickly, Sean.'

Filling like a sail in a hurricane, swollen and hard and tight, stretched beyond its limit until it burst and was blown to shreds in the wind and was gone. Everything gone. The wind and the sail, the tension and the wanting, all gone. There was left only the great nothingness which is peace. Perhaps a kind of death; perhaps death is like that. But, like death, not an ending – for even death contains the seeds of resurrection. So they came back from peace to a new beginning, slowly at first and then faster until they were two people again. Two people on a blanket among reeds with the sunlight white on the sand about them.

'Each time it's better and better – isn't it, Sean?'

'Ah!' Sean stretched, arching his back and spreading his arms.

'Sean, you do love me, don't you?'

'Sure. Sure I love you.'

'I think you must love me to have done' – she hesitated – 'to do what you did.'

'I just said so, didn't I?' Sean's attention wandered to the basket. He selected an apple and polished it on the blanket.

'Tell me properly. Hold me tight and tell me.'

'Hell, Anna, how many times have I got to say it?' Sean bit into the apple. 'Did you bring any of your Ma's shortbread?'

It was coming on night when Sean got back to Theunis Kraal. He turned his horse over to one of the grooms and went into the house. His body tingled from the sun, and he felt the emptiness and sadness of after-love, but it was a good sadness, like the sadness of old memories.

Garrick was in the dining-room, eating alone. Sean walked into the room and Garrick looked up nervously.

'Hello, Garry.' Sean smiled at him and Garrick was momentarily dazzled by it. Sean sat down in the chair beside him and punched him lightly on the arm.

'Have you left any for me?' His hatred was gone.

'There's plenty,' Garrick nodded eagerly. 'Try some of the potatoes, they're jolly good.'

83

14

'They say the Governor sent for your Pa while he was in Pietermaritzburg. Had him alone for nearly two hours.' Stephen Erasmus took the pipe out of his mouth and spat down onto the railway lines. In his brown homespun and *veldschoen* he did not look like a rich cattleman. 'Well, we don't need a prophet to tell us what it was about, do we?'

'No, sir,' Sean agreed vaguely. The train was late and Sean wasn't listening. He had an entry in the stock register to explain to his father and he was mentally rehearsing his speech.

'*Ja*, we know what it's about all right.' Old Erasmus put the pipe back between his teeth and spoke around it. 'It's been two weeks now since the British Agent was recalled from Cetewayo's kraal at Gingindhlovu. *Liewe Here*! in the old days we'd have called out the Commando long ago.' He packed his pipe, pushing down onto the glowing tobacco with a calloused forefinger. Sean noticed that the finger was twisted and scarred by the trigger-guards of a hundred heavy rifles.

'You've never been on commando have you, *Jong*?'

'No, sir.'

'About time you did then,' said Erasmus, 'about bledy time.'

Up on the escarpment the train whistled and Sean started guiltily.

'There she is.' Erasmus stood up from the bench on which they were sitting and the station master came out from his office with a rolled red flag in his hand. Sean felt his stomach sink slowly until it stopped somewhere just above his knees.

The train ran in past them, whooshing steam and brakes whining. The single passenger coach stopped precisely opposite the wooden platform. Erasmus came forward and took Waite's hand.

'*Goeie More*, Steff.'

'*More*, Waite. They tell me you're the new chairman now. Well done, man.'

'Thanks. Did you get my telegram?' Waite spoke in Afrikaans.

'*Ja*. I got it. I told the others, we'll all be out at Theunis Kraal tomorrow.'

'Good,' Waite nodded. 'You'll stay for lunch, of course. We've got a lot to talk about.'

'Is it what I think it is?' Erasmus grinned wickedly. The tobacco had stained his beard yellow around his mouth and his face was brown and wrinkled.

'I'll tell you all about it tomorrow, Steff.' Waite winked at him, 'But in the meantime you'd better get that old muzzle-loader of yours out of moth-balls.'

They laughed, one deep down and the other a rusty old laugh.

'Grab the bags, Sean. Let's get home.' Waite took Ada's arm and they walked with Erasmus to the buggy. Ada had on a new dress, blue with leg o'mutton sleeves and a picture hat; she looked lovely but a little worried as she listened to them talking. It's strange how women can never face the prospect of war with the same boyish enthusiasm as their men.

'Sean!' Waite Courtney's roar carried clearly from his study along the corridor and through the closed door of the sitting-room. Ada dropped her knitting into her lap and her features set into an expression of unnatural calm. Sean stood up from his chair.

'You should have told him earlier,' Garrick said in a small voice. 'You should have told him during lunch.'

'I didn't get a chance.'

'Sean!' Another blast from the study.

'What's happened now?' asked Ada quietly.

'It's nothing, Ma. Don't worry about it.'

Sean crossed to the door.

'Sean,' Garrick's stricken voice, 'Sean, you won't – I mean you don't have to tell—' He stopped and sat hunched in his chair, his eyes full of desperate appeal.

'It's all right, Garry, I'll fix it.'

Waite Courtney stood over the desk. Between his clenched fists the stock register lay open. He looked up as Sean came in and closed the door.

'What's this?' He prodded the page with a huge square-tipped finger. Sean opened his mouth and then closed it again.

'Come on. I'm listening.'

'Well, Pa—'

'Well, Pa – be buggered. Just tell me how you've managed to massacre half the cattle on this farm in a little over a week?'

'It's not half the cattle – it's only thirteen.' Sean was stung by the exaggeration.

'Only thirteen,' bellowed Waite, '*only* thirteen. God Almighty, shall I tell you how much that is in cash? Shall I tell you how much that is in hard work and time and worry?'

'I know, Pa.'

'You know,' Waite was panting. 'Yes, you know everything. There's nothing anyone can tell you, is there? Not even how to kill thirteen head of prime oxen.'

'Pa—'

'Don't Pa me, by Jesus.' Waite slammed the heavy book closed. 'Just explain to me how you managed it. What's "dip poisoning"? What the bloody hell is "dip poisoning"?

Did you give it to them to drink? Did you stick it up their arses?'

'The dip was too strong,' said Sean.

'And why was the dip too strong? How much did you put in?'

Sean took a deep breath. 'I put in four drums.'

There was silence and then Waite asked softly, '*How much?*'

'Four drums.'

'Are you mad? Are you raving bloody mad?'

'I didn't think it would harm them.' His carefully rehearsed speech forgotten, Sean unconsciously repeated the words he had heard from Garrick. 'It was getting late and my leg was—' Sean bit the sentence off and Waite stared at him, then the confusion cleared from his face.

'Garry!' he said.

'No,' shouted Sean. 'It wasn't him, I did it.'

'You're lying to me.' Waite came round from behind the desk. There was a note of disbelief in his voice. To his knowledge it was the first time it had ever happened. He stared at Sean and then his anger was back more violently than before. He had forgotten the oxen – it was the lie that concerned him now. 'By Christ, I'll teach you to tell the truth.' He snatched up his sjambok from the desk.

'Don't hit me, Pa,' Sean warned him, backing away. Waite threw up the sjambok and swung it down overarm. It hissed softly and Sean twisted away from it, but the tip of the lash caught his shoulder. Sean gasped at the pain and lifted his hand to it.

'You lying little bastard!' shouted Waite and swung the whip sideways as though he were scything wheat, and this time it curled around Sean's chest under his uplifted arm. It split his shirt like a razor cut and the cloth fell away to expose the red ridged welt across his ribs and around his back.

'Here's some more!' Waite lifted the sjambok again and as he stood with his arm thrown back and his body turned off balance he knew he had made a mistake. Sean was no longer clutching the whip marks; his hands were held low and his fists were bunched. At the corners his eyebrows were lifted, giving an expression of satanical fury to his face. He was pale and his lips were drawn back tight, showing his teeth. His eyes, no longer blue but burning black, were on a level with Waite's.

'He's coming for me.' Waite's surprise slowed his reflexes, he couldn't bring his whip-arm down before Sean was on him. Sean hit him, standing solidly on both feet, bringing the full weight of his body into the punch, hurling it into the middle of Waite's exposed chest.

Heart punched, strength oozing out of him, Waite staggered back against the desk. The sjambok fell out of his hand and Sean went after him. Waite had the sensation of being a beetle in a saucer of treacle: he could see and think but he could barely move. He saw Sean take three quick paces forward, saw his right hand cocked like a loaded rifle, saw it aimed at his defenceless face.

In that instant, while his body moved in slow motion but his mind raced, the scales of paternal blindness dropped from Waite Courtney's eyes and he realized that he was fighting a man who matched him in strength and height, and who was his superior in speed. His only advantage lay in the experience he had gathered in forty years of brawling.

Sean threw his punch: it had all the power of the first one and Waite knew that he could not survive that in his face – and yet he could not move to avoid it. He dropped his chin onto his chest and took Sean's fist on the top of his head. The force of it flung him backwards over the desk, but as it hit he heard the brittle crackle of Sean's fingers breaking.

Waite dragged himself to his knees, using the corner of the desk as a support, and looked at his son. Sean was doubled up with pain, holding his broken hand against his stomach. Waite pulled himself to his feet and sucked in big breaths of air, he felt his strength coming back.

'All right,' he said, 'if you want to fight – then we fight.' He came round the desk, moving slowly, his hands ready, no longer underestimating his man.

'I am going to knock the daylights out of you,' announced Waite. Sean straightened up and looked at him. There was agony in his face now, but the anger was there also. Something surged up inside Waite when he saw it.

He can fight and he's game. Now we'll see if he can take a beating. Rejoicing silently Waite moved in on him, watching Sean's left hand, disregarding the broken right for he knew what pain was in it. He knew that no man could use a hand in that condition.

He shot out his own left hand, measuring with it, trying to draw Sean. Sean side-stepped, moving in past it. Waite was wide open for Sean's right, his broken right, the hand he could not possibly use – and Sean used it with all his strength into Waite's face.

Waite's brain burst into bright colours and darkness, he spun sideways, falling, hitting the leopard-skin rug with his shoulder and sliding with it across the floor into the fireplace. Then in the darkness he felt Sean's hands on him and heard Sean's voice.

'Pa, oh, my God, Pa. Are you all right?'

The darkness cleared a little and he saw Sean's face, the anger gone from it and in its place worry that was almost panic.

'Pa, oh, my God! Please, Pa.'

Waite tried to sit up, but he could not make it. Sean had to help him. He knelt next to Waite holding him, fumbling helplessly with his face, trying to brush the hair back off his forehead, stroking the rumpled beard into place. 'I'm sorry, Pa, truly I'm sorry. Let me help you to the chair.'

Waite sat in the chair and massaged the side of his jaw. Sean hovered over him, his own hand forgotten.

'What you want to do – kill me?' asked Waite ruefully.

'I didn't mean it. I just lost my temper.'

'I noticed,' said Waite, 'I just happened to notice that.'

'Pa – about Garry. You don't have to say anything to him, do you?'

Waite dropped his hand from his face and looked at Sean steadily.

'I'll make a bargain with you,' he said. 'I'll leave Garry out of it if you'll promise me two things. One: You never lie to me again.'

Sean nodded quickly.

'Two: If anybody ever takes a whip to you again you swear to me you'll give him the same as you just gave me.'

Sean started to smile and Waite went on gruffly, 'Now let's have a look at your hand.'

Sean held it out and Waite examined it, moving each finger in turn. Sean winced.

'Sore?' asked Waite. *He hit me with that. Sweet Jesus, I've bred me a wild one.*

'A little.' Sean was white-faced again.

'It's a mess,' said Waite. 'You'd better get into town right away and let Doctor Van have a go at it.'

Sean moved towards the door.

'Hold on.' Sean stopped and Waite pulled himself out of his chair. 'I'll come with you.'

'I'll be all right, Pa, you stay and rest.'

Waite ignored this and walked towards him.

'Really, Pa, I'll be all right on my own.'

'I'm coming with you,' Waite said harshly; and then softly, almost inaudibly, 'I want to, dammit.'

He lifted his arm as though to put it around Sean's shoulders, but before it touched him he let it drop back to his side and together they went out into the corridor.

– 15 –

With two fingers in splints Sean handled his knife awkwardly at lunch the next day, but his appetite was unimpaired. As was only right and fitting he took no part in the conversation except on the rare occasions that a remark was addressed directly to him. But he listened, his jaws chewing steadily and his eyes moving from speaker to speaker. He and Garry sat side by side in a backwater of the luncheon board while the guests were grouped in order of seniority around Waite.

Stephen Erasmus by age and wealth was in the right-hand seat; opposite him Tim Hope-Brown, just as wealthy but ten years younger; below him Gunther Niewenhuizen, Sam Tingle and Simon Rousseau. If you added it all together you could say that Waite Courtney had about a hundred thousand acres of land and half a million sterling sitting around his table. They were brown men – brown clothing, brown boots and big brown, calloused hands. Their faces were brown and battered-looking and now that the meal was in its closing stages their usual reserve was gone and there was a tendency among them to talk all at the same time and to perspire profusely. This was not entirely a consequence of the dozen bottles of good Cape Mossel that Waite had provided nor of the piles of food they had eaten – it was more than that. There was a sense of expectancy among them, an eagerness they were finding it difficult to suppress.

'Can I tell the servants to clear away, Waite?' Ada asked from the end of the table.

'Yes, thank you, my dear. We'll have coffee in here, please.'

He stood up and fetched a box of cigars from the sideboard and carried it to each of his guests in turn. When the ends were cut and the tips were glowing, every man leaning back in his chair with a recharged glass and a cup of coffee in front of him, Ada slipped out of the room and Waite cleared his throat for silence.

'Gentlemen.' They were all watching him. 'Last Tuesday I spent two hours with the Governor. We discussed the recent developments across the Tugela.'

Waite lifted his glass and sipped at it, then held it by the stem and rolled it between his fingers as he went on.

'Two weeks ago the British Agent at the Zulu king's kraal was recalled. Recalled is perhaps the wrong word – the king offered to smear him with honey, and tie him over an ant-hill, an offer that Her Britannic Majesty's Agent declined with thanks. Shortly thereafter he packed his bags and made for the border.'

There was a small ruffle of laughter.

'Since then Cetewayo has collected all his herds which were grazing near the Tugela and driven them into the north; he has commanded a buffalo hunt for which he has decided he will need *all* his impis – twenty thousand spears. This hunt is to be held along the banks of the Tugela, where the last buffalo was seen ten years ago.' Waite sipped at his glass, watching their faces. 'And he has ordered that all wounded game is to be followed across the border.'

There was a sigh then, a murmur from them. They all knew that this was the traditional Zulu declaration of war.

'So, man, what are we going to do about it. Must we sit here and wait for them to come and burn us out?'

Erasmus leaned forward watching Waite.

'Sir Bartle Frere met Cetewayo's Indunas a week ago. He has given them an ultimatum. They have until January the eleventh to disband the impis and take the Queen's Agent back into Zululand. In the event that Cetewayo disregards the ultimatum, Lord Chelmsford is to command a punitive column of regulars and militia. The force is being assembled now and will leave Pietermaritzburg within the next ten days. He is to cross the Tugela at Rorke's Drift and engage the impis before they break out. It is intended to end this constant threat to our border and break the Zulu nation for ever as a military power.'

'It's about bledy time,' said Erasmus.

'His Excellency has gazetted me full colonel and ordered me to raise a commando from the Ladyburg district. I have promised him at least forty men fully armed, mounted and provisioned who will be ready to join Chelmsford at the Tugela. Unless any of you object I am appointing you gentlemen as my captains and I know I can rely upon you to help me make good my promise to His Excellency.'

Suddenly Waite dropped his stilted manner and grinned at them. 'You will collect your own pay. It will be in cattle, as usual.'

'How far north has Cetewayo driven his herds?' asked Tim Hope-Brown.

'Not far enough, I'll warrant,' cackled Stephen Erasmus.

'A toast,' said Simon Rousseau jumping to his feet and holding up his glass. 'I give you a toast: the Queen, Lord Chelmsford and the Royal Herds of Zululand.'

They all stood and drank it, and then suddenly embarrassed by their display they sat down again, coughing awkwardly and shuffling their feet,

'All right,' said Waite, 'let's get down to details. Steff, you'll be coming and your two eldest boys?'

'Ja, three of us and my brother and his son. Put down five, Erasmus.'

'Good. What about you, Gunther?'

They began the planning. Men, horses and wagons were marshalled on paper; each of the captains was allotted a series of tasks. There was question, answer and argument that filled the hours before the guests left Theunis Kraal. They rode in a bunch, trippling their horses, sitting slack and long-legged in the saddles, moving up the far slope along the road to Ladyburg. Waite and his sons stood on the front step and watched them go.

'Pa—' Garry tried tentatively for Waite's attention.

'Yes, boy?' Waite kept his eyes on the group. Steff Erasmus turned in the saddle and waved his hat above his head, Waite waved back.

'Why do we have to fight them, Pa? If the Governor just sent somebody to talk to them, then we wouldn't have to fight.'

Waite glanced at him, frowning slightly.

'Anything worth having is worth fighting for, Garry. Cetewayo has raised twenty thousand spears to take this from us—' Waite swept his arm in a circle that took in the whole of Theunis Kraal. 'I think it's worth fighting for – don't you, Sean?'

'You bet,' Sean nodded eagerly.

'But couldn't we just make a treaty with them?' Garry persisted.

'Another cross on a piece of paper.' Waite spoke with fierce disdain. 'They found one like that on Piet Retrief's body – hell of a lot of good it did him.'

Waite walked back into the house with his sons following him.

He lowered himself into his armchair, stretched his legs out in front of him and smiled at Ada. 'Damn good lunch, my dear.' He clasped his hands over his stomach, belched involuntarily and was immediately contrite. 'I beg your pardon – it just slipped out.'

Ada bent her head over her sewing to hide her smile.

'We've got a lot to do in the next few days.' He turned his attention back to his sons. 'We'll take one mule wagon and a pair of horses each. Now about ammunition . . .'

'But, Pa, couldn't we just – ?' Garry started again.

'Shut up,' said Waite, and Garry subsided miserably into one of the other chairs.

'I've been thinking,' announced Sean.

'Not you as well,' growled Waite. 'Damn it to hell, here's your chance to win your own cattle and . . .'

'That's just what I've been thinking,' Sean cut in. 'Everybody will have more cattle than they know what to do with. The prices will drop way down.'

'They will at first,' admitted Waite, 'but in a year or two they'll climb back again.'

'Shouldn't we sell now? Sell everything except the bulls and breeding cows, then after the war we'll be able to buy back at half the price.'

For a moment Waite sat stunned and then slowly his expression changed.

'My God, I never thought of that.'

'And Pa,' Sean was twisting his hands together in his enthusiasm, 'we'll need more land. When we bring the herds back across the Tugela there won't be enough grazing to go round. Mr Pye has called the mortgages on Mount Sinai and Mahoba's Kloof. He's not using the land. Couldn't we lease them from him now before everybody starts looking for grazing?'

'We had a lot to do before you started thinking,' said Waite softly, 'but now we've really got to work.'

He searched his pockets, found his pipe and while he filled it with tobacco he looked at Sean. He tried to keep his face neutral but the pride kept showing.

'You keep thinking like that and you'll be a rich man one day.' Waite could not know how true his prophecy would prove – the time was still remote when Sean could drop the purchase price of Theunis Kraal across a gaming table, and laugh at the loss.

– 16 –

The Commando was moving out on New Year's Day. New Year's Eve was set down for a double celebration: 'Welcome 1879', and 'God speed the Ladyburg Mounted Rifles'. The whole district was coming into town for the *braaivleis* and dancing that was being held in the square. Feast the warriors – laugh, dance and sing, then form them up and march them out to war.

Sean and Garry rode in early. Ada and Waite were to follow later in the afternoon. It was one of those bright days of a Natal summer: no wind and no clouds, the kind of day when the dust from a wagon hangs heavy in the air. They crossed the Baboon Stroom and from the farther ridge looked down across the town and saw the wagon dust on every road leading into Ladyburg.

'Look at them come,' said Sean; he screwed up his eyes against the glare and stared at the north road. 'That will be the Erasmus wagon. Karl will be with them.'

The wagons looked like beads on a string.

'That's the Petersens',' said Garry, 'or the Niewehuisens'.'

'Come on,' shouted Sean, and slapped the free end of his reins across his horse's neck. They galloped down the road. The horses they rode were big glossy animals, with their manes cropped like English hunters.

They passed a wagon. There were two girls sitting beside mama on the box seat, the Petersen sisters. Dennis Petersen and his father were riding ahead of the wagon.

Sean whooped as he raced past the wagon and the girls laughed and shouted something that was lost in the wind.

'Come on, Dennis,' howled Sean as he swept past the two sedately trotting outriders. Dennis's horse reared and then settled in to run, chasing Sean. Garry trailed them both.

They reached the crossroads, lying flat along their horses' necks, pumping the reins like jockeys. The Erasmus wagon was trundling down to meet them.

'Karl,' Sean called as he held his horse a little to stand in the stirrups. 'Karl. Come on, man, catch a wayo, Cetewayo!'

They rode into Ladyburg in a bunch. They were all flush-faced and laughing, excited and happy at the prospect of dancing and killing.

The town was crowded, its streets congested with wagons and horses and men and women and girls and dogs and servants.

'I've got to stop at Pye's store,' said Karl, 'come with me – it won't take long.'

They hitched their horses and went into the store; Sean, Dennis and Karl walked noisily and talked aloud. They were men, big sun-burned raw-boned men, muscled from hard work, but uncertain of the fact that they were men. Therefore, walk with a swagger and laugh too loud, swear when Pa isn't listening and no one will know you have your doubts.

'What are you going to buy, Karl?'

'Boots.'

'That'll take all day – you'll have to try them on. We'll miss half the fun.'

'There'll be nothing doing for another couple hours,' protested Karl. 'Wait for me, you chaps.'

Karl sitting on the counter, trying boots on his large feet, was not a spectacle that could hold Sean's interest for long. He drifted away amongst the piles of merchandise that cluttered Pye's store. There were stacks of pick handles, piles of blankets, bins of sugar and salt and flour, shelves of groceries and clothing, overcoats and women's dresses and hurricane-lamps and saddles hanging from the roof, and all of it was permeated by the peculiar smell of a general dealer's store: a mixture of paraffin, soap and new cloth.

Pigeon to its coop, iron to magnet ... Sean's feet led him to the rack of rifles against the far wall of the room. He lifted down one of the Lee Metford carbines and worked the action; he stroked the wood with his fingertips, then he weighed it in his hands to feel the balance and finally brought it up to his shoulder.

'Hello, Sean.' His ritual interrupted, Sean looked up at the shy voice.

'It's Strawberry Pie,' he said smiling. 'How's school?'

'I've left school now. I left last term.'

Audrey Pye had the family colouring but with a subtle difference – instead of carrot her hair was smoked copper with glints in it. She was not a pretty girl, her face was too broad and flat, but she had that rare skin that too seldom goes with red hair: creamy unfreckled purity.

'Do you want to buy anything, Sean?'

Sean placed the carbine back in the rack.

'Just looking,' he said. 'Are you working in the store now?'

'Yes.' She dropped her eyes from Sean's scrutiny. It was a year since he'd last seen her. A lot can change in a year; she now had that within her blouse which proved she was no longer a child. Sean eyed it appreciatively and she glanced up and saw the direction of his eyes; the cream of her skin clouded red. She turned quickly towards the trays of fruit.

'Would you like a peach?'

'Thanks,' said Sean and took one.

'How's Anna?' asked Audrey.

'Why ask me?' Sean frowned.

'You're her beau, aren't you?'

'Who told you that?' Sean's frown became a scowl.

'Everybody knows that.'

'Well, everybody's wrong.' Sean was irritated by the suggestion that he was one of Anna's possessions. 'I'm nobody's beau.'

'Oh!' Audrey was silent a moment, then, 'I suppose Anna will be at the dance tonight?'

'Most probably.' Sean bit into the furry golden peach and studied Audrey. 'Are you going, Strawberry Pie?'

'No,' Audrey answered wistfully. 'Pa won't let me.'

How old was she? Sean made a quick calculation ... three years younger than he was. That made her sixteen. Suddenly Sean was sorry she wouldn't be at the dance.

'That's a pity,' he said. 'We could have had some fun.' Linking them together, with the plural 'we', Sean threw her into confusion again. She said the first words she could think of, 'Do you like the peach?'

'Hmm.'

'It's from our orchard.'

'I thought I recognized the flavour.' Sean grinned and Audrey laughed. Her mouth was wide and friendly when she laughed. 'I knew you used to pinch them. Pa knew it was you. He used to say he'd set a mantrap in that hole in the hedge.'

'I didn't know he'd found that hole – we used to cover it up each time.'

'Oh, yes,' Audrey assured him, 'we knew about it all the time. It's still there. Some nights when I can't sleep I climb out of my bedroom window and go down through the orchard, through the hedge into the wattle plantation. It's so dark and quiet in the plantation at night – scary, but I like it.'

'You know something,' Sean spoke thoughtfully. 'If you couldn't sleep tonight and came down to the hedge at ten o'clock, you might catch me pinching peaches again.'

It took a few seconds for Audrey to realize what he had said. Then the colour flew up her face again and she tried to speak but no words came. She turned with a swirl of skirt and darted away among the shelves. Sean bit the last of the flesh off the peach pip and dropped it on the floor. He was smiling as he walked across to join the others.

'Hell's teeth, Karl, how much longer are you going to be?'

– 17 –

There were fifty or more wagons outspanned around the perimeter of the square but the centre was left open, and here the braaivleis pits were burning, the flames already sinking to form glowing beds. Trestle-tables stood in two lines near the fires and the women worked at them cutting meat and boerwors, buttering bread, arranging platoons of pickle bottles, piling the food on trays and sweetening the evening with their voices and laughter.

In a level place a huge buck-sail was spread for the dancing and at each corner a lantern hung on a pole. The band was tuning with squeaks from the fiddles and preliminary asthma from the single concertina.

The men gathered in knots amongst the wagons or squatted beside the braaivleis pits, and here and there a jug pointed its base briefly at the sky.

'I don't like to be difficult, Waite,' Petersen came across to where Waite was standing with his captains, 'but I see you've put Dennis in Gunther's troop.'

'That's right.' Waite offered him the jug and Petersen took it and wiped the neck with his sleeve.

'It's not you, Gunther,' Petersen smiled at Gunther Niewehuisen, 'but I would be much happier if I could have Dennis in the same troop as myself. Keep an eye on him, you know.'

They all looked at Waite to hear what he would say. 'None of the boys are riding with their fathers. We've purposely arranged it that way. Sorry, Dave.'

'Why?'

Waite Courtney looked away, over the wagons at the furious red sunset that hung above the escarpment. 'This isn't going to be a bushbuck shoot, Dave. You may find that you'll be called upon to make decisions that will be easier for you if you're not making them about your own son.'

There was a murmur of agreement and Steff Erasmus took his pipe out of his mouth and spat into the fire. 'There are some things it is not pretty for a man to see. They are too hard for him to forget. He should not see his son kill his first man, also he should not see his son die.'

They were silent then, knowing this truth. They had not spoken of it before because too much talk softens a man's stomach, but they knew death and understood what Steff had said. One by one their heads turned until they were all staring across the square at the gathering of youngsters beyond the fires. Dennis Petersen said something but they could not catch the words and his companions laughed.

'In order to live a man must occasionally kill,' said Waite, 'but when he kills too young, he loses something . . . a respect for life: he makes it cheap. It is the same with a woman, a man should never have his first woman until he understands about it. Otherwise that too becomes cheap.'

'I had my first when I was fifteen,' said Tim Hope-Brown.

'I can't say it made them any cheaper; in fact I've known them to be bloody expensive.'

Waite's big boom led the laughter.

'I know your old man pays you a pound a week but what about us, Sean?' protested Dennis. 'We aren't all millionaires.'

'All right, then,' Sean agreed, 'five shillings in the pool. Winner takes the lot.'

'Five bob is reasonable,' Karl opined, 'but let's get the rules clear so there's no argument afterwards.'

'Kills only, woundings don't count,' said Sean.

'And they have to be witnessed,' insisted Frikkie Van Essen. He was older than the others; his eyes were already a little bloodshot for he had made a start on the evening's drinking.

'All right, dead Zulus only and a witness to each kill. The highest score takes the pool.' Sean looked around the circle of faces for their assent. Garry was hanging back on the fringe. 'Garry will be banker. Come on, Garry, hold out your hat.'

They paid the money into Garrick's hat and he counted it.

'Two pounds – from eight of us. That's correct.'

'Hell, the winner will be able to buy his own farm.'

They laughed.

'I've got a couple of bottles of smoke hidden in my saddle bags,' Frikkie said. 'Let's go and try them.'

The hands of the clock on the church tower showed quarter before ten. There were silver-edged clouds around the moon, and the night had cooled. Rich meaty smelling steam from the cooking pits drifted across the dancers, fiddles sawed and the concertina bawled the beat, dancers danced and the watchers clapped in time and called

encouragement to them. Someone whooped like a High-
lander in the feverish pattern of movement, in the fever of
fun. Dam the dribble of minutes with laughter, hold the
hour, lay siege against the dawn!

'Where are you going, Sean?'

'I'll be back just now.'

'But where are you going?'

'Do you want me to tell you, Anna, do you really want
to know?'

'Oh, I see. Don't be long. I'll wait for you by the band.'

'Dance with Karl.'

'No, I'll wait for you, Sean. Please don't be long. We've
got such a little time left.'

Sean slipped through the circle of wagons. He kept in
the tree shadow along the sidewalk, round the side of Pye's
store and down the lane, running now, jumped the ditch
and through the barbed wire fence. It was dark in the
plantation and quiet as she had said; dead leaves rustled
and a twig popped under his feet. Something ran in the
darkness, scurry of small feet. Sean's stomach flopped over:
nerves, only a rabbit. He came to the hedge and searched
for the hole, missed it and turned back, found it and
through into the orchard. He stood with his back against
the wall of vegetation and waited. The trees were moon
grey and black below. He could see the roof of the house
beyond them. He knew she'd come, of course. He had told
her to.

The church clock chimed the hour and then later the
single stroke of the quarter hour. Angry now, damn her! He
went up through the orchard, cautiously staying in shadow.
There was a light in one of the side windows, he could see
it spilling out into a yellow square on the lawn. He circled
the house softly.

She was at the window with the lamp behind her. Her
face was dark but lamplight lit the edges of her hair into a

coppery halo. There was something of yearning in her attitude, leaning forward over the sill. He could see the outline of her shoulders through the white cloth of her gown.

Sean whistled, pitching it low to reach her only, and she started at the sound. A second longer she stared out from light into the dark and then she shook her head, slowly and regretfully from side to side. She closed the curtains and through them Sean saw her shadow move away. The lamp went out.

Sean went back through the orchard and the plantation. He was trembling with anger. From the lane he heard the music in the square and he quickened his pace. He turned the corner and saw the lights and movement.

'Silly little fool,' he said out loud, anger still there but something else as well. Affection? Respect?

'Where have you been? I've waited nearly an hour.' Possessive Anna.

'There and back to see how far it is.'

'Funny! Sean Courtney, where have you been?'

'Do you want to dance?'

'No.'

'All right, don't then.'

Karl and some of the others were standing by the cooking pits. Sean started for them.

'Sean, Sean, I'm sorry.' Penitent Anna. 'I'd love to dance, please.'

They danced, jostled by other dancers, but neither of them spoke until the band stopped to wipe their brows and wet dry throats.

'I've got something for you, Sean.'

'What is it?'

'Come, I'll show you.'

She led him from the light among the wagons and

stopped by a pile of saddles and blankets. She knelt and opened one of the blankets and stood up again with the coat in her hands.

'I made it for you. I hope you like it.'

Sean took it from her. It was sheepskin, tanned and polished, stitched with love, the inside wool bleached snowy white.

'It's beautiful,' Sean said. He recognized the labour that had gone into it. It made him feel guilty: gifts always made him feel guilty.

'Thank you very much.'

'Try it on, Sean.'

Warm, snug at the waist, room to move in the shoulders; it enhanced his considerable bulk. Anna stood close to him, arranging the collar.

'You look nice in it,' she said. Smug pleasure of the giver.

He kissed her and the mood changed. She held him tight around the neck. 'Oh, Sean, I wish you weren't going.'

'Let's say goodbye properly.'

'Where?'

'My wagon.'

'What about your parents?'

'They've gone back to the farm. Pa's coming in tomorrow morning. Garry and I are sleeping here.'

'No, Sean, there are too many people. We can't.'

'You don't want to,' Sean whispered. 'It's a pity because it might be the last time ever.'

'What do you mean?' She was suddenly still and small in his arms.

'I'm going away tomorrow. You know what might happen?'

'No. Don't talk like that. Don't even think it.'

'It's true.'

105

'No, Sean, don't. Please don't.'

Sean smiled in the darkness. So easy, so very easy.

'Let's go to my wagon.' He took her hand.

– 18 –

Breakfast in the dark, cooking fires around the square, voices quiet, men standing with their wives, holding the small children in farewell. The horses saddled, rifles in the scabbards and blanket rolls behind, four wagons drawn up in the centre of the square with the mules in the traces.

'Pa should be here any minute. It's nearly five o'clock,' said Garry.

'They're all waiting for him,' agreed Sean. He shrugged at the weight of the bandolier strapped over his shoulder.

'Mr Niewehuizen has made me one of the wagon drivers.'

'I know,' said Sean. 'Can you handle it?'

'I think so.'

Jane Petersen came towards them.

'Hello, Jane. Is your brother ready yet?'

'Nearly. He's just saddling up.'

She stopped in front of Sean and shyly held out a scrap of green-and-yellow silk.

'I've made you a cockade for your hat, Sean.'

'Thanks, Jane. Won't you put it on for me?' She pinned up the brim of Sean's hat; he took it back from her and set it at a jaunty angle on his head.

'I look like a general now,' he said and she laughed at him. 'How about a goodbye kiss, Jane?'

'You're terrible,' said little Jane and went away quickly, blushing. Not so little, Sean noticed. There were so many of them you hardly knew where to start.

106

'Here's Pa,' announced Garry, as Waite Courtney rode into the square.

'Come on,' said Sean and untied his horse. From all around the square, men were leading out their horses.

'See you later,' said Garry and limped off towards one of the waiting mule wagons.

Waite rode at the head of the column. Four troops of fifteen men in double file, four wagons behind them, and then the loose horses driven by black servants.

They moved out across the square, through the litter of the night's festivities, and into the main street. The women watched them in silence, standing motionless with the children gathered around them. These women had seen men ride out before against the tribes; they did not cheer for they too were wise in the ways of death, they had learned that there is no room for glory in the grave.

Anna waved to Sean. He did not see her for his horse was skittish and he was past her before he had it under control. She let her hand drop back to her side and watched him go. He wore the skeepskin coat.

Sean did see the coppery flash and the swiftly-blown kiss from the upstairs window of Pye's store. He saw it because he was looking for it. He forgot his injured pride sufficiently to grin and wave his hat.

Then they were out of the town, and at last even the small boys and dogs that ran beside them fell back and the column trotted out along the road to Zululand.

The sun came up and dried the dew. The dust rose from under the hooves and drifted out at an angle from the road. The column lost its rigidity as men spurred ahead or dropped back to ride with their friends. They rode in groups and straggles, relaxed and cheerfully chatting, as informal as a party out for a day's shooting. Each man had taken to the field in the clothing he considered most suitable. Steff

Erasmus wore his church suit, but he was the most formally attired of the group. They had only one standard item of uniform among them: this was the green-and-yellow cockade. However, even here there was scope for individual taste: some wore them on their hats, some on their sleeves and others on their chests. They were farmers, not fighting men, but their rifle scabbards were battered with use, their bandoliers worn with easy familiarity and the wood of their gun butts was polished from the caress of their hands.

It was middle afternoon before they reached the Tugela.

'My God, look at that!' whistled Sean. 'I've never seen so many people in one place in my life before.'

'They say there are four thousand,' said Karl.

'I know there are four thousand.' Sean ran his eyes over the camp. 'But I didn't know four thousand was that many.'

The column was riding down the last slope to Rorke's Drift. The river was muddy brown and wide, rippling over the shallows of the crossing place. The banks were open and grassy with a cluster of stone-walled buildings on the near side. In a quarter-mile radius around the buildings Lord Chelmsford's army was encamped. The tents were laid out in meticulous lines, row upon row with the horses picketed between them. The wagons were marshalled by the Drift, five hundred at least, and the whole area swarmed with men.

The Ladyburg Mounted Rifles, in a solid bunch that overflowed the road behind their Colonel, came down to the perimeter of the camp and found their passage blocked by a sergeant in a dress coat and with a fixed bayonet.

'And who be you, may I ask?'

'Colonel Courtney – and a detachment of the Ladyburg Mounted Rifles.'

'What's that? Didn't catch it.'

Waite Courtney stood in his stirrups and turned to face his men.

'Hold on there, gentlemen. We can't all talk at once.'

The hubbub of conversation and comment behind him faded and this time the sergeant heard him.

'Ho! Beg your pardon, sir. I'll call the orderly officer.'

The orderly officer was an aristocrat and a gentleman. He came and looked at them. 'Colonel Courtney?' There was a note of disbelief in his voice.

'Hello,' said Waite with a friendly smile. 'I hope we are not too late for the fun.'

'No, I don't believe you are.' The officer's eyes fastened on Steff Erasmus. Steff lifted his top hat politely. '*More, Meneer.*' The bandoliers of ammunition looked a little out of place slung across his black frockcoat.

The officer tore his eyes away from him. 'You have your own tents, Colonel?'

'Yes, we've got everything we need.'

'I'll get the sergeant here to show you where to make camp.'

'Thank you,' said Waite.

The officer turned to the sergeant. So carried away was he that he took the man by the arm. 'Put them far away. Put them on the other side of the Engineers—' he whispered frantically. 'If the General sees this lot . . .' He shuddered, but in a genteel fashion.

– 19 –

Garrick first became conscious of the smell. Thinking about it served as a rallying point for his attention and he could start to creep out of the hiding-place in his mind. For Garrick, these returns to reality were always accompanied by a feeling of light-headedness and a heightening of the senses. Colours were vivid, skin sensitive to the touch, tastes and smells sharp and clear.

He lay on a straw mattress. The sun was bright, but he was in shade. He lay on the veranda of the stone-walled hospital above Rorke's Drift. He thought about the smell that had brought him back. It was a blending of corruption and sweat and dung, the smell of ripped bowels and congealing blood.

He recognized it as the smell of death. Then his vision came into focus and he saw the dead. They were piled along the wall of the yard where the cross-fire from the store and the hospital had caught them; they were scattered between the buildings, and the burial squads were busy loading them onto the wagons. They were lying down the slope to the Drift, they were in the water and on the far bank. Dead Zulus, with their weapons and shields strewn about them. Hundreds of them, Garrick thought with astonishment: no, thousands of them.

Then he was aware that there were two smells; but both of them were the smells of death. There was the stink of the black, balloon-bellied corpses swelling in the sun and there was the smell from his own body and the bodies of the men about him, the same smell of pain and putrefaction but mixed with the heaviness of disinfectant. Death wearing antiseptic – the way an unclean girl tries to cover her menstrual odour.

Garrick looked at the men around him. They lay in a long row down the veranda, each on his own mattress. Some were dying and many were not but on all of them the bandages were stained with blood and iodine. Garrick looked at his own body. His left arm was strapped across his bare chest and he felt the ache start beating within him, slow and steady as a funeral drum. There were bandages around his head. I'm wounded – again he was astonished. How? But how?

'You've come back to us, Cocky,' said a cheerful cockney from beside him. 'We thought you'd gone clean bonkers.'

Garrick turned his head and looked at the speaker; he was a small monkey-faced man in a pair of flannel underpants and a mummy suit of bandages.

'Doc said it was shock. He said you'd come out of it soon enough.' The little man raised his voice, 'Hey, Doc, the hero is completely mentos again.' The doctor came quickly, tired-looking, dark under the eyes, old with overwork.

'You'll do,' he said, having groped and prodded. 'Get some rest. They're sending you back home tomorrow.' He moved away for there were many wounded, but then he stopped and looked back. He smiled briefly at Garrick. 'I doubt it will ease the pain at all but you've been recommended for the Victoria Cross. The General endorsed your citation yesterday. I think you'll get it.' Garrick stared at the doctor as memory came back patchily.

'There was fighting,' Garrick said.

'You're bloody well tooting there was!' the little man beside him guffawed.

'Sean!' said Garrick. 'My brother! What happened to my brother?' There was silence then and Garrick saw the quick shadow of regret in the doctor's eyes. Garrick struggled into a sitting position.

'And my Pa. What happened to my father?'

'I'm sorry,' said the doctor with simplicity, 'I'm afraid they were both killed.'

Garrick lay on his mattress and looked down at the Drift. They were clearing the corpses out of the shallows now, splashing as they dragged them to the bank. He remembered the splashing as Chelmsford's army had crossed. Sean and his father had been among the scouts who had led the column, three troops of the Ladyburg Mounted Rifles and sixty men of the Natal Police. Chelmsford had used these men who knew the country over which the initial advance was to be made.

Garrick had watched them go with relief. He could

hardly believe the good fortune that had granted him a squirting dysentery the day before the ultimatum expired and the army crossed the Tugela.

'The lucky bastards,' protested one of the other sick as they watched them go. Garrick was without envy: he did not want to go to war, he was content to wait here with thirty other sick men and a garrison of sixty more to hold the Drift while Chelmsford took his army into Zululand.

Garrick had watched the scouts fan out from the Drift and disappear into the rolling grassland, and the main body of men and wagons follow them until they too had crawled like a python into the distance and left a well-worn road behind them through the grass.

He remembered the slow slide of days while they waited at the Drift. He remembered grumbling with the others when they were made to fortify the store and the hospital with bags and biscuit tins filled with sand. He remembered the boredom.

Then, his stomach tightening, he remembered the messenger.

'Horseman coming.' Garrick had seen him first. Recovered from his dysentery he was doing sentry duty above the Drift.

'The General's left his toothbrush behind, sent someone back for it,' said his companion. Neither of them stood up. They watched the speck coming across the plain towards the river.

'Coming fast,' said Garrick. 'You'd better go and call the Captain.'

'I suppose so,' agreed the other sentry. He trotted up the slope to the store and Garrick stood up and walked down to the edge of the river. His peg sank deep into the mud.

'Captain says to send him up to the store when he gets here.' Garrick's companion came back and stood beside him.

'Something funny about the way he's riding,' said Garrick, 'he looks tired.'

'He must be drunk. He's falling about in the saddle like it's Saturday night.'

Garrick gasped suddenly, 'He's bleeding, he's wounded.'

The horse plunged into the Drift and the rider fell forward onto its neck; the side of his shirt was shiny black with blood, his face was pale with pain and dust. They caught his horse as it came out of the water and the rider tried to shout but his voice was a croak. 'In the name of God prepare yourselves. The Column's been surrounded and wiped out. They're coming – the whole black howling pack of them. They'll be here before nightfall.'

'My brother,' said Garrick. 'What happened to my brother?'

'Dead,' said the man. 'Dead, they're all dead.' He slid sideways off his horse.

They came, the impis of Zulu in the formation of the bull, the great black bull whose head and loins filled the plain and whose horns circled left and right across the river to surround them. The bull stamped with twenty thousand feet and sang with ten thousand throats until its voice was the sound of the sea on a stormy day. The sunlight reflected brightly from the spear blades as it came singing to the Tugela.

'Look! Those in front are wearing the helmets of the Hussars,' one of the watchers in the hospital exclaimed. 'They've been looting Chelmsford's dead. There's one wearing a dress coat and some are carrying carbines.'

It was hot in the hospital for the roof was corrugated-iron and the windows were blocked with sandbags. The rifle slits let in little air. The men stood at the slits, some in pyjamas, some stripped to the waist and sweating in the heat.

'It's true then, the Column has been massacred.'

113

'That's enough talking. Stand to your posts and keep your mouths shut.'

The impis of Zulu crossed the Tugela on a front five hundred yards wide. They churned the surface to white with their crossing.

'My God! Oh, my God!' whispered Garrick as he watched them come. 'We haven't got a chance, there are so many of them.'

'Shut up. Damn you,' snapped the sergeant at the Gatling machine-gun beside him and Garry covered his mouth with his hand.

> '—Grabbed O'Riley by the neck
> Shoved his head in a pail of water
> Rammed that pistol up his—'

sang one of the malaria cases in delirium and somebody else laughed, shrill hysteria in the sound.

'Here they come!'

'Load!'

The metallic clashing of rifle mechanism. 'Hold your fire, men. Fire on command only.'

The voice of the bull changed from a deep sonorous chant to the shrill ululation of the charge – high-pitched frenzy of the blood squeal.

'Steady, men. Steady. Hold it. Hold your fire.'

'Oh, my God!' whispered Garrick softly, watching them come back up the slope. 'Oh, my God! – please don't let me die.'

'Ready!'

The van had reached the wall of the hospital yard. Their plumed head-dresses were the frothy crest of a black wave as they came over the wall.

'Aim!'

Sixty rifles lifted and held, aimed into the press of bodies.

'Fire!'

Thunder, then the strike of bullets into flesh, a sound as though a handful of gravel had been flung into a puddle of mud. The ranks reeled from the blow. The clustered barrels of the Gatling machine-gun jump – jump – jumped as they swung, cutting them down so they fell upon each other, thick along the wall. The stench of burnt black powder was painful to breathe.

'Load!'

The bullet-ravaged ranks were re-forming as those from behind came forward into the gaps.

'Aim!'

They were coming again, solid black and screaming halfway across the yard.

'Fire!'

Garrick sobbed in the shade of the veranda and pressed the fingers of his right hand into his eye sockets to squeeze out the memory.

'What's the trouble, Cocky?' The Cockney rolled painfully onto his side and looked at Garrick.

'Nothing!' said Garrick quickly. 'Nothing!'

'Coming back to you, is it?'

'What happened? I can only remember pieces of it.'

'What happened!' The man echoed his question, 'What didn't happen!'

'The doctor said—' Garrick looked up quickly. 'He said the General had endorsed my citation. That means Chelmsford's alive. My brother and my father – they must be alive as well!'

'No such luck, Cocky. The Doc's taken a fancy to you – you with one leg doing what you did – so he made inquiries about your folk. It's no use.'

'Why?' asked Garrick desperately. 'Surely if Chelmsford's alive they must be too?'

The little man shook his head. 'Chelmsford's made a

base camp at a place called Isandhlwana. He left a garrison there with all the wagons and supplies. He took a flying column out to raid, but the Zulus circled around him and attacked the base camp, then they came on here to the Drift. As you know, we held them for two days until Chelmsford's flying column came to help us.'

'My folk – what happened to them?'

'Your father was at the Isandhlwana camp. He didn't escape. Your brother was with Chelmsford's column but he was cut off and killed in one of the skirmishes before the main battle.'

'Sean dead?' Garrick shook his head. 'No, it's not possible. They couldn't have killed him.'

'You'd be surprised how easily they did it,' said the Cockney. 'A few inches of blade in the right place is enough for the best of them.'

'But not Sean – you didn't know him. You couldn't understand.'

'He's dead, Cocky. Him and your Pa and seven hundred others. The wonder is we aren't too.' The man wriggled into a more comfortable position on his mattress. 'The General made a speech about our defence here. Finest feat of arms in the annals of British courage – or something like that.'

He winked at Garrick. 'Fifteen citations for the old V.C. – you's one of them. I ask you, Cocky, isn't that something? What's your girl friend going to do when you come home with a mucking great gong clanking around on your chest, hey?'

He stared at Garrick and saw the tears oozing in oily lines down his cheeks.

'Come on, Cock. You're a bloody hero.' He looked away from Garrick's grief. 'Do you remember that part – do you remember what you did?'

'No,' Garrick's voice was husky. *Sean. You can't leave me alone. What am I going to do, now that you're gone?*

'I was next to you. I saw it all. I'll tell you about it,' said the Cockney.

As he talked so the events came back and fitted into sequence in Garrick's mind.

'It was on the second day, we'd held off twenty-three charges.'

Twenty-three, was it as many as that? Garrick had lost count; it might have been but a single surging horror. Even now he could taste the fear in the back of his throat and smell it rancid in his own sweat.

'Then they piled wood against the hospital wall and set fire to it.' Zulus coming across the yard carrying bundles of faggots, falling to the rifles, others picking up the bundles and bringing them closer until they too died and yet others came to take their place. Then flames pale yellow in the sunlight, a dead Zulu lying on the bonfire his face charring, and the smell of him mingled with the smoke.

'We knocked a hole in the back wall and started to move the sick and wounded out through it and across to the store.'

The boy with the assegai through his spine had shrieked like a girl as they lifted him.

'Them bloody savages came again as soon as they saw we were pulling out. They came from that side.' He pointed with his bandaged arm, 'Where the chaps in the store couldn't reach them, and there was only you and I and a couple of others at the loopholes – everyone else was carrying the wounded.'

There had been a Zulu with the blue heron feathers of an Induna in his head-dress. He had led the charge. His shield was dried oxhide dappled black and white, and at his wrists and ankles were bunches of war rattles. Garrick had

117

fired at the instant the Zulu half-turned to beckon to his warriors – the bullet sliced across the tensed muscles of his belly and unzipped it like a purse. The Zulu went down on his hands and knees with his entrails bulging out in a pink and purple mass.

'They reached the door of the hospital and we couldn't fire on them from the angle of the windows.'

The wounded Zulu started to crawl towards Garrick, his mouth moving and his eyes fastened on Garrick's face. He still had his assegai in his hand. The other Zulus were beating at the door and one of them ran his spear blade through a crack in the woodwork and lifted the bar. The door was open.

Garrick watched the Zulu crawling towards him through the dust with his pink wet bowels swinging like a pendulum under him. The sweat was running down Garrick's cheeks and dripping off the end of his chin, his lips were trembling. He lifted his rifle and aimed into the Zulu's face. He could not fire.

'That's when you moved, Cocky. I saw the bar lifted out of its brackets and I knew that in the next second there'd be a mob of them in through the door and we'd stand no chance against their spears at close range.'

Garrick let go his rifle and it rattled on the concrete floor. He turned away from the window. He could not watch that crippled, crawling thing. He wanted to run, to hide. That was it – to hide. He felt the fluttering start behind his eyes, and his sight began to grey.

'You were nearest to the door. You did the only thing that could have saved us. Though I know I wouldn't have had the guts to do it.'

The floor was covered with cartridge cases – brass cylinders shiny and treacherous under foot. Garrick stumbled; as he fell he put out his arm.

'Christ,' the little Cockney shuddered, 'to put your arm into the brackets like that – I wouldn't have done it.'

Garrick felt his arm snap as the mob of Zulus threw themselves against the door. He hung there staring at his twisted arm, watching the door tremble and shake as they beat against it. There was no pain and after a while everything was grey and warm and safe.

'We fired through the door until we had cleared them away from the other side. Then we were able to get your arm free, but you were out cold. Been that way ever since.'

Garrick stared out across the river. He wondered if they had buried Sean or left him in the grass for the birds.

Lying on his side Garrick drew his legs up against his chest, his body was curled. Once as a brutal small boy he had cracked the shell of a hermit crab. Its soft fat abdomen was so vulnerable that its vitals showed through the transparent skin. It curled its body into the same defensive attitude.

'I'll reckon you'll get your gong,' said the Cockney.

'Yes,' said Garrick. He didn't want it. He wanted Sean back.

– 20 –

D octor Van Rooyen gave Ada Courtney his arm as she stepped down from the buggy. In fifty years he had not obtained immunity from other people's sorrow. He had learned only to conceal it: no trace of it in his eyes, or his mouth, or his lined and whiskered face.

'He's well, Ada. They did a good job on his arm: that is, for military surgeons. It will set straight.'

'When did they arrive?' asked Ada.

'About four hours ago. They sent all the Ladyburg wounded back in two wagons.'

Ada nodded, and he looked at her with the professional shield of indifference, hiding the shock he felt at the change in her appearance. Her skin was as dry and lifeless as the petals of a pressed flower, her mouth had set determinedly against her grief and her widow's weeds had doubled her age.

'He's waiting for you inside.' They walked up the steps of the church and the small crowd opened to let them pass. There were subdued greetings for Ada and the usual funereal platitudes. There were other women there wearing black, with swollen eyes.

Ada and the doctor went into the cool gloom of the church. The pews had been pushed against the wall to make room for the mattresses. Women were moving about between them and men lay on them.

'I'm keeping the bad ones here, where I can watch them,' the doctor told her. 'There's Garry.'

Garrick stood up from the bench on which he was sitting. His arm was slung awkwardly across his chest. He limped forward to meet them, his peg tapped loudly on the stone floor.

'Ma, I'm—' he stopped. 'Sean and Pa—'

'I've come to take you home, Garry.' Ada spoke quickly, flinching at the sound of those two names.

'They can't just let them lie out there, they should—'

'Please, Garry. Let's go home,' said Ada. 'We can talk about it later.'

'We are all very proud of Garry,' said the doctor.

'Yes,' said Ada. 'Please, let's go home, Garry.' She could feel it there just below the surface and she held it in: so much sorrow confined in so small a place. She turned back towards the door, she mustn't let them see it. She mustn't cry here in front of them, she must get back to Theunis Kraal.

Willing hands carried Garrick's bags out to the buggy

and Ada took the reins. Neither of them spoke again until they crossed the ridge and looked down at the homestead.

'You're the master of Theunis Kraal now, Garry,' said Ada softly and Garrick stirred uneasily on the seat beside her. He didn't want it, he didn't want the medal. He wanted Sean.

– 21 –

'I hope you don't mind me coming,' said Anna, 'but I had to talk to you.'

'No. I'm glad you did. Truly I'm glad,' Garrick assured her earnestly. 'It's so good to see you again, Anna. It feels like forever since we left.'

'I know, and so much – so much has happened. My Pa and yours. And – and Sean.' She stopped. 'Oh, Garry, I just can't believe it yet. They've told me and told me but I can't believe it. He was so – so alive.'

'Yes,' said Garrick, 'he was so alive.'

'He talked about dying the night before he left. I hadn't even thought about it until then.' Anna shook her head in disbelief, 'And I never dreamed it could happen to him. Oh, Garry, what am I going to do?'

Garrick turned and looked at Anna. The Anna he loved, Sean's Anna. But Sean was dead. He felt an idea move within him, not yet formed in words, but real enough to cause a sick spasm of conscience. He shied away from it.

'Oh, Garry. What can I do?'

She was asking for help, the appeal was apparent in her voice. Her father killed at Isandhlwana, her elder brothers still with Chelmsford at Tugela, her mother and the three small children to feed. How blind of him not to see it!

'Anna, can I help you? Just tell me.'

'No, Garry. I don't think anyone can.'

'If it's money—' He hesitated discreetly. 'I'm a rich man now. Pa left the whole of Theunis Kraal to Sean and I, and Sean isn't—' She looked at him without answering.

'I can lend you some to tide you over—' blushed Garrick, 'as much as you need.'

She went on staring at him while her mind adjusted itself. Garrick master of Theunis Kraal, he was rich, twice as rich as Sean would have been. And Sean was dead.

'Please, Anna. Let me help you. I want to, really I do.'

He loved her, it was pathetically obvious – and Sean was dead.

'You will let me, Anna?'

She thought of hunger and bare feet, dresses washed until you could see through them when you held them to the light, petticoats patched and cobbled. And always the fear, the uncertainty you must live with when you are poor. Garry was rich and alive, Sean was dead.

'Please tell me you will.' Garrick leaned forward and took her arm, he gripped it fiercely in his agitation and she looked into his face. You could see the resemblance, she thought, but Sean had strength where here there was softness and uncertainty. The colour was wrong also, pale sand and paler blue instead of brutal black and indigo. It was as though an artist had taken a portrait and with a few subtle strokes had altered its meaning completely so as to make it into an entirely different picture. She did not want to think about his leg.

'It's sweet of you, Garry,' she said, 'but we've got a little in the bank and the plot is free of debt. We've got the horses; we can sell them if we have to.'

'What is it then? Please tell me.'

She knew then what she was going to do. She could not lie to him – it was too late for that. She would have to tell him, but she knew that the truth would not make any

122

difference to him. Well, perhaps a little – but not enough to prevent her getting what she wanted. She wanted to be rich, and she wanted a father for the child she carried within her.

'Garry, I'm going to have a baby.'

Garrick's chin jerked up and his breathing jammed and then started again.

'A baby?'

'Yes, Garrick. I'm pregnant.'

'Whose? Sean's?'

'Yes, Garry. I'm going to have Sean's baby.'

'How do you know, are you sure?'

'I'm sure.'

Garrick pulled himself out of his chair and limped across the veranda. He stopped against the railing and gripped it with his good hand; the other was still in the sling. His back was turned to Anna and he stared out across the lawns of Theunis Kraal to the lightly-forested slope beyond.

Sean's baby. The idea bewildered him. He knew that Sean and Anna did that together. Sean had told him and Garrick had not resented it. He was jealous, but only a little, for Sean had let him share in it by telling him and so some of it had belonged to him also. But a baby. Sean's baby.

Slowly the full implication came to him. Sean's baby would be a living part of his brother, the part that had not been cut down by the Zulu blades. He had not completely lost Sean. Anna – she must have a father for her child, it was unthinkable that she could go another month without marrying. He could have both of them, everything he loved in one package. Sean and Anna. She must marry him, she had no other choice. Triumph surged up within him and he turned to her.

'What will you do, Anna?' He felt sure of her now. 'Sean's dead. What will you do?'

'I don't know.'

'You can't have the baby. It would be a bastard.' He saw her wince at the word. He felt very certain of her.

'I'll have to go away – to Port Natal.' She spoke without expression in her voice. Looking calmly at him, knowing what he would say, 'I'll leave soon,' she said, 'I'll be all right. I'll find some way out.'

Garrick watched her face as she spoke. Her head was small on shoulders wide for a girl, her chin was pointed, her teeth were slightly crooked but white – she was very pretty despite the catlike set of her eyes.

'I love you, Anna,' he said. 'You know that, don't you?'

She nodded slowly and her hair moved darkly on her shoulders. The cat eyes softened contentedly. 'Yes, I know, Garry.'

'Will you marry me?' He said it breathlessly.

'You don't mind? You don't mind about Sean's baby?' she said, knowing he did not.

'I love you, Anna.' He came towards her clumsily and she looked up at his face. She did not want to think about the leg.

'I love you, nothing else matters.' He reached for her and she let him hold her.

'Will you marry me, Anna?' He was trembling.

'Yes.' Her hands were quiescent on his shoulders. He sobbed softly and her expression changed to one of distaste. She made the beginnings of a movement to push him away but stopped herself.

'My darling, you won't regret it. I swear you won't,' he whispered.

'We must do it quickly, Garry.'

'Yes. I'll go into town this afternoon and speak to Padre—'

'No! Not here in Ladyburg,' Anna cut in sharply. 'People will have too much to say. I couldn't stand it.'

'We'll go up to Pietermaritzburg,' Garrick acquiesced.

'When, Garry?'

'As soon as you like.'

'Tomorrow,' she said. 'We'll go tomorrow.'

– 22 –

The Cathedral in Pietermaritzburg stands on Church Street. Grey stone with a bell-tower and iron railings between the street and the lawns. Pigeons strut puff-chested on the grass.

Anna and Garrick went up the paved path and into the semi-dark of the Cathedral. The stained glass window had the sun behind it, making the interior glow weirdly with colour. Because they were both nervous they held hands as they stood in the aisle.

'There's no one here,' whispered Garrick.

'There must be,' Anna whispered back. 'Try through that door there.'

'What shall I say?'

'Just tell him we want to get married.'

Garrick hesitated.

'Go on.' Anna still whispered, pushing him gently towards the door of the vestry.

'You come with me,' said Garrick. 'I don't know what to say.'

The priest was a thin man with steel-rimmed spectacles. He looked over the top of them at the nervous pair in the doorway and shut the book on the desk in front of him.

'We want to get married,' Garrick said and blushed crimson.

'Well,' said the priest drily, 'you have the right address. Come in.'

He was surprised at their haste and they argued a little,

then he sent Garrick down to the Magistrates' Court for a special licence. He married them, but the ceremony was hollow and unreal. The drone of the priest's voice was almost lost in the immense cavern of the Cathedral as they stood small and awed before him. Two old ladies who came in to pray stayed on gleefully to witness for them, and afterwards they both kissed Anna and the priest shook Garrick's hand. Then they went out again into the sunlight. The pigeons still strutted on the lawn and a mule wagon rattled down Church Street with the coloured driver singing and cracking his whip. It was as though nothing had happened.

'We're married,' said Garrick doubtfully.

'Yes,' agreed Anna, but she sounded as though she didn't believe it either.

They walked back to the hotel side by side. They didn't talk or touch each other. Their luggage had been taken up to their room and the horses had been stabled. Garrick signed the register and the clerk grinned at him.

'I've put you in Number Twelve, sir, it's our honeymoon suite.' One of his eyelids drooped slightly and Garrick stammered in confusion.

After dinner, an excellent dinner, Anna went up to the room and Garrick sat on in the lounge drinking coffee. It was almost an hour later that he mustered the courage to follow her. He crossed the drawing-room of their suite, hesitated at the bedroom door then went in. Anna was in bed. She had pulled the bedclothes up to her chin and she looked at him with her inscrutable cat's eyes.

'I've put your nightshirt in the bathroom, on the table,' she said.

'Thank you,' said Garrick. He stumbled against a chair as he crossed the room. He closed the door behind him, undressed quickly and leaning naked over the basin splashed water onto his face; then he dried and pulled the nightshirt over his head. He went back into the bedroom: Anna lay with her face turned away from him. Her hair was loose on the pillow, shining in the lamplight.

Garrick sat on the edge of the chair. He lifted the hem of his nightshirt above his knee and unfastened the straps of his leg, laid the peg carefully beside the chair and massaged the stump with both hands. It felt stiff. He heard the bed creak softly and he looked up. Anna was watching him, staring at his leg. Hurriedly Garrick pulled down his nightshirt to cover the protruding, slightly enlarged end with its folded line of scar-tissue. He stood up, balancing, and then hopped one-legged across to the bed. He was blushing again.

He lifted the edge of the blankets and slipped into the bed and Anna jerked violently away from him.

'Don't touch me,' she said hoarsely.

'Anna. Please don't be scared.'

'I'm pregnant, you mustn't touch me.'

'I won't. I swear I won't.'

She was breathing hard, making no attempt to hide her revulsion.

'Do you want me to sleep in the drawing-room, Anna? I will if you say so.'

'Yes,' she said, 'I want you to.'

He gathered his dressing-gown from the chair and stooping picked up his leg. He hopped to the door and turned back to face her. She was watching him still.

'I'm sorry, Anna, I didn't mean to frighten you.' She did not answer him and he went on.

'I love you. I swear I love you more than anything in the world. I wouldn't hurt you, you know that, don't you? You know I wouldn't hurt you?'

Still she did not answer and he made a small gesture of

appeal, the wooden leg clutched in his hand and the tears starting to fill his eyes. 'Anna. I'd kill myself rather than frighten you!'

He went quickly through the door and closed it behind him. Anna scrambled out of the bed and with her nightdress flurrying around her legs she ran across the room to the door and turned the key in the lock.

– 23 –

In the morning Garrick was bewildered to find Anna in a mood of girlish gaiety. She had a green ribbon in her hair and her green frock was faded but pretty. She chattered happily through breakfast and while they were having their coffee she leaned across the table and touched Garrick's hand. 'What shall we do today, Garry?'

Garrick looked surprised, he hadn't thought that far ahead. 'I suppose we'd better catch the afternoon train back to Ladyburg,' he said.

'Oh, Garry,' Anna pouted effectively. 'Don't you love me enough to give me a honeymoon?'

'I suppose—' Garrick hesitated and then, 'of course, I didn't think of it.' He grinned excitedly. 'Where can we go?'

'We could take the mail boat down the coast to Cape-town,' Anna suggested.

'Yes!' Garrick adopted the idea immediately. 'It'll be fun.'

'But, Garry—' Anna's eagerness faded. 'I only have two old dresses with me.' She touched her clothes. Garrick sobered also while he grappled with this new problem. Then he found the solution.

'We'll buy you some more!'

'Oh, Garry, could we? Could we really?'

'We'll buy you all you can use, more than you can use. Come on, finish your coffee and we'll go into town and see what they have.'

'I'm finished.' Anna stood up from the table ready to go.

– 24 –

They had a stateroom on the *Dunottar Castle* from Port Natal to Capetown. There were other young people aboard. Anna, in her elegant new clothing and sparkling with excitement, formed the centrepiece of a gay little group that played deck games, dined, danced and flirted as the mailboat drove south through the sunny, golden days of early autumn.

At first Garrick was content to stay unobtrusively close to Anna. He was there to hold her coat, fetch a book or carry a rug. He watched her fondly, revelling in her success, hardly jealous when she almost disappeared behind a palisade of attentive young men, not resenting the sofa which formed his uncomfortable bed in the drawing-room of their suite.

Then gradually there came a realization among their travelling companions that Garrick was paying for most of the refreshments and other little expenses that came up each day. They became aware of him and of the fact that he appeared to be the richest of the group. From there it needed only a small adjustment to their thinking to admit Garrick to the circle. The men addressed remarks directly at him and some of the other girls flirted with him openly and sent him on small errands. Garrick was at once overjoyed and appalled by these attentions, for he could not cope with the lightning exchange of banter that flickered around him and left him stammering and blushing. Then Garrick found how easy it really was.

'Have a dram, old chap?'

'No, really. I don't, you know.'

'Nonsense, everybody does. Steward, bring my friend here a whisky.'

'Really, no really I won't.'

And of course Garrick did. It tasted foul and he spilt a little on Anna's evening dress; while he wiped it up with his handkerchief she whispered a barbed reprimand and then laughed gaily at a joke from the moustached gentleman on her right. Garrick shrank miserably back in his chair and forced down the rest of the whisky. Then slowly and exquisitely the glow came upon him, starting deep down inside him and spreading out warmly to the very tips of his fingers.

'Have another one, Mr Courtney?'

'Yes, thanks. I'll have the same again, but I think it's my round.' He had the next drink. They were sitting in deck-chairs on the upper deck in the shelter of the superstructure, there was a moon and the night was warm. Someone was talking about Chelmsford's Zulu campaign.

'You're wrong on that point,' Garrick said clearly. There was a small silence.

'I beg your pardon!' the speaker glanced at him with surprise. Garrick leaned forward easily in his chair and began talking. There was a stiffness at first but he made a witticism and two of the women laughed. Garrick's voice strengthened. He gave a quick and deep-sighted résumé of the causes and effects of the war. One of the men asked a question. It was a sharp one but Garrick saw the essence of it and answered neatly. It was all very clear and he found the words without effort.

'You must have been there,' one of the girls hazarded.

'My husband was at Rorke's Drift,' said Anna quietly, looking at him as though he were a stranger. 'Lord Chelmsford has cited him for the award of the Victoria Cross. We are waiting to hear from London.'

The party was silent again, but with new respect.

'I think it's my round, Mr Courtney. Yours is whisky, isn't it?'

'Thank you.'

The dry musty taste of the whisky was less offensive this time; he sipped it thoughtfully and found that there was a faint sweetness in the dry.

As they went down to their staterooms later that night Garrick put his arm around Anna's waist.

'What fun you were tonight!' she said.

'Only a reflection of your charm, my darling, I am your mirror.' He kissed her cheek and she pulled away, but not violently.

'You're a tease, Garry Courtney.'

Garrick slept on his back on the sofa with a smile on his face and no dreams, but in the morning his skin felt tight and dry and there was a small ache behind his eyes. He went through to the bathroom and cleaned his teeth; it helped a little but the ache behind his eyes was still there. He went back to the drawing-room and rang for the cabin steward.

'Good morning, sir.'

'Can you bring me a whisky and soda?' Garry asked hesitantly.

'Certainly, sir.'

Garry did not put the soda into it but drank it neat, like medicine. Then afterwards miraculously the glow was there again, warming him. He had hardly dared to hope for it.

He went through to Anna's cabin. She was rosy with sleep, her hair a joyous tangle on the pillow.

'Good morning, my darling.' Garrick stooped over her and kissed her, and his hand moved to cover one of her breasts through the silk of her gown.

'Garry, you naughty boy.' She slapped his wrist, but jokingly.

There was another honeymoon couple aboard returning to their farm near Capetown – seventy-five acres of the finest vines on the whole of the Cape Peninsula, the man's own words. Anna and Garrick were forced by sheer persistence to accept their invitation to stay with them.

Peter and Jane Hugo were a delightful pair. Very much in love, rich enough, popular and in demand with Capetown society. With them Anna and Garrick spent an enchanted six weeks.

They went racing at Milnerton.

They swam at Muizenberg in the warm Indian Ocean. They picnicked at Clifton and ate crayfish, fresh caught and grilled over open coals. They rode to hounds with the Cape Hunt and caught two jackals after a wild day's riding over the Hottentots' Holland. They dined at the Fort and Anna danced with the Governor.

They went shopping in the bazaars that were filled with treasures and curiosities from India and the Orient. Whatever Anna wanted she was given. Garry bought himself something as well – a silver flask, beautifully worked and set with cornelians. It fitted into the inside pocket of his coat without showing a bulge. With its help Garrick was able to keep pace with the rest of the company.

Then the time came for them to leave. The last night there were only the four of them for dinner and it was sad with the regret of present parting, but happy with the memory of shared laughter.

Jane Hugo cried a little when she kissed Anna goodnight. Garry and Peter lingered on downstairs until the bottle was finished and then they walked upstairs together and shook hands outside Garry's bedroom. Peter spoke gruffly. 'Sorry to see you two go. We've got used to having you round. I'll wake you early and we can go out for a last early morning ride before the boat leaves.'

Garry changed quietly in the bathroom and went through to the bedroom. His peg made no sound on the heavily carpeted floor. He crossed to his own bed and sat down to unstrap his peg.

'Garry,' Anna whispered.

'Hullo, I thought you were asleep.'

There was a stirring and Anna's hand came out from under the bedclothes, held towards him in invitation.

'I was waiting to say goodnight to you.'

Garry crossed to her bed, suddenly awkward again.

'Sit down for a minute,' said Anna and he perched on the edge of her bed. 'Garry, you don't know how much I've enjoyed these last weeks. They've been the happiest days of my whole life. Thank you so much, my husband.'

She reached up and touched his cheek. She looked small and warm curled up in the bed.

'Kiss me goodnight, Garry.'

He leaned forward to touch her forehead with his lips but she moved quickly and took it full on her mouth.

'You can come in, if you like,' she whispered, her mouth still against his. She opened the bedclothes with one hand.

So Garry came to her when the bed was warm, and the wine still sang a little in her head and she was ready in the peculiar passion of early pregnancy. It should have been so wonderfully good.

Impatient now, ready to lead him, she reached down to touch and then stilled into surprised disbelief. Where there should have been hardness, male and arrogant, there was slackness and uncertainty.

Anna started to laugh. Not even the shotgun blast had hurt as deeply as that laugh.

'Get out,' she said through the cruel laughter. 'Go to your own bed.'

Anna and Garrick had been married two full months when they came back to Theunis Kraal. Garrick's arm was out of plaster, Peter Hugo's doctor had fixed that for him.

They took the road that by-passed the village and crossed the Baboon Stroom bridge. At the top of the rise Garry pulled the horses to a halt and they looked out across the farm.

'I can't understand why Ma moved into town,' said Garrick. 'She didn't have to do that. There's plenty of room for everybody at Theunis Kraal.'

Anna sat silently and contentedly beside him. She had been relieved when Ada had written to them at Port Natal after they had telegraphed her the news of their marriage. Young as she was Anna was woman enough to recognize the fact that Ada had never liked her. Oh, she was sweet enough when they met, but Anna found those big dark eyes of hers disconcerting. They looked too deep and she knew they found the things she was trying to hide.

'We'll have to go and see her as soon as we can. She must come back to the farm – after all Theunis Kraal is her home too,' Garrick went on. Anna moved slightly in her seat, *let her stay in the house in Ladyburg, let her rot there,* but her voice was mild as she answered, 'Theunis Kraal belongs to you now, Garry, and I'm your wife. Perhaps your stepmother knows what's best.' Anna touched his arm and smiled at him, 'Anyway we'll talk about it some other time. Let's get home now, it's been a long drive and I'm very tired.'

Immediately concerned, Garrick turned to her. 'I'm terribly sorry, my dear. How thoughtless of me.' He touched the horses with the whip and they went down the slope towards the homestead.

The lawns of Theunis Kraal were green and there were cannas in bloom, red and pink and yellow.

It's beautiful, thought Anna, *and it's mine. I'm not poor any more.* She looked at the gabled roof and the heavy yellow wood shutters on the windows as the carriage rolled up the drive.

There was a man standing in the shade of the veranda. Anna and Garrick saw him at the same time. He was tall with shoulders as wide and square as the crosstree of a gallows. He stepped out of the shadow and came down the front steps into the sunlight. He was smiling with white teeth in a brown burnt face; it was the old irresistible smile.

'Sean,' whispered Anna.

– 26 –

Sean really noticed him for the first time when they stopped to water the horses. They had left Chelmsford's Column the previous noon to scout towards the north-east. It was a tiny patrol – four mounted white men and a half-a-dozen Nongaai, the loyal Native troops from Natal.

He took the reins from Sean's hands. 'I will hold your horse while you drink.' His voice had a resonance to it and Sean's interest quickened. He looked at the man's face and liked it immediately. The whites of the eyes had no yellow in them and the nose was more Arabic than negroid. His colour was dark amber and his skin shone with oil.

Sean nodded. There is no word in the Zulu language for 'thank you', just as there are no words for 'I am sorry'.

Sean knelt beside the stream and drank. The water tasted sweet for he was thirsty; when he stood again there were damp patches on his knees and water dripping from his chin.

He looked at the man who was holding his horse. He wore only a small kilt of civet-cat tails: no rattles nor cloak, no head-dress. His shield was black rawhide and he carried two short stabbing spears.

'How are you called?' Sean asked, noticing the breadth of the man's chest and the way his belly muscles stood out like the static ripples on a windswept beach.

'Mbejane.' Rhinoceros.

'For your horn?' The man chuckled with delight, his masculine vanity tickled.

'How are you called, Nkosi?'

'Sean Courtney.'

Mbejane's lips formed the name silently and then he shook his head.

'It is a difficult name.' He never said Sean's name – not once in all the years that were to follow.

'Mount up,' called Steff Erasmus. 'Let's get moving.'

They swung up onto the horses, gathered the reins and loosened the rifles in the scabbards. The Nongaai who had been stretched out resting on the bank stood up.

'Come on,' said Steff. He splashed through the stream. His horse gathered itself and bounded up the far bank and they followed him. They moved in line abreast across the grassland, sitting loose and relaxed in their saddles, the horses trippling smoothly.

At Sean's right stirrup ran the big Zulu, his long extended stride easily pacing Sean's horse. Once in a while Sean dropped his eyes from the horizon and looked down at Mbejane; it was a strangely comforting feeling to have him there.

They camped that night in a shallow valley of grass.

There were no cooking fires; they ate biltong for supper, the black strips of dried salt meat, and washed it down with cold water.

'We're wasting our time. There hasn't been a sign of Zulu in two days' riding,' grumbled Bester Klein, one of the troopers.

'I say we should turn back and rejoin the Column. We're getting farther and farther away from the centre of things – we're going to miss the fun when it starts.'

Steff Erasmus wrapped his blanket more closely about his shoulders: the night's first chill was on them.

'Fun, is it?' He spat expertly into the darkness. 'Let them have the fun, if we find the cattle.'

'Don't you mind missing the fighting?'

'Look, you, I've hunted bushmen in the Karroo and the Kalahari, I've fought Xhosas and Fingoes along the Fish river, I went into the mountains after Moshesh and his Basutos. Matabele, Zulu, Bechuana – I've had fun with all of them. Now four or five hundred head of prime cattle will be payment enough for any fun we miss.' Steff lay back and adjusted his saddle behind his head. 'Anyway what makes you think there won't be guards on the herds when we find them. You'll get your fun – I promise you.'

'How do you know they've got the cattle up here?' insisted Sean.

'They're here,' said Steff, 'and we'll find them.' He turned his head towards Sean. 'You've got the first watch, keep your eyes open.' He tilted his top hat forward over his face, groped with his right hand to make sure his rifle lay beside him and then spoke from under the hat, 'Goodnight.' The others settled down into their blankets: fully-dressed, boots on, guns at hand. Sean moved out into the darkness to check the Nongaai pickets.

There was no moon, but the stars were fat and close to earth; they lit the land so that the four grazing horses were

137

dark blobs against the pale grass. Sean circled the camp and found two of his sentries awake and attentive. He had posted Mbejane on the north side and now he went there. Fifty yards in front of him he picked up the shape of the small bush beside which he had left Mbejane. Suddenly Sean smiled and sank down onto his hands and knees, he cradled his rifle across the crooks of his elbows and began his stalk. Moving flat along the ground silently, slowly he closed in on the bush. Ten paces from it he stopped and lifted his head, careful to keep the movement inchingly slow. He stared, trying to find the shape of the Zulu among the scraggy branches and bunches of leaves. The point of a stabbing spear pricked him below the ear in the soft of his neck behind the jaw bone. Sean froze but his eyes rolled sideways and in the starlight he saw Mbejane kneeling over him holding the spear.

'Does the Nkosi seek me?' asked Mbejane solemnly, but there was laughter deep down in his voice. Sean sat up and rubbed the place where the spear had stung him.

'Only a night ape sees in the dark,' Sean protested.

'And only a fresh caught catfish flops on its belly,' chuckled Mbejane.

'You are Zulu,' Sean stated, recognizing the arrogance, although he had known immediately from the man's face and body that he was not one of the bastard Natal tribes who spoke the Zulu language but were no more Zulu than a tabby-cat is a leopard.

'Of Chaka's blood,' agreed Mbejane, reverence in his voice as he said the old king's name.

'And now you carry the spear against Cetewayo, your king?'

'My king?' The laughter was gone from Mbejane's voice. 'My king?' he repeated scornfully.

There was silence and Sean waited. Out in the darkness

a jackal barked twice and one of the horses whickered softly.

'There was another who should have been king, but he died with a sharpened stick thrust up into the secret opening of his body, until it pierced his gut and touched his heart. That man was my father,' said Mbejane. He stood up and went back into the shelter of the bush and Sean followed him. They squatted side by side, silent but watchful. The jackal cried again up above the camp and Mbejane's head turned towards the sound.

'Some jackals have two legs,' he whispered thoughtfully. Sean felt the tingle along his forearms.

'Zulus?' he asked. Mbejane shrugged, a small movement in the darkness.

'Even if it is, they will not come for us in the night. In the dawn, yes, but never in the night.' Mbejane shifted the spear in his lap. 'The old one with the tall hat and grey beard understands this. Years have made him wise, that's why he sleeps so sweetly now but mounts up and moves in the darkness before each dawn.'

Sean relaxed slightly. He glanced sideways at Mbejane.

'The old one thinks that some of the herds are hidden near here.'

'Years have made him wise,' repeated Mbejane. 'Tomorrow we will find the land more broken, there are hills and thick thorn bush. The cattle will be hidden among them.'

'Do you think we'll find them?'

'Cattle are difficult to hide from a man who knows where to look.'

'Will there be many guards with the herds?'

'I hope so,' answered Mbejane, his voice a purr. His hand crept to the shaft of his assegai and caressed it. 'I hope there will be very many.'

'You would kill your own people, your brothers, your cousins?' asked Sean.

'I would kill them as they killed my father.' Mbejane's voice was savage now. 'They are not my people. I have no people. I have no brothers – I have nothing.'

Silence settled between them again, but slowly the ugliness of Mbejane's mood evaporated and in its place came a sense of companionship. Each of them felt comforted by the other's presence. They sat on into the night.

– 27 –

Mbejane reminded Sean of Tinker working a bird, he had the same half-crouched gait and the same air of complete absorption. The white men sat their horses in silence watching him. The sun was well up already and Sean unbuttoned his sheepskin coat and pulled it off. He strapped it onto the blanket roll behind him.

Mbejane had moved out about fifty yards from them and now he was working slowly back towards them. He stopped and minutely inspected a wet pat of cow dung.

'*Hierdie Kaffir verstaan wat hy doen,*' opined Steff Erasmus approvingly, but no one else spoke. Bester Klein fidgeted with the hammer of his carbine; his red face was already sweaty in the rising heat.

Mbejane had proved right, they were in hilly country. Not the smoothly rounded hills of Natal but hills with rocky crests, deeply gullied and ravined between. There was thorn forest and euphorbia covering the sides of the hills with a lattice work of reptile grey trunks, and the grass was coarse and tall.

'I could use a drink,' said Frikkie Van Essen and wiped his knuckles across his lips.

'Chee peep, chee peep,' a barbet called stridently in the

branches of the kaffir boom tree under which they waited. Sean looked up; the bird was brown and red among the scarlet flowers which covered the tree.

'How many?' asked Steff and Mbejane came to stand at his horse's head.

'Fifty – no more,' he answered.

'When?'

'Yesterday, after the heat of the day they moved slowly down the valley. They were grazing. They cannot be more than half an hour's ride ahead of us.'

Steff nodded. Fifty head only, but there would be more.

'How many men with them?'

Mbejane clucked his tongue disgustedly. 'Two *umfaans*.' He pointed with his spear at a dusty place where the print of a half grown boy's bare foot showed clearly. 'There are no men.'

'Good,' said Steff. 'Follow them.'

'They told us that if we found anything we must go back and report,' protested Bester Klein quickly. 'They said we shouldn't start anything on our own.'

Steff turned in his saddle. 'Are you frightened of two *umfaans*?' he asked coldly.

'I'm not frightened of anything, it's just what they told us.' Klein flushed redder in his already red face.

'I know what they told us, thank you,' said Steff. 'I'm not going to start anything, we're just going to have a look.'

'I know you,' burst out Klein. 'If you see cattle you'll go mad for them. All of you, you're greedy for cattle like some men are for drink. Once you see them you won't stop.' Klein was a railway ganger.

Steff turned away from him. 'Come on, let's go.'

They rode out of the shade of the kaffir boom tree into the sunlight, Klein muttering softly to himself and Mbejane leading them down the valley.

The floor of the valley sloped gradually and on each side

141

of them the ground rose steep and rocky. They travelled quickly with Mbejane and the other Nongaai thrown out as a screen and the horsemen cantering in a line with their stirrups almost touching.

Sean levered open the breech of his rifle and drew out the cartridge. He changed it for another from the bandolier across his chest.

'Fifty head is only ten apiece,' complained Frikkie.

'That's a hundred quid – as much as you earn in six months.' Sean laughed with excitement and Frikkie laughed with him.

'You two keep your mouths shut and your eyes open.' Steff's voice was phlegmatic, but he couldn't stop the excitement from sparkling in his eyes.

'I knew you were going to raid,' sulked Klein. 'I knew it, sure as fate.'

'You shut up also,' said Steff and grinned at Sean.

They rode for ten minutes; then Steff called softly to the Nongaai and the patrol halted. No one spoke and every man stood with his head alert and his ears straining.

'Nothing,' said Steff at last. 'How close are we?'

'Very close,' Mbejane answered. 'We should have heard them from here.'

Mbejane's exquisitely muscled body was shiny with sweat and the pride of his stance set him apart from the other Nongaai. There was a restrained eagerness about him, for the excitement was infectious.

'All right, follow them,' said Steff. Mbejane settled the rawhide shield securely on his shoulder and started forward again.

Twice more they stopped to listen and each time Sean and Frikkie were more restless and impatient.

'Sit still,' snapped Steff. 'How can we hear anything with you moving about?'

Sean opened his mouth, but before he could answer they

142

all heard an ox low mournfully ahead of them among the trees.

'That's it!'

'We've got them!'

'Come on!'

'No, wait!' Steff ordered. 'Sean, take my farlookers and climb up that tree. Tell me what you can see.'

'We're wasting time,' argued Sean. 'We should—'

'We should learn to do as we're damn well told,' said Steff. 'Get up that tree.'

With the binoculars slung around his neck, Sean clambered upwards until he sat high in a crotch of two branches. He reached out and broke off a twig which obscured his vision, then exclaimed immediately, 'There they are, right ahead of us!'

'How many?' Steff called up to him.

'A small herd – two herdboys with them.'

'Are they among the trees?'

'No,' said Sean, 'they're in the open. Looks like a patch of swamp.'

'Make sure there aren't any other Zulus with them.'

'No—' Sean started to answer but Steff cut him short.

'Use the glasses, dammit. They'll be hiding if they're there.'

Sean brought up the glasses and focused them. The cattle were fat and sleek skinned, big horned and bodies dappled black on white. A cloud of white tick-birds hovered over them. The two herdboys were completely naked, youngsters with the thin legs and the disproportionately large genitals of the Africans. Sean turned the glasses slowly back and forth searching the patch of swamp and the surrounding bush. At last he lowered them.

'Only the two herdboys,' he said.

'Come down then,' Steff told him.

The herdboys fled as soon as the patrol rode out into the

open. They disappeared among the fever trees on the far side of the swamp.

'Let them go,' laughed Steff. 'The poor little buggers are going to be in enough trouble as it is.'

He spurred his horse forward into the vivid green patch of swamp grass. It was lush: thick and tall enough to reach his saddle.

The others followed him in with the mud squelching and sucking at the hooves of the horses. They could see the backs of the cattle showing above the grass a hundred yards ahead of them. The tick-birds circled squawking.

'Sean, you and Frikkie cut around to the left—' Steff spoke over his shoulder and before he could finish the grass around them was full of Zulus, at least a hundred of them in full war dress.

'Ambush!' yelled Steff. 'Don't try and fight, too many of them. Get out!' and they dragged him off his horse.

Horses panicked in the mud, whinnying as they reared. The bang of Klein's rifle was almost drowned in the triumphant roar of the warriors. Mbejane jumped to catch the bridle of Sean's horse; he dragged its head around.

'Ride, Nkosi, quickly. Do not wait.'

Klein was dead, an assegai in his throat and the blood bursting brightly from the corners of his mouth as he fell backwards.

'Hold on to my stirrup leather.' Sean felt surprisingly calm. A Zulu came at him from the side; Sean held his rifle across his lap and fired with the muzzle almost in the man's face. It cut the top off his head. Sean ejected the cartridge case and reloaded.

'Ride, Nkosi!' Mbejane shouted again. He had made no effort to obey Sean: his shield held high he barged into two of the attackers and knocked them down into the mud. His assegai rose and fell, rose and fell.

'Ngi Dhla,' howled Mbejane. 'I have eaten.' Fighting

madness on him, he jumped over the bodies and charged. A man stood to meet him and Mbejane hooked the edge of his shield under his and jerked it aside, exposing the man's left flank to his blade.

'*Ngi Dhla*,' Mbejane howled again.

He had torn an opening in the ring of attackers and Sean rode for it, his horse churning heavily through the mud. A Zulu caught at his reins and Sean fired with his muzzle touching the man's chest. The Zulu screamed.

'Mbejane,' shouted Sean. 'Take my stirrup!'

Frikkie Van Essen was finished; his horse was down and Zulus swarmed over him with red spears.

Leaning out of the saddle Sean circled Mbejane's waist with his arm and plucked him out of the mud. He struggled wildly but Sean held him. The ground firmed under his horse's hooves, they were moving faster. Another Zulu stood in their way with his assegai ready. With Mbejane kicking indignantly under one arm and his empty rifle in his other hand Sean was helpless to defend himself. He shouted an obscenity at the Zulu as he rode down on him. The Zulu dodged to one side and darted in again. Sean felt the sting of the blade across his shin and then the shock as it went on into his horse's chest. They were through, out of the swamp and into the trees.

Sean's horse carried him another mile before it fell. The assegai had gone in deep. It fell heavily but Sean was able to kick his feet out of the irons and jump clear. He and Mbejane stood looking down at the carcass – both of them were panting.

'Can you run in those boots?' asked Mbejane urgently.

'Yes.' They were light *veldschoen*.

'Those breeches will hold your legs.' Mbejane knelt swiftly and with his assegai cut away the cloth until Sean's legs were bare from the thighs down. He stood up again and listened for the first sounds of pursuit. Nothing.

'Leave your rifle, it is too heavy. Leave your hat and your bandolier.'

'I must take my rifle,' protested Sean.

'Take it then,' Mbejane flashed impatiently. 'Take it and die. If you carry that they'll catch you before noon.'

Sean hesitated a second longer and then he changed his grip, holding the rifle by the barrel like an axe. He swung it against the trunk of the nearest tree. The butt shattered and he threw it from him.

'Now we must go,' said Mbejane.

Sean glanced quickly across at his dead horse, the leather thongs held his sheepskin coat onto the saddle. All Anna's hard work wasted, he thought wryly. Then following Mbejane he started to run.

The first hour was bad; Sean had difficulty matching his step to that of Mbejane. He ran with his body tensed and soon had a stabbing stitch in his side. Mbejane saw his pain and they stopped for a few minutes while Mbejane showed him how to relax it away. Then they went on with Sean running smoothly. Another hour went by and Sean had found his second wind.

'How long will it take us to get back to the main army?' grunted Sean.

'Two days perhaps . . . don't talk,' answered Mbejane.

The land changed slowly about them as they ran. The hills not so steep and jagged, the forest thinned and again they were into the rolling grassland.

'It seems we are not being followed.' It was half an hour since Sean had last spoken.

'Perhaps,' Mbejane was non-committal. 'It is too soon yet to tell.'

They ran on side by side, in step so their feet slapped in unison on the hard-baked earth.

'Christ, I'm thirsty,' said Sean.

'No water,' said Mbejane, 'but we'll stop to rest a while at the top of the next rise.'

They looked back from the crest. Sean's shirt was soaked with sweat and he was breathing deeply but easily.

'No one following us,' Sean's voice was relieved. 'We can slow down a bit now.'

Mbejane did not answer. He also was sweating heavily but the way he moved and held his head showed he was not yet beginning to tire. He carried his shield on his shoulder and the blade of the assegai in his other hand was caked with black, dry blood. He stared out along the way they had come for fully five minutes before he growled angrily and pointed with his assegai.

'There! Close to that clump of trees. Can you see them?'

'Oh, hell!' Sean saw them: about four miles behind, on the edge of the forest where it thinned out, a black pencil line drawn on the brown parchment of grassland. But the line was moving.

'How many of them?' asked Sean.

'Fifty,' hazarded Mbejane. 'Too many.'

'I wish I had brought my rifle,' muttered Sean.

'If you had they would be much closer now – and one gun against fifty—' Mbejane left it unfinished.

'All right, let's get going again,' said Sean.

'We must rest a little longer. This is the last time we can stop before nightfall.'

Their breathing had slowed. Sean took stock of himself: he was aching a little in the legs, but it would be hours yet before he was really tired. He hawked a glob of the thick gummy saliva out of his throat and spat it into the grass. He wanted a drink but knew that would be fatal folly.

'Ah!' exclaimed Mbejane. 'They have seen us.'

'How do you know?' asked Sean.

'Look, they are sending out their chasers.' From the head

147

of the line a trio of specks had detached themselves and were drawing ahead.

'What do you mean?' Sean scratched the side of his nose uneasily. For the first time he was feeling the fear of the hunted – vulnerable, unarmed, with the pack closing in.

'They are sending their best runners ahead to force us beyond our strength. They know that if they push us hard enough – even though they break their own wind while they do it – we will fall easily to the others that follow.'

'Good God.' Sean was now truly alarmed. 'What are we going to do about it?'

'For every trick, there is a trick,' said Mbejane. 'But now we have rested enough, let us go.'

Sean took off down the hill like a startled duiker, but Mbejane pulled him up sharply.

'That is what they want. Run as before.' And once again they fell into the steady lope, swinging long-legged and relaxed.

'They're closer,' said Sean when they reached the top of the next hill. Three specks were now well ahead of the others.

'Yes.' Mbejane's voice was expressionless. They went over the crest and down the other side, the slap-slap-slap of their feet together and their breathing an unaltering rhythm: suck blow, suck blow.

There was a tiny stream in the bottom of the valley, clean water rippling over white sand. Sean jumped it with only a single longing glance and they started up the far slope. They were just short of the crest when behind them they heard a thin distant shout. He and Mbejane looked round. On the top of the hill they had just left, only a half a mile away, were the three Zulu runners, and as Sean watched they plunged down the slope towards him with their tall feather head-dresses bobbing and their leopard-tail kilts swirling about their legs. They had thrown aside their shields, but each man carried an assegai.

'Look at their legs,' exulted Mbejane. Sean saw that they ran with the slack, blundering steps of exhaustion.

'They are finished, they have run too hard.' Mbejane laughed. 'Now we must show them how afraid we are: we must run like the wind, run as though a hundred Toko-loshe* breathe on our necks.'

It was only twenty paces to the crest of the slope and they pelted panic-stricken up and over the top. But the instant they were out of sight Mbejane caught Sean's arm and held him.

'Get down,' he whispered. They sank into the grass and then crawled back on their stomachs until they lay just below the crest.

Mbejane held his assegai pointed forward, his legs were gathered up under him and his lips were drawn back in a half grin.

Sean searched in the grass and found a rock the size of an orange. It fitted neatly into his right hand.

They heard the Zulus coming, their horny bare feet pounding up the hill and then their breathing, hoarse hissing gasps, closer and closer until suddenly they came up over the crest. Their momentum carried them down to where Sean and Mbejane stood up out of the grass to meet them. Their fatigue-grey faces crumbled into expressions of complete disbelief; they had expected to find their quarry half a mile ahead of them. Mbejane killed one with his assegai, the man did not even lift his arms to parry the thrust; the point came out between his shoulders.

Sean hurled the rock into the face of another. It made a sound like a ripe pumpkin dropped on a stone floor; he fell backwards with his assegai spinning from his hand.

* A chimera of Zulu mythology.

The third man turned to run and Mbejane landed heavily on his back, bore him down and then sat astride his chest, pushed his chin back and cut his throat.

Sean looked down at the man he had hit; he had lost his head-dress and his face had changed shape. His jaw hung lopsided, he was still moving feebly.

I have killed three men today, thought Sean, *and it was so easy*.

Without emotion he watched Mbejane come across to his victim. Mbejane stooped over him and the man made a small gasping sound then lay still. Mbejane straightened up and looked at Sean.

'Now they cannot catch us before dark.'

'And only a night ape can see in the dark,' said Sean. Remembering the joke, Mbejane smiled; the smile made his face younger. He picked up a bunch of dry grass and wiped his hands on it.

The night came only just in time to save them. Sean had run all day and at last his body was stiffening in protest; his breathing wheezed painfully and he had no moisture left to sweat with.

'A little longer, just a little longer.' Mbejane whispered encouragement beside him.

The pack was spread out, the stronger runners pressing a scant mile behind them and the others dwindling back into the distance.

'The sun is going; soon you can rest.' Mbejane reached out and touched his shoulder; strangely, Sean drew strength from that brief physical contact. His legs steadied slightly and he stumbled less frequently as they went down the next slope. Swollen and red, the sun lowered itself below the land and the valleys were full of shadow.

'Soon now, very soon.' Mbejane's voice was almost crooning. He looked back: the figures of the nearest Zulu were indistinct. Sean's ankle twisted under him and he fell heavily; he felt the earth graze the skin from his cheek and he lay on his chest with his head down.

'Get up,' Mbejane's voice was desperate. Sean vomited painfully, a cupful of bitter bile.

'Get up.' Mbejane's hands were on him, dragging him to his knees.

'Stand up or die here,' threatened Mbejane. He took a handful of Sean's hair and twisted it mercilessly. Tears of pain ran into Sean's eyes and he swore and lashed out at Mbejane.

'Get up,' goaded Mbejane and Sean heaved to his feet.

'Run,' said Mbejane, half-pushing him and Sean's legs began to move mechanically under him. Mbejane looked back once more. The nearest Zulu was very close but almost merged into the fading twilight. They ran on, Mbejane steadying Sean when he staggered, Sean grunting in his throat with each step, his mouth hanging open, sucking air across a swollen tongue.

Then quickly, in the sudden African transition from day to night, all colour was gone from the land and the darkness shut down in a close circle about them. Mbejane's eyes flicked restlessly back and forth, picking up shapes in the gloom, judging the intensity of the light. Sean reeled unseeing beside him.

'We will try now,' decided Mbejane aloud. He checked Sean's run and turned him right at an acute angle on their original track, now they were heading back towards the hunters at a tangent that would take them close past them but out of sight in the darkness.

They slowed to a walk, Mbejane holding Sean's arm across his shoulders to steady him, carrying his assegai ready in his other hand. Sean walked dully, his head hanging.

They heard the leading pursuers passing fifty paces away in the darkness and a voice called in Zulu, 'Can you see them?'

'*Aibo!*' Negative answered another.

'Spread out, they may try to turn in the dark.'

'*Yeh-bo!*' Affirmative.

Then the voices were passed and silence and night closed about them once more. Mbejane made Sean keep walking. A little bit of moon came up and gave them light and they kept going with Mbejane gradually working back onto a course towards the southeast. They came to a stream at last with trees along its bank. Sean drank with difficulty, for his throat was swollen and sore. Afterwards they curled together for warmth on the carpet of leaves beneath the trees and they slept.

– 28 –

They found Chelmsford's last camp on the following afternoon: the neat lines of black camp fires and the flattened areas where the tents had stood, the stakes which had held the horse pickets and the piles of empty bully-beef tins and five-pound biscuit tins.

'They left two days ago,' said Mbejane.

Sean nodded, not doubting the correctness of this. 'Which way did they go?'

'Back towards the main camp at Isandhlwana.'

Sean looked puzzled.

'I wonder why they did that.'

Mbejane shrugged. 'They went in haste – the horsemen galloped ahead of the infantry.'

'We'll follow them,' said Sean.

The spoor was a wide road for a thousand men had passed along it and the wagons and gun carriages had left deep ruts.

They slept hungry and cold beside the spoor and the

next morning there was frost in the low places when they started out.

A little before noon they saw the granite dome of Isandhlwana standing out against the sky and unconsciously they quickened their pace. Isandhlwana, the Hill of the Little Hand. Sean was limping for his boot had rubbed the skin from one heel. His hair was thick and matted with sweat and his face was plastered with dust.

'Even army bully beef is going to taste good,' said Sean in English, and Mbejane did not answer for he did not understand, but he was looking ahead with a vaguely worried frown on his face.

'Nkosi, we have seen no one for two days' march. It comes to me that we should have met patrols from the camp before now.'

'We might have missed them,' said Sean without much interest, but Mbejane shook his head. In silence they went on. The hill was closer now so they could make out the detail of ledge and fissure that covered the dome in a lacework pattern.

'No smoke from the camp,' said Mbejane. He lifted his eyes and started visibly.

'What is it?' Sean felt the first tingle of alarm.

'N'yoni,' said Mbejane softly and Sean saw them. A dark pall, turning like a wheel slowly, high above the hill of Isandhlwana, still so far off that they could not distinguish the individual birds: only a shadow, a thin dark shadow in the sky. Watching it Sean was suddenly cold in the hot noonday sun. He started to run.

There was movement below them on the plain. The torn canvas of an overturned wagon flapped like a wounded bird, the scurry and scuffle of the jackals and higher up the slope of the kopje the hunch-shouldered trot of a hyena.

'Oh, my God!' whispered Sean. Mbejane leaned on his

153

spear; his face was calm and withdrawn but his eyes moved slowly over the field.

'Are they dead? Are they all dead?' The question required no answer. He could see the dead men in the grass, thick about the wagons and then scattered more thinly back up the slope. They looked very small and inconsequential. Mbejane stood quietly waiting. A big black kolbes vulture planed across their front, the feathers in its wing-tips flated like the fingers of a spread hand. Its legs dropped, touched and it hopped heavily to rest among the dead, a swift transformation from beautiful flight to obscene crouching repose. It bobbed its head, ruffled its feathers and waddled to dip its beak over a corpse that wore the green Hunting Tartan of the Gordons.

'Where is Chelmsford? Was he caught here also?'

Mbejane shook his head. 'He came too late.'

Mbejane pointed with his spear at the wide spoor that skirted the battlefield and crossed the shoulder of Isandhlwana towards the Tugela. 'He has gone back to the river. He has not stopped even to bury his dead.'

Sean and Mbejane walked down towards the field. On the outskirts they picked their way through the debris of Zulu weapons and shields; there was rust forming on the blades of the assegais. The grass was flattened and stained where the dead had lain, but the Zulu dead were gone – sure sign of victory.

They came to the English lines. Sean gagged when he saw what had been done to them. They lay piled upon each other, faces already black, and each one of them had been disembowelled. The flies crawled in their empty stomach cavities.

'Why do they do that?' he asked. 'Why do they have to hack them up like that?'

He walked on heavily past the wagons. Cases of food and drink had been smashed open and scattered in the

154

grass, clothing and paper and cartridge cases lay strewn around the dead, but the rifles were gone. The smell of putrefaction was so thick that it coated his throat and tongue like castor oil.

'I must find Pa,' Sean spoke quietly in almost a conversational tone. Mbejane walked a dozen paces behind him. They came to the lines where the Volunteers had camped. The tents had been slashed to tatters and trampled into the dust. The horses had been stabbed while still tethered to their picket lines; they were massively bloated. Sean recognized Gypsy, his father's mare. He crossed to her.

'Hello, girl,' he said. The birds had taken her eyes out; she lay on her side, her stomach so swollen that it was as high as Sean's waist. He walked around her. The first of the Ladyburg men lay just beyond. He recognized all fifteen of them although the birds had been at them also. They lay in a rough circle, facing outwards. Then he found a sparse trail of corpses leading up towards the shoulder of the mountain. He followed the attempt that the Volunteers had made to fight their way back towards the Tugela and it was like following a paper chase. Along the trail, thick on each side of it, were the marks where the Zulus had fallen.

'At least twenty of them for every one of us,' whispered Sean, with a tiny flicker of pride. He climbed on up and at the top of the shoulder, close under the sheer rock cliff of Isandhlwana, he found his father.

There were four of them, the last four: Waite Courtney, Tim Hope-Brown, Hans and Nile Erasmus. They lay close together. Waite was on his back with his arms spread open, the birds had taken his face away down to the bone, but they had left his beard and it stirred gently on his chest as the wind touched it. The flies, big metallic green flies, crawled thick as swarming bees in the open pit of his belly.

Sean sat down beside his father. He picked up a discarded felt hat that lay beside him and covered his terribly mutilated face. There was a green-and-yellow silk cockade on the hat, strangely gay in the presence of so much death. The flies buzzed sullenly and some came to settle on Sean's face and lips. He brushed them away.

'You know this man?' asked Mbejane.

'My father,' said Sean, without looking up.

'You too.' Compassion and understanding in his voice, Mbejane turned away and left them alone.

'I have nothing,' Mbejane had said. Now Sean also had nothing. There was hollowness: no anger, no sorrow, no ache, no reality even. Staring down at this broken thing, Sean could not make himself believe that this was a man. Meat only; the man had gone.

Later Mbejane came back. He had cut a sheet of canvas from one of the unburned wagons and they wrapped Waite in it. They dug his grave. It was hard work for the soil was thick with rock and shale. They laid Waite in the grave, with his arms still widespread in *rigor mortis* beneath the canvas for Sean could not bring himself to break them. They covered him gently and piled rocks upon the place. They stood together at the head of the grave.

'Well, Pa – ' Sean's voice sounded unnatural. He could not make himself believe he was talking to his father.

'Well, Pa – ' he started again, mumbling self-consciously. 'I'd like to say thanks for everything you've done for me.' He stopped and cleared his throat. 'I reckon you know I'll look after Ma and the farm as best I can – and Garry also.' His voice trailed away once more and he turned to Mbejane.

'There is nothing to say.' Sean's voice was surprised, hurt almost.

'No,' agreed Mbejane. 'There is nothing to say.'

For a few minutes longer Sean stood struggling to grapple with the enormity of death, trying to grasp the utter finality of it, then he turned away and started walking towards the

Tugela. Mbejane walked a little to one side and a pace behind him. *It will be dark before we reach the river*, thought Sean. He was very tired and he limped from his blistered heel.

– 29 –

'Not much farther,' said Dennis Petersen.

'No,' Sean grunted. He was irritated at the statement of the obvious; when you come out of Mahoba's Kloof and have the Baboon Stroom next to the road on your left hand, then it is five miles to Ladyburg. As Dennis had said: not much farther.

Dennis coughed in the dust. 'That first beer is going to turn to steam in my throat.'

'I think we can ride ahead now.' Sean wiped at his face, smearing the dust. 'Mbejane and the other servants can bring them in the rest of the way.'

'I was going to suggest it.' Dennis was obviously relieved. They had almost a thousand head of cattle crowding the road ahead of them and raising dust for them to breathe. It had been two days' drive from Rorke's Drift where the Commando had disbanded.

'We'll hold them in the sale pens tonight and send them out tomorrow morning – I'll tell Mbejane.'

Sean clapped his heels into his horse and swung across to where the big Zulu trotted at the heels of the herd. A few minutes' talk and then Sean signalled to Dennis. They circled out on each side of the herd and met again on the road ahead of it.

'They've lost a bit of condition,' grumbled Dennis looking back.

'Bound to,' said Sean. 'We've pushed them hard for two days.'

A thousand head of cattle, five men's share of Cetewayo's herds – Dennis and his father, Waite, Sean and Garrick – for even dead men drew a full share.

'How far ahead of the others do you reckon we are?' asked Dennis.

'Dunno,' said Sean. It wasn't important and any answer would be only a guess: pointless question is just as irritating as obvious statement. It suddenly occurred to Sean that but a few months previously a question like that would have started a discussion and argument that might have lasted half an hour. What did that mean? It meant that he had changed. Having answered his own question, Sean grinned sardonically.

'What're you laughing at?' asked Dennis.

'I was just thinking that a lot has changed in the last few months.'

'Ja,' said Dennis and then silence except for the broken beat of their hooves. 'It's going to seem funny without Pa,' Dennis said wistfully. Mr Petersen had been at Isandhlwana. 'It's going to seem funny being just Ma, the girls and me on the farm.'

They didn't speak again for a while. They were thinking back across the brief months and the events that had changed their lives.

Neither of them yet twenty years of age, but already head of his family, a holder of land and cattle, initiated into grief and a killer of men. Sean was older now with new lines in his face, and the beard he wore was square and spade-shaped. They had ridden with the Commandos who had burned and plundered to avenge Isandhlwana. At Ulundi they had sat their horses behind the ranks of Chelmsford's infantry in the hot sun, quietly waiting as Cetewayo massed his impis and sent them across open ground to overwhelm the frail square of men. They had waited through the din of the regular, unhurried volleys and watched the great black bull of Zulu tearing itself to shreds against the square. Then at the end the ranks of infantry had opened and they had ridden out, two thousand horsemen strong, to smash for ever the power of the Zulu empire. They had chased and hunted until the darkness had stopped them and they had not kept score of the kill.

'There's the church steeple,' said Dennis.

Sean came back slowly out of the past. They were at Ladyburg.

'Is your stepmother out at Theunis Kraal?' asked Dennis.

'No, she's moved into town – the cottage on Protea Street.'

'I suppose she doesn't want to be in the way now that Anna and Garry are married,' said Dennis.

Sean frowned quickly.

'How do you like old Garry getting Anna?' Dennis chuckled and shook his head. 'I reckon you could have got twenty-to-one odds he didn't have a chance.'

Sean's frown became a scowl. Garry had made him look such a damn fool – Sean hadn't finished with Anna.

'Have you heard from them yet? When are they coming home?'

'The last time we heard was from Pietermaritzburg; they sent a wire to Ma just to say they were married. She got it a couple of days before I arrived home from Isandhlwana. That was two months ago; as far as I know we haven't heard since.'

'I suppose Garry's so firmly settled on the nest they'll have to prise him off with a crowbar.' Dennis chuckled again, lewdly. Sean had a sudden and shockingly vivid mental picture of Garry on top of Anna; her knees were up high, her head was thrown back and her eyes were closed; she was making that little mewing sound.

'Shut up, you dirty bastard,' snarled Sean.

Dennis blinked. 'Sorry, I was only joking.'

159

'Don't joke about my family, he's my brother.'

'And she was your girl, hey?' murmured Dennis.

'Do you want a punch?'

'Cool down, man, I was joking.'

'I don't like that kind of joke, see?'

'All right. All right. Cool down.'

'It's dirty, that's dirty talk.' Sean was trying desperately to shut out the picture of Anna; she was in wild orgasm, her hands pleading at the small of Garrick's back.

'Jesus, since when have you become a saint?' asked Dennis and, urging his horse into a gallop, drew ahead of Sean; he kept going along the main street towards the hotel. Sean considered calling him back, but finally let him go.

Sean turned right into a shady side street. The cottage was the third house down. Waite had purchased it three years before as an investment. It was a charming little place, set among trees in a small green garden with flowers: thatched, whitewashed and surrounded by a wooden picket fence. Sean hitched his horse at the gate and went up the path.

There were two women in the sitting-room when he pushed the door open. They both stood up, surprise instantly becoming delight as they recognized him. It warmed him inside to see it – it's good to be welcome.

'Oh Sean, we weren't expecting you.' Ada came quickly to him. He kissed her and saw that sorrow had left its marks on her. He felt vaguely guilty that Waite's death had not wrought so obvious a change in him. He held her away at arm's length.

'You're beautiful,' he said. She was thin. Her eyes were too big for her face and the grief was in them like shadows in the forest, but she smiled and laughed at him.

'We thought you'd be back on Friday. I'm so glad you've come earlier.'

Sean looked past Ada.

'Hello, Strawberry Pie.' She was hovering impatiently for his attention.

'Hello, Sean.' She flushed a little with his eyes on her, but she did not drop hers.

'You look older,' she said, hardly noticing the dust that caked his skin, powdered his hair and eyelashes, and reddened his eyes.

'You've just forgotten what I look like,' he said, turning back to Ada.

'No, I'd never do that,' whispered Audrey so softly that neither of them heard her. She felt swollen up inside her chest.

'Sit down, Sean.' Ada led him to the big armchair across from the fireplace. There was a daguerreotype of Waite on the mantel.

'I'll get you a cup of tea.'

'How about a beer, Ma?' Sean sank into the chair.

'Of course – I'll get it.'

'No.' Audrey flew across the room towards the kitchen. 'I'll get it.'

'They're in the pantry, Audrey,' Ada called after her, and then to Sean, 'She's such a sweet child.'

'Look again,' Sean smiled. 'She's no child.'

'I wish Garry—' Ada cut herself short.

'What do you wish?' Sean prompted her. She was quiet for a moment, wishing that Garrick could have found a girl like Audrey instead of –

'Nothing,' she said to Sean and came to sit near him.

'Have you heard from Garry again?' asked Sean.

'No. Not yet, but Mr Pye says he had a cheque come through the bank – cashed in Capetown.'

'Capetown?' Sean raised a dusty eyebrow. 'Our boy's living life to the hilt.'

'Yes,' said Ada, remembering the size of that cheque. 'He is.'

Audrey came back into the room: she had a large bottle and a glass on a tray. She crossed to Sean's chair. Sean touched the bottle; it was cold.

'Quickly, wench,' Sean encouraged her. 'I'm dying of thirst.'

The first glass emptied in three swallows. Audrey poured again and, with the replenished glass in his fist, Sean settled back comfortably in the chair.

'Now,' said Ada, 'tell us all about it.'

In the warmth of their welcome – his muscles aching pleasantly, the glass in his hand – it was good to talk. He had not realized that there was so much to tell. At the first hint of slackening in his flow of speech either Ada or Audrey was ready with a question to keep him going.

'Oh, my goodness,' gasped Audrey at last. 'It's nearly dark outside, I must go.'

'Sean,' Ada stood up. 'Will you see that she gets home safely?'

They walked side by side in the half darkness, under the flamboyants. They walked in silence until Audrey spoke.

'Sean, were you in love with Anna?' She blurted out the question and Sean experienced his standard reaction: quick anger. He opened his mouth to blast her, then checked. It was a nice question. Had he been in love with Anna? He thought about it now for the first time, phrasing the question with care that he might answer it with truth. He felt a sudden rush of relief and he was smiling when he told her.

'No, Strawberry Pie, no, I was never in love with Anna.' The tone of his voice was right, he wasn't lying. She walked on happily beside him.

'Don't bother to come up to the house.' She noticed for the first time his stained and dirty clothing that might embarrass him in front of her parents. She wanted it to be right from the start.

'I'll watch you till you get to the door,' said Sean.

'I suppose you'll be going out to Theunis Kraal tomorrow?' she asked.

'First thing in the morning,' Sean assured her. 'There's a hell of a lot of work to do.'

'But you'll be coming to the store?'

'Yes,' said Sean and the way he looked at her made her blush and hate her redhead's skin which betrayed her so easily. She went quickly up the path and then stopped and looked back.

'Sean, please don't call me Strawberry Pie any more.'

Sean chuckled. 'All right, Audrey, I'll try to remember.'

– 30 –

Six weeks had gone since his return from the Zulu Campaign, Sean reflected, six weeks that had passed in a blur of speed. He sipped coffee from a mug the size of a German beer *stein*, sitting in the centre of his bed with his nightshirt hitched up to his waist and his legs crossed in comfortable Buddha fashion. The coffee was hot; he sipped noisily and then exhaled steam from his mouth.

The last six weeks had been full – too full for brooding grief or regret, although in the evenings, when he sat in the study with Waite's memory all about him, the ache was still there.

The days seemed to pass before they had fairly begun. There were three farms now: Theunis Kraal and the other two rented from old man Pye. He had stocked them with the looted cattle and the purchases he had made since his return. The price of prime beef had dropped to a new low, with nearly a hundred thousand cattle brought back from Zululand and Sean could afford to be selective in his buying. He could also afford to wait while the price climbed up again.

Sean swung his legs off the bed and walked across the room to the washstand. He poured water from the jug into the basin and tested it tentatively with one finger. It was so cold it stung. He stood hesitating in his ridiculously feminine nightshirt, with dark chest hairs curling out above the elaborately embroidered front. Then he mustered his courage and plunged his face into the basin; he scooped water with both hands and poured it over the back of his neck, massaged it into his hair with hooked fingers and emerged at last blowing heavily with water dripping down onto his nightshirt. He towelled, stripped off the damp garment and stood naked peering out of the window. It had lightened enough for him to make out the smoky swirl of drizzle and mist beyond the pane.

'A hell of a day,' he grumbled aloud, but his tone was deceptive. He felt excitement for this day; he was fresh and sharp-edged, hungry for breakfast, ready to go for there was work to do.

He dressed, hopping on one leg as he got into his breeches, stuffing in the tails of his shirt and then sitting on the bed to pull on his boots. Now he was thinking about Audrey – he must try and get into town tomorrow to see her.

Sean had decided on matrimony. He had three good reasons. He had found that it was easier to get into the Bank of England's vaults than to get under Audrey's petticoats without marrying her. When Sean wanted something no price was too high to pay.

Living at Theunis Kraal with Garry and Anna, Sean had decided that it would be pleasant to have his own woman to cook for him, mend his clothes and listen to his stories, for Sean was feeling a little left out.

The third consideration, by no means the least signif-

164

icant, was Audrey's connections with the local bank. She was one of the very few weaknesses in old man Pye's armour. He might even weigh in with Mahoba's Kloof Farm as a wedding present, though even the optimist in Sean realized that this hope was extravagant. Pye and his money were not easily parted.

Yes, Sean decided, he would have to find time to get into town and tell Audrey – in Sean's mind it wasn't a question of asking her. Sean brushed his hair, combed his beard, winked at himself in the mirror and went out into the passage. He could smell breakfast cooking and his mouth started to water.

Anna was in the kitchen. Her face was flushed from the heat of the stove.

'What's for breakfast, little sister?'

She turned to him, quickly brushing the hair off her forehead with the back of her hand.

'I'm not your sister,' she said. 'I wish you wouldn't call me that.'

'Where's Garry?' Sean asked as though he had not heard her protest.

'He's not up yet.'

'The poor boy's exhausted, no doubt.' Sean grinned at her and she turned away in confusion. Sean looked at her bottom without desire. Strange that Anna being Garry's wife should kill his appetite for her. Even the memory of what they had done before was vaguely obscene, incestuous.

'You're getting fat,' he said noticing the new heaviness of her body. She ducked her head but did not answer and Sean went on, 'I'll have four eggs, please, and tell Joseph not to dry them out completely.'

Sean went through into the dining-room and Garry came in through the side door at the same moment. His face was still vacant from sleep. Sean got a whiff of his breath; it smelled of stale liquor.

'Good morning, Romeo,' said Sean and Garry grinned sheepishly. His eyes were bloodshot and he hadn't shaved.

'Hello, Sean. How did you sleep?'

'Beautifully, thank you. I take it that you did also.' Sean sat down and spooned porridge from the tureen.

'Have some?' he asked Garry.

'Thanks.' Sean passed him the plate. He noticed how Garry's hand shook. *I'll have to talk to him about letting up on the bottle a trifle.*

'Hell, I'm hungry.' They talked the jerky, disconnected conversation of the breakfast table. Anna came through and joined them. Joseph brought the coffee.

'Have you told Sean yet, Garry?' Anna spoke suddenly, clearly and with decision.

'No.' Garry was taken by surprise, he spluttered his coffee.

'Told me what?' Sean asked. They were silent and Garrick fluttered his hand nervously. This was the moment he had been dreading – what if Sean guessed, what if he knew it was his baby and took them away, Anna and the baby, took them away and left Garry with nothing. Haunted by wild unreasonable fears, Garrick stared fixedly across the table at his brother.

'Tell him, Garry,' commanded Anna.

'Anna's going to have a baby,' he said. He watched Sean's face, saw the surprise change slowly to delight, felt Sean's arm close round his shoulders in a painful hug, almost crushing him.

'That's great,' Sean exulted, 'that's wonderful. We'll have the house full of kids in no time if you keep that up, Garry. I'm proud of you.'

Grinning stupidly with relief Garrick watched Sean hug Anna more gently and kiss her forehead.

'Well done, Anna, make sure it's a boy. We need cheap labour around here.'

166

He hasn't guessed, thought Garrick, *he doesn't know and it will be mine. No one can take it away from me now.*

That day they worked in the south section. They stayed together, Garry laughing in happy confusion at Sean's banter. It was delightful to have Sean give him so much attention. They finished early; for once Sean was in no mood for work.

'My reproductive brother, every barrel loaded with buckshot.' Sean leaned across and punched Garry's shoulder. 'Let's knock it off and go into town. We can have a few quick ones to celebrate at the hotel and then go and tell Ada.'

Sean stood up in the stirrup and yelled above the moo and mill of the herd.

'Mbejane, bring those ten sick ones up to the house and don't forget that tomorrow we are going to fetch cattle from the sale pens.'

Mbejane waved in acknowledgement and Sean turned back to Garrick.

'Come on, let's get the hell out of here.'

They rode side by side, globules of moisture covering their oilskins and shining on Sean's beard. It was still cold and the escarpment was hidden in the wet mist.

'It's real brandy-drinking weather,' said Sean and Garrick did not answer. He was frightened again. He didn't want to tell Ada. She would guess. She guessed everything, she would know it was Sean's child. You couldn't lie to her.

The horses' hooves plopped wetly in the mud. They reached the spot where the road forked and climbed over the ridge to Ladyburg.

'Ada's going to love being a grandma,' chuckled Sean, and at that moment his horse stumbled slightly, broke its gait and started favouring its near fore. Sean dismounted, lifted the hoof and saw the splinter driven deep into the frog.

167

'Damn it to hell,' he swore. He bent his head, gripped the hilt of the splinter with his teeth and drew it out.

'Well, we can't go into Ladyburg now, that leg will be sore for days.' Garry was relieved; it put off the time when he must tell Ada.

'Your horse isn't lame. Off you go, man, give her my love.' Sean looked up at him.

'We can tell her some other time. Let's get back home,' Garry demurred.

'Go on, Garry, it's your baby. Go and tell her.'

Garrick argued until he saw Sean's temper rising, then with a sigh of resignation he went and Sean led his own horse back to Theunis Kraal. Now that he was walking the oilskin was uncomfortably hot and heavy, Sean took it off and slung it over the saddle.

Anna was standing on the *stoep* as he came up to the homestead.

'Where's Garry?' she called.

'Don't worry. He's gone into town to see Ada. He'll be back by supper-time.'

One of the stable boys came to take Sean's horse. They talked together and then Sean stooped to lift the injured hoof. His breeches tightened across his buttocks and enhanced the long moulded taper of his legs. Anna looked at him. He straightened up and his shoulders were wide beneath the damp white linen of his shirt. He smiled at her as he came up the steps of the *stoep*. The rain had made his beard curl and he looked like a mischievous pirate.

'You must take better care of yourself now.' He put his hand on her upper arm to lead her inside. 'You can't stand around in the cold any more.' They went in through the glass doors. Anna looked up at him, the top of her head on a level with his shoulder.

'You're a damn fine woman, Anna, and I'm sure you're going to make a fine baby.' It was a mistake, for as he said it his eyes softened and his face turned down towards her. He let his arm drop around her shoulders.

'Sean!' She said his name as though it were an exclamation of pain. She moved quickly, fiercely within the circle of his arm, her body flattened itself against his and her hands went up to catch in the thick hair at the back of his head. She pulled his face down and her mouth opened warm and wet across his lips, her back arched and thrust her thighs against his legs. She moaned softly as she kissed him. For startled seconds Sean stood imprisoned in her embrace, then he tore his face away.

'Are you mad?' He tried to push her from him, but she fought her way back through his fending hands. She locked her arms around him and pressed her face against his chest.

'I love you. Please, please. I love you. Just let me hold you, that's all. I just want to hold you.' Her voice was muffled by the damp cloth of his shirt. She was shivering.

'Get away from me.' Roughly Sean broke her hold and almost threw her backwards onto the couch beside the fireplace.

'You're Garry's wife now, and you'll soon be the mother of his child. Keep your hot little body for him.' Sean stood back from her with his anger starting to mount.

'But I love you, Sean. Oh, my God, if I could only make you understand how I've suffered, living here with you and not being able to touch you even.'

Sean strode across to where she sat. 'Listen to me.' His voice was harsh. 'I don't want you. I never loved you, but now I could no more touch you than I could go with my own mother.' She could see the revulsion in his face. 'You're Garry's wife; if ever again you look at another man I'll kill you.'

He lifted his hands, holding them with the fingers crooked ready. 'I'll kill you with my bare hands.'

His face was close to hers. She could not bear the

expression in his eyes: she lashed out at him. He pulled back in time to save his eyes, but her nails gouged bloody lines across his cheek and down the side of his nose. He caught her wrists and held her while a thin trickle of blood dribbled down into his beard. She twisted in his hands, jerking her body from side to side, and she screamed at him.

'You swine, you dirty, dirty swine. Garry's wife, you say. Garry's baby, you say.' She threw her head back and laughed wildly through her screaming. 'Now I'll tell you the truth. What I have within me you gave me. It's yours! Not Garry's!' Sean let go her wrists and backed away from her.

'It can't be,' he whispered, 'you must be lying.' She followed him.

'Don't you remember how you said goodbye to me before you went to war? Don't you remember that night in the wagon? Don't you remember – don't you? Don't you?' She was talking quietly now, using her words to wound him.

'That was months ago. It can't be true,' Sean stammered, still moving away from her.

'Three and a half months,' she told him. 'Your brother's baby will be a little early, don't you think? But lots of people have premature babies—' Her voice droned on steadily, she was shivering uncontrollably now and her face was ghostly pale. Sean could stand it no longer.

'Leave me, leave me alone. I've got to think. I didn't know.' He brushed past her and went out into the passage. She heard the door of Waite's study slam shut and she stood still in the centre of the floor. Gradually her panting came under control and the storm surf of her anger abated to expose the black reefs of hatred beneath. She crossed the floor, went down the passage and into her own bedroom. She stood in front of the mirror and looked at herself.

'I hate him.' Her lips formed the words in the mirror. Her face was still pale. 'There's one thing I can take from him. Garry's mine now, not his.'

She pulled the pins from her hair and let them drop onto the floor; her hair fell down her back. She shook it onto her shoulders then lifted her hands and tangled it into confusion. Her teeth closed on her own lips, she bit until she tasted blood.

'Oh, God, I hate him, I hate him,' she whispered through the pain. Her hands came down onto the front of her dress. She tore it open, then in the mirror looked without interest at the round bosses of her nipples that were already darkening with the promise of fruition. She kicked off her shoes.

'I hate him.' She stooped and her hands went up under her skirts into the petticoats. She loosened her pantaloons and stepped out of them; she held them across her chest to tear them, then threw them next to the bed. She swept her arm across the top of her dressing-table: one of the bowls hit the floor and burst with a splash of face-powder and there was the sudden pungent reek of spilled perfume. She crossed to the bed and dropped onto it. She lifted her knees and her petticoats fell back like the petals of a flower: her white legs and lower body were the stamen.

Just before nightfall there was a shy knock on her door.

'What is it?' she asked.

'The Nkosikazi has not told me what I should cook for dinner.' Old Joseph's voice was raised respectfully.

'There will be no dinner tonight. You and all the servants may go.'

'Very well, Nkosikazi.'

Garrick came home in the dark. He had been drinking; she heard him stagger as he crossed the *stoep*, and his voice slur as he called.

'Hallo. Where's everybody? Anna! Anna! I'm back.' Silence for a while as he lit one of the lamps and then the hurried thump, thump of his peg along the passage and his voice again edged with alarm.

171

'Anna, Anna, where are you?'

He pushed the door open and stood with the lamp in his hand. Anna rolled away from the light, pressing her face into the pillow and hunching her shoulders. She heard him set the lamp down on the dressing-table, felt his hands pulling down her skirts to cover her nakedness, then gently turn her to face him. She looked into his face and saw the uncomprehending horror in it.

'My darling, oh Anna, my darling, what's happened?' He started at her broken lips and her breasts. Bewildered he turned his head and looked at the bottles on the floor, at her torn pantaloons. His face hardened and came back to her.

'Are you hurt?' She shook her head.

'Who? Tell me who did it.' She turned away from him again, hiding her face.

'My darling, my poor darling. Who was it – one of the servants?'

'No,' her voice stifled with shame.

'Please tell me, Anna. What happened?'

She sat up quickly and threw her arms about him, holding him hard so her lips were near his ear. 'You know, Garry. You know who did it.'

'No, I swear I don't, please tell me.'

Anna drew her breath in deep, held it a second then breathed it out. 'Sean!'

Garrick's body convulsed in her arms, she heard him grunt as though he had been hit. Then he spoke. 'This too. Now this too.'

He loosened her hands from his neck and pushed her gently down onto the pillows. He crossed to the cupboard, opened one of the drawers and took out Waite's service pistol.

He's going to kill Sean, she thought. Garrick went out of the room without looking at her again. She waited with

172

her hands clenched at her sides and her whole body stretched tightly. When the shot came at last it was surprisingly muted and unwarlike. Her body relaxed, her hands opened and she began to cry softly.

– 31 –

Garry limped down the passage. The pistol was heavy and the checkered grip rough in his hand. There was light showing under the study door at the end of the passage. It was unlocked. Garrick went in.

Sean sat with his elbows on the desk and his face in his hands but he looked up as Garrick came in through the door. The scratches had already dried black across his cheek, but the flesh around them was red and inflamed. He looked at the pistol in Garrick's hand.

'She has told you.' There was no question or expression in his voice.

'Yes.'

'I hoped that she wouldn't,' said Sean. 'I wanted her to spare you that at least.'

'Spare me?' Garrick asked. 'What about her? Did you think of her?'

Sean did not answer, instead he shrugged and laid back tiredly in his chair.

'I never realized before what a merciless swine you are,' choked Garrick. 'I have come to kill you.'

'Yes.' Sean watched the pistol come up. Garrick was holding it with both hands, his sandy hair hung forward onto his forehead.

'My poor Garry,' Sean said softly and immediately the pistol started to shake. It sank until Garrick held it, still with both hands between his knees. He crouched over it, blubbering – chewing at his lips to stop himself. Sean started out of his chair to go to him, but Garrick recoiled against the door-jamb.

'Keep away from me,' he yelled, 'don't touch me.' He threw the pistol, the sharp edge of the hammer cut across Sean's forehead, jerking his head back. The pistol glanced off and hit the wall behind him. It fired and the bullet splintered the panelled woodwork.

'We're finished,' Garrick screamed. 'We're finished for ever.' He groped wildly for the door and stumbled out into the passage, through the kitchens into the rain. He fell many times as the grass caught his peg, but each time he scrambled up and kept running. He sobbed with each step in the utter darkness of the night.

At last the growl of the rain-engorged Baboon Stroom blocked his way. He stood on the bank with the drizzle blowing into his face.

'Why me, why always me?' He screamed his agony into the darkness. Then with a rush of relief as strong as the torrent in the river-bed below him he felt the moth flutter its wings behind his eyes. The warmth and the greyness closed about him and he sank down onto his knees in the mud.

– 32 –

Sean took very little with him: his bedroll, a rifle and a spare horse. Twice in the darkness he lost the path to Mbejane's kraal but each time his horse found it again. Mbejane had built his big grass beehive hut well away from the quarters of the other servants, for he was Zulu of royal blood. When at last Sean came to it there were a few minutes of sleepy stirring and muttering within before Mbejane, with a blanket draped around his shoulders and an old paraffin lamp in his hand, came out to Sean's shouts.

'What is it, Nkosi?'

'I am going, Mbejane.'

'Where to?'

'Wherever the roads lead. Will you follow?'

'I will get my spears,' said Mbejane.

Old man Pye was still in his office behind the bank when they reached Ladyburg. He was counting the sovereigns and stacking them in neat golden piles and his hands were as gentle on them as a man's hands on the body of the woman he loves, but he reached quickly for the open drawer at his side as Sean shouldered the door open.

'You don't need that,' said Sean and Pye lifted his hand guiltily off the pistol.

'Good gracious! I didn't recognize you, my boy.'

'How much have I got credited to my account?' Sean cut through the pleasantries.

'This isn't banking hours, you know.'

'Look here, Mr Pye, I'm in a hurry. How much have I got?'

Pye climbed out of his chair and crossed to the big iron safe. Shielding it with his body he tumbled the combination and swung open the door. He brought the ledger across to the desk.

'Carter – Cloete – Courtney,' he muttered as he turned the pages. 'Ah – Ada – Garrick – Sean. Here we are. Twelve hundred and ninety-six pounds eight and eight pence; of course, there are last month's accounts at the store still unpaid.'

'Call it twelve hundred then,' said Sean. 'I want it now and while you are counting it you can give me pen and paper.'

'Help yourself, there on the desk.'

Sean sat at the desk, pushed the piles of gold out of his way, dipped the pen and wrote. When he had finished he looked up at old Pye.

'Witness that, please.'

Pye took the paper and read it through. His face went limp with surprise.

'You're giving your half share of Theunis Kraal and all the cattle to your brother's first born!' he exploded.

'That's right, please witness it.'

'You must be mad,' protested Pye. 'That's a fortune you're giving away. Think what you're doing – think of your future. I had hoped that you and Audrey—' He stopped himself and went on. 'Don't be a fool, man.'

'Please witness it, Mr Pye,' said Sean and, muttering under his breath, Pye signed quickly.

'Thank you.' Sean folded the document, slipped it into an envelope and sealed it. He put it away inside his coat.

'Where's the money?' he asked.

Pye pushed a canvas bag across to him. His expression was one of disgust; he wanted no truck with fools.

'Count it,' he said.

'I'll take your word for it,' said Sean and signed the receipt.

Sean rode out past the sale-pens and up the escarpment along the road to Pietermaritzburg. Mbejane trotted at his stirrup leading the spare horse. They stopped at the top of the escarpment. The wind had blown the clouds open and the starlight came through. They could see the town below them with here and there a lighted window.

I should have said goodbye to Ada, Sean thought. He looked down the valley towards Theunis Kraal. He could see no light. He touched the letter in the inside pocket of his coat.

'I'll post it to Garry from Pietermaritzburg,' he spoke aloud.

'Nkosi?' asked Mbejane.

'I said, "It's a long road, let us begin."'

'Yes,' agreed Mbejane. 'Let us begin.'

– II –
Witwatersrand

– 1 –

They turned north from Pietermaritzburg and climbed steadily up across bleak grassland towards the mountains. On the third day they saw the Drakensberg, jagged and black as the teeth of an ancient shark along the skyline.

It was cold; wrapped in his kaross Mbejane trailed far behind Sean. They had exchanged perhaps two dozen words since they left Pietermaritzburg for Sean had his thoughts and they were evil company. Mbejane was keeping discreetly out of his way. Mbejane felt no resentment, for a man who had just left his home and his cattle was entitled to brood. Mbejane was with sadness himself – he had left a fat woman in his bed to follow Sean.

Mbejane unplugged his small gourd snuff-box, picked a pinch and sniffed it delicately. He looked up at the mountains. The snows upon them were turning pink in the sunset and in a little while now they would make camp, and then again perhaps they would not. It made no difference.

Sean rode on after dark. The road crossed another fold in the veld and they saw the lights in the valley below.

'Dundee,' Sean thought without interest. He made no effort to hasten his horse but let it amble down towards the town. Now he could smell the smoke from the coal mine, tarry and thick in the back of his throat. They entered the main street. The town seemed deserted in the cold. Sean did not intend stopping – he would camp on the far side;

but when he reached the hotel he hesitated. There was warmth in there and laughter and the sound of men's voices and he was suddenly aware that his fingers were stiff with cold.

'Mbejane, take my horse. Find a place to camp beyond the town and make a fire so I won't miss you in the dark.'

Sean climbed down and walked into the bar. The room was full, miners most of them – he could see the grey coal dust etched into their skins. They looked at him incuriously as he crossed to the counter and ordered a brandy. He drank it slowly, making no attempt to join the loud talk around him.

The drunk was a short man but built like Table Mountain, low, square and solid. He had to stand on tiptoe to put his arm around Sean's neck.

'Have a drink with me, *Boetie*.' His breath smelt sour and old.

'No thanks.' Sean was in no mood for drunks.

'Come on, come on,' the drunk insisted; he staggered and Sean's drink slopped onto the counter.

'Leave me alone.' Sean shrugged the arm away.

'You've got something against me?'

'No. I just feel like drinking alone.'

'You don't like my face, maybe?' The drunk held it close to Sean's. Sean didn't like it.

'Push off, there's a good fellow.'

The drunk slapped the counter.

'Charlie, give this big ape a drink. Make it a double. If he don't drink it, I ram it down his throat.'

Sean ignored the proffered glass. He swallowed what remained in his own and turned for the door. The drunk threw the brandy in his face. The spirit burned his eyes and he hit the man in the stomach. As his head came down Sean hit him again – in the face. The drunk spun sideways, fell and lay bleeding from his nose.

'What you hit him for?' Another miner was helping the drunk into a sitting position.

'It wouldn't cost you nothing to have a drink with him.' Sean felt the hostility in the room; he was the outsider.

'This boy is looking for trouble.'

'He's a tough monkey. We know how to handle tough monkeys.'

'Come on, let's sort this bastard out.'

Sean had hit the man as a reflex action. He was sorry now, but his guilt evaporated as he saw them gathering against him. Gone too was his mood of depression and in its place was a sense of relief. This was what he needed.

There were six of them moving in on him in a pack. Six was a fairly well-rounded number. One of them had a bottle in his hand and Sean started to smile. They were talking loudly, spreading courage and waiting for one of their fellows to start it.

Sean saw movement out of the side of his eye and jumped back to cover it with his hands ready.

'Steady on there,' a very English voice soothed him. 'I have come to offer my services. It seems to me you have adversaries and to spare.' The speaker had stood up from one of the tables behind Sean. He was tall, with a gauntly ravaged face and an immaculate grey suit.

'I want them all,' said Sean.

'Damned unsporting.' The newcomer shook his head. 'I'll buy the three gentlemen on the left if your price is reasonable.'

'Take two as a gift and consider yourself lucky.' Sean grinned at him and the man grinned back. They had almost forgotten the impending action in the pleasure of meeting.

'Very decent of you. May I introduce myself – Dufford Charleywood.' He shifted the light cane into his left hand and extended his right to Sean.

'Sean Courtney.' Sean accepted the hand.

181

'Are you bastards going to fight or what?' protested one of the miners impatiently.

'We are, dear boy, we are,' said Duff and moved lightly as a dancer towards him, swinging the cane. Thin as it was it made a noise like a well-hit baseball along the man's head.

'Then there were five,' said Duff. He flicked the cane and, weighted with lead, it made a most satisfactory swish. Like a swordsman he lunged into the throat of the second miner. The man lay on the floor and made a strangling noise.

'The rest are yours, Mr Courtney,' said Duff regretfully.

Sean dived in low, spreading his arms to scoop up all four pairs of legs at once. He sat up in the pile of bodies and started punching and kicking.

'Messy, very messy,' murmured Duff disapprovingly. The yelps and thuds gradually petered into silence and Sean stood up. His lip was bleeding and the lapel was torn off his jacket.

'Drink?' asked Duff.

'Brandy, please.' Sean smiled at the elegant figure against the bar. 'I won't refuse another drink this evening.'

They took the glasses to Duff's table, stepping over the bodies as they went.

'Mud in your eye!'

'Down the old red lane!'

Then they studied each other with frank interest, ignoring the clearing up operations being conducted around them.

'You are travelling?' asked Duff.

'Yes, are you?'

'No such luck. I am in the permanent employ of Dundee Collieries Ltd.'

'You work here?' Sean looked incredulous for Duff was a peacock among pigeons.

'Assistant Engineer,' nodded Duff. 'But not for long; the taste of coal-dust sticks in my craw.'

'May I suggest something to wash it out?'

'A splendid idea,' agreed Duff.

Sean brought the drinks to the table.

'Where are you headed?' asked Duff.

'I was facing north when I started,' shrugged Sean, 'I just kept going that way.'

'Where did you start from?'

'South.' Sean answered abruptly.

'Sorry, I didn't mean to pry.' Duff smiled. 'Yours is brandy, isn't it?'

The barman came round from behind the counter and crossed to their table.

'Hello, Charlie,' Duff greeted him. 'I take it you require compensation for the damage to your fittings and furniture?'

'Don't worry about it, Mr Charleywood. Not often we have a good barney like that. We don't mind the odd table and chair as long as it's worth watching. Have it on the house.'

'That's extremely good of you.'

'That's not what I came across for, Mr Charleywood. I've got something I'd like you to take a look at, you being a mining chap and all. Could you spare a minute, sir?'

'Come on, Sean. Let's see what Charlie's got for us. My guess is it's a beautiful woman.'

'It's not actually, sir,' said Charlie seriously and led the way through into the back room. Charlie reached up and took a lump of rock down from one of the shelves. He held it out to Duff. 'What do you make of that?'

Duff took it and weighed it in his hand, then peered closely at it. It was glassy grey, blotched with white and dark-red and divided by a broad black stripe.

'Some sort of conglomerate.' Duff spoke without enthusiasm. 'What's the mystery?'

'Friend of mine brought it down from Kruger's Republic on the other side of the mountains. He says it's gold bearing. They've made a big strike at a place called Witwatersrand just outside Pretoria. Of course, I don't put much store by these rumours 'cos you hear them all the time: diamonds and gold, gold and diamonds.'

Charlie laughed and wiped his hands on his apron.

'Anyway my friend says the Boers are selling mining licences to them as want to dig for the stuff. Thought I'd just get you to have a look.'

'I'll take this with me, Charlie, and pan it in the morning. Right now my friend and I are drinking.'

– 2 –

S ean opened his eyes the next morning to find the sun burning in through the window above his bed. He closed them again hurriedly and tried to remember where he was. There was a pain in his head that distracted him and a noise. The noise was a regular croaking rattle; it sounded as though someone was dying. Sean opened his eyes and turned his head slowly. Someone was in the bed across the room. Sean groped for a boot and threw it; there was a snort and Duff's head came up. For a second he regarded Sean through eyes as red as a winter sunset and then he subsided gently back into the blankets.

'Keep it down to a bellow,' whispered Sean. 'You are in the presence of grave illness.'

A long time later a servant brought coffee.

'Send word to my office that I am sick,' commanded Duff.

'I have done so.' The servant clearly understood his master. He went on, 'There is one outside who seeks the other Nkosi.' He glanced at Sean. 'He is greatly worried.'

'Mbejane. Tell him to wait,' said Sean.

They drank coffee in silence, sitting on the edge of their beds.

'How did I get here?' asked Sean.

'Laddie, if you don't know, then nobody does.' Duff stood up and crossed the room to find fresh clothing. He was naked and Sean saw that although he was slim as a boy his body was finely muscled.

'My God, what does Charlie put in his liquor?' complained Duff as he picked up his jacket.

He found the lump of rock in the pocket, brought it out and tossed it onto the packing-case that served as a table. He regarded it sourly as he finished dressing, then he went to the great pile of bachelor debris that filled one corner of the room. He scratched around and came out with a steel pestle-and-mortar and a battered black gold pan.

'I feel very old this morning,' he said as he started to crush the rock to powder in the mortar. He poured the powder into the pan, carried it out to the corrugated iron water tank beside the front door and filled the pan from the tap.

Sean followed him and they sat together on the front step. Duff worked the pan, using a practised dip and swing that set the contents spinning like a whirlpool and slopped a little over the front lip with each turn. He filled it again with clean water.

Suddenly Sean felt Duff stiffen beside him. He glanced at his face and saw that his hangover had gone; his lips were shut in a thin line and his bloodshot eyes were fastened on the pan.

Sean looked down and saw the gleam through the water, like the flash of a trout's belly as it turns to take the fly. He felt the excitement prickle up his arms and lift the hair on his neck.

Quickly Duff splashed fresh water into the pan; three

more turns and he flicked it out again. They sat still, not speaking, staring at the golden tail curved round the bottom of the pan.

'How much money have you got?' Duff asked without looking up.

'Little over a thousand.'

'As much as that. Excellent! I can raise about five hundred but I'll throw in my mining experience. Equal partners – do you agree?'

'Yes.'

'Then why are we sitting here? I'm going down to the bank. Meet me on the edge of town in half an hour.'

'What about your job?' Sean asked.

'I hate the smell of coal – the hell with my job.'

'What about Charlie?'

'Charlie is a poisoner – the hell with Charlie.'

– 3 –

They camped that night in the mouth of the pass with the mountains standing up before them. They had pushed the pace all that afternoon and the horses were tired – they turned their tails to the wind and cropped at the dry winter grass.

Mbejane built a fire in the shelter of a red stone outcrop and they huddled beside it brewing coffee, trying to keep out of the snow-cold wind, but it came down off the mountains and blew a plume of sparks from the fire. They ate; then Mbejane curled up beside the fire, pulled his kaross over his head and did not move again until morning.

'How far is it to this place?' Sean asked.

'I don't know,' Duff admitted. 'We'll go up through the pass tomorrow – fifty or sixty miles through the mountains

– and then we'll be out into the high veld. Perhaps another week's riding after that.'

'Are we chasing rainbows?' Sean poured more coffee into the mugs.

'I'll tell you when we get there.' Duff picked up his mug and cupped his hands around it. 'One thing's certain – that sample was stinking with gold. If there's much of that stuff around somebody's going to get rich.'

'Us, perhaps?'

'I've been on gold stampedes before. The first ones in make the killings. We might find the ground for fifty miles around as thick with claim pegs as quills on a porcupine's back.' Duff sipped noisily at his coffee. 'But we've got money – that's our ace in the hole. If we peg a proposition we've got capital to work it. If we're too late we can buy claims from the brokers. If we can't, well, there're other ways of getting gold than grubbing for it – a store, a saloon, a transport business, take your pick.'

Duff flicked the coffee grounds out of his mug. 'With money in your pocket you're somebody; without it anyone can kick you in the teeth.' He took a long black cheroot out of his top pocket and offered it to Sean. Sean shook his head and Duff bit the tip from the cheroot and spat it into the fire. He picked up a burning twig and lit it, sucking with content.

'Where did you learn mining, Duff?'

'Canada.' The wind whipped the smoke away from his mouth as Duff exhaled.

'You've been around?'

'I have, laddie. It's too damn cold to sleep; we'll talk instead. For a guinea I'll tell you the story of my life.'

'Tell me first, I'll see if it's worth it!' Sean pulled the blanket up around his shoulders and waited.

'Your credit is good,' agreed Duff. He paused dramatically.

'I was born thirty-one years ago, fourth and youngest son to the sixteenth Baron Roxby – that is, not counting the others who never made it to puberty.'

'Blue blood,' said Sean.

'Of course, just look at my nose. But please don't interrupt. Very early in the game my father, the sixteenth Baron, dispelled with a horsewhip any natural affection we may have owed him. Like Henry the Eighth he preferred children in the abstract. We kept out of his way and that suited everybody admirably. A sort of armed truce.

'Dear father had two great passions in life: horses and women. During his sixty-two glorious years he acquired a fine collection of both. My fifteen-year-old cousin, a comely wench as I recall, was his last and unattained ambition. He took her riding every day and fingered her most outrageously as he helped her in and out of the saddle. She told me about it with giggles.

'However father's horse, a commendably moral creature, cut short the pursuit by kicking father on the head, presumably in the middle of one of these touching scenes. Poor father was never the same again. In fact so much was he altered by this experience that two days later, to the doleful clangour of bells and a collective sigh of relief from his sons and his neighbours who owned daughters, they buried him.'

Dufford leaned forward and prodded the fire.

'It was all very sad. I or any of my brothers could have told father that not only was my cousin comely but she had the family sporting instincts developed to a remarkable degree. After all who should know better than we? We were her cousins and you know how cousins will be cousins. Anyway father never found out and to this day I feel guilty – I should have told him. He would have died happier . . . Do I bore you?'

'No, go on. I've had half a guinea's worth already,' Sean laughed.

'Father's untimely decease made no miraculous changes in my life. The seventeenth Baron, brother Tom, once he had the title was every bit as tight-fisted and unpleasant as father had been. There I was at nineteen on an allowance too small to enable me to pursue the family hobbies, gathering mould in a grim old castle forty miles from London, with the development of my sensitive soul being inhibited by the undiluted company of my barbaric brothers.

'I left with three months' advance allowance clutched in my sweaty palm and the farewells of my brothers ringing in my ears. The most sentimental of these was "don't bother to write".

'Everybody was going to Canada: it seemed like a good idea so I went too. I made money and spent it. I made women and spent them also, but the cold got to me in the end.'

Duff's cheroot had died; he re-lit it and looked at Sean.

'It was so cold you couldn't urinate without getting frostbite on your equipment, so I began to think of lands tropical, of white beaches and sun, of exotic fruits and even more exotic maidens. The peculiar circumstances that finally decided me to leave are painful to recall and we will not dwell upon them. I left, to say the least, under a cloud. So here you see me freezing slowly to death, with a bearded ruffian for company and not an exotic maiden within a day's ride.'

'A stirring tale – well told,' applauded Sean.

'One story deserves another – let's hear your tale of woe.'

Sean's smile slid off his face. 'Born and bred here in Natal. Left home a week or so ago, also in painful circumstances.'

189

'A woman?' asked Duff with deep compassion.

'A woman,' agreed Sean.

'The sweet bitches,' sighed Duff. 'How I love them.'

– 4 –

The pass ran like a twisted gut through the Drakensberg. The mountains stood up sheer and black on each side of them, so they rode in shadow and saw the sun only for a few hours in the middle of the day. Then the mountains dropped away and they were out into the open.

Open was the word for the high veld. It stretched away flat and empty, grass and brown grass dwindling to a distant meeting with the pale empty sky. But the loneliness could not blunt the edge of their excitement: each mile covered, each successive camp along the ribbon road ground it sharper until at last they saw the name in writing for the first time. Forlorn as a scarecrow in a ploughed land the signpost pointed right and said, 'Pretoria', pointed left and said, 'Witwatersrand'.

'The Ridge of White Waters,' whispered Sean. It had a ring to it that name – a ring like a hundred millions in gold.

'We're not the first,' muttered Duff. The left-hand fork of the road was deeply scored by the passage of many wagons.

'No time to worry about that.' Sean had the gold sickness on him now. 'There's a little speed left in these mokes – let's use it.'

It came up on the horizon as a low line above the emptiness, a ridge of hills like a hundred others they had crossed. They went up it and from the top looked down.

Two ridges ran side by side, north and south, four miles or so apart. In the shallow valley between they could see the flash of the sun off the swamp pools that gave the hills their name.

'Look at them,' groaned Sean.

The tents and wagons were scattered along the length of the valley and in between them the prospect trenches were raw wounds through the grass. The trenches were concentrated along a line down the centre of the valley.

'That's the strike of the reef,' said Duff, 'and we're too late – it's all pegged!'

'How do you know?' protested Sean.

'Use your eyes, laddie. It's all gone.'

'There might be some they've overlooked.'

'These boys overlook nothing. Let's go down and I'll show you.' Duff prodded his horse and they started down. He spoke over his shoulder to Sean. 'Look up there near that stream – they aren't wasting time. They've got a mill going already. It's a four-stamp rig by the looks of it.'

They rode into one of the larger encampments of tents and wagons; there were women at work around the fires and the smell of food brought saliva jetting from under Sean's tongue. There were men also, sitting among the wagons waiting for their suppers.

'I'm going to ask some of these characters what's going on here,' said Sean. He climbed down off his horse and tossed the reins to Mbejane. Duff watched him with a wry grin as he tried in succession to engage three different men in conversation. Each time Sean's victim avoided his eyes, mumbled vaguely and withdrew. Sean finally gave up and came back to the horses.

'What's wrong with me?' he asked plaintively. 'Have I got a contagious clap?'

Duff chuckled. 'They've got gold sickness,' he said.

'You're a potential rival. You could die of thirst and not one of them would spit on you, lest it gave you strength to crawl out and peg something they hadn't noticed.'

He sobered. 'We're wasting time. There's an hour left before dark, let's go and have a look for ourselves.'

They trotted out towards the area of mauled earth. Men were working pick and shovel in the trenches, some of them lean and tough-looking with a dozen natives working beside them; others fat from an office stool, sweating and gritting teeth against the pain of blistered palms, their faces and arms burnt angry red by the sun. All of them greeted Sean and Duff with the same suspicious hostility.

They rode slowly towards the north and every hundred yards with sickening regularity they came across a claim peg with a cairn of stones around its foot and the scrap of canvas nailed to it. Printed in crude capitals on the canvas was the owner's name and his licence number.

Many of the claims were as yet untouched and on these Duff dismounted and searched in the grass, picking up pieces of rock and peering at them before discarding them again. Then once more they moved on with sinking spirits and increasing exhaustion. They camped after dark on the open windy ridge and while the coffee brewed they talked.

'We're too late.' Sean scowled into the fire.

'We've got money, laddie, just remember that. Most of these gentlemen are broke – they are living on hope, not beef and potatoes. Look at their faces and you'll see despair starting to show. It takes capital to work reef gold: you need machinery and money for wages, you have to pipe in water and pile rock, you need wagons and time.'

'Money's no good without a claim to work,' brooded Sean.

'Stay with me, laddie. Have you noticed how many of these claims haven't been touched yet? They belong to speculators and my guess is that they are for sale. In the next few weeks you'll see the men sorted out from the boys—'

'I feel like packing up. This isn't what I expected.'

'You're tired. Sleep well tonight and tomorrow we'll see how far this reef runs – then we'll start some scheming.'

Duff lit one of his cheroots and sucked on it: in the firelight his face was as gaunt as a Red Indian's. They sat on in silence for a while, then Sean spoke.

'What's that noise?' It was a dull tom-tom beat in the darkness.

'You'll get used to that if you stay around here much longer,' said Duff. 'It's the stamps on that mill we saw from the high ground. It's a mile or so farther up the valley; we'll pass it in the morning.'

They were on the move again before the sun was up and they came to the mill in the morning's uncertain light. The mill crouched black and ugly on the smooth curve of the ridge, defiant as a quixotic monster. Its jaws thumped sullenly as it chewed the rock; it snorted steam and screeched metallically.

'I didn't realize it was so big,' said Sean.

'It's big all right,' agreed Duff, 'and they cost money, they don't give them away. Not many men around here can afford a set-up like that.'

There were men moving around the mill, tending its needs, feeding it rock and fussing about the copper tables over which its gold-laden faeces poured. One of the men came forward to offer them the usual hospitality. 'This is private ground. We don't want sightseers around here – keep on going.'

He was a dapper little man with a round brown face and a derby hat pulled down to his ears. His moustache bristled like the whiskers of a fox terrier.

'Listen, Francois, you miserable bloody earthworm, if you talk to me like that I'll push your face around the back of your head,' Duff told him, and the dapper one blinked uncertainly and came closer, peering up at them.

'Who are you? Do I know you?'

Duff pushed his hat back so the man could see his face.

'Duff!' crowed the little man delightedly. 'It's old Duff.' He bounced forward to take Duff's hand as he dismounted. Sean watched the orgy of reunion with amusement. It lasted until Duff managed to bring it under control and lead the little Afrikander across to make the introduction.

'Sean, this is Francois du Toit. He's an old friend of mine from the Kimberley diamond fields.'

Francois greeted Sean and then relapsed once more into the excited chorus of 'Gott, it's good to see you, old Duff.' He pounded Duff's back despite the nimble footwork that Duff was using to spoil his aim. Another few minutes of this passed before Francois composed himself to make his first coherent statement.

'Listen, old Duff, I'm just in the middle of cleaning the amalgam tables. You and your friend go down to my tent. I'll be with you in half an hour, tell my servant to make you some breakfast. I won't be long, man. Gott, man, it's good to see you.'

'An old lover of yours?' asked Sean when they were alone.

Duff laughed. 'We were on the diamond fields together. I did him a favour once – pulled him out of a caving drive when the rock fall had broken his legs. He's a good little guy and meeting him here is the proverbial answer to a prayer. What he can't tell us about this goldfield no one else can.'

Francois came bustling into the tent well under the promised half hour and during breakfast Sean was an outsider in a conversation where every exchange began, 'Do you remember – ?' or 'What happened to old so and so?'

Then, when the plates were empty and the coffee mugs

filled, Duff asked, 'So, what are you doing here, Franz? Is this your own outfit?'

'No, I'm still with the Company.'

'Not that whoreson Hradsky?' Duff registered mock alarm. 'Tha – tha that's ta – ta – terrible,' he imitated a stutter.

'Cut it out, Duff.' Francois looked nervous. 'Don't do that, you want me to lose my job?'

Duff turned to Sean with an explanation. 'Norman Hradsky and God are equals, but in this part of the world God takes his orders from Hradsky.'

'Cut it out, Duff.' Francois was deeply shocked but Duff went on imperturbably.

'The organization through which Hradsky exercises his divine powers is referred to with reverently bated breath as "The Company". In actual fact its full and resounding title is The South African Mining and Lands Company. Do you get the picture?'

Sean nodded smiling and Duff added as an afterthought, 'Hradsky is a bastard and he stutters.'

It was too much for Francois. He leaned across and caught Duff's arm. 'Please, man. My servant understands English, cut it out, Duff.'

'So the Company has started on these fields, hey? Well, well, it must be pretty big,' mused Duff and Francois followed with relief onto safer ground.

'It is! You just wait and see, it's going to make the diamond fields look like a church bazaar!'

'Tell me about it,' said Duff.

'They call it the Rotten Reef or the Banket or the Heidelberg Reef – but in fact there are three reefs, not one. They run side by side like layers in a sandwich cake.'

'All three have pay gold?' Duff shot the question and Francois shook his head. There was a light in his eyes; he was happy talking gold and mining.

'No – you can forget about the outer reef, just traces there. Then there's the Main Reef. That's a bit better, it's as much as six feet thick in places and giving good values, but it's patchy.'

Francois leaned eagerly across the table; in his excitement his thick Afrikaans accent was very noticeable.

'The bottom reef is the winner, we call it the Leader Reef. It's only a few inches thick and some places it fades out altogether, but it's rich. There's gold in it like plums in a pudding. It's rich, Duff, I'm telling you that you won't believe it until you see it!'

'I'll believe you,' said Duff. 'Now tell me where I can get some of this Leader Reef for myself.'

Francois sobered instantly, a shutter dropped over his eyes and hid the light that had shone there a moment before.

'It's gone. It's all gone,' he said defensively. 'It's all been pegged, you've come too late.'

'Well, that's that,' said Duff and a big silence settled on the gathering. Francois fidgeted on his stool, chewing at the ends of his moustache and scowling into his mug. Duff and Sean waited quietly; it was obvious that Francois was wrestling with himself, two loyalties tearing him down the middle. Once he opened his mouth and then closed it again; he blew on his coffee to cool it and the heat came off it in steam.

'Have you got any money?' He fired the question with startling violence.

'Yes,' said Duff.

'Mr Hradsky has gone down to Capetown to raise money. He has a list of a hundred and forty claims that he will buy when he gets back.' Francois paused guiltily. 'I'm only telling you this because of what I owe you.'

'Yes, I know.' Duff spoke softly. Francois took an audible breath and went on.

'On the top of Mr Hradsky's list is a block of claims that belongs to a woman. She is willing to sell and they are the most likely-looking propositions on the whole field.'

'Yes?' Duff encouraged him.

'This woman has started an eating-house about two miles from here on the banks of the Natal Spruit. Her name is Mrs Rautenbach, she serves good food. You could go and have a meal there.'

'Thanks, Francois.'

'I owed it to you,' Francois said gruffly, then his mood changed quickly and he chuckled. 'You'll like her, Duff, she's a lot of woman.'

Sean and Duff went to eat lunch at Mrs Rautenbach's. It was an unpainted corrugated-iron building on a wooden frame and the sign above the veranda said in letters of red and gold 'Candy's Hotel. High-class cuisine. Free toilet facilities. No drunks or horses admitted. Proprietor Mrs Candella Rautenbach.'

They washed off the dust in the enamel basin which stood on the veranda, dried themselves on the free towel and combed in the free mirror on the wall.

'How do I look?' asked Duff.

'Ravishing,' said Sean, 'but you don't smell so good. When did you last bath?'

They went into the dining-room and found it almost full, but there was an empty table against the far wall. The room was hot and thick with pipe smoke and the smell of cabbage. Dusty, bearded men laughed and shouted or ate silently and hungrily. They crossed the room to the table and a coloured waitress came to them.

'Yes?' she asked. Her dress was damp at the armpits.

'May we have the menu?'

The girl looked at Duff with faint amusement. 'Today we got steak and mashed potatoes with pudding afterwards.'

'We'll have it,' Duff agreed.

197

'You sure as hell won't get nothing else,' the girl assured him and trotted back to the kitchen.

'The service is good,' Duff enthused. 'We can only hope that the food and the proprietress are of the same high standard.'

The meat was tough but well flavoured and the coffee was strong and sweet. They ate with appreciation until Sean, who was facing the kitchen, stopped his fork on its way to his mouth. A hush was on the room.

'Here she is,' he said.

Candy Rautenbach was a tall and bright, shiny blonde and her skin was Nordic flawlessness as yet unspoiled by the sun. She filled the front of her blouse and the back of her skirt with a pleasant abundance. She was well aware of and yet not disconcerted by the fact that every eye in the room was on one of those areas. She carried a ladle which she twitched threateningly at the first hand that reached out to pinch her rump, the hand withdrew and Candy smiled sweetly and moved on among the tables. She stopped occasionally to chat with her customers and it was clear that many of these lonely men came here not only to eat. They watched her avidly, grinning with pleasure when she spoke to them. She reached their table and Sean and Duff stood up. Candy blinked with surprise.

'Sit down, please.' The small courtesy had touched her. 'You are new here?'

'We got in yesterday,' Duff smiled at her. 'And the way you cook a steak makes me feel as though I were home again.'

'Where are you from?' Candy looked at the two of them with perhaps just a shade more than professional interest.

'We've come up from Natal to have a look around. This is Mr Courtney – he is interested in new investments and he thought that these goldfields might provide an outlet for some of his capital.'

Sean just managed to stop his jaw dropping open and then quickly assumed the slightly superior air of a big financier as Duff went on.

'My name is Charleywood. I am Mr Courtney's mining adviser.'

'Pleased to meet you. I am Candy Rautenbach.' She was impressed.

'Won't you join us for a few minutes, Mrs Rautenbach?' Duff drew back a chair for her and Candy hesitated.

'I have to check up in the kitchen – perhaps later.'

'Do you always lie so smoothly?' Sean spoke with admiration when Candy had gone.

'I spoke no untruths,' Duff defended himself.

'No, but the way you tell the truth! How the hell am I going to play up to the role you have created for me?'

'You'll learn to live with it, don't worry. Just look wise and keep your mouth shut,' Duff advised. 'What do you think of her anyway?'

'Toothsome,' said Sean.

'Decidedly palatable,' agreed Duff.

When Candy came back Duff kept the conversation light and general for a while, but when Candy started asking some sharp questions it was immediately apparent that her knowledge of geology and mining was well above average and Duff remarked on it.

'Yes, my husband was in the game. I picked it up from him.' She reached into one of the pockets of her blue and white checked skirt and brought out a small handful of rock samples. She put them down in front of Duff. 'Can you name those?' she asked. It was the direct test, she was asking him to prove himself.

'Kimberlite. Serpentine. Feldspar.' Duff reeled them off and Candy relaxed visibly.

'As it happens I have a number of claims pegged along the Heidelberg Reef. Perhaps Mr Courtney would care to have a look at them. Actually, I am negotiating at the moment with The South African Mining and Lands Company who are very interested.'

Sean made his solitary but valuable contribution to the conversation. 'Ah yes,' he nodded sagely. 'Good old Norman.'

Candy was shaken – not many men used Hradsky's Christian name. 'Will tomorrow morning be convenient?' she asked.

– 5 –

That afternoon they bought a tent from a disillusioned hopeful who had thrown up his job on the Natal Railways to make the pilgrimage to Witwatersrand and now needed money to get home. They pitched it near the Hotel and went down to the Natal Spruit to take a long overdue bath. That night they held a mild celebration on the half bottle of brandy that Duff produced from his saddlebag and the next morning Candy took them out to the claims. She had twenty of them pegged right along the Banket. She led them to a spot where the reef outcropped.

'I'll leave you two to look around. If you're interested we can talk about it when you come to the Hotel. I've got to get back now, there'll be hungry mouths to feed.'

Duff escorted Candy to her horse, giving her his arm across the rough ground and helping her into the saddle in a manner he must have learned from his father. He watched her ride away then came back to Sean. He was elated.

'Tread lightly, Mr Courtney, walk with reverence for beneath your feet lies our fortune.'

They went over the ground, Sean like a friendly bloodhound and Duff cruising with the restless circling of a tiger

200

shark. They inspected the claim notices, paced out the boundaries and filled their pockets with chips of rock, then they rode back to their tent and Duff brought out his pestle, mortar and pan. They took them down to the bank of the Natal Spruit and all afternoon crushed the rock and worked the pan. When they had tested the last sample Duff gave his judgement.

'Well, there's gold – and I'd say it's payable gold. It's not nearly as rich as the one we panned at Dundee but that must have been a selected piece of the Leader Reef!' He paused and looked seriously at Sean. 'I think it's worth a try. If the Leader Reef is there we'll find it and in the meantime we won't lose money by working the main reef.'

Sean picked up a pebble and tossed it into the stream in front of him. He was learning for the first time the alternate thrill and depression of gold sickness when one minute you rode the lightning and the next you dropped abruptly into the depths. The yellow tails in the pan had looked pathetically thin and undernourished to him.

'Supposing you're right and supposing we talk Candy into selling her claims, how do we go about it? That four-stamp mill looked a devilishly complicated and expensive bit of machinery to me, not the kind of thing you can buy over the counter in every general dealer's store.'

Duff punched his shoulder and smiled lopsidedly at him. 'You've got your Uncle Duff looking after you. Candy will sell her claims – she trembles when I touch her, a day or two more and she'll be eating out of my hand. As for the mill . . . When I came out to this country I fell in with a rich Cape farmer whose lifelong ambition had been to have his own gold mine. He selected a ridge which in his undisputed wisdom as a grower of grapes he considered to be an ideal place for his mine. He hired me to run it for him, purchased a mill of the latest and most expensive vintage and prepared himself to flood the market with gold.

After six months when we had processed vast quantities of assorted quartz, schist and earth and recovered sufficient gold to fit into a mouse's ear without touching the sides, my patron's enthusiasm was somewhat dampened and he dispensed with my invaluable services and closed the circus down. I left for the diamond fields and as far as I know the machinery is still lying there waiting for the first buyer with a couple of hundred pounds to come and pick it up.' Duff stood up and they walked back towards the tent. 'However, first things first. Do you agree that I should continue the negotiations with Mrs Rautenbach?'

'I suppose so.' Sean was feeling more cheerful again. 'But are you sure your interest in Mrs Rautenbach is strictly line of duty?'

Duff was shocked. 'Don't think for a minute that my intentions are anything but to further the interests of our partnership. You can't believe that my animal appetite plays any part in what I intend doing?'

'No, of course not,' Sean assured him. 'I hope you can force yourself to go through with it.'

Duff laughed. 'While we are on the subject I think this is as good a time as any for you to develop a stomach ailment and retire to your lonely bed. From now on until we've got the agreement signed your boyish charm will be of no great value in the proceedings. I'll tell Candy that you've given me authority to act on your behalf.'

Duff combed his curls, put on the clothes that Mbejane had washed for him and disappeared in the direction of Candy's Hotel. Time passed slowly for Sean; he sat and chatted with Mbejane, drank a little coffee and when the sun went down retired to his tent. He read one of Duff's books by the light of the hurricane lamp but could not concentrate on it; his mind kept straying to thoughts of blonde hair. When someone scratched on the canvas door he leapt up with a confused hope that Candy had decided to come and deal with him direct. It was the coloured girl from the Hotel, her crinkly black hair at odds with what he had been thinking.

'Madame says she's sorry to hear about your sickness and to tell you to have two spoons of this,' she told him and offered Sean the bottle of castor oil.

'Tell your mistress, thank you very much.'

Sean accepted the medicine and started to close the tent flap again.

'Madame told me to stay and make sure that you took two full spoons – I have to take the bottle back and show her how much you've had.'

Sean's stomach cringed. He looked at the coloured girl standing resolute in the doorway, determined to carry out her instructions. He thought of poor Duff doing his duty like a man – he could do no less. He swallowed down the thick clinging oil with his eyes closed then went back to his book. He slept uneasily, starting up occasionally to look at the empty bed across the tent. The medicine drove him out into the cold at half past two in the morning. Mbejane was curled up next to the fire and Sean scowled at him. His regular contented snoring seemed a calculated mockery. A jackal yelped miserably up on the ridge, expressing Sean's feelings exactly, and the night wind fanned his bare buttocks.

Duff came home in the dawning. Sean was wide awake.

'Well, what happened?' he demanded.

Duff yawned. 'At one stage I began to doubt whether I was man enough. However, it worked out to the satisfaction of all concerned. What a woman!' He pulled off his shirt and Sean saw the scratches across his back.

'Did she give you any castor oil?' Sean asked bitterly.

'I'm sorry about that.' Duff smiled at him sympathetically. 'I tried to dissuade her – truly I did. She's a very motherly person. Most concerned about your stomach.'

'You still haven't answered my question. Did you make any progress with the claims?'

'Oh that—' Duff pulled the blankets up under his chin. 'We disposed of that early on in the proceedings. She'll take a down payment of ten pounds each on them and give us an option to buy the lot at any time during the next two years for ten thousand. We arranged that over dinner. The rest of the time was devoted, in a manner of speaking, to shaking hands over the deal. Tomorrow afternoon – or rather this afternoon – you and I'll ride across to Pretoria and get a lawyer to write up an agreement for her to sign. But right now I need some sleep. Wake me at lunch time. Goodnight, laddie.'

Duff and Sean brought the agreement back from Pretoria the following evening. It was an impressive four-page document full of 'in so much as' and 'party of the first part'. Candy led them to her bedroom and they sat around anxiously while she read it through twice.

She looked up at last and said, 'That seems all right – but there is just one other thing.' Sean's heart sank and even Duff's smile was strained. It had all been too easy so far.

Candy hesitated and Sean saw with faint surprise that she was blushing. It was a pleasant thing to see the peach of her cheeks turning to ripe apple and they watched it with interest, their tension lessening perceptibly. 'I want the mine named after me.'

They nearly shouted with relief.

'An excellent idea! How about the Rautenbach Reef Mine?'

Candy shook her head. 'I'd rather not be reminded of him – we'll leave him out of it.'

'Very well – let's call it the Candy Deep. A little premature, I suppose, as we are still at ground level, but pessimism never pays,' suggested Duff.

'Yes, that's lovely,' Candy enthused, flushing again but this time with pleasure. She scrawled her name across the bottom of the document while Sean fired out the cork of the champagne which Duff had bought in Pretoria. They clinked glasses and Duff gave the toast 'To Candy and the Candy Deep – may one grow sweeter and the other deeper with each passing day.'

– 6 –

'We'll need labour, about ten natives to start with. That'll be your problem,' Duff told Sean. It was the following morning and they were eating breakfast in front of the tent. Sean nodded but didn't try to answer until he had swallowed his mouthful of bacon.

'I'll get Mbejane onto that right away. He'll be able to get us Zulus, even if he has to drive them here with a spear at their backs.'

'Good – in the meantime you and I'll ride back to Pretoria again to buy the basic equipment. Picks, shovels, dynamite and the like.' Duff wiped his mouth and filled his coffee cup. 'I'll show you how to start moving the overburden and stacking the ore in a dump. We'll pick a site for the mill and then I'll leave you to get on with it while I head south for the Cape to see my farmer friend. God and the weather permitting ours will be the second mill working on these fields.'

They brought their purchases back from Pretoria in a small ox wagon. Mbejane had done his work well. There were a dozen Zulus lined up for Sean's approval next to the tent with Mbejane standing guard over them like a cheerful sheepdog. Sean walked down the line, stopping to ask each man his name and joke with him in his own language. He came to the last in the line. 'How are you called?'

'My name is Hlubi, Nkosi.'

Sean pointed at the man's well-rounded paunch bulging out above his loincloth.

'If you come to work for me, we'll soon have you delivered of your child.'

They burst out in delighted laughter and Sean smiled at them affectionately: proud simple people, tall and big-muscled, completely defenceless against a well-timed jest. Through his mind flashed the picture of a hill in Zululand, a battlefield below it and the flies crawling in the pit of an empty stomach. He shut the picture out quickly and shouted above their laughter.

'So be it then – sixpence a day and all the food you can eat. Will you sign on to work for me?'

They chorused their assent and climbed up onto the back of the wagon. Sean and Duff took them out to the Candy Deep and they laughed and chattered like children going on a picnic.

It took another week for Duff to instruct Sean in the use of dynamite, to explain how he wanted the first trenches dug and to mark out the site for the mill and the dump. They moved the tent up to the mine and worked twelve hours every day. At night they rode down to Candy's Hotel to eat a full meal and then Sean rode home alone. He was so tired by evening that he hardly envied Duff the comfort of Candy's bedroom; instead he found himself admiring Duff's stamina. Each morning he looked for signs of fatigue in his partner but, although his face was lean and gaunt as ever, his eyes were just as clear and his lopsided smile just as cheerful.

'How you do it beats me,' Sean told him the day they finished marking out the mill site.

Duff winked at him. 'Years of practice, laddie, but between you and me the ride down to the Cape will be a welcome rest.'

'When are you going?' Sean asked.

'Quite frankly I think that every day I stay on here increases the risk of someone else getting in before us. Mining machinery is going to be at a premium from now on. You have got things well in hand now . . . What do you say?'

'I was starting to think along the same lines,' Sean agreed. They walked back to the tent and sat down in the camp chairs, from where they could look down the length of the valley. The week before about two dozen wagons had been outspanned around Candy's Hotel, but now there were at least two hundred and from where they sat they could count another eight or nine encampments, some even larger than the one around Candy's place. Wood and iron buildings were beginning to replace the canvas tents and the whole veld was criss-crossed with rough roads along which mounted men and wagons moved without apparent purpose.

The restless movement, the dust clouds raised by the passage of men and beasts, and the occasional deep crump, crump of dynamite firing in the workings along the Banket – all heightened the air of excitement, of almost breathless expectancy that hung over the whole goldfield.

'I'll leave at first light tomorrow,' Duff decided. 'Ten days' riding to the railhead at Colesberg and another four days by train will get me there. With luck I'll be back in under two months.' He wriggled round in his chair and looked directly at Sean. 'After paying Candy her two hundred pounds and with what I spent in Pretoria I've only got about a hundred and fifty left. Once I get to Paarl I'll have to pay out three or four hundred for the mill, then I'll need to hire twenty or thirty wagons to bring it up here – say eight hundred pounds altogether to be on the safe side.'

Sean looked at him. He had known this man a few short weeks. Eight hundred was the average man's earnings for three years. Africa was a big land, a man could disappear easily. Sean loosened his belt and dropped it onto the table; he unbuttoned the money pouch.

'Give me a hand to count it out,' he told Duff.

'Thanks,' said Duff and he was not talking about the money. With trust asked for so simply and given so spontaneously the last reservations in their friendship shrivelled and died.

– 7 –

When Duff had gone Sean drove himself and his men without mercy. They stripped the overburden off the Reef and exposed it across the whole length of the Candy claims, then they broke it up and started stacking it next to the mill site. The dump grew bigger with every twelve-hour day worked. There was still no trace of the Leader Reef but Sean found little time to worry about that. At night he climbed into bed and slept away his fatigue until another morning called him back to the workings. On Sundays he rode across to Francois's tent and they talked mining and medicines. Francois had an enormous chest of patent medicines and a book titled *The Home Physician*. His health was his hobby and he was treating himself for three major ailments simultaneously. Although he was occasionally unfaithful, his true love was sugar diabetes. The page in *The Home Physician* which covered this subject was limp and grubby from the touch of his fingers. He could recite the symptoms from memory and he had all of them. His other favourite was tuberculosis of the bone; this moved around his body with alarming rapidity taking only a week to leave his hip and reach his wrist. Despite his failing health, however, he was an expert on mining and Sean picked his brain shamelessly. Francois's sugar diabetes did not prevent him from sharing a bottle of brandy with Sean on Sunday evenings. Sean kept away from Candy's Hotel – that shiny blonde hair and peach skin would have been too much temptation. He couldn't trust himself not to wreck his new friendship with Duff by another importunate affair, so instead he sweated away his energy in the trenches of the Candy Deep.

Every morning he set his Zulus a task for the day, always just a little more than the day before. They sang as they worked and it was very seldom that the task was not complete by nightfall. The days blurred into each other and turned to weeks which quadrupled like breeding amoebae and became months. Sean began to imagine Duff giving the Capetown girls a whirl with his eight hundred pounds. One evening he rode south for miles along the Cape road, stopping to question every traveller he met and when he finally gave up and returned to the goldfields he went straight to one of the canteens to look for a fight. He found a big, yellow-haired German miner to oblige him. They went outside and for an hour they battered each other beneath a crisp Transvaal night sky surrounded by a ring of delighted spectators. Then he and the German went back into the canteen, shook each other's bleeding hands, drank a vow of friendship together and Sean returned to the Candy Deep with his devil exorcized for the time being.

The next afternoon Sean was working near the north boundary of the claims; at this point they had burrowed down about fifteen feet to keep contact with the reef. Sean had just finished marking the shot holes for the next blast and the Zulus were standing around him taking snuff and spitting on their hands before attacking the rock once more.

'Mush, you shag-eared villains. What's going on here, a trade union meeting?' The familiar voice came from above their heads. Duff was looking down at them. Sean scrambled straight up the side of the trench and seized him in a bear hug. Duff was thinner, his jowls covered with a pale stubble and his curly hair white with dust. When the fury of greeting had subsided a little Sean demanded, 'Well, where's the present you went to fetch me?'

Duff laughed. 'Not far behind, all twenty-five wagons full of it.'

'You got it then?' Sean roared.

'You're damn right I did! Come with me and I'll show you.'

Duff's convoy was strung out four miles across the veld, most of the wagons double-teamed against the enormous weight of the machinery. Duff pointed to a rust-streaked cylinder that completely filled one of the leading wagons.

'That is my particular cross, seven tons of the most spiteful, stubborn and evil boiler in the world. If it's broken the wagon axle once it's broken it a dozen times since we left Colesberg, not to mention the two occasions on which it capsized itself – once right in the middle of a river.'

They rode along the line of wagons.

'Good God! I didn't realize there'd be so much.' Sean shook his head dubiously. 'Are you sure you know how it all fits together?'

'Leave it to your Uncle Duff. Of course, it's going to need a bit of work done on it, after all it's been lying out in the open for a couple of years. Some of it was rusted up solid, but the judicious use of grease, new paint and the Charleywood brain will see the Candy Deep plant breaking rock and spitting out gold within a month.' Duff broke off and waved to a horseman coming towards them. 'This is the transport contractor. Frikkie Malan – Mr Courtney, my partner.'

The contractor pulled up next to them and acknowledged the introduction. He wiped the dust off his face with the sleeve of his shirt.

'Gott, man, Mr Charleywood, I don't mind telling you

210

that this is the hardest money I've ever worked for. Nothing personal – but I'll be *vragtig* glad to see the last of this load.'

– 8 –

Duff was wrong; it took much longer than a month. The rust had eaten deep into parts of the machinery and each bolt they twisted open was red with the scaly cancer. They worked the usual twelve-hour day chipping and scraping, filing and greasing, knuckles knocked raw against steel and palms wet and red where the blisters had burst. Then one day suddenly and miraculously they were finished. Along the ridge of the Candy Deep, neat and sweet smelling in its new paint, thick with yellow grease and waiting only to be fitted together, lay the dismembered mill.

'How long has it taken us so far?' Duff asked.

'It seems like a hundred years.'

'Is that all?' Duff feigned surprise. 'Then I declare a holiday – two days of meditation.'

'You meditate, brother – I'm going to do some carousing.'

'That's an excellent alternative – let's go!'

They started at Candy's place but she threw them out after the third fight so they moved on. There were a dozen places to drink at and they tried them all. Others were celebrating, because the day before old Kruger, the President of the Republic, had given official recognition to the goldfields. This had the sole effect of diverting the payments for mining licences from the pockets of the farmers who owned the land into the Government coffers. No one worried about that, except possibly the farmers. Rather it was an excuse for a party. The canteens were packed with swearing, sweating men. Duff and Sean drank with them.

The Crown and Anchor boards were doing a steady business in every bar and the men who crowded around them were the new population of the goldfields. Diggers bare to the waist and caked with dirt, salesmen with loud clothes and louder voices selling everything from dynamite to dysentery cure, an evangelist peddling salvation, gamblers mining pockets, gentlemen trying to keep the tobacco juice off their boots, boys new-flown from home and wishing themselves back, Boers bearded and drab-suited, drinking little but watching with inscrutable eyes the invaders of their land. Then there were the others, the clerks and farmers, the rogues and contractors listening greedily to the talk of gold.

The coloured girl, Martha, came to find Sean and Duff on the afternoon of the second day. They were in a mud-brick and thatch hut called The Tavern of the Bright Angels. Duff was doing a solo exhibition of the Dashing White Sergeant partnered by a chair; Sean and the fifty or so other customers were beating the rhythm on the bar counter with glasses and empty bottles.

Martha skittered across to Sean, slapping at the hands that tried to dive up her skirts and squealing sharply every time her bottom was pinched. She arrived at Sean's side flushed and breathless.

'Madame says you must come quickly – there's big trouble,' she gasped and started to run the gauntlet back to the door. Someone flipped up her dress behind and a concerted masculine roar approved the fact that she wore nothing under the petticoats.

Duff was so engrossed in his dancing that Sean had to carry him bodily out of the bar and dip his head in the horse trough outside before he could gain his attention.

'What the hell did you do that for?' spluttered Duff and swung a round-arm punch at Sean's head. Sean ducked under it and caught him about the body to save him falling on his back.

'Candy wants us – she says there's big trouble.'

Duff thought about that for a few seconds, frowning with concentration, then he threw back his head and sang to the tune of 'London's Burning',

> 'Candy wants us – Candy wants us
> We don't want Candy, we want brandy.'

He broke out of Sean's grip and headed back for the bar. Sean caught him again and pointed him in the direction of the Hotel. Candy was in her bedroom. She looked at the two of them as they swayed arm-in-arm in the doorway.

'Did you enjoy your debauch?' she asked sweetly. Duff mumbled and tried to straighten his coat. Sean tried to steady him as his feet danced an involuntary sideways jig.

'What happened to your eye?' she asked Sean and he fingered it tenderly; it was puffed and blue. Candy didn't wait for an answer but went on, still sweetly:

'Well, if you two beauties want to own a mine by tomorrow you'd better sober up.'

They stared at her and Sean spoke deliberately but nevertheless indistinctly.

'Why, what's the matter?'

'They're going to jump the claims, that's the matter. This new proclamation of a State goldfield has given the drifters the excuse they've been waiting for. About a hundred of them have formed a syndicate. They claim that the old titles aren't legal any more; they are going to pull out the pegs and put in their own.'

Duff walked without a stagger across to the washbasin beside Candy's bed; he splashed his face, towelled it vigorously then stooped and kissed her. 'Thanks, my sweet.'

'Duff, please be careful,' Candy called after them.

'Let's see if we can't hire a few mercenaries,' Sean suggested.

'Good idea, we'll try and find a few sober characters – there should be some in Candy's dining-room.'

They made a short detour on their way back to the mine and stopped at Francois's tent; it was dark by then and Francois came out in a freshly ironed nightshirt. He raised an eyebrow when he saw the five heavily armed men with Sean and Duff.

'You going hunting?' he asked.

Duff told him quickly and Francois was hopping with agitation before he had finished.

'Steal my claims, the thunders, the stinking thunders!' He rushed into his tent and came out again with a double-barrelled shotgun.

'We'll see, man, we'll see how they look full of buckshot.'

'Francois, listen to me,' Sean shouted him down. 'We don't know which claims they'll go to first. Get your men ready and if you hear shooting our way come and give us a hand – we'll do the same for you.'

'Ja, ja, we'll come all right – the dirty thunders.' His nightshirt flapping around his legs Francois trotted off to call his men.

Mbejane and the other Zulus were cooking dinner, squatting round the three-legged pot. Sean rode up to them.

'Get your spears,' he told them. They ran for their huts and almost immediately came crowding back.

'Nkosi, where's the fight?' they pleaded, food forgotten.

'Come on, I'll show you.'

They placed the hired gunmen amongst the mill machinery from where they could cover the track which led up to the mine. The Zulus they hid in one of the prospect trenches. If it developed into a hand-to-hand fight the syndicate was in for a surprise. Duff and Sean walked a little

214

way down the slope to make sure their defenders were all concealed.

'How much dynamite have we got?' Sean asked thoughtfully. Duff stared at him a second, then he grinned.

'Sufficient, I'd say. You're full of bright ideas this evening.' He led the way back to the shed which they used as a storeroom.

In the middle of the track a few hundred yards down the slope they buried a full case of explosive and placed an old tin can on top of it to mark the spot. They went back to the shed and spent an hour making grenades out of bundles of dynamite sticks, each with a detonator and a very short fuse. Then they settled down huddled into their sheepskin coats, rifles in their laps and waited.

They could see the lights of the encampments straggled down the valley and hear an occasional faint burst of singing from the canteens, but the moonlit road up to the mine remained deserted. Sean and Duff sat side by side with their backs against the newly painted boiler.

'How did Candy find out about this, I wonder?' Sean asked.

'She knows everything. That hotel of hers is the centre of this goldfield and she keeps her ears open.'

They relapsed into silence again while Sean formed his next question.

'She's quite a girl – our Candy.'

'Yes,' agreed Duff.

'Are you going to marry her, Duff?'

'Good God!' Duff straightened up as though someone had stuck a knife into him. 'You going mad, laddie, or else that was a joke in the worst possible taste.'

'She dotes on you and from what I've seen you're fairly well disposed towards her.' Sean was relieved at Duff's quick rejection of the idea. He was jealous, but not of the woman.

'Yes, we've got a common interest, that I won't deny –

but marriage!' Duff shivered slightly, not altogether from the cold. 'Only a fool makes the same mistake twice.'

Sean turned to him with surprise. 'You've been married before?' he asked.

'With a vengeance. She was half Spanish and the rest Norwegian, a smoking bubbly mixture of cold fire and hot ice.' Duff's voice went dreamy. 'The memory has cooled sufficiently for me to think of it with a tinge of regret.'

'What happened?'

'I left her.'

'Why?'

'We only did two things well together and one of them was fight. If I close my eyes I can still see the way she used to pout with those lovely lips and bring them close to my ear before she hissed out a particularly foul word, then – hey ho! back to bed for the reconciliation.'

'Perhaps you made the wrong choice. You look around, you'll see millions of happily married people.'

'Name me one,' challenged Duff and the silence lengthened as Sean thought.

Then Duff went on, 'There's only one good reason for marriage, and that's children.'

'And companionship – that's another good reason.'

'Companionship from a woman?' Duff cut in incredulously. 'Like perfume from garlic. They're incapable of it. I suppose it's the training they get from their mothers, who are after all women themselves, but how can you be friends with someone who suspicions every little move you make, who takes your every action and weighs it on the balance of he loves me, he loves me not?' Duff shook his head unhappily. 'How long can a friendship last when it needs an hourly declaration of love to nourish it? The catechism of matrimony, "Do you love me, darling?" "Yes, darling, of course I do, my sweet." It's got to sound convincing every time otherwise tears.'

Sean chuckled.

'All right, it's funny – it's hilarious until you have to live with it,' Duff mourned. 'Have you ever tried to talk to a woman about anything other than love? The same things that interest you leave them cold. It comes as a shock the first time you try talking sense to them and suddenly you realize that their attention is not with you – they get a slightly fixed look in their eyes and you know they are thinking about that new dress or whether to invite Mrs Van der Hum to the party, so you stop talking and that's another mistake. That's a sign; marriage is full of signs that only a wife can read.'

'I hold no brief for matrimony, Duff, but aren't you being a little unfair, judging everything by your own unfortunate experience?'

'Select any woman, slap a ring on her third finger and she becomes a wife. First she takes you into her warm, soft body, which is pleasant, and then she tries to take you into her warm, soft mind, which is not so pleasant. She does not share, she possesses – she clings and she smothers. The relation of man to woman is uninteresting in that it conforms to an inescapable pattern, nature has made it so for the very good reason that it requires us to reproduce; but in order to obtain that result every love, Romeo and Juliet, Bonaparte and Josephine not excepted, must lead up to the co-performance of a simple biological function. It's such a small thing – such a short-lived, trivial little experience. Apart from that man and woman think differently, feel differently and are interested in different things. Would you call that companionship?'

'No, but is that a true picture? Is that all there is between them?' Sean asked.

'You'll find out one day. Nature in her preoccupation with reproduction has planted in the mind of man a barricade; it has sealed him off from the advice and experience of his fellowmen, inoculated him against it. When your time comes you'll go to the gallows with a song on your lips.'

'You frighten me.'

'It's the sameness of it all that depresses me – the goddamn monotony of it.' Duff shifted his seat restlessly then settled back against the boiler. The interesting relationships are those in which sex the leveller takes no hand – brothers, enemies, master and servant, father and son, man and man.'

'Homosexuals?'

'No, that's merely sex out of step and you're back to the original trouble. When a man takes a friend he does it not from an uncontrollable compulsion but in his own free choice. Every friendship is different, ends differently or goes on for ever. No chains bind it, no ritual or written contract. There is no question of forsaking all others, no obligation to talk about it – mouth it up and gloat on it the whole time.' Duff stood up stiffly. 'It's one of the good things in life. How late is it?'

Sean pulled out his watch and tilted its face to catch the moonlight. 'After midnight – it doesn't look as if they're coming.'

'They'll come – there's gold here, another uncontrollable compulsion. They'll come. The question is when.'

The lights along the valley faded out one by one, the deep singsong voices of the Zulus in the prospect trench stilled and a small cold wind came up and moved the grass along the ridge of the Candy Deep. Sitting together, sometimes drowsing, sometimes talking quietly, they waited the night away. The sky paled, then pinked prettily. A dog barked over near Hospital Hill and another joined it. Sean stood up and stretched, he glanced down the valley towards Ferrieras Camp and saw them. A black moving blot of horsemen, overflowing the road, lifting no dust from the dew-damp earth, spreading out to cross the Natal Spruit then bunching together on the near bank before coming on.

'Mr Charleywood, we have company.'

Duff jumped up.

'They might miss us and go on to the Jack and Whistle first.'

'We'll see which road they take when they come to the fork. In the meantime let's get ready. Mbejane,' shouted Sean and the black head popped out of the trench.

'Nkosi?'

'Are you awake? They are coming.'

The blackness parted in a white smile. 'We are awake.'

'Then get down and stay down until I give the word.'

The five mercenaries were lying belly down in the grass, each with a newly-opened packet of cartridges at his elbow. Sean hurried back to Duff and they crouched behind the boiler.

'The tin can shows up clearly from here. Do you think you can hit it?'

'With my eyes closed,' said Sean.

The horsemen reached the fork and turned without hesitation towards the Candy Deep, quickening their paces as they came up the ridge. Sean rested his rifle across the top of the boiler and picked up the speck of silver in his sights.

'What's the legal position, Duff?' he asked out of the corner of his mouth.

'They've just crossed our boundary – they are now officially trespassers,' Duff pronounced solemnly.

One of the leading horses kicked over the tin can and Sean fired at the spot on which it had stood. The shot was indecently loud in the quiet morning and every head in the syndicate lifted with alarm towards the ridge, then the ground beneath them jumped up in a brown cloud to meet the sky. When the dust cleared there was a struggling tangle of downed horses and men. The screams carried clearly up to the crest of the ridge.

'My God,' breathed Sean, appalled at the destruction.

'Shall we let them have it, boss?' called one of the hired men.

'No,' Duff answered him quickly. 'They've had enough.'

The flight started, riderless horses, mounted men and others on foot were scattering back down the valley. Sean was relieved to see that they left only half a dozen men and a few horses lying in the road.

'Well, that's the easiest fiver you've ever earned,' Duff told one of the mercenaries. 'I think you can go home now and have some breakfast.'

'Wait, Duff.' Sean pointed. The survivors of the explosion had reached the road junction again and there they were being stopped by two men on horseback.

'Those two are trying to rally them.'

'Let's change their minds, they're still within rifle range.'

'They are not on our property any more,' disagreed Sean. 'Do you want to wear a rope?'

They watched while those of the syndicate who had had enough fighting for one day disappeared down the road to the camps and the rest coagulated into a solid mass at the crossroad.

'We should have shot them up properly while we had the chance,' grumbled one of the mercenaries uneasily. 'Now they'll come back – look at that bastard talking to them like a Dutch uncle.'

They left their horses and spread out, then they started moving cautiously back up the slope. They hesitated just below the line of boundary pegs then ran forward, tearing up the pegs as they came.

'All together, gentlemen, if you please,' called Duff

politely and the seven rifles fired. The range was long and the thirty or so attackers ran doubled up and dodging. The bullets had little effect at first, but as the distance shortened men started falling. There was a shallow donga running diagonally down the slope and as each of the attackers reached it he jumped down into it and from its safety started a heated reply to the fire of Sean's men. Bullets spanged off the machinery, leaving bright scars where they struck.

Mbejane's Zulus were adding their voices to the confusion.

'Let us go down to them now, Nkosi.'

'They are close – let us go.'

'Quiet down, you madmen, you'd not go a hundred paces against those rifles,' Sean snarled impatiently.

'Sean, cover me,' whispered Duff. 'I'm going to sneak round the back of the ridge, rush them from the side and lob a few sticks of dynamite into that donga.'

Sean caught his arm, his fingers dug into it so that Duff winced.

'You take one step and I'll break a rifle butt over your head – you're as bad as those Blacks. Now keep shooting and let me think.' Sean peered over the top of the boiler but ducked again as a bullet rang loudly against it, inches from his ear. He stared at the new paint in front of his nose, put his shoulder against it; the boiler rocked slightly. He looked up and Duff was watching him.

'We'll walk down together and lob that dynamite,' Sean told him. 'Mbejane and his bloodthirsty heathens will roll the boiler in front of us. These other gentlemen will cover us, we'll do this thing in style.'

Sean called the Zulus out of the trench and explained to them. They chorused their approval of the scheme and jostled each other to find a place to push against the boiler.

Sean and Duff filled the front of their shirts with the dynamite grenades and lit a short length of tarred rope each.

Sean nodded to Mbejane.

'Where are the children of Zulu?' sang Mbejane, shrilling his voice in the ancient rhetorical question.

'Here,' answered his warriors braced ready against the boiler.

'Where are the spears of Zulu?'

'Here.'

'How bright are the spears of Zulu?'

'Brighter than the Sun.'

'How hungry are the spears of Zulu?'

'Hungrier than the locust.'

'Then let us take them to the feeding.'

'*Yeh-bo.*' Explosive assent and the boiler revolved slowly to the thrust of black shoulders.

'*Yeh-bo.*' Another reluctant revolution.

'*Yeh-bo.*' It moved more readily.

'*Yeh-bo.*' Gravity caught it. Ponderously it bumped down the slope and they ran behind it. The fire from the donga doubled its volume, rattling like hail against the huge metal cylinder. The singing of the Zulus changed its tone also; the deep-voiced chanting quickened, climbed excitedly, and became the blood trill. That insane, horrible squealing made Sean's skin crawl, tickled his spine with the ghost fingers of memory, but it inflamed him also. His mouth opened and he squealed with them. He touched the first grenade with the burning rope then flung it in a high spluttering sparking arc. It burst in the air above the donga. He threw again. Crump, crump. Duff was using his explosive as well. The boiler crashed over the lip of the donga and came to rest in a cloud of dust; the Zulus followed it in, spreading out, still shrieking, and now their assegais were busy. The white men broke, clawed frantically out of the ravine and fled, the Zulus hacking at them as they ran.

When Francois arrived with fifty armed diggers following him the fight was over.

'Take your boys down to the camps. Comb them out carefully. We want every one of those that got away,' Duff told him. 'It's about time we had a little law and order on this field.'

'How will we pick out the ones that were in on it?' asked Francois.

'By their white faces and the sweat on their shirts you will know them,' Duff answered.

Francois and his men went, leaving Sean and Duff to clean up the battlefield. It was a messy job – the stabbing spears had made it so. They destroyed those horses that the blast had left still half alive and they gleaned more than a dozen corpses from the donga and the slope below it. Two of them were Zulus. The wounded, and there were many, they packed into a wagon and took them down to Candy's Hotel.

It was early afternoon by the time they arrived. They threaded the wagon through the crowd and stopped it in front of the Hotel. It seemed the entire population of the goldfield was there, packed around the small open space in which Francois was holding his prisoners.

Francois was almost hysterical with excitement. He was sweeping the shotgun around in dangerous circles as he harangued the crowd. Then he darted back to prod one of the prisoners with the twin muzzles.

'You thunders,' he screamed. 'Steal our claims – hey – steal our claims.'

At that moment he caught sight of Duff and Sean bringing the wagon through the press.

'Duff, Duff. We got them. We got the whole lot of

them.' The crowd backed respectfully away from the menace of that circling shotgun and Sean flinched as it pointed directly at him for a second.

'So I see, Francois,' Duff assured him. 'In fact, I have seldom seen anyone more completely had.'

Francois's prisoners were swathed in ropes; they could move only their heads and as additional security a digger with a loaded rifle stood over each of them. Duff climbed down off the wagon.

'Don't you think you should slacken those ropes a little?' Duff asked dubiously.

'And have them escape?' Francois was indignant.

'Do you think they'd get very far?'

'No, I don't suppose so.'

'Well, another half hour and they'll all have gangrene – look at that one's hand already, a beautiful shade of blue.'

Reluctantly Francois conceded and told his men to untie them.

Duff pushed his way through the crowd and climbed the steps of the Hotel. From there he held up his hands for silence.

'There have been a lot of men killed today – we don't want it to happen again. One way we can prevent it is to make sure that this lot get what they deserve.' Cheers were led by Francois.

'But we must do it properly. I suggest we elect a committee to deal with this affair and with any other problems that crop up on these fields. Say ten members and a chairman.'

More cheers.

'Call it the Diggers' Committee,' shouted someone and the crowd took up the name enthusiastically.

'All right, the Diggers' Committee it is. Now we want a chairman, any suggestions?'

'Mr Charleywood,' shouted Francois.

'Yes, Duff – he'll do.'

'Yes, Duff Charleywood.'

'Any other suggestions?'

'No,' roared the crowd.

'Thank you, gentlemen.' Duff smiled at them. 'I am sensible of the honour. Now, ten members.'

'Jock and Trevor Heyns.'

'Karl Lochtkamper.'

'Francois du Toit.'

'Sean Courtney.'

There were fifty nominations. Duff baulked at counting votes so the committee was elected by applause. He called the names one at a time and judged the strength of the response to each. Sean and Francois were among those elected. Chairs and a table were brought out onto the veranda and Duff took his seat. With a water-jug he hammered for silence, declared the first session of the Diggers' Committee open and then immediately fined three members of the crowd ten pounds each for discharging firearms during a meeting – gross contempt of Committee. The fines were paid and a proper air of solemnity achieved.

'I'll ask Mr Courtney to open the case for the prosecution.'

Sean stood up and gave a brief description of the morning's battle, ending, 'You were there, Your Honour, so you know all about it anyway.'

'So I was,' agreed Duff. 'Thank you, Mr Courtney. I think that was a very fair picture you presented. Now,' he looked at the prisoners, 'who speaks for you?'

There was a minute of shuffling and whispering, then one of them was pushed forward. He pulled off his hat and blushed purple.

'Your Worship,' he began, then stopped, wriggling with embarrassment.

'Your Worship.'

'You've said that already.'

'I don't rightly know where to begin, Mr Charleywood – I mean Your Honour, sir.'

Duff looked at the prisoners again.

'Perhaps you'd like to reconsider your choice.'

Their first champion was withdrawn in disgrace and a fresh one sent forward to face the Committee. He had more fire.

'You bastards got no right to do this to us,' he started and Duff promptly fined him ten pounds. His next attempt was more polite.

'Your Honour, you can't do this to us. We had our rights, you know, that new proclamation and all, I mean, them old titles wasn't legal no more now, was they? We just came along as peaceful as you please, the old titles not being legal, we got a right to do what we done. Then you bastards, I mean Your Honour, dynamited us and like we had a right to protect ourselves, I mean after all, didn't we, sir?'

'A brilliant defence most ably conducted. Your fellows should be grateful to you,' Duff complimented him, then turned to his Committee. 'Well now, how say you merry gentlemen. Guilty or not guilty?'

'Guilty.' They spoke together and Francois added for emphasis, 'The dirty thunders.'

'We will now consider sentence.'

'String them up,' shouted someone and instantly the mood changed. The mob growled: an ugly sound.

'I'm a carpenter, I'll whip you up a handsome set of gallows in no time at all.'

'Don't waste good wood on them. Use a tree.'

'Get the ropes.'

'String them up.'

The crowd surged in, lynch mad. Sean snatched Francois's shotgun and jumped up onto the table.

'So help me God, I'll shoot the first one of you that

touches them before this court says so.' They checked and Sean pressed his advantage. 'At this range I can't miss. Come on, try me – there's two loads of buckshot in here. Someone will get cut in half.' They fell back still muttering.

'Perhaps you've forgotten, but there's a police force in this country and there's a law against killing. Hang them today and it'll be your turn tomorrow.'

'You're right, Mr Courtney, it'll be cruel, heartless murder. That it will,' wailed the spokesman.

'Shut up, you bloody fool,' Duff snarled at him and someone in the crowd laughed. The laughter caught on and Duff sighed silently with relief. That had been very close.

'Give them the old tar and feathers.'

Duff grinned. 'Now you're talking sense. Who's got a few barrels of tar for sale?' He looked round. 'What, no offers? Then we'll have to think of something else.'

'I've got ten drums of red paint – thirty shillings each, good imported brand.' Duff recognized the speaker as a trader who had opened a general dealer's store down at Ferrieras Camp.

'Mr Tarry suggests paint. What about it?'

'No, it comes off too easily – that's no good.'

'I'll let you have it cheap – twenty-five shillings a drum.'

'No – stick your ruddy paint,' the crowd booed him.

'Give them a twist on Satan's Roulette Wheel,' shouted another voice, and the crowd clamoured agreement.

'That's it – give them the wheel.'

'Round and round and round she goes – where she stops nobody knows,' roared a black-bearded digger from the roof of the shanty across the road. The crowd howled.

Sean watched Duff's expression – the smile had gone. He was weighing it up. If he stopped them again they might lose all patience and risk the shotgun. He couldn't chance it.

'All right. If that's what you want.' He faced the terrified cluster of prisoners. 'The sentence of this court is that you play roulette with the devil for one hour and that you then leave this goldfield – if we catch you back here again you'll get another hour of it. The wounded are excused the first half of the sentence. I think they've had enough. Mr du Toit will supervise the punishment.'

'We'd prefer the paint, Mr Charleywood,' pleaded the spokesman again.

'I bet you would,' said Duff softly, but the crowd was carrying them away already, out towards the open veld beyond the Hotel. Most of them had staked claims of their own and they didn't like claim jumpers. Sean climbed down off the table.

'Let's go and have a drink,' Duff said to him.

'Aren't you going to watch?' asked Sean.

'I've seen it done once before down in the Cape. That was enough.'

'What do they do?'

'Go and have a look, I'll be waiting for you at the Bright Angels. I'll be surprised if you stay the full hour.'

By the time Sean joined the crowd most of the wagons had been gathered from the camps and drawn up in a line. Men swarmed round them fitting jacks under the axles to lift the big back wheels clear of the ground. Then the prisoners were hustled forward – one to each wheel. Eager hands lifted them and held them while their wrists and ankles were lashed to the rim of the wheel with the hub in the middle of their backs and their arms and legs spread-eagled like stranded starfish. Francois hurried along the line checking the ropes and placing four diggers at each wheel, two to start it and another two to take over when those were tired. He reached the end, came back to the centre again, pulled his watch from his pocket, checked the time, then shouted.

'All right – turn them, *kerels*.'

228

The wheels started moving, slowly at first then faster as they built up momentum. The bodies strapped to them blurred with the speed.

'Round and round and round she goes – round and round and round she goes,' chanted the crowd gleefully.

Within minutes there was a burst of laughter from the end of the line of wagons. Someone had started vomiting, it sprayed from him like yellow sparks from a catherine wheel. Then another and another joined in. Sean could hear them retching and gasping as the centrifugal force flung the vomit up against the back of their throats and out of their noses. He waited a few more minutes but when their bowels started to empty he turned away gagging and headed for the Bright Angel.

'Did you enjoy it?' asked Duff.

'Give me a brandy,' answered Sean.

– 9 –

With the Diggers' Committee dispensing rough justice a semblance of order came to the camps. President Kruger wanted no part in policing the nest of ruffians and cut-throats which was growing up just outside his Capital and he contented himself with placing his spies among them and leaving them to work out their own salvation. After all, the field was far from proved and the chances were that in another year the veld would again be as deserted as it had been nine months before. He could afford to wait; in the meantime the Diggers' Committee had his tacit sanction.

While the ants worked, cutting down into the reef with pick and with dynamite, the grasshoppers waited in the bars and shanties. So far only the Jack and Whistle mill was turning out gold, and only Hradsky and Francois du Toit knew how much gold was coming out of it. Hradsky was still in Capetown crusading for capital and Francois spoke to no one, not even to Duff, about the mill's productivity.

The rumours flew like sand in a whirlwind. One day it seemed that the reef had pinched out fifty feet below the surface, and the next the canteens buzzed with the news that the Heyns brothers had gone down a hundred feet and were pulling out nuggets the size of musket balls. Nobody knew but everybody was prepared to guess.

Up at the Candy Deep, Duff and Sean worked on relentlessly. The mill took shape on its concrete platform, its jaws open for the first bite at the rock. The boiler was swung up onto its cradle by twenty sweating, singing Zulus. The copper tables were fitted up ready to be smeared with quicksilver. There was no time to worry about the reef nor the dwindling store of money in Sean's cash belt. They worked and they slept – there was nothing else. Duff took to sharing Sean's tent up on the ridge and Candy had her featherbed to herself again.

On the twentieth of November they fired the boiler for the first time. Tired and horny-handed, their bodies lean and tempered hard with toil, they stood together and watched the needle creek up round the pressure gauge until it touched the red line at the top.

Duff grunted. 'Well, at least we've got power now.' Then he punched Sean's shoulder. 'What the hell are you standing here for – do you think this is a Sunday School picnic? There's work to do, laddie.'

On the second of December they fed the mill its first meal and watched the powdered rock flow across the amalgam tables. Sean threw his arm round Duff's neck in an affectionate half-Nelson, Duff hit him in the stomach and pulled his hat down over his eyes, they drank a glass of brandy each at supper and laughed a little but that was all. They were too tired to celebrate. From now on one of them must be in constant attendance on that iron monster. Duff took the first night shift and when Sean went up to the mill next morning he found him weaving on his feet, his eyes sunk deep in dark sockets.

'By my reckoning we've run ten tons of rock through her. Time to clean the tables and see just how much gold we've picked up.'

'You go and get some sleep,' said Sean and Duff ignored him.

'Mbejane, bring a couple of your savages here, we're going to change the tables.'

'Listen, Duff, it can wait an hour or two. Go and get your head down.'

'Please stop drivelling – you're as bad as a wife.'

Sean shrugged. 'Have it your own way, show me how you do it then.'

They switched the flow of powdered rock onto the second table that was standing ready; then with a broad bladed spatula Duff scraped the mercury off the copper top of the first table, collecting it in a ball the size of a coconut.

'The mercury picks up the tiny particles of gold,' he explained to Sean as he worked, 'and lets the grains of rock wash across the table and fall off into the dump. Of course it doesn't collect it all, some of it goes to waste.'

'How do you get the gold out again?'

'You put the whole lot in a retort and boil off the mercury – the gold stays behind.'

'Hell of a waste of mercury, isn't it?'

'No, you catch it as it condenses and use it again. Come on, I'll show you.'

Duff carried the ball of amalgam down to the shed, placed it in the retort and lit the blow-lamp. With the heat on it the ball dissolved and started to bubble. Silently they stared at it. The level in the retort fell.

'Where's the gold?' Sean asked at last.

'Oh, shut up,' Duff snapped impatiently, and then, repentant, 'Sorry, laddie, I feel a bit jaded this morning.'

The last of the mercury steamed off and there it was, glowing bright, molten yellow. A drop of gold the size of a pea. Duff shut off the blow-lamp and neither of them spoke for a while. Then Sean asked, 'Is that all?'

'That, my friend, is all,' agreed Duff wearily. 'What do you want to do with it – fill a tooth?'

He turned towards the door with a droop to his whole body.

'Keep the mill running, we might as well go down with our colours flying.'

– 10 –

It was a miserable Christmas dinner. They ate it at Candy's Hotel. They had credit there. She gave Duff a gold signet ring and Sean a box of cigars. Sean had never smoked before but now the sting of it in his lungs gave him a certain masochistic pleasure. The dining-room roared with men's voices and cutlery clatter, the air was thick with the smell of food and tobacco smoke while in one corner – marooned on a little island of gloom – sat Sean, Duff and Candy.

Once Sean lifted his glass at Duff and spoke like an undertaker's clerk. 'Happy Christmas.'

Duff's lips twitched back in a dead man's grin. 'And the same to you.'

They drank. Then Duff roused himself to speak. 'Tell me again – how much have we got left? I like to hear you say it; you have a beautiful voice, you should have played Shakespeare.'

'Three pounds and sixteen shillings.'

'Yes, yes, you got it just right that time – three pounds

and sixteen shillings – now to really make me feel Christmassy, tell me how much we owe.'

'Have another drink.' Sean changed the subject.

'Yes, I think I will, thank you.'

'Oh please, you two, let's just forget about it for today,' pleaded Candy. 'I planned for it to be such a nice party – look, there's Francois! Hey, Francois – over here!'

The dapper du Toit bustled across to their table.

'Happy Christmas, kerels, let me buy you a drink.'

'It's nice to see you.' Candy gave him a kiss. 'How are you? You're looking fine.'

Francois sobered instantly. 'It's funny you should say that, Candy. As a matter of fact I'm a bit worried.' He tapped his chest and sank down into an empty chair. 'My heart, you know, I've been waiting for it to happen, and then yesterday I was up at the mill, just standing there, you understand, when suddenly it was as though a vice was squeezing my chest. I couldn't breathe – well, not very well anyway. Naturally I hurried back to my tent and looked it up. Page eighty-three. Under "Diseases of the Heart".' He shook his head sadly. 'It's very worrying. You know I wasn't a well man before, but now this.'

'Oh, no,' wailed Candy. 'I can't stand it – not you too.'

'I'm sorry, have I said something wrong?'

'Just in keeping with the festive spirit at this table.' She pointed at Duff and Sean. 'Look at their happy faces – if you'll excuse me I'm going to check up in the kitchen.' She went.

'What's wrong, old Duff?'

Duff flashed his death's head grin across the table at Sean.

'The man wants to know what's wrong – tell him.'

'Three pounds sixteen shillings,' said Sean and Francois looked puzzled.

'I don't understand.'

'He means we're broke – flat broke.'

'*Gott*, I'm sorry to hear that, Duff, I thought you were going good. I've heard the mill running all this month, I thought you'd be rich by now.'

'The mill's been running all right and we've recovered enough gold to block a flea's backside.'

'But why, man? You are working the Leader Reef, aren't you?'

'I'm beginning to think this Leader Reef of yours is a bedtime story.'

Francois peered into his glass thoughtfully.

'How deep are you?'

'We've got one incline shaft down about fifty feet.'

'No sign of the Leader?' Duff shook his head and Francois went on.

'You know when I first spoke to you a lot of what I said was just guessing.'

Duff nodded.

'Well, I know a bit more about it now. What I am going to tell you is for you alone – I'll lose my job if it gets out, you understand?'

Duff nodded again.

'So far the Leader Reef has only been found at two places. We've got it on the Jack and Whistle and I know the Heyns brothers have struck it on the Cousin Jock Mine. Let me draw it for you.' He picked up a knife and drew in the gravy on the bottom of Sean's plate. 'This is the Main Reef running fairly straight. Here I am, here is the Cousin Jock and here you are in between us. Both of us have found the Leader and you haven't. My guess is it's there all right – you just don't know where to look.

'At the far end of the Jack and Whistle claims the Main Reef and the Leader are running side by side two feet apart but by the time they reach the boundary nearest to the Candy Deep they've opened up to seventy feet apart. Now on the boundary of the Cousin Jock they're back to fifty feet apart. To me it seems that the two reefs form the shape of a long bow, like this.' He drew it in. 'The Main Reef is the string and the Leader Reef is the wood. I'm telling you, Duff, if you cut a trench at right-angles to the Main Reef you'll find it – and when you do you can buy me a drink.'

They listened gravely and when Francois finished Duff leaned back in his chair. 'If we'd known this a month ago! Now how are we going to raise the money to cut this new trench and still keep the mill running?'

'We could sell some of our equipment,' suggested Sean.

'We need it, every scrap of it, and besides if we sold one spade the creditors would be on us like a pack of wolves, howling for their money.'

'I'd make you a loan if I had it – but with what Mr Hradsky pays me—' Francois shrugged. 'You'll need about two hundred pounds. I haven't got it.'

Candy came back to the table in time to hear Francois's last remark.

'What's this all about?'

'Can I tell her, Francois?'

'If you think it will do any good.'

Candy listened, then thought for a moment. 'Well, I've just bought ten plots of ground in Johannesburg, this new Government village down the valley, so I'm short myself. But I could let you have fifty pounds if that would help.'

'I've never borrowed money from a lady before – it'll be a new experience. Candy, I love you.'

'I wish you meant that,' said Candy, but luckily for Duff his hearing failed him completely just as Candy spoke. He went on hurriedly.

'We'll need another hundred and fifty or so – let's hear your suggestions, gentlemen.'

There was a long silence, then Duff started to smile and he was looking at Sean.

'Don't tell me, let me guess.' Sean forestalled him. 'You're going to put me out to stud?'

'Close – but not quite right. How are you feeling, laddie?'

'Thank you, I'm all right.'

'Strong?'

'Yes.'

'Brave?'

'Come on, Duff, let's have it. I don't like that look in your eye.'

Duff pulled a notebook out of his pocket and wrote in it with a stump of pencil. Then he tore out the page and handed it to Sean. 'We'll have posters like this put up in every canteen on the goldfields.'

Sean read it:

ON NEW YEAR'S DAY MR SEAN COURTNEY HEAVY-WEIGHT CHAMPION OF THE TRANSVAAL REPUBLIC WILL STAND TO MEET ALL COMERS IN FRONT OF CANDY'S HOTEL FOR
A PURSE OF FIFTY POUNDS ASIDE.
Spectators' Fee, 2s. All Welcome.

Candy was reading it over his shoulder. She squeaked.

'That's wonderful. I'll have to hire extra waiters to serve drinks and I'll run a buffet luncheon. I suppose I could charge two shillings a head?'

'I'll fix the posters,' Francois was not to be outdone, 'and I'll send a couple of my chaps down to put up a ring.'

'We'll close the mill down until New Year – Sean will have to get a lot of rest. We'll put him on light training only. No drinking, of course, and plenty of sleep,' said Duff.

'It's all arranged then, is it?' asked Sean. 'All I've got to do is go in there and get beaten to a pulp?'

'We're doing this for you, laddie, so that you can be rich and famous.'

'Thank you, thank you very much.'

'You like to fight, don't you?'

'When I'm in the mood.'

'Don't worry, I'll think up some dirty names to call you – get you worked up in no time.'

– 11 –

'How are you feeling?' Duff asked for the sixth time that morning.

'No change since five minutes ago,' Sean reassured him.

Duff pulled out his watch, stared at it, held it to his ear and looked surprised that it was still ticking.

'We've got the challengers lined up on the veranda. I've told Candy to serve them free drinks – as much as they want. Every minute we can wait here gives them a little longer to take on a load of alcohol. Francois is collecting the gate money in my valise; as you win each bout the stakes will go into it as well. I've got Mbejane stationed at the mouth of the alley beside the Hotel. If there's a riot one of us will throw the bag to him and he'll head for the long grass.'

Sean was stretched out on Candy's bed with his hands behind his head. He laughed. 'I can find no fault with your planning. Now for pity's sake calm down, man. You're making me nervous.'

The door burst open and Duff leapt out of his chair at the crash. It was Francois, he stood in the doorway holding his chest.

'My heart,' he panted. 'This is doing my heart no good.'

'What's happening outside?' Duff demanded.

'We've collected over fifty pounds gate money already.

There's a mob up on the roof that haven't paid, but every time I go near them they throw bottles at me.'

Francois cocked his head on one side. 'Listen to them.' The noise of the crowd was barely softened by the flimsy walls of the Hotel. 'They won't wait much longer – you'd better come out before they start looking for you.'

Sean stood up. 'I'm ready.'

Francois hesitated.

'Duff, you remember Fernandes, that Portuguese from Kimberley?'

'Oh no!' Duff anticipated him. 'Don't tell me he's here.'

Francois nodded. 'I didn't want to alarm you but some of the local boys clubbed in and telegraphed south for him. He arrived on the express coach half an hour ago. I had hoped he wasn't going to make it in time, but—' He shrugged.

Duff looked at Sean sadly.

'Bad luck, laddie.'

Francois tried to soften the blow. 'I told him it was first come first served. He's sixth in the line so Sean will be able to make a couple of hundred quid anyway – then we can always say he's had enough and close the contest.'

Sean was listening with interest. 'This Fernandes is dangerous?'

'They were thinking of him when they invented that word,' Duff told him.

'Let's go and have a look at him.'

Sean led the way out of Candy's room and down the passage.

'Did you get hold of a scale to weigh them with?' Duff asked Francois as they hurried after Sean.

'No, there's not one on the fields that goes over a hundred and fifty pounds – but I have Gideon Barnard outside.'

'How does that help us?'

'He's a cattle dealer – all his life he's been judging animals on the hoof. He'll give us the weights to within a few pounds.'

Duff chuckled. 'That'll have to do then. Besides I doubt we'll be claiming any world titles.'

Then they were out on the veranda blinking in the brightness of the sun and the thunder of the crowd.

'Which is the Portuguese?' whispered Sean – he needn't have asked. The man stood out like a gorilla in a cage of monkeys. A shaggy coating of hair began on his shoulders and continued down his back and chest, completely hiding his nipples and exaggerating the bulge of his enormous belly.

The crowd opened a path for Sean and Duff and they walked along it to the ring. Hands slapped Sean's back but the well-wishes were drowned in the churning sea of sound. Jock Heyns was the referee – he helped Sean through the ropes and ran his hands over his pockets.

'Just checking,' he apologized. 'We don't want any scrap iron in the ring.' Then he beckoned to a tall, brown-faced fellow who was leaning on the ropes chewing tobacco.

'This is Mr Barnard our weighing steward. Well, what do you say, Gideon?'

The steward hosed a little juice from the side of his mouth.

'Two hundred and ten.'

'Thank you.' Jock held up his hands and after a few minutes was rewarded with a comparative silence.

'Ladies and Gentlemen.'

'Who you talking to, Guvnor?'

'We are privileged to have with us today – Mr Sean Courtney.'

'Wake up, *Boet*, he's been with us for months.'

'The heavyweight champion of the Republic.'

'Why not make it the world, cock, he's got just as much right to that title.'

'Who will fight six bouts—'

'If it lasts that long.'

' – for his title and a purse of fifty pounds each.'

Sustained cheering.

'The first challenger – at two hundred and ten pounds – Mr Anthony—'

'Hold on,' Sean shouted, 'who says he's first?'

Jock Heyns had taken a deep breath to bellow the name. He let it escape with a hiss. 'It was arranged by Mr du Toit.'

'If I fight them, then I pick them – I want the Port . . .'

Duff's hand whipped over Sean's mouth and his whisper was desperate. 'Don't be a bloody fool – take the easy ones first. Use your head – we aren't doing this for fun, we're trying to finance a mine, remember?'

Sean clawed Duff's hand off his mouth. 'I want the Portuguese,' he shouted.

'He's joking,' Duff assured the crowd, then turned on Sean fiercely. 'Are you mad? That dago's a man-eater, we're fifty pounds poorer before you start.'

'I want the Portuguese,' repeated Sean with all the logic of a small boy picking the most expensive toy in the shop.

'Let him have the dago,' shouted the gentlemen on the hotel roof and Jock Heyns eyed them nervously; it was clear that they were about to add a few more bottles to the argument.

'All right,' he agreed hastily. 'The first challenger, at—' he glanced at Barnard and repeated after him, 'two hundred and fifty-five pounds – Mr Felezardo da Silva Fernandes.'

In a storm of hoots and applause the Portuguese waddled down off the veranda and into the ring. Sean had seen Candy at the dining-room window and he waved to her. She blew him a two-handed kiss and at that instant Trevor

Heyns, the timekeeper, hit the bucket which served as a gong and Sean heard Duff's warning shout. Instinctively he started to duck. There was a flash of lightning inside his skull and he found himself sitting in amongst the legs of the first line of spectators.

'The bastard King hit me,' Sean complained loudly. He shook his head and was surprised to find it still attached to his body. Someone poured a glass of beer over him and it steadied him. He felt his anger flaming up through his body.

'Six,' counted Jock Heyns.

The Portuguese was standing at the ropes. 'Come back, Leetle Sheet, I haf some more for you, not half.'

Sean's anger jumped in his throat.

'Seven, eight.'

Sean gathered his legs under him.

'I kiss your mother.' Fernandes puckered his lips and smacked them. 'I love your sister, like this.' He demonstrated graphically.

Sean charged. With the full weight of his run behind it, his fist thudded into the Portuguese's mouth, then the ropes caught Sean and catapulted him back into the crowd once more.

'You weren't even in the ring, how could you hit him?' protested one of the spectators who had broken Sean's fall. He had money on Fernandes.

'Like this!' Sean demonstrated. The man sat down heavily and had nothing further to say. Sean hurdled the ropes. Jock Heyns was halfway through his second count when Sean interrupted him by lifting the reclining Portuguese to his feet, using the tangled bush of his hair as a handle. He balanced the man on his unsteady legs and hit him again.

'One, two, three . . .' resignedly Jock Heyns began his third count, this time he managed to reach ten.

There was a howl of protest from the crowd and Jock Heyns struggled to make himself heard above it.

'Does anyone want to lodge a formal objection?'

It seemed that there were those who did.

'Very well, please step into the ring. I can't accept shouted comments.' Jock's attitude was understandable – he stood to lose a considerable sum if his decision were reversed. But Sean was patrolling the ropes as hungrily as a lion at feeding time. Jock waited a decent interval, then held up Sean's right arm.

'The winner – ten minutes for refreshments before the next bout. Will the keepers please come and fetch their property.' He gestured towards the Portuguese.

'Nice going, laddie, unorthodox perhaps but beautiful to watch.' Duff took Sean's arm and led him to a chair on the veranda.

'Three more to go, then we can call it a day.' He handed Sean a glass.

'What's this?'

'Orange juice.'

'I'd prefer something a little stronger.'

'Later, laddie.'

Duff collected the Portuguese purse and dropped it into the valise while that gentleman was being carried from the ring by his straining sponsors and laid to rest at the far end of the veranda.

Mr Anthony Blair was next. His heart was not in the encounter. He moved prettily enough on his feet but always in the direction best calculated to keep him out of reach of Sean's fists.

'The boy's a natural long-distance champ.'

'Watch it, Courtney, he'll run you to death.'

'Last lap, Blair, once more round the ring and you've done five miles.'

The chase ended when Sean, now sweating gently, herded him in a corner and there dispatched him.

The third challenger had by this time developed a pain in his chest.

'It hurts like you wouldn't believe it,' he announced through gritted teeth.

'Does it sort of gurgle in your lungs as you breathe?' asked Francois.

'Yes, that's it – gurgles like you wouldn't believe it.'

'Pleurisy,' diagnosed du Toit with more than a trace of envy in his voice.

'Is that bad?' the man asked anxiously.

'Yes it is. Page one hundred and sixteen. The treatment is—'

'Then I won't be able to fight. Hell, that's bad luck,' the invalid complained cheerfully.

'It's exceptionally bad luck,' agreed Duff. 'It means you'll have to forfeit your purse money.'

'You wouldn't take advantage of a sick man?'

'Try me,' Duff suggested pleasantly.

The fourth contestant was a German. Big, blond and happy-faced. He stumbled three or four times on his way to the ring, tripped over the ropes and crawled to his corner on hands and knees; once there he was able to regain his feet with a little help from the ring post. Jock went close to him to smell his breath and before he could dodge, the German caught him in a bear hug and led him into the opening steps of a waltz. The crowd loved it and there were no objections when at the end of the dance Jock declared Sean the winner on a technical knockout. More correctly the decision should have gone to Candy who had provided the free drinks.

'We can close down the circus now if you want to, laddie,' Duff told Sean. 'You've made enough to keep the Candy Deep afloat for another couple of months.'

'I haven't had a single good fight out of the lot of them. But I like the looks of this last one. The others were for business; this one I'll have just for the hell of it.'

'You've been magnificent – now you deserve a little fun,' agreed Duff.

'Mr Timothy Curtis. Heavyweight champion of Georgia, U.S.A.' Jock introduced him.

Gideon Barnard put his weight at two hundred and ten pounds, the same as Sean's. Sean shook his hand and from the touch of it knew he was not going to be disappointed.

'Glad to know you.' The American's voice was as soft as his grip was hard.

'Your servant, sir,' said Sean and hit the air where the man's head had been an instant before. He grunted as a fist slogged into his chest under his raised right arm and backed away warily. A soft sigh blew through the crowd and they settled down contentedly. This was what they had come to see.

The red wine was served early; it flew in tiny drops every time a punch was thrown or received. The fight flowed smoothly around the square of trampled grass. The sound of bone on flesh was followed immediately by the growl of the crowd and the seconds between were filled with the hoarse breathing of the two men and the slither, slither of their feet.

'Yaaaa!' Through the tense half silence ripped a roar like that of a mortally wounded foghorn. Sean and the American jumped apart startled, and turned with everyone else to face Candy's Hotel. Fernandes was with them again; his mountain-wide hairiness seemed to fill the whole veranda. He picked up one of Candy's best tables and holding it across his chest tore off two of its legs as though they were the wings of a roasted chicken.

'Francois, the bag!' shouted Sean. Francois snatched it up and threw it high over the heads of the crowd. Sean held his breath as he followed its slow trajectory, then he blew out again with relief as he saw Mbejane field the pass and vanish around the corner of the Hotel.

'Yaaaa!' Fernandes gave tongue again. With a table leg in each hand he charged the crowd that stood between him and Sean; it scattered before him.

'Do you mind if we finish this some other time?' Sean asked the American.

'Of course not. Any time at all. I was just about to leave myself.'

Duff reached through the ropes and caught Sean's arm.

'There's someone looking for you – or had you noticed?'

'It might just be his way of showing friendliness.'

'I wouldn't bet on it – are you coming?'

Fernandes rumbled to a halt, braced himself and threw. The table leg whirred like a rising pheasant an inch over Sean's head, ruffling his hair with the wind of its passage.

'Lead on, Duff.' Sean was uncomfortably conscious of the fact that Fernandes was again in motion towards him, still armed with a long oak, and that three very thin ropes were all that stood between them. The speed that Sean and Duff turned on them made Mr Blair's earlier exhibition seem like that of a man with both legs in plaster. Fernandes, carrying top weight as he was, never looked like catching them.

Francois came up to the Candy Deep just after midday with the news that the Portuguese, after beating three of his sponsors into insensibility, had left on the noon coach back to Kimberley.

Duff uncocked his rifle. 'Thanks, Franz, we were waiting lunch for him. I thought he might call on us.'

'Have you counted the takings?'

'Yes, your commission is in that paper bag on the table.'

'Thanks, man, let's go down and celebrate.'

'You go and have one for us.'

'Hey, Duff, you promised—' Sean started.

'I said later – in three or four weeks' time. Now we've got a little work to do, like digging a trench fifty feet deep and three hundred yards long.'

'We could start first thing tomorrow.'

'You want to be rich, don't you?' asked Duff.

'Sure, but—'

'You want nice things, like English suits, French champagne and—'

'Yes, but—'

'Well, stop arguing, get off your fat arse and come with me.'

– 12 –

The Chinese use firecrackers to keep the demons away. Duff and Sean applied the same principle. They kept the mill running; as long as its clunking carried across the valley to the ears of their creditors all was well. Everyone accepted the fact that they were working a payable reef and left them alone, but the money they fed into the front of the mill had halved its value by the time it came out of the other side in those pathetic little yellow pellets.

In the meantime they cut their trench, tearing into the earth in a race against Settlement Day. They fired dynamite and as the last stones dropped back out of the sky they were in again, coughing with the fumes, to clear the loosened rock and start drilling the next set of holes. It was summer, the days were long, and while it was light they worked. Some evenings they lit the last fuses by lantern light.

Sand fell through the hour-glass faster than they had bargained for, the money dribbled away and on the fifteenth of February Duff shaved himself, changed his shirt and went to see Candy about another loan. Sean watched him walk away down the slope. They had sold the horses a week before, and he said a small prayer – the first for many years.

Duff came back in the late morning. He stood on the edge of the trench and watched Sean tamping in the charges for the next cut. Sean's back was shiny with sweat; each individual muscle standing out in relief, swelling and subsiding as he moved.

'That's the stuff, laddie, keep at it.'

Sean looked up with dust-reddened eyes. 'How much?' he asked.

'Another fifty, and this is the last – or so she threatens.'

Sean's eyes fastened on the package Duff held under his arm.

'What's that?'

He could see the stains seeping through the brown paper and the saliva flooded out from under his tongue.

'Prime beef chops – no mealie meal porridge for lunch today.' Duff grinned at him.

'Meat.' Sean caressed the word. 'Underdone – bleeding a little as you bite it, a trace of garlic, just enough salt.'

'And you beside me, singing in the wilderness,' agreed Duff. 'Cut out the poetry, light those fuses and let's go and eat.'

An hour later they walked side by side along the bottom of their trench, Mbejane and his Zulus crowding behind them. Sean belched. 'Ah, pleasant memory, I'll never be able to look another plate of mealie meal in the face again.'

They reached the end, where the freshly broken earth and rock lay piled. Sean felt the thrill start in his hands, tingle up his arms and squeeze his lungs. Then Duff's fingers were biting into his shoulder; he could feel them trembling.

It looked like a snake, a fat grey python crawling down one wall of the trench, disappearing under the heap of new rubble and out the other side.

Duff moved first, he knelt and picked up a piece of the reef, a big grey mottled lump of it and he kissed it.

'It must be it, hey, Duff? It must be the Leader?'

'It's the end of the rainbow.'

'No more mealie meal,' Sean said softly and Duff laughed. Then Sean laughed. Wildly, crazily, together they howled their triumph.

– 13 –

'L et me hold it again,' said Sean.

Duff passed it across to him.

'Hell, it's heavy.'

'There's nothing heavier,' agreed Duff.

'Must be all of fifty pounds.'

Sean held the bar in two hands, it was the size of a cigar box. 'More!'

'We've retrieved all our losses in two days' working.'

'And some to spare, I'd say.'

Sean placed the gold bar on the table between them. It shone with little yellow smiles in the lantern light and Duff leaned forward and stroked it, its surface felt knobbly from the rough casting.

'I can't keep my hands off it,' he confessed sheepishly.

'I can't either!' Sean reached out to touch it. 'We'll be able to pay Candy out for the claims in another week or two.'

Duff started. 'What did you say?'

'I said we'd be able to pay Candy out.'

'I thought I wasn't hearing things.' Duff patted his arm indulgently. 'Listen to me, laddie, I'll try and put it simply. How long have we got the option on these claims for?'

'Three years.'

'Correct – now the next question. How many people on these fields have any money?'

Sean looked mystified. 'Well, we have now and – and . . .'

'No one else, that is until Hradsky gets back,' Duff finished for him.

'What about the Heyns brothers? They've cut open the Leader Reef.'

'Certainly, but it won't do them any good, not until their machinery arrives from England.'

'Go on!' Sean wasn't quite sure where Duff was leading.

'Instead of paying Candy out now we are going to use this' – he patted the gold bar – 'and all its little brothers to buy up every likely claim we can lay our hands on. For a start there are Doc Sutherland's claims between us and the Jack and Whistle. Then we are going to order a couple of big ten-stamp mills and when those are spilling out gold we'll use it to buy land, finance brick works, engineering shops, transport companies and the rest. I've told you before there are more ways of making gold than digging for it.'

Sean was staring at him silently.

'Have you got a head for heights?' asked Duff.

Sean nodded.

'You're going to need it, because we are going up where the eagles fly – you are about to be a party to the biggest financial killing this country has ever seen.'

Sean lit one of Candy's cigars; his hand was a little unsteady.

'Don't you think it would be best to – well – not try and go too quickly. Hell, Duff, we've only been working the Leader for two days—'

'And we've made a thousand pounds,' Duff interrupted him. 'Listen to me, Sean, all my life I've been waiting for an opportunity like this. We're the first in on this field, it's

249

as wide open as the legs of a whore. We're going to go in and take it.'

The next morning Duff had the good fortune to find Doc Sutherland early enough to talk business with him, before he began the day's drinking. Another hour would have been too late. As it was Doc knocked over his glass and fell out of his chair before he finally signed away twenty-five claims to Sean and Duff. The ink was hardly dry on the agreement before Duff was riding down to Ferrieras Camp to look for Ted Reynecke who held the claims on the other side of the Cousin Jock. Up on the Candy Deep Sean nursed the mill and bit his nails. Within seven days Duff had bought over one hundred claims and committed them to forty thousand pounds in debts.

'Duff, you're going mad.' Sean pleaded with him. 'We'll lose everything again.'

'How much have we pulled out of the Candy Deep so far?'

'Four thousand.'

'Ten per cent of what we owe in ten days – and with a miserable little four-stamp mill at that. Hold on to your hat, laddie, tomorrow I'm going to sign up for the forty claims on the other side of the Jack and Whistle. I would have had them today but that damned Greek is holding out for a thousand pounds apiece. I'll have to give it to him, I suppose.'

Sean clutched his temples.

'Duff – please, man, we're in over our necks already.'

'Stand back, laddie, and watch the wizard work.'

'I'm going to bed – I suppose I'll have to take your shift again in the morning if you're determined to spend tomorrow ruining us.'

'That's not necessary, I've hired that Yankee – Curtis. You know, your sparring partner. It turns out he's a miner and he's willing to work for thirty a month. So you can come to town with me and watch me make you rich. I'm meeting the Greek at Candy's Hotel at nine o'clock.'

At nine o'clock Duff was talking and Sean sat silently on the edge of his chair; at ten the Greek had still not put in an appearance. Duff was moody and Sean was garrulous with relief. At eleven Sean wanted to go back to the mine.

'It's an omen, Duff, God looked down and he saw us sitting here all ready to make a terrible mistake. "No," he said, "I can't let them do it – I'll have the Greek break a leg – I can't let it happen to such nice boys."'

'Why don't you go and join a Trappist monastery?' Duff checked his watch. 'Come on, let's go!'

'Yes, sir!' Sean stood up with alacrity. 'We'll get back in plenty of time to clean the tables before lunch.'

'We're not going home, we're going to look for the Greek.'

'Now listen, Duff.'

'I'll listen later – come on.'

They rode across to the Bright Angels, left the horses outside and walked in together. It was dark in the canteen after the sunshine outside, but even in the gloom a group at one of the tables caught their attention immediately. The Greek sat with his back to them; the line of his parting seemed to be drawn with white chalk and a ruler through the oily black waves of his hair. Sean's eyes switched from him to the two men that sat across the table from him. Jews, there was no mistaking it, but there any similarity ended. The younger one was thin with smooth olive skin drawn tight across the bold bones of his cheeks; his lips were very red and his eyes, fringed with girl's lashes, were toffee-brown and melting. In the chair beside him was a man with a body that had been shaped in wax then held near a hot flame. Shoulders rounded to the verge of deformity drooped down over a pear-shaped body; with difficulty they supported the great Taj Mahal domed head. His hair was styled in the fashion of Friar Tuck, thick only around the ears. But the eyes – the flickering yellow eyes – there was nothing comical about them.

'Hradsky,' hissed Duff, then his expression changed. He smiled as he walked across to the table.

'Hello, Nikky, I thought we had an appointment.'

The Greek twisted quickly in his chair.

'Mr Charleywood, I'm sorry, I was held up.'

'So I see, the woods are full of highwaymen.'

Sean saw the flush start to come up out of Hradsky's collar then sink back again.

'Have you sold?' Duff asked.

The Greek nodded nervously.

'I'm sorry, Mr Charleywood, but Mr Hradsky paid my price and no haggling – cash money, too!'

Duff let his eyes wander across the table.

'Hello, Norman. How's your daughter?'

This time the flush escaped from Hradsky's shirt and flooded over his face. He opened his mouth, his tongue clucked twice, then he closed it again.

Duff smiled, he looked at the younger Jew. 'Say it for him, Max.'

The toffee eyes dropped to the table top. 'Mr Hradsky's daughter is very well.'

'I believe she married soon after my involuntary departure from Kimberley.'

'That is correct.'

'Wise move, Norman, much wiser than having your bully boys run me out of town. That wasn't very nice of you.'

252

No one spoke.

'We must get together some time and have a chat about old times. Until then, fa – fa – fare ye we – we – well.'

On the way back to the mine Sean asked, 'He's got a daughter? If she looks like him you were lucky to escape.'

'She didn't – she was like a bunch of ripe grapes with the bloom on them.'

'I can hardly credit it.'

'Neither could I. The only conclusion I could reach was that Max did that job for him as well.'

'What's the story about Max?'

'He's the Court Jester. Rumour has it that after Hradsky has finished hanging it out, Max shakes it for him.'

Sean laughed and Duff went on, 'But don't underestimate Hradsky. His stutter is his only weakness and with Max to talk for him he's overcome that. Beneath that monumental skull is a brain as quick and merciless as a guillotine. Now that he's arrived on this goldfield there's going to be some action; we'll have to gallop to keep up with him.'

Sean thought for a few seconds, then, 'Talking about action, Duff, now that we've lost the Greek's claims and won't have to use all our ready money satisfying him, let's give some thought to ordering new machinery to work the claims we have got.'

Duff grinned at him.

'I sent a telegram to London last week. There'll be a pair of brand new ten-stamp mills on the water to us before the end of the month.'

'Good God, why didn't you tell me?'

'You were worried enough as it was – I didn't want to break your heart.'

Sean opened his mouth to blast Duff out of the saddle. Duff winked at him before he could talk and Sean's lips trembled. He felt the laughter in his throat, he tried to stop it but it swamped him.

'How much is it going to cost us?' he howled through his mirth.

'If you ask that question once more, I'll strangle you,' Duff laughed back at him. 'Rest content in the knowledge that if we're going to have enough to honour the bills of lading when those mills arrive at Port Natal, we'll have to run a mountain of Leader Reef through our little rig during the next few weeks.'

'What about the payments on the new claims?'

'That's my department – I'll worry about that.'

And so their partnership crystallized; their relationship was established over the weeks that followed. Duff with his magic tongue and his charming, lopsided grin was the one who negotiated, who poured the oil on the storm waters churned up by impatient creditors. He was the storehouse of mining knowledge which Sean tapped daily, he was the conceiver of schemes, some wild, others brilliant. But his fleeting nervous energy was not designed to bring them to fruition. He lost interest quickly and it was Sean who finally rejected the least likely Charleywood brain children and adopted the others that were more deserving; once he had made himself stepfather to them he reared them as though they were his own. Duff was the theorist, Sean the practician. Sean could see why Duff had never found success before, but at the same time he recognized that without him he would be helpless. He watched with profound admiration the way that Duff used the barely sufficient flow of gold from the Candy Deep to keep the mill running, pay the tradesmen, meet the claim monies as they fell due and still save enough for the new machinery. He was a man juggling with live coals: hold one too long and it burns, let one fall and all fall. And Duff, deep-down-uncertain Duff, had a wall to put his back against. His speech never showed it but his eyes did when he looked at Sean. Sometimes he felt small next to Sean's big body and bigger determination, but it was a good feeling: like being on a friendly mountain.

They put up new buildings around the mill: storerooms, a smelting house and cabins for Sean and Curtis. Duff was sleeping at the Hotel again. The location for the Natives sprawled haphazard down the back slope of the ridge, retreating a little each week as the white mountain of the mine dump grew and pushed it back. The whole valley was changing. Hradsky's new mills arrived and stood up along the ridge, tall and proud until their own dumps dwarfed them. Johannesburg, at first a mere pattern of surveyors' pegs, sucked the scattered encampments onto her grassy chequerboard and arranged them in a semblance of order along her streets.

The Diggers' Committee, its members tired of having to scrape their boots every time they went indoors, decreed public latrines be erected. 'Then, flushed with their own audacity, they built a bridge across the Natal Spruit, purchased a water cart to lay the dust on the streets of Johannesburg and passed a law prohibiting burials within half a mile of the city centre. Sean and Duff as members of the Committee felt it their duty to demonstrate their faith in the goldfield, so they bought twenty-five plots of ground in Johannesburg, five pounds each to be paid within six months. Candy recruited all her customers and in one weekend of frantic effort they razed her Hotel to the ground, packed every plank and sheet of iron onto their wagons, carried it a mile down the valley and re-erected it on her own land in the centre of the township. During the party she gave them on that Sunday night they nearly succeeded in dismantling it for the second time. Each day the roads from Natal and the Cape fed more wagons, more men into the Witwatersrand goldfield. Duff's suggestion that the Diggers' Committee levy a guinea a head from all newcomers to help finance the public works was reluctantly rejected, the general feeling being that if it led to civil rebellion there were more newcomers than Committee members and no one fancied being on the losing side.

One morning, when he came out to the mine, Duff brought a telegram with him. He handed it to Sean without comment. Sean read it. The machinery had arrived.

'Good God, it's three weeks early.'

'They must have had a downhill sea, or a following wind or whatever it is that makes ships go faster,' muttered Duff.

'Have we got enough to pay the bill?' asked Sean.

'No.'

'What are we going to do?'

'I'll go and see the little man at the bank.'

'He'll throw you out in the street.'

'I'll get him to give us a loan on the claims.'

'How the hell are you going to do that – we haven't paid for them yet.'

'That's what you call financial genius. I'll simply point out to him that they're worth five times what we bought them for.' Duff grinned. 'Can you and Curtis carry on here without me for today while I go and arrange it?'

'You arrange it and I'll happily give you a month's holiday.'

When Duff came back that afternoon he carried a paper with him. It had a red wax seal in the bottom corner, across the top it said 'Letter of Credit' and in the middle, standing out boldly from the mass of small print, was a figure that ended in an impressive string of noughts.

'You're a bloody marvel,' said Sean.

'Yes, I am rather, aren't I?' agreed Duff.

The Heyns brothers' machinery was on the same ship. Jock and Duff rode down to Port Natal together, hired a hundred wagons and brought it all back in one load.

'I'll tell you what I'll do with you, Jock, I'll wager you that we get our mills producing before you do. Loser pays for the transport on the whole shipment,' Duff challenged him when they reached Johannesburg where, in Candy's new bar-room, they were washing the dust out of their throats.

'You're on!'

'I'll go further, I'll put up a side bet of five hundred.'

Sean prodded Duff in the ribs.

'Gently, Duff – we can't afford it.' But Jock had already snapped up the bet.

'What do you mean we can't afford it?' whispered Duff. 'We've got nearly fifteen hundred pounds left on the letter of credit.'

Sean shook his head. 'No, we haven't.'

Duff pulled the paper from his inside pocket and tapped Sean's nose with it. 'There – read for yourself.'

Sean took it out of Duff's hand.

'Thanks, old chap, I'll go and pay the man now.'

'What man?'

'The man with the wagons.'

'What wagons?'

'The wagons that you and Jock hired in Port Natal. I've bought them.'

'The hell you say!'

'It was your idea to start a transport business. Just as soon as they've offloaded they'll be on their way again to pick up a shipment of coal from Dundee.'

Duff grinned at him. 'Don't you ever forget an idea? All right, laddie, off you go – we'll just have to win the bet, that's all.'

One of the mills they placed on the Candy Deep, the other on the new claims beyond the Cousin Jock Mine. They hired two gangs from among the unemployed in Johannesburg. Curtis supervised one of them and Sean the other, while Duff darted back and forth keeping an eye on both. Each time he passed the Cousin Jock he spent a few minutes checking Trevor and Jock's progress.

'They've got the edge on us, Sean; their boilers are up and holding pressure already,' he reported fretfully, but the next day he was smiling again.

'They didn't mix enough cement in the platform – it started to crumble as soon as they put the crusher on it. They'll have to cast it again. That set them back three or four days.'

The betting down in the canteens fluctuated sharply with each change of fortune. Francois came up to the Candy Deep one Saturday afternoon. He watched them work, made a suggestion or two, then remarked, 'They're giving three-to-one against you at the Bright Angels; they reckon the Heynses will be finished by next weekend.'

'Go down and put another five hundred pounds on for me,' Duff told him, and Sean shook his head despairingly.

'Don't worry, laddie, we can't lose – that amateur mining engineer, Jock Heyns, has assembled his crusher jaws all arse-about-face. I only noticed it this morning – he's in for a surprise when he tries to start up. He'll have to strip the whole damn rig.'

Duff was right – they brought both their mills into production a comfortable fifteen hours before the Heyns brothers. Jock rode over to see them with his jaw on his chest. 'Congratulations.'

'Thanks, Jock, did you bring your cheque book?'

'That's what I came to talk about. Can you give me a little time?'

'Your credit's good,' Sean assured him, 'come and have a drink and let me sell you some coal.'

'Ah, yes, I heard your wagons arrived back this morning. What price are you charging?'

'Fifteen pounds a hundredweight.'

'Good God. You bloody bandit, I bet it cost you less than five shillings a hundredweight.'

'A man's entitled to a reasonable profit,' protested Sean.

It had been a long hard pull up to the top of the hill but Sean and Duff had arrived at last and from there it was downhill all the way. The money poured in.

The geological freak that had bowed the Leader Reef away from the Main across the Candy Deep claims had, at the same time, enriched it – injected it full of the metal. Francois was there one evening when they put the ball of amalgam into the retort. His eyes bulged as the mercury boiled away; he stared at the gold the way a man watches a naked woman.

'*Gott!* I'm going to have to call you two thunders "Mister" from now on.'

'Have you ever seen richer reef, Francois?' Duff gloated.

Francois shook his head slowly. 'You know my theory about the reef being the bed of an old lake – well this bears it out. The kink in your reef must have been a deep trench along the bottom of the lake. It would have acted as a natural gold trap. Hell, man, what luck. With your eyes closed you have picked the plum out of the pudding. The Jack and Whistle is half as rich as this.'

Their overdraft at the bank dropped like a barometer in a hurricane; the tradesmen started greeting them with a smile; they gave Doc Sutherland a cheque which would have kept even him in whisky for a hundred years. Candy kissed them both when they paid her out in full, plus interest at seven per cent. Then she built herself a new Hotel, double storied, with a crystal chandelier in the dining-room and a magnificent bedroom suite on the second floor done out in maroon and gold. Duff and Sean rented it immediately but with the express understanding that if ever the Queen visited Johannesburg they would allow her to use it. In anticipation Candy called it the Victoria Rooms.

Francois, with a little persuasion, agreed to take over the running of the Candy Deep. He moved his possessions, one chest of clothes and four chests of patent medicines, across from the Jack and Whistle. Timothy Curtis was the manager of the mill on the new claims; they named it the Little Sister Mine. Although not nearly as rich as the Candy Deep it was producing a sweet fortune each month, for Curtis worked as well as he fought.

By the end of August Sean and Duff had no more creditors: the claims were theirs, the mills were theirs and they had money to invest.

'We need an office of our own here in town. We can't run this show from our bedrooms,' complained Sean.

'You're right,' agreed Duff, 'we'll build on that corner plot nearest the market square.' The plan was for a modest little four-room building, but it finally expanded to two stories, stinkwood floors, oak panelling and twenty rooms. What they couldn't use they rented.

'The price of land has trebled in three months,' said Sean, 'and it's still moving.'

'You're right – now's the time to buy,' Duff agreed. 'You're starting to think along the right lines.'

'It was your idea.'

'Was it?' Duff looked surprised.

'Don't you remember your "up where the eagles fly" speech?'

'Don't you forget anything?' asked Duff.

They bought land: one thousand acres at Orange Grove

and another thousand around Hospital Hill. Their transport wagons, now almost four hundred strong, plied in daily from Port Natal and Lourenço Marques. Their brickfields worked twenty-four hours a day, seven days a week, to try to meet the demand for building materials.

It took Sean almost a week to dissuade Duff from building an Opera House but he succeeded and instead they joined most of the other members of the Diggers' Committee in financing a different type of pleasure palace. At Duff's suggestion they called it the Opera House. They recruited the performers not from the great companies of Europe but from the dock areas of Capetown and Port Natal and chose as the conductor a Frenchwoman of vast experience named Blue Bessie after the colour of her hair. The Opera House provided entertainment on two levels. For the members of the Committee and the other emergent rich there was a discreet side entrance, a lavishly furnished lounge where one could buy the finest champagne and discuss the prices on the Kimberley Stock Exchange, and beyond the lounge were a series of tastefully decorated retiring-rooms. For the workers there was a bare corridor to queue in, no choice for your money and a five-minute time limit. In one month the Opera House produced more gold than the Jack and Whistle mine.

By December there were millionaires in Johannesburg: Hradsky, the Heyns brothers, Karl Lochtkamper, Duff Charleywood, Sean Courtney and a dozen others. They owned the mines, the land, the buildings and the city: the aristocracy of the Witwatersrand, knighted with money and crowned with gold.

A week before Christmas, Hradsky, their unacknowledged but undoubted king, called them all to a meeting in one of the private lounges of Candy's Hotel.

'Who the hell does he think he is,' complained Jock Heyns, 'ordering us round like a bunch of kaffirs.'

'*Verdammt Juden!*' agreed Lochtkamper.

But they went, every last man of them, for whatever Hradsky did had the smell of money about it and they could no more resist it than a dog can resist the smell of a bitch in season.

Duff and Sean were the last to arrive and the room was already hazed with cigar smoke and tense with expectation. Hradsky sagged in one of the polished leather armchairs with Max sitting quietly beside him; his eyes flickered when Duff walked in but his expression never changed. When Duff and Sean had found chairs Max stood up. 'Gentlemen, Mr Hradsky has invited you here to consider a proposition.'

They leaned forward slightly in their chairs and there was a glitter in their eyes like hounds close upon the fox.

'From time to time it is necessary for men in your position to find capital to finance further ventures and to consolidate past gains; on the other hand those of us who have money lying idle will be seeking avenues for investment.' Max cleared his throat and looked at them with his sad brown eyes.

'Up to the present there has been no meeting-place for these mutual needs such as exists in the other centres of the financial world. Our nearest approach to it is the Stock Exchange at Kimberley which, I'm sure you will agree, is too far removed to be of practical use to us here at Johannesburg. Mr Hradsky has invited you here to consider the possibility of forming our own Exchange and, if you accept the idea, to elect a chairman and governing body.'

Max sat down and in the silence that followed they took up the idea, each one fitting it into his scheme of thinking, testing it with the question 'How will I benefit?'.

'*Ja*, it's dom fine idea.' Lochtkamper spoke first.

'Yes, it's what we need.'

'Count me in.'

While they schemed and bargained, setting the fees, the

place and the rules, Sean watched their faces. The faces of bitter men, happy men, quiet ones and big bull-roarers but all with one common feature – that greedy glitter in the eyes. It was midnight before they finished.

Max stood up again.

'Gentlemen, Mr Hradsky would like you to join him in a glass of champagne to celebrate the formation of our new enterprise.'

'This I can't believe; the last time he paid for drinks was back in 'sixty,' declared Duff. 'Quickly somebody – find a waiter before he changes his mind.'

Hradsky hooded his eyes to hide the hatred in them.

– 16 –

With its own Stock Exchange and bordel Johannesburg became a city. Even Kruger recognized it; he deposed the Diggers' Committee and sent in his own police force, sold monopolies for essential mining supplies to members of his family and Government, and set about revising his tax laws with special attention to mining profits. Despite Kruger's efforts to behead the gold-laying goose, the city grew, overflowed the original Government plots and spread brawling and blustering out into the surrounding veld.

Sean and Duff grew with it. Their way of life changed swiftly; their visits to the mines fell to a weekly inspection and they left it to their hired men. A steady river of gold poured down from the ridge to their offices on Eloff Street, for the men they hired were the best that money could find.

Their horizons closed in to encompass only the two panelled offices, the Victoria Rooms and the Exchange. Yet within that world Sean found a thrill that he had never dreamed existed. He had been oblivious to it during the first feverish months; he had been so absorbed in laying the foundations that he could spare no energy for enjoying or even noticing it.

Then one day he felt the first voluptuous tickle of it. He had sent to the bank for a land title document he needed, expecting it to be delivered by a junior clerk – but instead the sub-manager and a senior clerk filed respectfully into his office. It was an exquisite physical shock and it gave him a new awareness. He noticed the way men looked at him as he passed them on the street. He realized suddenly that over fifteen hundred human beings depended on him for their livelihood.

There was satisfaction in the way a path cleared for him and Duff as they crossed the floor of the Exchange each morning to take their places in the reserved leather armchairs of the members' lounge. When Duff and he leaned together and talked quietly before the trading began, even the other big fish watched them. Hradsky with his fierce eyes hooded by sleepy lids, Jock and Trevor Heyns, Karl Lochtkamper – any of them would have given a day's production from their mines to overhear those conversations.

'Buy!' said Sean.

'Buy! Buy! Buy!' clamoured the pack and the prices jumped as they hit them, then slumped back as they sucked their money away and put it to work elsewhere.

Then one March morning in 1886 the thrill became so acute it was almost an orgasm. Max left the chair at Norman Hradsky's side and crossed the lounge towards them. He stopped in front of them, lifted his sad eyes off the patterned carpet and almost apologetically proffered a loose sheaf of papers.

'Good morning, Mr Courtney. Good morning, Mr Charleywood. Mr Hradsky has asked me to bring this new share

264

issue to your attention. Perhaps you would be interested in these reports, which are, of course, confidential, but he feels they are worthy of your support.'

You have power when you can force a man who hates you to ask for your favours. After the first advance by Hradsky they worked together often. Hradsky never acknowledged their existence by word or look. Each morning Duff called a cheerful greeting across the full width of the lounge, 'Hello, chatterbox,' or 'Sing for us, Norman.'

Hradsky's eyes would flicker and he would sag a little lower into his chair, but before the bell started the day's trading Max would stand up and come across to them, leaving his master staring into the empty fireplace. A few soft sentences exchanged and Max would walk back to Hradsky's side.

Their combined fortunes were irresistible: in one wild morning's trading alone they added another fifty thousand to their store of pounds.

An untaught boy handles his first rifle like a toy. Sean was twenty-two. The power he held was a more deadly weapon than any rifle, and much sweeter, more satisfying to use. It was a game at first with the Witwatersrand as a chessboard, men and gold for pieces. A word or a signature on a slip of paper would set the gold jingling and the men scampering. The consequences were remote and all that mattered was the score, the score chalked up in black figures on a bank statement. Then in that same March he was made to realize that a man wiped off the board could not be laid back in the box with as much compassion as a carved wooden knight.

Karl Lochtkamper, the German with a big laugh and a happy face, laid himself open. He needed money to develop a new property on the east end of the Rand; he borrowed and signed short-term notes on his loans, certain that he

265

could extend them if necessary. He borrowed secretly from men he thought he could trust. He was vulnerable and the sharks smelt him out.

'Where is Lochtkamper getting his money?' asked Max.

'Do you know?' asked Sean.

'No, but I can guess.'

Then the next day Max came back to them again.

'He has eight notes out. Here is the list,' he whispered sadly. 'Mr Hradsky will buy the ones that have a cross against them. Can you handle the rest?'

'Yes,' said Sean.

They closed on Karl on the last day of the quarter; they called the loans and gave him twenty-four hours to meet them. Karl went to each of the three banks in turn.

'I'm sorry, Mr Lochtkamper, we have loaned over our budget for this quarter.'

'Mr Hradsky is holding your notes – I'm sorry.'

'I'm sorry, Mr Lochtkamper, Mr Charleywood is one of our directors.'

Karl Lochtkamper rode back to the Exchange. He walked across the floor and into the lounge for the last time. He stood in the centre of the big room, his face grey, his voice bitter and broken.

'Let Jesus have this much mercy on you when your time comes. Friends! My friends! Sean, how many times haf we drunk together? And you, Duff, was it yesterday you shook my hand?'

Then he went back across the floor, out through the doors. His suite in the Great North Hotel wasn't fifty yards from the Exchange. In the members' lounge they heard the pistol shot quite clearly.

That night Duff and Sean got drunk together in the Victoria rooms.

'Why did he have to do it? Why did he have to kill himself?'

'He didn't,' answered Duff. 'He was a quitter.'

'If I'd known he was going to do that – my God, if only I'd known.'

'Damn it, man, he took a chance and lost – it's not our fault. He would have done the same to us.'

'I don't like this – it's dirty. Let's get out, Duff.'

'Someone gets knocked down in the rush and you want to cry "enough!"'

'It's different now somehow, it wasn't like this at the start.'

'Yes, and it'll be different in the morning. Come on, laddie, I know what you need.'

'Where are we going?'

'To the Opera House.'

'What will Candy say?'

'Candy doesn't have to know.'

Duff was right; it was different in the morning. There was the usual hurly-burly of work at the office and some tense action at the Exchange. He thought about Karl only once during the day and somehow it didn't seem to matter so much. They sent him a nice wreath.

He had faced the reality of the game he was playing. He had considered the alternative which was to get out with the fortune he had already made; but to do that would mean giving up the power he held. The addiction was already seated too deeply, he could not deny it. So his subconscious opened, sucked in his conscience and swallowed it deep down into its gut. He could feel it struggling there sometimes, but the longer it stayed swallowed the more feeble those struggles became. Duff comforted him: Duff's words were like a gastric juice that helped to digest that lump in the gut and he had not yet learned that what Duff said and what Duff did were not necessarily what Duff believed.

Play the game without mercy, play to win.

17

D uff stood with his back to the fireplace in Sean's office smoking a cheroot while they waited for the carriage to take them up to the Exchange. The fire behind him silhouetted his slimly tapered legs with the calves encased in polished black leather. He still wore his top coat, for the winter morning was cold. It fell open at his throat to show a diamond that sparkled and glowed in his cravat.

'. . . you get used to a woman somehow,' he was saying. 'I've known Candy four years now and yet it seems I've been with her all my life.'

'She's a fine girl,' Sean agreed absently as he dipped his pen and scribbled his signature on the document in front of him.

'I'm thirty-five now,' Duff went on. 'If I'm ever to have a son of my own . . .'

Sean laid down the pen deliberately and looked up at him; he was starting to grin.

'The man said to me once "They take you into their soft little minds" and again he said "They don't share, they possess". Is this a new tune I hear?'

Duff shifted uneasily from one foot to the other.

'Things change,' he defended himself. 'I'm thirty-five . . .'

'You're repeating yourself,' Sean accused and Duff smiled weakly.

'Well, the truth is . . .'

He never finished the sentence; hooves beat urgently in the street outside and both their faces swung in the direction of the window.

'Big hurry!' said Sean coming quickly to his feet. 'Big trouble!' He crossed to the window. 'It's Curtis, and by his face it's not good news he brings.'

There were voices outside the door raised in agitation and the quick rush of feet, then Timothy Curtis burst into the room without knocking. He wore a miner's overall and splattered gumboots. 'We've hit a mud rush on the ninth level.'

'How bad?' Duff snapped.

'Bad enough – it's flooded right back to number eight.'

'Jesus, that will take two months at least to clear,' Sean exclaimed. 'Does anyone else in town know – have you told anyone?'

'I came straight here – Cronje and five men were up at the face when it blew.'

'Get back there immediately,' ordered Sean, 'but ride quietly, we don't want the whole world to know there's trouble. Don't let a soul off the property. We must have time to sell out.'

'Yes, Mr Courtney.' Curtis hesitated. 'Cronje and five others were hit by the rush. Shall I send word to their wives?'

'Can't you understand English? I don't want a whisper of this to get out before ten o'clock. We've got to have time.'

'But, Mr Courtney—' Curtis was appalled. He stood staring at Sean and Sean felt the sick little stirring of guilt. Six men drowned in treacle-thick mud … He made an irresolute gesture with his hands.

'We can't—' He stopped and Duff cut in.

'They're dead now, and they'll be just as dead when we tell their wives at ten o'clock. Get going, Curtis.'

They sold their shares in the Little Sister within an hour of the start of trading and a week later they bought them back at half the price. Two months later the Little Sister was back on full production again.

18

They split their land at Orange Grove into plots and sold them, all but a hundred acres and on that they started building a house. Into the designing of it they poured their combined energy and imagination. With money Duff seduced the horticulturist of the Capetown Botanical Gardens and brought him up by express coach. They showed him the land.

'Make me a garden,' said Duff.

'The whole hundred acres?'

'Yes.'

'It'll cost a pretty penny.'

'That is no problem.'

The carpets came from Persia, the wood from the Knysna forests and the marble from Italy. On the gates at the entrance to the main drive they engraved the words 'At Xanadu did Kublai Khan a stately pleasure dome decree'. As the gardener had predicted, it all cost a pretty penny. Each afternoon when the Exchange closed they would drive up together and watch the builders at work. One day Candy came with them and they showed it off to her like two small boys.

'This will be the ballroom.' Sean bowed to her. 'May I have the pleasure of this dance?'

'Thank you, sir.' She curtsied, then swept away on his arm across the unsanded boards.

'This will be the staircase,' Duff told her, 'marble – black and white marble – and there on the main landing in a glass case will be Hradsky's head, beautifully mounted with an apple in his mouth.'

They climbed laughing up the rough concrete ramp.

'This is Sean's room – the bed is being made of oak,

thick oak to withstand punishment.' They trooped with linked arms down the passage.

'And this is my room – I was thinking of a solid gold bath but the builder says it's too heavy and Sean says it's too vulgar. Look at that view; from here you can see out across the whole valley. I could lie in bed in the mornings and read the prices on the Exchange floor with a telescope.'

'It's lovely,' Candy said dreamily.

'You like it?'

'Oh, yes.'

'It could be your room too.'

Candy started to blush and then her face tightened with annoyance. 'He was right – you are vulgar.'

She started for the door and Sean fumbled for his cigars to cover his embarrassment. With two quick steps Duff caught her and turned her to face him. 'You sweet idiot, that was a proposal.'

'Let me go.' Near to tears she twisted in his hands. 'I don't think you're funny.'

'Candy – I'm serious. Will you marry me?'

The cigar dropped out of Sean's mouth but he caught it before it hit the ground. Candy was standing very still, her eyes fastened on Duff's face.

'Yes or no – will you marry me?'

She nodded once slowly and then twice very fast.

Duff looked at Sean over his shoulder. 'Leave us, laddie.'

On the way back to town Candy had regained her voice. She chattered happily and Duff answered her with his lopsided grin. Sean hunched morosely in one corner of the carriage. His cigar was burning unevenly and he threw it out of the window.

'You'll let me keep the Victoria rooms, I hope, Candy.'

There was a silence.

'What do you mean?' asked Duff.

'Two's company,' Sean answered.

'Oh, no,' Candy exclaimed.

'It's your house as well.' Duff spoke sharply.

'I give it to you – a wedding present.'

'Oh, shut up,' Duff grinned, 'it's big enough for all of us.'

Candy crossed quickly to Sean's seat and put her hand on his shoulder.

'Please – we've been together a long time. We'd be lonely without you.'

Sean grunted.

'Please!'

'He'll come,' said Duff.

'Please.'

'Oh, well—' Sean frowned ungraciously.

– 19 –

They went racing at Milnerton. Candy with a hat full of ostrich feathers, Sean and Duff with pearl grey toppers and gold heads on their canes.

'You can pay for your wedding gown by putting fifty guineas on Trade Wind! She can't lose—' Duff told Candy.

'What about Mr Hradsky's new filly? I've heard she's a good bet,' Candy asked and Duff frowned.

'You want to go over to the enemy?'

'I thought you and Hradsky were almost partners.' Candy twirled her parasol. 'From the rumours I've heard you work with him all the time.'

Mbejane slowed the carriage as they ran into the crush of pedestrians and coaches outside the Turf Club gates.

'Well you've heard wrong both times. His Sun Dancer will never hold Trade Wind over the distance, she's bred too light in the legs. Frenchified with Huguenot blood; she'll fade within the mile. And as far as Hradsky being our partner, we throw him an occasional bone. Isn't that right, Sean?'

Sean was watching Mbejane's back. The Zulu, in loin clothes only and his spears laid carefully on the boards at his feet, was handling the horses with an easy familiarity. They cocked their ears back to catch his voice, deep and soft, as he talked to them.

'Isn't that right, Sean?' Duff repeated.

'Of course,' agreed Sean vaguely. 'You know – I think I'll get Mbejane a livery. He looks out of place in those skins.'

'Well, some of the other horses from the same stud were stayers. Sun Honey won the Cape Derby twice and Eclipse showed up the English stock in the Metropolitan Handicap last year,' Candy argued.

'Huh,' Duff smiled his superiority, 'well, you can take my word for it that Trade Wind will walk the main race today and he'll be back in his stable before Sun Dancer sees the finishing post.'

'Maroon and gold – the same as our racing colours,' Sean muttered thoughtfully. 'That would go very well with his black skin, perhaps a turban with an ostrich feather in it.'

'What the hell are you talking about?' complained Duff.

'Mbejane's livery.'

They left the carriage in the reserved area and went through to the members' grandstand, Candy sailing prettily between her escorts.

'Well, Duff, we've got the nicest looking woman here today.'

'Thank you.' Candy smiled up at Sean.

'Is that why you keep trying to look down the front of her dress?' challenged Duff.

'You filthy-minded beast.' Sean was shocked.

'Don't deny, it,' Candy teased, 'but I find it very flattering – you're welcome.'

They moved through the throng of butterfly-coloured dresses and stiffly-suited men. A ripple of greetings moved with them.

'Morning, Mr Courtney.' The accent was on the 'Mister'. 'How's your Trade Wind for the big race?'

'Put your pants on him.'

'Hello, Duff, congratulations on your engagement.'

'Thanks, Jock, it's time you took the plunge as well.'

They were rich, they were young, they were handsome and all the world admired them. Sean felt good, with a pretty girl on his arm and a friend walking beside him.

'There's Hradsky – let's go across and engage in a little hog-baiting,' Duff suggested.

'Why do you hate him so much?' Candy asked softly.

'Look at him and answer your own question. Have you ever seen anything more pompous, joyless and unlovable?'

'Oh, leave him alone, Duff, don't spoil the day. Let's go down to the paddock.'

'Come on!' Duff steered them across to where Hradsky and Max were standing alone by the rail of the track.

'Salome, Norman, and peace to you also, Maximilian.' Hradsky nodded and Max murmured sadly; his lashes touched his cheeks as he blinked.

'I noticed you two chatting away and thought I would come across and listen to your stimulating repartee.'

He received no answer and went on. 'I saw your new filly exercising on the practice track yesterday evening and I said to myself, Norman's got a girl friend – that's what it is – he's bought a hack for his lady. But now they tell me you are going to race her. Oh, Norman, I wish you'd consult me before you do these silly things. You're an impetuous little devil at times.'

'Mr Hradsky is confident that Sun Dancer will make a reasonable showing today,' Max murmured.

'I was about to offer you a side bet, but being a naturally

kind-hearted person, I feel it would be taking an unfair advantage.'

A small crowd had gathered round them listening with anticipation. Candy tugged gently at Duff's elbow trying to lead him away.

'I thought five hundred guineas would be acceptable to Norman.' Duff shrugged. 'But let's forget it.'

Hradsky made a fierce little sign with his hands and Max interpreted smoothly. 'Mr Hradsky suggests a thousand.'

'Rash, Norman, extremely rash.' Duff sighed. 'But I suppose I must accommodate you.'

They walked down to the refreshment pavilion. Candy was quiet awhile, then she said, 'An enemy like Mr Hradsky is a luxury that even you two gods can't afford. Why don't you leave him alone?'

'It's a hobby of Duff's,' explained Sean as they found seats at one of the tables. 'Waiter – bring us a bottle of Pol Roger.'

Before the big race they went down to the paddock. A steward opened the wicket gate for them and they passed into the ring of circling horses. A gnome in silk of maroon and gold came to meet them and touched his cap then stood awkwardly, fingering his whip.

'He looks good this morning, sir.' The little man nodded at Trade Wind. There was a dark patch of sweat on the horse's shoulder and he mouthed the snaffle, lifting his feet delicately. Once he snorted and rolled his eyes in mock terror.

'He's got an edge on him, sir, eager kind of – if you follow me.'

'I want you to win, Harry,' said Duff.

'So do I, sir, I'll do my best.'

'There's a thousand guineas for you if you do.'

'A thousand—' the jockey repeated on an outgoing breath.

Duff looked across to where Hradsky and Max were standing talking to their trainer. He caught Hradsky's eye, glanced significantly at Hradsky's honey-coloured filly and shook his head sympathetically.

'Win for me, Harry,' he said softly.

'That I will, sir!'

The groom led the big stallion across to them and Sean flicked the jockey up into the saddle.

'Good luck.'

Harry settled his cap and gathered up the reins; he winked at Sean, his hobgoblin face wrinkling in a grin.

'There's no better luck than a thousand guineas, sir, if you follow me.'

'Come on.' Duff caught Candy's arm. 'Let's get a place at the rail.'

They hustled her out of the paddock and across the members' enclosure. The rail was crowded but a place opened for them respectfully and no one jostled them.

'I can't understand you two,' Candy laughed breathlessly. 'You make an extravagant bet, then you fix it so you can get nothing even if you win.'

'Money's not the problem,' Duff assured her.

'He won that much from me at Klabejas last night,' Sean commented. 'If Trade Wind beats the filly his prize will be the look on Hradsky's face – the loss of a thousand guineas will hurt him like a kick between the legs.'

The horses came parading past, stepping high next to the grooms who held them, then they turned free and cantered back, dancing sideways, throwing their heads, shining in the sunlight like the bright silk upon their backs. They moved away round the curve of the track.

The crowd rustled with excitement, a bookmaker's voice carried over the buzz.

'Twenty-to-one bar two. Sun Dancer at fives. Trade Wind even money.'

Duff showed his teeth as he smiled. 'That's right, you tell the people.'

Candy twisted her gloves nervously and looked up at Sean.

'You there in the grandstand – can you see what they're doing?'

'They're in line now, moving up together – it looks as though they'll get away first time,' Sean told her without taking his binoculars from his eyes. 'Yes, there they go – they're away!'

'Tell me, tell me,' commanded Candy, pounding Sean's shoulder.

'Harry's showing in front already – can you see the filly, Duff?'

'I saw a flash of green in the pack – yes, there she is lying sixth or seventh.'

'What horse is that next to Trade Wind?'

'That's Hamilton's gelding, don't worry about him, he won't last to the turn.'

The frieze of horses, their heads going like hammers and the dust lifting pale and thin behind them, were framed by the guide rail and the white mine dumps beyond them. Like a string of dark beads they moved up the back stretch and then bunched in the straight.

'Trade Wind's still there – I think he's making ground – the gelding's finished and no sign of the filly yet.'

'Yes! There she is, Duff, wide on the outside. She's moving up.'

'Come on, my darling—' Duff half whispered. 'Let's see you foot it now.'

'She's clear of the pack – she's coming up, Duff, she's coming up fast,' Sean warned.

'Come on, Trade Wind, hold her off,' Duff pleaded. 'Keep her there, boy.'

The pounding of the hooves reached them now, a sound

277

like distant surf, but rising sharply. The colours showed, emerald green above a honey skin and maroon and gold leading on the bay.

'Trade Wind – come on Trade Wind,' shrieked Candy. Her hat flopped over her eyes as she hopped; she ripped it off impatiently and her hair tumbled to her shoulders.

'She's catching him, Duff!'

'Give him the whip, Harry, for Christ's sake – the whip, man.'

The hoof beats crescendoed, thundered up to them, then passed. The filly's nose was at Harry's boot, creeping steadily forward, now level with Trade Wind's heaving shoulder.

'The whip, God damn you,' screamed Duff, 'give him the whip.'

Harry's right arm moved, fast as a mamba – crack, crack; they heard the whip above the howling crowd, above the drumming of hooves and the bay jumped at its sting. Like a pair in harness the two horses swept over the finishing line.

'Who won?' Candy asked as though she were in pain.

'I couldn't see, damn it,' Duff answered.

'Nor could I—' Sean took out his handkerchief and wiped his forehead. 'That didn't do my heart any good – as Francois would say. Have a cigar, Duff.'

'Thanks – I need one.'

Everyone in the crowd was turned to face the board above the judges' box and an uneasy silence held them.

'Why do they take such a long time to make up their minds?' complained Candy. 'I'm so upset that I can only last a minute before I visit the Ladies' Room.'

'The numbers are going up,' shouted Sean.

'Who is it?' Candy jumped to try and see over the heads of the crowd then stopped hurriedly with an expression of alarm on her face.

'Number Sixteen,' bellowed Duff and Sean together, 'it's Trade Wind!'

Sean punched Duff in the chest and Duff leaned over and snapped Sean's cigar in half. Then they caught Candy between them and hugged her. She let out a careful shriek and fought her way out of their arms. 'Excuse me,' she said and fled.

'Let me buy you a drink.' Sean lit the mutilated stump of his cigar.

'No, it's my honour, I insist.' Duff took his arm and they walked with big satisfied grins towards the pavilion. Hradsky was sitting at one of the tables with Max. Duff walked up behind him, lifted his top hat off his head with one hand and with the other ruffled Hradsky's few remaining hairs.

'Never mind, Norman, you can't win all the time.'

Hradsky turned slowly. He retrieved his hat and smoothed back his hair, his eyes glittered yellow.

'He's going to talk,' whispered Duff excitedly.

'I agree with you, Mr Charleywood, you can't win all the time,' said Norman Hradsky. It came out quite clearly with only a small catch on the 'c's' – they were always difficult letters for him. He stood up, put his hat back on his head and walked away.

'I will have a cheque delivered to your office early on Monday morning,' Max told them quietly without taking his eyes off the table. Then he stood up and followed Hradsky.

Sean came through from the bathroom, his beard in wild disorder and a bath-towel round his waist.

> 'The famous Duke of York
> He had ten thousand men
> He marched them up to the top of the hill
> And he marched them down again.'

He sang as he poured bay rum from a cut-glass bottle into his cupped hands and rubbed it into his hair. Duff sat in one of the gilt chairs watching him. Sean combed his hair carefully then smiled at himself in the mirror.

'You magnificent creature,' Sean told his reflection.

'You're getting fat,' Duff grunted.

Sean looked hurt. 'It's muscle.'

'You've got a backside on you like a hippopotamus.'

Sean removed his towel and turned his back to the mirror; he surveyed it over his shoulder.

'I need a heavy hammer to drive a long nail,' he protested.

'Oh, no,' groaned Duff. 'Your wit at this time of the morning is like pork for breakfast, heavy on the stomach.'

Sean took a silk shirt out of his drawer, held it like a toreador's cape, made two passes and swirled it onto his back with a half veronica.

'*Olé!*' applauded Duff wryly. Sean pulled on his trousers and sat to fit his boots.

'You're in a nice mood this morning,' he told Duff.

'I've just come through an emotional hurricane!'

'What's the trouble?'

'Candy wants a church wedding.'

'Is that bad?'

'Well, it's not good.'

'Why?'

'Is your memory so short?'

'Oh, you mean your other wife.'

'That's right, my other wife.'

'Have you told Candy about her?'

'Good God, no.' Duff looked horrified.

'Yes, I see your problem – what about Candy's husband? Doesn't that even the score between you?'

'No, he has gone to his reward.'

'Well, that's convenient. Does anyone else know you're married already?' Duff shook his head.

'What about Francois?'

'No, I never told him.'

'Well, what's your problem – take her down to the church and marry her.'

Duff looked uncomfortable.

'I don't mind marrying a second time in a magistrate's court, it would only be a couple of old Dutchmen I'd be cheating, but to go into a church—' Duff shook his head.

'I'd be the only one who'd know,' said Sean.

'You and the headman.'

'Duff,' Sean beamed at him. 'Duff, my boy, you have scruples – this is amazing!'

Duff squirmed a little in his chair.

'Let me think.' Sean held his forehead dramatically. 'Yes, yes, it's coming to me – that's it.'

'Come on, tell me.' Duff sat on the edge of his chair.

'Go to Candy and tell her it's all fixed, not only are you prepared to marry her in a church but you're even going to build your own church.'

'That's wonderful,' Duff murmured sarcastically, 'that's the way out of my difficulties all right.'

'Let me finish.' Sean started filling his silver cigar case. 'You also tell her that you want a civil ceremony as well – I

281

believe that's what royalty do. Tell her that, it should win her over.'

'I still don't follow you.'

'Then you build your own chapel up at Xanadu – we can find a distinguished-looking character, dress him up in a dog collar and teach him the right words. That keeps Candy happy. Immediately after the service the priest takes the coach for Capetown. You take Candy down to the magistrate's office and that keeps you happy.'

Duff looked stunned then slowly his face broke into a great happy smile. 'Genius – pure inspired genius.'

Sean buttoned his waistcoat. 'Think nothing of it. And now if you'll excuse me I'll go and do some work – one of us has to make sufficient to allow you to indulge these strange fancies of yours.'

Sean shrugged on his coat, picked up his cane and swung it. The gold head gave it a balance like a handmade shotgun. The silk next to his skin and the halo of bay rum round his head made him feel good.

He went down the stairs. Mbejane had the carriage waiting for him in the Hotel yard. The body tilted slightly at Sean's weight and the leather upholstery welcomed him with a yielding softness. He lit his first cigar of the day and Mbejane smiled at him.

'I see you, Nkosi.'

'I see you also, Mbejane, what is that lump on the side of your head?'

'Nkosi, I was a little drunk, otherwise that ape of Basuto would never have touched me with his fighting stick.'

Mbejane rolled the carriage smoothly out of the yard and into the street.

'What were you fighting about?'

Mbejane shrugged. 'Must a man have a reason to fight?'

'It is usual.'

'It is in my memory that there was a woman,' said Mbejane.

'That is also usual – who won this fight?'

'The man bled a little, his friends took him away. The woman, when I left, was smiling in her sleep.'

Sean laughed, then ran his eyes over the undulating plain of Mbejane's bare back. It was definitely not in keeping. He hoped his secretary had remembered to speak to the tailor. They pulled up in front of his offices. One of his clerks hurried down off the veranda and opened the door of the carriage.

'Good morning, Mr Courtney.'

Sean went up the stairs with his clerk running ahead of him like a hunting dog.

'Good morning, Mr Courtney,' another polite chorus from the row of desks in the main office. Sean waved his cane at them and went through into his own office. His portrait leered at him from above the fireplace and he winked at it.

'What have we this morning, Johnson?'

'These requisitions, sir, and the pay cheques, sir, and development reports from the engineers, sir, and . . .'

Johnson was a greasy-haired little man in a greasy-looking alpaca coat; with each 'sir' he made a greasy little bow. He was efficient so Sean hired him, but that didn't mean he liked him.

'You got a stomach ache, Johnson?'

'No, sir.'

'Well, for God's sake, stand up straight, man.'

Johnson shot to attention.

'Now let's have them one at a time.'

Sean dropped into his chair. At this time of the day came the grind. He hated the paper work and so he tackled it with grim concentration, making random checks on the

283

long rows of figures, trying to associate names with faces and querying requisitions that appeared exorbitant until finally he wrote his signature between the last of Johnson's carefully pencilled crosses and threw his pen onto the desk.

'What else is there?'

'Meeting with Mr Maxwell from the Bank at twelve-thirty, sir.'

'And then?'

'The agent for Brooke Bros. at one, and immediately after that Mr MacDougal, sir, then you're expected up at the Candy Deep mine.'

'Thank you, Johnson, I'll be at the Exchange as usual this morning if anything out of the ordinary comes up.'

'Very good, Mr Courtney. Just one other thing.' Johnson pointed at the brown paper parcel on the couch across the room. 'From your tailor.'

'Ah!' Sean smiled. 'Send my servant in here.' He walked across and opened the parcel. Within a few minutes Mbejane filled the doorway.

'Nkosi?'

'Mbejane – your new uniform.' Sean pointed at the clothes laid out on the couch. Mbejane's eyes switched to the gold and maroon finery, his expression suddenly dead.

'Put it on – come on, let's see how you look.'

Mbejane crossed to the couch and picked up the jacket. 'These are for me?'

'Yes, come on, put it on.' Sean laughed.

Mbejane hesitated, then slowly he loosened his loin cloth and let it drop. Sean watched him impatiently as he buttoned on the jacket and pantaloons, then he walked in a critical circle around the Zulu.

'Not bad,' he muttered, and then in Zulu, 'Is it not beautiful?'

Mbejane wriggled his shoulders against the unfamiliar feel of the cloth and said nothing.

'Well, Mbejane, do you like it?'

'When I was a child I went with my father to trade cattle at Port Natal. There was a man who went about the town with a monkey on a chair, the monkey danced and the people laughed and threw money to it. That monkey had such a suit as this. Nkosi, I do not think he was a very happy monkey.'

The smile slipped off Sean's face. 'You would rather wear your skins?'

'What I wear is the dress of a warrior of Zululand.'

There was still no expression on Mbejane's face. Sean opened his mouth to argue with him but before he could speak he lost his temper.

'You'll wear that uniform,' he shouted. 'You'll wear what I tell you to wear and you'll do it with a smile, do you hear me?'

'Nkosi, I hear you.' Mbejane picked up his loin cloth of leopard tails and left the office. When Sean went out to the carriage Mbejane was sitting on the driver's seat in his new livery. All the way to the Exchange his back was stiff with protest and neither of them spoke. Sean glared at the doorman of the Exchange, drank four brandies during the morning, rode back to his office again at noon scowling at Mbejane's still protesting back, shouted at Johnson, snapped at the bank manager, routed the representative from Brooke Bros. and drove out to the Candy Deep in a high old rage. But Mbejane's silence was impenetrable and Sean couldn't re-open the argument without sacrifice of pride. He burst into the new administrative building of the Candy Deep and threw the staff into confusion.

'Where's Mr du Toit?' he roared.

'He's down the Number Three shaft, Mr Courtney.'

'What the hell is he doing down there? He's supposed to be waiting for me here.'

'He didn't expect you for another hour, sir.'

'Well, get me some overalls and a mining helmet, don't just stand there.'

He clapped the tin hat on his head and stamped his heavy gumboots across to the Number Three shaft. The skip dropped him smoothly five hundred feet into the earth and he climbed out at the tenth level.

'Where's Mr du Toit?' he demanded of the shift boss at the lift station.

'He's up at the face, sir.'

The floor of the drive was rough and muddy; his gumboots squelched as he set off down the tunnel. His carbide lamp lit the uneven rock walls with a flat white light and he felt himself starting to sweat. Two natives pushing a cocopan back along the railway lines forced him to flatten himself against one wall to allow them to pass and while he waited he felt inside his overalls for his cigar case. As he pulled it out it slipped from his hand and plunked into the mud. The cocopan was gone by that time so he stooped to pick up the case. His ear came within an inch of the wall and a puzzled expression replaced his frown of annoyance. The rock was squeaking. He laid his ear against it. It sounded like someone grinding his teeth. He listened to it for a while trying to guess the cause; it wasn't the echo of shovels or drills, it wasn't water. He walked another thirty yards or so down the drive and listened again. Not so loud here but now the grinding noise was punctuated with an occasional metallic snap like the breaking of a knife blade. Strange; very strange; he had never heard anything like it before. He walked on down the drive, his bad mood lost in his preoccupation with this new problem. Before he reached the face he met Francois.

'Hello, Mr Courtney.' Sean had long since given up

trying to stop Francois calling him that. 'Gott, I'm sorry I wasn't there to meet you. I thought you were coming at three.'

'That's all right, Francois, how are you?'

'My rheumatism's been giving me blazes, Mr Courtney, but otherwise I'm all right. How's Mr Charleywood?'

'He's fine.' Sean couldn't restrain his curiosity any longer. 'Tell me something, Franz, just now I put my ear against the wall of the drive and I heard an odd noise, I couldn't make out what it was.'

'What kind of noise?'

'A sort of grinding, like – like . . .' Sean searched for words to describe it, 'like two pieces of glass being rubbed together.'

Francois's eyes flew wide open and then began to bulge, the colour of his face changed to grey and he caught Sean's arm.

'Where?'

'Back along the drive.'

The breath jammed in Francois's throat and he struggled to speak through it, shaking Sean's arm desperately.

'Cave-in!' he croaked. 'Cave-in, man!'

He started to run but Sean grabbed him. Francois struggled wildly.

'Francois, how many men up at the face?'

'Cave-in.' Francois's voice was now hysterically shrill. 'Cave-in.' He broke Sean's grip and raced away towards the lift station, the mud flying from his gumboots. His terror infected Sean and he ran a dozen paces after Francois before he stopped himself. For precious seconds he wavered with fear slithering round like a reptile in his stomach; go back to call the others and perhaps die with them or follow Francois and live. Then the fear in his belly found a mate, a thing just as slimy and cold; its name was shame, and shame it was that drove him back towards the face. There

287

were five blacks and a white man there, bare-chested and shiny with sweat in the heat. Sean shouted those two words at them and they reacted the way bathers do when someone on the beach shouts 'shark'. The same moment of paralysed horror, then the panic. They came stampeding back along the tunnel. Sean ran with them, the mud sucked at his heavy boots and his legs were weak with easy living and riding in carriages. One by one the others passed him.

'Wait for me,' he wanted to scream. 'Wait for me.' He slipped on the greasy footing, scraping his shoulder on the rough wall as he fell, and dragged himself up again, mud plastered in his beard, the blood humming in his ears. Alone now he blundered on down the tunnel. With a crack like a rifle shot one of the thick shoring timbers broke under the pressure of the moving rock and dust smoked from the roof of the tunnel in front of him. He staggered on and all around him the earth was talking, groaning, protesting, with little muffled shrieks. The timbers joined in again, crackling and snapping, and as slowly as a theatre curtain the rock sagged down from above him. The tunnel was thick with dust that smothered the beam of his lamp and rasped his throat. He knew then that he wasn't going to make it but he ran on with the loose rock starting to fall about him. A lump hit his mining helmet and jarred him so that he nearly fell. Blinded by the swirling dust fog he crashed at full run into the abandoned cocopan that blocked the tunnel, he sprawled over the metal body of the trolley with his thighs bruised from the collision.

'Now I'm finished,' he thought, but instinctively he pulled himself up and started to grope his way around the cocopan to continue his flight. With a roar the tunnel in front of him collapsed. He dropped on his knees and crawled between the wheels of the cocopan, wriggling under the sturdy steel body just an instant before the roof above him collapsed also. The noise of the fall around him seemed to last for ever, but then it was over and the rustling and grating of the rock as it settled down was almost silence in comparison. His lamp was lost and the darkness pressed as heavily on him as the earth squeezed down on his tiny shelter. The air was solid with dust and he coughed; he coughed until his chest ached and he tasted salty blood in his mouth. There was hardly room to move, the steel body of the trolley was six inches above him, but he struggled until he managed to open the front of his overalls and tear a piece off the tail of his shirt. He held the silk like a surgical mask across his mouth and nose. It strained the dust out of the air so he could breathe. The dust settled; his coughing slowed and finally stopped. He felt surprise that he was still alive and cautiously he started exploring. He tried to straighten out his legs but his feet touched rock. He felt with his hands, six inches of head room and perhaps twelve inches on either side, warm mud underneath him and rock and steel all around. He took off his helmet and used it as a pillow. He was in a steel coffin buried five hundred feet deep. He felt the first flutter of panic. 'Keep your mind busy, think of something, think of anything but the rock around you, count your assets,' he told himself. He started to search his pockets, moving with difficulty in the cramped space.

'One silver cigar case with two Havanas.' He laid it down next to him.

'One box of matches, wet.' He placed it on top of the case.

'One pocket watch.'

'One handkerchief, Irish linen, monogrammed.'

'One comb, tortoiseshell – a man is judged by his appearance.' He started to comb his beard but found immediately that though this occupied his hands it left his mind free. He put the comb down next to his matches.

'Twenty-five pounds in gold sovereigns—' He counted

them carefully, 'yes, twenty-five. I shall order a bottle of good champagne.' The dust was chalky in his mouth so he went on hurriedly, 'And a Malay girl from the Opera. No, why be mean – ten Malay girls. I'll have them dance for me, that'll pass the time. I'll promise them a sovereign each to bolster their enthusiasm.'

He continued the search, but there was nothing else. 'Gumboots, socks, well-cut trousers, shirt torn I'm afraid, overalls, a tin hat, and that's all.'

With his possessions laid out carefully beside him and his cell explored he had to start thinking. First he thought about his thirst. The mud in which he lay was too thick to yield water. He tried straining it through his shirt without success, and then he thought about air. It seemed quite fresh and he decided that sufficient was filtering in from the loosely packed rock around him to keep him alive.

To keep him alive – alive until the thirst killed. Until he died curled up like a foetus in the warm womb of the earth. He laughed, a worm in a dark warm womb. He laughed again and recognized it as the beginnings of panic, he thrust his fist into his mouth to stop himself, biting down hard on his knuckles. It was very quiet, the rock had stopped moving.

'How long will it take? Tell me, Doctor. How long have I got?'

'Well, you are sweating. You'll lose moisture quite rapidly. I'd say about four days,' he answered himself.

'What about hunger, Doctor?'

'Oh, no, don't worry about that, you'll be hungry, of course, but the thirst will kill you.'

'And typhoid, or is it typhus, I can never remember. What about that, Doctor?'

'If there were dead men trapped in here with you there'd be a good chance, but you're alone, you know.'

'Do you think I'll go mad, Doctor, not immediately, of course, but in a few days?'

'Yes, you'll go mad.'

'I've never been mad before, not that I know of anyway, but I think it will help to go mad now, don't you?'

'If you mean, will it make it easier, well, I don't know.'

'Ah! now you're being obscure – but I follow you. You mean in that sleep of madness what dreams will come? You mean, will madness be more real than reality? You mean, will dying mad be worse than dying thirsty? But then I may beat the madness. This cocopan might buckle under the strain, after all there must be thousands of tons of rock bearing down on it. That's quite clever, you know, Doctor; as a medical man you should appreciate it. Mother Earth was saved but, alas, the child was stillborn, she bore down too hard.' Sean had spoken aloud, and now he felt foolish. He picked up a piece of stone and tapped the cocopan with it.

'It sounds firm enough. A most pleasing noise, really.' He beat harder on the metal body – one, two, three, one, two, three – then dropped the stone. Soft as an echo, distant as the moon, he heard his taps repeated. His whole body stiffened at the sound, and he started to shiver with excitement. He snatched up the stone: three times he rapped, and three times the answer came back to him.

'They heard me, sweet merciful Christ, they heard me.' He laughed breathlessly. 'Dear Mother Earth, don't bear down, please don't bear down. Just be patient. Wait a few days and by Caesarian they'll take this child out of your womb.'

Mbejane waited until Sean disappeared down the Number Three shaft before he took off his new jacket. He folded it carefully on the driver's seat next to him. He sat and enjoyed the feel of the sun on his skin for a while, then he climbed off the carriage and went to the horses. He took them one at a time to the trough for water then returned them to their harnesses, buckling them in loosely. He picked up his spears from the footboard and moved across to a patch of short grass next to the administrative building. He sat down and went to work on the blade, humming softly to himself as he honed. At last he ran an expert thumb along each edge, grunted, shaved a few hairs off his forearm, smiled contentedly and laid his spears beside him in the grass. He lay back and the sun warmed him to sleep.

The shouting woke him. He sat up and automatically checked the height of the sun. He had slept an hour or more. Duff was shouting and Francois, mud-splattered and frightened-looking, was answering him. They were standing together in front of the administrative building. Duff's horse was sweating. Mbejane stood up and went across to them; he listened closely, trying to understand their staccato voices. They went too fast for him, but something was wrong, that much he knew.

'It's caved in almost to the Number Ten lift station,' Francois said.

'You left him in there,' accused Duff.

'I thought he was following me, but he turned back.'

'What for – why did he turn back?'

'To call the others—'

'Have you started clearing the drive?'

'No, I was waiting for you.'

'You stupid bloody idiot, he might be alive in there . . . every minute is vital.'

'But he hasn't a chance, Mr Charleywood, he must be dead.'

'Shut up, damn you.'

Duff swung away from him and started running towards

292

the shaft. There was a crowd gathered beneath the high steel structure of the head gear, and suddenly Mbejane knew it was Sean. He caught up with Duff before he reached the shaft.

'Is it the Nkosi?'

'Yes.'

'What has happened?'

'The rock has fallen on him.'

Mbejane pushed his way into the skip next to Duff and neither of them spoke again until they reached the tenth level. They went down the drive, only a short way before they reached the end. There were men there with crowbars and shovels standing undecided, waiting for orders, and Mbejane shouldered a path through them. He and Duff stood together in front of the new wall of broken rock that sealed the tunnel, and the silence went on and on. Then Duff turned on the white shift-boss.

'Were you at the face?'

'Yes.'

'He went back to call you, didn't he?'

'Yes.'

'And you left him there?'

The man couldn't look at Duff.

'I thought he was following us,' he muttered.

'You thought only of your own miserable skin,' Duff told him, 'you filthy little coward, you slimy yellow bastard, you . . .'

Mbejane caught Duff's arm and Duff stopped his tirade. They all heard it then – clink, clink, clink.

'It's him – it must be him,' whispered Duff, 'he's alive!' He snatched a crowbar from one of the natives and knocked against the side of the tunnel. They waited, their breathing the only sound, until the answer came back to them louder and sharper than before. Mbejane took the crowbar out of Duff's hands. He thrust it into a crack in the rock jam and his back muscles bunched as he heaved. The bar bent like a liquorice stick, he threw it away and went at the stone with his bare hands.

'You!' Duff snapped at the shift-boss. 'We'll need timber to shore up as we clear the fall – get it.' He turned to the natives. 'Four of you working on the face at one time – the rest of you carry the stone away as we loosen it.'

'Do you want any dynamite?' asked the shift-boss.

'And bring the rock down a second time? Use your brains, man. Go and get that timber and call Mr du Toit while you're at the surface.'

In four hours they cleared fifteen feet of tunnel, breaking the larger slabs of stone with sledge hammers and prising the pieces out of the jam. Duff's body ached and his hands were raw. He had to rest. He walked slowly back to the lift station and there he found blankets and a huge dish of soup.

'Where did this come from?'

'Candy's Hotel, sir. Half Johannesburg is waiting at the head of the shaft.'

Duff huddled into a blanket and drank a little of the soup. 'Where's du Toit?'

'I couldn't find him, sir.'

Up at the face Mbejane worked on. The first four natives came back to rest and fresh men took their place. Mbejane led them, grunting an order occasionally but otherwise reserving his strength for the assault on the rock. For an hour Duff rested and when he returned to the head of the tunnel Mbejane was still there. Duff watched him curl his arms round a piece of stone the size of a beer keg, brace his legs and tear the stone out of the jam. Earth and loose rock followed it, burying Mbejane's legs to the knees, and Duff jumped forward to help him.

Another two hours and Duff had to rest again. This time he led Mbejane back with him, gave him a blanket and made him drink a little soup. They sat next to each other with their backs against the wall of the tunnel and blankets over their shoulders. The shift-boss came to Duff.

'Mrs Rautenbach sent this down for you, sir.'

It was a half-bottle of brandy.

'Tell her, thank you.' Duff pulled the cork with his teeth and swallowed twice. It brought the tears into his eyes – he offered the bottle to Mbejane.

'It is not fitting,' Mbejane demurred.

'Drink.'

Mbejane drank, wiped the mouth of the bottle carefully on his blanket and handed it back. Duff took another swallow and offered it again but Mbejane shook his head.

'A little of that is strength, too much is weakness. There is work to do now.'

Duff corked the bottle.

'How long before we reach him?' asked Mbejane.

'Another day, maybe two.'

'A man can die in two days,' mused the Zulu.

'Not one with a body like a bull and a temper like a devil,' Duff assured him. Mbejane smiled and Duff went on groping for his words in Zulu.

'You love him, Mbejane?'

'Love is a woman's word.'

Mbejane inspected one of his thumbs; the nail was torn loose, standing up like a tombstone; he took it between his teeth, pulled it off and spat it onto the floor of the drive. Duff shuddered as he watched.

'Those baboons will not work unless they are driven.' Mbejane stood up. 'Are you rested?'

'Yes,' lied Duff, and they went back to the face.

Sean lay in the mud with his head on the hard pillow of the helmet. The darkness was as solid as the rock around him. He tried to imagine where the one ended and the other began – by doing that he could stop himself feeling his thirst so strongly. He could hear the ring of hammer on stone and the rattle of rock falling free but it never seemed to come any closer. The whole side of his body was stiff and sore but he could not turn over, his knees caught on the cocopan every time he tried and the air in his little cave was starting to taste stale – his head ached. He moved again, restlessly, and his hand brushed the small pile of sovereigns. He struck at them, scattering them into the mud. They were the bait that had led him into this trap. Now he would give them, and all the millions of others, for just the feel of the wind in his beard and the sun in his face. The darkness clung to him, thick and cloying as black treacle; it seemed to fill his nose, his throat and eyes, smothering him. He groped and found the matchbox. For a few seconds of light he would burn up most of the precious oxygen in his cave and call it fair exchange – but the box was sodden. He struck match after match but the wet heads crumbled without a spark and he threw them away and clenched his eyelids to keep the darkness out. Bright colours formed in front of his closed eyes, moving and rearranging themselves until suddenly and very clearly they formed a picture of Garrick's face. He hadn't thought about his family for months, he had been too busy reaping the golden harvest, but now memories crowded back. There were so many things he had forgotten. Everything else had become unimportant when compared with power and gold – even lives, men's lives, had meant nothing. But now it was his own life, teetering on the edge of the black cliff.

The sound of the sledge-hammers broke into his thoughts again. There were men on the other side of the blocked tunnel trying to save him, working their way into the treacherous rock pile which might collapse again at any minute. People were more valuable than the poisonous metal, the little gold discs that lay smugly beside him in the mud while men struggled to save him.

He thought of Garry, crippled by his careless shotgun, father to the bastard he had sired, of Ada whom he had left without a word of goodbye, of Karl Lochtkamper with the pistol in his hand and half his head splattered across the floor of his bedroom, of other nameless men dead or broken because of him.

Sean ran his tongue across his lips and listened to the hammers; he was certain they were nearer now.

'If I get out of here, it'll be different. I swear it.'

Mbejane rested for four hours in the next thirty-six. Duff watched the flesh melt off him in sweat. He was killing himself. Duff was worn out; he could no longer work with his hands but he was directing the teams who were shoring up the reclaimed tunnel. By the second evening they had cleared a hundred feet of the drive. Duff paced it out and when he reached the face he spoke to Mbejane.

'How long since you last signalled to him?'

Mbejane stepped back with a sledge-hammer in his tattered hands; its shaft was sticky and brown with blood.

'An hour ago and even then it sounded as though there were but the length of a spear between us.'

Duff took a crowbar from one of the other natives and tapped the rock. The answer came immediately.

'He's hitting something made of iron,' Duff said. 'It sounds as though he's only a few feet away. Mbejane, let these other men take over. If you wish you can stay and watch but you must rest again now.'

For answer Mbejane lifted the hammer and swung it against the face. The rock he hit cracked and two of the natives stepped up and levered it loose with their crowbars. At the back of the hole it left in the wall they could see the corner of the cocopan. Everyone stared at it, then Duff shouted.

'Sean, Sean, can you hear me?'

'Stop talking and get me out of here.' Sean's voice was hoarse with thirst and dust, and muffled by the rock.

'He's under the cocopan.'

'It's him.'

'Nkosi, are you all right?'

'We've found him.'

The shouts were picked up by the men working behind them in the drive and passed back to those waiting at the lift station.

'They've found him – he's all right – they've found him.'

Duff and Mbejane jumped forward together, their exhaustion completely forgotten. They cleared the last few lumps of rock and with their shoulders touching knelt and peered under the cocopan.

'Nkosi, I see you.'

'I see you also, Mbejane, what took you so long?'

'Nkosi, there were a few small stones in the way.'

Mbejane reached under the cocopan and with his hands under Sean's armpits pulled him out.

'What a hell of a place you chose to go to ground in, laddie. How are you feeling?'

'Give me some water and I'll be all right.'

'Water – bring water,' shouted Duff.

Sean gulped it, trying to drink the whole mug in one mouthful. He coughed and it shot out of his nose.

'Easy, laddie, easy.' Duff thumped his back. Sean drank the next mugful more slowly and finished panting from the effort.

'That was good.'

'Come on, we've got a doctor waiting up on top.' Duff draped a blanket over his shoulders. Mbejane picked Sean up across his chest.

'Put me down, damn you, I haven't forgotten how to walk.'

Mbejane set him down gently, but his legs buckled like those of a man just out of bed from a long illness and he clutched at Mbejane's arm. Mbejane picked him up again and carried him down to the lift station. They rode up in the skip into the open.

'The moon's shining. And the stars – my God, they're beautiful.' There was wonder in Sean's voice; he sucked the night air into his lungs but it was too rich for him and he started coughing again. There were people waiting at the head of the shaft and they crowded round them as they stepped out of the skip.

'How is he?'

'Are you all right, Sean?'

'Doc Symmonds is waiting in the office.'

'Quickly, Mbejane,' said Duff, 'get him out of the cold.'

One on either side of him they hurried Sean across to the administrative building and laid him on the couch in Francois's office. Symmonds checked him over, looked down his throat and felt his pulse.

'Have you got a closed carriage here?'

'Yes,' Duff answered.

'Well, wrap him up warmly and get him home to bed. With the dust and bad air he's been breathing there's serious danger of pneumonia. I'll come down with you and give him a sedative.'

'I won't need one, Doc,' Sean grinned at him.

'I think I know what's best for you, Mr Courtney.' Doctor Symmonds was a young man. He was the fashionable doctor among the rich of Johannesburg and he took it very seriously.

'Now if you please, we'll get you to your hotel.' He started to pack his instruments back into his valise.

'You're the doctor,' Sean agreed, 'but before we go will

you have a look at my servant's hands, they're in a hell of a mess. There's hardly any meat left on them.'

Doctor Symmonds did not look up from what he was doing. 'I have no Kaffir practice, Mr Courtney, I'm sure you'll find some other doctor to attend to him when we get back to town.'

Sean sat up slowly, he let the blankets slip off his shoulders. He walked across to Doctor Symmonds and held him by the throat against the wall. The doctor had a fine pair of waxed moustaches and Sean took one of them between the thumb and forefinger of his free hand: he plucked it out like feathers from the carcass of a dead fowl and Doctor Symmonds squealed.

'Starting now, Doctor, you have a Kaffir practice,' Sean told him. He pulled the handkerchief out of Symmonds' top pocket and dabbed at the little drops of blood on the doctor's bare upper lip.

'Be a good fellow – see to my servant.'

– 21 –

When Sean woke the next morning the hands of the grandfather clock across the bedroom pointed at the top of their dial. Candy was in the room opening the curtains and with her were two waiters, each with a loaded tray.

'Good morning, how is our hero this morning?' The waiters put down their trays and went out as she came across to Sean's bed.

Sean blinked the sleep out of his eyes. 'My throat feels as though I've just finished a meal of broken glass.'

'That's the dust,' Candy told him and laid her hands on his forehead. Sean's hand sneaked round behind her and she squeaked as he pinched her. Standing well away from the bed she rubbed her bottom and made a face at him.

'There's nothing wrong with you!'

'Good, then I'll get up.' Sean started to pull back the bedclothes.

'Not until the doctor's had a look at you, you won't.'

'Candy, if that bastard puts one foot in this room I'll punch him so hard in the mouth his teeth will march out of his backside like soldiers.'

Candy turned to the breakfast trays to cover her smile. 'That's no way to talk in front of a lady. But don't worry, it isn't Symmonds.'

'Where's Duff?' Sean asked.

'He's having a bath, then he's coming to eat breakfast with you.'

'I'll wait for him, but give me a cup of coffee in the meantime, there's a sweetheart.'

She brought the coffee to him. 'Your savage has been camping on my trail all morning, he wants to see you. I've just about had to put an armed guard on this room to keep him out.'

Sean laughed. 'Will you send him in, Candy?'

She went to the door and stopped with a hand on the latch.

'It's nice to have you back, Sean, don't do anything silly like that again, will you?'

'That's a promise,' Sean assured her.

Mbejane came quickly and stood in the doorway. 'Nkosi, is it well with you?'

Sean looked at the iodine-stained bandages on his hands and the maroon and gold livery without answering. Then he rolled on his back and stared at the ceiling. 'I sent for my servant and instead there comes a monkey on a chain.'

Mbejane stood still, his face expressionless but for the hurt in his eyes.

301

'Go – find my servant. You will know him by his dress which is that of a warrior of Zululand.'

It took a few seconds for the laughter to start rolling around in Mbejane's belly; it shook his shoulders and creased the corners of his mouth. He closed the door very softly behind him and when he came back in his loin cloth Sean grinned at him.

'Ah! I see you, Mbejane.'

'And I see you also.'

He stood by the bed and they talked. They spoke little of the cave-in and not at all of Mbejane's part in the rescue. Between them it was understood, words could only damage it. Perhaps they would talk of it later, but not now.

'Tomorrow, will you need the carriage?' Mbejane asked at last.

'Yes – go now. Eat and sleep.' Sean reached out and touched Mbejane's arm. Just that small physical contact – that almost guilty touching – and Mbejane left him.

Then Duff came in in a silk dressing-gown and they ate eggs and steak from the trays and Duff sent down for a bottle of wine just to rinse the dust out of their throats once more.

'They tell me Francois is still down at the Bright Angels – he's been on the drink ever since he got out of that shaft. When he sobers up he can come to the office and collect his pay packet.'

Sean sat up. 'You're going to fire him?'

'I'm going to fire him so high he'll only touch ground when he reaches Capetown.'

'What the hell for?' demanded Sean.

'What for?' Duff echoed. 'What for? For running – that's what for.'

'Duff, he was in a cave-in at Kimberley, wasn't he?'

'Yes.'

'Broke his legs, didn't you say?'

'Yes.'

'Shall I tell you something? If it were to happen to me a second time I'd run as well.'

Duff filled his wine glass without answering.

'Send down to the Bright Angels, tell him alcohol is bad for the liver – that should sober him – tell him unless he's back at work by tomorrow morning we'll dock it off his pay,' Sean said. Duff looked at him with a puzzled expression. 'What is this?'

'I had some time to think while I was down in that hole. I decided that to get to the top you don't have to stamp on everyone you meet.'

'Ah, I understand.' Duff gave his lopsided grin. 'A good resolution – New Year in August. Well, that's all right, you had me worried there, I thought a rock had fallen on your head. I also make good resolutions.'

'Duff, I don't want Francois fired.'

'All right, all right – he stays on. If you like we can open a soup kitchen at the office and turn Xanadu into a home for the aged.'

'Oh, go and burst. I just don't think it's necessary to fire Francois, that's all.'

'Who's arguing? I agreed with you, didn't I? I have deep respect for good resolutions. I make them all the time.'

Duff pulled his chair up to the bed. 'Quite by chance I happen to have a pack of cards with me.' He took them out of his dressing-gown pocket. 'Would you care for a game of Klabejas?'

Sean lost fifty pounds before he was saved by the arrival of the new doctor. The doctor tapped his chest and tut-tutted, looked down his throat and tut-tutted, wrote out a prescription and confined him to bed for the rest of the day.

He was just leaving when Jock and Trevor Heyns arrived. Jock had a bunch of flowers which he presented to Sean in an embarrassed fashion.

Then the room began to fill in earnest: the rest of the crowd from the Exchange arrived, someone had brought a case of champagne, a poker game started in one corner and a political meeting in another.

'Who does this Kruger think he is, anyway – God or something? You know what he said last time we went to see him about getting the vote, he said "Protest, protest – I have the guns and you have not!"'

'Three Kings wins – you *are* holding cards!'

' – you wait and see. Consolidated Wits. will hit thirty shillings by the end of the month.'

' – and the taxes – they're putting another twenty per cent on dynamite.'

' – a new piece at the Opera, Jock's got a season ticket on her – no one else has had a look in yet.'

'All right, you two – stop that. If you want to fight go outside – this is a sick room.'

'This bottle's empty – break open a new one, Duff.'

Sean lost another hundred to Duff and then a little after five Candy came in. She was horrified. 'Out, all of you, out!'

The room emptied as quickly as it had filled and Candy wandered around picking up cigar butts and empty glasses.

'The vandals! Someone's burnt a hole in the carpet and look at this – champagne spilt all over the table.'

Duff coughed and started pouring himself another drink.

'Don't you think you've had enough of that, Dufford?'

Duff put down his glass. 'And it's time you went and changed for dinner.' Duff winked sheepishly at Sean, but he went.

Duff and Candy came back to his room after supper and had a liqueur with him.

'Now to sleep,' Candy commanded and went across to draw the curtains.

'It's still early,' protested Duff with no effect. Candy blew the lamp out.

Sean was not tired, he had lain in bed all day and now his brain was overactive. He lit a cigar and smoked, listening to the street noises below his window and it was past midnight before he finally drifted off. When he woke, he woke screaming, for the darkness was on him again and the blankets pressed down on him suffocating him. He fought them off and stumbled blindly across the room. He had to have air and light. He ran into the thick velvet curtains and they closed around his face; he tore himself free and hit the french windows with his shoulder; they burst open and he was out on the balcony, out in the cold air with the moon fat and yellow in the sky above him. His gasping slowed until he was breathing normally again. He went back inside and lit the lamp, then he went through to Duff's empty bedroom. There was a copy of *Twelfth Night* on the bedside table and he took it back to his own room. He sat with the lamp at his elbow and forced his eyes to follow the printed words even though they made no sense. He read until the dawn showed grey through the open windows, then he put down the book. He shaved, dressed and went down the back stairs into the hotel yard. He found Mbejane in the stables.

'Put a saddle on the grey.'

'Where are you going, Nkosi?'

'To kill a devil.'

'Then I will come with you.'

'No, I will be back before midday.'

He rode up to the Candy Deep and tied his horse outside the administration buildings. There was a sleepy clerk in the front offices.

'Good morning, Mr Courtney. Can I help you?'

'Yes. Get me overalls and a helmet.'

Sean went to the Number Three shaft. There was a frost on the ground that crunched as he walked on it and the sun had just cleared the eastern ridge of the Witwatersrand. Sean stopped at the hoist shed and spoke to the driver.

'Has the new shift gone on yet?'

'Half an hour ago, sir.' The man was obviously surprised to see him. 'The night shift finished blasting at five o'clock.'

'Good – drop me down to the fourteenth level.'

'The fourteenth is abandoned now, Mr Courtney, there's no one working there.'

'Yes, I know.'

Sean walked across to the head of the shaft. He lit his carbide lamp and while he waited for the skip he looked out across the valley. The air was clear and the sun threw long shadows. Everything stood out in sharp relief. He had not been up this early in the morning for many months and he had almost forgotten how fresh and delicately coloured a new day was. The skip stopped in front of him. He took a deep breath and stepped into it. When he reached the fourteenth level he got out and pushed the recall signal for the skip and he was alone in the earth again. He walked up the tunnel and the echo of his footsteps went with him. He was sweating and a muscle in his cheek started to jerk; he reached the face and set the carbide lamp down on a ledge of rock. He checked to make sure his matches were in his pocket, then he blew out the lamp. The darkness came squeezing down on him. The first half hour was the worst. Twice he had the matches in his hand ready to strike but he stopped himself. The sweat formed cold wet patches under his arms and the darkness filled his open mouth and choked him. He had to fight for each lungful of air, suck in, hold it, breathe out. First he regulated his breathing and then slowly, slowly his mind came under control and he knew he had won. He waited another ten minutes breathing

306

easily and sitting relaxed with his back against the side of the tunnel, then he lit the lamp. He was smiling as he went back to the lift station and signalled for the skip. When he reached the surface he stepped out and lit a cigar; he flicked the match into the square black opening of the shaft.

'So much for you, little hole.'

He walked back towards the administration building. What he could not know was that the Number Three shaft of the Candy Deep was to take something from him just as valuable as his courage and that, next time, what it took it would not give back. But that was many years ahead.

– 22 –

By October Xanadu was nearly finished. The three of them drove out to it as usual one Saturday afternoon.

'The builder is only six months behind schedule – now he says he'll be finished by Christmas and I haven't found the courage yet to ask him which Christmas,' Sean remarked.

'It's all the alterations Candy has thought up,' Duff said. 'She's got the poor man so confused he doesn't know whether he's a boy or a girl.'

'Well, if you'd consulted me in the first place it would have saved a lot of trouble,' Candy told them.

The carriage turned in through the marble gates and they looked around them. Already the lawns were smooth and green and the jacaranda trees lining the drive were shoulder high.

'I think it's going to live up to its name – that gardener's doing a good job,' Sean spoke with satisfaction.

'Don't you call him a gardener to his face or we'll have a strike on our hands. He's a horticulturist,' Duff smiled across at him.

'Talking about names,' Candy interrupted, 'don't you think Xanadu is – well, a bit outlandish?'

'No, I do not,' Sean said. 'I picked it myself. I think it's a damn good name.'

'It's not dignified – why don't we call it Fair Oaks?'

'Firstly, because there isn't an oak tree within fifty miles and secondly because it's already called Xanadu.'

'Don't get cross, it was just a suggestion.'

The builder met them at the top of the drive and they began the tour of the house. That took an hour, then they left the builder and went out into the garden. They found the gardener with a gang of natives near the north boundary.

'How's it going, Joubert?' Duff greeted him.

'Not bad, Mr Charleywood, but it takes time you know.'

'You've done a damn fine job so far.'

'It's kind of you to say so, sir.'

'When are you going to start laying out my maze?'

The gardener looked surprised; he glanced at Candy, opened his mouth, closed it again and looked once more at Candy.

'Oh, I told Joubert not to worry about the maze.'

'Why did you do that? I wanted a maze – ever since I visited Hampton Court as a child I've wanted my own maze.'

'They're silly things,' Candy told him. 'They just take up a lot of space and they're not even nice to look at.'

Sean thought Duff was going to argue, but he didn't. They talked to the gardener a little longer, then they walked back across the lawns in front of the house towards the chapel.

'Dufford, I've left my parasol in the carriage, would you mind getting it for me?' Candy asked.

When Duff was gone Candy took Sean's arm.

'It's going to be a lovely home. We're going to be very happy here.'

'Have you two decided on a date yet?' Sean asked.

'We want the house finished first so we can move straight in. I think we'll make it some time in February next year.'

They reached the chapel and stopped in front of it.

'It's a sweet little church.' Candy spoke dreamily. 'And such a nice idea of Dufford's – a special church of our own.'

Sean shuffled uncomfortably. 'Yes,' he agreed, 'it's a very romantic idea.' He glanced over his shoulder and saw Duff coming back with the parasol.

'Candy – it's none of my business. I don't know anything about marriage, but I know about training horses – you break them to the halter before you put the saddle on their backs.'

'I don't follow you.' Candy looked puzzled. 'What are you trying to say?'

'Nothing – just forget it. Here comes Duff.'

When they got back to the hotel there was a note at the reception desk for Sean. They went through into the main lounge and Candy went off to check the menu for dinner. Sean opened the envelope and read the note:

'I should like to meet you and Mr Charleywood to discuss a matter of some importance. I will be at my hotel after dinner this evening and hope that it will be convenient for you to call on me then. N. Hradsky.'

Sean passed the note across to Duff.

'What do you suppose he wants?'

'He has heard of your deadly skill as a Klabejas player. He wants to take lessons,' Duff answered.

'Shall we go?'

'Of course. You know I can't resist Norman's exhilarating company.'

It was a superb dinner. The crayfish, packed in ice, had come up from Capetown by express coach.

'Candy – Sean and I are going across to see Hradsky. We might be back a little late,' Duff told her when they were finished.

'As long as it's Hradsky,' Candy smiled at him. 'Don't get lost – I have my spies at the Opera House you know.'

'Shall we take the carriage?' Duff asked Sean, and Sean noticed that he hadn't laughed at Candy's joke.

'It's only two blocks, we might as well walk.'

They walked in silence. Sean felt his dinner settling down comfortably inside him, he belched softly and took another puff from his cigar. When they had almost reached the Grand National Hotel Duff spoke.

'Sean . . .' He stopped.

'Yes?' Sean prompted him.

'About Candy . . .' He stopped again.

'She's a fine girl,' Sean prompted again.

'Yes, she's a fine girl.'

'Is that all you wanted to say?'

'Well – oh! never mind. Let's go and see what Saul and David want.'

Max met them at the door of Hradsky's suite.

'Good evening, gentlemen, I am so pleased you could come.'

'Hello, Max.' Duff went past him to where Hradsky was standing in front of the fireplace.

'Norman, my dear fellow, how are you?'

Hradsky nodded an acknowledgement and Duff took hold of the lapels of Hradsky's coat and adjusted them carefully; then he picked an imaginary piece of fluff off his shoulder.

'You have a way with clothes, Norman. Don't you agree that Norman has a way with clothes, Sean? I know of no one else who can put on a twenty-guinea suit and make it look like a half-filled bag of oranges.' He patted Hradsky's arm affectionately. 'Yes, thank you – I will have a drink.' He went across to the liquor cabinet and poured one for himself. 'Now, what can you gentlemen do for me?'

Max glanced at Hradsky and Hradsky nodded.

'I will come to the point immediately,' said Max. 'Our two groups of companies are the largest on the Witwatersrand.'

Duff put his glass back on top of the cabinet and dropped his grin. Sean sat down in one of the armchairs, his expression also serious; both of them could guess what was coming.

'In the past,' continued Max, 'we have worked together on numerous occasions and we have both benefited from it. The next logical step, of course, is to combine our strength, pool our resources and go on together to new greatness.'

'I take it that you are proposing a merger?'

'Precisely, Mr Courtney, a merger of these two vast financial ventures.'

Sean leaned back in his chair and started to whistle softly. Duff picked up his glass again and took a sip.

'Well, gentlemen, what are your feelings on the subject?' asked Max.

'Have you got a proposal worked out, Max, something definite for us to think about?'

'Yes, Mr Courtney, I have.' Max went to the stinkwood desk which filled one corner of the room and picked up a sheaf of papers. He carried it across to Sean. Sean scanned through it.

'You've done quite a bit of work here, Max. It's going to take us a day or two to work out exactly what you are offering.'

'I appreciate that, Mr Courtney. Take as long as you

wish. We have worked for a month to draw up that scheme and I hope our labours have not been in vain. I think you will find our offer very generous.'

Sean stood up.

'We'll contact you again in the next few days, Max. Shall we go, Duff?'

Duff finished his drink.

'Goodnight, Max, look after Norman. He's very precious to us, you know.'

They went to their building on Eloff Street. Sean let them in through one of the side doors, lit the lamps in his office and Duff pulled up an extra chair to the desk. By two o'clock the following morning they understood the essentials of Hradsky's offer. Sean stood up and went to open one of the windows, for the room was thick with cigar smoke. He came back and flopped onto the couch, arranged a cushion behind his head and looked at Duff.

'Let's hear what you've got to say.'

Duff tapped his teeth with a pencil while he arranged his words.

'Let's decide first if we want to join with him.'

'If he makes it worth our while, we do,' Sean answered.

'I agree with you – but only if he makes it worth our while.' Duff laid back in his chair. 'Now the next point. Tell me, laddie, what is the first thing that strikes you about this scheme of Norman's?'

'We get nice-sounding titles and fat cash payments and Hradsky gets control,' Sean answered.

'You have laid your finger on the heart of it – Norman wants control. More than money, Norman wants control, so that he can sit at the top of the pile, look down on everyone else and say, "All right, you bastards, what if I do stutter?"'

Duff stood up, he walked round the desk and stopped in front of Sean's couch.

'Now for my next question. Do we give him control?'

'If he pays our price, then we give him control,' Sean answered. Duff turned away and went across to the open window.

'You know I rather like the feeling of being top man myself,' he said thoughtfully.

'Listen, Duff, we came here to make money. If we go in with Hradsky we'll make more,' Sean said.

'Laddie, we've got so much now that we could fill this room waist deep in sovereigns. We've got more than we'll ever be able to spend and I like being top man.'

'Hradsky's more powerful than we are – let's face up to that. He's got his diamond interests as well, so you're not top man even now. If we join him you still won't be top man but you'll be a damn sight richer.'

'Unassailable logic,' Duff nodded. 'I agree with you then. Hradsky gets control but he pays for it; we'll put him through the wringer until he's dry.'

Sean swung his legs off the couch. 'Agreed – now let's take this scheme of his by the throat, tear it to pieces and build it up again to suit ourselves.'

Duff looked at his watch. 'It's after two o'clock. We'll leave it now and start on it when we're fresh in the morning.'

They had their lunch brought down to the office the next day, and ate it at the desk. Johnson, who had been sent up to the Stock Exchange with instructions to keep an eye on prices and call them immediately if anything out of the ordinary happened, reported back after high change.

'It's been as quiet as a graveyard all day, sir, there's all sorts of rumours flying about. Seems someone saw the lights burning in this office at two o'clock this morning. Then when you didn't come to the Exchange but sent me instead – well, I can tell you, sir, there were a lot of questions asked.' Johnson hesitated, then his curiosity got the better of him.

'Can I help you at all, sir?' He started sidling across towards the desk.

'I think we can manage on our own, Johnson. Shut the door as you go out, please.'

At half-past seven they decided it was enough for one day and they went back to the hotel. As they walked into the lobby Sean saw Trevor Heyns disappear into the lounge and heard his voice.

'Here they are!'

Almost immediately Trevor appeared again with his brother.

'Hello, boys.' Jock appeared surprised to see them. 'What are you doing here?'

'We live here,' said Duff.

'Oh, yes, of course. Well, come and have a drink with us.' Jock smiled expansively.

'And then you can pump us and find out what we've been doing all day,' Duff suggested.

Jock looked embarrassed. 'I don't know what you mean, I just thought we'd have a drink together, that's all.'

'Thanks all the same, Jock, we've had a hard day. I think we'll just go on up to bed,' Duff said. They were halfway across the lobby before Duff turned back to where the two brothers were standing.

'I'll tell you boys something,' he said in a stage whisper. 'This is really big – it's so big it takes a while for the mind to grasp it. When you two realize that it's been right there under your noses all the time, you're going to kick yourselves.'

They left the Heyns brothers in the lobby staring after them and went up the stairs.

'That wasn't very kind,' Sean laughed. 'They won't sleep for a week.'

W hen neither Sean nor Duff put in an appearance at the Exchange the next morning, the rumours surged round the members' lounge and the prices started running amok. Reliable information that Sean and Duff had struck a rich new goldfield across the vaal sent the prices up like rocketing snipe; then twenty minutes later the denial came in and clipped fifteen shillings a share off the Courtney-Charleywood stock. Johnson ran backwards and forwards between the office and the Exchange all morning. By eleven he was so tired he could hardly talk.

'Don't worry any more, Johnson,' Sean told him. 'Here's a sovereign – go down to the Grand National and buy yourself a drink, you've had a hard morning.'

One of Jock Heyns's men, who had been detailed off to watch the Courtney-Charleywood offices, followed Johnson down to the Grand National and heard him place his order with the barman. He raced back to the Exchange and reported to Jock.

'Their head clerk has just gone and ordered himself a bottle of French champagne,' he panted.

'Good God!' Jock nearly jumped out of his chair and beside him Trevor signalled frantically for his clerk.

'Buy,' he whispered in the man's ear. 'Buy every scrap of their script you can lay your hands on.'

Across the lounge Hradsky settled down a little further in his chair; he clasped his hands contentedly over the front of his stomach and he very nearly smiled.

By midnight Sean and Duff had completed their counter-proposal to Hradsky's offer.

'How do you think Norman will react to it?' asked Sean.

'I hope his heart is strong enough to stand the shock,'

Duff grinned. 'The only reason that his jaw won't hit the floor is that his great gut will be in the way.'

'Shall we go down to his hotel now and show him?' suggested Sean.

'Laddie, laddie.' Duff shook his head sorrowfully. 'After all the time I've spent on your education, and you still haven't learned.'

'What do we do then?'

'We send for him, laddie, we make him come to us. We play him on the home ground.'

'How does that help?' Sean asked.

'It gives us an advantage immediately – it makes him remember that he's the one doing the asking.'

Hradsky came down to their office at ten o'clock the next morning; he came in state driven behind a four-in-hand and attended by Max and two secretaries. Johnson met them at the front door and ushered them into Sean's office.

'Norman, dear old Norman, I'm delighted to see you,' Duff greeted him and, fully aware of the fact that Hradsky never smoked, Duff thrust a cheroot between his lips. When everyone was seated Sean opened the meeting.

'Gentlemen, we have spent some time examining your proposition and in the main we find it just, fair and equitable.'

'Hear, hear,' Duff agreed politely.

'At the outset I want to make it quite clear,' Sean went on, 'that Mr Charleywood and myself feel strongly that the union of our two ventures is desirable – nay! essential. If you will forgive the quotation, "*ex unitate vires*".'

'Hear, hear – hear, hear.' Duff lit his cigar.

'As I was saying, we have examined your proposition and we accept it readily and happily, with the exception of a few minor details which we have listed.' Sean picked up the thick pile of paper. 'Perhaps you would care to glance

316

through it and then we can proceed to the drawing-up of a formal agreement.'

Max accepted the sheaf gingerly. 'If you want privacy, Mr Charleywood's office which adjoins this room is at your disposal.'

Hradsky took his band next door and an hour later when he led them back again they looked like a party of pallbearers. Max was on the verge of tears, he cleared the lump from his throat.

'I think we should examine each item separately,' he said sadly, and three days later they shook hands on the deal.

Duff poured the drinks and gave each man a glass. 'To the new company, Central Rand Consolidated. It has been a long confinement, gentlemen, but I think we have given birth to a child of which we can be proud.'

Hradsky had control, but it had cost him dearly.

Central Rand Consolidated had its christening party on the main floor of the Johannesburg Stock Exchange; ten per cent of the shares were put out for sale to the public. Before the day's dealings began the crowd had overflowed the Stock Exchange building and jammed in the street for a block in each direction. The President of the Exchange read the prospectus of Central Rand Consolidated; in the cathedral hush his every word carried clearly to the members' lounge. The bell rang and still the hush persisted. Hradsky's authorized clerk broke the silence timidly. 'I sell C.R.C.'s.'

It was nearly a massacre; two hundred men were trying to buy shares from him simultaneously. First his jacket and then his shirt disintegrated beneath the clutching hands; he lost his spectacles, crushed to powdered glass beneath the trampling feet. Ten minutes later he managed to fight his way out of the crowd and report to his masters, 'I was able to sell them, gentlemen.'

Sean and Duff laughed. They had reason to laugh, for in

317

those ten minutes their thirty per cent holding in C.R.C. had appreciated in value by half a million pounds.

– 24 –

That year Christmas dinner at Candy's Hotel was considerably better than it had been five years previously. Seventy-five people sat down to it at one table and by three o'clock, when it ended, only half of them were able to stand up. Sean used the banisters to get up the stairs and at the top he told Candy and Duff solemnly, 'I love you – I love you both desperately – but now I must sleep.' He left them and set off down the corridor bouncing against the walls like a trick billiard shot until he ricocheted through the door into his suite.

'You'd better make sure he's all right, Dufford.'

'A case of the blind drunk leading the blind drunk,' said Duff indistinctly, and also employing the wall to wall route followed Sean down the corridor. Sean was sitting on the edge of his bed wrestling with one of his boots.

'What you trying to do, laddie, break your ankle?'

Sean looked up and smiled beatifically. 'Come in, come in – all four of you. Have a drink.'

'Thanks, I brought my own.'

Duff closed the door behind him like a conspirator and produced a bottle from under his coat. 'She didn't see me – she didn't know her little Dufford had a big beautiful bottle in his inside pocket.'

'Would you mind helping me with this damn boot?' Sean asked.

'That's a very good question,' said Duff seriously as he set a course across the room for one of the armchairs. 'I'm glad you asked it.' He reached the chair and dropped into it. 'The answer, of course, is, Yes! I would mind.'

318

Sean let his foot drop and lay back on the bed.

'Laddie, I want to talk to you,' Duff said.

'Talk's free – help yourself.'

'Sean, what do you think of Candy?'

'Lovely pair of titties,' Sean opined.

'Sure, but a man cannot live by titties alone.'

'No, but I suppose she's also got the other basic equipment,' Sean said drowsily.

'Laddie, I'm being serious now – I want your help. Do you think I am doing the right thing – this marriage business, I mean.'

'Don't know much about marriage.' Sean rolled over on his face.

'She's calling me Dufford already – did you notice that, laddie? That's an omen, that's an omen of the most frightful portent. Did you notice, hey?' Duff waited a second for an answer which he didn't receive. 'That's what the other one used to call me. "Dufford," she'd say – I can hear it now – "Dufford, you're a pig".'

Duff looked hard at the bed. 'Are you still with me?'

No answer.

'Sean, laddie, I need your help.'

Sean snored softly.

'Oh, you drunken oaf,' said Duff miserably.

– 25 –

Xanadu was finished by the end of January and the wedding was set for the twentieth of February. Duff sent the Commandant and the entire police force of Johannesburg an invitation: in return they put a twenty-four hour a day guard on the ballroom of Xanadu where the wedding gifts were laid out on long trestle tables. Sean drove up with Duff and Candy on the afternoon of the tenth, as Duff put it, to make the latest count of the booty. Sean gave the constable on duty a cigar and then they went through into the ballroom.

'Look, oh look,' squealed Candy. 'There's a whole lot of new presents!'

'This one's from Jock and Trevor.' Sean read the card.

'Open quickly, please, Dufford, let's see what they've given us.'

Duff prised the lid off the case and Sean whistled softly.

'A solid gold dinner service,' gasped Candy. She picked up one of the plates and hugged it to her chest. 'Oh, I just don't know what to say.'

Sean examined the other boxes. 'Hey, Duff, this one will make you specially happy – "Best wishes, N. Hradsky".'

'This I must see,' said Duff with the first enthusiasm he had shown in a month. He unwrapped the parcel.

'A dozen of them!' Duff hooted gleefully. 'Norman, you priceless little Israelite, a whole dozen dish towels.'

'It's the thought that counts,' laughed Sean.

'Dear old Norman, how it must have hurt him to shell out for them! I'll have him autograph them and I'll frame them and hang them in the front hall.'

They left Candy to arrange the presents and they went out into the garden.

'Have you got this mock priest organized?' asked Duff.

'Yes, he's at a hotel in Pretoria. He's in training now – he'll be able to rattle through the service like an old hand when the time comes.'

'You don't think that faking it is just as bad as doing it properly?' asked Duff dubiously.

'It's a hell of a time to think of that now,' said Sean.

'Yes, I suppose it is.'

'Where are you going for the honeymoon?' Sean asked.

'We'll coach down to Capetown and take the mail boat

to London, then a month or so on the Continent. Be back here about June.'

'You should have a good time.'

'Why don't you get married as well?'

'What for?' Sean looked surprised.

'Well, don't you feel as though you're letting the old firm down a bit – me going into this alone?'

'No,' said Sean. 'Anyway, who is there to marry?'

'What about that lass you brought to the races last Saturday; she's a lovely piece of work.'

Sean raised an eyebrow. 'Did you hear her giggle?'

'Yes, I did,' admitted Duff. 'You couldn't very well miss it.'

'Can you imagine that giggle coming at you across the breakfast table?' Sean asked.

Duff shuddered. 'Yes, I see your point. But as soon as we get back I'll have Candy start picking you out a suitable female.'

'I've got a better idea, you let Candy run your life and I'll run my own.'

'That, laddie, is what I'm very much afraid is going to happen.'

Hradsky reluctantly agreed that the activities of the group – the mines, the workshops, the transport companies, all of them – should be suspended on the twentieth to allow their employees to attend Duff's nuptials. This meant that half the businesses on the Witwatersrand would shut down for the day. Consequently, most of the independent companies decided to close as well. On the eighteenth the wagons carrying the food and liquor started caravanning up the hill to Xanadu. Sean, in a burst of benevolence, that night invited the entire company from the Opera House to the wedding. He remembered it vaguely the next morning and went down to cancel the invitation but Blue Bessie told him that most of the girls had already gone into town to buy new dresses.

'The hell with it then – let them come. I just hope Candy doesn't guess who they are, that's all.'

On the night of the nineteenth Candy gave them the use of the dining-room and all the downstairs lounges of the Hotel for Duff's bachelor party. Francois arrived with a masterpiece made up in the mine workshops – an enormous ball and chain. This was formally locked onto Duff's leg and the party began.

Afterwards there was a school of thought that maintained that the building contractor commissioned to repair the damage to the Hotel was a bandit and that the bill for just under a thousand pounds that he presented was nothing short of robbery. However, none of them could deny that the Bok-Bok game in the dining-room, played by a hundred men, had done a certain amount of damage to the furniture and fittings; nor that the chandelier had not been able to support Mr Courtney's weight and on the third swing had come adrift from the ceiling and knocked a moderately large hole through the floor. Neither did anyone dispute the fact that after Jock Heyns had tried unsuccessfully for half an hour to shoot a glass off the top of his brother's head with champagne corks, the resulting ankle-deep lake of wine in the one lounge made it necessary for the floor to be relaid. Nevertheless they felt that a thousand was a little bit steep. On one point, however, everyone agreed – it was a memorable party.

At the beginning Sean was worried that Duff's heart wasn't in it for Duff stood by the bar with the metal ball under one arm listening to the lewd comments with a lopsided grin fixed on his face. After seven or eight drinks Sean stopped worrying about him and went off to have his way with the chandelier. At midnight Duff talked Francois into releasing him from his chains and he slipped out of the room. No one – least of all Sean – noticed him go.

Sean could never remember how he got up to bed that night but next morning he was tactfully awakened by a waiter with a coffee tray and a note.

'What time is it?' asked Sean as he unfolded the note.

'Eight o'clock, baas.'

'No need to shout,' muttered Sean. His eyes focused with difficulty for the pain in his head was pushing them out of their sockets.

'Dear Best Man,
     This serves as a reminder that you and Duff have an
     appointment at eleven o'clock. I am relying on you to
     get him there, whole or in pieces. Love Candy.'

The brandy fumes in the back of his throat tasted like chloroform, he washed them out with coffee and lit a cigar which started him coughing, and every cough nearly took the top off his head. He stubbed out the cigar and went to the bathroom. Half an hour later he felt strong enough to wake Duff. He went across the sitting-room and pushed open Duff's door; the curtains in the room were still drawn. He pulled them open and was nearly blinded by the sunlight that poured in through them. He turned to the bed and frowned with surprise. He walked slowly across and sat on the edge of it.

'He must have slept in Candy's room,' Sean muttered as he looked at the unused pillows and neatly tucked blankets. It took a few seconds for him to find the fault in his reasoning.

'Then why did she write that note?' He stood up, feeling the first twinge of alarm. A picture of Duff, drunk and helpless lying out in the yard or knocked over the head by one of the busy Johannesburg footpads came very clearly to mind. He ran across the bedroom and into the sitting-room. Halfway to the door he saw the envelope propped up on the mantelpiece and he took it down.

'What is this, a meeting of the authors' guild?' he muttered. 'The place is thick with letters.'

The paper crackled as he opened it and he recognized Duff's back sloping hand.

'The first the worst, the second the same. I'm not going through with it. You're the best man so make my excuses to all the nice people. I'll be back when the dust has settled a little. D.'

Sean sat down in one of the armchairs, he read through it twice more. Then he exploded.

'Damn you, Charleywood – "make my excuses". You craven bastard. Walk out and leave me to sweep up the mess.'

He rushed across the room with his dressing-gown flapping furiously round his legs. 'You'll make your own damned excuses – even if I have to drag you back on the end of a rope.'

Sean ran down the back stairs. Mbejane was in the stable yard talking to three of the grooms.

'Where is Nkosi Duff?' Sean roared.

They stared at him blankly.

'Where is he?' Sean's beard bristled.

'The baas took a horse and went for a ride,' answered one of the grooms nervously.

'When?' bellowed Sean.

'In the night – perhaps seven, eight hours ago. He should be back soon.'

Sean stared at the groom, breathing heavily. 'Which way did he go?'

'Baas, he did not say.'

Eight hours ago – he could be fifty miles away by now. Sean turned and went back to his room. He threw himself on the bed and poured another cup of coffee.

'This is going to break her up badly—' He imagined the tears and the chaos of undisciplined grief.

'Oh, hell – damn you to hell, Charleywood.' He sipped the coffee and thought about going as well – taking a horse and getting as far away as possible. 'It's no mess of my making – I want no part of it.' He finished the coffee and started dressing. He looked in the mirror to comb his hair and saw Candy standing alone in the chapel, waiting while the silence turned to murmuring and then to laughter.

'Charleywood, you pig,' Sean scowled. 'I can't let her go up there – it'll be bad enough without that. I'll have to tell her.'

He picked up his watch from the dressing-table, it was past nine.

'Damn you, Charleywood.'

He went down the passage and stopped outside Candy's door. He could hear women's voices inside and he knocked before he went in. There were two of Candy's friends and the coloured girl Martha. They stared at him.

'Where's Candy?'

'In the bedroom – but you mustn't go in. It's bad luck.'

'It's the worst bloody luck in the world,' agreed Sean. He knocked on the bedroom door.

'Who is it?'

'Sean.'

'You can't come in – what do you want?'

'Are you decent?'

'Yes, but you mustn't come in.'

He opened the door and looked in on a confusion of squealing females.

'Get out of here' – he said harshly – 'I have to speak to Candy alone.'

They fled and Sean closed the door behind them. Candy was in a dressing-gown. Her face was quick with anticipation; her hair was pulled back and hung shiny and soft. She was beautiful, Sean realized. He looked at the frothy pile of her wedding-dress on the bed.

'Candy, bad news – I'm afraid. Can you take it?' He spoke almost roughly – hating it, hating every second of it.

He saw the bloom on her face wither until her expression was dead – blank and dead as a statue.

'He's gone,' said Sean. 'He's run out on you.'

Candy picked up a brush from her dressing-table and started stroking it listlessly through her hair. It was very quiet in the room.

'I'm sorry, Candy.'

She nodded without looking at him; instead she was looking down the lonely corridor of the future. It was worse than tears would have been, that silent acceptance. Sean scratched the side of his nose – hating it.

'I'm sorry – I wish I could do something about it.' He turned to the door.

'Sean, thank you for coming and telling me.' There was no emotion in her voice; like her face it was dead.

'That's all right,' Sean said gruffly.

He rode up to Xanadu. There were people clustered about the marquees on the lawn; by the quality of their laughter he could tell they were drinking already. The sun was bright and as yet not too hot, the band was playing from the wide veranda of the mansion, the women's dresses were gay against the green of the lawns. 'Gala day' fluttered the flags above the tents. 'Gala day' shouted the laughter.

Sean rode up the drive, lifting his hand in brief acknowledgement of the greetings that were shouted to him. From

326

the vantage point of his horse's back he spotted Francois and Martin Curtis, glasses in hand, standing near the house talking to two of the Opera girls. He gave his horse to one of the native grooms and strode across towards them.

'Hello, boss,' called Curtis. 'Why so glum – you're not the one getting married.' They all laughed.

'Francois, Martin, come with me please.'

'What's the trouble, Mr Courtney?' Francois asked as he led them aside.

'The party's over,' Sean said grimly. 'There'll be no wedding.'

They gaped at him.

'Go around and tell everybody. Tell them they'll get their presents back.'

He turned to leave them.

'What's happened, boss?' Curtis asked.

'Just tell them that Candy and Duff changed their minds.'

'Do you want us to send them home?'

Sean hesitated. 'Oh, the hell with it – let them stay – let them all get sick drunk. Just tell them there'll be no wedding.'

He went up to the house. He found the pseudo-priest waiting nervously in the downstairs study. The man's Adam's apple had been rubbed raw by the starch-stiff dog collar.

'We won't need you,' Sean told him.

He took out his cheque book, sat down at the desk and filled in a cheque form.

'That's for your trouble. Now get out of town.'

'Thank you, Mr Courtney, thank you very much.' The man looked mightily relieved; he started for the door.

'My friend,' Sean stopped him. 'If you ever breathe a word about what we planned to do today, I'll kill you. Do I make myself clear?'

Sean went through to the ballroom, he slipped a small stack of sovereigns into the constable's hand.

'Get all these people out of here.' He gestured with his head at the crowds that were wandering among the tables looking at the gifts. 'Then lock the doors.'

He found the chef in the kitchen. 'Take all this food outside – give it to them now. Then lock up the kitchens.'

He went round the house closing the doors and drawing the curtains. When he walked into the study there was a couple on the big leather couch and the man's hand was under the girl's skirts; she was giggling.

'This isn't a whore house,' Sean shouted at them and they left hurriedly. He sank into one of the chairs. He could hear the voices and the laughter from outside on the lawn, the band was playing a Strauss waltz. It irritated him and he scowled at the marble fireplace. His head was aching again and the skin of his face felt dry and tight from the night's debauch.

'What a mess – what a bloody mess,' he said aloud. After an hour he went out and found his horse. He rode out along the Pretoria Road until he had passed the last houses, then he turned off into the veld. He cantered into the sea of grass with his hat pushed back on his head so the sun and the wind could find his face. He sat relaxed and loose in the saddle and let his horse pick its own way. In the late afternoon he came back to Johannesburg and left his horse with Mbejane in the stableyard. He felt better; the exercise and the fresh air had cleared his head and helped him to see things in truer perspective. He ran himself a deep hot bath, climbed into it and while he soaked the last of his anger at Duff smoothed out. He had control of himself again. He got out of the bath and towelled, then he slipped on his gown and went through to the bedroom. Candy was sitting on his bed.

'Hello, Sean.' She smiled at him, a brittle smile. Her hair was a little tangled now, her face was pale and unrouged. She had not changed from the dressing-gown he had seen her in that morning.

'Hello, Candy.' He picked up the cut-glass bottle of bay rum and rubbed some into his hair and beard.

'You don't mind me coming to see you, do you?'

'No, of course not.' He started combing his hair. 'I was about to come and see you myself.'

She drew her legs up under her in the double-jointed manner of women that is impossible for a man to copy.

'Can I have a drink, please?'

'I'm sorry – I thought you never touched the stuff.'

'Oh, today is special.' She laughed too gaily. 'It's my wedding day, you know.'

He poured the brandy without looking at her. He hated this suffering and he felt his anger at Duff coming back strongly. Candy took the drink and sipped it. She pulled a face. 'It tastes awful.'

'It'll do you good.'

'To the bride,' she said and drank it down quickly.

'Another one?' asked Sean.

'No thanks.' She stood up and went across to the window. 'It's getting dark now – I hate the darkness. Darkness distorts things so; what is bad in the daylight is unbearable at night.'

'I'm sorry, Candy, I wish I could help you.'

She whirled and came to him, her arms circled tight round his neck and her face pale and frightened pressed to his chest.

'Oh, Sean, please hold me – I'm so afraid.'

He held her awkwardly.

'I don't want to think about it. Not now, not now in the darkness,' she whispered. 'Please help me. Please help me not to think about it.'

329

'I'll stay with you. Don't get yourself upset. Come and sit down. I'll get you another drink.'

'No, no,' she clung to him desperately. 'I don't want to be alone. I don't want to think. Please help me.'

'I can't help you – I'll stay with you but that's all I can do.' Anger and pity mixed together in Sean like charcoal and saltpetre; his fingers tightened hard on her shoulders, digging into the flesh until they met bone.

'Yes, hurt me. That way I'll forget for a while. Take me to the bed and hurt me, Sean, hurt me deep.'

Sean caught his breath. 'You don't know what you're saying, that's crazy talk.'

'It's what I want – to forget for a little. Please, Sean, please.'

'I can't do that, Candy, Duff's my friend.'

'He's finished with me and I with him. I'm your friend too. Oh, God, I'm so alone. Don't you leave me too. Help me, Sean, please help me.'

Sean felt his anger slide down from his chest and flare up, cobra-headed, from his thighs. She felt it also.

'Yes, oh please, yes.'

He picked her up and carried her to the bed. He stood over her while he tore off his gown. She moved on the bed, shedding her clothing and spreading herself to meet him, to take him in and let him fill the emptiness. He covered her quickly bayoneting through the soft veil and into the warmth of her body. There was no desire in it, it was cruel and hard drawn out to the frontiers of endurance. For him an expression of anger and pity; for her an act of renunciation. Once was not enough. Again and yet again he took her, until there were brown smudges on the bedclothes from his bleeding back, until her body ached and they lay entwined, wet and tired from the fury of it. In the quiescence of after-passion Sean spoke softly. 'It didn't help, did it?'

'Yes, it did.' Physical exhaustion had weakened the barriers that held back her grief. Still holding onto him, she started to cry.

A street lamp outside the room threw a silver square of light on the ceiling. Sean laid on his back and watched it, listening to Candy's sobs. He recognized the moment they reached their climax and followed their decline into silence. They slept then and later before the day woke together as if by arrangement.

'You are the only one who can help him now,' Candy said.

'Help him do what?' asked Sean.

'Find what he is looking for. Peace, himself – whatever you want to call it. He's lost, you know, Sean. He's lost and lonely, almost as lonely as I am. I could have helped him, I'm sure I could.'

'Duff lost?' Sean asked cynically. 'You must be mad!'

'Don't be so blind, Sean, don't be misled by the big talk and the grand manner. Look at the other things.'

'Like what?' asked Sean.

She didn't answer for a while. 'He hated his father, you know.'

'I guessed as much from the little he told me.'

'The way he revolts at any discipline. His attitude to Hradsky, to women, to life. Think about it, Sean, and then tell me if he acts like a happy man.'

'Hradsky did him a disservice once – he just doesn't like him,' Sean defended Duff.

'Oh, no – it's much deeper than that. In a way Hradsky is an image of his father. He's so broken up inside, Sean, that's why he clings to you. You can help him.'

Sean laughed outright. 'Candy, my dear, we like each other that's all, there are no deep and dark motives in our friendship. Don't you start getting jealous of me now.'

Candy sat up and the blankets slipped down to her waist.

She leaned towards Sean and her breasts swung forward, heavy, round and silver-white in the half light.

'There's a strength in you, Sean, a kind of solid sureness in you that you haven't discovered yet. Duff has recognized it and so will other unhappy people. He needs you, he needs you very badly. Look after him for me, help him to find what he seeks.'

'Nonsense, Candy,' Sean muttered with embarrassment.

'Promise me you'll help him.'

'It's time you went back to your room,' Sean told her. 'People will start talking.'

'Promise me, Sean.'

'All right, I promise.'

Candy slipped out of the bed. She dressed quickly. 'Thank you, Sean, goodnight.'

– 26 –

For Sean, Johannesburg was poorer without Duff: the streets were not so busy, the Rand Club was drearier and the thrills at the Stock Exchange not so intense. However, there was work to do; his share and Duff's as well.

It was late every evening when the conferences with Hradsky and Max ended and he went back to the Hotel. In the reaction from the day's tension, when his brain was numb and his eyes burned, there was little energy to spare for regret. Yet he was lonely. He went to the Opera House and drank champagne with the crowd there. One of the girls did the Can-Can on the big table in the centre of the room and when she stopped in front of Sean and Trevor Heyns, with her forehead touching her knees and her petticoats hanging forward over her shoulders, Sean let Trevor whip her pants down – a week before he would have punched Trevor in the nose rather than concede the honour. It wasn't so much fun any more. He went home early.

The following Saturday noon Curtis and Francois came into the office for the weekly progress meeting. When they had finished and Hradsky had left, Sean suggested, 'Come along with me, we'll go and have a pot or twelve at the Grand National Bar, baptize the weekend so to speak.'

Curtis and Francois fidgeted in their chairs.

'We had arranged to meet some of the other boys down at the Bright Angels, boss.'

'That's fine, I'll come along with you,' said Sean eagerly, the prospect of being with ordinary men again was suddenly very attractive to him. He felt sickened of the company of those who shook his hand and smiled at him while they waited for a chance to wipe him off the board. It would be good to go along with these two and talk mining and not stocks and shares, to laugh with men who didn't give a damn if C.R.C.'s hit sixty shillings on Monday. He'd get a little drunk with Francois and Curtis; later on perhaps he'd have a fight – an honest, snorting, stand-up fight. God, yes, it would be good to be with men who were clean inside – even if there was dirt under their nails and the armpits of their shirts were stained with sweat.

Curtis glanced quickly at Francois. 'There'll be just a crowd of roughnecks down there, boss, all the diggers come in on a Saturday.'

'That's fine,' said Sean. 'Let's go.'

He stood up and buttoned his dove-grey coat; the lapels were edged in black watered silk and matched the black pearl pin in his tie. He picked up his cane from the desk.

'Come on – let's get moving.'

They ran into the noise from the Bright Angels a block before they reached the building. Sean grinned and quickened his step like an old gun dog with the scent of the bird in its nostrils again. Francois and Curtis hurried along on either side of him. There was a big digger standing on the bar counter. Sean recognized him as one of his men from the Little Sister Mine; the man's body was tilted back to balance the weight of the demijohn he held to his lips and his throat jerked regularly as he swallowed. The crowd around his feet were chanting:

'Drink it, down, down, down, down.'

The digger finished, he threw the bottle against the far wall and belched like an air-locked geyser. He bowed to acknowledge the applause and then he caught sight of Sean standing in the doorway. He wiped his mouth guiltily with the back of his hand and jumped down off the counter. The other men in the crowd turned and saw Sean and the noise tapered off. They spread out along the bar in silence. Sean led Francois and Curtis into the room. He placed a pile of sovereigns on the counter.

'Set them up, barman, take the orders. Today is Saturday and it's time to tie the dog loose.'

'Cheers, Mr Courtney.'

'Good luck, sir.'

'*Gezondheid*, Mr Courtney.'

Their voices were subdued with respect.

'Drink up, men, there's plenty more where that came from.' Sean stood with Francois and Curtis at the bar. They laughed at his jokes. His voice was loud with good fellowship and his face flushed with happiness. He bought more drinks. After a while his bladder started making its presence felt and he went through the back door into the washrooms. There were men talking in there; he stopped before he rounded the edge of the screen into the room. '. . . what's he want to come here for, hey? This isn't the mucking Rand Club.'

'Shh! He'll hear you, man, do you want to lose your job?'

'I don't give a damn. Who does he think he is – "Drink up, boys, there's plenty more where that came from – I'm

334

the boss, boys, do as you're told, boys, kiss my arse, boys.'"
Sean stood paralysed.

'Pipe down, Frank, he'll go just now.'

'The sooner the better, say I, the big dandy bastard with his ten-guinea boots and gold cane. Let him go back where he belongs.'

'You're drunk, man, don't talk so loud.'

'Sure I'm drunk, drunk enough to go in there and tell him to his face . . .'

Sean backed out through the door and walked slowly across the bar to François and Curtis.

'I hope you'll excuse me; I've just remembered there's something I've got to do this afternoon.'

'That's too bad, boss.' Curtis looked relieved. 'Perhaps some other time, hey?'

'Yes, perhaps some other time.'

They were pleased to see him when he went up to the Rand Club. Three men nearly fought one another to buy him a drink.

– 27 –

He had dinner with Candy that night and over the liqueurs he told her about it. She listened without interruption until he finished.

'They didn't want me there, I don't see what I've done to them that they should dislike me that way.'

'And it worries you?' she asked.

'Yes, it worries me. I've never had people feel like that towards me before.'

'I'm glad it worries you.' She smiled gently at him. 'One day you're going to grow into quite a nice person.'

'But why do they hate me?' Sean followed his original line of thought.

'They're jealous of you – you say this man said, "ten-guinea boots and gold cane" – that is what's behind it. You're different from them now, you're rich. You can't expect them to accept that.'

'But I've never done anything to them,' he protested.

'You don't have to. One thing I've found in this life – for everything you get you have to pay a price. This is part of the payment you have to make for success.'

'Hell, I wish Duff was here,' said Sean.

'Then Duff would explain to you that it doesn't matter, wouldn't he?' said Candy. '"Who gives a damn for them, laddie, the unwashed herd? We can do without them,"' she mimicked. Sean scratched the side of his nose and looked down at the table.

'Please, Sean, don't ever let Duff teach you that people don't matter. He doesn't believe it himself – but he's so convincing. People are important. They are more important than gold or places or – or anything.'

Sean looked up at her. 'I realized that once; when I was trapped in the Candy Deep. I saw it very clearly then in the darkness and the mud. I made a resolution.' He grinned sheepishly. 'I told myself I'd never hurt anyone again if I could help it. I really meant it, Candy. I felt it so strongly at the time – but, but . . .'

'Yes, I think I understand. That's a big resolution to make and a much bigger one to keep. I don't think any single experience is enough to change a person's way of thinking. It's like building a wall brick by brick. You add to it a little at a time until at last it's finished. I've told you before, Sean, that you have a strength in you. I think one day you'll finish building your wall – and when you do, it will have no weak spots.'

The next Tuesday Sean rode up to Xanadu for the first time since Duff had left. Johnson and four of the clerks from the office were at work in the ballroom, packing and labelling the presents.

'Nearly finished, Johnson?'

'Just about, Mr Courtney, I'll send a couple of wagons up tomorrow morning to fetch this lot.'

'Yes, do that. I don't want them lying around here any longer.'

He went up the marble staircase and stood on the top landing. The house had a dead feeling to it: new and sterile, it was waiting for people to come into it and bring it to life. He went down the corridor, stopping to look at the paintings that Candy had chosen. They were oils in soft pastels, woman's colours.

'We can do without these – I'll get some with fire in them, scarlets and blacks and bright blues.'

He pushed open the door to his own bedroom. This was better: vivid Persian rugs on the floor, walls panelled in dark satiny wood and a bed like a polo field. He lay on the bed and looked up at the scrolled ornate plaster ceiling.

'I wish Duff were back – we can do some real living in this house.' He went downstairs again.

Johnson was waiting at the foot of the stairs. 'All finished, sir.'

'Good man! Off you go, then.'

He went through into the study and walked across to the gun rack. He took down a Purdey shotgun, carried it to the french windows and looked at it in the light. His nostrils flared a little at the nostalgic smell of gun oil. He brought the gun up to his shoulder, felt the true exciting balance of it and enjoyed it. He swung the barrels in an arc across the room, following the flight of an imaginary bird, and suddenly Duff's face was in his sights. Sean was taken so by surprise that he stood with the gun trained at Duff's head.

'Don't shoot, I'll come quietly,' said Duff solemnly.

Sean lowered the shotgun and carried it back to the rack.

'Hello.'

'Hello,' Duff answered, still standing in the doorway. Sean made a pretence of fitting the gun into the rack with his back to Duff.

'How are you, laddie?'

'Fine! Fine!'

'How's everybody else?'

'To whom do you refer, in particular?' Sean asked.

'Candy, for one.'

Sean considered the question. 'Well, you could have damaged her more by feeding her into a stamp mill.'

'Bad, hey?'

'Bad,' agreed Sean.

They stood in silence for a while.

'I take it that you are not very well disposed towards me either,' Duff said at last.

Sean shrugged his shoulders and moved across to the fireplace.

'Dufford, you're a pig,' he said conversationally.

Duff winced. 'Well, it was nice knowing you, laddie. I suppose from here on our paths diverge?'

'Don't drivel, Duff, you're wasting time. Pour the drinks and then you can tell me what it feels like being a pig. Also I want to discuss with you those paintings Candy has plastered along the upstairs corridor. I don't know whether to give them away or burn them.'

Duff straightened up from leaning against the door jamb; he tried to stop the relief showing on his face but Sean went on quickly, 'Before we close the lid on the subject and bury it, I want to tell you this. I don't like what you did. I can see why you did it, but I don't like it. That's my piece said. Have you got anything to add to it?'

'No,' said Duff.

'All right then. I think you'll find a bottle of Courvoisier right at the back of the cabinet behind the whisky decanter.'

Sean went down to Candy's Hotel that evening and found Candy in her office.

'He's back, Candy.'

'Oh!' Candy caught her breath. 'How is he, Sean?'

'A little chastened, but not much.'

'I didn't mean that – I meant is he well?'

'The same as ever. He had the grace to ask how you were,' said Sean.

'What did you tell him?' asked Candy.

Sean shrugged and sat down in the chair next to her desk. He looked at the tall stacks of sovereigns that Candy was counting.

'Is that last night's bar takings?' he asked, avoiding her question.

'Yes,' she answered absently.

'You're rich – will you marry me?' he smiled.

Candy stood up and walked across to the window.

'I suppose you two will be moving up to Xanadu now,' she said. Sean grunted and she went on quickly. 'The Heyns brothers will take over the Victoria rooms – they've spoken to me about it already, so don't worry about that. You'll have fun up there, it will be marvellous for you. I bet you'll have parties every night and crowds of people. I don't mind, I've gotten used to the idea now.'

Sean stood up and went to her, he took her gently by the elbow and turned her to face him. He gave her the silk handkerchief out of his top pocket to blow her nose.

'Do you want to see him again, Candy?'

She shook her head, not trusting her voice.

'I'll look after him like I promised.' He gave her a hug and turned to go.

'Sean,' she called after him. He looked back. 'You'll come to see me sometimes. We could have dinner and talk a little. You'll still be my friend, won't you?'

'Of course, Candy, of course, my dear.'

She smiled damply. 'If you pack your things and Duff's I'll have them sent up to Xanadu for you.'

– 29 –

Sean looked across the boardroom table at Duff, seeking his support. Duff blew a thick ring of cigar smoke. It spun and expanded like a ripple in a pond before it hit the table top and disintegrated. Duff wasn't going to back him up, Sean realized bitterly. They had argued half the previous night. He had hoped that Duff might still change his mind. Now he knew he wouldn't. He made one last appeal.

'They have asked for a ten per cent wage increase. I believe they need it – prices have soared in this town, but wages have remained the same. These men have wives and children, gentlemen, can't we take that into account?'

Duff blew another smoke ring and Hradsky pulled his watch from his pocket and looked at it pointedly. Max coughed and interrupted. 'I think we've been over that before, Mr Courtney. Could we put it to the vote now?'

Sean watched Hradsky's hand go up against him. He

didn't want to look at Duff. He didn't want to see him vote with Hradsky, but he forced himself to turn his head. Duff's hands were on the table in front of him. He blew another smoke ring and watched it hit the table top.

'Those in favour of the motion?' asked Max, and Duff and Sean raised their right hands together. Sean realized then how much it would have meant if Duff had voted against him. Duff winked at him and he couldn't help grinning.

'That is thirty votes for, and sixty against,' declared Max. 'Therefore Mr Courtney's motion falls to the ground. I will inform the Mineworkers' Union of the decision. Now is there any other business before we close the meeting?'

Sean walked with Duff back to his own office.

'The only reason I supported you was because I knew Hradsky would win anyway,' said Duff pleasantly. Sean snorted.

'He's right, of course,' Duff went on unperturbed as he held open the door to Sean's office. 'A ten per cent wage increase would jump the group working costs up ten thousand a month.'

Sean kicked the door closed behind them and didn't answer.

'For God's sake, Sean, don't carry this goodwill-towards-men attitude to absurdity. Hradsky's right – Kruger is likely to slap another one of his taxes on us at any moment and we've got to finance all that new development on the East Rand. We can't let production costs creep up now.'

'All right,' gruffed Sean. 'It's all settled. I just hope we don't have a strike on our hands.'

'There are ways of dealing with strikes. Hradsky has got the police on our side and we can have a couple of hundred men up from Kimberley in no time at all,' Duff told him.

'Damn it, Duff, it's wrong. You know it's wrong. That

grotesque Buddha with the little eyes knows it's wrong. But what can I do? Damn it, what can I do?' Sean exploded. 'I feel so bloody helpless.'

'Well, you're the one who wanted to give him control.' Duff laughed at him. 'Stop trying to change the world and let's go home.'

Max was waiting for them in the outer office. He looked nervous. 'Excuse me, gentlemen, could I have a word with you?'

'Who's talking,' Sean asked abruptly, 'you or Hradsky?'

'It's a private matter, Mr Courtney.' Max dropped his voice.

'Can't it wait until tomorrow?' Sean pushed past him and kept going for the door.

'Please, Mr Courtney, it's of the utmost importance.' Max plucked desperately at Sean's arm.

'What is it, Max?' Duff asked.

'I have to speak to you alone,' Max dropped his voice again and glanced unhappily at the street door.

'Well, speak then,' Duff encouraged him. 'We're alone now.'

'Not here. Can you meet me later?'

Duff raised an eyebrow. 'What is this, Maximilian, don't tell me you are selling dirty pictures.'

'Mr Hradsky is waiting for me at the hotel. I told him I was coming to find some papers, he'll get suspicious if I don't go back immediately.' Max was nearly in tears; his Adam's apple played hide-and-seek behind his high collar, bobbing out and disappearing again. Duff was suddenly very interested in what Max had to say.

'You don't want Norman to know about this?' he asked.

'My goodness, no.' Max came closer to tears.

'When do you want to meet us?'

'Tonight, after ten o'clock when Mr Hradsky has retired.'

342

'Where?' asked Duff.

'There's a side road round the east end of the Little Sister Mine dump. It's not used any more.'

'I know it,' said Duff. 'We'll ride along there about half past ten.'

'Thank you, Mr Charleywood, you won't regret it.' Max scampered for the door and disappeared.

Duff adjusted his beaver at the correct angle, then he prodded Sean in the belly with the point of his cane.

'Smell it – suck it in.' Duff sniffed appreciatively and Sean did the same.

'I don't smell a thing,' Sean declared.

'The air is thick with it,' Duff told him. 'The sweet smell of treachery.'

They left Xanadu just after half past nine. Duff insisted on wearing a black opera cloak.

'Atmosphere is vital, laddie, you can't go to a rendezvous like this dressed in dirty khaki pants and *veldschoen*. It would ruin the whole thing.'

'Well, I'm damned if I'm going to get into fancy dress. This is a very good suit. It will have to do.'

'Can't I persuade you to wear a pistol in your belt?' asked Duff wistfully.

'No,' laughed Sean.

'No?' Duff shook his head. 'You're a barbarian, laddie. No taste, that's your trouble.'

They avoided the main streets on their way through Johannesburg and met the Cape road half a mile beyond the town. There was only a minute slice of moon left in the dark bowl of the sky. The stars, however, were big and by their light the white mine dumps, each the size of a large hill, stood out like pustules on the earth's face.

Despite himself, Sean felt a little breathless with excitement – Duff's zest was always infectious. They cantered with their stirrups almost touching, Duff's cloak billowing out behind him and the breeze of their passage fanning the tip of Sean's cigar to a fierce red spark.

'Slow down, Duff, the turning's just about here somewhere. It's overgrown, we'll miss it.'

They reined to a walk.

'What's the time?' asked Duff.

Sean drew on his cigar and held his watch close to the glow. 'A quarter after ten. We're early.'

'My bet is Maximilian will be there before us – here's the road.' Duff turned his horse onto it and Sean followed him. The Little Sister Mine dump rose up next to them, steep and white in the starlight. They skirted it but its bulk threw a shadow over them. Duff's horse snorted and shied and Sean gripped with his knees as his own horse danced sideways. Max had stepped out from a scraggy cluster of bushes next to the road.

'Well met by moonlight, Maximilian,' Duff greeted him.

'Please bring your horses off the road, gentlemen.' Max was still showing signs of the afternoon's agitation. They tied their horses next to Max's among the bushes and walked across to join him.

'Well, Max, what's new? How are the folks?' Duff asked.

'Before we go any further in this matter, I want you gentlemen to give me your word of honour that, whether anything comes of it or not, you will never say a word to anybody of what I tell you tonight.' Max was very pale, Sean thought, or perhaps it was just the starlight.

'I agree to that,' said Sean.

'Cross my heart,' said Duff.

Max opened the front of his coat and brought out a long envelope. 'I think if I show you these first it will make it easier to explain my proposition.'

Sean took the envelope from him. 'What are they, Max?'

344

'The latest statements from all four banks at which Mr Hradsky deals.'

'Matches, Sean, give us a light, laddie,' said Duff eagerly.

'I have a lantern with me,' Max said and he squatted down to light it. Sean and Duff squatted with him and spread the bank statements in the circle of yellow light. They examined them in silence until at last Sean rocked back on his heels and lit another cigar.

'Well, I am glad I don't owe that much money,' Sean announced. Sean folded up the sheets and put them back in the envelope. He slapped the envelope into the palm of his free hand and started chuckling. Max reached across, took it from him and placed it carefully back inside his coat.

'All right, Max, spell it out for us,' said Sean. Max leaned forward and blew out the lantern. What he had to say was easier said in darkness.

'The large cash payment that Mr Hradsky had to make to you gentlemen and the limitation of output from his diamond mines in terms of the new cartel agreements in the diamond industry have forced him to borrow heavily on all his banks.' Max stopped and cleared his throat. 'The extent of this borrowing you have seen. Of course, the banks demanded security for the loans and Mr Hradsky has given them his entire holding of C.R.C. shares. The banks have set a limit on the shares of thirty-five shillings each. As you know C.R.C.'s are currently quoted at ninety shillings, which leaves a wide margin of safety. However, if the shares were to suffer a setback and fall in price to thirty-five shillings the banks would sell. They would dump every single share that Mr Hradsky owns in C.R.C.'s onto the market.'

'Go on, Max,' said Duff. 'I'm beginning to like the sound of your voice.'

'It occurred to me that if Mr Hradsky were temporarily absent from Johannesburg – say if he went on a trip to England to buy new machinery or something of that nature – it would be possible for you gentlemen to force the price of C.R.C.'s down to thirty-five shillings. Done correctly it would only take three or four days to accomplish. You could sell short and start rumours that the Leader Reef had pinched out at depth. Mr Hradsky would not be here to defend his interests and as soon as C.R.C.'s hit thirty-five shillings the banks would off-load his shares. The price would crash and you, with ready cash available, would be in a position to buy up C.R.C. shares at a fraction of their actual value. There is no reason why you shouldn't gain control of the group and make a couple of million to boot.'

There was another silence. It lasted a long time before Sean asked, 'What do you get out of it, Max?'

'Your cheque for one hundred thousand pounds, Mr Courtney.'

'Wages are going up,' remarked Sean. 'I thought the standard pay for this type of work was thirty pieces of silver. The rate, I believe, was set by a countryman of yours.'

'Shut up,' snapped Duff, then more pleasantly to Max, 'Mr Courtney likes his little jokes. Tell me, Max, is that all you want – just the money? I'll be frank with you – it doesn't ring true. You must be a moderately rich man as it is.'

Max stood up quickly and started towards the horses. He hadn't reached them before he swung around. His face was in darkness but his voice was naked as he screamed at them.

'Do you think I don't know what they call me – "The Court Jester", "Hradsky's tongue", "Lick-arse". Do you think I like it? Do you think I enjoy crawling to him every minute of every day? I want to be free again. I want to be a man again.' His voice choked off and his hands came up and covered his face. He was sobbing. Sean couldn't watch him

and even Duff looked down at the ground in embarrassment. When Max spoke again it was in his usual soft and
sad voice.

'Mr Courtney, if you wear your yellow waistcoat to the
office tomorrow, I will take it as a sign that you intend to
follow my suggestion and that my terms are acceptable to
you. I will then make the necessary arrangements to ensure
Mr Hradsky's absence from the country.' He untied his
horse, mounted and rode away down the track towards the
Cape Road. Neither Sean nor Duff moved to stand up.
They listened to the hoof-beats of Max's horse fade into
the darkness, before Duff spoke. 'Those bank statements
were genuine – I had a good look at the seals.'

'And even more genuine was Max's emotion.' Sean
flicked his cigar away into the bushes. 'No one could act
that well. It made me feel quite sick listening to him. Hell,
how can a man so cold-bloodedly betray his trust?'

'Laddie, let's not turn this into a discussion of Max's
morals. Let's concern ourselves with the facts. Norman has
been delivered into our hands, neatly trussed, spiced with
garlic and with a sprig of parsley behind each ear. I say let's
cook him and eat him.'

Sean smiled at him. 'Give me a few good reasons. I want
you to convince me. The way I feel towards him after that
meeting this afternoon, I shouldn't be surprised if I convince easily.'

'One.' Duff held up a finger. 'Norman deserves it.'

Sean nodded.

'Two.' Another of Duff's fingers came up. 'If we gain
control we can run things the way we want. You can
indulge your good resolution and give everybody a pay rise
and I'll be top man again.'

'Yes!' Sean tugged at his moustache thoughtfully.

'Three. We came here to make money, we'll never get
another opportunity like this. And my last reason, but the

347

most potent – you look so beautiful in that yellow waistcoat, laddie, I wouldn't miss seeing you in it tomorrow morning, not for a thousand C.R.C. shares.'

'It is rather natty,' admitted Sean. 'But listen, Duff, I don't want another Lochtkamper business. Messy, you know.'

Duff stood up.

'Norman's a big boy, he wouldn't do that. Anyway, he'll still be rich – he's got his diamond mines. We'll only be relieving him of his responsibilities on the Witwatersrand.'

They walked across to the horses. Sean had his foot in the stirrup when he stiffened and exclaimed, 'My God, I can't do it. It's all off.'

'Why?' Duff was alarmed.

'I spilt gravy on that waistcoat – I can't possibly wear it tomorrow. My tailor would murder me.'

– 30 –

There was no problem in arranging for Hradsky's absence – someone had to go to London. There was machinery to buy for the new areas on the East Rand and they had to select two engineers from the hundred or so applicants waiting in England. Not ungraciously, Hradsky allowed himself to be elected for the job.

'We'll give him a farewell party,' Duff suggested to Sean during dinner that night. 'Well, not really a farewell party – but a wake.'

Sean started whistling the 'Dead March' and Duff tapped it out on the table with the handle of his knife.

'We'll have it at Candy's Hot—' Duff cut himself short. 'We'll have it here. We'll really lay it on for poor old Norman so afterwards he'll be able to say, "The bastards may have cleaned me out, but they certainly gave me a grand party".'

'He doesn't like parties,' said Sean.

'That's an excellent reason why we should give him one,' agreed Duff.

A week later when Hradsky and Max left on the morning coach for Port Natal there were fifty members of the Johannesburg Stock Exchange still in full evening dress from the night's party to wave him goodbye. Duff made a touching, if somewhat slurred, little speech and presented Hradsky with a bouquet of roses. Nervous of the crowd that milled about them, the horses bolted when the driver cracked his whip and Max and Hradsky were thrown together in an undignified heap on the rear seat of the coach. The crowd cheered them out of sight. With an arm around his shoulder Sean led Duff across the street to the office and deposited him in one of the deep leather armchairs.

'Are you sober enough to talk sense?' Sean asked dubiously.

'Sure. Always at your service as the lady said to the customer.'

'I managed to have a word with Max last night,' Sean told him. 'He will send us a telegram from Port Natal when he and Hradsky are safely on the mailboat. We won't start anything until we receive it.'

'Very wise – you're the wisest chap I know,' Duff grinned happily.

'You'd better go to bed,' Sean told him.

'Too far,' said Duff. 'I'll sleep here.'

It was another ten days before Max's telegram arrived. Sean and Duff were eating lunch in the Rand Club when it was delivered to their table. Sean slit open the envelope and read the message to Duff.

'Sailing four o'clock this afternoon. Good luck. Max.'

'I'll drink to that.' Duff lifted his wine glass.

'Tomorrow,' said Sean, 'I'll go up to the Candy Deep and tell Francois to pull all the men out of the bottom levels of the mine. No one's to be allowed in.'

'Put a guard at the fourteenth level,' suggested Duff. 'That'll make it more impressive.'

'Good idea,' agreed Sean. He looked up as someone passed their table and suddenly he started to smile. 'Duff, do you know who that is?'

'Who are you talking about?' Duff looked bewildered.

'That chap who's just gone out into the lounge – there he is, going into the lavatories.'

'Isn't that Elliott, the newspaper fellow?'

'Editor of the *Rand Mail*,' nodded Sean. 'Come with me, Duff.'

'Where are we going?'

'To get a bit of cheap publicity.'

Duff followed Sean out of the dining-room, across the lounge and into the men's lavatories. The door of one of the closets was closed and as they walked in someone farted softly behind it. Sean winked at Duff and went across to the urinal. As he addressed himself to it he said, 'Well, all we can hope for now, Duff, is that Norman will be able to work a miracle in England. Otherwise—' He shrugged his shoulder. Duff picked up his cue.

'We're taking a hell of a chance relying on that. I still say we should sell out now. C.R.C.'s were at ninety-one shillings this morning so it's obvious that the story hasn't leaked out yet. But when it does you won't be able to give the bloody shares away. I say we should get out while the going's good.'

'No,' Sean disagreed. 'Let's wait until we hear from Norman. It's taking a bit of a chance, I know, but we have a responsibility to the men working for us.' Sean took Duff's arm and led him out of the lavatory again; at the door he added the cherry to the top of the pie. 'If and when C.R.C. collapses there are going to be thousands of men out of work – do you realize that?'

Sean closed the door behind them and they grinned delightedly at each other.

'You're a genius, laddie,' whispered Duff.

'I'm happy to say I agree with you,' Sean whispered back.

The next morning Sean woke with the knowledge that something exciting was going to happen that day. He lay and savoured the feeling before he sent his mind out to hunt for the reason. Then he sat up suddenly and reached for the newspaper that lay folded on the coffee tray beside his bed. He shook it open and found what he was looking for on the front page, big headlines: *Is all well with the Central Rand Consolidated? Norman Hradsky's mystery journey.* The story itself was a masterpiece of journalistic evasion. Seldom had Sean seen anyone write so fluently or convincingly on a subject about which he knew nothing. 'It is suggested', 'Usually reliable sources report' and 'There is reason to believe' – all the old phrases of no significance. Sean groped for his slippers and padded down the corridor to Duff's room.

Duff had all the blankets and most of the bed; the girl was curled up like a pink anchovy on the outskirts. Duff was snoring and the girl whimpered a little in her sleep. Sean tickled Duff's lips with the tassel of his dressing-gown cord; Duff's nose twitched and his snores gurgled into silence. The girl sat up and looked at Sean with eyes wide but vacant from sleep.

'Quickly, run,' Sean shouted at her, 'the rebels are coming.'

She leapt straight into the air and landed three feet from the bed quivering with panic. Sean ran a critical eye over her. A pretty filly, he decided, and made a mental note to take her for a trot just as soon as Duff put her out to grass.

'All right,' he reassured her, 'they've gone away now.'

She became aware of her nakedness and Sean's frank appraisal of it. She tried to cover it with hands too small for the task. Sean picked up Duff's gown from the foot of the bed and handed it to her.

'Go and have a bath or something, sweetheart, I want to talk to Mr Charleywood.'

With the gown on she recovered her composure and told him severely, 'I didn't have any clothes on, Mr Courtney.'

'I would never have guessed,' said Sean politely.

'It's not nice.'

'You are too modest – I thought it was better than average. Off you go now, there's a good girl.' With a saucy flick of her head she disappeared into the bathroom and Sean transferred his attention to Duff. Duff had held grimly onto the threads of sleep throughout the exchange but he let go when Sean whacked him across the backside with the folded newspaper. Like a tortoise coming out of its shell his head emerged from the blankets. Sean handed him the paper and sat down on the edge of the bed. He watched Duff's face crease into laughter lines before he spoke.

'You better get down to the Editor's office and shout at him a little – just to confirm his suspicions. I'll go up to the Candy Deep and close all the bottom levels. I'll meet you back at the Exchange at opening time and don't forget to clean that grin off your face before you show it round town. Try and look haggard, it shouldn't be difficult for you.'

When Sean arrived at the Stock Exchange building the crowd had filled the street outside. Mbejane eased the landau into it and it opened to give them a passage. Sean scowled straight ahead and ignored the questions which were shouted at him from all around. Mbejane stopped the carriage outside the main entrance and four police constables held back the mob while Sean hurried across the pavement and through the double doors. Duff was there

352

ahead of him, the centre of a turbulent circle of members and brokers. He saw Sean and waved frantically over the heads of his inquisitors. That was sufficient to switch their attention from Duff to Sean and they flocked to him, ringing him in with anxious angry faces. Sean's hat was knocked forward over his eyes and a button popped off his coat as one of them caught hold of his lapels.

'Is it true?' the man shouted, spittle flying from his lips into Sean's face. 'We've got a right to know if it's true.'

Sean swung his cane in a full overarm stroke onto the man's head and sent him tottering backwards into the arms of those behind him.

'Back, you bastards,' he roared at them using both the point and the edge of his cane to beat them away, scattering them across the floor until he stood alone, glowering at them with the cane still twitching restlessly in his hand.

'I'll make a statement later on. Until then, behave yourselves.' He adjusted his hat, picked the loose thread where the button had been from his coat and stalked across to join Duff. He could see Duff's grin starting to lift the corner of his mouth and he cautioned him silently with his eyes. Grim-faced they walked through into the members' lounge.

'How's it going your end?' Duff kept his voice low.

'Couldn't be better.' Sean contrived a worried expression. 'I've got an armed guard on the fourteenth level. When this bunch hear about that, they'll really start frothing at the mouth.'

'When you make your statement, let it ring with obvious false confidence,' Duff instructed. 'If it goes on like this we'll have the shares down to thirty-five shillings within an hour of opening.'

Five minutes before opening time Sean stood in the President's box and made his address to his fellow members, Duff listened to him with mounting admiration. Sean's hearty reassurances and verbal side-stepping were enough to strike despair into the souls of the most hardened optimists. Sean finished his speech and climbed down from the box amid a gloomy lack of applause. The bell rang and the brokers stood singly or in small disconsolate groups about the floor. The first tentative offer was made. 'I sell C.R.C.'

But there was no rush to buy. Ten minutes later there was a sale recorded at eighty-five shillings, six shillings lower than the previous day's closing price. Duff leaned across to Sean. 'We'll have to start selling some of our own shares to get things moving, otherwise everybody's going to keep sitting on the fence.'

'That's all right,' Sean nodded, 'we'll buy them back later at a quarter of the price. But wait until the news about the Candy Deep gets out.'

It was just before ten o'clock when that happened. The reaction was sharp. In one quick burst of selling C.R.C.'s dropped to sixty shillings. But there they hung, fluctuating nervously in the chaos of hope and doubt.

'We'll have to sell now,' whispered Duff, 'they are short of script. We'll have to give it to them otherwise the price will stick here.'

Sean felt his hands trembling and he clenched them in his pockets. Duff was showing signs of the strain as well, there was a nerve jumping in his cheek and his eyes had receded into their sockets a little. This was a game with high stakes.

'Don't overdo it – sell thirty thousand.'

The price of C.R.C.'s sagged under the weight but levelled out at forty-five shillings. There was still another hour until high change and Sean's whole body was screwed up tight with tension. He felt the cold patches of sweat under his arms.

'Sell another thirty thousand,' he ordered his clerk and

even to himself his voice sounded wheezy. He stubbed out his cigar in the copper ashtray next to his chair; it was already half full of butts. It was no longer necessary for either of them to act worried. This time the price stuck at forty shillings and the sale of sixty thousand more of their shares failed to move it down more than a few shillings.

'Someone's buying up,' muttered Sean uneasily.

'It looks like it,' agreed Duff. 'I'll lay odds it's that bloody Greek Efthyvoulos. It looks as if we'll have to sell enough to glut him before they'll drop any further.'

By high change Duff and Sean had sold three-quarters of their holdings in C.R.C.'s and the price still stood stubbornly at thirty-seven and sixpence. So tantalizingly close to the magic figure that would release a flood of Hradsky's shares onto the unprepared market, but now they were nearing the stage when they would no longer have any shares with which to force the price down that last two and sixpence.

The market closed and left Duff and Sean sitting limply in their armchairs, shaken and tired as prizefighters at the end of the fifteenth round. Slowly the lounge emptied but still they sat on. Sean leaned across and put his hand on Duff's shoulder. 'It's going to be all right,' he said. 'Tomorrow it will be all right.'

They looked at each other and they exchanged strength, each of them drawing it from the other until they were both smiling. Sean stood up. 'Come on, let's go home.'

Sean went to bed early and alone. Although he felt drained of energy, sleep was a long time coming to him and when it did it was full of confused dreams and punctuated with sharp jerks back into wakefulness. It was almost a relief to see the dawn define the windows as grey squares and to be released from his unrewarding rest. At breakfast he drank a cup of coffee and found that his stomach was unable to accept the plateful of steak and eggs that was offered it for it was already screwing up tight in anticipation of the day ahead. Duff was edgy and tired-looking as well; they spoke only a little during the meal and not at all in the carriage when Mbejane drove them down to the Exchange.

The crowd was outside the Stock Exchange again. They forced their way through it and into the building; they took their seats in the lounge and Sean looked round at the faces of his fellow members. In each of them were the marks of worry, the same darkness round the eyes and the jerkiness in movement. He watched Jock Heyns yawn extravagantly and had to do the same; he lifted his hand to cover his mouth and found it was trembling again. He laid the hand on the arm of his chair and kept it still. Across the lounge Bonzo Barnes caught Sean's eye and looked away quickly, then he also gaped into a cavernous yawn. It was the tension. In the years ahead Sean would see men yawn like that while they waited for the dawn to send them against the Boer guns. Duff leaned across to him and broke his line of thought.

'As soon as the trading starts, we'll sell. Try and panic them. Do you agree?'

'Sudden death,' Sean nodded. He couldn't face another morning of that mental agony. 'Couldn't we offer shares at thirty-two shillings and sixpence and get it over with?' he asked.

Duff grinned at him. 'We can't do that, it's too obvious – we'll just have to go on offering to sell at best and let the price fall on its own.'

'I suppose you're right – but we'll play our high cards now and dump the rest of our shares as soon as the market opens. I don't see how the price can possibly hold after that.'

Duff nodded. He beckoned to their authorized clerk who was waiting patiently at the door of the lounge and when the man came up to them he told him, 'Sell one hundred thousand C.R.C.'s at best.'

The clerk blinked but he jotted the order down on his pad and went out onto the main floor where the other brokers were gathering. It was a few minutes from the bell.

'What if it doesn't work?' Sean asked. The tightness in his belly was nauseating him.

'It must work – it's got to work,' Duff whispered as much to himself as to Sean. He was twisting his fingers round the head of his cane and chewing against clenched teeth. They sat and waited for the bell and when it rang Sean jumped then reached sheepishly for his cigar case. He heard their clerk's voice, raised sharply, 'I sell C.R.C.'s,' and then the confused mumble of voices as the trading started. Through the lounge door he saw the recorder chalk up the first sale. 'Thirty-seven shillings.'

He drew hard on his cigar and lay back in his chair forcing himself to relax, ignoring the restless tapping of Duff's fingers on the arm of the chair next to him. The recorder wiped out the figures and wrote again. 'Thirty-six shillings.'

Sean blew out cigar smoke in a long jet. 'It's moving,' he whispered and Duff's hand clenched on the arm of the chair, his knuckles paling from the pressure of his grip.

'Thirty-five.' The elusive number at last. Sean heard Duff sigh next to him and his voice, 'Now! watch it go, laddie, now the banks will come on. Get ready, laddie, get ready now.'

'Thirty-four and six,' wrote the recorder.

'They must come in now,' said Duff again. 'Get ready to get rich, laddie.'

Their clerk was coming back across the floor and into the lounge. He stopped in front of their chairs. 'I managed to sell them, sir.'

Sean straightened up quickly. 'So soon?' he asked.

'Yes, sir, three big sales and I got rid of them all. I'm afraid the last was only at thirty-four and sixpence.'

Sean stared back at the board. The figure was still at thirty-four and sixpence.

'Duff, something's going on here. Why haven't the banks come in yet?'

'We'll force them to off-load.' Duff's voice was unnaturally hoarse. 'We'll force the bastards.' He pulled himself half out of his chair and snarled at the clerk.

'Sell another one hundred thousand at thirty shillings.' The man's face went slack with surprise. 'Hurry, man, do you hear me? What are you waiting for?' The clerk backed away from Duff, then he turned and scurried out of the lounge.

'Duff, for God's sake.' Sean grabbed his arm. 'Have you gone mad?'

'We'll force them,' muttered Duff. 'They'll have to sell.'

'We haven't got another hundred thousand shares.' Sean jumped up. 'I'm going to stop him.' He ran across the lounge but before he reached the door he saw the sale being chalked up on the board at thirty shillings. He pushed his way across the crowded floor until he reached his clerk. 'Don't sell any more,' he whispered.

The man looked surprised. 'I've sold them already, sir.'

'The whole hundred thousand?' There was horrified disbelief in Sean's voice.

'Yes, sir, someone took the lot in one batch.'

Sean walked back across the floor in a daze. He sank into the chair beside Duff.

'They're sold already.' He spoke as though he didn't believe himself.

'We'll force them, we'll force them to sell,' muttered Duff again and Sean turned to him with alarm. Duff was sweating in little dewdrops across his forehead and his eyes were very bright.

'Duff, for God's sake,' Sean whispered to him, 'steady, man.' Sean knew that they were watched by everybody in the lounge. The watching faces seemed as large as those seen through a telescope and the buzz of their voices echoed strangely in his ears. Sean felt confused: everything seemed to be in slow motion like a bad dream. He looked through into the trading floor and saw the crude number thirty still chalked accusingly against C.R.C. Where were the banks? Why weren't they selling?

'We'll force them, we'll force the bastards,' Duff said again. Sean tried to answer him but the words wouldn't come. He looked back across the trading floor and now he knew it was a bad dream for Hradsky and Max were there, walking across the floor towards the members' lounge. Men were crowding around them and Hradsky was smiling and holding up his hands as if to fend off their questions. They came through into the lounge and Hradsky went to his chair by the fireplace. He lowered himself into it with his shoulders sagging forward and his waistcoat wrinkled tightly around the full bag of his belly. He was still smiling and Sean thought that his smile was one of the most unnerving things he had ever seen. He watched it with flesh-crawling fascination and beside him Duff was just as still and stricken. Max spoke quickly to Hradsky and then he stood up and walked across to Sean and Duff. He stopped in front of them.

'The clerk informs us that you have contracted to sell to Mr Hradsky five hundred thousand shares in C.R.C.'s at an average price of thirty-six shillings.' Max's lashes drooped sadly onto his cheeks. 'The total issue of C.R.C.'s, as you know, is one million shares. During the last two days Mr Hradsky was able to purchase another seventy-five thousand shares apart from the ones you sold to him. This makes his total holdings of C.R.C.'s almost six hundred thousand shares. It seems therefore that you have sold shares that don't exist. Mr Hradsky foresees that you will have some difficulty in fulfilling your contract.'

Sean and Duff went on staring at him. He turned to leave them and Duff blurted out. 'But the banks – why didn't the banks sell?'

Max smiled a mournful little smile. 'The day he reached Port Natal Mr Hradsky transferred sufficient funds from his accounts there to liquidate his overdrafts in Johannesburg. He sent you that telegram and returned here immediately. We only arrived an hour ago.'

'But – but, you lied to us. You tricked us!'

Max inclined his head. 'Mr Charleywood, I will not discuss honesty with a man who does not understand the meaning of the word.' He went back to Hradsky's side. Everyone in the lounge had heard him and while Duff and Sean went on sitting amongst the ruins of their fortune the struggle to buy C.R.C. shares started on the main floor. In five minutes the price was over ninety shillings and still climbing. When it reached one hundred shillings, Sean touched Duff's arm.

'Let's go.' They stood up together and started for the door of the members' lounge. As they passed Hradsky's chair he spoke.

'Yes, Mr Charleywood, you can't win all the time.' It came out quite clearly with only a slight catch on the 'c's' – they were always difficult letters for Norman Hradsky.

Duff stopped, he turned to face Hradsky, his mouth open as he struggled to find a reply. His lips moved, groping, groping for words – but there were none. His shoulders drooped, he shook his head and turned away. He stumbled once at the edge of the floor. Sean held his arm and guided him through the excited jabber of brokers. No one took any notice of the two of them. They were bumped and jostled before they were through the crush and out onto the pavement. Sean signalled Mbejane to bring the carriage.

They climbed into it and Mbejane drove them up to Xanadu.

They went through into the drawing-room.

'Get me a drink, please, Sean.' Duff's face was grey and crumpled-looking. Sean poured two tumblers half full of brandy and carried one across to Duff. Duff drank and then sat staring into the empty glass.

'I'm sorry – I lost my head. I thought we'd be able to buy those shares for dirt, when the banks started selling.'

'It doesn't matter,' Sean's voice was tired. 'We were smashed before that happened. Christ! What a well-laid trap it was!'

'We couldn't have known. It was so damn cunning, we couldn't have guessed, could we, Sean?' Duff was trying to excuse himself.

Sean kicked off his boots and loosened his collar. 'That night up at the mine dump – I would have staked my life Max wasn't lying.' He lay back in the chair and stirred his brandy with a circular movement of his hand. 'Christ, how they must have laughed to see us stampede into the pitfall!'

'But we aren't finished, Sean, we aren't completely finished, are we?' Duff was pleading with him, begging for a peg to hang his hope on. 'We'll come out of this all right, you know we will, don't you? We'll save enough out of the wreckage to start again. We'll build it all up again, won't we, Sean?'

'Sure,' Sean laughed brutally. 'You can get a job down at the Bright Angels cleaning out the spittoons and I'll get one at the Opera House playing the piano.'

'But – but – there'll be something left. A couple of thousand even. We could sell this house.'

'Don't dream, Duff, this house belongs to Hradsky. Everything belongs to him.' Sean flicked the brandy that was left in his glass into his mouth and swallowed it. He stood up quickly and went across to the liquor cabinet. 'I'll explain it to you. We owe Hradsky a hundred thousand shares that don't exist. The only way we can deliver them is to buy them from him first and he can set his own price on them. We're finished, Duff, do you know what that means? Smashed! Broken!' Sean poured brandy into his glass, slopping a little on the sideboard. 'Have another drink on Hradsky, it's his brandy now.' Sean swept his arm round the room, pointing at the rich furniture and heavy curtains. 'Take a last look at this lot. Tomorrow the Sheriff will be here to attach it; then through the due processes of the law it will be handed to its rightful owner – Mr Norman Hradsky.' Sean started back towards his chair and then he stopped.

'The due processes of the law,' he repeated softly. 'I wonder – it might just work.'

Duff sat up eagerly in his chair. 'You've got an idea?'

Sean nodded. 'Well, half an idea anyway. Listen, Duff, if I can save a couple of thousand out of this do you agree that we get out of here?'

'Where to – where will we go?'

'We were facing north when we started. It's as good a direction as any. They say there's gold and ivory beyond the Limpopo for those who want it.'

'But, why can't we stay here? We could play the stock market.' Duff looked uncertain, almost afraid.

'Damn it, Duff, we're finished here. It's a different story playing the market when you are paying the fiddler and calling the tune, but with a mere thousand or so we'd be among the dogs fighting for the scraps under Hradsky's table. Let's get out and start again. We'll go north, hunt ivory and prospect for a new reef. We'll take a couple of wagons and find another fortune. I bet you've forgotten how it feels to sit on a horse and handle a rifle, to have the wind in your face and not a whore or a stockbroker within five hundred miles.'

'But it means leaving everything we've worked for,' Duff groaned.

'Sweet merciful heavens, man, are you blind or just plain stupid?' Sean stormed at him. 'You don't own anything, so how the hell can you leave something you haven't got? I'm going down to see Hradsky and try to make a deal with him. Are you coming?'

Duff looked at him without seeing him, his lips were trembling and he was shaking his head. At last he was realizing the position they were in and the impact of it had dazed him. The higher you ride the further there is to fall.

'All right,' said Sean. 'Wait for me here.'

Hradsky's suite was full of talking, laughing men. Sean recognized most of them as the courtiers who used to cluster round the throne on which he and Duff had sat. The King is dead, long live the King! They saw him standing in the doorway and the laughter and loud voices fizzled out. He saw Max take two quick steps to the stinkwood desk in the corner, pull open the top drawer and drop his hand into it. He stood like that watching Sean. One by one the courtiers picked up their hats and canes and hurried out of the room. Some of them mumbled embarrassed greetings as they brushed passed Sean. Then there were only the three of them left: Sean standing quietly in the doorway, Max behind the desk with his hand on the pistol and Hradsky in the chair by the fireplace watching through yellow, half-hooded eyes.

'Aren't you going to invite me in, Max?' Sean asked and Max glanced quickly at Hradsky, saw his barely perceptible nod and looked back at Sean. 'Come in, please, Mr Courtney.'

Sean pushed the door shut behind him. 'You won't need the gun, Max, the game is over.'

'And the score is in our favour, is it not, Mr Courtney?'

Sean nodded. 'Yes, you've won. We are prepared to make over to you all the C.R.C. shares we hold.'

Max shook his head unhappily. 'I'm afraid it's not quite as easy as that. You have undertaken to sell us a certain number of shares and we must insist upon delivery in full.'

'Just where do you suggest we get them?' Sean asked.

'You could buy them on the Stock Exchange.'

'From you?'

Max shrugged but made no reply.

'So you are going to twist the knife, are you?'

'You put it very poetically, Mr Courtney,' agreed Max.

'Have you considered the consequences of forcing us into bankruptcy?'

'I will admit freely that the consequences to you do not concern us.'

Sean smiled. 'That was not very nice, Max, but I was talking about it from your point of view. Sequestration orders, creditors' meetings – you can rest assured that the liquidator appointed will be a member of the *Volksraad* or a relative of one. There will be court actions and counter actions, enforced sale of the shares in the estate and costs to pay. A liquidator with any sense at all could string it out for three or four years, all the time drawing a handsome commission. Have you thought about that, Max?'

The narrowing of Max's eyes showed that he hadn't. He looked at Hradsky with a trace of helplessness in his face, and Sean took a little comfort from that look.

'Now what I suggest is this – you let us draw ten thousand, take our horses and personal belongings. We in exchange will give you the rest. Shares, bank accounts, property, everything. You cannot possibly get more out of it if you force us into bankruptcy.'

Hradsky gave Max a message in their private facial code and Max interpreted it to Sean.

'Would you mind waiting outside, please, while we discuss this offer of yours.'

'I'll go down and have a drink in the bar,' said Sean. He pulled his watch from his waistcoat pocket and checked the time. 'Will twenty minutes be enough?'

'Ample, thank you, Mr Courtney.'

Sean had his drink by himself although the bar was nowhere near empty. This was not an arrangement of his own choosing, but he was flying the fever flag of failure and so he had to take an isolation berth at one end of the bar while all the other ships steered wide of him. No one looked in his direction and the conversation that went on round him was carefully arranged so as to exclude him. While he waited out the twenty minutes he amused himself by imagining the reactions of these his friends if he were to ask them for a loan. This helped to take the sting out of their snubs but still he felt it rankling. He looked at his watch again. The twenty minutes were up. Sean walked back along the counter towards the door. Jock and Trevor Heyns saw him coming, they turned away abruptly and immediately became absorbed in staring at the bottle-lined shelves behind the bar counter. Sean stopped level with Jock and cleared his throat deferentially. 'Jock, could you spare a minute?'

Jock turned slowly. 'Ah, Sean. Yes, what is it?'

'Duff and I are leaving the Rand. I have something for you, just something to remember us by. I know Duff would want you to have it too.'

Jock reddened with embarrassment. 'That's not necessary,' he said and started to turn back to his drink.

'Please, Jock.'

'Oh, all right,' Jock's voice was irritable. 'What is it?'

'This,' Sean said and stepped forward, moving his weight behind the fist. Jock's large and whisky-flushed nose was a target to dream about. It was not one of Sean's best punches, he was out of training, but it was good enough to send Jock in a spectacular back-somersault over the counter. Dreamily Sean picked up Jock's glass and emptied it over Trevor's head.

'Next time you meet me smile and say "Hello",' he told Trevor. 'Until then – stay out of mischief.'

He went up the stairs to Hradsky's suite in much better spirits. They were waiting for him.

'Give me the word, Max,' Sean could even grin at him.

'Mr Hradsky has very generously—'

'How much?' Sean cut him short.

'Mr Hradsky will allow you to take fifteen hundred and your personal effects. As part of the agreement you will give an undertaking not to embark on any business venture on the Witwatersrand for a period of three years.'

'That will be too soon,' said Sean. 'Make it two thousand and you've got a deal.'

'The offer is not open to discussion.'

Sean could see they meant it. They didn't have to bargain; it was a statement.

'All right, I accept.'

'Mr Hradsky has sent for his lawyer to draw up the agreement. Would you mind waiting, Mr Courtney?'

'Not at all, Max, you forget I am a gentleman of leisure now.'

Sean found Duff still sitting in the chair where he had left him in the drawing-room of Xanadu. The bottle clutched in his hand was empty and he was unconscious. He had spilt brandy down the front of his waistcoat and three of the buttons were undone. Huddled in the big chair, his body seemed to have shrunk and the curly hair hanging onto his forehead softened the gaunt lines of his face. Sean loosened his fingers from the neck of the bottle and Duff moved restlessly, muttering and twisting his head.

'Bedtime for small boys,' said Sean. He lifted him out of the chair and hung him over one shoulder.

Duff sicked up copiously.

'That's the way, show Hradsky what you think of his bloody carpet,' Sean encouraged him. 'Give him another one for luck, but not on my boots.'

Duff did as he was bid and, chuckling, Sean carried him up the stairs. At the top he stopped and with Duff still bundled over one shoulder tried to analyse his own feelings. Damn it, he felt happy. It was ridiculous to feel so happy in the midst of disaster. He went on down the passage still wondering at himself and into Duff's room. He dropped Duff on the bed and stripped his clothes off, then he rolled him under the blankets. He brought the enamel wash basin from the bathroom and placed it next to the bed.

'You may need this – sleep well. There's a long ride ahead of us tomorrow.'

He stopped again at the top of the stairs and looked down their marble slope into the splendour of the lobby. He was leaving all of it and that was nothing to feel happy about. He laughed aloud. Perhaps it was because he had faced complete annihilation and at the last instant had changed it into something less; by avoiding the worst he had made defeat into a victory. A pathetic little victory to be sure, but at least they were no worse off now than they had been when they had arrived on the Rand. Was that the reason? Sean thought about it and found that it wasn't the whole truth. There was also a feeling of release. That was another part of it. To go on his way: north to a new land. He felt the tingle of anticipation.

'Not a whore or a stockbroker within five hundred miles,' he said aloud and grinned. He gave up trying to find words for his feeling. Emotion was so damned elusive: as soon as you cornered it, it changed its shape and the net of words which you had ready to throw over it was no longer suitable. He let it go free to range through his body, accepting and enjoying it. He ran down the stairs, out through the kitchens and into the stableyard.

'Mbejane!' he shouted, 'where the hell are you?'

The clatter of a stool overturning in the servants' quarters and the door of one of the rooms burst open.

'Nkosi – what is it?' The urgency of Sean's voice had alarmed Mbejane.

'Which are the six best horses we have?'

Mbejane named them, making no attempt to hide his curiosity.

'Are they all salted against the Nagana?'*

'All of them, Nkosi.'

'Good – have them ready before tomorrow's light. Two with saddles, the others to carry the packs.'

Mbejane turned on his smile. 'Could it be we are going hunting, Nkosi?'

'It could easily be,' Sean agreed.

'How long will we be gone, Nkosi?'

'How long is for ever? Take leave of all your women,

---

* Sleeping sickness. Salting involved deliberate exposure to the sting of the tsetse fly. Animals that recovered were then immune.

bring your kaross and your spears and we will see where the road leads.'

Sean went back to his bedroom. It took him half an hour to pack. The pile of discarded clothing in the centre of the room grew steadily and what he kept made only half a horseload. He crammed it into two leather valises. He found his sheepskin coat in the back of one of the closets and threw it over a chair with his leather breeches and slouch hat, ready to wear in the morning. He went down to the study and made his selection from the gun rack, ignoring the fancy doubles and obscure calibres. He took down a pair of shotguns and four Mannlichers.

Then he went to tell Candy goodbye. She was in her suite but she opened quickly to his knock.

'Have you heard?' he asked her.

'Yes, the whole town knows. Oh! Sean, I'm so sorry – please come in.' She held the door open for him. 'How is Duff?'

'He'll be all right – right now he's both drunk and asleep.'

'I'll go to him,' she said quickly. 'He'll need me now.'

For answer Sean raised an eyebrow and looked at her until she dropped her eyes.

'No, you're right, I suppose. Perhaps later, when he's got over the first shock.' She looked up at Sean and smiled. 'I suppose you need a drink. It must have been hell for you as well.' She went across to the cabinet. She had on a blue gown and it clung to the womanish thrust of her hips and did not go high enough to cover the cleft of her breasts. Sean watched her pour his drink and bring it to him. She was lovely, he thought.

'Till we meet again, Candy.' Sean lifted his glass.

Her eyes went wide and very blue. 'I don't understand. Why do you say that?'

'We're going, Candy, first thing tomorrow.'

369

'No, Sean – you're joking.' But she knew he wasn't. There wasn't much to say after that. He finished his drink and they talked for a while, then he kissed her.

'Be happy, please,' he ordered her.

'I'll try. Come back one day soon.'

'Only if you promise to marry me.' He smiled at her and she caught hold of his beard and tugged his head from side to side.

'Get away with you – before I hold you to that.' He left her then because he knew she was going to weep and he didn't want to watch it.

The next morning Duff packed his gear under Sean's direction. He followed each instruction with a dazed obedience, answering when Sean spoke but otherwise withdrawn in a protective shell of silence. When he had finished Sean made him pick up his bags and marched him down to where the horses waited in the chill gloom of not-yet day. With the horses were men, four shapes in the darkness. Sean hesitated before going out into the yard.

'Mbejane,' he called. 'Who are these with you?'

They came forward into the light that poured through the doorway and Sean chuckled.

'Hlubi, of the noble belly! Nonga! And is it you, Kandhla?' Men who had worked beside him in the trenches of the Candy Deep, had plied the spades that had uncovered his fortune, had plied the spears that protected it from the first predators. Happy at his recognition of them, for it had been many years, they crowded forward smiling as widely and whitely as only a Zulu can.

'What brings you three rogues together so early in the day?' Sean asked, and Hlubi answered for them.

'Nkosi, we heard talk of a trek and our feet burned, we heard talk of hunting and we could not sleep.'

'There is no money for wages,' Sean spoke gruffly to cover the sudden rush of affection he felt for them.

370

'We made no talk of wages,' Hlubi answered with dignity. Sean nodded, it was the reply he had expected. He cleared his throat and went on.

'You would come with me when you know that I have the Tagathi on me?' He used the Zulu word for witchcraft. 'You would follow me knowing that behind me I leave a spoor of dead men and sorrow?'

'Nkosi,' Hlubi was grave as he answered. 'Something always dies when the lion feeds – and yet there is meat for those that follow him.'

'I hear the chatter of old women at a beer drink,' Mbejane observed drily. 'There is no more to say and the horses grow restless.'

They rode down the driveway of Xanadu between the jacaranda trees and the smooth wide lawns. Behind them the mansion was grey and unlighted in the half darkness. They took the Pretoria road, climbed to the ridge and checked their horses at the crest. Sean and Duff looked back across the valley. The valley was filled with early morning mist, and the mine headgears probed up out of it. They watched the mists turn to gold as the low sun touched them and a mine hooter howled dismally.

'Couldn't we stay for just a week longer – perhaps we could work something out?' Duff asked softly.

Sean sat silently staring at the golden mist. It was beautiful. It hid the scarred earth and it hid the mills – it was a most appropriate cloak for that evil, greedy city. Sean turned his horse away towards Pretoria and slapped the loose end of his reins across its neck.

– III –

The Wilderness

– 1 –

They stayed five days in Pretoria, just long enough to buy the wagons and commission them, and when they left on the morning of the sixth day they went north on the Hunters Road. The wagons moved in column urged on by the Zulus and a dozen new servants that Sean had hired. They were followed by a mixed bag of black and white urchins and stray dogs; men called good luck after them and women waved from the verandas of the houses which lined the road. Then the town was behind them and they were out into the veld with only a dozen of the more adventurous mongrels still following them.

They made fifteen miles the first day and when they camped that night beside the ford of a small stream, Sean's back and legs ached from his first full day in the saddle in over five years. They drank a little brandy and ate steaks grilled over wood embers, then they let the fire die and sat and looked at the night. The sky was a curtain at which a barrel of grape-shot had been fired, riddling it with the holes through which the stars shone. The voices of the servants made a hive murmur as a background to the wailing of a jackal in the darkness beyond the firelight. They went to their living wagon early and for Sean the feel of rough blankets instead of silk sheets and the hardness of a straw mattress were not sufficient to keep him long from sleep.

From an early start the following morning they put another twenty miles behind them before outspan that night and twenty more the next day. The push and urgent drive were habits Sean had acquired on the Rand when every minute was vital and the loss of a day was a disaster. They were habits that stuck, and he pushed the caravan northward as impatiently as he would have chivvied the men on the Candy Deep who were cutting a drive to intersect the Reef. Then one morning, when they were inspanning the oxen at the usual hour of dawn, Mbejane asked him, 'Do we go to meet someone, Nkosi?'

'No. Why do you ask?'

'When a man moves fast there is usually a reason. I was seeking the reason for our haste.'

'The reason is—' Sean stopped. He looked around him quickly as if to find it, then he cleared his throat and scratched the side of his nose, ' – outspan an hour before high sun,' he finished abruptly and went to his horse. He and Duff rode out a mile or two ahead of the wagons that day, then instead of keeping to the track or hurrying back to chase up the caravan Sean suggested, 'Let's ride across to that kopje over there. We'll leave the horses at the bottom and climb up to the top.'

'What for?' asked Duff.

'For the hell of it – come on.'

They hobbled the horses and set off up the steep side of the kopje, picking their way over the tumbled boulders and through the tangle of tree trunks. They were sweating and blowing hard when they came out on the summit and found a place with shade and a flat rock ledge on which to sit. Sean gave Duff a cheroot and they smoked and looked out across the land that was spread like a map below them.

Here the grasslands of the high veld were starting to blend into the forests and hilly country of the bushveld. There were vleis open as wheatfields, ending suddenly against a hill or bounded by haphazard plantations of tall trees. From the height at which they sat they could trace the courses of underground rivers by the dark green and superior height of the trees that grew above them. Everything else was the colour of Africa – brown, a thousand different shades of brown. Pale brown grass on red brown soil, with twisted, chocolate-brown tree trunks reaching up to the moving masses of brown leaves at their tips. Flickering indefinite brown were the herds of springbok that fed amongst the trees and on the slopes of the bare bulging brown hills, and the brown land reached away vast and unhurried into immeasurable distance, unmarred by the scratchings of man: tranquil and dignified in its immensity.

'It makes me feel small, but sort of safe – as though no one will notice me here,' said Duff, then laughed self-consciously.

'I know what you mean,' Sean answered him. He saw that for the first time since they had left the Rand the strain was gone from Duff's face. They smiled at each other and leaned back against the rock face behind them. They watched their wagons, far below them, coil into the tight circle of the laager and the cattle turned free move out to graze. The sun sank and the shadows stretched out longer and longer across the land. At last they went down the hill and found their horses. That night they stayed later than usual next to the fire and though they talked little there was the old feeling between them again. They had discovered a new reef that was rich with the precious elements of space and time. Out here there was more of those two treasures than a man could use in a dozen lifetimes. Space to move, to ride or to fire a rifle; space spread with sunlight and wind, grass and trees, but not filled with them. There was also time. This was where time began: it was a quiet river, moving but not changed by movement; draw on it as much as you would and still it was always full. It was measured by the seasons but not restricted by them, for the summer that was now standing back to let autumn pass was

377

the same summer that had flamed a thousand years before and would flame again a thousand years hence. In the presence of so much space and time all striving was futile.

From then on their lives took their tempo from the leisurely turning of wagon-wheels. Sean's eyes which had been pointing straight ahead along the line of travel now turned aside to look about him. Each morning he and Duff would leave the wagons and wander out into the bush. Sometimes they would spend the day panning for gold in the sands of a stream, another day they would search for the first signs of elephant, but mostly they just rode and talked or lay hidden and watched the herds of game that daily became more numerous. They killed just enough to feed themselves, their servants and the pack of dogs that had followed them when they left Pretoria. They passed the little Boer settlement at Pietersburg and then the Zoutpansberg climbed up over the horizon, its sheer sides dark with rain forest and high rock cliffs. Here under the mountains they spent a week at Louis Trichardt, the most northerly permanent habitation of white men.

In the town they spoke with men who had hunted to the north of the mountains, across the Limpopo. These were taciturn brown-faced Boers with tobacco-stained beards – big men with the peace of the bush in their eyes. In their courteous, unhurried speech Sean sensed a fierce possessive love of the animals that they hunted and the land through which they moved so freely. They were a different breed from the Natal Afrikanders and those he had met on the Witwatersrand, and he conceived the respect for them that would grow stronger in the years ahead when he would have to fight them.

There was no way through the mountains, they told him, but wagons could pass around them. The western passage skirted the edge of the Kalahari desert and this was bad country where the wagon wheels sank into the sandy

378

soil and the marches between water became successively longer. To the east there was good rich forest land, well watered and stocked with game: low country, hotter the nearer one went to the coast, but the true bushveld where a man could find elephant.

So Sean and Duff turned east and, holding the mountains always in sight at their left hand, they went down into the wilderness.

– 2 –

Within a week's trek they saw elephant sign: trees broken and stripped of their bark. Although it was months old – the trees already dried out – nevertheless Sean felt the thrill of it and that night spent an hour cleaning and oiling his rifles. The forest thickened until the wagons had to weave continually between the trunks of the trees. But there were clearings in the forest – open vleis filled with grass where buffalo grazed like herds of domestic cattle and white tick birds squawked about them. This country was well watered with streams as clear and merry as a Scottish trout stream, but the water was blood-warm and the banks thick with bush. Along the rivers, in the forest and in the open were the herds of game: impala twisting and leaping away at the first approach with their crumpled horns laid back, kudu with big ears and soft eyes, black sable antelope with white bellies and horns curved like a naval cutlass, zebra trotting with the dignity of fat ponies, while about them frolicked their companions, the gnu, waterbuck, nyala, roan antelope and – at last – elephant.

Sean and Mbejane were ranging a mile ahead of the wagons when they found the spoor. It was fresh, so fresh that sap still oozed from the mahoba-hoba tree where the bark had been prised loose with the tip of a tusk and then stripped off. The wood beneath was naked and white.

'Three bulls,' said Mbejane. 'One very big.'

'Wait here.' Sean spun his horse and galloped back to the column. Duff lay on the driver's seat of the first wagon rocking gently to its motion, his hat covering his face and his hands behind his head.

'Elephant! Duff,' Sean yelled. 'Not an hour ahead of us. Get saddled up, man!'

Duff was ready in five minutes. Mbejane was waiting for them; he had already worked the spoor a short distance and picked up the run of it and now he went away on it. They followed him, riding slowly side by side.

'You've hunted elephant before, laddie?' asked Duff.

'Never,' said Sean.

'Good grief!' Duff looked alarmed. 'I thought you were an expert. I think I'll go back and finish my sleep, you can call me when you've had a little more experience.'

'Don't worry,' Sean laughed with excitement. 'I know all about it; I was raised on elephant stories.'

'That sets my heart at ease,' Duff murmured sarcastically and Mbejane glanced over his shoulder at them, not trying to conceal his irritation.

'Nkosi, it is not wise to talk now for we will soon come up with them.'

So they went on in silence: passing a knee-high pile of yellow dung that looked like the contents of a coir mattress, following the oval pad marks in the dust and the trail of torn branches.

It was a good hunt, this first one. The small breeze held steadily into their faces and the spoor ran straight and hot. They closed in, each minute strengthening the certainty of the kill. Sean sat stiff and eager in the saddle with his rifle across his lap, his eyes restlessly moving over the frieze of bush ahead of him. Mbejane stopped suddenly and came back to Sean's stirrup.

'Here they halted for the first time. The sun is hot and they will rest but this place was not to their liking and they have moved on. We will find them soon now.'

'The bush becomes too thick,' Sean grunted; he eyed the untidy tangle of catbush into which the spoor had led them. 'We will leave the horses here with Hlubi and go in on foot.'

'Laddie,' Duff demurred. 'I can run much faster on horseback.'

'Off!' said Sean and nodded to Mbejane to lead. They moved forward again. Sean was sweating and the drops clung heavily to his eyebrows and trickled down his cheeks; he brushed them away. The excitement was an indigestible ball in his stomach and a dryness in his throat.

Duff sauntered casually next to Sean with that small half smile on his face, but there was a quickness in his breathing. Mbejane cautioned them with a gesture of his hand and they stopped. Minutes passed slowly and then Mbejane's hand moved again, pink-palmed eloquence.

'It was nothing,' said the hand. 'Follow me.'

They went on again. There were Mopani flies swarming at the corners of Sean's eyes, drinking the moisture, and he blinked them away. Their buzzing was so loud in his ears that he thought it must carry to their quarry. His every sense was tuned to its limit: hearing magnified, vision sharp and even his sense of smell so clear that he could pick up the taint of dust, the scent of a wild flower and Mbejane's faintly musky body-smell.

Suddenly in front of him Mbejane was still; his hand moved again gently, unmistakably.

'They are here,' said the hand.

Sean and Duff crouched behind him, searching with eyes

that could see only brown bush and grey shadows. The tension coarsened their breathing and Duff was no longer smiling. Mbejane's hand came up slowly and pointed at the wall of vegetation in front of them. The seconds strung together like beads on the string of time and still they searched.

An ear flapped lazily and instantly the picture jumped into focus. Bull elephant, big and very close, grey among grey shadow. Sean touched Mbejane's arm. 'I had seen it,' said that touch.

Slowly Mbejane's hand swivelled and pointed again. Another wait, another searching and then a belly rumbled, a great grey belly filled with half-digested leaves. It was a sound so ridiculous in the silence that Sean wanted to laugh – a gurgling sloshy sound – and Sean saw the other bull. It was standing in shadow also, with long yellow ivory and small eyes tight-closed. Sean put his lips to Duff's ear.

'This one is yours,' he whispered. 'Wait until I get into position for the other,' and he began moving out to the side, each step exposing a little more of the second bull's flank until the shoulder was open to him and he could see the point of the elbow beneath the baggy, wrinkled skin. The angle was right; from here he could reach the heart. He nodded at Duff, brought his rifle up – leaning forward against the recoil, aiming close behind the massive shoulder – and he fired.

The gunfire was shockingly loud in the confined thorn bush; dust flew in a spurt from the bull's shoulder and it staggered from the strike of the bullet. Beyond it the third elephant burst from sleep into flight and Sean's hands moved neatly on his weapon, ejecting and reloading, swinging up and firing again. He saw the bullet hit and he knew it was a mortal wound. The two bulls ran together and the bush opened to them and swallowed them: they were gone, crashing away wounded, trumpeting in pain.

Sean ran after them, dodging through the catbush, oblivious to the sting of the thorns that snatched at him as he passed.

'This way, Nkosi,' Mbejane shouted beside him. 'Quickly or we will lose them.' They sprinted after the sounds of flight – a hundred yards, two hundred, panting now and sweating in the heat. Suddenly the catbush ended and in front of them was a wide riverbed with steep banks. The river sand was blindingly white and in the middle was a sluggish trickle of water. One of the bulls was dead, lying in the stream with the blood washing off him in a pale brown stain. The other bull was trying to climb the far bank; it was too steep for him and he slid back wearily. The blood dripped from the tip of his trunk, and he swung his head to look at Sean and Mbejane. His ears cocked back defiantly and he began his charge, blundering towards them through the soft river sand.

Sean watched him come and there was sadness in him as he brought up his rifle, but it was the proud regret that a man feels when he watches hopeless courage. Sean killed with a brain shot, quickly.

They climbed down the bank into the riverbed and went to the elephant; it knelt with its legs folded under it and its tusks driven deep into the sand with the force of its fall. The flies were already clustering at the little red mouths of the bullet wounds. Mbejane touched one of the tusks and then he looked up at Sean.

'It is a good elephant.' He said no more, for this was not the time to talk. Sean leaned his rifle against the bull's shoulder; he felt in his top pocket for a cheroot and stood with it unlit between his teeth. He would kill more elephant, he knew, but always this would be the one he would remember. He stroked his hand over the rough skin and the bristles were stiff and sharp.

'Where is Nkosi Duff?' Sean remembered him suddenly. 'Did he also kill?'

'He did not shoot,' answered Mbejane.

'What!' Sean turned quickly to Mbejane. 'Why not?'

Mbejane sniffed a pinch of snuff and sneezed, then he shrugged his shoulders.

'It is a good elephant,' he said again, looking down at it.

'We must go back and find him.' Sean snatched up his rifle and Mbejane followed him. They found Duff sitting alone in the catbush with his rifle propped beside him and a water-bottle to his lips. He lowered the bottle as Sean came up and saluted him with it.

'Hail! the conquering hero comes.' There was something in his eyes that Sean could not read.

'Did you miss yours?' Sean asked.

'Yes,' said Duff, 'I missed mine.' He lifted the bottle and drank again. Suddenly and sickeningly Sean was ashamed for him. He dropped his eyes, not wanting to acknowledge Duff's cowardice.

'Let's get back to the wagons,' he said. 'Mbejane can come with packhorses for the tusks.'

They did not ride together on the way home.

– 3 –

It was almost dark when they arrived back at the laager. They gave their horses to one of the servants and washed in the basin that Kandhla had ready for them, then they went to sit by the fire. Sean poured the drinks, fussing over the glasses to avoid looking at Duff. He felt awkward. They'd have to talk about it and he searched his brain for a way to bring it into the open. Duff had shown craven and Sean started to find excuses for him – he may have had a misfire or he may have been unsighted by Sean's shot. At all events Sean determined not to let it stay like this, sour and brooding between them. They'd talk it out then forget it. He carried Duff's glass to him and smiled at him.

'That's right, try and cover it with a grin,' Duff lifted his glass. 'To our big brave hunter. Dammit, laddie, how could you do it?'

Sean stared at Duff. 'What do you mean?'

'You know what I mean, you're so damned guilty you can't even look me in the face. How could you kill those bloody great animals – but even worse how could you *enjoy* doing it?'

Sean subsided weakly into his chair. He couldn't tell which of his emotions was uppermost – relief or surprise. Duff went on quickly.

'I know what you're going to say, I've heard the arguments before – from my dear father. He explained it to me one evening after we'd ridden down a fox. When I say "we", I mean twenty horsemen and forty hounds.'

Sean had not yet rallied from the shock of finding himself in the dock after preparing himself to play the role of prosecutor.

'Don't you like hunting?' he asked incredulously. The way he might have asked, 'don't you like eating?'

'I'd forgotten what it was like. I was carried away by your excitement, but when you started to kill them it all came back to me.' Duff sipped his brandy and stared into the fire. 'They never had a chance. One minute they were sleeping and the next you were ripping them with bullets the way the hounds ripped that fox. They didn't have a chance.'

'But, Duff, it wasn't meant to be a contest.'

'Yes, I know, my father explained that to me. It's a ritual – a sacred rite to Diana. He should have explained it to the fox as well.'

Sean was getting angry now. 'We came out here to hunt ivory – and that's what I'm doing.'

'Tell me that you killed those elephant only for their

teeth, laddie, and I'll call you a liar. You loved it. Christ! You should have seen your face and the face of your damned heathen.'

'All right! I like hunting and the only other man I ever met who didn't was a coward,' Sean shouted at him.

Duff's face paled and he looked up at Sean. 'What are you trying to say?' he whispered. They stared at each other and in the silence Sean had to choose between letting his temper run or keeping Duff's friendship, for the words that would spoil it for ever were crowding into his mouth. He made his hands relax their grip on the arms of his chair.

'I didn't mean that,' he said.

'I hope you didn't.' Duff's grin came precariously back onto his face. 'Tell me why you like hunting, laddie. I'll try and understand but don't expect me to hunt with you again.'

It was like explaining colour to a blind man, describing the lust of the hunter to someone who was born without it. Duff listened in agonized silence as Sean tried to find the words for the excitement that makes a man's blood sing through his body, that heightens his senses and allows him to lose himself in an emotion as old as the urge to mate. Sean tried to show him how the nobler and more beautiful was the quarry, the stronger was the compulsion to hunt and kill it, that it had no conscious cruelty in it but was rather an expression of love: a fierce possessive love. A devouring love that needed the complete and irrevocable act of death for its consummation. By destroying something, a man could have it always as his own: selfish perhaps, but then instinct knows no ethics. It was all very clear to Sean, so much a part of him that he had never tried to voice it before and now he stumbled over the words, gesticulating in helpless inarticulateness, repeating himself, coming at last to the end and knowing by the look on Duff's face that he had failed to show it to him.

'And you were the gentleman who fought Hradsky for the rights of man,' Duff said softly, 'the one who always talked about not hurting people.'

Sean opened his mouth to protest but Duff went on. 'You get ivory for us and I'll look for gold – each of us to what he is best suited. I'll forgive you your elephants as you forgave me my Candy – still equal partners. Agreed?'

Sean nodded and Duff held up his glass.

'It's empty,' he said. 'Do me a favour, laddie.'

– 4 –

There was never any after-taste to their disputes, no rankling of unspoken words or lingering of doubt. What they had in common they enjoyed, where there were differences they accepted them. So when after each hunt the packhorses brought the tusks into the camp there was no trace of censure in Duff's face or voice; there was only the genuine pleasure of having Sean back from the bush. Sometimes it was a good day and Sean would cut the spoor, follow, kill and be back in the laager the same night. But more often, when the herd was moving fast or the ground was hard or he could not kill at the first approach, he would be gone for a week or more. Each time he returned they celebrated, drinking and laughing far into the night, lying late in bed the next morning, playing Klabejas on the floor of the wagon between their cots or reading aloud out of the books that Duff had brought with him from Pretoria. Then a day or two later Sean would be gone again, with his dogs and his gunboys trotting behind him.

This was a different Sean from the one who had whored it up at the Opera House and presided over the panelled offices in Eloff Street. His beard, no longer groomed and shaped by a barber, curled onto his chest. The doughy colour of his face and arms had been turned by the sun to the rich brown of a newly-baked loaf. The seat of his pants that had been stretched to danger point across his rump now hung loosely; his arms were thicker and the soft swell of fat had given way to the flatness and bulge of hard muscle. He walked straighter, moved quicker and laughed more easily.

In Duff the change was less noticeable. He was lean and gaunt-faced as ever, but now there was less of the restlessness in his eyes. His speech and movements were slower and the golden beard he was growing had the strange effect of making him appear younger. Each morning he left the wagons, taking one of the servants with him, and spent the days wandering in the bush, tapping with his prospecting hammer at the occasional outcrops of rock or squatting beside a stream and spinning the gravel in his pan. Every evening he came back to camp and analysed the bag of rock samples he had collected during the day; then he threw them away, bathed and set out a bottle and two glasses on the table beside the fire. While he ate his supper he listened and waited for the dogs to bark, for the sound of horses in the darkness and Sean's voice. If the night remained silent he put the bottle away and climbed up into his wagon. He was lonely then, not with a deep loneliness but just enough to add relish to Sean's return.

Always they moved east, until gradually the silhouette of the Zoutpansberg softened as the mountains became less steep and began to fade into the tail of the range. Scouting along their edge Sean found a pass and they took the wagons up and over and down into the Limpopo valley beyond. Here the country changed character again; it became flat, the monotony of thorn scrub relieved only by the baobab trees with their great, swollen trunks crowned in a little halo of branches. Water was scarce and Sean rode ahead from each camp to find the next waterhole before they moved. However, the hunting was good for the game was concentrated on the isolated drinking places, and before they were halfway from the mountains to the Limpopo Sean had filled another wagon with ivory.

'We'll be coming back this way, I suppose?' Duff asked.

'I suppose so,' agreed Sean.

'Well then, I don't see any point in carrying a ton of ivory with us. Let's bury it and we can pick it up on our way back.'

Sean looked at him thoughtfully. 'About once in every year you come up with a good idea – we'll do exactly that.'

The next camp was a good one. There was water – an acre of muddy liquid not as heavily salted with elephant urine as some of the previous ones had been; there was shade provided by a grove of wild fig trees and the grazing was of a quality that promised to restore the condition that the oxen had lost since crossing the mountains. They decided to make it a rest camp: bury the ivory, do some repairs and maintenance on the wagons and let the servants and animals fatten up a little. The first task was to dig a hole large enough to contain all the hundred-odd tusks they had accumulated and it was evening on the third day before they finished.

– 5 –

Sean and Duff sat together inside the laager and watched the sun go down, bleeding below the land, and after it had gone the clouds were oyster and lilac-coloured in the brief twilight. Kandhla threw wood on the fire and it burnt up fiercely. They ate grilled kudu liver, and thick steaks with a rind of yellow fat on them, and they drank brandy with their coffee. The conversation lagged into contented silence for they were both tired. They sat staring into the fire, too lazy to make the effort required for bed. Sean watched the fire pictures form in the coals, the faces and the phantoms flickering and fading. He saw a tiny temple have its columns pulled out from under it by a fiery Samson and collapse in a shower of sparks – a burning horse changed magically into a dragon of blue flame. He looked away to rest his eyes and when he turned back there was a small black scorpion scuttling out from under the loose bark on one of the logs. It lifted its tail like the arm of a flamenco dancer and the flames that ringed it shone on its glossy body armour. Duff was also watching it, leaning forward with his elbows on his knees.

'Will he sting himself to death before the flames reach him?' he asked softly. 'I have heard that they do.'

'No,' said Sean.

'Why not?'

'Only man has the intelligence to end the inevitable; in all other creatures the instinct of survival is too strong,' Sean answered him, and the scorpion crabbed sideways from the nearest flames and stopped again with its raised sting jerking slightly. 'Besides he's immune to his own poison so he has no choice.'

'He could jump down into the fire and get it over with,' murmured Duff, subdued by the little tragedy.

The scorpion started its last desperate circuit of the closing ring. Its tail drooped and the grip of its claws was unsteady on the rough bark; it was shrivelling with the heat, its legs curling up and its tail subsiding. The flames caressed it with swift yellow hands and smeared its shiny body with the dullness of death. The log tipped sideways and the speck was gone.

'Would you?' asked Sean. 'Would you have jumped?'

Duff sighed softly. 'I don't know,' he said and stood up. 'I'm going to pump out my bilges and crawl into bed.' He walked away and went to stand at the edge of the circle of firelight.

Since they had left Pretoria the small voices of the jackals had yapped discreetly around each outspan – they were so much a part of the African night that they went unnoticed – but now suddenly there was a difference. Only one jackal spoke, and with a voice that stammered shrilly – a sound of pain, a crazy hysterical shrieking that made Sean's skin prickle. He scrambled to his feet and stood staring undecided into the darkness. The jackal was coming towards the camp, coming fast – and suddenly Sean knew what was happening.

'Duff!' he called. 'Come back here! Run, man, run!'

Duff looked back at Sean helplessly, his hands held low in front of him and his water arcing down, curving silver in the firelight from his body to the ground.

'Duff!' Sean's voice was a shout. 'It's a rabid jackal. Run, damn you, run!' The jackal was close now, very close, but at last Duff started to move. He was halfway back to the fire before he tripped. He fell and rolled over and brought his feet up under his body to rise. His head turned to face the darkness from which it would come. Then Sean saw it. It flitted out of the shadows like a grey moth in the bad light and went straight for where Duff knelt. Sean saw him try to cover his face with his hands as the jackal sprang at him. One of the dogs twisted out of Mbejane's hand and brushed past Sean's legs. Sean snatched up a piece of firewood and sprinted after it, but already Duff was on his back, his arms flailing frantically as he tried to push away the terrier-sized animal that was slashing at his face and hands. The dog caught it and dragged it off, worrying it, growling through locked jaws. Sean hit the jackal with the club – breaking its back. He swung again and again, beating its body into shapelessness before he turned to Duff. Duff was on his feet now. He had unwound the scarf from his neck and was mopping with it at his face but the blood dribbled down his chin and blotched the front of his shirt. His hands were trembling. Sean led him close to the fire, pulled Duff's hands down and examined the bites. His nose was torn and the flesh of one cheek hung open in a flap.

'Sit down!'

Duff obeyed, holding the scarf to his face again. Sean went quickly to the fire: with a stick he raked embers into a pile, then he drew his hunting-knife and thrust the blade into the coals.

'Mbejane,' he called, without taking his eyes off the knife. 'Throw that jackal onto the fire. Put on plenty of wood. Do not touch its body with your hands. When you have done that tie up that dog and keep the others away from it.' Sean turned the knife in the fire. 'Duff, drink as much of that brandy as you can.'

'What are you going to do?'

'You know what I've got to do.'

'He bit my wrist as well.' Duff held up his hand for Sean to see the punctures, black holes from which the blood oozed watery and slow.

'Drink.' Sean pointed at the brandy bottle. For a second they looked at each other and Sean saw the horror moving in Duff's eyes: horror of the hot knife and horror of the germs which had been injected into him. The germs that must be burnt out before they escaped into his blood, to breed and ferment there until they ate into his brain and rode him to a screaming, gibbering death.

'Drink,' said Sean again. Duff took up the bottle and lifted it to his mouth. Sean stooped and pulled the knife out of the fire. He held the blade an inch from the back of his hand. It was not hot enough. He thrust it back into the coals.

'Mbejane, Hlubi, stand on each side of the Nkosi's chair.

392

Be ready to hold him.' Sean loosened his belt, doubled the thick leather and handed it to Duff. 'Bite on this.'

He turned back to the fire and this time when he drew the knife its blade was pale pink. 'Are you ready?'

'The work you are about to do will break the hearts of a million maids.' A last hoarse attempt at humour from Duff.

'Hold him,' said Sean.

Duff gasped at the touch of the knife – a great shuddering gasp – and his back arched, but the two Zulus held him down remorselessly. The edges of the wound blackened and hissed as Sean ran the blade in deeper. The stink of burning brought the vomit into his throat. He clenched his teeth. When he stepped back Duff hung slackly in the Zulus' hands, sweat had soaked his shirt and wet his hair. Sean heated the knife again and cleaned the bites in Duff's wrist while Duff moaned and writhed weakly in the chair. He smeared axle grease over the burns and bandaged the wrist loosely with strips torn from a clean shirt. They lifted Duff into the wagon and laid him on his cot. Sean went out to where Mbejane had tied the dog. He found scratches beneath the hair on its shoulder. They put a sack over its head to stop it biting and Sean cauterized its wounds also.

'Tie it to the far wagon, do not let the other dogs near it, see it has food and water,' he told Mbejane.

Then he went back to Duff. Delirious with pain and brandy Duff did not sleep at all that night and Sean stayed by his cot until the morning.

About fifty yards from the laager under one of the wild fig trees the servants built Duff a hut. The framework was of poles and over it they stretched a tarpaulin. They made a bed for him and brought his mattress and blankets from the wagon. Sean joined four trekchains together, forging new links and hammering them closed. He passed one end of the chain round the base of the fig tree and riveted it back up on itself. Duff sat in the shade of a wagon and watched them work. His hurt hand was in a sling and his face was swollen, the wound crusty-looking and edged in angry red. When he was finished with the chain, Sean walked across to him.

'I'm sorry, Duff, we have to do it.'

'They abolished the slave trade some time ago – just in case you didn't know.' Duff tried to grin with his distorted face. He stood up and followed Sean to the hut. Sean looped the loose end of the chain round Duff's waist. He locked it with a bolt through two of the links then flattened the end of the bolt with a dozen strokes of the hammer.

'That should hold you.'

'An excellent fit,' Duff commended him. 'Now let us inspect my new quarters.'

Sean followed him into the hut. Duff lay down on the bed. He looked very tired and sick.

'How long will it take before we know?' he asked quietly.

Sean shook his head. 'I'm not sure. I think you should stay here at least a month – after that we'll allow you back into society.'

'A month – it's going to be fun. Lying here expecting any minute to start barking like a dog and lifting my leg against the nearest tree.'

Sean didn't laugh. 'I did a thorough job with the knife.

It's a thousand to one you'll be all right. This is just a precaution.'

'The odds are attractive – I'll put a fiver on it.' Duff crossed his ankles and stared up at the roof. Sean sat down on the edge of the bed. It was a long time before Duff ended the silence.

'What will it be like, Sean? Have you ever seen someone with rabies?'

'No.'

'But you've heard about it, haven't you? Tell me what you've heard about it,' Duff persisted.

'For Chrissake, Duff, you're not going to get it.'

'Tell me, Sean, tell me what you know about it.' Duff sat up and caught hold of Sean's arm.

Sean looked steadily at him for a moment before he answered. 'You saw that jackal, didn't you?'

Duff sank back onto his pillows. 'Oh, my God!' he whispered.

Together they started the long wait. They used another tarpaulin to make an open shelter next to the hut and under it they spent the days that followed.

In the beginning it was very bad. Sean tried to pull Duff out of the black despair into which he had slumped, but Duff sat for hours at a time gazing out into the bush, fingering the scabs on his face and only occasionally smiling at the banquet of choice stories that Sean spread for him. But at last Sean's efforts were rewarded – Duff began to talk. He spoke of things he had never mentioned before and listening to him Sean learned more about him than he had in the previous five years. Sometimes Duff paced up and down in front of Sean's chair with the chain hanging down behind him like a tail; at other times he sat quietly, his voice filled with longing for the mother he had never known.

' – there was a portrait of her in the upper gallery, I used to spend whole afternoons in front of it. It was the kindest face I had ever seen—'

Then it hardened again as he remembered his father, 'that old bastard'.

He talked of his daughter. ' – she had a fat chuckle that would break your heart. The snow on her grave made it look like a big sugar-iced cake, she would have liked that—'

At other times his voice was puzzled as he examined some past action of his, angry as he remembered a mistake or a missed opportunity. Then he would break off and grin self-consciously. 'I say, I am talking a lot of drivel.'

The scabs on his face began to dry up and come away, and more often now his old gaiety bubbled to the surface.

On one of the poles that supported the tarpaulin roof he started a calendar, cutting a notch for each day. It became a daily ceremony. He cut each notch with the concentration of a sculptor carving marble and when he had finished he would stand back and count them aloud as if by doing so he could force them to add up to thirty, the number that would allow him to shed his chain.

There were eighteen notches on the pole when the dog went mad. It was in the afternoon. They were playing Klabejas. Sean had just dealt the cards when the dog started screaming from among the wagons. Sean knocked over his chair as he jumped up. He snatched his rifle from where it leant against the wall and ran down to the laager. He disappeared behind the wagon to which the dog was tied and almost immediately Duff heard the shot. In the abrupt and complete stillness that followed, Duff slowly lowered his face into his hands.

It was nearly an hour before Sean came back. He picked up his chair, set it to the table and sat down.

'It's you to call – are you going to take on?' he asked as he picked up his cards. They played with grim intensity, fixing their attention on the cards, but both of them knew that there was a third person at the table now.

'Promise you'll never do that to me,' Duff blurted out at last.

Sean looked up at him. 'That I'll never do what to you?'

'What you did to that dog.'

The dog! The bloody dog. He should never have taken a chance with it, he should have destroyed it that first night.

'Just because the dog got it doesn't mean that you—'

'Swear to me,' Duff interrupted fiercely, 'swear you won't bring the rifle to me.'

'Duff, you don't know what you're asking. Once you've got it—' Sean stopped; anything he said would make it worse.

'Promise me,' Duff repeated.

'All right, I swear it then.'

– 7 –

It was worse now than it had been in the beginning. Duff abandoned his calendar and with it the hope that had been slowly growing stronger. If the days were bad then the nights were hell, for Duff had a dream. It came to him every night – sometimes two or three times. He tried to keep awake after Sean had left, reading by the light of a lantern; or he lay and listened to the night noises, the splash and snort of buffalo drinking down at the waterhole, the liquid half-warble of night birds or the deep drumming of a lion. But in the end he would have to sleep and then he dreamed.

He was on horseback riding across a flat brown plain: no hills, no trees, nothing but lawnlike grass stretching away on all sides to the horizon. His horse threw no shadow – he always looked for a shadow and it worried him that there never was one. Then he would find the pool – clear water, blue and strangely shiny. The pool frightened him but he could not stop himself going to it. He would kneel beside it and look into the water; the reflection of his own face looked up at him – animal-snouted, shaggy-brown with wolf teeth, white and long. He would wake then and the horror of that face would last until morning.

Nearly desperate with his own utter helplessness, Sean tried to help him. Because of the accord they had established over the years and because they were so close to each other, Sean had to suffer with him. He tried to shut himself off from it; sometimes he succeeded for an hour or even half a morning, but then it came back with a stomach-swooping shock. Duff was going to die – Duff was going to die an unspeakable death. Was it a mistake to let someone get too deep inside you, so that you must share his agony in every excruciating detail? Didn't a man have enough of his own that he must share the full measure of another's suffering?

By then the October winds had started, the heralds of the rain: hot winds full of dust, winds that dried the sweat on a man's body before it had time to cool him, thirsty winds that during daylight brought the game to the water-hole in full view of the camp.

Sean had half a case of wine hoarded under his cot. That last evening he cooled four bottles, wrapping them in wet sacking. He took them up to Duff's shelter just before supper and set them on the table. Duff watched him. The scars on his face were almost completely healed now, glassy red marks on his pale skin.

'Chateau Olivier,' said Sean and Duff nodded.

'It's a good wine – most probably travel-sick.'

'Well, if you don't want it, I'll take it away again,' said Sean.

'I'm sorry, laddie,' Duff spoke quickly. 'I didn't mean to be ungrateful. This wine suits my mood tonight. Did you know that wine is a sad drink?'

'Nonsense!' Sean disagreed as he twisted the corkscrew into the first cork. 'Wine is gay.' He poured a little into Duff's glass and Duff picked it up and held it towards the fire so the light shone through it.

'You see only the surface, Sean. A good wine has the elements of tragedy within it. The better the wine the more sad it is.'

Sean snorted. 'Explain yourself,' he invited.

Duff put his glass down on the table again and stared at it. 'How long do you suppose this wine has taken to reach its present perfection?'

'Ten or fifteen years, I suppose,' Sean answered.

Duff nodded. 'And now all that remains is to drink it – the work of years destroyed in an instant. Don't you think that is sad?' Duff asked softly.

'My God, Duff, don't be so damned morbid.'

But Duff wasn't listening to him. 'Wine and mankind have this in common. They can find perfection only in age, in a lifetime of seeking. Yet in the finding they find also their own destruction.'

'So you think that if a man lives long enough he will reach perfection?' Sean challenged him, and Duff answered him still staring at the glass.

'Some grapes grew in the wrong soil, some were diseased before they went to the press and some were spoiled by a careless vintner – not all grapes make good wine.' Duff picked up his glass and tasted from it, then he went on. 'A man takes longer and he must find it not within the quiet confines of the cask but in the cauldron of life; therefore his is the greater tragedy.'

'Yes, but no one can live for ever,' Sean protested.

'So you think that makes it less sad?' Duff shook his

head. 'You're wrong, of course. It does not detract from it, it enhances it. If only there were some escape, some way of ensuring that what is good could endure instead of this complete hopelessness.'

Duff lay back in his chair, his face pale and gaunt-looking. 'Even that I could accept, if only they had given me more time.'

'I've had enough of this talk. Let's discuss something else. I don't know what you're worrying about. You're not fit to drink yet, you've got another twenty or thirty years to go,' Sean said gruffly and Duff looked up at him for the first time.

'Have I, Sean?'

Sean couldn't meet his eyes. He knew Duff was going to die. Duff grinned his lopsided grin and looked down again at his glass. Slowly the grin disappeared and he spoke again.

'If only I had more time, I could have done it. I could have found the weak places and fortified them. I could have seen the answers.' His voice rose higher. 'I could have! I know I could have! Oh God, I'm not ready yet. I need more time.' His voice was shrill and his eyes wild and haunted. 'It's too soon – it's too soon!'

Sean couldn't stand it, he jumped up and caught Duff's shoulders and shook him.

'Shut up, God damn you, shut up,' he shouted at him. Duff was panting, his lips were parted and quivering. He touched them with the tips of his fingers as though to stop them.

'I'm sorry, laddie, I didn't mean to let go like that.' Sean dropped his hands from Duff's shoulders.

'Both of us are too damned edgy,' he said. 'It's going to be all right, you wait and see.'

'Yes – it will be all right.' Duff ran his fingers through his hair, combing it back from his eyes. 'Open another bottle, laddie.'

8

That night after Sean had gone to bed, Duff had his dream again. The wine he had drunk slowed him down and prevented him from waking. He was trapped in his fancy, struggling to escape into wakefulness but only reaching the surface before he sank back to dream that dream again.

Sean went up to Duff's shelter the next morning early. Although the night's coolness still lingered under the spreading branches of the wild figs the rising day promised to blow dry and burn hot. The animals could sense it. The trek oxen were clustered among the trees and a small herd of eland was moving from the waterhole. The bull, with his short thick horns and the dark tuft on his forehead, was leading his cows away to find shade. Sean stood in the doorway of the hut and waited while his eyes adjusted themselves to its gloom. Duff was awake.

'Get out of bed or you'll have bed sores to add to your happiness.'

Duff swung his feet off the litter and groaned.

'What did you put in that wine last night?' He massaged his temples gently. 'I've got a hundred hobgoblins doing a Cossack dance around the roof of my skull.'

Sean felt the first twinge of alarm. He put his hand on Duff's shoulder feeling for the heat of fever, but Duff was quite cool. He relaxed.

'Breakfast's ready,' said Sean. Duff played with his porridge and barely tasted the grilled eland liver. He kept screwing his eyes up against the glare of the sun and when they had finished their coffee he pushed back his chair.

'I'm going to take my tender head to bed.'

'All right.' Sean stood up as well. 'We're a bit short of meat. I'll go and see if I can get a buck.'

'No, stay and talk to me,' Duff said quickly. 'We can have a few hands of cards.'

They hadn't played in days and Sean agreed readily. He sat on the end of Duff's bed and within half an hour he had won thirty-two pounds from him.

'You must let me teach you this game sometime,' he gloated.

Petulantly, Duff threw his hand in. 'I don't feel like playing any more.' He pressed his fingers to his closed eyelids. 'I can't concentrate with this headache.'

'Do you want to sleep?' Sean gathered up the cards and put them in their box.

'No. Why don't you read to me?'

Duff picked up a leather-bound copy of *Bleak House* from the table beside the bed and tossed it into Sean's lap.

'Where shall I start?' Sean asked.

'It doesn't matter, I know it almost by heart.' Duff lay back and closed his eyes. 'Start anywhere.'

Sean read aloud. He stumbled on for half an hour with his tongue never quite catching the rhythm of the words. Once or twice he glanced up at Duff, but Duff lay still with a faint sheen of sweat on his face and the scars very noticeable. He was breathing easily. Dickens is a powerful sleeping-draught for a hot morning and Sean's eyelids sagged down and his voice slowed and finally stopped. The book slid off his lap.

The small tinkle of Duff's chain disturbed him; he awoke and looked at the bed. Duff crouched apelike. The madness was a fire in his eyes and his cheeks twitched. A yellowish froth coated his teeth and formed a thin line of scum along his lips.

'Duff—' Sean said, and Duff lunged at him with fingers hooked and a noise in his throat that was not human nor yet animal. It was a sound that jellied Sean's stomach and took the strength from his legs.

'Don't!' screamed Sean, and the chain caught on one of the posts of the bed, jerking Duff back sprawling onto the bed before he could sink his teeth into Sean's paralysed body.

Sean ran. He ran out of the hut and into the bush. He ran with terror trembling in his legs and choking his breath. He ran with his heart taking its beat from his racing feet and his lungs pumping in disordered panic. A branch ripped across his cheek and the sting of it served to steady him. His feet slowed – he stopped and stood gasping, staring back towards the camp. He waited while his body settled and he forced his terror down until it was only a sickening sensation in his stomach. Then he circled through the thorn bush and approached the laager from the side farthest away from Duff's shelter. The camp was empty, the servants had fled in the same terror that had driven Sean. He remembered that his rifle was still in the hut beside Duff's bed. He slipped into his wagon and quickly opened the case of unused rifles. His hands were unsteady again as he fumbled with the locks, for the chain might have parted and at every second he expected to hear that inhuman sound behind him. He found his bandolier hanging on the end of his cot and he took cartridges from it. He loaded the rifle and cocked it. The weight of steel and wood in his hands gave him comfort. It made him a man again.

He jumped down out of the wagon and with the rifle held ready he went cautiously out of the circle of wagons. The chain had held. Duff stood in the shade of the wild fig plucking at it. He was making a sound like a new-born puppy. His back was turned to Sean and he was naked, his torn clothing scattered about him. Sean walked slowly towards him. He stopped outside the reach of the chain.

'Duff!' Sean called uncertainly. Duff spun and crouched, the froth was thick in his golden beard; he looked at Sean and his teeth bared. Then he charged screaming until the chain caught him and threw him onto his back once more. He scrambled to his feet and fought the chain, his eyes fastened hungrily on Sean. Sean backed away. He brought up the rifle and aimed between Duff's eyes.

Swear to me. Swear to me you won't bring the rifle to me.

Sean's aim wavered. He kept moving backwards. Duff was bleeding now. The steel links had smeared the skin off his hips, but still he pulled against them fighting to get at Sean – and Sean was shackled just as effectively by his promise. He could not end it. He lowered the rifle and watched in impotent pity.

Mbejane came to him at last.

'Come away, Nkosi. If you will not end it, come away. He no longer has need of you. The sight of you inflames him.'

Duff still struggled and screamed against his chain. From his torn waist the blood trickled down and clung in the hair of his legs with the stickiness of molten chocolate. With each jerk of his head the froth sprayed from his mouth and splattered his chest and arms.

Mbejane led Sean back into the laager. The other servants were there and Sean roused himself to give orders.

'I want everyone away from here. Take blankets and food – go camp on the far side of the water. I will send for you when it is over.' He waited until they had gathered their belongings and as they were leaving he called Mbejane back. 'What must I do?' he asked.

'If a horse breaks a leg?' Mbejane answered him with a question.

'I gave him my word,' Sean shook his head desperately, still facing towards the sound of Duff's raving.

'Only a rogue and a brave man can break an oath,' Mbejane answered simply. 'We will wait for you.' He turned and followed the others. When they were gone Sean hid in one of the wagons and through a tear in the canvas he

404

watched Duff. He saw the idiotic shaking of his head, the curious shambling gait as he moved around the circle of the chain. He watched when the pain made him roll on the ground and claw at his head, tearing out tufts of hair and leaving long scratches down his face. He listened to the sounds of insanity: the bewildered bellows of pain, the senseless giggling and that growl, that terrible growl.

A dozen times he sighted along the rifle barrel, holding his aim until the sweat ran into his eyes and blurred them and he had to take the butt from his shoulder and turn away.

Out there on the end of the chain, its exposed flesh reddening in the sun a piece of Sean was dying. Some of his youth, some of his laughter, some of his carefree love of life – so he had to creep back to the hole in the canvas and watch.

The sun reached its peak and started down again and the thing on the chain grew weaker. It fell and was a long time crawling on its hands and knees before it regained its feet again.

An hour before sunset Duff had his first convulsion. He was standing facing Sean's wagon, swinging his head from side to side, his mouth working silently. The convulsion took him and he stiffened; his lips pulled up grinning, showing his teeth, his eyes rolled back and disappeared leaving only the whites, and his body started to bend backwards. That beautiful body, still slim as a boy's with the long moulded legs, bending tighter and tighter until with a brittle crack the spine snapped and he fell. He lay wriggling, moaning softly and his trunk was twisted at an impossible angle from the broken spine.

Sean jumped from the wagon and ran to him: standing over him he shot Duff in the head and turned away. He flung his rifle from him and heard it clatter on the hard earth. He walked back to his wagon and took a blanket off

Duff's cot. He came back and wrapped Duff in it, averting his eyes from the mutilated head. He carried him to the shelter and laid him on the bed. The blood soaked through the blanket, spreading on the cloth, like ink spilled on blotting-paper. Sean sank down on the chair beside the bed.

Outside the darkness gathered and became complete. Once in the night a hyena came and snuffled at the blood outside on the earth, then it moved away. There was a pride of lions hunting in the bush beyond the waterhole; they killed two hours before dawn and Sean sat in the darkness and listened to their jubilant roaring.

In the morning, Sean stood up stiffly from his chair and went down to the wagons. Mbejane was waiting beside the fire in the laager.

'Where are the others?' Sean asked.

Mbejane stood up. 'They wait where you sent them. I came alone – knowing you would need me.'

'Yes,' said Sean. 'Get two axes from the wagon.'

They gathered wood, a mountain of dry wood, and packed it around Duff's bed – then Sean put fire to it. Mbejane saddled a horse for Sean and he mounted up and looked down at the Zulu.

'Bring the wagons on to the next waterhole. I will meet you there.'

Sean rode out of the laager. He looked back only once and saw that the breeze had spread the smoke from the pyre in a mile long smudge across the tops of the thorn trees.

9

Like a bag of pus at the root of an infected tooth the guilt and grief rotted in Sean's mind. His guilt was double-edged. He had betrayed Duff's trust, and he had lacked the courage to make the betrayal worthwhile. He had waited too long. He should have done it at the beginning, cleanly and quickly, or he should not have done it at all. He longed with every fibre of his body to be given the chance to do it again, but this time the right way. He would gladly have lived once more through all that horror to clear his conscience and clean the stain from the memory of their friendship.

His grief was a thing of emptiness, an aching void – so immense that he was lost in it. Where before there had been Duff's laughter, his twisted grin and his infectious zest there was now only a grey nothingness. No glimmer of sun penetrated it and there were no solid shapes in it.

The next waterhole was shallow soup in the centre of a flat expanse of dry mud the size of a polo field. The mud was cracked in an irregular chequered pattern forming small brickettes, each the size of a hand. A man could have jumped across the water without wetting his feet. Scattered thickly round its circumference were the droppings of the animals that had drunk there. Back and forth across its surface, changing direction as the wind veered, a few loose feathers sailed. The water was brackish and dirty. It was a bad camp. On the third day Mbejane went to Sean's wagon. Sean lay in his cot. He had not changed his clothes since leaving Duff. His beard was beginning to mat, sticky with sweat for it was hot as an oven under the wagon canvas.

'Nkosi, will you come and look at the water. I do not think we should stay here.'

'What is wrong with it?' Sean asked without interest.

'It is dirty, I think we should go on towards the big river.'

'Do whatever you think is right.' Sean rolled away from him, his face towards the side of the wagon.

So Mbejane took the wagon-train down towards the Limpopo. It was two days later that they found the ribbon of dark green trees that lined the banks. Sean stayed in his cot throughout the trek, jolting over the rough ground, sweating in the heat but oblivious to all discomfort. Mbejane put the wagons into laager on the bank above the riverbed, then he and all the other servants waited for Sean to come to life again. Their talk round the fire at nights was baited with worry and they looked often towards Sean's living wagon, where it stood unlit by lantern, dark as the mood of the man that lay within.

Like a bear coming out of its cave at the end of winter, Sean came out of the wagon at last. His clothes were filthy. The dogs hurried to meet him, crowding round his knees, begging for attention and he did not notice them. Vaguely he answered the greetings of his servants. He wandered down the bank into the riverbed.

The summer had shrunk the Limpopo into a sparse line of pools strung out down the centre of the watercourse. The pools were dark olive green. The sand around them was white, glaring snowfield white, and the boulders that choked the barely moving river were black and polished smooth. The banks were steep, half a mile apart and walled in with trees. Sean walked through the sand, sinking to his ankles with each step. He reached the water and sat down at the edge, he dabbled his hand in it and found it warm as blood. In the sand next to him was the long slither mark of a crocodile, and a troop of monkeys were shaking the branches of a tree on the far bank and chattering at him. A pair of Sean's dogs splashed across the narrow neck between two pools and went off to chase the monkeys. They went half-heartedly with their tongues flapping at the corners of their mouths for it was very hot in the whiteness of the riverbed. Sean stared into the green water. It was lonely without Duff; he had only his guilt and his sorrow for company. One of the dogs that had stayed with him touched his cheek with its cold nose. Sean put his arm round its neck and the dog leaned against him. He heard footsteps in the sand behind him, he turned and looked up. It was Mbejane.

'Nkosi, Hlubi has found elephant not an hour's march up stream. He has counted twenty who show good ivory.'

Sean looked back at the water. 'Go away,' he said.

Mbejane squatted down beside him with his elbows on his knees. 'For whom do you mourn?' he asked.

'Go away, Mbejane, leave me alone.'

'Nkosi Duff does not need your sorrow – therefore I think that you mourn for yourself.' Mbejane picked up a pebble and tossed it into the pool.

'When a traveller gets a thorn in his foot,' Mbejane went on softly, 'and he is wise he plucks it out – and he is a fool who leaves it and says "I will keep this thorn to prick me so that I will always remember the road upon which I have travelled." Nkosi, it is better to remember with pleasure than with pain.' Mbejane lobbed another pebble into the pool, then he stood up and walked back to the camp. When Sean followed him ten minutes later he found a saddle on his horse, his rifle in the scabbard and Mbejane and Hlubi waiting with their spears. Kandhla handed him his hat, he held it by the brim, turning it in his hands. Then he clapped it onto his head and swung up onto the horse.

'Lead,' he ordered.

During the next weeks Sean hunted with a single-mindedness that left no time for brooding. His returns to the wagons were short and intermittent; his only reasons for returning at all were to bring in the ivory and change his horse. At the end of one of these brief visits to camp and as Sean was about to mount up for another hunt, even Mbejane complained. 'Nkosi, there are better ways to die than working too hard.'

'You look well enough,' Sean assured him, although Mbejane was now as lean as a greyhound and his skin shone like washed anthracite.

'Perhaps all men look healthy to a man on horseback,' Mbejane suggested and Sean stopped with one foot in the stirrup. He looked at Mbejane thoughtfully, then he lowered his leg again. 'We hunt on foot now, Mbejane, and the first to ask for mercy earns the right to be called "woman" by the other.'

Mbejane grinned; the challenge was to his liking. They crossed the river and found spoor before midday – a small herd of young bulls. They followed it until nightfall and slept huddled together under one blanket, then they went on again next morning. On the third day they lost the spoor in rocky ground and they cast back towards the river. They picked up another herd within ten miles of the wagons, went after them and killed that evening – three fine bulls, not a tusk between them under fifty pounds weight. A night march back to the wagons, four hours' sleep and they were away again. Sean was limping a little now and on the second day out, during one of their infrequent halts, he pulled off his boot. The blister on his heel had burst and his sock was stiff with dried blood. Mbejane looked at him expressionlessly. 'How far are we from the wagons?' asked Sean.

'We can be back before dark, Nkosi.' Mbejane carried Sean's rifle for him on the return. Not once did his mask of solemnity slip. Back in camp Kandhla brought a basin of hot water and set it in front of Sean's chair. While Sean soaked his feet in it his entire following squatted in a circle about him. Every face wore an expression of studied concern and the silence was broken only by the clucking sounds of

410

Bantu sympathy. They were loving every minute of it and Mbejane, with the timing of a natural actor, was building up the effect, playing to his audience. Sean puffed at a cheroot, scowling to stop himself laughing. Mbejane cleared his throat and spat into the fire. Every eye was on him; they waited breathlessly.

'Nkosi,' said Mbejane, 'I would set fifty head of oxen as your marriage price – if you were my daughter.'

One instant more of silence, then a shout of laughter. Sean laughed with them at first, but after a while when Hlubi had nearly staggered into the fire and Nonga was sobbing loudly on Mbejane's shoulder with tears of mirth streaming down his cheeks, Sean's own laughter stopped. It wasn't *that* funny.

He looked at them sourly – at their wide open pink mouths and their white teeth, at their shaking shoulders and heaving chests and suddenly it came to him very clearly that they were no longer laughing at him. They were laughing for the joy of it. They were laughing because they were alive. A chuckle rattled up Sean's throat and escaped before he could stop it, another one bounced around inside his chest and he lay back in his chair, opened his mouth and let it come. The hell with it, he was alive, too.

In the morning when he climbed out of his wagon and limped across to see what Kandhla was cooking for breakfast, there was a faint excitement in him again, the excitement of a new day. He felt good. Duff's memory was still with him, it always would be, but now it was not a sickening ache. He had plucked out the thorn.

10

They moved camp three times in November, keeping to the south bank of the river, following it back towards the west. Slowly the wagons which they had emptied of ivory beside the waterhole began to fill again, for the game was concentrated along the river. The rest of the land was dry but now each day there was promise of relief.

The clouds that had been scattered across the sky began to crowd together, gathering into rounded dark-edged masses or rearing proudly into thunderheads. All of nature seemed impressed by their growing importance. In the evenings the sun dressed them in royal purple and during the day the whirlwinds did dervish dances for their entertainment. The rains were coming. Sean had to make a decision, cross the Limpopo and cut himself off from the south when the river flooded, or stay where he was and leave the land beyond undisturbed. It wasn't a difficult decision. They found a place where the banks flattened out a little on both sides of the river. They unloaded the first wagon and double-teamed it; then with everybody shouting encouragement the oxen galloped down the steep slope into the riverbed. The wagon bounced behind them until it hit the sand where it came to a halt, tilted at an abandoned angle, with its wheels sunk axle-deep into the sand.

'Onto the spokes,' shouted Sean. 'They flung themselves on the wheels and strained to keep them turning, but half the oxen were down on their knees, powerless in the loose footing.

'Damn it to hell.' Sean glared at the wagon. 'Outspan the oxen and take them back. Get out the axes.'

It took them three days to lay a bridge of corduroyed branches across the river and another two to get all the wagons and ivory to the far bank. Sean declared a holiday when the last wagon was manhandled into the laager and the whole camp slept late the next morning. The sun was high by the time Sean descended from his wagon. He was still muzzy and a little liverish from lying abed. He yawned wide and stretched like a crucifix. He ran his tongue round his mouth and grimaced at the taste, then he scratched his chest and the hair rasped under his fingers.

'Kandhla, where's the coffee? Don't you care that I am near dead from thirst?'

'Nkosi, the water will boil very soon.'

Sean grunted and walked across to where Mbejane squatted with the other servants by the fire watching Kandhla.

'This is a good camp, Mbejane.' Sean looked up at the roof of leaves above them. It was a place of green shade, cool in the late morning heat. Christmas beetles were squealing in the wide stretched branches.

'There is good grazing for the cattle,' Mbejane agreed; he stretched out his hand towards Sean.

'I found this in the grass – someone else has camped here.' Sean took it from him and examined it, a piece of broken china with a blue fig-leaf pattern. It was a shock to Sean, that little fragment of civilization in the wilderness; he turned it in his fingers and Mbejane went on. 'There are the ashes of an old fire there against the shuma tree and I found the ruts where wagons climbed the bank at the same place as ours.'

'How long ago?'

Mbejane shrugged. 'A year perhaps. Grass has grown in the wagon tracks.'

Sean sat down in his chair, he felt disturbed. He thought about it and grinned as he realized he was jealous; there were strangers here in the land he was coming to regard as his own, those year-old tracks gave him a feeling of being in a crowd. Also there was the opposite feeling, that of longing for the company of his own kind. The sneaking desire to see a white face again. It was strange that he could resent something and yet wish for it simultaneously.

'Kandhla, am I to have coffee now or at supper tonight?'

'Nkosi, it is done.' Kandhla poured a little brown sugar into the mug, stirred it with a stick and handed it to him. Sean held the mug in both hands, blowing to cool it, then sipping and sighing with each mouthful. The talk of his Zulus passed back and forth about the circle and the snuff-boxes followed it, each remark of worth being greeted with a solemn chorus of 'It is true, it is true,' and the taking of snuff. Small arguments jumped up and fell back again into the leisurely stream of conversation. Sean listened to them, occasionally joining in or contributing a story until his stomach told him it was time to eat. Kandhla started to cook, under the critical supervision and with the helpful suggestions of those whom idleness had made garrulous. He had almost succeeded in grilling the carcass of a guinea-fowl to the satisfaction of the entire company, although Mbejane felt that he should have added a pinch more salt, when Nonga, sitting across the fire from him, jumped to his feet and pointed out towards the north. Sean shaded his eyes and looked.

'For Chrissake,' said Sean.

'Ah! ah! ah!' said his servants.

A white man rode towards them through the trees; he cantered with long stirrups, slouched comfortably, close enough already for Sean to make out the great ginger beard that masked the bottom half of his face. He was a big man; the sleeves of his shirt rolled high around thick arms.

'Hello,' shouted Sean and went eagerly to meet him. The rider reined in at the edge of the laager. He climbed stiffly out of the saddle and grabbed Sean's outstretched hand. Sean felt his finger-bones creak in the grip.

414

'Hello, man! How goes it?' He spoke in Afrikaans. His voice matched the size of his body and his eyes were on a level with Sean's. They pumped each other's arms mercilessly, laughing, putting sincerity into the usual inanities of greeting.

'Kandhla – get out the brandy bottle,' Sean called over his shoulder, then to the Boer, 'Come in, you're just in time for lunch. We'll have a dram to celebrate. Hell, it's good to see a white man again!'

'You're on your own, then?'

'Yes – come in, man, sit down.'

Sean poured drinks and the Boer took one up.

'What's your name?' he asked.

'Courtney – Sean Courtney.'

'I'm Jan Paulus Leroux – glad to meet you, meneer.'

'Good health, meneer,' Sean answered him and they drank. Jan Paulus wiped his whiskers on the palm of his hand and breathed out heavily, blowing the taste of the brandy back into his mouth.

'That was good,' he said and held out his mug. They talked excitedly, tongues loose from loneliness, trying to say everything and ask all the questions at once – meetings in the bush are always like this. Meanwhile the tide was going out in the bottle and the level dropped quickly.

'Tell me, where are your wagons?' Sean asked.

'An hour or two behind. I came ahead to find the river.'

'How many in your party?' Sean watched his face, talking just for the sound of it.

'Ma and Pa, my little sister and my wife – which reminds me – you had better move your wagons.'

'What?' Sean looked puzzled.

'This is my outspan place,' the Boer explained to him. 'See, there are the marks of my fire – this is my camp.'

The smile went out of Sean's voice. 'Look around you,

415

Boer, there is the whole of Africa. Take your pick – anywhere except where I am sitting.'

'But this is my place.' Jan Paulus flushed a little. 'I always camp at the same place when I return along a spoor.'

The whole temper of their meeting had changed in a few seconds. Jan Paulus stood abruptly and went to his horse. He stooped and tightened the girth, hauling so savagely on the strap that the animal staggered off balance. He flung himself onto its back and looked down at Sean.

'Move your wagons,' he said. 'I camp here tonight.'

'Would you like to bet on that?' Sean asked grimly.

'We'll see!' Jan Paulus flashed back.

'We certainly shall,' agreed Sean.

The Boer wheeled his horse and rode away. Sean watched his back disappear among the trees and only then did he let his anger slip. He rampaged through the laager working himself into a fury, pacing out frustrated circles, stopping now and then to glare out in the direction from which the Boer's wagons would come – but under all the external signs of indignation was his unholy anticipation of a fight. Kandhla brought him food, hurrying along behind him with the plate. Sean waved him away impatiently and continued his pugnacious patrol. At last a trek whip popped in the distance and an ox lowed faintly, to be answered immediately by Sean's cattle. The dogs started barking and Sean crossed to one of the wagons on the north side of the laager and leaned against it with assumed nonchalance. The long line of wagons wound out of the trees towards him. There were bright blobs of colour on the high box seat of the lead wagon. Women's dresses! Ordinarily they would have made Sean's nostrils flare like those of a stud stallion, but now his whole attention was concentrated on the larger of the two outriders. Jan Paulus cantered ahead of his father, and Sean, with his fists clenched into bony hammers at his sides, watched him come. Jan Paulus sat straight in the saddle; he stopped his horse a dozen paces from Sean and shoved his hat onto the back of his head with a thumb as thick and as brown as a fried sausage; he tickled his horse a little with his spurs to make it dance and he asked with mock surprise, 'What, *Rooi Nek*, still here?'

Sean's dogs had rushed forward to meet the other pack and now they milled about in a restrained frenzy of mutual bottom-smelling, stiff-limbed with tension, backs abristle and legs cocking in the formal act of urination.

'Why don't you go and climb a tree? You'll feel more at home there,' Sean suggested mildly.

'Ah! so?' Jan Paulus reared in his stirrups. He kicked loose his right foot, swung it back over his horse's rump to dismount and Sean jumped at him. The horse skittered nervously, throwing the Boer off balance and he clutched at the saddle. Sean reached up, took a double handful of his ginger beard and leaned back on it with all his weight. Jan Paulus came over backwards with his arms windmilling, his foot caught in the stirrup and he hung suspended like a hammock, held at one end to the plunging horse and at the other by his chin to Sean's hands. Sean dug his heels in, revelling in the Boer's bellows.

Galvanized into action by Sean's example, the dogs cut short the ceremony and went at each other in a snarling, snapping shambles; the fur flew like sand in a Kalahari dust-storm.

The stirrup-leather snapped; Sean fell backwards and rolled to his feet just in time to meet Jan Paulus's charge. He smothered the punch that the Boer bowled overarm at him, but the power behind it shocked him; then they were chest to chest and Sean felt his own strength matched. They strained silently with their beards touching and their eyes inches apart. Sean shifted his weight quickly and tried for a fall, but smoothly as a dancer Jan Paulus met and held him. Then it was his turn; he twisted in Sean's arms and

Sean sobbed with the effort required to stop him. Oupa Leroux joined in by driving his horse at them, scattering the dogs, his hippo-hide sjambok hissing as he swung it.

'Let it stand! you thunders, give over – hey! Enough, let it stand!'

Sean shouted with pain as the lash cut across his back and at the next stroke Jan Paulus howled as loudly. They let go of each other and massaging their whip-weals retreated before the skinny old white-beard on the horse.

The first of the wagons had come up now and two hundred pounds of woman, all in one package, called out from the box seat, 'Why did you stop them, Oupa?'

'No sense in letting them kill each other.'

'Shame on you – so you must spoil the boys' fun. Don't you remember how you loved to fight? Or are you now so old you forget the pleasures of your youth? Leave them alone!'

Oupa hesitated, swinging the sjambok and looking from Sean to Jan Paulus.

'Come away from there, you old busybody,' his wife ordered him. She was solid as a granite kopje, her blouse packed full of bosom and her bare arms brown and thick as a man's. The wide brim of her bonnet shaded her face but Sean could see it was pink and pudding-shaped, the kind of face that smiles more easily than it frowns. There were two girls on the seat beside her but there was no time to look at them. Oupa had pulled his horse out of the way and Jan Paulus was moving down on him. Sean went up on his toes, crouching a little, preoccupied with the taste he had just had of the other's strength, watching Jan Paulus close in for the main course and not too certain he was going to be able to chew this mouthful.

Jan Paulus tested Sean with a long right-hander but Sean rolled his head with it and the thick pad of his beard

418

cushioned the blow; he hooked Jan Paulus in the ribs under his raised arm and Jan Paulus grunted and circled away.

Forgetting his scruples, Oupa Leroux watched them with rising delight. It was going to be a good fight. They were well matched – both big men, under thirty, quick and smooth on their feet. Both had fought before and that often; you could tell it by the way they felt each other out, turning just out of reach, moving in to offer an opening that a less experienced man might have attempted and regretted, then dropping back.

The fluid, almost leisurely pattern of movement exploded. Jan Paulus jumped in, moving left, changed direction like the recoil of a whip lash and used his right hand again; Sean ducked under it and laid himself open to Jan Paulus's left. He staggered back from its kick, bleeding where it had split the flesh across his cheek-bone, and Jan Paulus followed him eagerly, his hands held ready, searching for the opening. Sean kept clear, instinct moving his feet until the blackness faded inside his head and he felt the strength in his arms again. He saw Jan Paulus following him and he let his legs stay rubbery; he dropped his hands and waited for Jan Paulus to commit himself. Too late Jan Paulus caught the cunning in Sean's eyes and tried to break from the trap, but clenched bone raked his face. He staggered away and now he was bleeding also.

They fought through the wagons with the advantage changing hands a dozen times. They came together and used their heads and their knees, they broke and used their fists again. Then locked chest to chest once more they rolled down the steep bank into the riverbed of the Limpopo. They fought in the soft sand and it held their legs, it filled their mouths when they fell and clung like white icing-sugar to their hair and beards. They splashed into one of the pools and they fought in the water, coughing

419

with the agony of it in their lungs, floundering like a pair of bull hippos, their movements slowing down until they knelt facing each other, no longer able to rise, the water running from them and the only sound their gasping for air.

Not sure whether the darkness was actuality or a fantasy of fatigue, for the sun had set by the time they were finished, Sean watched Jan Paulus starting to puke, retching with a tearing noise to bring up a small splash of yellow bile. Sean crawled to the edge of the pool and lay with his face in the sand. There were voices echoing in his ears and the light of a lantern – the light was red – filtered through the blood that had trickled into his eyes. His servants lifted him and he hardly felt them. The light and the voices faded into blackness as he slipped over the edge of consciousness.

The sting of iodine woke him and he struggled to sit up but hands pushed him down.

'Gently, gently, the fight is over.' Sean focused his one eye to find the voice. The pinkness of Ouma Leroux hung over him. Her hands touched his face and the antiseptic stung him again. He exclaimed through puffed lips.

'So! Just like a man,' Ouma chuckled. 'Your head nearly knocked off without a murmur but one touch of medicine and you cry like a baby.'

Sean ran his tongue round inside his mouth; one tooth loose but all the others miraculously present. He started to lift his hand to touch his closed eye but Ouma slapped it down impatiently and went on working over him.

'Glory, what a fight!' She shook her head happily. 'You were good, *kerel*, you were very good.'

Sean looked beyond her and saw the girl. She was standing in shadow, a silhouette against the pale canvas. She was holding a basin. Ouma turned and dipped the cloth in it, washing out the blood before she came back to his face. The wagon rocked under her weight and the lantern that hung from the roof swung, lighting the girl's face from

420

the side. Sean's legs straightened on his cot and he moved his head slightly to see her better.

'Be still, *jong*,' Ouma commanded. Sean looked past her at the girl at the full serene line of her lips and the curve of her cheek. He saw the pile of her hair fluff up in happy disarray and then, suddenly – penitent – slide down behind her neck, curl over her shoulder and hang to her waist in a plait as thick as his wrist.

'Katrina, do you expect me to reach right across to the basin each time? Stand closer, girl.'

She stepped into the light and looked at Sean. Green, laughing, almost bubbling green was the colour of her eyes. Then she dropped them to the basin. Sean stared at her, not wanting to miss the moment when she would look up again.

'My big bear,' Ouma spoke with grudging approval. 'Steal our camp site, fight my son and ogle my daughter. If you go on like this I might have to knock the thunder out of you myself. Glory, but you are a dangerous one! Katrina, you had better go back to our wagons and help Henrietta see to your brother. Leave the basin on the chest there.'

She looked at Sean once more before she left. There were secret shadows in the green – she didn't have to smile with her mouth.

– 11 –

Sean woke to the realization that something was wrong. He started to sit up but the pain checked him: the stiffness of bruised muscle and the catch of half-dried scab. He groaned and the movement hurt his lips. Slowly he swung his legs off the cot and roused himself to take stock of the damage. Dark through the hair of his chest showed a heel imprint of Jan Paulus's boot. Sean prodded round it gently, feeling for the give of a broken rib; then, satisfied with that area, he went on to inspect the raw graze that wrapped round onto his back, holding his left arm high and peering closely at the broken skin. He picked a bit of blanket fluff from the scab. He stood up, only to freeze as a torn muscle in his shoulder knifed him. He started to swear then softly, monotonously, and he kept it up all through the painful business of climbing down out of the wagon.

His entire following watched his descent – even the dogs looked worried. Sean reached the ground and started to shout.

'What the hell—' He stopped hurriedly as he felt his lip crack open again and start to bleed.

'What the hell' – he said again, keeping his lips still – 'are you doing standing round like a bunch of women at a beer drink – is there no work here? Hlubi, I thought I sent you out to look for elephant.' Hlubi went. 'Kandhla, where's breakfast? Mbejane, get me a basin of water and my shaving-mirror.' Sean sat in his chair and morosely inspected his face in the mirror.

'If a herd of buffalo had stampeded across it they would have done less damage.'

'Nkosi, it is nothing compared to his face,' Mbejane assured him.

'Is he bad?' Sean looked up.

'I have spoken to one of his servants. He has not left his bed yet and he lies there, growling like a wounded lion in a thicket; but his eyes are as tightly closed as those of a new cub.'

'Tell me more, Mbejane. Say truly, was it a good fight?'

Mbejane squatted down next to Sean's chair. He was silent a moment as he gathered his words.

'When the sky sends its cloud impis against the peaks of the Drakensberg, with thunder and the spears of lightning, it is a thing to thrill a man. When two bull elephants fight unto death there is no braver show in all the veld. Is this not so?'

Sean nodded, his eyes twinkling.

'Nkosi, hear me when I tell you these things were as the play of little children beside this fight.'

Sean listened to the praises. Mbejane was well versed in the oldest art of Zululand and when he had finished he looked at Sean's face. It was happy. Mbejane smiled and took a fold of paper out of his loin cloth. 'A servant from the other camp brought this while you slept.'

Sean read the note. It was written in a big round school-girl hand and worded in High Dutch. He liked that writing. It was an invitation to dinner.

'Kandhla, get out my suit and my number one boots.' He picked up the mirror again. There wasn't very much he could do about his face – trim the beard, perhaps, but that was all. He laid the mirror down and looked up stream to where the Leroux wagons were half hidden among the trees.

Mbejane carried a lantern in front of Sean. They walked slowly to enable Sean to limp with dignity. When they reached the other laager, Jan Paulus climbed stiffly out of his chair and nodded an equally stiff greeting. Mbejane had lied – except for a missing tooth there was little to choose between their faces. Oupa slapped Sean's back and pressed a tumbler of brandy into his hand. He was a tall man, but twenty thousand suns had burnt away his flesh and left only stringy muscle, had faded his eyes to a pale green and toughened his skin to the texture of a turkey's neck. His beard was yellowish-white with still a touch of ginger round the mouth. He asked Sean three questions without giving him time to answer the first, then he led him to a chair.

Oupa talked, Sean listened and Jan Paulus sulked. Oupa talked of cattle and hunting and the land to the north. After a few minutes Sean realized that he was not expected to take part in the conversation: his few tentative efforts were crushed under Oupa's verbal avalanche. So Sean listened half to him and half to the whisper of women's voices from the cooking fires behind the laager. Once he heard her laugh. He knew it was her for it was the rich sound of the thing that he had seen in her eyes. At last the women's business with food and pots was finished and Ouma led the girls to where the men sat. Sean stood up and saw that Katrina was tall, with shoulders like a boy. As she walked towards him the movement pressed her skirt against her legs – they were long but her feet were small. Her hair was red-black and tied behind her head in an enormous bun.

'Ah, my battling bear,' Ouma took Sean's arm, 'let me present my daughter-in-law, Henrietta – here is the man that nearly killed your husband.' Jan Paulus snorted from his chair and Ouma laughed, her bosom wobbling merrily. Henrietta was a small dark-eyed girl. *She doesn't like me*, Sean guessed instantly. He bowed slightly and took her hand. She pulled it away.

'This is my youngest daughter, Katrina. You met her last night.'

She does like me. Her fingers were long and square-tipped in his. Sean risked his lips with a smile.

'Without her ministrations I might have bled to death,' he said. She smiled straight back at him but not with her mouth.

'You wear your wounds well, maneer, the blue eye has an air of distinction.'

'That will be enough from you, girl,' Oupa spoke sharply. 'Go and sit by your mother.' He turned to Sean. 'I was telling you about this horse – I said to the fellow, "He's not worth five pounds let alone fifteen, look at those hocks, thin as sticks." So he says to me, trying to get me away, you follow, he says, "Come and look at the saddle." But I can see he's worried—'

The thin cotton of the girl's blouse could hardly contain the impatient push of her breasts. Sean thought that he had never seen anything so wonderful.

There was a trestle-table next to the cooking fire; they went to it at last. Oupa said grace. Sean watched him through his lashes. Oupa's beard waggled as he spoke and at one point he thumped the table to emphasize the point he was making to the Almighty. His 'amen' had such an impressive resonance that Sean had to make an effort to stop himself applauding and Oupa fell back spent.

'Amen,' said Ouma and ladled stew from a pot the size of a bucket. Henrietta added pumpkin fritters and Katrina stacked slices of fresh mealie bread on each plate. A silence fell on the table, spoiled only by the clank of metal on china and the sound of Oupa breathing through his nose.

'Mevrouw Leroux, I have waited a long time to taste food like this again.' Sean mopped up the last bit of gravy with a piece of mealie bread. Ouma beamed.

'There's plenty more, meneer. I love to see a man eat. Oupa used to be a great trencherman. My father made him take me away for he could not afford to feed him every time he came courting.' She took Sean's plate and filled it. 'You look to me like a man who can eat.'

'I think I'll hold my own in most company,' Sean agreed.

'So?' Jan Paulus spoke for the first time. He passed his plate to Ouma. 'Fill it up, please, Mother, tonight I am hungry.'

Sean's eyes narrowed, he waited until Jan Paulus had his plate back in front of him, then he took up his fork deliberately. Jan Paulus did the same.

'Glory,' said Ouma happily. 'Here we go again. Oupa, you may have to go out and shoot a couple of buffalo before dinner is finished tonight.'

'I will bet one sovereign on Jan Paulus,' Oupa challenged

his wife. 'He is like an army of termites. I swear that if there was nothing else he'd eat the canvas off the wagons.'

'All right,' agreed Ouma. 'I've never seen the Bear eat before, but it seems to me he has plenty of room to put it.'

'Your woollen shawl against my green bonnet that Jan Paulus gives up first,' Katrina whispered to her sister-in-law.

'When Jannie has finished the stew he'll eat the English man,' Henrietta giggled. 'But it's a pretty bonnet – I'll take the wager.'

Plateful for plateful, Ouma measuring out each ladle with scrupulous fairness, they ate against each other. The talk round the table dwindled and halted.

'More?' asked Ouma each time the plates were clean, and each time they looked at each other and nodded. At last the ladle scraped the bottom of the pot.

'That's the end of it, my children, we will have to call it another draw.'

The silence went on after she had spoken. Sean and Jan Paulus sat very still looking at their respective plates. Jan Paulus hiccupped, his expression changed. He stood up and went into the darkness.

'Ah! listen! listen!' crowed Ouma. They waited and then she exploded into laughter. 'The ungrateful wretch, is that what he thinks of my food? Where's your sovereign, Oupa?'

'Wait, you greedy old woman, the game's not finished yet.' He turned and stared at Sean. 'To me it looks as though your horse is nearly blown.'

Sean closed his eyes. The sounds of Jan Paulus's distress came to him very clearly.

'Thank you for a—' He didn't have time to finish. He wanted to get far away so the girl couldn't hear him.

12

T he following morning during breakfast Sean thought about his next move. He would write an invitation to dinner and then he would deliver it himself. They would have to ask him to stay for coffee and then, if he waited, there would be a chance. Even Oupa would have to stop talking sometime and Ouma might relax her vigilance. He was sure there'd be a chance to talk to the girl. He didn't know what he would say to her but he'd worry about that when the time came. He climbed into the wagon and found pencil and paper in his chest. He went back to the table and spread the paper in front of him. He chewed the end of the pencil and stared out into the bush. Something moved against the trees. Sena put the pencil down and stood up. The dogs barked then stopped as they recognized Hlubi. He was coming at a trot – he was coming with news. Sean waited for him.

'A big herd, Nkosi, with many showing ivory. I saw them drink at the river and then go back into the bush, feeding quietly.'

'When?' asked Sean to gain time. He was searching for a plausible excuse to stay in camp – it would have to be good to satisfy Mbejane who was already saddling one of the horses.

'Before the sun this morning,' answered Hlubi and Sean was trying to remember which was his sore shoulder – he couldn't hunt with a sore shoulder. Mbejane led the horse into the laager. Sean scratched the side of his nose and coughed.

'The tracker from the other camp follows close behind me, Nkosi, he too has seen the herd and brings the news to his master. But I, being as swift as a springbok when I run, have outdistanced him,' Hlubi ended modestly.

'Is that so?' For Sean it changed the whole problem, he couldn't leave the herd to that red-headed Dutchman. He ran across to the wagon and snatched his bandolier from the foot of the cot. His rifle was already in the scabbard.

'Are you tired, Hlubi?' Sean buckled the heavy ammunition belt across his chest. The sweat had run in oily streaks down the Zulu's body; his breathing was deep and quick.

'No, Nkosi.'

'Well, then, lead us to these elephant of yours, my fleet-footed springbok.' Sean swung up onto his horse. He looked over his shoulder at the other camp. She would still be there when he came back.

Sean was limited to the speed of Hlubi's feet while the two Leroux had only to gallop along the easy spoor left by Sean's party and they caught up with him before he had gone two miles.

'Good morning to you,' Oupa greeted him as he drew level and pulled his horse in to a trot. 'Out for a morning's ride, I see.'

Sean made the best of it with a grin. 'If we are all to hunt then we must hunt together. Do you agree?'

'Of course, meneer.'

'And we must share the bag equally, one third to each man.'

'That is always the way.' Oupa nodded.

'Do you agree?' Sean turned in his saddle towards Jan Paulus. Jan Paulus grunted. He showed little inclination to open his mouth since he had lost his tooth.

They found the spoor within an hour. The herd had wrecked a road through the thick bush along the river. They had stripped the bark from the saplings and left them naked and bleeding. They had knocked down bigger trees to reach the tender top leaves and they had dropped their great piles of dung in the grass.

'We need no trackers to follow this.' Jan Paulus had the first excitement on him. Sean looked at him and wondered how many elephant had died in front of his rifle. A thousand perhaps, and yet the excitement was on him again now.

'Tell your servants to follow us. We'll go ahead. We'll catch them within an hour.' He smiled at Sean, gap-toothed, and Sean felt the excitement lift the hair on his own forearms. He smiled back.

They cantered in a rough line abreast, slack-reined to let the horses pick their own way among the fallen trees. The river bush thinned out as they moved north and soon they were into parkland. The grass brushed their stirrups and the ground beneath it was firm and smooth.

They rode without talking, leaning forward in their saddles, looking ahead. The rhythmic beat of hooves was a war drum. Sean ran his fingers along the row of bullets strapped across his chest, then he drew his rifle, checked the load and thrust it back into its scabbard.

'There!' said Oupa and Sean saw the herd. It was massed among a grove of fever trees a quarter of a mile ahead.

'Name of a name,' Paulus whistled. 'There must be two hundred at least.'

Sean heard the first pig-squeal of alarm, saw ears fan out and trunks lift. Then the herd bunched together and ran with their backs humped, a thin screen of dust trailing behind them.

'Paulus take the right flank. You, meneer, in the middle and I'll ride left,' shouted Oupa.

Sean jammed his hat down over his ears and his horse jumped under him as he hit it with his heels. Like a thrown trident the three horsemen hurled themselves at the herd. Sean rode into the dust. He picked an old cow elephant from the moving mountain range in front of him and pressed his horse so close upon her that he could see the bristles in her tail tuft and the erosion of her skin, wrinkled as an old man's scrotum. He touched his hand to his horse's neck and it plunged – from full gallop to standstill in half a dozen strides. Sean threw his feet free of the stirrups and hit the ground, loose-kneed to ride the shock. The cow's spine was a line of lumps beneath the grey skin – Sean broke it with his first bullet and she dropped, sliding on her hindquarters like a dog with worms. His horse started to run again before he was properly in the saddle and everything became movement and noise, dust and the smell of burnt powder. Chase them, coughing in the dust. Close with them. Off the horse and shoot. Wet blood on grey skin. Slam, slam of the rifle – its barrel hot, recoiling savagely. Sweat in the eyes, stinging. Ride. Shoot again. Two more down, screaming, anchored by paralysed legs. Blood-red as a flag. Load, cramming cartridges into the rifle. Ride. Chase them, shoot again and again. The bullets striking on flesh with a hollow sound, then up and ride again. Ride – until the horse could no longer keep up with them and he had to let them go. He stood holding his horse's head, the dust and the thirst closed his throat. He could not swallow. His hands trembled in reaction. His shoulder was aching again. He untied his silk scarf, wiped his face with it and blew the mud out of his nose, then he drank from his water-bottle. The water tasted sweet.

The hunt had led from parkland into mopani bush. It was very thick, shiny green leaves hanging to the ground and pressing close around him. The air was still and warm to breathe. He turned back along the line of the chase. He found them by their squealing. When they saw him they tried to charge, dragging themselves towards him – using the front legs only and groping with their trunks. They sagged into stillness after the head shot. This was the bad part. Sean worked quickly. He could hear the other rifles in the mopani forest around him and when he came to one of

the long clearings among the trees he saw Jan Paulus walking towards him, leading his horse.

'How many?' called Sean.

'*Gott*, man, I didn't count. What a killing, hey? Have you got a drink for me? I dropped my water-bottle somewhere.'

Jan Paulus's rifle was in its saddle scabbard. The reins were slung over his shoulder and his horse followed him with its head drooping from exhaustion. The clearing was walled in with the dense mopani trees and a wounded elephant broke into the open. It was lung shot – the side of its chest painted with froth – and when it squealed the blood sprayed in a pink spout from the end of its trunk. It went for Jan Paulus, streaming the black battle ensigns of its ears. His horse reared, the reins snapped, it turned free and galloped away, leaving him full in the path of the charge. Sean went up onto his horse's back without touching stirrups. His horse threw its head, dancing in a tight circle, but he dragged it around and drove it to intercept the charge.

'Don't run, for God's sake, don't run!' he shouted as he cleared his rifle from the scabbard. Jan Paulus heard him. He stood with his hands at his sides, his feet apart and his body braced. The elephant heard Sean shout also and it swung its head and Sean saw the first hesitation in its run. He fired, not trying to pick his shot, hoping only to hurt it, to bring it away from Jan Paulus. The bullet slapped into it with the sound of a wet towel flicked against a wall. The elephant turned, clumsy with the weakness of its shattered lungs. Sean gathered his horse beneath him and wheeled it away and the elephant followed him.

Sean fumbled as he reloaded, his hands were slippery with sweat. One of the brass shells slipped through his fingers, tapped against his knee and dropped into the grass under his horse's hooves. The elephant gained on him. He loosened his bed-roll from the saddle and let it fall – they would sometimes stop to savage even a fallen hat, but not this one. He turned in the saddle and fired into it. It squealed again so close upon him that the blown blood splattered into his face. His horse was almost finished; he could feel its legs flopping with every stride and they were nearly at the end of the clearing racing towards the solid wall of green mopani. He pushed another round into the breech of his rifle and swung his body across the saddle. He slid down until his feet touched the ground and he was running next to his horse. He let go and was flung forward, but he fought to keep his balance, his body jarring with the force of his run. Then, still on his feet, he turned for his first steady shot. The elephant was coming in fast, almost on top of him, hanging over him like a cliff. Its trunk coiled on its chest and the curves of its ivory were lifted high.

It's too close, much too close, I can't hit the brain from here.

He aimed at the hollow in its forehead just above the level of its eyes. He fired and the elephant's legs folded up; its brain burst like an overripe tomato within the bone castle of its skull.

Sean tried to jump aside as the massive body came skidding down upon him, but one of its legs hit him and threw him face down into the grass. He lay there. He felt sick, for his stomach was still full of warm oily fear.

After a while he sat up and looked at the elephant. One of its tusks had snapped off flush with the lip. Jan Paulus came, panting from his run. He stopped next to the elephant and touched the wound in its forehead, then he wiped his fingers on his shirt.

'Are you all right, man?'

He took Sean's arm and helped him to his feet; then he picked up Sean's hat and dusted it carefully before handing it to him.

432

13

In the three-sided shelter formed by the belly and out-thrust legs of one of the dead elephants they made their camp that night. They drank coffee together and Sean sat between the two Leroux with his back against the rough skin of the elephant's belly. The silhouettes of the tree against the night sky were deformed by the shapes of the vultures that clustered in them and the darkness was ugly with the giggling of hyena. They had set a feast for the scavengers. They spoke little for they were tired, but Sean could feel the gratitude of the men who sat beside him and before they rolled into their blankets Jan Paulus said gruffly, 'Thank you, *kerel*.'

'You might be able to do the same for me one day.'

'I hope so, *ja*! I hope so.'

In the morning Oupa said, 'It's going to take us three or four days to cut out all this ivory.' He looked up at the sky. 'I don't like these clouds. One of us had better ride back to camp to fetch more men and wagons to carry the ivory.'

'I'll go.' Sean stood up quickly.

'I was thinking of going myself.' But Sean was already calling to Mbejane to saddle his horse and Oupa couldn't really argue with him, not after yesterday.

'Tell Ouma to take the wagons across the river,' he acquiesced. 'We don't want to be caught on this side when the river floods. Perhaps you wouldn't mind helping her.'

'No,' Sean assured him. 'I don't mind at all.'

His horse was still tired from the previous day's hunt and it was three hours before he reached the river.

He tied his horse on the bank and went down to one of the pools. He stripped off his clothes and lowered himself into the water. He scrubbed himself with handfuls of the coarse sand and when he waded out of the pool and dried on his shirt his skin was tingling. He rode along the bank and the temptation to gallop his horse was almost unbearable. He laughed to himself a little.

'The field's almost clear, though I wouldn't put it past that suspicious old Dutchman to follow me.'

He laughed again and thought about the colour of her eyes, green as *crème-de-menthe* in a crystal glass, and the shape of her bosom. The muscles in his legs tightened and the horse lengthened its stride in response to the pressure of his knees. 'All right, run then,' Sean encouraged it, 'I don't insist on it, but I would be grateful.'

He went to his own wagons first and changed his sweaty shirt for a fresh one, his leather breeches for clean calico and his scuffed boots for soft polished leather. He scrubbed his teeth with salt and dragged a comb through his hair and beard. He saw in the mirror that the battle damage to his face was fading and he winked at his image. 'How can she resist you?' He gave his moustache one more twirl, climbed out of the wagon and was immediately aware of a most uncomfortable feeling in his stomach. He walked towards the Leroux laager thinking about it, and he recognized it as the same feeling he used to have when Waite Courtney called him to the study to do penance for his boyhood sins.

'That's odd,' he muttered. 'Why should I feel like that?' His confidence faded and he stopped. 'I wonder if my breath smells – I think I'd better go back and get some cloves.' He turned with relief, knew it as cowardice and stopped again. 'Get a grip on yourself. She's only a girl, an uneducated little Dutch girl. You've had fifty finer women.'

'Name me two,' he shot back at himself.

'Well, there was – Oh! for Chrissake, come on.' Resolutely he set off for the Leroux's laager again.

She was sitting in the sun within the circle of wagons. She was leaning forward on the stool and her newly-washed hair fell thickly over her face almost to the ground. With each stroke of the brush it leapt like a live thing and the sun sparkled the red lights in it. Sean wanted to touch it – he wanted to twist fistfuls of it round his hands and he wanted to smell it, it would smell warm and slightly milky like a puppy's fur. He stepped softly towards her but before he reached her she took the shiny mass with both hands and threw it back over her shoulders – a startled flash of green eyes, one despairing wail, 'Oh, no! not with my hair like this.' A swirl of skirts that sent the stool flying and she was gone into her wagon. Sean scratched the side of his nose and stood awkwardly.

'Why are you back so soon, meneer?' she called through the canvas. 'Where are the others? Is everything all right?'

'Yes, they're both fine. I left them and came to fetch wagons to carry the ivory.'

'Oh, that's good.' Sean tried to interpret the inflection of her voice: was it good that they were fine, or good that he had left them? So far the indications were favourable; her confusion at seeing him boded well.

'What's wrong?' Ouma bellowed from one of the other wagons. 'It's not Oupa, don't tell me something has happened to him?' The wagon rocked wildly and her pink face, puckered with sleep, popped out of the opening. Sean's reassurances were smothered by her voice.

'Oh, I knew this would happen. I had a feeling. I shouldn't have let him go.'

'Paulus, oh, Jan Paulus – I must go to him. Where is he?'

Henrietta came running from the cooking fire behind the wagons and then the dogs started barking and the servants added their chatter to the confusion. Sean tried to shout them all down and watch Katrina emerging from her wagon at the same time. She had disciplined her hair now – it had a green ribbon in it and hung down her back. She was laughing and she helped him to quieten Ouma and Henrietta.

They brought him coffee, then they sat round him and listened to the story of the hunt. Sean went into detail on the rescue of Jan Paulus and was rewarded by a softening of the dislike in Henrietta's eyes. By the time Sean had finished talking it was too late to start moving the wagons across the river. So he talked some more, it was most agreeable to have three women as an attentive audience, and then they ate supper.

With ostentatious tact Ouma and Henrietta retired early to their respective living wagons and left Sean and Katrina sitting by the fire. At carefully-spaced intervals there was a stage cough from Ouma's wagon, a reminder that they were not entirely alone. Sean lit a cheroot and frowned into the fire searching desperately for something intelligent to say, but all his brain could dredge up was, 'Thank God, Oupa isn't here.' He sneaked a glance at Katrina: she was staring into the fire as well and she was blushing. Instantly Sean felt his own cheeks starting to heat up. He opened his mouth to talk and made a squawking noise. He shut it again.

'We can speak in English if you like, meneer.'

'You speak English?' Sean's surprise brought his voice back.

'I practise every night – I read aloud out of my books.'

Sean grinned at her delightedly – it was suddenly very important that she could speak his language. The dam, holding back all the questions that there were to ask and all the things there were to say, burst and the words came pouring out over each other. Katrina fluttered her hands when she couldn't find the word she wanted and then lapsed back into Afrikaans. They killed the short taut silences with a simultaneous rush of words, then laughed together in confusion. They sat on the edges of their chairs and watched each other's faces as they talked. The moon came up, a red rain moon, and the fire faded into a puddle of ashes.

'Katrina, it's long past the time decent people were asleep. I'm sure Meneer Courtney is tired.'

They dropped their voices to a whisper, drawing out the last minutes.

'In just one minute, girl, I'm coming out to fetch you to bed.'

They walked to her wagon and with each step her skirts brushed against his leg. She stopped with one hand on the wagon step. She wasn't as tall as he'd imagined, the top of her head came to his chin. The seconds slid by as he hesitated, reluctant to touch, strangely frightened to test the delicate thread they had spun together lest he destroy it before it became strong. Slowly he swayed towards her and something surged up inside him as he saw her chin lift slightly and the lashes fall over her eyes.

'Goodnight, Meneer Courtney.' Ouma's voice again, loud and with an edge to it. Sean started guiltily.

'Goodnight, mevrouw.'

Katrina touched his arm just above the elbow, her fingers were warm.

'Goodnight, meneer, I shall see you in the morning.'

She rustled up the steps and slipped through the opening of the canvas. Sean scowled at Ouma's wagon.

'Thanks very much – and if there is ever anything I can do for you, please don't hesitate to ask.'

– 14 –

They started moving the wagons early next morning. There was no time to talk to Katrina in the bustle of inspanning and working the wagons across the corduroy bridge. Sean spent most of the morning in the riverbed and the white sand bounced the heat up at him. He threw off his shirt and sweated like a wrestler. He

437

trotted beside Katrina's wagon when they ran it through the riverbed. She looked once at his naked chest and arms; her cheeks darkened in the shadow of her bonnet and she dropped her eyes and didn't look at him again. With only the two wagons that were going back to fetch the ivory still on the north bank and the rest safely across, Sean could relax. He washed in one of the pools, put on his shirt and went across to the south bank looking forward to a long afternoon of Katrina's company.

Ouma met him. 'Thank you, my dear, the girls have made you a parcel of cold meat and a bottle of coffee to eat on your way.' Sean's face went slack. He had forgotten all about that stinking ivory; as far as he was concerned Oupa and Paulus could keep the lot of it.

'Don't worry about us any more now, maneer. I know how it is with a man who is a man. When there's work to do everything else comes after.'

Katrina put the food in his hands. Sean looked for a sign from her. One sign and he'd defy even Ouma.

'Don't be too long,' she whispered. The thought that he might shirk work had obviously not even occurred to her. Sean was glad he hadn't suggested it.

It was a long ride back to the elephant.

'You've taken your time, haven't you?' Oupa greeted him with sour suspicion. 'You'd better get to work if you don't want to lose some of your share.'

Taking out the tusks was a delicate task: a slip of the axe would scar the ivory and halve its value. They worked in the heat with a blue haze of flies around their faces, settling on their lips and crawling into their nostrils and eyes. The carcasses had started to rot and the gases ballooned their bellies and escaped in posthumous belches. They sweated as they worked and the blood caked their arms to the elbows, but each hour the wagons filled higher until on the

438

third day they loaded the last tusk. Sean reckoned his share at twelve hundred pounds, the equivalent of a satisfactory day on the Stock Exchange.

He was in a good mood on the morning that they started back to the camp, but it deteriorated as the day wore on and they struggled with the heavily-loaded wagons. The rain seemed to have made up its mind at last and now the sky's belly hung down as heavily as that of a pregnant sow. The clouds trapped the heat beneath them and the men panted and the oxen complained mournfully. At mid-afternoon they heard the first far thunder.

'It will be on us before we pass the river,' fretted Oupa. 'See if you can't get some pace out of those oxen.'

They reached Sean's camp an hour after dark and threw his share of the ivory out of the wagons almost without stopping; then they went down to the river and across the bridge to the south bank.

'My mother will have food ready,' Jan Paulus called back to Sean. 'When you have washed come across and eat with us.'

Sean had supper with the Leroux, but his attempts to get Katrina by herself were neatly countered by Oupa whose suspicions were now confirmed. The old man played his trump card immediately after supper and ordered Katrina to bed. Sean could only shrug helplessly in reply to Katrina's appealing little glance. When she had gone Sean went back to his own camp. He was dizzy with fatigue and he fell onto his cot without bothering to undress.

The rains opened their annual offensive with a midnight broadside of thunder. It startled Sean to his feet before he was awake. He pulled open the front of the wagon and heard the wind coming.

'Mbejane, get the cattle into the laager. Make sure all the canvas is secure.'

'It is done already, Nkosi. I have lashed the wagons together so the oxen cannot stampede and I have—' Then the wind whipped his voice away.

It came out of the east and it frightened the trees so they thrashed their branches in panic; it drummed on the wagon canvas and filled the air with dust and dry leaves. The oxen turned restlessly within the laager. Then came the rain: stinging like hail, drowning the wind and turning the air to water. It swamped the sloping ground that could not drain it fast enough, it blinded and it deafened. Sean went back to his cot and listened to its fury. It made him feel drowsy. He pulled the blankets up to his chin and slept.

In the morning he found his oilskins in the chest at the foot of his cot. They crackled as he pulled them on. He climbed out of the wagon. The cattle had churned the inside of the laager to calf-deep mud and there was no chance of a fire for breakfast. Although the rain was still falling the noise was out of proportion to its strength. Sean paused in his inspection of the camp; he thought about it and suddenly he knew that it was the flood voice of the Limpopo that he heard. Sliding in the mud, he ran out of the laager and stood on the bank of the river. He stared at the mad water. It was so thick with mud it looked solid and it raced so fast it appeared to be standing still. It humped up over piles of submerged rock, gullied through the deeps and hissed in static waves through the shallows. The branches and tree trunks in it whisked past so swiftly that they did little to dispel the illusion that the river was frozen in this brown convulsion.

Reluctantly Sean lifted his eyes to the far bank. The Leroux's wagons were gone.

'Katrina,' he said with the sadness of the might-have-been, then again, 'Katrina,' with the sense of his loss melting in the flame of his anger; and he knew that his wanting was not just the itch that is easily scratched and forgotten, but that it was the true ache, the one that gets into your hands and your head and your heart as well as your loins. He couldn't let her go. He ran back to his wagon and threw his clothes onto the cot.

'I'll marry her,' he said and the words startled him. He stood naked, with an awed expression on his face.

'I'll marry her,' he said again; it was an original thought and it frightened him a little. He took a pair of shorts out of his chest and put his legs into them; he pulled them up and buttoned the fly.

'I'll marry her!' He grinned at his own daring. 'I'm damned if I won't!' He buckled his belt on and tied a pair of *veldschoen* to it by their laces. He jumped down into the mud. The rain was cold on his bare back and he shivered briefly. Then he saw Mbejane coming out of one of the other wagons and he ran.

'Nkosi, Nkosi, what are you doing?' Sean put his head down and ran faster with Mbejane chasing him out onto the bank of the river.

'It's madness ... let us talk about it first,' Mbejane shouted. 'Please, Nkosi, please.' Sean slipped in the mud and slithered down the bank. Mbejane jumped down after and caught him at the edge of the water, but the mud had coated Sean's body like grease and Mbejane couldn't hold him. Sean twisted out of his hands and sprang far out. He hit the water flat and swam on his back trying to avoid the undertow. The river swept him away. A wave slapped into his mouth and he doubled up to cough; immediately the river caught him by the heels and pulled him under the surface. It let him go again, just long enough to snatch air then it stirred him in a whirlpool and sucked him under once more. He came up beating at the water with his arms, then it tumbled him over a cascade and he knew by the pain in his chest that he was drowning. He swooped down a chute of swift water between rocks and it didn't matter

441

anymore. He was too tired. Something scraped against his chest and he put out his hand to protect himself; his fingers closed round a branch and his head lifted out of the water. He drank air and then he was clinging to the branch, still alive and wanting to live. He started kicking, edging across the current, riding the river with his arms around the log.

One of the eddies beneath the south bank swung the log in, under the branches of a tree. He reached up, caught them and dragged himself out. He knelt in the mud and water came gushing up out of him, half through his mouth and half through his nose. He had lost his *veldschoen*. He belched painfully and looked at the river. How fast was it moving, how long had he been in the water? He must be fifteen miles below the wagons. He wiped his face with his hand. It was still raining. He stood shakily and faced upstream.

It took him three hours to reach the spot opposite his wagons. Mbejane and the others waved in wild relief when they saw him, but their shouts could not carry across the river. Sean was cold now and his feet were sore. The tracks of the Leroux wagons were dissolving in the rain. He followed them and at last the pain in his feet healed as he saw the flash of canvas in the rain mist ahead of him.

'Name of a name,' shouted Jan Paulus. 'How did you cross the river?'

'I flew, how else?' said Sean. 'Where's Katrina?'

Paulus started to laugh, leaning back in the saddle. 'So that's it then, you haven't come all this way to say goodbye to me.'

Sean flushed. 'All right, laughing boy. That's enough merriment for today . . . Where is she?'

Oupa came galloping back towards them. He asked his first question when he was fifty yards away and his fifth as he arrived. From experience Sean knew there was no point in trying to answer them. He looked beyond the two Leroux and saw her coming. She was running back from the lead wagon, her bonnet hanging from its ribbon around her throat and her hair bouncing loosely with each step. She held her skirts out of the mud, her cheeks flushed darker than the brown of her face and her eyes were very green. Sean ducked under the neck of Oupa's horse and went wet, muddy and eager to meet her.

Then the shyness stopped them and they stood paces apart. 'Katrina, will you marry me?'

She went pale. She stared at him then turned away, she was crying and Sean felt the bottom drop out of his stomach.

'No,' shouted Oupa furiously. 'She won't marry you. Leave her alone, you big baboon. You've made her cry. Get out of here. She's only a baby. Get out of here.' He forced his horse between them.

'You hold your mouth, you old busybody.' Ouma came panting back to join the discussion. 'What do you know about it anyway? Just because she's crying doesn't mean she doesn't want him.'

'I thought he was going to let me go,' sobbed Katrina. 'I thought he didn't care.'

Sean whooped and tried to dodge around Oupa's horse.

'You leave her alone,' shouted Oupa desperately, manoeuvring his horse to cut Sean off. 'You made her cry. I tell you she's crying.'

Katrina was undoubtedly crying. She was also trying to get around Oupa's horse.

'*Vat haar*,' shouted Jan Paulus. 'Get her, man, go and get her!'

Ouma caught the horse by the reins and dragged it away: she was a powerful woman. Sean and Katrina collided and held tight.

'Hey, that's it, man.' Jan Paulus jumped off his horse and pounded Sean's back from behind. Unable to protect himself Sean was driven forward a pace with each blow.

Much later Oupa muttered sulkily, 'She can have two wagons for her dowry.'

'Three!' said Katrina.

'Four!' said Ouma.

'Very well, four. Take your hands off him, girl. Haven't you any shame?' Hastily Katrina dropped her arm from Sean's waist. Sean had borrowed a suit of clothing from Paulus and they were all standing round the fire. It had stopped raining but the low clouds were prematurely bringing on the night.

'And four of the horses,' Ouma prompted her husband.

'Do you want to beggar me, woman?'

'Four horses,' repeated Ouma.

'All right, all right ... four horses.' Oupa looked at Katrina, his eyes were stricken. 'She's only a baby, man, she's only fifteen years.'

'Sixteen,' said Ouma.

'Nearly seventeen,' said Katrina, 'and anyway you've promised, Pa, you can't go back on your word now.'

Oupa sighed; then he looked at Sean and his face hardened.

'Paulus, get the Bible out of my wagon. This big baboon is going to swear an oath.'

Jan Paulus put the Bible on the tailboard of the wagon. It was thick and the cover was of black leather, dull with use.

'Come here,' Oupa said to Sean. 'Put your hand on the book ... don't look at me. Look up, man, look up. Now say after me, "I do most solemnly swear to look after this woman" – don't gobble, speak slower – "until I can find a priest to say the proper words. Should I fail in this then I ask you, God, to blast me with lightning, sting me with serpents, burn me in eternal fire – "' Oupa completed the list of atrocities, then he grunted with satisfaction and tucked the Bible under his arm. 'He won't have a chance to do all that to you . . . I'll get you first.'

Sean shared Jan Paulus's wagon that night; he wasn't in a mood for sleep and anyway Jan Paulus snored. It was raining again in the morning, depressing weather for farewells. Jan Paulus laughed, Henrietta cried and Ouma did both. Oupa kissed his daughter.

'Be a woman like your mother,' he said, then he scowled at Sean.

'Remember, just you remember!'

Sean and Katrina stood together and watched the trees and the curtain of rain hide the wagon train. Sean held Katrina's hand. He could feel the sadness on her; he put his arm round her and her dress was damp and cold. The last wagon disappeared and they were alone in a land as vast as solitude. Katrina shivered and looked up at the man beside her. He was so big and overpoweringly male; he was a stranger. Suddenly she was frightened. She wanted to hear her mother's laugh and see her brother and father riding ahead of her wagon, the way it had always been.

'Oh, please, I want . . .' She pulled out from his arm. She never finished that sentence, for she looked at his mouth and his lips were full and burnt dark by the sun – they were smiling. Then she looked at his eyes and her panic smoothed away. With those eyes watching over her she was never to feel frightened again, not until the very end and that was a long time away. Going into his love was like going into a castle, a thick-walled place. A safe place where no one else could enter. The first feeling of it was so strong that she could only stand quietly and let the warmth wrap her.

That evening they outspanned Katrina's wagons back at the south bank of the river. It was still raining. Sean's servants waved and signalled to them, but the brown water bellowed down between them cutting off all sound and hope of passage. Katrina looked at the water. 'Did you really swim that, meneer?'

'So fast that I hardly got wet.'

'Thank you,' she said.

Despite the rain and smoky fire Katrina served up a meal as good as one of Ouma's. They ate it in the shelter of the tarpaulin beside her wagon. The wind guttered the hurricane lamp, flogged the canvas and blew a fine haze of rain in on them. It was so uncomfortable that when Sean suggested that they go into the wagon Katrina barely hesitated before agreeing. She sat on the edge of her cot and Sean sat on the chest opposite her. From an awkward start their conversation was soon running as fast as the river outside the wagon.

'My hair is still wet,' Katrina exclaimed at last. 'Do you mind if I dry it while we talk?'

'Of course not.'

'Then let me get my towel out of the chest.'

They stood up at the same time. There was very little space in the wagon. They touched. They were on the cot. The movement of his mouth on hers, the warm taste of it, the strong pleading of his fingers at the nape of her neck and along her spine – all these things were strangely confusing. She responded slowly at first, then faster with bewildered movements of her own body and little graspings at his arms and shoulders. She did not understand and she did not care. The confusion spread through her whole body and she could not stop it, she did not want to. She reached up and her fingers went into his hair. She pulled his face down on hers. His teeth crushed her lips – sweet, exciting pain. His hand came round from her back and enclosed a fat round breast. Through the thin cotton he found the erectness of her nipple and rolled it gently between his fingers. She reacted like a filly feeling the whip for the first time. One instant she lay under the shock of his touch and then her convulsive heave caught him by surprise. He went backwards off the cot and his head cracked against the wooden chest. He sat on the floor and stared up at her, too surprised even to rub the lump on his head. Her face was flushed and she pushed the hair back from her forehead with both hands. She was shaking her head wildly in her effort to speak through her gasping. 'You must go now, meneer – the servants have made a bed for you in one of the other wagons.'

Sean scrambled to his feet. 'But, I thought . . . surely we are . . . well, I mean.'

'Keep away from me,' she warned anxiously. 'If you touch me again tonight, I'll . . . I'll bite you.'

'But, Katrina, please, I can't sleep in the other wagon.' The thought appalled him.

'I'll cook your food, mend your clothes . . . everything! But until you find a priest . . .' She didn't go on, but Sean got the idea. He started to argue. It was his introduction to Boer immovability and at last he went to find his own bed. One of Katrina's dogs was there before him – a three-quarters-grown brindle hound. Sean's attempts to persuade it to leave were as ill-fated as had been his previous arguments with its mistress. They shared the bed. During the night a difference of opinion arose between them as to what constituted a half-share of the blankets. From it the dog earned its name – Thief.

Sean determined to show Katrina just how strongly he resented her attitude. He would be polite but distant. Five minutes after they had sat down to breakfast the next morning this demonstration of disapproval had deteriorated to the stage where he was unable to take his eyes off her face and he was talking so much that breakfast lasted an hour.

The rain held steady for three more days and then it stopped. The sun came back, as welcome as an old friend, but it was another ten days before the river regained its sanity. Time, rain or river meant very little to the two of them. They wandered out into the bush together to pick mushrooms; they sat in camp and when Katrina was working Sean followed her around. Then, of course, they talked. She listened to him. She laughed at the right places and gasped with wonder when she was meant to. She was a good listener. As for Sean, if she had repeated the same word over and over the sound of her voice alone would have held him entranced. The evenings were difficult. Sean would start getting restless and make excuses to touch her. She wanted him to, but she was frightened of the confusion that had so nearly trapped her the first night. So she drew up a set of rules and put them to him. 'Do you promise not to do anything more than kiss me?'

'Not unless you say I can,' Sean agreed readily.

'No.' She saw the catch in that.

'You mean, I must never do anything but kiss you even if you say I can?'

She started to blush. 'If I say so in the daytime, that's different . . . but anything I say at night doesn't count, and if you break your promise I'll never let you touch me again.'

Katrina's rules stood unchanged by the time the river

had dropped enough for the wagons to be taken across to the north bank. The rains were resting, gathering their strength, but soon they would set in once more. The river was full but no longer murderous. Now was the time to cross. Sean took the oxen across first, swimming them in a herd. Holding on to one of their tails he had a Nantucket sleigh-ride across the river and when he reached the north bank there was a joyous welcome awaiting him.

They took six thick coils of unused rope from the stores wagon and joined them together. With the end of the rope round his waist Sean made one of his horses tow him back across the river, Mbejane paying out the line to him as he went. Then Sean supervised Katrina's servants as they emptied all the water barrels and lashed them to the sides of the first wagon to serve as floats. They ran the wagon into the water, tied on the rope and adjusted the barrels so that the wagon floated level. Sean signalled to Mbejane and waited until he had made the other end of the rope fast to a tree on the north bank. Then they pushed the wagon into the current and watched anxiously as it swung across the river like a pendulum, the current driving it but the tree anchoring it. It hit the north bank a distance the exact width of the river downstream of the tree, and Sean's party cheered as Mbejane and the other servants ran down the bank to retrieve it. Mbejane had a team of oxen standing ready and they dragged it out. Sean's horse towed him across the river again to fetch the rope.

Sean, Katrina and all her servants rode across on the last wagon. Sean stood behind Katrina with his arms round her waist, ostensibly to steady her, and the servants shouted and chattered like children on a picnic.

The water piled up brown against the side of the wagon, tilting it and making it roll, and with an exhilarating swoop they shot across the river and crashed into the far bank. The impact tumbled them overboard, throwing them into the knee-deep water beside the bank. They scrambled ashore. The water streamed out of Katrina's dress, her hair melted wetly over her face; she had mud on one cheek and she was gasping with laughter. Her sodden petticoats clung to her legs, tripping her, and Sean picked her up and carried her to his own laager. His servants shouted loud encouragement after him and Katrina shrieked genteelly to be put down, but held tight round his neck with both arms.

– 17 –

Now that the rains had changed every irregularity in the land into a waterhole and sowed new green grass where before had been dust and dry earth, the game scattered away from the river. Every few days Sean's trackers came into camp to report that there were no elephant. Sean condoled with them and sent them out again. He was well satisfied; there was a new quarry now, more elusive and therefore more satisfying than an old bull elephant with a hundred and fifty pounds of ivory on each side of his face. Yet to call Katrina his quarry was a lie. She was much more than that.

She was a new world – a place of endless mysteries and unexpected delights, an enchanting mixture of woman and child. She supervised the domestic routine with deceptive lack of fuss. With her there, suddenly his clothes were clean and had their full complement of buttons; the stew of boots and books and unwashed socks in his wagon vanished. There were fresh bread and fruit preserves on the table; Kandhla's eternal grilled steaks gave way to a variety of dishes. Each day she showed a new accomplishment. She could ride astride, though Sean had to turn his back when she mounted and dismounted. She cut Sean's hair and made as good a job of it as his barber in Johannesburg. She had a medicine chest in her wagon from which she produced remedies for every ailing man or beast in the company. She handled a rifle like a man and could strip and clean Sean's Mannlicher. She helped him load cartridges, measuring the charges with a practised eye. She could discuss birth and procreation with a clinical objectivity and a minute later blush all over when he looked at her that way. She was as stubborn as a mule, haughty when it suited her, serene and inscrutable at times and at others a little girl. She would push a handful of grass down the back of his shirt and run for him to chase her, giggle for minutes at a secret thought, play long imaginative games in which the dogs were her children and she talked to them and answered for them. Sometimes she was so naive that Sean thought she was joking until he remembered how young she was. She could drive him from happiness to spitting anger and back again within the space of an hour. But, once he had won her confidence and she knew that he would play to the rules, she responded to his caresses with a violence that startled them both. Sean was completely absorbed in her. She was the most wonderful thing he had ever found and, best of all, he could talk to her. He told her about Duff. She saw the extra cot in his wagon and found clothing that was obviously too small for him. She asked about it and he told her all of it and she understood.

The days became weeks. The cattle grew fat, their skins sleek and tight. Katrina planted a small vegetable garden and reaped a crop from it. Christmas came and Katrina baked a cake. Sean gave her a kaross of monkey skins that Mbejane had worked on in secret. Katrina gave Sean handsewn shirts, each with his initials embroidered on the top pocket, and she relaxed the rules a fraction.

Then when the new year had begun and Sean hadn't killed an elephant in six weeks, Mbejane headed a deputation from the gunboys. The question he had to ask, though tactfully disguised, was simply, 'Did we come here to hunt, or what?'

They broke camp and moved north again and the strain was showing on Sean at last. He tried to sweat it out by long days of hunting but this didn't help for conditions were so bad that they added to his irritability. The grass in most places was higher than a mounted man's head, its sharp edges cut as he passed through it. But the grass seeds were the worst: half an inch long and barbed like an arrow they worked their way quickly through clothing and into the skin. In the humid heat the small wounds they made festered within hours. Then there were the flies. Hippo-flies, greenheaded flies, sand-flies all with one thing in common – they stung. The soft skin behind the ears was their favourite place. They'd creep upon him, settle so lightly he wouldn't feel it – then, ping with the red-hot needle. Always wet, sometimes with sweat, other times with rain, Sean would close with a herd of elephant. He would hear them moving in the long grass around him and see the white canopy of egrets fluttering over them, but it was seldom he could get a shot at them. If he did he had to stand in the centre of a storm of blundering bodies. Often they would be following a herd, almost upon them, when Sean would lose interest and they'd all go back to camp. He couldn't keep away.

He was miserable, his servants were miserable, and Katrina was happy as a bird at daybreak. She had a man, she was mistress of a household which she ran with confidence and, because her senses were not yet as seasoned as Sean's, she was physically content. Even with Sean's strict adherence to the rules, their evenings in her wagon would end for her with a sigh and a shudder and she would go dreamy-eyed to bed and leave Sean with a burning devil inside of him. The only person Sean could complain to was Thief. He would lie with his snout buried in Sean's armpit,

452

with at least his share of the blankets over him, and listen quietly.

The Zulus could see what the trouble was but they didn't understand it. They didn't discuss it, of course, but if one of them spread his hands expressively or coughed in a certain way the others knew what he meant. Mbejane came closest to actually putting it into words. Sean had just thrown a tantrum. It was a matter of a lost axe and who was responsible. Sean lined them up and expressed doubts as to their ancestry, present worth and future prospects, then he stormed off to his wagon. There was a long silence and Hlubi offered his snuff-box to Mbejane.

Mbejane took a pinch and said, 'It's a stupid stallion that doesn't know how to kick down a fence.'

'It is true, it is true,' they agreed, and there the matter rested.

– 18 –

A week later they reached the Sabi river. The mountains on the far side were blue-grey with distance and the river was full – brown and full.

The next morning was fresh and cool from the night's rain. The camp smelt of wood-smoke, cattle and wild mimosa. From one of the ostrich eggs that Mbejane had found the day before, Katrina made an omelette the size of a soup-plate. It was flavoured with nutmeg and chunks of mushroom, yellow and rich. Afterwards there were scones and wild honey, coffee and a cheroot for Sean.

'Are you going out today?' Katrina asked.

'Uh huh.'

'Oh!'

'Don't you want me to?'

'You haven't stayed in camp for a week.'

453

'Don't you want me to go?'

She stood up quickly and started clearing the table. 'Anyway you won't find any elephant . . . you haven't found anything for ages.'

'Do you want me to stay?'

'It's such a lovely day.' She signed to Kandhla to take the plates away.

'If you want me to stay, ask me properly.'

'We could look for mushrooms.'

'Say it,' said Sean.

'All right then, please!'

'Mbejane! Take the saddle off that horse, I won't be using him.'

Katrina laughed. She ran to her wagon, skirts swirling around her legs, calling to the dogs. She came back with her bonnet on and a basket in her hand. The dogs crowded round them, jumping up and barking.

'Go on . . . seek up then,' Sean told them and they raced ahead, circling back barking, chasing one another. Sean and Katrina walked holding hands. The brim of Katrina's bonnet kept her face in shadow, but even then her eyes when she looked at him were bright green. They picked the new mushrooms, round and hard, brown and slightly sticky on top, fluted underneath delicately as a lady's fan. In an hour they had filled the basket and they stopped under a marula tree. Sean lay on his back. Katrina broke off a blade of grass and tickled his face with it until he caught her wrist and pulled her down onto his chest. The dogs watched them, sitting around them in a circle, their tongues hanging out pink and wet.

'There's a place in the Cape, just outside Paarl. The mountains stand over it and there's a river . . . the water's very clear, you can see the fish lying on the bottom,' said Katrina. Her ear was against his chest and she was listening to his heart. 'Will you buy me a farm there one day?'

'Yes,' said Sean.

'We'll build a house with a wide veranda and on Sundays we'll drive to church with the girls and the little ones in the back and the bigger boys riding next to the buggy.'

'How many will there be?' asked Sean. He lifted the side of her bonnet and looked at her ear. It was a very pretty ear, in the sunlight he could see the fine fur on the lobe.

'Oh lots . . . boys mostly, but a few girls.'

'Ten?' suggested Sean.

'More than that.'

'Fifteen?'

'Yes, fifteen.'

They lay and thought about it. To Sean it seemed a fairly well-rounded number.

'And I'll keep chickens, I want lots of chickens.'

'All right,' said Sean.

'You don't mind?'

'Should I?'

'Some people mind chickens, some people don't like them at all,' said Katrina. 'I'm glad you don't mind them. I've always wanted them.'

Stealthily Sean advanced his mouth towards her ear but she felt him move and sat up.

'What are you doing?'

'This,' said Sean and his arm shot out.

'No, Sean, they're watching us.' She waved her hand at the dogs.

'They'll understand,' said Sean and then they were both quiet for a long time.

The dogs burst out together in full hunting chorus. Katrina sat up and Sean turned his head and saw the leopard. It stood fifty yards away on the edge of the thick bush along the river bank watching them, poised elegantly in tights of black and gold, long and small-bellied. It moved then, blurring with speed, touching the ground as lightly as a swallow touches the water when it drinks in flight. The dogs went after it in a pack, Thief leading them, his voice cracking with excitement.

'Back, come back,' shouted Sean. 'Leave it, damn you, come back.'

'Stop them, Sean, go after them. We'll lose them all.'

'Wait here,' Sean told her.

He ran after the sound of the pack. Not shouting, saving his wind. He knew what would happen and he listened for it. He heard the tone of the hunt change – sharper now. Sean stopped and stood panting, peering ahead. The dogs were not moving. The sound of their barking was steady in volume.

'The swine has stopped; he's going to take them.'

He started running again and almost immediately heard the first dog scream. He kept running. He found the dog lying where the leopard had flung it – the old bitch with white ears, her stomach was stripped out. Sean went on. The tan ridgeback next, disembowelled, still alive and crawling to meet him. He ran on; always the hunt was out of sight ahead of him but he kept after it. He no longer stopped to help the dogs that had been mauled. Most of them were dead before he reached them. The saliva thickened in his mouth, his heart jumped against his ribs and he reeled as he ran.

Suddenly he was in the open and the hunt was spread out before him. There were three dogs left. One of them was Thief. They were circling the leopard, belling him, darting in at his back legs, snapping, then jumping back as the leopard spun snarling. The grass was short and green in the clearing. The sun was directly overhead: it threw no shadow, it lit everything with a flat, even light. Sean tried to shout but his throat wouldn't let the sound out. The leopard dropped onto its back and lay with the sprawled grace of a sleeping cat, its legs open and its belly exposed.

The dogs hung back, hesitating. Sean shouted again but his voice still would not carry. That creamy yellow belly, soft and fluffy, was too much temptation. One of the dogs went for it, dipping its head, its mouth open. The leopard closed on it like a spring trap. It caught and held the dog with its front paws and its back legs worked quickly. The dog yammered at the swift surgeon strokes and then it was thrown aside, its bowels hanging out. The leopard relaxed again to show the yellow bait of its belly. Sean was close now and this time the two dogs heard his shout. The leopard heard it also. It flashed to its feet and tried to break, but the instant it turned Thief was at it, slashing at its back legs forcing it to swing and crouch.

'Here, boy, leave him! Here, Thief, come here!'

Thief took Sean's shout as encouragement. He danced just out of reach of the flicking paws, shrilly taunting the leopard. The hunt was finely balanced now. Sean knew if he could get the dogs to slacken their attack the leopard would run. He went forward a pace, stooped to pick up a stone to throw at Thief and his movement tipped the balance. When he straightened up the leopard was watching him and he felt the eel of fear move in his stomach. It was going to come for him. He knew it by the way its ears flattened against its head and its shoulders bunched like loaded springs. Sean dropped the stone and reached for the knife on his belt.

The leopard's lips peeled back. Its teeth were yellow, its head with the ears flattened was like a snake's. It came fast and low against the ground, brushing the dogs aside. Its run was long-reaching, smoothly beautiful. It snaked towards him, fast over the short grass. It came into the air, lifting high, very fast and very smoothly. Sean felt the shock and the pain together. The shock threw him backwards and the pain sucked the breath from his lungs. Its claws hooked into his chest, he felt them scrape his ribs. He held its mouth from his face, his forearm against its throat and he smelt the overripe grave smell of its breath. They rolled together in the grass, its front claws still holding in the flesh of his chest, and he felt its back legs coming up to rake his stomach. He twisted desperately to keep clear of them, using his knife at the same time, slipping the blade into its back. The leopard screamed, its back legs came up again; he felt the claws go into his hip and tear down his thigh. The pain was deep and strong and he knew he was badly hurt. The legs came up again. This time they would kill him.

Thief locked his teeth in the leopard's leg before the claws could catch in Sean's flesh, he dragged back, digging in with his front feet, holding the leopard stretched out across Sean's body. Sean's vision was dissolving into blackness and bright lights. He pushed the knife into the leopard's back, close to the spine and pulled it down between the ribs the way a butcher cuts a chop. The leopard screamed again with its body shuddering and its claws curling in Sean's flesh. Sean cut again, deep and long – and again, then again. Tearing at it, mad with the pain, its blood gushed out and mixed with his and he rolled away from it. The dogs were worrying it, growling. It was dead. Sean let the knife slip out of his hand and touched the tears in his leg. The blood was dark red, pouring with the thickness of treacle, much blood. He was looking down a funnel of darkness. The leg was far away, not his – not his leg.

'Garry,' he whispered. 'Garry, oh God! I'm sorry. I slipped, I didn't mean it, I slipped.' The funnel closed and there was no leg – only darkness. Time was a liquid thing, all the world was liquid, moving in darkness. The sun was dark and only the pain was steady, steady as a rock in the dark moving sea. He saw Katrina's face indistinct in the darkness. He tried to tell her how sorry he was. He tried to tell her it was an accident, but the pain stopped him. She was crying. He knew she would understand so he went back into the dark sea. Then the surface of the sea boiled and he choked in the heat, but always the pain was there like a rock to hold onto. The steam from the sea coiled up around him and it hardened into the shape of a woman and he thought it was Katrina, then he saw its head was a leopard's head and its breath stank like the rotting of a gangrenous leg.

'I don't want you – I know who you are,' he shouted at it. 'I don't want you. It's not my child,' and the thing broke into steam, twisting grey steam, and came back gibbering at him on a chain that tinkled, frothing yellow from the grey misty mouth, and terror came with it. He twisted and covered his face, holding onto the pain for the pain was real and steady.

Then after a thousand years the sea froze and he walked on it and the white ice stretched away wherever he looked. It was cold and lonely on the ice. There was a small wind, a cold small wind, the wind whispered across the ice and its whispering was a sad sound, and Sean held his pain, hugging it close to him for he was lonely and only the pain was real. Then there were other figures moving around him on the ice, dark figures all hurrying one way, crowding him, pushing him along with them and he lost his pain, lost it in the desperate hurrying press. And though they had no faces, some of the figures wept and others laughed and they hurried forward until they came to the place where the crevasse split across the ice in front of them. The crevasse was wide and deep and its sides were white, then pale-green shading to blue and at last to infinite blackness, and some of the figures threw themselves joyfully into it singing as they fell. Others clung to edges, their formless faces full of fear, and still others stepped off into the void, tiredly, like travellers at the end of a long journey. When Sean saw the crevasse he began to fight, throwing himself back against the crowd that bore him forward, carrying him to the edge of the pit, and his feet slid over the edge. He clawed with his fingers at the slippery edge of the ice. He fought and he shouted as he fought for the dark drop sucked at his legs. Then he lay quietly and the crevasse had closed and he was alone. He was tired – wasted and terribly tired. He closed his eyes and the pain came back to him, throbbing softly in his leg.

He opened his eyes and he saw Katrina's face. She was pale and her eyes were big and heavily underscored in blue. He tried to lift his hand to touch her face but he couldn't move.

'Katrina,' he said. He saw her eyes go green with surprise and happiness.

'You've come back. Oh, thank God. You've come back.'

Sean rolled his head and looked at the canvas of the wagon tent.

'How long?' he asked. His voice was a whisper.

'Five days . . . Don't talk – please, don't talk.'

Sean closed his eyes. He was very tired so he slept.

– 19 –

Katrina washed him when he woke. Mbejane helped her lift and turn him, his big pink-palmed hands very gentle as he handled the leg. They washed the smell of fever off him and changed the dressings. Sean watched Katrina as she worked and every time she looked up they smiled at each other. Once he used a little of his strength to ask Mbejane, 'Where were you when I needed you?'

'I slept in the sun, Nkosi, like an old woman,' Mbejane half-laughed, half-apologized. Katrina brought him food and when he smelt it he was hungry. He ate it all and then he slept again.

Mbejane built a shelter with open sides and a roof of thatch. He sited it in the shade on the bank of the Sabi. Then he made a bed of poles and laced leather thongs. They carried Sean from the wagon, Katrina fussing around them until they had laid him in the shelter. Katrina went back to the wagon for pillows and when she returned she found Thief and Sean settling down comfortably.

'Sean, get that monster out of there – those blankets have just been washed.'

Thief flattened his body and hid his head in Sean's armpit.

'It's all right, he's quite clean,' Sean protected him.

'He smells.'

'He does not.' Sean sniffed at Thief. 'Well, not much anyway.'

'You two!' She put the pillows under Sean's head and went round to his leg. 'How does it feel?'

'It's fine,' said Sean. Thief inched himself up the bed until he reached the pillows.

In the slow slide of days Sean's body healed and the well of his strength filled. The moving air under the shelter dried the scabs off his chest and leg, but there would be scars. In the mornings, after breakfast, Sean held court from his couch. Katrina sat on the end of the bed and his servants squatted around him. First they talked over domestic matters – the health of the oxen, mentioning them by name, discussing their eyes, hooves and stomachs. There was a tear in the canvas of one wagon. The single remaining bitch was in season – was Thief man enough for the job yet? There was meat to kill – perhaps the Nkosikaze would take the rifle later today. Hlubi had caught four barbel of medium size in his fish trap, and here the talk turned to the bush around them. A lion had killed a buffalo below the first bend in the river – there you could see the vultures. During the night a herd of cow elephant had drunk a mile upstream. Each item was considered by the meeting. Everyone felt free to comment or argue against any view which conflicted with his own. When everything had been said Sean gave them their tasks for the day and sent them away. Then he and Katrina could be alone.

From the shelter they could see the full sweep of the river, with the crocodiles lying on the white sandbars and the kingfishers plopping into the shallows. They sat close to each other and they talked of the farm they would have. Sean would grow grapes and breed horses and Katrina would keep chickens. By the next rainy season they would have filled all the wagons; one more trip after that and they would have enough to buy the farm.

Katrina kept him in bed long after he was strong enough to leave it. She mothered him and he loved it. Shamelessly, in the fashion of the male, he accepted her attentions and even exaggerated his injuries a little. Finally but reluctantly Katrina let him up. He stayed in camp a week more, until his legs stopped wobbling, then one evening he took his rifle and went with Mbejane to shoot fresh meat. They went slowly, Sean favouring his leg, and he shot a young eland not far from the laager. Sean sat against a msasa tree and smoked a cheroot while Mbejane went back to fetch servants to carry the meat. Sean watched them butcher the carcass; there were slabs of white fat on the meat. They slung it on poles and carried it between them, two men to a pole, and when they got back to camp Sean found Katrina in one of her inscrutable moods. When he talked to her at supper she answered him from far away and afterwards by the fire she sat detached from him. She was very lovely and Sean was puzzled and a little resentful. At last he stood up.

'It's time for bed – I'll see you to your wagon.'

'You go. I'll sit a little longer.'

Sean hesitated. 'Is there something wrong? Have I done something wrong?'

'No,' she said quickly. 'No. I'm all right. You go to bed.'

He kissed her cheek. 'If you need me I'll be close. Goodnight, sleep sweet.'

He straightened up. 'Come on, Thief,' he said. 'Time for bed.'

'Leave Thief with me, please.' Katrina caught the skin at the back of the dog's neck and restrained him.

'Why?'

'I just feel like company.'

'Then I'll stay as well.' Sean moved to sit down again.

'No, you go to bed.' She sounded desperate and Sean looked hard at her.

'Are you sure you're all right?'

'Yes, please go.'

He went to his wagon and looked back at her. She was sitting very straight, holding the dog. He climbed into the wagon. The lamp was lit and he stopped in surprise when he saw his cot. There were sheets on it, not just the rough blankets. He ran his hand over the smooth fabric; it was crisp from new ironing. He sat on the cot and pulled off his boots. He undid his shirt and threw it onto the chest, then he lay back and looked up at the lamp.

'There's something bloody funny going on here,' he said.

'Sean' – her voice just outside the wagon. Sean jumped up and opened the flap. 'Can I come in?'

'Yes, of course.' He gave her his hand and lifted her into the wagon. He looked at her face. She was frightened.

'There *is* something wrong,' he said.

'No, don't touch me. There's something I've got to tell you. Sit down on the cot.'

Sean watched her face. He was worried.

'I thought I loved you when I came away with you. I thought we had for ever to be together.' She swallowed painfully. 'Then I found you there in the grass – torn and dead. Before our life together had begun you were dead.'

Sean saw the pain come back into her eyes; she was living it again. He put out his hand to her but she held his wrist.

'No, wait ... please let me finish. I have to explain to you. It's very important.'

Sean dropped his hand and she went on speaking quickly.

'You were dead and I, too, was dying inside. I felt empty. There was nothing left. Nothing ... just the hollowness inside and the dry dead feeling on the outside. I touched your face and you looked at me. I prayed then, Sean, and I prayed through the days when you fought the rotting of your body.'

She knelt in front of him and held him around the waist.

'Now we are alive and together again, but I know that it cannot be for ever. A day more, a year, if we are lucky, twenty. But not for ever. I see how small I have been to us. I want to be your wife.'

He bent to her quickly but she pulled away and stood up. She slipped the buttons and her clothing fell away. She loosed her hair and let it drop shiny bright down the whiteness of her body.

'Look at me, Sean, I want you to look at me. This and my love I can give you ... is it enough?'

There was smoothness, hollow and swell, hair like black fire and soft light on soft skin. He saw the flush from her cheeks spread onto her breasts until they glowed, pink and shy but proud in their perfection. He looked no further. He took her to him and covered her nakedness with his big body. She was trembling and he put her between the sheets and gentled her with his voice until the trembling stopped and she lay with her face pressed up under his beard into his neck.

'Show me how ... I want to give everything to you. Please show me how,' she whispered.

So they married each other and their marriage was a comingling of many things. There was the softness of the wind in it and wanting, the way the baked earth wants the rain. There was pain sharp and swift, movement like running horses, sound low as voices in the night but glad as a greeting, joy climbing on eagles' wings, the triumphant surge and burst of wild water on a rock shore and then there was stillness and warmth within and the snuggling of drowsy puppies, and sleep. Yet it did not end in the sleep, it went on to another seeking and finding, another union and a stranger mystery in the secret depths of her body.

– 20 –

In the morning she brought her Bible to him.

'Hey, hey,' protested Sean, 'I've already sworn one oath.' Katrina laughed at him, the memory of the night still warm and happy inside her. She opened the book at its fly leaf.

'You've got to write your name in it ... here, next to mine.'

She watched him, standing next to his chair with her hip touching his shoulder.

'And your date of birth,' she said.

Sean wrote: 'Ninth Jan. 1862.' Then he said: 'What's this "date of death" ... do you want me to fill that in as well?'

'Don't talk like that,' she said quickly and touched the wooden table.

Sean was sorry he'd said it. He tried to cover up. 'There's only space for six children.'

'We can write the others in the margin. That's what Ma

did . . . hers even go over onto the first page of Genesis. Do you think we'll get that far, Sean?'

Sean smiled at her. 'The way I feel now we should reach the New Testament without much trouble.'

They had made a good start. By June the rains were over and Katrina walked with her shoulders back to balance her load. There was a good feeling in the camp. Katrina was more woman than child now. She was big and radiant, pleased with the awe her condition inspired in Sean. She sang to herself often and sometimes in the night she would let him share in it. She would let him pull the nightdress back from the mound of her stomach and lay his ear against the tight-stretched, blue-veined skin. He listened to the suck and gurgle and felt the movement against his cheek. When he sat up his eyes would be full of the wonder of it and she would smile proudly at him and take his head on her shoulder and they would lie together quietly. In the daytime things were right as well. Sean laughed with the servants and hunted without the intensity of before.

They moved north along the Sabi river. Sometimes they camped for a month at one place. The game came back to the rivers as the veld dried out and once more the ivory started piling up in the wagons.

One afternoon in September Sean and Katrina left the camp and walked along the bank. The land was brown again and smelt of dry grass. The river was pools and white sand.

'Hell, it's hot.' Sean took off his hat and wiped the sweat off his forehead. 'You must be cooking under all those clothes.'

'No, I'm all right.' Katrina was holding his arm.

'Let's have a swim.'

'You mean with no clothes on?' Katrina looked shocked.

'Yes, why not?'

'It's rude.'

466

'Come on.' He took her down the bank protesting every step and at a place where boulders screened the water he prised her out of her dress. She was laughing and gasping and blushing all at the same time. He carried her into the pool and she sat down thankfully with the water up to her chin.

'How's that feel?' Sean asked.

She let her hair down and it floated out round her, she wriggled her toes in the sand and her stomach showed through the water like the back of a white whale.

'It's nice,' she admitted. 'It feels like silk underwear against my skin.'

Sean stood over her with only his hat on. She looked at him.

'Sit down,' she said uncomfortably and looked away from him.

'Why?' he asked.

'You know why . . . you're rude, that's why.'

Sean sat down beside her.

'You should be used to me by now.'

'Well, I'm not.'

Sean put his arm round her under the water.

'You're lovely,' he said. 'You're my fancy.'

She let him kiss her ear.

'What's it going to be?' He touched the ripe swelling. 'Boy or girl?' This was currently the favourite topic of conversation.

'Boy.' She was very definite.

'What shall we call him?'

'Well, if you don't find a *predikant* soon we'll have to call him the name you're always giving to the servants.'

Sean stared at her. 'What do you mean?'

'You know what you call them when you're cross.'

'Bastard,' said Sean, then really concerned, 'Hell, I hadn't thought of that! We'll have to find a priest. No child

467

of mine will be a bastard. We'll have to go back to Louis Trichardt.'

'You've got about a month,' Katrina warned him.

'My God, we'll never make it. We've left it too late.' Sean's face was ghastly. 'Wait, I've got it. There are Portuguese settlements across the mountains on the coast.'

'Oh, Sean, but they're Roman Catholics.'

'They all work for the same boss.'

'How long will it take to cross the mountains?' Katrina asked doubtfully.

'I don't know. Perhaps two weeks to reach the coast on horseback.'

'On horseback?' Katrina looked still more doubtfully.

'Oh hell ... you can't ride!' Sean scratched the side of his nose. 'I'll have to go and fetch one. Will you stay on your own? I'll leave Mbejane to look after you.'

'Yes, I'll be all right.'

'I won't go if you don't want me to. It's not that important.'

'It is important, you know it is. I'll be all right, truly I will.'

Before he left the next morning Sean took Mbejane aside. 'You know why you're not coming with me, don't you?'

Mbejane nodded, but Sean answered his own question. 'Because there is more important work for you to do here.'

'At night,' said Mbejane, 'I will sleep beneath the Nkosikazi's wagon.'

'You'll sleep?' asked Sean threateningly.

'Only once in a while and then very lightly,' Mbejane grinned.

'That's better,' said Sean.

Sean said goodbye to Katrina. There were no tears, she understood necessity and helped him to a quiet acceptance of it. They stood a long while beside their wagon, holding each other, their lips almost touching as they whispered together and then Sean called for his horse. Hlubi followed him leading the packhorse when he crossed the Sabi and when Sean reached the far bank he turned and looked back. Katrina was still standing by their wagon and behind her hovered Mbejane. In her bonnet and green dress she looked very young. Sean waved his hat over his head and then set off towards the mountains.

The forests dwindled into grassland as they climbed and each night was colder than the last. Then, in its turn the grassland conceded to the sheer bluffs and misty gorges of the mountain back. Sean and Hlubi struggled upwards, following the game trails, losing them, turning back from impassable cliffs, scouting for a pass, leading the horses over the steep pitches and at night sitting close to the fire and listening to the baboons barking in the kranses around them. Then suddenly, in the middle of a morning that was bright as a cut diamond, they were at the top. To the west the land lay spread out like a map and the distance they had travelled in a week was pathetically small. By straining his eyes and his imagination Sean could make out the dark-green belt of the Sabi watercourse. To the east the land merged with a blueness that was not the sky and for a while he failed to recognize it. Then – 'The sea,' he shouted and Hlubi laughed with him for it was a godlike feeling to stand above the world. They found an easier route down the eastern slopes and followed it onto the coastal plain. At the bottom of the mountains they came to a native village. To see cultivated lands and human dwellings again was a small shock to Sean. He had come to accept the fact that he and his retinue were the only people left on earth.

The entire population of the village fled when they saw him. Mothers snatched up a child in each hand and ran as fast as their menfolk – memories of the slave-traders still persisted in this part of Africa. Within two minutes of his arrival Sean again had the feeling that he was the only person left on earth. With the contempt of the Zulu for every other tribe in Africa, Hlubi shook his head sadly.

'Monkeys,' he said.

They dismounted and tied their horses under the big tree that was the centre of the village. They sat in the shade and waited. The huts were grass beehives, their roofs blackened with smoke, and a few chickens picked and scratched at the bare earth between them. Half an hour later Sean saw a black face watching him from the edge of the bush and he ignored it. Slowly the face emerged, followed closely by a reluctant body. With a twig, Sean went on drawing patterns in the dust between his feet. Out of the corner of his eye he watched the hesitant approach. It was an old man with stork thin legs and one eye glazed into a white jelly by tropical ophthalmia. Sean concluded that his fellows had picked him to act as ambassador on the grounds that of all their number he would be the least loss.

Sean looked up and gave him a radiant smile. The old man froze and then his lips twitched into a sickly grin of relief. Sean stood up, dusted his hands on the sides of his breeches and went to shake the old man's hand. Immediately the bush around them swarmed with people, they poured back into the village jabbering and laughing: they crowded round Sean and felt his clothing, peered into his face and exclaimed delightedly. It was obvious that most of them had never seen a white man before. Sean was trying to shake off One-Eye, who still had a possessive hold on Sean's right hand, and Hlubi leaned disdainfully against the

470

tree, taking no part in the welcome. One-Eye ended the confusion by screeching at them in a voice rusty with age. The courage he had displayed earlier now earned its reward. At his command a dozen of the younger women scampered off and came back with a carved wooden stool and six earthenware pots of native beer. By the hand, on which he had not for an instant relaxed his grip, One-Eye led Sean to the stool and made him sit; the rest of the villagers squatted in a circle round him and one of the girls brought the biggest beer-pot to Sean. The beer was yellow and it bubbled sullenly. Sean's stomach shied at the sight of it. He glanced at One-Eye who was watching him anxiously, he lifted the pot and sipped. Then he smiled with surprise; it was creamy and pleasantly tart.

'Good,' he said.

'Goot,' chorused the villagers.

'Your health,' said Sean.

''ealt,' said the village as one man, and Sean drank deep. One of the girls took another beer-pot to Hlubi. She knelt in front of him and shyly offered it. She had a plaited-grass string around her waist from which a small kilt hung down in front, but her stern was completely exposed and her bosoms were the size and shape of ripe melons. Hlubi looked at them until the girl hung her head, then he lifted the beer-pot.

Sean wanted a guide to the nearest Portuguese settlement. He looked at One-Eye and said, 'Town? Portagee?'

One-Eye was almost overcome by Sean's attention. He grabbed Sean's hand again before he could pull it away and shook it vigorously.

'Stop that, you bloody fool,' said Sean irritably and One-Eye grinned and nodded, then without releasing Sean's hand he began an impassioned speech to the other villagers. Sean meanwhile was searching his memory for the name of one of the Portuguese ports on this coast.

471

'Nova Sofala,' he shouted as he got it.

One-Eye broke off his speech abruptly and stared at Sean.

'Nova Sofala,' said Sean again pointing vaguely towards the east and One-Eye showed his gums in his biggest grin yet.

'Nova Sofala,' he agreed pointing with authority and then it was only a matter of minutes before it was understood between them that he would act as guide. Hlubi saddled the horses, One-Eye fetched a grass sleeping mat and a battle-axe from one of the huts. Sean mounted and looked at Hlubi to do the same but Hlubi was acting strangely.

'Yes?' Sean asked with resignation. 'What is it?'

'Nkosi.' Hlubi was looking at the branches of the tree above them. 'The Old One could lead the packhorse.'

'You can take it in turns,' said Sean.

Hlubi coughed and transferred his eyes to the fingernails of his left hand.

'Nkosi, is it possible that you will return to this village on the way back from the sea?'

'Yes, of course,' said Sean, 'we'll have to leave the Old One here. Why do you ask?'

'I have a thorn in my foot, Nkosi, it gives me pain. If you do not require me I will wait here for you. Perhaps the thorn wound will have healed by then.' Hlubi looked up at the tree again and shuffled his feet with embarrassment. Sean had not noticed him limping and he was puzzled as to why Hlubi should start malingering now. Then Hlubi could not stop himself from glancing at where the girl stood in the circle of villagers. Her kilt was very small and from the sides gave her no cover at all. Understanding came to Sean and he chuckled.

'The thorn you have is painful, but it's not in your foot.'

472

Hlubi shuffled his feet again. 'You said they were monkeys . . . have you changed your mind?' Sean asked.

'Nkosi, they are indeed monkeys,' Hlubi sighed. 'But very friendly monkeys.'

'Stay then . . . but do not weaken yourself too much. We have mountains to cross on the way home.'

– 22 –

One-Eye led the packhorse – this made him very proud. Through tall grass, mangrove swamp and thick hot jungle, then through white coral sand and the curving stems of palm trees, they came at last to the sea. Nova Sofala was a fort with brass cannon and thick walls. The sea beyond it was muddy brown from the estuary that flowed into it.

The sentry at the gates said, '*Madre de Dio*' when he saw Sean, and took him to the Commandant. The Commandant was a small man with fever-yellowed face and a tired, sweat-darkened tunic. The Commandant said, '*Madre de Dio*,' and shot his chair back from his desk. It took some time for him to realize that contrary to appearance this dirty, bearded giant was not dangerous. The Commandant could speak English and Sean laid his problem before him.

For a certainty he could be of assistance. There were three Jesuit missionaries in the fort, freshly arrived from Portugal and eager for employment. Sean could take his pick but first he must bath, eat dinner with the Commandant and help him sample the wines that had arrived on the same boat as the missionaries. Sean thought that was a good idea.

At dinner he met the missionaries. They were young men, pink-faced still, for Africa had not yet had a chance

473

to mark them. All three of them were willing to go with him and Sean selected the youngest – not for his appearance but rather for his name. 'Father Alphonso' had a heroic ring to it. The Jesuits went early to bed and left the Commandant, the four junior officers and Sean to the port. They drank toasts to Queen Victoria and her family and to the King of Portugal and his family. This made them thirsty so they drank to absent friends, then to each other. The Commandant and Sean swore a mutual oath of friendship and loyalty and this made the Commandant very sad. He cried and Sean patted his shoulder and offered to dance the Dashing White Sergeant for him. The Commandant said that he would esteem it as a very great honour and furthermore he would be delighted. He himself did not know this dance but perhaps Sean would instruct him. They danced on the table. The Commandant was doing very well until in his enthusiasm he misjudged the size of the table. Sean helped the junior officers put him to bed and in the morning Sean, Father Alphonso and One-Eye started back towards the mountains.

Sean was impatient of any delay now; he wanted to get back to Katrina. Father Alphonso's English was on a par with Sean's Portuguese. This made conversation difficult, so Alphonso solved the problem by doing all the talking. At first Sean listened but when he decided that the good father was trying to convert him he no longer bothered. Alphonso did not seem put out – he just went on talking and clinging to the horse with both hands while his cassock flapped about his legs and his face sweated in the shade of his wide-brimmed hat. One-Eye followed them like an ancient stork.

It took them two days back to One-Eye's village and their entry was a triumphal procession. Father Alphonso's face lit up when he saw so many prospective converts. Sean could see him mentally rubbing his hands together, and he decided to keep going before Alphonso forgot the main object of the expedition. He gave One-Eye a hunting-knife in payment for his services. One-Eye sat down under the big tree in the centre of the village, his own thin legs no longer able to support his weight and the knife clutched to his chest.

'Hlubi, you've had enough of that . . . come on now!' Sean had not dismounted and was restlessly waiting for Hlubi to say his farewells to three of the village girls. Hlubi had displayed traditional Zulu taste – all three of them were big-breasted, big-bottomed and young. They were also crying.

'Come on, Hlubi . . . what's the trouble?'

'Nkosi, they believe that I have taken them for my wives.'

'What made them think that?'

'Nkosi, I do not know.' Hlubi broke the armhold that the plumpest and youngest had around his neck, he snatched up his spears and fled. Sean and Alphonso galloped after him. The villagers shouted farewells and Sean looked back and saw One-Eye still sitting at the base of the big tree.

The pace which Sean set was at last telling on Alphonso. His verbal spring-tides slackened and he showed a measure of reluctance to let his backside touch the saddle; he rode crouched forward on his horse's neck with his buttocks in the air. They crossed the mountains and went down the other side; the ground levelled out into the Sabi Valley and they rode into the forest. On the ninth day out from Nova Sofala they reached the Sabi river. It was late afternoon. Flocks of guinea-fowl were drinking in the riverbed. They went up in a blue haze of whirling wings as Sean led his party down the bank. While the horses watered Sean spoke with Hlubi.

'Do you recognize this part of the river?'

'Yes, Nkosi, we are two hours' march upstream from the wagons ... we held too far to the north coming through the forest.'

Sean looked at the sun, it was on the tree-tops.

'Half an hour's light left ... and there's no moon tonight.'

'We could wait until morning,' Hlubi suggested hopefully. Sean ignored him and motioned to Alphonso to mount up. Alphonso was prepared to debate the advisability of moving on. Sean took a handful of his cassock and helped him into the saddle.

– 23 –

In the darkness the lantern burning in Katrina's wagon glowed through the canvas and guided them the last half mile into camp. Thief bayed them welcome and Mbejane ran out at the head of the other servants to take Sean's horse. His voice was loud with worry and relief.

'Nkosi, there is little time ... it has begun.'

Sean jumped off his horse and ran to the wagon. He tore open the canvas flap.

'Sean.' She sat up. Her eyes were very green in the lantern light, but they were dark-ringed. 'Thank God, you've come.'

Sean knelt beside her cot and held her. He said certain things to her and she clung to him and moved her lips across his face. The world receded and left one wagon standing in darkness, lit by a single lamp and the love of two people.

Suddenly she stiffened in his arms and gasped. Sean held her, his face suddenly helpless and his big hands timid and uncertain on her shoulders.

'What can I do, my fancy? How can I help you?'

Her body relaxed slowly and she whispered, 'Did you find a priest?'

'The priest!' Sean had forgotten about him. Still holding onto her he turned his head and bellowed, 'Alphonso ... Alphonso. Hurry, man.'

Father Alphonso's face in the opening of the wagon was pale with fatigue and grimy with dust.

'Marry us,' said Sean. 'Quickly, man, che-cha, chop-chop ... you savvy?'

Alphonso climbed into the wagon. The skirts of his cassock were torn and his knees were white and bony through the holes. He stood over them and opened his book. 'Ring?' he asked in Portuguese.

'I do,' said Sean.

'No! No! Ring?' Alphonso held up a finger and made an encircling gesture. 'Ring?'

'I think he wants a wedding ring,' whispered Katrina.

'Oh, my God,' said Sean. 'I'd forgotten about that.' He looked round desperately. 'What can we use? Haven't you got one in your chest or something?'

Katrina shook her head, opened her lips to answer but closed them again as another pain took her. Sean held her while it lasted and when she relaxed he looked up angrily at Alphonso.

'Marry us ... damn you. Don't you see there's no time for all the trimmings?'

'Ring?' said Alphonso again. He looked very unhappy.

'All right, I'll get you a ring.' Sean leapt out of the wagon and shouted at Mbejane.

'Bring my rifle, quickly.'

If Sean wanted to shoot the Portuguese that was his business and Mbejane's duty was to help him. He brought Sean the rifle. Sean found a gold sovereign in the pouch on his belt, he threw it on the ground and held the muzzle of the rifle on it. The bullet punched a ragged hole through it.

He tossed the rifle back to Mbejane, picked up the small gold circle and scrambled back into the wagon.

Three times during the service the pains made Katrina gasp and each time Sean held her tight and Alphonso increased the speed of his delivery. Sean put the punctured sovereign on Katrina's finger and kissed her. Alphonso gabbled out the last line of Latin and Katrina said, 'Oh, Sean, it's coming.'

'Get out,' Sean told Alphonso and made an expressive gesture towards the door – thankfully Alphonso went.

It did not take long then, but to Sean it was an eternity – like that time when they had taken Garrick's leg. Then in a slippery rush it was finished. Katrina lay very quiet and pale, while on the cot below her, still linked to her, purple-blotched and bloody lay the child that they had made.

'It's dead,' croaked Sean. He was sweating and he had backed away against the far wall of the wagon.

'No.' Katrina struggled up fiercely. 'No, it's not . . . Sean, you must help me.'

She told him what to do and at last the child cried.

'It's a boy,' said Katrina softly. 'Oh, Sean . . . it's a boy.' She was more beautiful than he had ever seen her before; pale and tired and beautiful.

– 24 –

Sean's protests were in vain – Katrina left her bed the next morning and squeezed into one of her old dresses. Sean hovered between her and the child on the cot.

'I'm still so *fat*,' she lamented.

'Fancy, please stay in bed another day or two.'

She pulled a face at him and went on struggling with the lacing of her bodice.

'Who's going to look after the baby?'

'I will!' said Sean earnestly. 'You can tell me what to do.'

Arguing with Katrina was like trying to pick up quick-silver with your fingers, not worth the effort. She finished dressing and took up the child.

'You can help me down the steps.' She smiled at him. Sean and Alphonso set a chair for her in the shade of one of the big shuma trees and the servants came to see the child. Katrina held him in her lap and Sean stood over them in uncertain possession. For Sean it seemed unreal yet ... too much for his mind to digest in so short a time. He grinned dazedly at the steady stream of comment from his servants and his arm was limp when Alphonso shook his hand for the twentieth time that morning.

'Hold your child ... Nkosi. Let us see you with him on your arm,' called Mbejane and the other Zulus took up the cry. Sean's expression changed slowly to one of apprehension.

'Pick him up, Nkosi.'

Katrina proffered the bundle and a hunted look came into Sean's eyes.

'Have no fear, Nkosi, he has no teeth, he cannot harm you,' Hlubi encouraged him. Sean held his first-born awkwardly and assumed the hunchbacked posture of the new father. The Zulus cheered him and slowly Sean's face relaxed and his smile was a glow of pride.

'Mbejane, is he not beautiful?'

'As beautiful as his father,' Mbejane agreed.

'Your words are a blade with two edges,' laughed Sean. He looked at the child closely. It wore a cap of dark hair, its nose was flat as a bulldog's, its eyes were milky-grey and its legs were long, skinny and red.

'How will you name him?' asked Hlubi. Sean looked at Katrina.

'Tell them,' he said.

'He shall be called Dirk,' she said in Zulu.

'What is the meaning?' asked Hlubi, and Sean answered him.

'It means a dagger . . . a sharp knife.'

There was immediate nodded approval from all the servants. Hlubi produced his snuff-box and passed it among them and Mbejane took a pinch.

'That,' he said, 'is a good name.'

– 25 –

Paternity, the subtle alchemist, transformed Sean's attitude to life within twelve hours. Never before had anything been so utterly dependent upon him, so completely vulnerable. That first evening in their wagon he watched Katrina sitting cross-legged on her cot, stooping forward over the child to give it her breast. Her hair hung in a soft wing across one cheek, her face was fuller, more matronly and the child in her lap fed with a red face and small wheezings. She looked up at him and smiled and the child tugged her breast with its tiny fists and hunting mouth.

Sean crossed to the cot, sat beside them and put his arm around them. Katrina rubbed her cheek against his chest and her hair smelt warm and clean. The boy went on feeding noisily. Sean felt vaguely excited as though he were on the threshold of a new adventure.

A week later, when the first rain clouds built up in the sky, Sean took the wagons across the Sabi and onto the slopes of the mountains to escape the heat of the plains. There was a valley he had noticed when he and Hlubi had made their journey to the coast. The valley bottom was covered with short sweet grass and cedar trees grew along a stream of clean water. Sean took them to this place.

Here they would wait out the rainy season and when it was finished and the baby was strong enough to travel they could take the ivory south and sell it in Pretoria. It was a happy camp. The oxen spread out along the valley, filling it with movement and the contented sound of their lowing; there was laughter among the wagons and at night when the mist slumped down off the mountains the camp fire was bright and friendly. Father Alphonso stayed with them for nearly two weeks. He was a pleasant young man and although he and Sean never understood what the other was saying yet they managed well enough with sign language. He left at last with Hlubi and one of the other servants to escort him back over the mountains, but before he did he managed to embarrass Sean by kissing him goodbye. Sean and Katrina were sorry to see him go. They had grown to like him and Katrina had almost forgiven him his religion.

The rains came with the usual flourish and fury. Weeks drifted into months. Happy months, with life centring around Dirk's cot. Mbejane had made the cot for him out of cedarwood and one of Katrina's chests produced the sheets and blankets for it. The child grew quickly: each day he seemed to occupy more of his cot, his legs filled out, his skin lost its blotchy-purple look and his eyes were no longer a vague milky-blue. There was green in them now – they would be the same colour as his mother's.

To fill the long lazy days Sean started to build a cabin beside the stream. The servants joined in and from a modest first plan it grew into a thing of sturdy plastered walls and neatly thatched roof with a stone fireplace at one end. When it was finished Sean and Katrina moved into it. After their wagon with its thin canvas walls, the cabin gave a feeling of permanence to their love. One night, when the rain hissed down in darkness outside and the wind whined at the door like a dog wanting to be let in, they spread a mattress in front of the fireplace and there in the moving firelight they started another baby.

Christmas came, and after it the New Year. The rains stuttered and stopped and still they stayed on in their valley. Then at last they had to go, for their supplies of basic stores – powder, salt, medicines, cloth – were nearly finished. They loaded the wagons, inspanned and left in the early morning. As the line of wagons wound down the valley towards the plains Katrina sat on the box-seat of the lead wagon holding Dirk on her lap and Sean rode beside her. She looked back – the roof of their cabin showed brown through the branches of the cedar trees. It seemed forlorn and lonely.

'We must come back one day, we've been so happy here,' she said softly. Sean leaned out of the saddle towards her and touched her arm.

'Happiness isn't a place, my fancy, we aren't leaving it here, we're taking it with us.'

She smiled at him. The second baby was starting to show already.

– 26 –

They reached the Limpopo river at the end of July and found a place to cross. It took three days to unload the wagons, work them through the soft sand and then carry the ivory and stores across. They finished in the late afternoon of the third day and by then everyone was exhausted. They ate an early supper and an hour after sunset the Zulus were rolled in their blankets, and Sean and Katrina were sleeping arms-around and head-on-chest in the wagon. In the morning Katrina was quiet and a little pale. Sean didn't notice it until she told him that she felt tired and was going to lie down – immediately he was all attentive. He helped her into the wagon and settled the pillows under her head.

'Are you sure you're all right?' he kept asking.

'Yes . . . it's nothing, I'm just a bit tired. I'll be all right,' she assured him. She appreciated his concern but was relieved when finally he went to see to the business of reloading the wagons for Sean's ministrations were always a little clumsy. She wanted to be left alone, she felt tired and cold.

By midday the wagons were loaded to Sean's satisfaction. He went to Katrina's wagon, lifted the canvas and peeped in. He expected her to be asleep. She was lying on the cot with her eyes open and two of the thick grey blankets wrapped around her. Her face was as pale as a two-day corpse. Sean felt the first leap of alarm. He scrambled into the wagon.

'My dear, you look ghastly. Are you sick?' He put his hand on her shoulder and she was shivering. She didn't answer him, instead her eyes moved from his face to the floor near the foot of the bed and Sean's eyes followed hers. Katrina's luxury was her chamberpot; it was a massive china thing with red roses hand-painted on it. She loved it dearly and Sean used to tease her when she was perched on top of it. Now the pot stood near the foot of the bed and when Sean saw what was in it his breathing stopped. It was half full of a liquid the colour of milk stout. 'Oh, my God,' he whispered. He went on staring at it, standing very still while a gruesome snatch of doggerel he remembered hearing sung in the canteens of the Witwatersrand began trotting through his brain like an undertaker's hack.

Black as the Angel,
Black as disgrace
When the fever waters flow
They're as black as the ace.

483

Roll him in a blanket
Feed him on quinine
But all of us we know
It's the end of the line.

Black as the Angel
Black as disgrace
Soon we'll lay him down below
And chuck dirt in his face.

He raised his head and looked steadily at her, searching for the signs of fear. But just as steadily she looked back at him.

'Sean, it's blackwater.'

'Yes ... I know,' Sean said, for there was nothing to be gained by denial, no room for extravagant hope. It was blackwater fever: malaria in its most malignant form, attacking the kidneys and turning them to fragile sacks of black blood that the slightest movement could rupture. Sean knelt by her cot. 'You must lie very still.' He touched her forehead lightly with the tips of his fingers and felt the heat of her skin.

'Yes,' she answered him, but already the expression in her eyes was blurring and she made the first restless movement of delirium. Sean put his arm across her chest to hold her from struggling.

By nightfall Katrina was deep in the nightmare of malaria. She laughed, she screamed in senseless terror, she shook her head and fought him when he tried to make her drink. But she had to drink, it was her one chance, to flush out her kidneys that she might live. Sean held her head and forced her.

Dirk started crying, hungry and frightened by the sight of his mother.

'Mbejane!' shouted Sean, his voice pitched high with

desperation. Mbejane had waited all afternoon at the entrance of the wagon.

'Nkosi, what can I do?'

'The child . . . can you care for him?'

Mbejane picked up the cot with Dirk still in it. 'Do not worry about him again. I will take him to the other wagon.'

Sean turned his whole attention back to Katrina. The fever built up steadily within her. Her body was a furnace, her skin was dry and with every hour she was wilder and her movements more difficult to control.

An hour after dark Kandhla came to the wagon with a pot of steaming liquid and a cup. Sean's nose wrinkled as he caught the smell of it.

'What the hell is that?'

'I have stewed the bark from a maiden's breast tree . . . the Nkosikazi must drink it.'

It had the same musty smell as boiling hops and Sean hesitated. He knew the tree. It grew on high ground, it had a diseased-looking lumpy bark and each lump was the size and shape of a breast surmounted by a thorn.

'Where did you get it? I have seen none of these trees near the river.' Sean was marking time while he decided whether to make Katrina drink the brew. He knew these Zulu remedies, what they didn't kill they sometimes cured.

'Hlubi went back to the hills where we camped four days ago . . . he brought the bark into the camp an hour ago.'

A thirty-mile round journey in something under six hours – even in his distress Sean could smile.

'Tell Hlubi the Nkosikazi will drink his medicine.'

Kandhla held her head and Sean forced the evil-smelling liquid between her lips – he made her finish the whole potful. The juice of the bark seemed to relieve the congestion of her kidneys; four times before morning she passed frothy black water. Each time Sean held her gently, cushioning her body from any movement that might have killed her. Gradually her delirium became coma; she lay huddled and still in the cot, shaken only by the brief fits of shivering. When the morning sun hit the wagon canvas and lit the interior, Sean saw her face, and he knew that she was dying. Her skin was an opaque yellowish white, her hair had lost its glow and was lifeless as dry grass. Kandhla brought another pot of the medicine and they fed it to her. When the pot was empty Kandhla said, 'Nkosi, let me lay a mattress on the floor beside the Nkosikazi's bed. You must sleep and I will stay here with you and wake you if the Nkosikazi stirs.'

Sean looked at him with haunted eyes. 'There will be time to sleep later, my friend.' He looked down at Katrina and went on softly. 'Perhaps, very soon there will be time.'

Suddenly Katrina's body stiffened and Sean dropped on his knees beside her cot. Kandhla hovered anxiously behind him. It took Sean a while to understand what was happening and then he looked up at Kandhla.

'Go! Go quickly!' he said and the suffering in his voice sent Kandhla stumbling blindly from the wagon. Sean's second son was born that morning and while Kandhla watched over Katrina Sean wrapped the child in a blanket, took him into the veld and buried him. Then he went back to Katrina and stayed with her while days and nights blended together into a hopeless muddle of grief. As near as Katrina was to death, that near was Sean to insanity. He never moved out of the wagon, he squatted on the mattress next to her cot, wiping the perspiration from her face, holding a cup to her lips or just sitting and watching her. He had lost his child and before his eyes Katrina was turning into a wasted yellow skeleton. Dirk saved him. Mbejane brought the boy to him and he romped on the mattress, crawling into Sean's lap and pulling his beard. It was the one small glimmer of light in the darkness.

27

Katrina survived. She came back slowly from the motionless coma that precedes death and with her hesitant return Sean's despair changed to hope and then to a wonderful relief. Her water was no longer black but dark pink and thick with sediment. She was aware of him now and, although she was so weak that she could not lift her head off the pillow, her eyes followed him as he moved about the wagon. It was another week before she learned about the baby. She asked him, her voice a tired whisper, and Sean told her with all the gentleness of which he was capable. She did not have the strength for any great show of emotion; she laid quietly staring up at the canvas above her head and her tears slid down across her yellow cheeks.

The damage that the fever had done to her body was hardly credible. Her limbs were so thin that Sean could completely encircle her thigh with one hand. Her skin hung in loose yellow folds from her face and body and pink blood still stained her water. This was not all: the fever had sucked all the strength from her mind. She had nothing left to resist the sorrow of her baby's death, and the sorrow encased her in a shell through which neither Sean nor Dirk could reach her. Sean struggled to bring her back to life, to repair the terrible damage to her mind and body. Every minute of his time he employed in her service.

He and the servants scoured the veld for thirty miles around the laager to find delicacies to tempt her appetite, wild fruits, honey, giraffe marrows, the flesh of a dozen animals: kabobs of elephant heart and duiker liver, roasted iguana lizard as white and tender as a plump pullet, golden fillets of the yellow-mouthed bream from the river. Katrina picked at them listlessly then turned away and lay staring at the canvas wall of the cot.

Sean sat beside her and talked about the farm they would buy, trying vainly to draw her into a discussion of the house they would build. He read to her from Duff's books and the only reaction he received was a small quivering of her lips when he read the words 'death' or 'child'. He talked about the days on the Witwatersrand, searching his mind for stories that might amuse her. He brought Dirk to her and let him play about the wagon. Dirk was walking now, his dark hair had started to curl and his eyes were green. Dirk, however, could not be too long confined in the wagon. There was too much to do, too much to explore. Before long he would stagger to the entrance and issue the imperial summons: 'Bejaan! Bejaan!'

Almost immediately Mbejane's head would appear in the opening and he would glance at Sean for permission.

'All right, take him out then . . . but tell Kandhla not to stuff him full of food.'

Quickly, before Sean changed his mind, Mbejane would lift Dirk down and lead him away. Dirk had nearly two dozen Zulus to spoil him. They competed hotly for his affections, no effort was too much – dignified Mbejane down on his hands and knees being ridden mercilessly in and out among the wagons, Hlubi scratching himself under the arms and gibbering insanely in his celebrated imitation of a baboon while Dirk squealed with delight, fat Kandhla raiding Katrina's store of fruit preserves to make sure Dirk was properly fed and the others keeping in the background, anxious to join the worship but fearful of incurring the jealousy of Mbejane and Hlubi. Sean knew what was happening but he was powerless to prevent it. His time was completely devoted to Katrina.

For the first time in his life Sean was giving more than just a superficial part of himself to another human being. It was not an isolated sacrifice: it went on throughout the months it took for Katrina to regain sufficient of her strength to enable her to sit up in bed without assistance; it continued through the months that she needed before Sean judged it safe to resume the trek towards the south. They built a litter for her – Sean would not risk the jarring of the wagon – and the first day's trek lasted two hours. Four of the servants carried the litter and Katrina lay in it, protected from the sun by a strip of canvas spread above her head. Despite the gentleness with which the Zulus handled her, at the end of the two hours Katrina was exhausted. Her back ached and she was sweating in small beads from her yellow skin. The next week they travelled two hours daily and then gradually increased the time until they were making a full day's journey.

They were halfway to the Magaliesberg, camped at a muddy waterhole in the thorn flats, when Mbejane came to Sean.

'There is still one wagon empty of ivory, Nkosi.'

'The others are full,' Sean pointed out.

'Four hours' march from this place there is enough ivory buried to fill those wagons.'

Sean's mouth twisted with pain. He looked away towards the south-east and he spoke softly. 'Mbejane, I am still a young man and yet already I have stored up enough ugly memories to make my old age sad. Would you have me steal from a friend not only his life but his share of ivory also?'

Mbejane shook his head. 'I asked, that is all.'

'And I have answered, Mbejane. It is his . . . let it lie.'

28

They crossed the Magaliesberg and turned west along the mountain range. Then, two months after they had left the Limpopo river, they reached the Boer settlement at Louis Trichardt. Sean left Mbejane to outspan the wagons on the open square in front of the church and he went to search for a doctor. There was only one in the district. Sean found him in his surgery above the general dealer's store and took him to the wagons. Sean carried his bag for him and the doctor, a greybeard and unused to such hardships, trotted to keep up with Sean. He was panting and pouring sweat by the time they arrived. Sean waited outside while the doctor completed his examination and when he finally made his descent from the wagon Sean fell on him impatiently. 'What do you think, man?'

'I think, meneer, that you should give hourly thanks to your Maker.' The doctor shook his head in amazement. 'It seems hardly possible that your wife could have survived both the fever and the loss of the child.'

'She is safe then, there's no chance of a relapse?' Sean asked.

'She is safe now . . . but she is still a very sick woman. It may take a year before her body is fully mended. There is no medicine I can give you. She must be kept quiet, feed her well and wait for time to cure her.' The doctor hesitated. 'There is other damage—' He tapped his forehead with his forefinger. 'Grief is a terrible destroyer. She will need love and gentleness and after another six months she will need a baby to fill the emptiness left by the one she lost. Give her those three things, meneer, but most of all give her love.' The doctor hauled his watch from his waistcoat and looked at it. 'Time! There is so little time. I must go, there

490

are others who need me.' He held out his hand to Sean. 'Go with God, meneer.'

Sean shook his hand. 'How much do I owe you?'

The doctor smiled, he had a brown face and his eyes were pale blue; when he smiled he looked like a boy. 'I make no charge for words. I wish I could have done more.' He hurried away across the square and when he walked you could see that his smile lied, he was an old man.

'Mbejane,' said Sean. 'Get a big tusk out of the wagon and take it to the doctor's room above the store.'

Katrina and Sean went to the morning service in the church next day. Katrina could not stand through the hymns. She sat quietly in her pew, watching the altar, her lips forming the words of the hymn and her eyes full of her sorrow.

They stayed on for three more days in Louis Trichardt and they were made welcome. Men came to drink coffee with them and see the ivory and the women brought them eggs and fresh vegetables, but Sean was anxious to move south. So on the third day they started the last stage of their trek.

Katrina regained her strength rapidly now. She took over the management of Dirk from the servants, to their ill-concealed disappointment, and soon she left her litter and rode on the box seat of the lead wagon again. Her body filled out and there was colour showing once more through the yellow skin of her cheeks. Despite the improvement to her body the depression of her mind still persisted and there was nothing that Sean could do to lift it.

A month before the Christmas of 1895 Sean's wagon train climbed the low range of hills above the city and they looked down into Pretoria. The jacaranda trees that filled every garden were in bloom – masses of purple – and the busy streets spoke well of the prosperity of the Transvaal

Republic. Sean outspanned on the outskirts of the city, simply pulling the wagons off the road and camping beside it, and once the camp was established and Sean had made certain that Katrina no longer needed his help he put on his one good suit and called for his horse. His suit had been cut to the fashion of four years previously and had been made to encompass the belly he had acquired on the Witwatersrand. Now it hung loosely down his body but bunched tightly around his thickened arms. His face was burnt black by the sun and his beard bushed down onto his chest and concealed the fact that the stiff collar of his shirt could no longer close around his neck. His boots were scuffed almost through the uppers, there was not a suspicion of polish on them and they had completely lost their shape. Sweat had soaked through his hat around the level of the band and left dark greasy marks; the brim drooped down over his eyes so he had to wear it pushed onto the back of his head. There was, therefore, some excuse for the curious glances that followed him that afternoon as he rode down Church Street with a great muscular savage trotting at his one stirrup and an overgrown brindle hound at the other. They pushed their way between the wagons that cluttered the wide street; they passed the Raadsaal of the Republican Parliament, passed the houses standing back from the road in their spacious purple and green gardens and came at last to the business area of the city that crowded round the railway station. Sean and Duff had bought their supplies at a certain general dealer's stores and now Sean went back to it. It was hardly changed – the signboard in front had faded a little but still declared that I. Goldberg, Importer & Exporter, Dealer in Mining Machinery, Merchant & Wholesaler, was prepared to consider the purchase of gold, precious stone, hides and skins, ivory and other natural produce. Sean swung down from the saddle and tossed his reins to Mbejane. 'Unsaddle, Mbejane. This may take time.'

Sean stepped up onto the sidewalk, lifted his hat to two passing ladies and went through into the building where Mr Goldberg conducted his diverse activities. One of the assistants hurried to meet him, but Sean shook his head and the man went back behind the counter. He had seen Mr Goldberg with two customers at the far end of the store. He was content to wait. He browsed around among the loaded shelves of merchandise, feeling the quality of a shirt, sniffing at a box of cigars, examining an axe, lifting a rifle down off the rack and sighting at a spot on the wall, until Mr Goldberg bowed his customers through the door and turned to Sean. Mr Goldberg was short and fat. His hair was cropped short and his neck bulged over the top of his collar. He looked at Sean and his eyes were expressionless while he rifled through the index cards of his memory for the name. Then he beamed like a brilliant burst of sunlight. 'Mr Courtney, isn't it?'

Sean grinned. 'That's right. How are you, Izzy?' They shook hands. 'How's business?'

Mr Goldberg's face fell. 'Terrible, terrible, Mr Courtney. I'm a worried man.'

'You look well enough on it.' Sean prodded his stomach. 'You've put on weight.'

'You can joke, Mr Courtney, but I'm telling you it's terrible. Taxes and worry, taxes and worry.' Mr Goldberg sighed, 'And now there's talk of war.'

'What's this?' Sean frowned.

'War, Mr Courtney, war between Britain and the Republic.'

Sean's frown dissolved and he laughed. 'Nonsense, man, not even Kruger could be such a bloody fool! Get me a cup of coffee and a cigar and we'll go through to your office and talk business.'

Mr Goldberg's face went blank and his eyelids drooped almost sleepily.

'Business, Mr Courtney?'

'That's right, Izzy, this time I'm selling and you're buying.'

'What are you selling, Mr Courtney?'

'Ivory!'

'Ivory?'

'Twelve wagon loads of it.'

Mr Goldberg sighed sadly. 'Ivory's no good now, the bottom's fallen out of it. You can hardly give it away.' It was very well done; if Sean had not been told the ruling prices two days before he might have been convinced.

'I'm sorry to hear that,' he said. 'If you're not interested, I'll see if I can find someone else.'

'Come along to my office anyway,' said Mr Goldberg. 'We can talk about it. Talk costs nothing.'

Two days later they were still talking about it. Sean had fetched his wagons and had off-loaded the ivory in the back yard of the store. Mr Goldberg had personally weighed each tusk and written the weights down on a sheet of paper. He and Sean had added the columns of figures and agreed on the total. Now they were in the last stages of agreeing the price.

'Come on, Izzy, we've wasted two days already. That's a fair price and you know it ... let's get it over with,' Sean growled.

'I'll lose money on this,' protested Mr Goldberg. 'I've got to make a living, every man's got to live.'

'Come on.' Sean held out his right hand. 'Let's call it a deal.'

Mr Goldberg hesitated a second longer, then he put his pudgy hand in Sean's fist and they grinned at each other, both well satisfied. One of Mr Goldberg's assistants counted out the sovereigns, stacking them in piles of fifty along the counter, then Sean and Mr Goldberg checked them and agreed once more. Sean filled two canvas bags with the gold, slapped Mr Goldberg's back, helped himself to another cigar and headed heavily laden for the bank.

'When are you going into the veld again?' Mr Goldberg called after him.

'Soon!' said Sean.

'Don't forget to get your supplies here.'

'I'll be back,' Sean assured him.

Mbejane carried one of the bags and Sean the other. Sean was smiling and streamers of cigar smoke swirled back from his head as he strode along the sidewalk. There's something in the weight of a sack of gold that makes the man who holds it stand eight feet tall.

That night as they lay together in the darkness of the wagon Katrina asked him.

'Have we enough money to buy the farm yet, Sean?'

'Yes,' said Sean. 'We've got enough for the finest farm in the whole Cape peninsular ... and, after one more trip, we'll have enough to build the house and the barns, buy the cattle, lay out the vineyard and still have some left over.'

Katrina was silent for a moment then, 'So we are going back into the bushveld again?'

'One more trip,' said Sean. 'Another two years and then we'll go down to the Cape.' He gave her a hug. 'You don't mind, do you?'

'No,' she said. 'I think I'd like that. When will we leave?'

'Not just yet awhile,' Sean laughed. 'First we're going to have some fun.' He hugged her again, her body was still painfully thin; he could feel the bones of her hips pressed against him.

'Some pretty clothes for you, my fancy, and a suit for me that doesn't look like a fancy dress. Then we'll go out and see what this burg has to offer in the way of entertainment—' He stopped as the idea swelled up in his mind. 'Damn it! I know what we'll do. We'll hire a carriage and go across to Jo'burg. We'll take a suite at the Grand National Hotel and do some living. Bath in a china bath, sleep in a real bed; you can have your hair prettied-up and I'll have my beard trimmed by a barber. We'll eat crayfish and penguin eggs ... I can't remember when I last tasted pork or mutton ... we'll wash it down with the old bubbling wine and waltz to a good band—' Sean raced on and when he stopped for breath Katrina asked softly, 'Isn't the waltz a very sinful dance, Sean?'

Sean smiled in the darkness. 'It certainly is!'

'I'd like to be sinful just once ... not too much; just a little with you to see what it's like.'

'We will be,' said Sean, 'as wicked as hell.'

– 29 –

The next day Sean took Katrina to the most exclusive ladies' shop in Pretoria. He chose the material of half a dozen dresses. One of them was to be a ball gown in canary-yellow silk. It was extravagance and he knew it, but he didn't care once he saw the flash of guilty delight in Katrina's cheeks and the old green sparkle in her eyes. For the first time since the fever she was living again. He spilled out his sovereigns with thankful abandon. The sales girls were delighted with him, they crowded round him with trays of feminine accessories.

'A dozen of those,' said Sean and, 'yes, those will do.' Then a flash of green on the racks across the room caught his eye – it was Katrina's green.

'What's that?' He pointed and two sales girls nearly knocked each other down in the rush to get it for him. The winner carried the shawl back to him and Sean took it and placed it around Katrina's shoulders. It was a beautiful thing.

'We'll take it,' said Sean and Katrina's lips quivered – then suddenly she was crying, sobbing brokenly. The excitement had been too much. There was immediate consternation among the shop assistants, they flapped around Sean like hens at feeding time while he picked Katrina up and carried her out to the hired carriage. At the door he paused and spoke over his shoulder.

'I want those dresses finished by tomorrow evening. Can you do it?'

'They'll be ready, Mr Courtney, even if my girls have to work all night on them.'

He took Katrina back to the wagons and laid her on her cot.

'Please forgive me, Sean, I've never done that in my life before.'

'It's all right, my fancy, I understand. Now you just go to sleep.'

The following day Katrina stayed at the camp resting, while Sean went to see Mr Goldberg again and buy from him the stores they would need for the next expedition. It took another day to load the wagons and by then Katrina seemed well enough to make the trip to Johannesburg.

They left in the early afternoon. Mbejane driving, Sean and Katrina sitting close together on the back seat holding hands under the travelling rug and Dirk bouncing round the interior of the carriage, pausing now and then to flatten his face against a window and keeping up a flow of comment in the peculiar mixture of English, Dutch and Zulu that Sean called Dirkese. They reached Johannesburg long before Sean expected to. In four years the town had doubled its size and had spread out into the veld to meet them. They followed the main road through the new areas and came to the centre. There were changes here as well but it was, in the main, the way he remembered it. They threaded their way through the babble of Eloff Street, and around them, mingling with the crowds on the sidewalks, were the ghosts of the past. He heard Duff laugh and twisted quickly in his seat to place the sound; a dandy in a boater hat with gold fillings in his teeth laughed again from a passing carriage and Sean heard that it was not Duff's laugh. Very close, but not the same. All of it was like that – similar but subtly changed, nostalgic but sad with the knowledge of loss. The past was lost – and he knew then that you can never go back. Nothing is the same, for reality can exist at one time only and in one place only. Then it dies and you have lost it and you must go on to find it at another time and in another place.

They took a suite at the Grand National, with a sitting-room and two bedrooms, a private bathroom and a balcony that looked out over the street – over the rooftops to where the headgears and white dumps stood along the ridge. Katrina was exhausted. They had supper sent up to the room early and when they had eaten Katrina went to bed and Sean went down alone to drink a nightcap at the bar. The bar-room was crowded. Sean found a seat in the corner and sat silently in the jabber of conversation. In it, but no longer a part of it.

They had changed the picture above the bar – it used to be a hunting print; but now it was a red-coated general, impressively splattered with blood, taking leave of his staff in the middle of a battlefield. The staff looked bored. Sean let his eyes wander on along the dark panelled walls. He remembered – there was so much to remember! Suddenly he blinked. Near the side door was a star-shaped crack in the wooden panelling. Sean started to grin and put down his glass and massaged the knuckles of his right hand. If Oakie Henderson hadn't ducked under that punch it would have taken his head off.

Sean signalled to the barman. 'Another brandy, please.'

While the man was pouring, Sean asked, 'What happened to that panel near the door?'

The man glanced up and then back at the bottle. 'Some fellow put his fist through it in the old days. Boss left it like that, sort of souvenir, you know.'

'He must have been quite a fellow ... that wood's an inch thick. Who was he?' Sean asked expectantly.

The man shrugged. 'One of the drifters. They come and they go. Make a few pounds, piss it against the wall and then go back where they came from.' He looked at Sean with bored eyes. 'That'll be half a dollar, mate.' Sean drank the brandy slowly, turning the glass in his hands between sips and watching the liquor cling to its sides like thin oil. By a cracked panel in a bar-room they shall remember you.

And now I shall go to bed, he decided, this is no longer my world. My world is upstairs sleeping – I hope! He smiled a little to himself and finished the brandy in his glass.

'Sean' – a voice at his ear and a hand on his shoulder as he turned to leave. 'My God, Sean, is it really you?'

Sean stared at the man beside him. He did not recognize the neatly clipped beard and the big sun-burned nose with the skin peeling off the tip, but suddenly he knew the eyes.

'Dennis, you old rogue. Dennis Petersen from Ladyburg. That's right isn't it?'

'You didn't recognize me!' laughed Dennis. 'So much for our friendship – you disappear without a word and ten years later you don't even know me!'

Now they were both laughing.

'I thought they would have hanged you long ago—' Sean defended himself. 'What on earth are you doing in Johannesburg?'

'Selling beef – I'm on the committee of the Beef Growers' Association.' There was pride in Dennis's voice. 'I have been up here negotiating the renewal of our contracts.'

'When are you going back?'

'My train leaves in an hour.'

'Well, there's time for a drink before you go – what will it be?'

'I'll have a small brandy, thanks.'

Sean ordered the drinks and they took them up and stood, suddenly awkward in the awareness that ten years were between their once complete accord.

'So, what have you been doing with yourself?' Dennis ended the pause.

'This and that, you know – a bit of mining, just come back from the bushveld. Nothing very exciting.'

'Well, it's good to see you again anyway. Your health.'

'And yours,' said Sean, and then suddenly he realized that here was news of his family – news he had been without for many years.

'How's everyone at Ladyburg – your sisters?'

'Both married – so am I, with four sons,' and the pride was in Dennis's voice again.

'Anyone I know?' asked Sean.

'Audrey – you know old Pye's daughter.'

'No!' Sean ripped out the word, and then quickly, 'That's wonderful, Dennis. I'm pleased for you – she was a lovely girl.'

'The best,' agreed Dennis complacently. He had the sleek well-fed, well-cared for look of a married man, fatter in the face and his stomach starting to show. I wonder if I have it yet, Sean thought. 'Of course, old man Pye's dead now – that's one creditor he couldn't buy off. Ronnie's taken over the bank and the store.'

'The bat-eared bush rat,' said Sean and knew immediately that he had said the wrong thing. Dennis frowned slightly. 'He's family now, Sean. A very decent chap really – and a clever business man.'

'I'm sorry, I was joking. How's my mother?' Sean changed

the subject by asking the question that had been in the forefront of his mind and he had picked the right topic. Dennis's expression softened immediately – you could see the warmth in his eyes.

'The same as ever. She's got a dress shop now, next door to Ronnie's store. It's a gold mine – no one would think of buying anywhere else but at Aunt Ada's. She's godmother to my two eldest, I guess she's godmother to half the kids in the district,' and then his expression hardened again. 'The least you could have done was write to her sometime, Sean. You can't imagine the pain you have caused her.'

'There were circumstances.' Sean dropped his eyes to his glass.

'That's no excuse – you have a duty which you neglected. There is no excuse for it.'

You little man. Sean lifted his head and looked at him without trying to disguise his annoyance. You pompous, preaching little man peering out at the world one-eyed through the keyhole of your own self-importance. Dennis had not noticed Sean's reaction and he continued. 'That's a lesson a man must learn before he grows up – we all have our responsibilities and our duties. A man grows up when he faces those duties, when he accepts the burdens that society places on him. Take my own case: despite the vast amount of work I have on the farms – I now own Mahoba's Kloof as well – and despite the demands made on me by my family, yet I have time to represent the district on the committee of the Beef Growers' Association, I am a member of the Church Council and the village management board, and I have every reason to believe that next month I will be asked to accept the office of mayor.' Then he looked steadily at Sean. 'What have *you* done with your life so far?'

'I've lived it,' Sean answered, and Dennis looked a little perplexed – then he gathered himself.

'Are you married yet?'

'I was – but I sold her to the Arab slavers up north.'

'You did what?'

'Well,' grinned Sean, 'she was an old wife and the price was good.'

'That's a joke, hey? Ha, ha!' You couldn't fool good old Dennis – Sean laughed out loud. This unbelievable little man!

'Have a drink, Dennis,' he suggested.

'Two is my limit, thanks, Sean.' Dennis pulled the gold hunter from his waistcoat pocket and inspected it. 'Time to go – I'm afraid. Nice seeing you again.'

'Wait,' Sean stopped him. 'My brother – how's Garry?'

'Poor old Garry.' Dennis shook his head solemnly.

'What's wrong with him?' Sean's voice was sharp with his sense of dread.

'Nothing – ' Dennis reassured him quickly. 'Well, I mean nothing more than ever was.'

'Why did you say "poor old Garry" then?'

'I don't really know – except that everybody says it. It's habit, I suppose – he's just one of those people you say *poor old* in front of.'

Sean suppressed his irritation, he wanted to know. He had to know.

'You haven't answered me – how is he?'

Dennis made a significant gesture with his right hand. 'Looking into the bottle quite a bit these days – not that I blame him with that woman he married. You were well out of it there if I may say so, Sean.'

'You may,' Sean acquiesced, 'but is he well? How are things at Theunis Kraal?'

'We all took a bit of a beating with the rindepest* but Garry – well, he lost over half of his herds. Poor old Garry, everything happens to him.'

* An epidemic cattle disease.

502

'My God – fifty per cent!'

'Yes – but, of course, Ronnie helped him out. Gave him a mortgage on the farm to tide him over.'

'Theunis Kraal bonded again,' groaned Sean. 'Oh Garry, Garry.'

'Yes – well.' Dennis coughed uneasily. 'Well, I think I'd better be going. *Totsiens*, Sean.' He held out his hand. 'Shall I tell them I saw you?'

'No,' said Sean quickly. 'Just leave it stand.'

'Very well then.' Dennis hesitated. 'Are you all right, Sean? I mean' – he coughed again – 'are you all right for money?'

Sean felt his unhappiness dissolve a little; this pompous little man was going to offer him a loan. 'That's very good of you, Dennis. But I've got a couple of pounds saved up – enough to eat on for a few days,' he spoke seriously.

'All right then.' Dennis looked mightily relieved. 'All right then – *totsiens*, Sean,' and he turned and walked quickly out of the bar. As he left the room so he went out of Sean's mind, and Sean was thinking of his brother again.

Then suddenly Sean decided. I will go back to Ladyburg when this next trip is over. The dream farm outside Paarl would not lose anything in being transplanted to Natal – and he suddenly longed to sit in the panelled study at Theunis Kraal again, and to feel the mist come cold down the escarpment in the mornings, and see the spray blowing off the white falls in the wind. He wanted to hear Ada's voice again and to explain to her, knowing she would understand and forgive.

But more, much more it was Garry – poor old Garry. I must go back to him – ten years is a long time and he will have lost the bitterness. I must go back to him – for his sake and for Theunis Kraal. With the decision made, Sean finished his drink and went up the stairs to his suite.

Katrina was breathing softly in her sleep, the dark mass

of her hair spread out on the pillow. While he undressed he watched her and slowly the melancholy dissolved. Gently he pulled back the blankets on his side of the bed and just then Dirk whimpered from the next room. Sean went through to him. 'All right, what's the trouble?'

Dirk blinked owlishly and searched for an excuse, then the relief flooded into his face and he produced the one that creaked with age. 'I want a drink a water.'

The delay while Sean went through to the bathroom gave Dirk an opportunity to rally his forces and when Sean came back he opened the offensive in earnest.

'Tell me a story, Daddy.' He was sitting up now, bright-eyed.

'I'll tell you a story about Jack and a Nory—' said Sean.

'Not that one—' protested Dirk. The saga of Jack and his brother lasted five seconds and Dirk knew it. Sean sat down on the edge of the bed and held the glass for him.

'How about this one? There once was a king who had everything in the world . . . but when he lost it he found out that he had never had anything and that he now had more than he ever had before.'

Dirk looked stunned.

'That's not a very good one,' he gave his opinion at last.

'No,' said Sean. 'It isn't . . . is it? But I think we should be charitable and admit that it's not too bad for this time of night.'

30

Sean woke feeling happy. Katrina was sitting up in bed filling cups from a pewter coffee pot and Dirk was hammering at the door to be let in. Katrina smiled at him. 'Good morning, meneer.'

Sean sat up and kissed her. 'How did you sleep, fancy?'

'Well, thank you,' but there were dark rings under her eyes. Sean went across to the bedroom door.

'Prepare to receive cavalry,' he said and swung it open. Dirk's charge carried him onto the bed and Sean dived after him. When two men are evenly matched, weight will usually decide and within seconds Dirk had straddled Sean's chest, pinning him helplessly and Sean was pleading for quarter.

After breakfast Mbejane brought the carriage round to the front of the hotel. When the three of them were settled in it, Sean opened the small window behind the driver's seat and told Mbejane, 'To the office first. Then we have to be at the Exchange by ten o'clock.'

Mbejane grinned at him. 'Yes, Nkosi, then lunch at the Big House.' Mbejane had never been able to master the word Xanadu.

They went to all the old places. Sean and Mbejane laughing and reminiscing at each other through the window. There was a panic at the Exchange, crowds on the pavement outside. The offices on Eloff Street had been refaced and a brass plate beside the front door carried the roll of the subsidiaries of Central Rand Consolidated. Mbejane stopped the carriage outside and Sean boasted to Katrina. She sat silently and listened to him, suddenly feeling inadequate for a man who had done so much. She misinterpreted Sean's enthusiasm and thought he regretted the past and wished he were back.

'Mbejane, take us up to the Candy Deep,' Sean called at last. 'Let's see what's happening there.'

The last five hundred yards of the road was overgrown and pitted with disuse. The administration block had been demolished and grass grew thick over the foundations. There were new buildings and headgears half a mile farther along the ridge, but here the reef had been worked out and abandoned. Mbejane pulled up the horses in the circular drive in front of where the offices had stood. He jumped down and held their heads while Sean helped Katrina out of the carriage. Sean lifted Dirk and sat him on his shoulder and they picked their way through the waist-high grass and piles of bricks and rubbish towards the Candy Deep Number Three Shaft.

The bare white concrete blocks that had held the machinery formed a neat geometrical pattern in the grass. Beyond them reared the white mine dump; some mineral in the powdered rock had leaked out in long yellow stains down its sides. Duff had once had the mineral identified. It was of little commercial value, used occasionally in the ceramics industry. Sean had forgotten the name of it; it sounded like the name of a star – Uranus perhaps.

They came to the shaft. The edges of it had crumbled and the grass hung into it, the way an unkempt moustache hangs into an old man's mouth. The headgear was gone and only a rusty barbed-wire fence ringed the shaft. Sean bent his knees: keeping his back straight for Dirk still sat on his shoulder, he picked up a lump of rock the size of a man's fist and tossed it over the fence. They stood quietly and listened to it clatter against the sides as it fell. It fell for a long time and when at last it hit the bottom the echo rang faintly up from a thousand feet below.

'Throw more!' commanded Dirk, but Katrina stopped him.

'No, Sean, let's go. It's an evil place.' She shuddered slightly. 'It looks like a grave.'

'It very nearly was,' said Sean softly, remembering the darkness and the rock pressing down upon him.

'Let's go,' she said again, and they went back to where Mbejane waited with the carriage.

Sean was gay at lunch, he drank a small bottle of wine, but Katrina was tired and more miserable than she had been since they left Louis Trichardt. She had begun to realize the type of life he had led before she met him and she was frightened that now he wanted to return to it. She had only known the bush and the life of the Trek-Boer. She knew she could never learn to live like this. She watched as he laughed and joked during the meal, she watched the easy assurance with which he commanded the white head waiter, the way he picked his way through the maze of cutlery that was spread out on the table before them and at last she could hold it in no longer.

'Let's go away, let's go back into the bush.'

Sean stopped with a loaded fork halfway to his mouth. 'What?'

'Please, Sean, the sooner we go the sooner we'll be able to buy the farm.'

Sean chuckled. 'A day or two more won't make any difference. We're starting to have fun. Tonight I'll take you dancing – we were going to be sinful, remember?'

'Who will look after Dirk?' she asked weakly.

'Mbejane will—' Sean looked at her closely. 'You have a good sleep this afternoon and tonight we'll go out and tie the dog loose.' He grinned at the memories that expression invoked.

When Katrina woke from her rest that evening she found the other part of the reason for her depression. For the first time since the baby her periodic bleeding had started again, the tides of her body and mind were at their lowest ebb. She said nothing to Sean, but bathed and put on the yellow gown. She brushed her hair furiously, dragging the brush through it until her scalp tingled, but still it hung dull and lifeless – as dull as the eyes that looked back at her out of the yellow face in the mirror.

Sean came up behind her and leaned over her to kiss her cheek. 'You look,' said he, 'like a stack of gold bars five-and-a-half feet high.' But he realized that the yellow gown had been a mistake: it matched too closely the fever colour of her skin. Mbejane was waiting in the sitting-room when they went through.

'It may be late before we return,' Sean told him.

'That is of no account, Nkosi.' Mbejane's face was as impassive as ever, but Sean caught a sparkle of anticipation in his eyes and realized that Mbejane could hardly wait to get Dirk to himself.

'You are not to go into his room,' Sean warned.

'What if he cries, Nkosi?'

'He won't . . . but if he does see what he wants, give it to him then leave him to sleep.'

Mbejane's face registered his protest.

'I'm warning you, Mbejane, if I come home at midnight and find him riding you round the room I'll have both your hides for a kaross.'

'His sleep shall be unspoiled, Nkosi,' lied Mbejane.

In the hotel lobby Sean spoke to the receptionist. 'Where can we find the best food in this town?' he asked.

'Two blocks down, sir, the Golden Guinea. You can't miss it.'

'It sounds like a gin palace.' Sean was dubious.

'I assure you, sir, that you'll have no complaint when you get there. Everyone goes there. Mr Rhodes dines there when he's in town, Mr Barnato, Mr Hradsky—'

'Dick Turpin, Cesare Borgia, Benedict Arnold,' Sean

continued for him. 'All right, you have convinced me. I'll take a chance on having my throat cut.'

Sean went out through the front entrance with Katrina on his arm. The splendour of the Golden Guinea subdued even Sean a little. A waiter with a uniform like a major-general's led them down a marble staircase, across the wide meadow of carpet between the group of elegant men and women to a table that even in the soft light dazzled with its bright silver and snowy linen. Chandeliers of crystal hung from the vaulted ceiling, the band was good, and the air was rich with the fragrance of perfume and expensive cigars.

Katrina stared helplessly at the menu until Sean came to her rescue and ordered the meal in a French accent that impressed her but not the waiter. The wine came and with it Sean's high spirits returned. Katrina sat quietly opposite him and listened. She tried to think of something witty to answer him with; in their wagon or alone in the veld they could talk for hours at a time but here she was dumb.

'Shall we dance?' Sean leaned across the table and squeezed her hand. She shook her head.

'Sean, I couldn't. Not with all these people watching. I'd only make a fool of myself.'

'Come on, I'll show you how . . . it's easy.'

'No, I couldn't, truly I couldn't.'

And to himself Sean had to admit that the dance floor of the Golden Guinea on a Saturday night was not the best place for a waltz lesson. The waiter brought the food, great steaming dishes of it. Sean addressed himself to it and the one-sided conversation wilted. Katrina watched him, picking at the too rich food herself, acutely conscious of the laughter and voices around them, feeling out of place and desperately miserable.

'Come on, Katrina,' Sean smiled at her. 'You've hardly touched your glass. Be a devil and get a little of that in you to warm you up.'

Obediently she sipped the champagne. She didn't like the taste. Sean finished the last of his crayfish thermidor and, leaning back in his chair glowing with wine and good food, said, 'Man . . . I only pray the chef can keep the rest of the meal up to that standard.' He belched softly behind his fingers and ran his eyes contentedly round the room. 'Duff used to say that a well-cooked crayfish was proof that—'

Sean stopped abruptly. He was staring at the head of the marble staircase – a party of three had appeared there. Two men in evening dress hovering attentively on each side of a woman. The woman was Candy Rautenbach. Candy with her blonde hair piled on top of her head. Candy with diamonds in her ears and at her throat, her bosom overflowing her gown as white as the frothy head on a beer tankard. Candy with bright blue eyes above a red mouth, Candy poised and lovely. Laughing, she glanced towards him and her eyes met his across the room. She stared in open disbelief, the laughter frozen on her lips, then suddenly her poise was gone and she was running down the stairs towards him, holding her skirts up to her knees, her escorts cantering after her in alarm, waiters scattering out of her path and every head in the room turning to watch her. Sean pushed back his chair, stood up to meet her and Candy reached him and jumped up to throw her arms around his neck. There was a long incoherent exchange of greetings and at last Sean prised her loose from his neck and turned her to face Katrina. Candy was flushed and panting with excitement; with every breath her bosom threatened to spring out of her bodice, and she was still holding on to Sean's arm.

'Candy, I want you to meet my wife, Katrina. My dear, this is Candy Rautenbach.'

'How do you do.' Katrina smiled uncertainly and Candy said the wrong thing.

'Sean, you're joking! You married?'

Katrina's smile faded. Candy noticed the change and went on quickly, 'But I must applaud your choice. I am so pleased to meet you, Katrina. We must get together some-time and I'll tell you all about Sean's terrible past.'

Candy was still holding Sean's arm and Katrina was watching her hand – the long tapered fingers against the dark cloth of Sean's suit. Sean saw the direction of Katrina's eyes and tried tactfully to disengage himself but Candy held on. 'Sean, these are my two current beaux.' They were standing to heel behind her like well-trained gundogs. 'They are both so nice I can't make up my mind about them. Harry Lategaan and Derek Goodman. Boys, this is Sean Courtney. You've heard lots about him.'

They shook hands all round.

'Do you mind if we join you?' asked Derek Goodman.

'I'd be upset if you didn't!' said Sean. The men spread out to find chairs while Candy and Katrina studied each other. 'Is this your first visit to Johannesburg, Mrs Court-ney?' Candy smiled sweetly. *I wonder where Sean found her, she's thin as a stick and that complexion! – that accent! He could have done better for himself – he could have had his pick.*

'Yes, we won't be here very long though.' *She's a harlot. She must be – her breasts half-naked and the paint on her face and the way she touches Sean. She must have been his mistress. If she touches him again I'll – I'll kill her.*

Sean came back to the table carrying a chair and set it down for Candy. 'Candy's one of my old friends, my dear, I'm sure you two will like each other.'

'I'm sure we will,' said Candy but Katrina didn't answer and Candy turned back to him. 'Sean, how wonderful it is to see you again. You look so well ... as sunburnt and handsome as the first time I met you. Do you remember that day you and Duff came to eat at the Hotel?'

A shadow fell across Sean's face at the mention of Duff's name. 'Yes, I remember.' He looked round and snapped his fingers for the waiter. 'Let's have some more champagne.'

'I'll get it,' Candy's escorts cut in simultaneously and then started wrangling good-naturedly as to whose turn it was.

'Is Duff with you tonight, Sean?' Candy asked.

'Candy, didn't Derek get the drinks last time? It's my turn now.' Harry sought her support. Candy ignored them and looked at Sean for a reply but he turned and went round the table to the seat beside Katrina.

'I say, old girl, can I have the first dance?' asked Derek.

'I'll spin you for it, Derek, winner pays but gets first dance,' Harry suggested.

'You're on.'

'Sean, I said is Duff here tonight?' Candy looked at him across the table.

'No, he's not. Listen, you two, how about letting me in on this.' Sean avoided her eyes and joined in the haggle with Harry and Derek. Candy bit her lip – she wanted to press Sean further. She wanted to know about Duff – then suddenly she turned on her smile again. She wasn't going to plead with him.

'What is this?' She tapped Harry's shoulder with her fan. 'Am I going to be the prize in a game of chance? Derek will pay for the wine and Sean gets first dance.'

'I say old girl, that's a bit rough, you know.' But Candy was already standing up.

'Come on, Sean, let's see if you can still tread a stately measure.'

Sean glanced at Katrina. 'You don't mind, do you . . . just one dance?'

Katrina shook her head.

I hate her. She's a harlot. Katrina had never in her life spoken the word out loud, she had seen it only in her Bible, but now it gave her a fierce pleasure to think it. She watched Sean and Candy walk arm-in-arm to the dance floor.

'Would you care to dance, Mrs Courtney?' said Derek. Katrina shook her head again without looking at him. She was staring at Sean and Candy. She saw Sean take her in his arms and a cold lump settled in her stomach. Candy was looking up into Sean's face, laughing at him, her arm on his shoulder, her hand in his.

She's a harlot. Katrina felt her tears very near the surface and thinking that word held them back. Sean swirled Candy into a turn – Katrina stiffened in her chair, her hands clenching in her lap – their legs were touching, she saw Candy arch her back slightly and press her thighs against Sean. Katrina felt as though she were suffocating, jealousy had spread up cold and tight through her chest.

I could go and pull him away, she thought. *I could stop him doing that. He has no right. It's as though the two of them are doing – doing it together. I know they have before, I know it now – Oh God, make them stop it. Please make them stop.*

At last Sean and Candy came back to the table. They were laughing together and when he reached her chair Sean dropped his hand on Katrina's shoulder. She moved away from it but Sean seemed not to notice. Everybody was having a good time. Everybody except Katrina. Harry and Derek were jostling for position. Sean's big laugh kept booming out and Candy was sparkling like the diamonds she wore. Every few minutes Sean turned to Katrina and tried to draw her into the conversation but Katrina stubbornly refused to be drawn. She sat there hating them all. Hating even Sean – for the first time she was unsure of him, jealous and frightened for him. She stared down at her hands on the tablecloth in front of her and saw how bony they were, chapped and reddened by the sun and wind, ugly compared to Candy's. She pulled them quickly into her lap

513

and leaned across towards Sean. 'Please, I want to go back to the hotel. I don't feel well.'

Sean stopped in the middle of a story and looked at her with a mixture of concern and dismay. He didn't want to leave and yet he knew she was still sick. He hesitated one second and then he said, 'Of course, my fancy, I'm sorry. I didn't realize—' He turned to the others. 'We'll have to be going ... my wife's not too strong ... she's just had one hell of a go of blackwater.'

'Oh, Sean, must you?' Candy couldn't hide her disappointment. 'There's still so much to talk about.'

'I'm afraid so. We'll get together another night.'

'Yes,' agreed Katrina quickly, 'next time we come to Johannesburg we'll see you.'

'Oh, I don't know ... perhaps before we go,' Sean demurred. 'Some night next week. How about Monday?'

Before Candy could answer Katrina interrupted. 'Please, Sean, can we go now. I'm very tired.' She started towards the stairs but looked back to see Candy jump up and take Sean's arm, hold her lips close to his ear and whisper a question. Sean answered her tersely and Candy turned back to the table and sat down. When they were out on the street Katrina asked, 'What did she say to you?'

'She just said goodbye,' muttered Sean and Katrina knew he was lying. They didn't talk again on the way back to the hotel. Katrina was preoccupied with her jealousy and Sean was thinking about what Candy had asked and what he had answered.

'Sean, where's Duff? You must tell me.'

'He's dead, Candy.'

The second before she turned back to the table Sean had seen her eyes.

31

Sean woke with a headache and Dirk's jumping on his chest did not help to ease it at all. Sean had to bribe him off with the promise of sweets. Dirk, sensing his advantage, raised his price to a packet of bull's eyes and two lollipops, the kind with red stripes, before he allowed Katrina to lead him away to the bathroom. Sean sighed and settled back under the blankets. The pain moved up and crouched just behind his eyes. He could taste stale champagne on his own breath and his skin smelt of cigar smoke. He drowsed back in half sleep and the ache faded a little.

'Sean, it's Sunday you know. Are you coming to church with us?' Katrina asked coldly from the bedroom door. Sean squeezed his eyelids tighter closed.

'Sean!' No answer.

'Sean!' He opened one eye.

'Are you going to get up?'

'I don't feel very well,' he croaked. 'I think I have a touch of malaria.'

'Are you coming?' Katrina demanded remorselessly. Her feelings towards him had not softened during the night.

'I don't feel up to it this morning, truly I don't. I'm sure the Good Lord will understand.'

'Thou shalt not take the Lord's name in vain,' Katrina warned him with ice in her voice.

'I'm sorry.' Sean pulled the blankets up to his chin defensively. 'But truly, fancy, I can't get up for another couple of hours. My head would burst.'

Katrina turned back into the sitting-room and Sean heard her speak to Dirk in a voice purposely pitched to reach him.

'Your father's not coming with us. We will have to go

down to breakfast by ourselves. Then we will have to go to church on our own.'

'But,' Dirk pointed out, 'he's going to buy me a packet of bull's eyes and *two* lollipops with red stripes.' In Dirk's opinion that levelled the score. Sean heard the door of the suite close and Dirk's voice receded down the passage. Sean relaxed slowly and waited for the ache behind his eyes to diminish. After a while he became aware of the coffee tray on the table beside the bed and he weighed the additional pain that the effort of sitting up would involve against the beneficial effect of a large cup of coffee. It was a difficult decision but in the end he carefully raised his body to a sitting position and poured a cupful. There was a small jug of fresh cream on the tray. He took it in his right hand and was just about to add a little to the cup when there was a knock on the sitting-room door.

'Come in!' called Sean. He supposed it was the waiter coming to collect the tray. Sean searched his mind for a really scathing remark to send him on his way. He heard the sitting-room door open.

'Who is it?' he asked. There were quick footsteps and then Sean started so violently that the cream slopped out of the jug onto his sheets and his new nightshirt.

'Good God, Candy, you shouldn't have come here.' Sean was in a frenzy of agitation. He put the jug back on the tray with nervous haste and wiped ineffectually at the mess on his nightshirt with his hands. 'If my wife ... Did anyone see you? You mustn't stay. If Katrina knows you've been here she'll ... well I mean, she won't understand.'

Candy's eyes were puffy and rimmed with red. She looked as though she hadn't slept. 'It's all right, Sean, I waited across the street until I saw your wife leave. One of my servants followed her, she went to the Dutch church on Commissioner Street and there the service lasts about fifty years.' She came into the room and sat down on the edge of his bed.

'I had to talk to you alone. I couldn't let you go without knowing about Duff. I want you to tell me about it ... everything about it. I promise not to cry, I know how you hate it.'

'Candy, let's not torture ourselves with it. He's dead. Let's remember him alive.' Sean had forgotten his headache for its place had been taken by pity for her and worry at the position in which she had placed him.

'Tell me, please. I must know. I'd never rest again if I didn't,' she said quietly.

'Candy, don't you see that it doesn't matter? The way in which he went is not important. All that you need to know is he's gone.' Sean's voice faded but went on softly almost to himself, 'He's gone, that is the only thing that matters, he's gone and left us richer for knowing him and a little poorer for having lost him.'

'Tell me,' she said again and they looked at each other, their emotions locked behind expressionless faces. Then Sean told her, his words limping at first, then faster and stronger as the horror of it came back to him. When he had finished she said nothing. She sat on the edge of the bed staring down at the patterned carpet. Sean moved closer to her and put his arm around her.

'There is nothing we can do. That's the thing about death, there is nothing you can do to make it change its mind.'

She leaned against him, against the comfort of his big body and they sat silently until suddenly Candy pulled away from him and smiled her gay brittle smile.

'And now tell me about you. Are you happy? Was that your son with Katrina? He's a lovely child.'

With relief Sean followed her away from the memory of

Duff. They talked about each other, filling in the blanks from the time they had last met until suddenly Sean returned to reality.

'Good God, Candy, we've been talking for ages. Katrina will be back at any moment. You had better run.'

At the door she turned, buried her fingers in his beard and tugged his head from side to side. 'If she ever throws you out, you magnificent brute, here's somebody who'll have a place for you.'

She stood up on her toes and kissed him. 'Be happy,' she commanded and the door closed softly behind her.

Sean rubbed his chin, then he pulled off his nightshirt, screwed it into a ball, tossed it through the open door of the bedroom and went to the bathroom. He was towelling himself and whistling the waltz that the band had played the night before, sweating a little in the steamy warmth of the bathroom when he heard the front door open. 'Is that you, Fancy?'

'Daddy! Daddy! Mummy got sweets for me.' Dirk hammered on the bathroom door, and Sean wrapped the towel round his waist before opening it.

'Look! Look at all my sweets,' gloated Dirk. 'Do you want one, Pa?'

'Thank you, Dirk,' Sean put one of the huge striped humbugs in his mouth, moved it to one side and spoke around it.

'Where's your Mummy?'

'There.' Dirk pointed at the bedroom. He closed the sweet packet carefully. 'I'll keep some for Bejaan,' he announced.

'He'll like that,' Sean said and went across to the bedroom. Katrina lay on the bed; as soon as he saw her he knew something was desperately wrong. She lay staring up at the ceiling, her eyes unseeing, her face as yellow and set as that of a corpse. Two quick strides carried him to her.

He touched her cheek with his fingers and the sense of dread settled on him again, heavily, darkly.

'Katrina?' There was no response. She lay still without a flicker of life in her eyes. Sean swung round and ran out of the suite, down the corridor to the head of the stairs. There were people in the lobby below him and he yelled over their heads to the clerk behind the desk.

'Get a doctor, man, as fast as you can ... my wife's dying.'

The man stared up at him blankly. He had a neck too thin for his high stiff collar and his black hair was parted down the centre and polished with grease.

'Hurry, you stupid bastard, get moving,' roared Sean. Everybody in the lobby was looking at him. He still wore only a small towel around his waist and, heavy with water, his hair hung down over his forehead.

'Move, man! Move!' Sean was dancing with impatience. There was a heavy stone vase on the banister at Sean's side, he picked it up threateningly and the clerk jerked out of his trance and scuttled for the front door. Sean ran back to the suite.

Dirk was standing by Katrina's bed, his face distorted by the humbug it contained and his eyes large with curiosity. Sean snatched him up, carried him through to the other bedroom and locked the door on his outraged howls. Dirk was unused to being handled in that manner. Sean went back to Katrina and knelt beside her bed. He was still kneeling there when the doctor arrived. Tersely Sean explained about the blackwater, and the doctor listened then sent him to wait in the sitting-room. It was a long wait before the doctor came through to him and Sean sensed that behind his professional poker face the man was puzzled.

'Is it a relapse?' Sean demanded.

'No, I don't think so. I've given her a sedative.'

519

'What's wrong with her? What is it?' Sean pursued him and the doctor hedged.

'Has your wife had some sort of shock ... some bad news, something that could have alarmed her? Has she been under nervous strain?'

'No ... she's just come back from church. Why? What's wrong?' Sean caught the doctor's lapels and shook him in his agitation.

'It appears to be some sort of paralytic hysteria. I've given her laudanum. She'll sleep now and I'll come back to see her this evening.'

The doctor was trying to loosen Sean's hands from his jacket. Sean let him go and pushed past him to the bedroom.

The doctor called again just before dark. Sean had undressed Katrina and put her into the bed, but apart from that she had not moved. Her breathing was shallow and fast despite the drug she had been given. The doctor was baffled.

'I can't understand it, Mr Courtney. There is nothing I can find wrong with her apart from her general run-down condition. I think we'll just have to wait and see. I don't want to give her any more drugs.'

Sean knew the man could be of no more help to him and he hardly noticed when he left with a promise to come again in the morning. Mbejane gave Dirk his bath, fed him and put him to bed and then he slipped quietly out of the suite and left Sean alone with Katrina. The afternoon of worry had tired Sean. He left the gas burning in the sitting-room and stretched out on his own bed. After a while he slept.

When the rhythm of his breathing changed Katrina looked across at him. Sean lay fully clothed on top of his blankets, one thickly-muscled arm thrown above his head and his tension betrayed by the twitching of his lips and the frown that puckered his face. Katrina stood up and moved across to stand over him, lonely as she had never been in the solitude of the bush, hurt beyond the limits of physical pain and with everything that she believed in destroyed in those few minutes that it had taken for her to discover the truth.

She looked down at Sean and with surprise realized that she still loved him, but now the security that she had found with him was gone. The walls of her castle had proved paper. She had felt the first cold draughts blowing in through them as she watched him reliving his past and regretting it. She had felt the walls tremble and the wind howl stronger outside when he danced with that woman – then, they had collapsed into ruin around her. Standing in the half-darkened room, watching the man she trusted so completely and who just as completely had betrayed her, she went carefully over the ground again to make sure there was no mistake.

That morning, she and Dirk had stopped at the sweet shop on the way back from church. It was almost opposite the hotel. It had taken Dirk a long time to select his tuppenny worth. The profusion of wares on display unmanned him and reduced him to a state of dithering indecision. Finally, with the assistance of the proprietor and a little prompting from Katrina, his purchases were made and packed into a brown paper bag. They were just about to go when Katrina looked out through the large front window of the shop and saw Candy Rautenbach leaving the hotel. She came quickly down the front steps, glanced about her, crossed the street to a waiting carriage and her coachman whisked her away. Katrina had stopped the instant she caught sight of her. A pang of last night's jealousy returned, for Candy looked very lovely even in the morning sunlight. It was not until Candy's carriage disappeared that Katrina began to question her presence at their hotel at eleven o'clock on a Sunday morning. Her jealousy was a bayonet thrust up under her ribs: it made her catch her breath. Vividly she remembered Candy's whispered question as they left the Golden Guinea the previous night. She remembered the way Sean had answered and the way he had lied about it afterwards. Sean knew that Katrina would go to church that morning. How simple it all was! Sean had arranged to meet her, he had refused to accompany Katrina and while Katrina was out of the way that harlot had gone to him.

'Mummy, you're hurting me.' Unconsciously she had tightened her grip on Dirk's hand. She hurried out of the shop, dragging Dirk with her. She almost ran across the hotel lobby, up the stairs and along the passage. The door was closed. She opened it and the smell of Candy's perfume met her. Her nostrils flared at it. There was no mistaking it, she remembered it from the previous evening – the smell of fresh violets. She heard Sean call from the bathroom, Dirk ran across the room and hammered on the door.

'Daddy! Daddy! Mummy got sweets for me.'

She put her Bible down on top of the writing desk and moved across the thick carpet with the smell of violets all around her. She stood in the doorway of the bedroom. Sean's nightshirt lay on the floor, there were still damp stains on it. She felt her legs begin to tremble. She looked up and saw the stains on the bed, grey on the white sheets. She felt giddy, her cheeks burned; she only just managed to reach her own bed.

32

She knew there was no mistake. Sean had taken that woman in such a casually blatant manner – in their own bedroom, almost before her eyes, that his rejection of her could hardly have been more final if he had slapped her face and thrown her into the street. Weakened by fever, depressed by the loss of her child and the phase of her cycle, she had not the resilience to fight against it. She had loved him but she had proved insufficient for him. She could not stay with him: the stubborn pride of her race would not allow it. There was only one alternative.

Timidly she bent over him and as she kissed him she smelt the warm man-smell of his body and felt his beard brush her cheek. Her determination wavered; she wanted to throw herself across his chest, lock her arms around his neck and plead with him. She wanted to ask for another chance. If he could tell her how she had failed him she could try to change, if only he could show her what she had done wrong. Perhaps if they went back into the bush again – She dragged herself away from his bed. She pressed her knuckles hard against her lips. It was no use. He had decided and even if she begged him to take her back there would always be this thing between them. She had lived in a castle and she would not change it now for a mud hut. Driven by the trek whip of her pride she moved quickly across to the wardrobe. She put on a coat and buttoned it – it reached to her ankles and covered her nightdress; she spread the green shawl over her head, winding the loose end around her throat. Once more she looked across at Sean. He slept with his big body sprawled and the frown still on his face.

In the sitting-room she stopped beside the writing desk. Her Bible lay where she had left it. She opened the front cover, dipped the pen and wrote. She closed the book and went to the door. There she hesitated once more and looked back at Dirk's bedroom. She could not trust herself to see him again. She lifted an end of the shawl to cover her mouth, then she went out into the passage and closed the door softly behind her.

– 33 –

Sean was surprised to find himself fully dressed and lying on top of his bed when he woke next morning. It was still half dark outside the hotel windows and the room was cold. He propped himself up on one elbow and rubbed at his eyes with the back of a clenched fist. Then he remembered and he swung his legs off the bed and looked at Katrina's bed. The blankets were thrown back and it was empty. Sean's first feeling was relief, she had recovered enough to get up on her own. He went through to the bathroom, stumbling a little from the stiffness of uneasy sleep. He tapped on the closed door.

'Katrina?' he questioned and then again louder. 'Katrina, are you in there?'

The handle turned when he tried it and the door swung open without resistance. He blinked at the empty room, white tiles reflecting the uncertain light, a towel thrown across a chair where he had left it. He felt the first twinge of alarm. Dirk's room – the door was still locked, the key on the outside. He flung it open. Dirk sat up in bed, his face flushed, his curls standing up like the leaves of a sisal bush. Sean ran out into the passage, along it and looked down into the lobby. There was a light burning behind the reception desk. The clerk slept with his head on his arms, sitting forward on his chair snoring. Sean went down the stairs three at a time. He shook the clerk.

'Has anybody been out through here during the night?' Sean demanded.

'I . . . I don't know.'

'Is that door locked?' Sean pointed at the front door.

'No, sir, there's a night latch on it. You can get out but not in.'

Sean ran out onto the pavement. Which way, which way to search for her? Which way had she gone? Back to Pretoria to the wagons? Sean thought not. She would need transport and she had no money to hire it. Why should she leave without waking him, leave Dirk, leave her clothing and disappear into the night? She must have been unbalanced by the drugs the doctor had given her. Perhaps there was something in his theory that she had suffered a shock, perhaps she was wandering in her nightdress through the streets with no memory, perhaps – Sean stood in the cold grey Transvaal morning, the city starting to murmur into wakefulness around him, the questions crowding into his head and finding there no answers with which to mate.

He turned and ran back through the hotel, out of the rear door into the stable yard.

'Mbejane,' he shouted. 'Mbejane, where the hell are you?'

Mbejane appeared quickly from the stall where he was currying one of the hired horses.

'Nkosi.'

'Have you seen the Nkosikazi?'

Mbejane's face creased into a puzzled frown. 'Yesterday—'

'No, man,' shouted Sean. 'Today, last night . . . have you seen her?'

Mbejane's expression was sufficient reply.

Sean brushed impatiently past him and ran into the stable. He snatched a saddle off the rack and threw it onto the back of the nearest horse. While he clinched the girth and forced a bit between its teeth he spoke to Mbejane.

525

'The Nkosikazi is sick. She has left during the night. It is possible that she walks as one who still sleeps. Go quickly among your friends and tell them to search for her, tell them that there's ten pounds in gold for the one who finds her. Then come back here and care for Dirk until I return.'

Sean led the horse from the stable and Mbejane hurried off to spread the word. Sean knew that within minutes half the Zulus in Johannesburg would be looking for Katrina – tribal loyalty and ten pounds in gold were strong incentives. He swung up onto the horse and galloped out of the yard. He tried the Pretoria road first. Three miles out of town a native herd boy grazing sheep beside the road convinced him that Katrina had not passed that way. He turned back. He paid a visit to the police station at Marshal Square. The Commandant remembered him from the old days; Sean could rely on his cooperation. Sean left him and rode fast through the streets that were starting to fill with the bustle of a working day. He hitched his horse outside the hotel and took the front steps three at a time. The clerk had no news for him. He ran up the stairs and along the passage to his suite. Mbejane was feeding Dirk his breakfast. Dirk beamed at Sean through a faceful of egg and spread his arms to be picked up but Sean had no time for him.

'Has she come back?'

Mbejane shook his head. 'They will find her, Nkosi. Fifty men are searching for her now.'

'Stay with the child,' said Sean and went down to his horse. He stood beside it ready to mount but not knowing which way to go. 'Where the hell has she got to?' he demanded aloud. In her night clothes with no money, where the hell had she gone?

He mounted and rode with aimless urgency through the streets, searching the faces of the people along the sidewalks, turning down the sanitary lanes and peering into backyards and vacant plots. By midday he had tired his

526

horse and worked himself into a ferment of worry and bad temper. He had searched every street in Johannesburg, made a nuisance of himself at the police station and sworn at the hotel clerk, but there was still no sign of Katrina. He was riding down Jeppe Street for the fifth time when the imposing double-storey of Candy's Hotel registered through his preoccupation.

'Candy,' he whispered. 'She can help.'

He found her in her office among Persian rugs and gilt furniture, walls covered with pink and blue patterned wallpaper, a mirrored ceiling hung with six crystal waterfalls of chandeliers and a desk with an Indian mosaic top. Sean pushed aside the little man in the black alpaca coat who tried to stop him entering and burst into the room. Candy looked up and her small frown of annoyance smoothed as she saw who it was.

'Sean . . . oh, how nice to see you.' She came round from behind the desk, the bell tent of her skirts covering the movement of her legs so she seemed to float. Her skin was smooth white and her eyes were happy blue. She held out her hand to him, but hesitated as she saw his face. 'What is it, Sean?'

He told her in a rush and she listened and when he had finished she rang the bell on her desk.

'There's brandy in the cabinet by the fireplace,' she said, 'I expect you are in need of one.'

The little man in the alpaca coat came quickly to the bell. Sean poured himself a large brandy and listened to Candy giving orders.

'Check the railway station. Telegraph the coach stages on each of the main roads. Send someone up to the hospital. Check the registers of every hotel and boarding-house in town.'

'Very well, madame.' The little man bobbed his head as he acknowledged each instruction and then he was gone.

Candy turned back to Sean.

'You can pour a drink for me also and then sit down and simmer down. You're behaving just the way she wanted you to.'

'What do you mean?' demanded Sean.

'You are being given a little bit of wifely discipline, my dear. Surely you have been married long enough to recognize that?'

Sean carried the glass across to her and Candy patted the sofa next to her.

'Sit down,' she said. 'We'll find your little Cinderella for you.'

'What do you mean ... wifely discipline?' he demanded again.

'Punishment for bad behaviour. You may have eaten with your mouth open, answered back, taken more than your share of the blankets, not said good morning with the right inflection or committed one of the other mortal sins of matrimony, but—' Candy sipped her drink and gasped slightly, 'I see that time has not given you a lighter hand with the brandy bottle. One Courtney tot always did equal an imperial gallon ... but, as I was saying, my guess is that little Katy is having an acute attack of jealousy. Probably her first, seeing that the two of you have spent your whole married life out in the deep sticks and she has never had an opportunity of watching the Courtney charm work on any other female before.'

'Nonsense,' said Sean. 'Who's she got to be jealous of?'

'Me,' said Candy. 'Every time she looked at me the other night I felt as though I'd been hit in the chest with an axe.' Candy touched her magnificent bosom with her fingertips, skilfully drawing Sean's attention to it. Sean looked at it. It was deeply cleft and smelt of fresh violets. He shifted restlessly and looked away.

'Nonsense,' he said again. 'We're just old friends, almost like—' he hesitated.

'I hope, my dear, that you weren't going to say "brother and sister" . . . I'll not be party to any incestuous relationship . . . or had you forgotten about that?'

Sean had not forgotten. Every detail of it was still clear. He blushed and stood up.

'I'd better be going,' he said. 'I'm going to keep looking for her. Thanks for your help, Candy, and for the drink.'

'Whatever I have is yours, m'sieur,' she murmured, lifting an eyebrow at him, enjoying the way he blushed. 'I'll let you know as soon as we hear anything.'

The assurance that Candy had given him wore thinner as the afternoon went by with no news of Katrina. By nightfall Sean was again wild with worry, it had completely swamped his bad temper and even anaesthetized his fatigue. One by one Mbejane's tribesmen came in to report a blank score, one by one the avenues Candy's men were exploring proved empty, and long before midnight Sean was the only hunter left. He rode hunched in the saddle, a lantern in his hand, riding the ground that had already been covered a dozen times, visiting the mining camps along the ridge, stopping to question late travellers he met along the network of roads between the mines. But the answer was always the same. Some thought he was joking: they laughed until they saw that his face was haunted and dark-eyed in the lantern light, then they stopped laughing and moved hurriedly on. Others had heard about the missing woman; they started to question him, but as soon as Sean realized they could not help him, he pushed past them and went on searching. At dawn he was back at the hotel. Mbejane was waiting for him.

'Nkosi, I have had food ready for you since last night. Eat now and sleep a little. I will send the men out to search again today, they will find her.'

'Tell them, I will give one hundred pounds to the one who finds her.' Sean passed his hand wearily across his face. 'Tell them to hunt the open veld beyond the ridges, she may not have followed a road.'

'I will tell them . . . but now you must eat.'

Sean blinked his eyes, they were red-veined and each had a little lump of yellow mucus in the corner.

'Dirk?' he asked.

'He is well, Nkosi, I have stayed with him all the while.'

Mbejane took Sean firmly by the arm. 'There is food ready. You must eat.'

'Saddle me another horse,' said Sean. 'I will eat while you do it.'

Without sleep, unsteady in the saddle as the day wore on, Sean widened the circle of his search until he was out into the treeless veld and the mine headgears were small spidery triangles on the horizon.

A dozen times he met Zulus from the city, big black men in loin cloths, moving at their businesslike trot, hunting the ground like hounds. There was a concealed sympathy behind their greetings.

'Mbejane has told us, Nkosi. We will find her.' And Sean left them and rode on alone, more alone than he had ever been in his life before. After dark he rode back into Johannesburg, the faint flutter of hope inside him stilled as he limped stiffly into the gas-lit lobby of the hotel and saw the pity in the reception clerk's face.

'No word, I'm afraid, Mr Courtney.'

Sean nodded. 'Thanks anyway. Is my son all right?'

'Your servant has taken good care of him, sir. I sent dinner up to him an hour ago.'

The stairs seemed endless as he climbed them. By God, he was tired – sick-tired and sick with worry. He pushed open the door of his suite and Candy stood up from a chair across the room. The hope flared up in him again.

'Have you—' he started eagerly.

'No,' she said quickly. 'No, Sean, I'm sorry.' He flopped into one of the chairs and Candy poured a drink for him from a decanter that was waiting on the writing desk. He smiled his thanks and took a big gulp at the glass. Candy lifted his legs one at a time and pulled off his boots, ignoring his faint protest. Then she took up her own glass and went to sit across the room from him.

'I'm sorry I joked yesterday,' she apologized softly. 'I don't think I realized how much you love her.' She lifted her glass to him. 'Here's a speedy end to the search.'

Sean drank again, half a glass at a swallow.

'You do love her, don't you?' Candy asked.

Sean answered her sharply. 'She's my wife.'

'But it's not only that,' Candy went on recklessly, knowing his anger was just below the surface of his fatigue.

'Yes, I love her. I'm just learning how much, I love her as I'll never be able to love again.' He drained his glass and stared at it, his face grey under the brown and his eyes dark with unhappiness. 'Love,' he said. 'Love,' mouthing the word, weighing it. 'They've dirtied that word ... they sell love at the Opera House ... they have used that word so much that now when I want to say "I love Katrina" it doesn't sound what I mean.' Sean hurled the glass against the far wall, it shattered with a crack and a tingle and Dirk stirred in the bedroom. Sean dropped his voice to a fierce whisper. 'I love her so it screws my gut, I love her so that to think of losing her now is like thinking of dying.'

He clenched his fists and leaned forward in his chair. 'I'll not lose her now, by Christ, I'll find her and when I do I'll tell her this. I'll tell her just like I'm telling you.' He stopped and frowned. 'I don't think I've ever said to her "I love you." I've never liked using that word. I've said "Marry me" and "You're my fancy," but I've never said it straight before.'

'Perhaps that's part of the reason she ran away, Sean,

531

perhaps because you never said it she thought you never felt it.' Candy was watching him with a strange expression – pity and understanding and a little yearning.

'I'll find her,' said Sean, 'and this time I'll tell her . . . if it's not too late.'

'You'll find her and it won't be too late. The earth can't have swallowed her, and she'll be glad to hear you say it.' Candy stood up. 'You must rest now, you have a hard day ahead of you.'

Sean slept fully dressed in the chair in the sitting-room. He slept brokenly, his mind struggling and kicking him back to half wakefulness every few minutes. Candy had turned the gas low before she left and its light fell in a soft pool onto the writing desk beneath it. Katrina's Bible lay where she had left it and each time Sean started awake the fat, leather-covered book caught his eye. Some time before dawn he woke for the last time and knew he could not sleep again.

He stood up and his body still ached and his eyes felt gritty. He moved across to the gas lamp and turned it up high, he let his hand drop from the lamp onto the Bible. Its leather was cool and softly polished beneath his fingers. He opened the front cover and caught his breath with a hiss.

Beneath Katrina's name, in her carefully rounded writing, the ink still freshly blue, *she had filled in the date of death*.

The page magnified slowly in front of his eyes until it filled the whole field of his vision. There was a rushing sound in his ears, the sound of a river in flood, but above it he heard voices, different voices.

'Let's go, Sean, it looks like a grave.'

'But more than anything she needs love.'

'The earth can't have swallowed her.'

And his own voice, 'If it's not too late, if it's not too late.'

The morning light was gathering strength as he reached the ruins of the old Candy Deep office block. He left his horse and ran through the grass towards the mine dump. The wind was small and cold; it moved the tops of the grass and went on to where Katrina's green shawl was caught on the barbed wire fence that ringed the shaft. In the wind the shawl flapped its wings like a big green bird of prey.

Sean reached the fence and looked down into the mouth of the shaft. At one place the grass had been torn away from the edge as though someone had snatched at it as they fell.

Sean loosed the shawl from the spikes of the barbed wire, he balled the heavy material in his fists, then he held it out over the shaft and let it drop. It spread out as it floated down into the blackness, and it was the bright green of Katrina's eyes.

'Why?' whispered Sean. 'Why have you done this to us, my fancy?' He turned away and walked back to his horse, stumbling carelessly in the rough footing.

Mbejane was waiting for him in the hotel suite.

'Get the carriage,' Sean told him.

'The Nkosikazi – ?'

'Get the carriage,' Sean repeated.

Sean carried Dirk downstairs. He paid his bill at the reception desk and went out to where Mbejane had the carriage ready. He climbed up into it and held Dirk on his lap.

'Drive back to Pretoria,' Sean said.

'Where's Mummy?' Dirk demanded.

'She's not coming with us.'

'Are we going alone?' Dirk insisted and Sean nodded wearily.

'Yes, Dirk, we are going alone.'

'Is Mummy coming just now?'

'No, Dirk. No, she's not.'

It was finished, Sean thought. It was all over – all the

533

dreams and the laughter and the love. He was too numbed to feel the pain yet – it would come later.

'Why are you squeezing me so hard, Daddy?'

Sean slackened his grip and looked down at the child on his lap. It was not finished, he realized; it was only a new beginning.

But first I must have time for this to heal: time – and a quiet place to lie up with this wound. The wagons are waiting and I must go back into the wilderness.

Perhaps after another year I will have healed sufficiently to start again, to go back to Ladyburg with my son, back to Ladyburg, and to Ada and to Garry – he thought. Then suddenly and sickeningly he felt the pain again, and the deep raw ache of it frightened him. *Please God*, prayed Sean who had never prayed before, *please God give me the strength to endure it.*

'Are you going to cry, Daddy? You look like you're going to cry.' Dirk was watching Sean's face with solemn curiosity. Sean pulled the child's head gently against his shoulder and held it there.

If tears could pay both our debts, thought Sean, if with my tears I could buy for you an indulgence from all pain, if by weeping now I could do all your weeping for you – then I would cry until my eyes were washed away.

'No, Dirk,' he answered. 'I am not going to cry – crying never helps very much.'

And Mbejane took them to where the wagons waited at Pretoria.